E. B. (Edward Bouverie) Pusey

First Letter To The Very Rev. J.H. Newman

E. B. (Edward Bouverie) Pusey

First Letter To The Very Rev. J.H. Newman

ISBN/EAN: 9783741130007

Manufactured in Europe, USA, Canada, Australia, Japa

Cover: Foto ©Andreas Hilbeck / pixelio.de

Manufactured and distributed by brebook publishing software
(www.brebook.com)

E. B. (Edward Bouverie) Pusey

First Letter To The Very Rev. J.H. Newman

FIRST LETTER

TO THE

VERY REV. J. H. NEWMAN, D.D.

In Explanation

CHIEFLY IN REGARD TO

THE REVERENTIAL LOVE DUE TO THE EVER-BLESSED THEOTOKOS,

AND

THE DOCTRINE OF HER IMMACULATE CONCEPTION;

WITH AN ANALYSIS OF CARDINAL DE TURRECREMATA'S WORK ON THE IMMACULATE CONCEPTION.

BY THE REV.

E. B. PUSEY, D.D.

REGIUS PROFESSOR OF HEBREW, AND CANON OF CHRIST CHURCH.

SOLD BY JAMES PARKER & CO., OXFORD,
AND 377, STRAND, LONDON;
RIVINGTONS, WATERLOO PLACE, LONDON,
HIGH STREET, OXFORD, AND TRINITY STREET, CAMBRIDGE.
1869.

CONTENTS.

a

viii *Contents.*

Contents.

APPENDIX.

ERRATA.

P. 250, line 18, *for* ought to be held as heretical, who *read* one who
    holds it ought to be accounted heretical, who
— —, — 20, *after* for ever ? *add* None certainly.
— —, note 2, *add* [printed wrongly for 118].
— 262, line 2, *for* She *read* The dawn ·
— 265, — 18, *for* went *read* goeth
— 266, — 3, *for* when *read* since
— 267, — 16, *for* waste *read* waste ⁹
— —, — 20, *for* consumption ⁹ *read* conception
— 268, — 21, *for* a Bishop *read* Archbishop
— 316, — 25, *for* ἄμωμον, *read* τανύμωμον,
— 340, — 17, *for* 304, *read* 384

LETTER,

&c.

MY DEAREST FRIEND,

First, let me thank you for the love shewn in your letter, a love which was such joy to my youth, and now is so cheering to my old age.

2. Next let me say, that I should indeed have thought it not rude only but insolent, to imply that "writing does not become" you. In the sentences which you quote, I was thinking, partly (as I said) of myself, "had the English Church, by accepting heresy, driven me out of it," partly, of an unpractical habit of mind of some who have gone over to the Roman Church, because they could accept the letter of the Council of Trent in their own sense. Nothing has been further from my mind than any criticism of yourself, whom I still admire as well as love.

3. But neither, on that account, have I ever meant to identify you, in your present position,

with any thing which I may say. In writing my
"historical preface" to Tract 90, which you kindly
permitted me to re-publish, "I purposely abstained
from consulting you upon the subject, in order not to
identify you with any thing in it." I dwell, indeed,
on the sunny memories of those bright days of early
or middle life, when we were fighting altogether
the same battle (for against unbelief we are fighting
the same battle still), when not our hearts only and
our affections were (as they now are) one, but our
thoughts also. But I did not mean to use your
name, in order to identify you in the least now
with any thing which I think or say.

4. In alleging those passages from the Fathers,
which "state or imply that the faith is contained in
Holy Scripture" (p. 336 sqq.), I had no idea of any
controversy with Rome. In the whole of this part
of my Eirenicon, I was purely on the defensive. It
is, I think, not uncommon with Roman Catholic
controversialists, to give to our VIth Article an un-
Catholic sense. I meant simply to maintain that
its teaching is identical with that of the Fathers.
It had been said that "the Church of England
weakens the hold of the truths which it teaches, by
detaching them from the Divine voice of the
Church." I meant to maintain that the Church of
England does hold a Divine authority in the Church,
to be exercised in a certain way, deriving the truth
from Holy Scripture, following Apostolical tradition,
under the guidance of God the Holy Ghost. I fully

believe that there is no difference between us in this. The "quod ubique, quod semper, quod ab omnibus," which our own Divines have so often inculcated, contains, I believe, the self-same doctrine as is laid down in the Council of Trent upon tradition. It was in pure honesty, and as a matter of fact, that I stated that, for some of the passages (which I did not know by my own reading), I was indebted to your most valuable notes on St. Athanasius.

But I am glad that this reference to yourself has brought out your own clear expression of the identity of the belief of Roman Catholics and Anglicans on this point. Your whole statement entirely expresses our belief. I may, in token of that agreement, transfer one clear sentence to these pages.

"We [you] mean—that not every article of faith is so contained there [in Holy Scripture], that it may thence be logically proved, *independently* of the teaching and authority of the Tradition; but Anglicans mean that every Article of faith is so contained there, that it may *thence* be proved, *provided* there be added the illustrations and compensations of Tradition [1]."

These explanations are towards yourself. There are three graver matters which concern myself: 1. That, in your own eyes and those of Roman Catholics, I have, under the name of an Eirenicon, been, in fact, to speak plainly, as aggressive as an Exeter-Hall [2] controversialist. 2. That I have withheld the expression of my faith in regard to

[1] Letter, p. 14. [2] Letter, p. 10.

the Mother of my Lord. 3. That in writing on a quasi-authoritative system in regard to her, which I set forth as our chief difficulty, I have, in fact, inserted more or less from persons who are of no weight.

All this you have said with your usual tenderness; but to this it comes in substance; and I am glad of the opportunity of explaining myself.

1. My book had necessarily a two-fold aspect. It was a defence of ourselves against what, amid all courteousness of language, was a root-and-branch attack upon the Church of England, ascribing to her more of evil, and less of good, than any publication I had happened to see. In answer to this, I claimed to her all the broad outlines of faith which you too have, and, (as I trust, truly,) I set aside many things which are the ordinary subjects of Protestant attack upon you. It has been so far said of my book, that, as far as it should have influence, it would change the character of the controversy.

But, having done this, I was bound in conscience to my own people to say why I remain where I am, and why I not only think the Church of England justified in not accepting the only terms now open to her—viz. simple and absolute submission, including the reception of that whole practical system, which is, I believe, the ground why she remains apart; but also trust that Almighty God has an office for her, in His over-ruling Providence, in regard to that same system. Yet I trusted that the exposition of this might still be without offence. For I pointed out, that those things which are a "crux" to me, and, I believe, to our people generally, are not *de fide* among you; so that I thought I could not be considered as attacking the Church of Rome itself. I called the whole an Eirenicon, to show what my real animus was; what, in my own mind, underlay the whole. I meant the name to be the key to what necessarily was very miscellaneous. Whatever else there was in the book, and whatever appearances some of it might wear, I wished to say, that although I had been put upon the defensive, and although, in parrying a death-thrust, I could hardly help wounding, what I *bonâ fide* aimed at, as the ultimate result of all, was "peace." Plainly, if the Roman Church were wholly in the right, we should be wholly in the wrong; which I could not think; else, of course, I should not be where I am. But (which is the centre of all) I meant to suggest, that this state of things was not irremediable; that there was a way, whereby peace and intercommunion might be restored, through mutual explanations, without calling upon the Church of Rome to abandon any thing which she had pronounced to be "de fide." The writer of the first article in the Weekly Register seized my meaning, and I am grateful to him for it.

At the same time seeing, in that remarkable collection of Episcopal letters [*] on the question of

---

[*] The Pareri dell' Episcopato Cattolico, &c.

defining, as "de fide," the doctrine of the Immaculate Conception, how tenderly many of the Bishops
felt towards those who are not in the Roman Communion, and how much they desired not to aggravate
their difficulties, I hoped that it would not be
taken amiss, if I stated, in all its breadth, what,
in that system which is our special difficulty,
startled and repelled us. I did not use (as you
will bear me witness) one word of declamation. I
meant the statements to be simply of historical
facts, if I may include under the term "historical,"
and simply *as* facts, the anticipations of influential
writers in the Roman Communion of a large developement of the cultus of the Blessed Virgin. In
putting together these facts, nothing was further
from my mind than to pass any opinion whatever,
as to the writers whom I quoted. I simply wished
to exhibit the picture of practical devotion to the
Blessed Virgin, as it was reflected to me in their
writings, and it did not even occur to me that I
could be thought thereby to pass any opinion as to
the inner life of those whose words were cited.
When I heard that my not expressing this was
thought to be unjust to holy men whom I quoted,
I took the first opportunity which occurred to say,
that I did not mean to impute to any of them
that "they took from our Lord any of the love
which they gave to His Mother."

In saying this, I may add, I hope without offence,
that their language does appear to me self-contra-

dictory.   They used it, doubtless, in the security
that they could not be misunderstood.   Perhaps, if
they had been writing for us English, or among us,
they would not have used it.   Still, the grammatical
meaning of the words does not, in many cases, bear
any softening.   When S. Alphonso quotes from
writers, following in part S. Thomas Aquinas, the
statement, " The Father gave all judgment to
the Son, and the whole office of mercy He gave to
the Mother⁴," this antithesis is not explained, but
contradicted by the statement, that " her tenderness and compassion for men are but a drop from
the boundless ocean of the infinite Mercy of Jesus
Christ, her Son and her God⁵." If it is said, "⁶The
greater luminary is Christ, who presides over the
just; the lesser luminary is Mary, who is set over
sinners;" the antithesis is misleading, if it be not
meant that Mary has some special office towards sinners which our Lord has not: the more so, when it is
added ; " since then Mary is this propitious moon
to sinners, if any miserable man finds himself
fallen into the night of sin, let him behold the
moon; let him pray to Mary." It is, of course,
not said " pray to her" exclusively; but the sinner
is said to have " lost the light of the Sun," i. e.
Jesus, " by losing Divine grace," and is not directed
to seek Him Whom he had lost, but Mary.   Or

---

⁴ Glories of Mary, T. i. p. 81.
⁵ Note of transl., Ibid.   (Not in former translations.)
⁶ Card. Hugo in Glories of Mary, C. 3. § 2. T. i. p. 184.

when it is said to her ', "Therefore hast thou been chosen from eternity to be the Mother of God, that thy mercy might procure salvation for those, whom the justice of thy Son could *not* save;" it seems to me, that the writer, in his vehement desire to set forth the privileges of Mary, contradicted the truth which he himself held, if he believed that the mercy of Jesus *could* save them.

If, by any choice of words, I could have softened the pain of such statements, you must know how gladly I would have done it. But the pain lay in the subject itself. And no other way occurred to me, than that which I adopted, of giving the statements which presented difficulties to me, in the words of the writers, with only so much of observation as should serve to indicate wherein the difficulty pressed upon us.

But my object was a practical one. I knew that in thousands of English minds (I doubt not, that in millions), this and the like language is the great barrier against re-union. I have often (though you will smile perhaps at the advocacy) had to defend the Roman Church against being idolatrous, and *that*, on the ground of this and the like language. I wished to make out our case *to* you, not *against* you. I held to what I had put down at the outset, that if the Roman Church could declare to be *de fide*, *that* only which the Council of Trent laid

---

' De Præs. Beatæ Virgin., quoted as S. Chrysostom's or S. Ignatius'.

down, as explained by Divines of repute among
you (especially in this country), one chief obstacle
to re-union would be removed. And so, as circumstances induced me to accumulate the evidence of
what we wished to be protected against, I thought
with myself, "Well, they have but to disown it,
and it will be so much gained."

But, let me say, that in three instances only (which
I will explain presently) I went to any book not
in use in England. The authorities which I
quote, the two Bernardines, Suarez, &c., were
all taken from S. Alphonso, just as they lay in his
book, only translated. And this book was in
English. The third edition of the English version
of his "Glories of Mary," came into my hands, (I
know not how,) just as I was finishing my defence
of Tract 90 in 1841. I had used Archbishop
Ussher's extracts, to illustrate what our Articles
meant by the Invocation of Saints which they condemned, but little thinking to impute them to Rome
at the present day. I thought that they belonged
to past times. I said that I had hoped that "they
were the exaggerations of individual minds, and that
it was not fair to charge them as teaching, now
received in the Roman Church." But in "the
Glories of Mary" I found the self-same quotations,
which I had before found in Archbishop Ussher,
so that not only the general system remained the
same, but there was a stream of authorities, which
flowed on from generation to generation. The

traditional system was sustained by the same traditional authorities.

The extracts I gave professedly on S. Liguori's authority, only here and there giving the name of the real author quoted (as Eadmer instead of St. Anselm); and this too (I may say) not on my own authority, but on that of the Benedictines. Indeed, although some Roman writers speak of me as laying down that "this is not genuine," &c., I believe that on one occasion only, and that not in controversy, I was obliged to use my own discrimination*. Else I have rested implicitly on the judgment of such critics as the Benedictines.

I did not rend the passages from their context. Whatever modification any of them may have had originally, from the circumstances under which they were written, this was entirely removed by the fact of their having been transplanted among us. Although written for Italians* chiefly, they were translated into English. The quotations from the Bernardines, &c., became, I thought, a sort of received sayings, or first principles on the subjects on which

---

* This one instance was in my work, " The Doctrine of the Real Presence from the Fathers," in which I extracted passages from those Sermons only of S. Augustine, published by Card. Mai, which I myself believed to be genuine. I could not do otherwise. But this was in defence of the " real objective Presence." In saying that *Ipsa* (Gen. iii. 15) was a mistake for *Ipse* (for which F. Gallwey censures me, " The Lady Chapel," &c., p. 51), I alleged the great Roman Catholic critic, De Rossi.

* Dr. Newman's Letter, p. 110.

they had written or preached. They *had been*
Italian devotions ; they now were naturalized in
England. Weary and sick of the controversy, I, so
far, did nothing in my Eirenicon, but extract anew
the passages which I had before quoted in my
defence of Tract 90, and in the notes to a sermon
on the Rule of faith, now fourteen years ago.

Principles, which had been enunciated of late, (I
thought, for the first time,) alone occasioned me to
do more. These principles were: 1) that it was
for the good of the Church, to decree honours to
the blessed Virgin, as gaining fresh favours from
her; 2) that there ought to be an *immense* increase
of devotion to her, and that Priests ought to incul-
cate it; 3) that whatever, being so inculcated,
became popularly received in the Church, was
infallibly true ; or, as some of the Bishops expressed
it, that the "quod ubique" was in itself a proof of
the "quod semper." For if, according to the
Council of Trent, the only sources of faith were
Holy Scripture and really Apostolic tradition, and
if what came to be taught popularly every where
in the Roman Church was infallibly true, then, if
it had not the authority of Holy Scripture, it must
of necessity be assumed to have that of tradition.
And there is a large body of teaching, against which
it would be difficult to find any opposed tradition,
on the ground that it did not bear directly on
any doctrine, which would occasion it to be
contradicted.

Now, in the official answers of Bishops of Italy, Sicily, Sardinia, Spain[1], I found that the doctrine, that the Blessed Virgin is our "co-Redemptress," was received in those countries which were of old most anxious that her Immaculate Conception should be declared to be matter of faith. Why should this too, I thought, not be declared to be matter of faith, since to honour the Blessed Virgin was considered an adequate ground for so declaring a belief, which was popularly received? And if so, this would be a fresh difficulty in the way of re-union.   But, as I did not understand the meaning of the title (with which I had become acquainted in studying those responses of the Bishops, as an index of the present mind in the Roman Church), I went to Salazar to learn it.

Almost the only other foreign writer, whom I quoted, Oswald, I quoted expressly as *not* representing Roman Theology, but as putting forth a fresh developement. I am thankful to hear that his book has been condemned. Of course, had I known this, I should not have quoted him. But I think it rather hard to be blamed for not knowing this[2], or for not looking in the Index to ascertain the fact, when I had no ground to imagine it. I met with quotations from Oswald in a German work; wishing to ascertain their correctness, I obtained his own book in the ordinary way of trade, and

[1] Eirenicon, pp. 151—153.
[2] By Mr. Rhodes in the Weekly Register.

read it. Why should I suspect a book to be in
the Index, which eminent Roman Divines, who
spoke of it, did not know to be there? But after
all, though he said strange things, the central
point, for which I quoted him, seems to me to lie
in what Faber reports to have been a revelation
to S. Ignatius Loyola [3].

I wished to see whether what I found in Oswald
and Faber, of the presence of something of the
Blessed Virgin in the Holy Eucharist, occurred in
other writers. And so I took up the third foreign
book, which I quoted, believing him to be popular
among your preachers, as he is, I think, among ours,
Corn. à Lapide. To me he seemed explicitly to
teach the same, on two grounds ; first, what seemed
to me an assertion of dogma. " The Blessed Virgin
feeds all with her own flesh, equally with the Flesh
of Christ in the Eucharist [4];" secondly, that from
this feeding with her own flesh is derived the
transfusion of the graces of the Blessed Virgin
into pious communicants. "And *hence*," (it is
from her so "feeding them with her own flesh
equally with the Flesh of Christ, ") "that love of
virginity and angelic purity in those who worthily
and frequently communicate." The maker of the
Index to à Lapide understood him, as I did [5].

[3] Eirenicon, pp. 171, 172.
[4] Ib., p. 171.
[5] " Ejus carnem in Ven. Eucharistia edimus," v. B.
Maria. I see that à Lapide's work is being re-published in a
cheap form.

This too Oakeley justifies : "In the same sense, surely, in which we say that the blood of our parents and ancestors flows in our veins (those physical changes notwithstanding), and with the necessary limitation expressed above, we may also say, and truly say, that the blood of the Blessed Virgin was in her Son from first to last, and is, therefore, in that wondrous communication of Himself which He makes to us in the Blessed Eucharist [*]."

I do not think that this is what those writers meant, since they insisted that the blood was unchanged, and it is open to the fatal objection urged by Raynaud, whom you quote [*], (and I think I remember the same in Suarez,) that then, (as Oakeley's defence too implies,) not the blood of the Blessed Virgin only, but that of her parents, and their parents in turn, must have been present too, the evil consequences of which theory Raynaud points out.

De Montfort I quoted, as being an approved writer, although recently published among us, and as one from whom a great impulse to that universal devotion, which was to characterize the new "age of Mary [*]," was expected. The Preface to his book contained the statement that "The MS. has been examined at Rome . . . most minutely examined as to

---

[*] Letter to Archbishop Manning, p. 23.
[*] Letter, p. 137.
[*] Faber, quoted Eirenicon, p. 116.

its doctrine, and declared to be exempt from all error which could be a bar to his canonization." So that I have been accused of presumption in demurring to any teaching[9], which had at least this negative sanction[1]. I know not how much this sanction amounts to. It could not, I suppose, involve an authoritative approbation of all in his book ; else, a similar sanction of the works of S. Thomas would involve a sanction of his denial of the Immaculate Conception. But if it did not authoritatively sanction all, neither, of necessity, did it sanction that which I cited; yet, with that general approbation and the strong commendation of Faber, it was no obscure nor uninfluential work, from which I extracted.

With regard to Faber himself, (whose memory I too cherish, and from whom I thankfully own that I have learned much,) I did not mean, that "the wide diffusion of" his "works, arose out of his particular sentiments about the Blessed Virgin[9];"

---

[9] Letter in the Weekly Register.

[1] Since this has been in type, Bishop Ullathorne has pointed out (Weekly Register, April 21), that one form of devotion recommended by De Montfort, has been condemned, that of "wearing little iron chains, as a badge of their loving slavery," by "those who made themselves slaves of Jesus and Mary." But the condemnation had no special reference to any devotion to the Blessed Virgin, since the use of such chains was equally prohibited, when employed to symbolize that the wearer was δοῦλος Ἰησοῦ Χριστοῦ, lit. "the slave of Jesus Christ," as St. Paul says (Rom. i. 1). It must have been, I suppose, something in the symbol, or its use, independent of the thing symbolized, which was condemned.

[9] Letter, p. 25.

I meant only, that he seemed to me to use the well-deserved influence, which he gained through that rich variety of natural and spiritual gifts wherewith God endowed him, to the promotion of an extreme cultus of the Blessed Virgin, and that, unless there were something to counterbalance it, the wide diffusion of his writings made him an important element in the future course of English and foreign Roman Catholic devotion to her.

My object was, as I said, *towards*, not *against* you. Speaking in the name of many (as I did), I hoped that those Roman Catholic Bishops, who, for love's sake, were unwilling to create any difficulty in the minds of those who wish to be one with them, might restrain those of their brethren who ignore us, or who look upon the healing of this division as hopeless.

But, in all this, I did not utter one word of censure. I could not but express my feeling of the seriousness of it. I wrote, as one in earnest for others who were in earnest. It was our case, why we wished to have some formula framed, which, by its very character, should tacitly shew that all this was not "de fide," that in case of re-union, we should be exempt from teaching, such as Faber was using all his well-merited influence to naturalize among us. Indeed I believe that the only "strong saying" in my book, is one which you say, I "bring to life, after it had long been in its grave." I thought that it had been interred so long, that

no one would know it again, or have guessed its
parent, else I would not have quoted it; and
now that you have revealed its author, I shall
take the first opportunity to remove it. I only
used it, as an illustration how deep the feeling
was among us, since "one who appreciated highly
what is good and holy in the Roman Church" had
used it.

Oakeley speaks of even the most extreme statements, which I quoted, as held to be " [3] doctrinally
defensible by many excellent Catholics, who yet would
hesitate to adopt them as the rule of their language
and habits of thought on the subject of our Blessed
Lady." He even anticipates their ultimate general
adoption, as the result of their having been brought
together. " [4] He [I] will lead many to the conclusion
that the love and cultus of the Blessed Virgin must
either be an extreme or a nullity ; that, unless we
are prepared to degrade her office, as the Mother of
our Redeemer and the great instrument of that
dispensation whence flow all blessings to the human
race, we cannot stop short of ascribing to her even
the most majestic of those titles [I suppose, "Co-
Redemptress," "Co-operatress," "Helper of Christ"
in our salvation,] which have been found for her in
the pious inventions of saintly love." But, if this
be so, I do not see where my supposed fault lies.

---

[3] Letter to the Weekly Register.
[4] Letter to the Most Rev. H. E. Manning, pp. 20, 21.

I set them down as *our* difficulties, and stated
what made them difficulties to us. Oakeley says
in fact, that they ought not to be difficulties, and
that, he thinks, they must one day be owned, as an
essential part of Christian truth[5]. But then I
see not what evil I can be supposed to have done,
in putting together, chiefly from a book in familiar
use in this country, passages which contain these
statements, with very little note except the
briefest indication wherein our difficulty lies.
And yet another, who dedicates his sermon to
Oakeley, has no other title for me than that of
"the Accuser[6]," ascribing to me, totidem verbis, the
character of Satan[7], while he himself puts into my

[5] Oakeley anticipates also, that the re-union of England in
visible communion with the Roman Church would, without
some provision, issue in our being involved in these and all the
other doctrines which I deprecated. He says, (Letter, p. 53,)
"Here Dr. P. is met by a serious practical difficulty. If the
Pope is to exercise in a re-united England the power which he
claims all over the world, of controlling the appointments to the
Episcopate, *it is quite certain that the Bishops* so nominated or
at least accepted by him *will, with the priests*, who are their
subjects, *be the instruments of flooding England* with *the devotions* to which Dr. P. conscientiously objects." And certainly,
to judge from the writing of him whom he addresses, this would
be so, if there should be no Concordat, and if this section of
Roman theology should be the accurate representative of Rome.

[6] Dr. Gallwey, "The Lady Chapel and Dr. P.'s Peacemaker,"
pp. 11—14, 18, 22, 26, 31.

[7] "Be not weary yet, for the accuser does not easily tire of
accusing. To the blessed St. John it was revealed that the
accusing spirit accused the brethren by day and by night. He
is not silenced then yet." p. 26.

mouth language which I never used[a]. Alas ! if I
have, unwittingly, (as you say half-playfully, in order
not to speak as would pain me,) "discharged my
olive branch as if from a catapult," he has wielded
"the lightning of the sword" of the judgment of
Almighty God.

2. But you think that I have been unjust to
myself in not stating what I do believe in regard to
the Blessed Virgin, as well as what I do not believe, and that, had I so done, my book would have
found less favour with Protestants[b]. Certainly, the
last thing which I imagined was, that my book
could find any thing but condemnation at the hands
of those who were really Protestants; and if it has
met with less disfavour than I expected, it is, I
think, owing to the powerful spell which those
words, "re-union of Christendom," must exercise
over every Christian heart. My omission of any
positive statements, in regard to the greatness of
the Blessed Virgin, was partly owing, I suppose,
to my not even imagining that any one could doubt
my belief, since the doctrine expressed by that great
title, *Theotokos*, is a matter of faith, an essential part
of the doctrine of the Incarnation. Partly too my
immediate subject was not her eminence, but the
"invocation of saints,"—in what way I thought
that the requests for the prayers of the saints would
find entrance among us, and what held us back

---

[a] e. g., p. 27.
[b] Letter, pp. 82, 88. 94.

from entering upon ⁻ the borders of the system. Englishmen are apt too much to concentrate themselves on the single point which they have in view; and I, I suppose, exaggerated an infirmity incidental to me as an Englishman.

Yet, in one respect, my own words have conveyed to you a meaning utterly different from what was in my mind. I said, "what was said of her [the Blessed Virgin] by the Fathers as the chosen vessel of the Incarnation, was [by later writers] applied personally to her." I seemed to you to be speaking of the Blessed Virgin as "the *physical* instrument only of the Incarnation." This had not occurred to me. The contrast in my own mind, which I expressed, I suppose, the less clearly, because I had expressed it so often, and presupposed it as known, was quite different from this. I meant two things; (1) that later writers apply to her present office, by virtue of her intercession, language which the Fathers used in regard to her office, which she through grace accepted, of becoming the Mother of her and our Redeemer; (2) that besides *this* co-operation in the salvation of mankind, which Holy Scripture speaks of as the result of her free and engraced will, Salazar and others speak (as I cited him) of a co-operation, all along, in our Lord's own proper work of our Redemption, in a way of which Holy Scripture and, I may add surely, tradition hint nothing.

But it never occurred to me to think of the

Blessed Virgin otherwise than as a *moral* instrument of our common redemption.   Almighty God employs His rational creatures only as moral instruments ; much more, in that central act whereby He restored our race, and, in us, united His creatures with Himself.

I have indeed thought it an exaggeration, when some writers of books of devotion have delighted to dwell on the Incarnation, as though our redemption depended upon the " fiat " of Mary.   For, although God,—in conformity with that His wondrous condescension, whereby He reverences (if I may so speak) the free will with which He has endowed us, and will not force our will—would not accomplish the Incarnation without the free will of His creature, yet, of course, there was nothing really in suspense.   Had He indeed, amid the manifold failures which He has allowed in His work of grace, willed to allow this scope also to free-will, that it should reject the privilege of being Theotokos, and so have offered it to one who would not accept it, the Incarnation might have been delayed for a while; it could not have failed.   But He did not so will.   He, in all eternity, we both believe, foreordained her who was to be Theotokos, Genitrix Dei, the Mother of God.   He, in time, created her; He endowed her with all those qualities, with which it was fitting that *she* should be endowed, in whom, " when Thou tookest upon Thee to deliver man, Thou didst not abhor the Virgin's womb."

It was indeed, in my young days, a startling thought, when it first flashed upon me, that it must be true, that one, of our nature, which is the last and lowest of God's rational creation, was raised to a nearness to Almighty God, above all the choirs of Angels or Archangels, Dominions or Powers, above the Cherubim, who seem so near to God, or the Seraphim with their burning love, close to His Throne [1]. Yet it was self-evident, as soon as stated, that she, of whom He deigned to take His Human Flesh, was brought to a nearness to Himself above all created beings; that she stood single and alone, in all creation or all possible creations, in that, in her womb, He Who, in His Godhead, is Consubstantial with the Father, deigned, as to His Human Body, to become Consubstantial with her. In S. Proclus' eloquent language, which you quote in part:—

"Traverse in thought, O man, the creation, and see if there is any thing equal to or greater than the holy Virgin, who bare God. Compass the earth, survey the sea, search the air, track the heavens in thought; consider all the invisible powers, and see whether there is any other such marvel in all creation. For the heavens declare the glory of God; the angels serve with fear; the archangels worship with trembling; the Cherubim, not sustaining, quiver; the Seraphim, flying around, approach not; and trembling cry, 'Holy, Holy, Holy, Lord of hosts; heaven and earth are full of His praise.' The clouds in awe became the chariot of the Resurrection; Hell in fear cast forth the dead;—count over the miracles, and admire the victory of the Virgin; for Whom all creation hymned with fear

---

[1] I see this in a sermon which I preached twelve years ago.

and trembling, she alone inexplicably housed. Blessed for her sake are all women. For womankind is no longer under a curse; for the race has received That wherefrom it shall surpass the Angels in glory. Eve is healed[2]," &c.

Yet she too had her trials. Nor, when I spoke of her as "the *chosen vessel* of the Incarnation," did I by that term, which I took from Holy Scripture, mean any other than a *moral* instrument. Great must that trial have been, whereby she believed what was, according to the laws of nature, impossible, and on the ground of what with God only was possible, risked the reproach[3] among men, with which the poor Jews still blaspheme her Son and revile herself. She too was perfected through trial, and her belief in God was the first step in the undoing of the evil brought upon us through Eve's unbelief in God and belief in the evil one.

And, doubtless, any imaginations of ours must come short of the truth, if we would picture to ourselves the superhuman, engraced beauty of the soul of her whom God vouchsafed to create, so alone in His whole creation, whose being ever lay in His eternal Counsels, who must have been in His Divine Mind, when, in all eternity, He contemplated the way in which He should unite His rational creation to Himself, redeeming our fallen race; from whom He, Who should be God and Man, was to derive

[2] Orat. vi. in S. Deip. pp. 342, 343.
[3] Celsus has it (in Orig. c. Cels. i. 20), and Origen himself has more, yet agreeing with the Talmud. (Ib. n. 32.)

His Human Flesh, and in His Sacred Childhood to be subject to her.

And in regard to that solemn act, whereby she became the mother of our Lord, with one addition, which you hold, though, as self-evident, you do not mention it, your words express my belief also.——

"'They [the Fathers] declare that she co-operated in our salvation, not merely by the descent of the Holy Ghost upon her body, but by specific holy acts, the effect of the Holy Ghost upon her soul; that, as Eve forfeited privileges by sin, so Mary earned privileges by the fruits of grace; that, as Eve was a cause of ruin to all, Mary was a cause of salvation to all; that, as Eve made room for Adam's fall, so Mary made room for our Lord's reparation of it; and thus, whereas the free gift was not as the offence, but much greater, it follows that, as Eve co-operated in effecting a great evil, Mary co-operated in effecting a much greater good."

That one self-evident addition is, that the Blessed Virgin, by her faith in Him Whom, on and through her faith, she conceived and bore, gained her own redemption as well as ministered to ours. I say this, because so many writers, in their zeal to exalt her, speak of her co-operating in our salvation, of her longing for it, as if they forgot that she needed redemption as much as we; that the Blood, shed for the redemption of the world, was shed for hers also.

Further, my only difficulty in adopting any of the great titles which, as you say, the Fathers have given to the Blessed Virgin, is my impression that,

⁴ Letter, pp. 38, 39.

in the popular devotions, those titles which alone would come into question here, have received a different meaning from that in which the Fathers used them; and so that I should be speaking the language of other days which would be understood as it has been moulded by later usage. I should be using coin which had been re-stamped. The titles which the Fathers give to the Blessed Virgin fall, I think, into two classes,—those which shadow her perpetual Virginity before, in, and after, the Birth, and those which speak of her as conceiving and bearing God. Of the first there is no question, and they, I think, seldom occur in modern books of devotion. Those other great terms, great as they were, were, I believe, but weaker expressions of that one word, Theotokos. They were so many colours evolved out of that central light. She was the Mother of our Redeemer, and so from her, as the fountain of His Human Birth, came all which He did and was to us. Thus she was "the Mother of Life," because she was the Mother of Him Who is our Life; she was "the gate of Paradise," because she bore Him Who restored us to our lost Paradise; "the gate of Heaven," because He, born of her, "opened the kingdom of Heaven to all believers;" she was "the all-undefiled Mother of holiness," because "the Holy One born of her was called the Son of God;" the "light-clad Mother of light," because He Who indwelt her and was born of her, was "the true Light, which lighteth every ·man that cometh into the world." And in like way, that other title, "staff of orthodoxy," has, I suppose, reference to that truth, which we suppose to lie as the foundation of the blessing to St. Peter, that the belief in the Incarnation, in our Lord, God and Man, which he has confessed, would be the impregnable strength of the Church. In the well-known words of S. Fulgentius, " ' It is certain that almost all the errors of heretical pravity have hence manifoldly stolen in upon some, that the great mystery of godliness, which was manifested in the flesh, justified in the spirit, appeared to Angels, preached to the Gentiles, believed in the world, received up in glory, some do not believe as it is, or altogether disbelieve."

And so, as to all the language which you have quoted from S. Cyril, I adopt it all, but I think, from the context, that I adopt it rightly, as expressing in different ways, that one central truth, of which S. Cyril was God's chosen champion, the

---

' ad Tras. i. 4. This, I understand to be the meaning of the Antiphone, "cunctas bæreses sola interemisti in universo mundo" (Off. Parv. B. M.). I did not criticise the Antiphone (Eiren. p. 124), as one of my critics has objected to me. The use of the past, "thou slewest," shows that the reference is to a past act, such as was the Incarnation, which, rightly believed, is the destruction of all heresies. I only spoke historically of its application to her present personal power, an expectation which I found repeated very often in the "Pareri," that she, "the destroyer of all heresies," would, on the declaration of her Immaculate Conception, destroy them. "I would she did!" said a very eminent foreign Divine; "but there they are, rife everywhere."

Incarnation;—that He Whom she bare, was not Man only, as Nestorius blasphemed, but the Very and Eternal God.

" ' Hail, holy Mother of God, majestic treasure of the whole world, the lamp unquenchable, the crown of virginity, the staff of orthodoxy, the indissoluble temple and dwelling-place of the Incomprehensible, Mother and Virgin, through whom He is named in the Gospels ' Blessed, Who cometh in the Name of the Lord.' Hail, thou who containedst in thy holy Virgin womb the Uncontainable; through whom the Holy Trinity is glorified and worshipped throughout the whole world; through whom heaven is gladdened; through whom Angels and Arch-angels are rejoiced; through whom devils are put to flight; through whom the devil, tempting, fell from heaven; through whom the fallen creature is received up into heaven; through whom the whole creation, bound by the madness of idolatry, has come to the knowledge of the truth; through whom holy Baptism accrueth to believers; through whom, the oil of gladness; through whom throughout the world churches are founded; through whom the Gentiles are brought to re-pentance; and why say more? through whom the Only-Begotten Son of God shone to them who sat in darkness and in the shadow of death."

Or, to take a much later, and to me unknown, writer, to whom I have already been referred, as though he were Hesychius of Jerusalem [7];

"Every well-meaning tongue greets, as is meet, the Virgin and Deipara, and imitates, as he may, the Archangel Gabriel. And one, bids her Hail; another addresses her, ' The Lord is from thee,' on account of Him Who was born from her, and ap-

---

[6] Opp. T. v. P. ii. pp. 355, 356. I have followed in some slight things a text amended from MSS. collated by my son, which I mention lest certain critics should accuse me of falsifying.

[7] Bibl. Vet. Patr., Paris, 1624, ii. 421.

peared in flesh to the race of man, the Lord.   One calleth her
'Mother of light;' another, 'Star of Life;' another calleth her
'Throne of God;' another, 'temple greater than the heavens;'
another, 'seat not less than the seat over the Cherubim;' another
again, 'garden, unsown, fruitful, untilled;' 'vine of goodly
cluster, flourishing intact;' 'pure turtle;' 'dove undefiled;'
'cloud of rain conceiving incorruptibly;' case, whose Pearl
was brighter than the sun; mine, from which the Stone, which
filleth the whole earth, goeth forth, no one cutting it out;
ship, full of its Burden, needing no pilot; enriching treasure.
Others, in like way, call her 'closed lamp, enkindled from
itself;' 'ark, wider, longer, more glorious than that of Noah;'
that was an ark of living creatures, this of Life; that of perish-
able being, this of imperishable Life; that bare Noah, this, the
Maker of Noah; that had second and third stories, this, the
whole fulness of the Trinity, since the Spirit came upon her
and the Father overshadowed her and the Son, borne in the
womb, indwelt her.   For he saith, 'The Holy Ghost shall come
upon thee, and the power of the Highest shall overshadow
thee; therefore also the Holy Thing born of thee, shall be
called the Son of God.'   Thou seest how great and what the
dignity of the Virgin Deipara.   For the Only-Begotten Son of
God, the Maker of the world, was carried by her as a Child,
and re-formed Adam and sanctified Eve, and destroyed the
serpent, and opened Paradise, and kept safe the seal of the
womb," &c.

Hence too S. Proclus, or whoever he was, calls
her "[a] the holy shrine of Sinlessness; the sanctified
temple of God; the golden altar of whole burnt
offerings; the precious alabaster of the pure ointment;—the gate looking eastward, which, through
the entrance and exit of the king, was closed for
ever;—the field, blessed of the Father, wherein the
Treasure of the dispensation of the Lord lay;—the

----

[a] Orat. vi. pp. 378—380.   Letter, pp. 72, 128.

beautiful spouse of the Canticles which modestly
received in her chamber the heavenly Bridegroom ;
the tabernacle of the faithful, which received the
living Ark of the covenant; the tabernacle of
witness, wherefrom the true Jesus, being God,
went forth after His nine months' sojourn ;—the
undefiled fleece, placed on the threshing-floor of the
world, wherein the saving rain, coming down from
heaven, dried the whole earth from the boundless
tide of evils;—the fruitful olive, planted in the
house of God, from which the Holy Ghost, taking
the branch of the Body of the Lord, brought It to
the tempest-tost race of man, announcing the peace
from above; the flourishing paradise of immortality,
wherein the Tree of life, being planted, yieldeth to
all, without hindrance, the fruits of immortality ;
the heavenly sphere of the new creation, wherein
the ever-shining Sun of righteousness chased from
every soul all darkness of night." And in the same
reference, I doubt not, he goes on to call her, " the
boast of virgins; the gladness of mothers; the
establishment of the faithful; the diadem of the
Church; the stamp of orthodoxy; the seal of piety;
the rule of truth; the garment of continency; the
vest of virtue; the munition of righteousness; *the
dwelling-place of the Holy Trinity;* according to the
Gospel relation, ' the Holy Ghost shall come upon
thee, and the power of the Highest shall overshadow
thee; wherefore also the Holy Thing born of thee
shall be called the Son of God;' to Him be glory," &c.

And Theodotus has much the same combination of images[9] :—

" Hail, saving and spiritual fleece; hail, light-clad Mother of the unsetting Light; hail, all undefiled Mother of Holiness; hail, most pellucid fountain of the life-giving Stream; hail, new Mother in whom the new Birth was moulded; hail, inexplicable mother of Incomprehensibility; hail, according to Isaiah, new tome of the new covenant, whereof the faithful witnesses are angels and men; hail, alabaster of the sanctifying ointment; hail, creation formed to embrace the Creator; hail, tiniest vessel, containing the Uncontainable," &c.

Such, also, I doubt not from the context, is the meaning of that highest title of all, which I am glad to add from your last edition[1], out of Basil of Seleucia, " mediatrix between God and Man." For the whole context is a paraphrase on the angelic salutation in reference to the Incarnation, and the fruits whereof he speaks, are the direct fruits of the Cross of Christ. " [2]Hail, engraced one! Bright be thy countenance! For from thee shall be born the Joy of all, and shall make cease their ancient curse, by loosing the power of death, and bestowing on all the hope of resurrection. Hail, engraced one! unfading paradise of chastity, planted wherein the. Tree of life shall bear the

[9] In S. Amphiloch. p. 40.
[1] Letter, p. 72, ed. 3.
[2] Orat. 39, p. 215.

fruits of salvation, whence the four-mouthed fountain of the Gospels shall well forth to believers streams of mercies. Hail, engraced one! mediating to God and men, that the middle wall of enmity may be destroyed, and the things on earth may be united to the things in heaven[1]."

Now, in all this, I suppose that there is nothing which any Anglican who reflected on the term "Theotokos," would hesitate about (except that we are unaccustomed to mystical interpretations of Holy Scripture), if only we were certain that we should be understood to use them in what I believe to have been their original meaning, and not to imply that she was "the gate of Heaven," &c. by virtue of her present Intercession. Not but that, of course, she with all the inhabitants of heaven, and she more eminently than all, does pray for us. The intercession of the saints departed and at rest, for *us* who are still militant, is part of the doctrine of the Communion of Saints, and would be a necessary consequence of God-given love, even if it did not appear from Holy Scripture. The contrary is inconceivable. "Not only does the High Priest," says Origen[1], "pray with those who pray aright, but the angels also, who ' rejoice in heaven over one sinner that repenteth, more than over ninety and nine just persons who need no repentance,' and the souls of the saints who have fallen asleep before

[1] Eph. ii. 14, 15.
[1] De Orat. n. 11. T. i. pp. 213, 214.

us. For seeing that knowledge is made manifest to
those who are worthy in this present life through
a glass darkly, but is there revealed face to face, it
were absurd not to conceive the like of the other
virtues too, that, which has been prepared beforehand
in this life, being perfected then. But one of the
very chiefest virtues, according to the Divine word,
is love to our neighbour, which we must needs conceive must exist in a far higher degree in the saints
who have fallen asleep before us towards those who
are militant in this life, than in those who are yet
beset with human weakness, and who labour together
with those who are deficient. For not here only
is *that* implanted in those who have brotherly love,
' if one member suffer, all the members suffer with
it, and if one member be glorified, all the members
rejoice with it.' For it beseemeth *that* love too,
which is external to this present life, to say, ' the
care of all the churches. Who is weak, and I am
not weak? Who is offended, and I burn not?'
Since Christ too confesseth that He is weak in each
of the saints who is weak, and in prison also and a
stranger and a hungered and athirst."

Great indeed is the thought of that glorious company in all their different orders, whether, as the
blessed Angels, they never fell, or as the Saints,
with whom God has been filling up their broken
ranks, they, "secure of their own safety, are anxious
as to our salvation [5]." And, as the world grows old

[5] S. Cyprian de mortal. fin.

and the strife with unbelief becomes more deadly;. and perhaps the last conflict is drawing on, year by year the number of *those* increaseth who, beholding God, pray for us militant on earth. " They that be with us are more than they that are against us." But the truth of the intercession of the inhabitants of Heaven is, as you observe, distinct from their "invocation." Nay, it would, in itself, rather seem to supersede it. For we do not ask any one to do, what we are *quite sure*, that he does without our asking. The asking for the prayers of any, living or departed, implies, that those so asked would pray for us, *if* asked, in a way in which otherwise they would not.

The intercession, then, upon which the difficulty turns, is not that general intercession of all the inhabitants of that realm of love and holiness and vision of our God, for all of us, who are struggling here, but the special intercession for individuals obtained by direct prayer to them.

Nor, again, does it turn on the mere fact of asking for their prayers especially, in the same way in which we should ask one another's prayers, it being always understood, (in your Bishop Milner's words which I have already quoted[*],) "That, as the saints in Heaven are free from every stain of sin and imperfection, and are confirmed in grace and glory, so their prayers are far more efficacious for obtaining what they ask for,

---

[*] Eirenicon, pp. 100, 101.

than are the prayers of us imperfect and sinful mortals." If this had been all, I have expressed my conviction that the difficulty never would have arisen.

The difficulty arose, I believe, in the change of the meaning of the great terms which the Fathers used of the Blessed Virgin, looking on to the Incarnation, in that she was the Mother of our Redeemer, God-Man, and the transference of those terms to describe her present influence and power with Him, her Son. Both interpretations are allowable among you. I am *not* accusing. I only say, from what we wish to be exempt. I am thankful to see in " The Crown of Jesus," to which you referred me, expositions of the great titles which are concentrated in the Litany of Loretto, such as every Christian must receive.

" *Mother of Divine Grace*, because she is the parent of Him Who is the Source and Author of all grace; *Seat of Wisdom*, as being replenished with this heavenly virtue, because she is the Mother of Him Who is Wisdom itself; *Cause of our Joy*, as being the instrument of that great blessing, which is the source of all our Christian consolations; *Tower of Ivory*, as being remarkable for the purity of innocence: ivory, by its whiteness, being the emblem of delicacy, whence that saying in the Canticles, ' Thy neck is as a tower of ivory;' *Ark of the Covenant*, as being the parent of Him, Who is the Mediator of the new Covenant; *Gate of Heaven*, as being, again, Mother of Him, Who has opened to us the gate of everlasting happiness ; *Morning Star*, as being the harbinger of that bright Day which has brought immortality to light '."

' pp. 653, 654.

Even with these explanations, there still, indeed, remain the difficulties of some titles, which do not occur in the Fathers, and which one would have expected rather to be given to our Lord ; *Health of the weak, Refuge of sinners, Comforter of the afflicted, Help of Christians.* For when a title is given to any one, we can hardly help thinking that it is meant "*par excellence*" to belong to that being to whom it is given ; that it must, at least, be his or her's, in some special way in which it can belong to no one else. Nothing short of this can justify the title. Even if, in some higher sense, it could belong to some one else, there must be some special way in which it must be believed to belong to that person ; else it would not be given at all. This title, "Refuge of sinners," is, accordingly, the text on which S. Liguori puts together the passages of middle-age writers, or such as are attributed wrongly to the Fathers, which speak of her as "*the* Hope of Sinners." Such sinners seem to be spoken of as out of the reach of Jesus, or hopeless of His help, and Mary seems to be held out to them as *the* way by which they are to approach to Jesus [a].

---

[a] See ab. pp. 9, 10. "In the ancient cities of refuge, all criminals did not find refuge ; but under the patronage of Mary, all sinners find protection, no matter what crimes they may have committed ; it is enough for them to take refuge under her mantle. 'I,' says St. John Damascene in the name of our queen, 'am the city of refuge of all who flee to me' (Or.

And with this fall in those explanations of the other titles, which are, I think, more common, as

2 de dorm. [said of the tomb, said not to be his]). It is enough to have recourse to Mary; for him who shall have the happiness to enter this city, it will not be necessary to speak in order to be saved. 'Assemble yourselves, and let us enter into the fenced city, and let us be silent there' (Jer. viii. 14). This fenced city is, according to B. Albertus Magnus, the Holy Virgin fortified in grace and glory. 'And let us be silent there,' i. e. says the gloss, 'because we do not dare to deprecate the Lord, whom we have offended, let her deprecate and ask.' Hence a devout author (Ben. Fernandez in Gen. iii.) exhorts all sinners to take shelter under the protection of Mary; 'Flee, O Adam, O Eve, flee ye their children, within the bosom of the Mother, Mary. She is the city of refuge, the only hope of sinners!' [S. Liguori adds, "after Jesus."] Thus she is called by St. Augustine, 'Only hope of sinners,' Serm. 18 de Sanct. [not his, see Bened. on T. v. Serm. 194 App.] Hence S. Ephrem says to Mary, 'Thou art the only advocate of sinners, and of those bereft of all succour.' Hence he salutes her, 'Hail, refuge and hospice of sinners, to whom namely sinners can fly,' de laud. V. [not his]. Richard of St. Lawrence also says, 'The Lord complained, before Mary [was born], "There is no one who riseth up and withholds Me" (Ezek. xxii.), until Mary was found, who held Him until He was softened' (Ric. i. 2, de laud. Virg.). The Blessed Virgin herself revealed to S. Brigit that 'there is not a sinner so cast off by God, who, if he invoke me, will not return to God.' Rev. i. 6 [wrong reference. "How much soever a man sins, if with his whole heart and true amendment he return to me [the Blessed Virgin], I am prepared forthwith to receive the penitent. Nor do I consider how much he have sinned, but with what intention and will he returns." Rev. ii. 23]. 'The world,' says the devout Blosius, 'has not so execrable a sinner that she should abominate him and repel him from her, and, if he pray for her help, not be able, know and will, to reconcile him to her most beloved Son' (Blos. de dictis PP. c. 5).

in the book which you also name, "The Key of Heaven." "*Tower of ivory*, for in the Canticles thou art that tower of ivory whereunto the fair neck of the Bride is likened; for *through thee all graces pass from Christ the Head unto the Church His Body: Gate of heaven*, since through thee salvation came into the world, and *none can enter into heaven but by thee*[1]."

This change in the meaning of titles, given by the Fathers, occasions devotions which (you will agree with me) the Fathers knew not, and furnishes their doctrinal basis. For when, instead of its being said, that "God will*ed* that we should have all through Mary," i. e. through the Incarnation, it came to be thought that "God will*eth* that we should have all through her," or that "through her," i. e., through her intercession, "God willeth that all graces should pass from Christ the Head unto the Church His Body," *that* doctrine involved the whole system of teaching as to the office of the B. V., as our access to our Redeemer, from which we wish to be exempt. For, setting aside cases of inculpable ignorance, then, if this were true, any one who should neglect to ask *her*, through

---

Justly then S. John Damascene salutes thee, 'Hail, hope of the hopeless!' S. Lawrence Justinian, 'Hope of criminals;' S. Ephrem, 'Safest harbour of the shipwrecked.' The same saint goes so far as to call thee the 'Protectress of those under sentence of damnation,'" &c. S. Lig. Gl. of M. iii. 2.

[1] P. 253.

whom God willed all His graces to come to His
creatures, would be shewing contempt to the
known will of God, and incurring the forfeiture of
all the graces necessary to his salvation. All the
strong language which I extracted from writers
quoted by S. Liguori in support of his thesis, "on
the *necessity* of invoking the intercession of Mary [2],"
"Mary is our life, because she obtains for us the
pardon of our sins[3];" "Mary is our life, because
she obtains for us the gift of perseverance[4];"
"Mary is the hope of all[5];" "Mary is the hope of
sinners[6];" "Mary is the peacemaker of sinners
with God[7]," are but applications of this one principle. Even Suarez goes beyond the Council of
Trent. "[8] The Church holds that the intercession
and prayer of the Virgin are useful and *necessary*
to her above all others [saints]; the Blessed Virgin
therefore is to be prayed by us above all." For
the Council of Trent only says that it is useful;
Suarez says, that "she *is* to be prayed to," because
her special intercession (for of this he is speaking), such intercession as is to be gained by prayer
to her, is *necessary*. And conversely, I suppose,
we may infer that S. Augustine and other Fathers
did not hold that there was any such necessity,
since, as you observe, no prayer to the Blessed

---

[2] C. v. s. 1. [3] C. ii. s. 1. [4] Ib. s. 2.
[5] C. iii. s. 1. [6] Ib. s. 2. [7] C. vi. s. 3.
[8] In P. iii. q. 37, disp. 23. s. 3. fin., the passage which I took
from S. Liguori.

Virgin is to be found in the voluminous works of St. Augustine.

As I said, I do not "accuse." I have never had any thought that the fact of your having such prayers would be " * compromising to those who propose entering into communion with" you. I was only thinking of ourselves, and, as a Priest, of our people, and I only wish that, in case of reunion, we should still be allowed to worship, as I believe that they did, who lived in the times nearest to our Lord and His Apostles.

The difference, then, does not relate to the greatness of the sanctification which we may well believe that God bestowed upon *her*, whom He willed to bring into so near a relation to Himself; nor to the singular eminence to which He willed thereby to raise her, alone in His whole creation; nor to the fact, that she, with all the saints in glory, intercedes for us; nor to its being permissible, in the way explained by your Bp. Milner above, to ask for her prayers as we ask for the prayers of other our fellow-creatures, only, of course, that she is far more exalted and acceptable to God; but to this, whether God has constituted her in such sort *the* Mediatrix with Him our Mediator, that as we have no approach to God, except through Jesus, so our approach to Jesus must be through her; or, again, as all grace comes to us through Jesus Alone and

---

* Letter, p. 155, said of seeking to enter into communion with the Greek Church.

for His merits, so all grace is transmitted from
Him through her; or whether, again, He have
delegated her as the dispensatrix of His graces, (as
the pictures of the Immaculate Conception represent her no longer, as in the representations of the
Catacombs, holding up her hands to God, but rain-
ing down graces upon us;) or whether she is "the
gate of Heaven" in such sort, that "no one can
enter heaven, unless he pass through Mary as
through a door[1];" or again, whether she be "the
hope of sinners," so that the first step for returning sinners is to betake themselves to her, as
their approach to Jesus; or whether "she restrains
her Son, that He may not inflict chastisement, and
saves sinners[2]."

It is my fear, that the system of extreme devotion to the B. V. is in the ascendancy.

It seems to me, and I am told, that there is a strong

---

[1] S. Bonav. in S. Lig. Gl. of M. v. i. p. 237.

[2] Gl. of M. c. iii. s. 2., quoting from S. Bonaventura, "She
takes hold of her Son, that He may not strike sinners." This
is set before the eyes in the picture of Rubens at Antwerp, in
which our Lord is represented as armed with lightning to dis-
charge it on the world for its wickedness (denoted by the serpent twined around it), and the Blessed Virgin as holding His
hand, and shewing her breasts, so shewing her claim, as His
Mother, to intercede with Him. S. Liguori, too, quotes (iii. 1.
p. 180.) from S. Bonaventura: "If my Redeemer cast me off
for my sins, I will throw myself at the feet of His mother, and
stay there, that she may obtain pardon for me. For *she* (ipsa)
knows not, how not to have mercy, and never knew, how not
to satisfy the miserable. And therefore, out of compassion,
she will incline her Son to pardon me."

tide setting in among you to extreme Marian devotions (I trust that the term is not offensive, since Bishops speak of Spain at least as "a Marian kingdom"). The tendency seemed and seems to me to be, to make matters to be "de fide," which have been taught so long undisputed, because they have been borne with patiently. And yet I was joyed to find some of your mind among foreign ecclesiastics. For while a Belgian divine of eminence defended the common saying, "If your Father [God] is angry with you, to whom should you go but to your Mother [Mary]?" as the voice of human nature, another very eminent Theologian condemned such language with uplifted hands. While one eminent French Bishop (not one of those, of whom the French papers reported, that they allowed me interviews) thought me gravely wrong in not believing that all graces came through Mary, an eminent Theologian quoted to me the remarkable (I fear antiquated) French proverb (to be found, he told me, in collections of French proverbs), "It is better to go to God than to all the saints." It appears to me that you are, on this and other points, in an unfixed state, analogous to ours; that God is leading you too somewhere, as all things among us are manifestly setting in two directions, and minds are rising to full Catholic belief (I mean, of course, primitive faith), or sinking to the abyss. Twenty or thirty years will, I suppose, see these, the two chief classes in England; twenty or thirty

years will, I suppose, determine whether very much
which is now matter of opinion among you, will be
erected into dogma, or whether there will be a
more pronounced body of Roman Catholics, who
will repress those excesses.   Oakeley anticipates
the former as to the Marian system.   I trust that
your voice, which once blew a deep trumpet-call
among us, will again occasion others also to speak,
who love truth and soberness.   I hope that I see
in your words and your disclaimers a dawn of a
hope of restored union, when yours shall not be a
single voice, and those, who think as you do, shall
by God's help prevail.   What we want is to have
it made clear by authority, in some way which God
the Holy Ghost may suggest, that these non-primi-
tive doctrines are not " de fide" or proximate to
faith, and are not to be required of any.   It has been
promised to certain individuals, on joining the
Roman communion, that it should not be required
of them to invoke the Blessed Virgin; one, some
twenty years ago, was allowed to say the Litany of
Jesus instead of the Litany of Loretto.   Why should
not what has been allowed to individuals be allowed
to a nation, or rather to many nations. (for such the
English are)?   Why should we not, in case of re-
union, be allowed to pray as the Fathers of the
Church and the holy army of martyrs prayed ?

3. The interpretation of Holy Scripture being
very seldom matter of faith, it will create no jar,
that I cannot interpret, as you do, the vision in the

Apocalypse of the woman clothed with the sun.
And this on the ground which, I suppose, determined the ancient interpreters to explain it of the
Church, that, after the " Child Who was to rule all
nations with a rod of iron, was caught up unto
God and to His throne," " the woman fled into the
wilderness, where she hath a place prepared of
God." The impossibility of explaining this as to
the Blessed Virgin has determined a modern Roman
Catholic interpreter too to adhere to the ancient
interpretation as the literal sense, and hold the
application to the Blessed Virgin to be nothing
more than allusive. But doctrine is only derived
from the literal sense. Here, however, nothing is
at issue, since the B. V. was undoubtedly more than
arrayed in the sun, when " the Sun of righteousness" dwelt in her.

4. The interpretation of the passage, upon which
Roman Catholics now generally rest the title of the
Blessed Virgin, " our mother," is, of course, much
graver. For this introduces a new personal relation
of the Blessed Virgin to us, not indirectly through
our Lord, but directly as given to her by Him. It
is a great change. In the two ancient passages,
where alone, as I believe, she is spoken of as hypo-
thetically the mother of any Christian, or mother
of Christians, it is because we are " members of
Christ [3]." Our relation to Christ is immediate;

[3] The two passages of which I know, are, the one of Origen,
the other S. Augustine's. Origen (in Joann. i. 6. p. 6. ed. de la

she is the Mother of Him our Head, of Whom we
have been made the members. She has not, in

Rue) is speaking of the greatness of St. John's Gospel, and
that no one could understand it, who was not himself another
St. John, and by the indwelling of Christ, a "Jesus from Jesus."
Having spoken of the other Evangelists as having reserved
something for St. John, he says, "We must venture to say,
that the Gospels are the first-fruits of all Scriptures, and that
that according to John is the first-fruits of the Gospels, whose
mind no one can gain, unless he lie upon the breast of Jesus,
and receives from Jesus, Mary becoming *his* mother also. Such
must one become who would be another John, so that like
John he might be shown to be a Jesus from Jesus. For if
there was, according to those who think soundly in regard to
her, no other son of Mary but Jesus, and Jesus says to His
mother, 'Behold thy son,' and not, 'Behold this too is thy son,'
He says as much as, 'This is Jesus whom thou barest.' For
every one who is perfected, it is no longer he who liveth, but
Christ liveth in him, and since Christ liveth in him, He saith
of him to Mary, 'See thy son, Christ.'" It is plain that Origen's
thought was that, to understand St. John, one must be another
St. John; that those who had the mind of Christ, and were
indwelt by Him, were, as some fathers boldly say, "Christs"
(Χριστοί), and were the sons of Mary, because members of
Him Who was the Son of Mary. S. Augustine's meaning is
plainly the same. He is consoling those who had given themselves to the virgin life, that they could not be also mothers,
and says that virgins too are spiritually mothers of Christ.
"That birth from the one holy Virgin is the glory of all holy
virgins. They too, with Mary, are mothers of Christ, if they
do the will of His Father. For hence was Mary too, in a
more praiseworthy and blessed way, Mother of Christ, according to this saying above-mentioned, 'Whosoever doeth the
will of My Father Which is in heaven, the same is My brother
and sister and mother.' All these kinships He forms for
Himself spiritually in the people which He has redeemed; for
brothers and sisters He hath holy men and holy women, since

this aspect, been assigned to men as a Mother to
bring them to Christ by her intercessions; her only

they are co-heirs with Him in the heavenly inheritance. His
mother is the whole Church, because she bears His members,
that is, His faithful through the grace of God. Also every
pious soul is His mother, doing the will of His Father in most
prolific charity, in those of whom it travaileth until He be
formed in them. Mary, then, doing the will of God, is corporally only mother of Christ, but spiritually both sister and
mother; and thereby that one woman is not only in spirit, but
also in body, both mother and virgin. And, indeed, mother in
spirit, not of our Head, of Whom rather she was spiritually
born, because all those who believed in Him, of whom she too
was one, are rightly called children of the Bridegroom; but
mother of His members, which we are, because she co-operated
by love that faithful should be born in the Church, who are
members of that Head, but, in the body, the Mother of the
Head Himself. For need was, that our Head, on account of
the wondrous miracle, should according to the flesh be born
of a virgin, that He might signify that, according to the spirit,
His members should be born of the Virgin Church. Mary
then alone is, in spirit and body, mother and virgin, and mother
of Christ and virgin of Christ. But the Church, which in the
saints shall possess the kingdom of God, is, in spirit, the whole
of her, mother of Christ; the whole of her, virgin of Christ;
but in the body, not the whole of her, but in some [members]
virgin of Christ, in others, mothers, but not of Christ" [viz. of
children who "are not born Christians of their flesh, but
become such"], [de sancta virginit. c. 5, 6]. It is plain, from
S. Augustine's speaking in past time, "she co-operated," that
he is speaking of the act of the Blessed Virgin in the Incarnation, by which she, through engraced love, became corporally
Mother of Him, of whom we, by grace and spiritually, are
members. Directly, he speaks of the Church as our Mother;
ultimately, she, whose virgin birth typified, he said, the virgin
maternity of the Church, is our mother, because mother of Him,
in Whom by grace we are.

relation to us is, in that we are already Christ's. It is remarkable, moreover, that no one of the early expositors of Scripture, as Origen, S. Chrysostom, S. Augustine, S. Cyril of Alexandria, (even such of them as explain our Lord's words to St. John and to His mother in the way of homilies,) or of those who comment on our Lord's words, although not on the Gospel, S. Hilary [4], S. Ambrose [5], or S. Siricius [6] (or Damasus); or Tertullian [7], who alludes to them, interprets the words, "Behold thy Son," "Behold thy Mother," of any relation of the Blessed Virgin, except that personal relation which is literally contained in the words, between the beloved disciple and herself. And this is the more remarkable in S. Ambrose, because he does in one place give a mystical interpretation of the words; yet it relates to the Church, not to the Blessed Virgin [8]. Some of these passages are but allusions; yet no one, I think,

[4] In S. Matt. c. i. pp. 611, 612.

[5] In S. Luc. ii. 4. vii. 5. x. 131. De instit. virg. vii. 47. Ep. 63. Eccl. Vere. n. i. 109. De obit. Valent. n. 39.

[6] Epist. ad Anys. et Epp. Illyr. Concil. T. ii. p. 1230. ed. Col.

[7] de Præscr. c. 22.

[8] "Thou sayest, How can I be a son of thunder? Thou canst, if thou recline, not on the earth, but on the breast of Christ. Thou canst be a son of thunder, if earthly things move thee not, but thou rather, by the power of thy mind, shatter the things of earth. Let the earth stand in awe of thee, not capture thee; let the flesh feel the power of thy mind, be shaken and subdued. Thou wilt be a son of thunder, if thou art a son of the Church. Let Christ say to thee from the Cross of suffering, 'Behold thy

can be otherwise than morally convinced that a modern Roman writer would have introduced the doctrine; nor can I myself think otherwise than that they did not introduce it because they were unacquainted with the doctrine, that they did not look upon St. John as a type of Christians, or think of any thing beyond the bare literal meaning. And yet S. Cyril, as you have observed, gave her the most exalted titles.

Yet those titles point to and culminate in our Lord; they are not reflected back, so as to have any relation directly to us. She was the Mother of Him Who is all in all to us; she has no personal office to us. So here. Her holy Motherhood terminates in Him: our relation is to Him Whom she bare, God-Man, our Redeemer, not to herself. And, although Roman Catholics now rest the relation chiefly on our Lord's words to St. John, and any other explanation of those words seems to them unnatural, not only is this interpretation not, I believe, found in antiquity, but in later times too the relation was rested equally on other mystical interpretations, in which few would probably now find it. Thus, on the same mis-interpretation which the Socinians, &c., adopt, that the words "she conceived her first-born son," not only declared our Lord's relation to her, but implied that she had other sons, it was

mother.' Let Him say to the Church, too, 'Behold thy son;' for then thou beginnest to be a son of the Church, when thou beholdest Christ conquer upon the cross." In S. Luc. vii. 5.

D +—

argued that, since piety forbade to think that she had other sons after the flesh, it must mean that she had spiritual sons [9]. Another, somehow, derived the doctrine from the words, "I am the Mother of fair love [1];" or from those in the Psalm, "Save the son of Thy handmaid [2]," as if David thereby called himself the son of Mary. On the other hand, I cannot think that, with any belief like that expressed by the name now, S. Athanasius could have called Mary "our sister." " [3] Nay, no phantasy is our salvation, nor of the body only; but of the whole man, soul and body in truth, was our salvation wrought in the Word Himself. Human, then, by nature, was That which was from Mary, according to the Sacred Scriptures, and true was the Body of the Lord. True it was, since it was the same with ours. For Mary was our sister, seeing also that we are all from Adam." I cannot but think that some other term or form of expression would have been used.

5. Your statement [4] about the doctrine of the Immaculate Conception opens a gleam of hope where the clouds seemed thickest before. It shews that the form of the doctrine, which brings it most proximately in connexion with that of the transmission

[9] Anonymous author in S. Lig. Glor. of M. i. pp. 94, 95; also S. Gertrude, as a "revelation." Ib.

[1] Ecclus. xxiv. 14. Ib. p. 98.   [2] Ps. lxxxv. 16.

[3] Ep. ad Epict. n. 7. Opp. i. 906. Ben.

[4] Letter, p. 52.

of original sin, is not declared to be de fide. Your
rejection of any such belief as, that the Blessed
Virgin did not die in Adam, that she did not come
under the penalty of the fall, that she was conceived in some way inconsistent with the verse in
the *Miserere* Psalm[5], if confirmed by authority,
would remove difficulties as to doctrine, which
the decree suggested to the Greeks as well as to
ourselves. Indeed, subsequently to the publication
of the Eirenicon, Mgr. Dupanloup had the goodness to explain to me his own belief, which is the
same as yours, and in explanation of which he quotes
the statement of Benedict XIV.:—

"[6] Conception may be taken in two ways: for it is either
active, wherein the parents of the B. V., coming together, supplied what related to the formation, organisation, and disposition of her body for receiving the rational soul, to be infused
therein by God, or it is *passive*, when the rational soul is united
with the body. For this infusion and union with the body is
commonly called the *passive* Conception, which itself takes place
at that very instant in which the rational soul is united with
the body, consisting of all its members and its organs[7]."

---

[5] Ps. li. 5.

[6] de festiv. D. N. J. C., B. M. V., et quorund. Sanctt. c. xv.

[7] I gave this same explanation in the Eirenicon, p. 146. A
critic (who reads awry all which I write) imputes my so doing
to my "own very imperfect acquaintance with the common
terms and distinctions of divines upon matters upon which I
undertake to write" (Month, Dec. 1865, p. 630). The same
critic, in the same page, imputes to me a grotesque ignorance
of the meaning of the words, "I believe one Catholic and
Apostolic Church," because I said, that in the words which
confess to God her being, I confessed also my belief in her
authority and my implicit submission to her teaching.

His own explanation is,

"'The Imm. Conc., in the mother of the Saviour, is the exemption from the original stain at the moment when the soul was created and united with her body, i. e. the dispensation, by Divine favour, for that blessed soul, of that mysterious solidarity, whereby we all come into existence, deprived of sanctifying grace, righteousness, primæval purity, and deprived of the friendship of God. We say that it was not thus with Mary. At the moment that her beautiful soul was united to the body, prepared naturally in her mother's womb to receive it, this soul, by the bounty of God, was supernaturally, even then, wholly pure, adorned with sanctifying grace, embellished (as the first man was formerly in the state of innocence, and even in a degree more excellent) with the interior gifts of righteousness and original holiness, exempt from all germ of concupiscence, as of the sin itself which is its source, and finally as the well-beloved daughter of Heaven, wherewith she was one day to be united by relations so amazing and so close."

The gift of sanctifying grace, at the first moment of existence, would be different in degree only, not in kind[1], from what Holy Scripture states in regard to Jeremiah, and St. John the Baptist. The sanctification of Jeremiah was in his mother's womb[2]. Of St. John Baptist the angel seems to prophesy that he should be sanctified, "then and thenceforward[3]." The sanctification, attributed to the Blessed Virgin under the term "Immaculate

---

[ ] Mandement, 1855, p. 3.

[1] This is not my statement only, but that of Mgr. Dupanloup.

[ ] Jer. i. 5.

[ ] St. Luke i. 15. Meyer (as cited by Alford on St. Luke) thinks that the sanctification in his mother's womb lies in the words ἔτι ἐκ κοιλίας μ. α.

Conception," would, on this explanation, be only
anterior in time; for, since Jeremiah and St. John
Baptist came into the world already sanctified,
they too were born free from the stain of original
sin.

Thus far there was no difficulty. It was natural
to believe that what Holy Scripture relates to
have been granted to Jeremiah and St. John Baptist was (even though not related) granted to *her*
whom our Lord willed to bring into so near a relation to Himself. The difficulty, as you know, arose
as to the doctrine of the transmission of original
sin, and related both to the (so-called) "active"
and "passive" "conception." S. Bernard states
both, while himself maintaining the sanctification
in her mother's womb.

"' She could not be holy before she was; since, before she
was conceived, she was not. Or did perchance holiness mingle
itself with the conception itself, so that she should be at once
sanctified and conceived? Neither will reason admit this.
For how could there be holiness without the hallowing Spirit?
or was the Holy Spirit associated with sin? or how was there
not sin, where concupiscence was not absent? unless some one
said, that she was conceived of the Holy Ghost and not of man;
but this hath hitherto been unheard of. It remains, that she be
believed to have received sanctification while already existing

---

* Ep. 174 ad Canon. Lugd. A story was circulated as to
S. Bernard, "that he retracted that opinion, at least after his
death; whence it is said that he appeared to a certain monk
after death with a spot on his breast, on account of the things
which he had said as to the Conception of the glorious Virgin."
Capreolus in Sent. 3. 3 q. 1. art. 1. fin.

in the womb, which, excluding sin, made her nativity holy, but not her conception also. Wherefore, although to some, though few, of the human race, it has been granted to be born with holiness, yet to be conceived so too has not been granted, in order that the prerogative of a holy Conception might be reserved for One Who should sanctify all, and, coming Alone without sin, should purge away sins. The Lord Jesus, then, Alone was conceived by the Holy Ghost, because He Alone was Holy, even before His Conception. Him excepted, *that* regards all who are born of Adam, which one humbly and truly said of himself, ' I was conceived in wickedness, and in sin did my mother conceive me. ' "

S. Bernard does not further express, in what way the defect, entailed upon the body through concupiscence, involved the soul.

Probably no explanation can be satisfactory. Möhler states the difficulties of each in turn, and says, on the authority of Payva ab Andrada, a Portuguese theologian present at the Council of Trent, that it purposely abstained from defining wherein original sin consisted [5], acting, Pallavicini adds, on the advice of the legates, " not to decide upon the nature of original sin, since divines were of different opinions thereon, Scripture and Tradition giving no results."

The Schoolmen indeed mostly seem to lay down, that there could have been no sanctification before animation, and, as they state it, it is self-evident. Thus Biel says [6]:

"The first conclusion, in which all agree, (is,) The Virgin

Symbolik, i. 2. p. 57.   [6] 3. 3 q. 1. art. 1.

Mary, before the second conception, whereby she was animated in her mother's womb, was not sanctified by grace. This is obvious, because that sanctification takes place through the infusion of grace, of which the intellectual soul alone is capable; therefore, where it existed not, sanctifying grace could not be; but, before the second conception, the soul was not, since it is created by infusing; therefore, &c. Also, to be sanctified pre-supposes being; whence what is not is not sanctified; but, before the second conception or animating of the Virgin, the Virgin was not; therefore she was not sanctified."

For, of course, as soon as it is laid down that sanctification is to be taken in the sense of "the infusion of grace," it is self-evident that such sanctification can take place only in the soul. We are here on grounds purely abstract. And, supposing (as the Schoolmen thought) that the body does ever exist without the soul, I see no reason why it should not have been sanctified then. For since the body, which has once been the temple of the Holy Ghost, even when resolved into its dust, is, in its dust, still holy, (as the common reverence of Christians thinks, not of Elisha's bones only, when the dead man woke to life at their touch, nor of the true remains of martyrs only, but, in their degree, as to the dust of those really asleep in Christ,) so I do not see any ground in the nature of things, why it should not have been sanctified before it received the soul. Durandus a S. Porciano, on the theory that "[1] by Adam's fall a destructive infectious quality worked its way into the human body, and,

' Möhler, l. c.

being propagated by generation, encompassed the soul at the moment of its union with the body, drew it down to itself, and communicated to it its own disorder," held it *possible* that the B. V. should " not have been conceived in original sin, but that at one and the same time she received her soul and grace was given her."

" * —— Although original sin is *formaliter* only in the soul, yet in the flesh there is a certain diseased quality or infection, by reason whereof original sin is contracted from the conjunction of the soul with the flesh having this diseased quality. Since then that diseased quality is different from the flesh itself, a given mass of flesh might be preserved by Divine power from being infected, or, if infected, might be cleansed before the infusion of the soul, so that, although on the part of the generator it was in itself flesh unclean and diseased, yet, by Divine virtue cleansing, it was made immaculate and clean, so that, from the union of the soul therewith, original sin should not be contracted by the soul."

The question of the immaculateness of the " active conception" was, of course, different from this. It was allowed that the act in itself might be pleasing to God, when done purely to fulfil the will of God, as in the case of Abraham. But they distinguished between " the act of the person, in which the will was the moving cause, and the act of nature, in which nature was the moving cause; in regard to the will, the act proceeded from charity; in regard to nature, from the disorderedness of concupiscence. But conception followed from nature, not from the

* In sent. 3. 8 q. 1.

will;" and therefore, following S. Bernard, they held that, "although on one side the act might be meritorious, the conception itself, following thereon, would not be, and so neither was there sanctification in conception [9]."

Yet, although this might be the thoughtful opinion, yet the popular mind would not enter into these distinctions. It was natural to understand by the "Immaculate Conception" conception in its widest sense. It seemed pious, too, to think that, when the will was holy, all which followed on that will was holy too. And, accordingly, in the "Revelations of S. Brigit," the exemption of the B. V. from original sin was connected with the propriety of the marital union of her parents. The Blessed Virgin is introduced as saying [1]:

" It is the truth, that I was conceived without original sin, because as my Son and I never sinned, so no marriage was ever more proper [nullum conjugium honestius] than that from which I proceeded."

Such conception of her body is also spoken of as the ground of the Festival of the Immaculate Conception [2];

" Wherefore also it would be very fitting and worthy, that that day should be held by all in great reverence, on which that matter was conceived and collected in the womb of Anna, from

---

[9] From Alex. Ales, P. 3. q. 9. memb. 2. art. 2.
[1] Revel. S. Brigit. vi. c. 49.
[2] Sermo Angel. B. Brigittæ, fin. p. 661.

which the blessed body of the Mother of God was to be formed,
which ["matter," "quam,"] God Himself and all His Angels
loved exceedingly in so great charity."

The Feast of the Nativity being Sept. 8, the day
of the Feast of the Immaculate Conception, Dec. 8,
was that day of which S. Brigit speaks.

In the first prayer, said to have been " [3] revealed
by God to the Bl. Brigit," in which " the glorious
Virgin is devoutly and beautifully praised for her
sacred Conception, &c." the conception spoken of
is, *not* the infusion of the soul but, the conception
of the body through her parents.

" ' Glory be to thee, my Lady, Virgin Mary, Mother of God,
who, by that same Angel by whom Christ was announced to
thee, wert announced to thy father and mother, and wert conceived and born of their most honourable marriage."

Of course, no believer would deny, on abstract
grounds, that God could miraculously have made
the " active conception" also absolutely holy, had
He so willed.   We only want the evidence, that He
has revealed that He did so.   But, unless some
authoritative explanation is given by the Roman
Church, it seems to me inevitable that under the
term " Immaculate Conception," which is declared
to be " of faith," the conception of the body of the

---

[3] Ib. p. 674.

[4] Ib. p. 764.   A like stress on the propriety [honestas] of
the marriage is laid in the Sermo Angel. c. 10. Ib. p. 661 ;
the absence of concupiscence is dwelt upon in Revel. i. 9. Ib.
p. 13.   At the close of Rev. L. v. God the Father is introduced,
saying, " She was conceived without sin, that My Son might be
conceived of her without sin."   p. 409.

Blessed Virgin will be included. Some Bishops, who were consulted about making " the Immaculate Conception" an article of faith, understood by the term " the conception of the body." Thus Alexander, Abp. of Urbino, said [s],

"Nay, although almost all theologians, distributing Conception into *active* and *passive*, contend that the *passive* only, and not the *active*, was immaculate in the B. V. yet, in the sense of the Church, I should believe either that this distinction was not really present, or that the *active* also was held to be immaculate. For this seemeth to be opposed neither to reason nor Scripture, and is supported also with some appearance of truth out of the revelations of S. Brigit, from which the Conception of the B. V. is inferred to have been therefore immaculate, because there was no marriage more decorous than that from which she proceeded."

This is, moreover, what, in common language, is meant by " conception," not in our own only but in other tongues. This is impressed upon our people by the language of Holy Scripture, in which the word " conceived" is uniformly used of what took place in the mother, as the result of the coming together of the parents [t]. The most probable original meaning of the Hebrew word, used in Holy

[s] Pareri, &c., iii. 43. Among the Schoolmen I see that Capreolus says, " There is a twofold inquiry as to this question [of the Immaculate Conception], because she had two sanctifications. The first inquiry is about the sanctification of the B. V. in the womb, while she was being conceived passively. The second, of the sanctification, while she was being conceived actively, of which sanctification I much doubt." In Sent. 3. 3. q. 1. art. 1. fin.

[t] e. g. Gen. iv. 1. 17. xvi. 4, &c.

Scripture, points to an act in which there was some, even if involuntary, human passion '. Holy Scripture speaks of conception without the distinctions of the schools. The distinction also which used to be made, whereby the reception of the rudiments of the body was separated by some long interval from the infusion of the soul, is now abandoned. It was part of the Aristotelian physics, when " the quickening," i. e. the moment when the child had strength to move in its mother's womb, was thought to be the real commencement of the animate existence of the human being, i. e. of the infusion of the soul ². This *date* of what was called " the passive conception" having been tacitly abandoned, it is probable that the distinction *of time* will be abandoned too. There is, of course, *a* distinction, as wide as heaven and earth. For the conception of the human body is through that which each parent supplieth; the infusion of the soul is from God. But the ground for detaching the two acts in time being gone, the wide distinction which used to be made formerly is gone too. Scripture says nothing; and, amid its silence, reason says nothing, physics nothing. There is an impenetrable veil over the

---

' The word הרה stands alone in the Semitic dialects. The only probable etymology which I have seen is that of Gesenius, that it is a softer pronunciation of חרה, " incalesco," according to the analogy of יחם, the word used in Ps. li. 7.

² The theory, I am told, still remains in our laws, in which the destruction of the fœtus before a given time is not accounted the destruction of a living being.

commencement of the undying life of the soul.
The two acts may as probably be simultaneous as
not. And when Holy Scripture says, "in sin did
my mother conceive me," it speaks not only of the
formless embryo, but of the whole being, "me."
When, on the other hand, Schoolmen wished to
express the reception of the soul as distinct from
the conception of the body, some of them, at least,
used separate terms, and spoke of the reception of
the soul as being "the second conception," or "the
animation [9]," which the Scotists declared to be im-

[9] Alexander de Hales, following S. Bernard, puts the same
questions as he, whether the B. V. was sanctified before her conception, i. e. in her parents; whether she could be sanctified
in the conception itself; whether, also, after the conception,
before the infusion of the soul, P. 3. q. 9. memb. 2. Art. 1, 2, 3.
S. Thomas proceeds in the same order, denying that she could
be sanctified before her conception, until *after* her conception,
or before her animation : but holding (like de Hales) that she
was sanctified before her birth (in 3 dist. 3. q. 1. art. 2). S.
Bonaventura follows S. Bernard, that the flesh of the Blessed
Virgin could not be sanctified before or in her conception, or
before animation; and holds "that it was more consonant to the
piety of faith and the authority of the saints, that her sanctification was after the contraction of original sin." L. 3. dist. 3.
art. 1. Albertus Magnus asks the same questions, "Whether
the flesh of the B. V. was sanctified in the womb or before the
womb ?" "Whether her flesh was sanctified before animation
or after it ? " He himself held that to say that she was sanctified before animation was a heresy condemned by S. Bernard
and all the masters of Paris (in 3. Dist. 3. Art. 3, 4). Dionysius Carth. quotes Udalric, (a celebrated disciple of Albert. M.,)
as saying (Summa L. v.), " We believe that the mother of Christ,
most worthy of all praise, was sanctified speedily after her
animation, i. e. the infusion of her soul. But John was sanctified

maculate in the Blessed Virgin.   It seems then the
more probable to me, that when this their limitation is dropped, the term "conception" must be
understood, in *this* case, of what every one understands it of in every other.   And that the more,
since the day, upon which the Immaculate Conception is celebrated, is that accounted to be the day
of the *first* Conception.   The term, also, used in
the Bull [1], still seems to me, unexplained, to favour
the same impression.   For S. Thomas Aquinas,
in one of the passages which I quoted [2], uses it
unmistakeably of the conception of the body.   For
although our Blessed Lord, when He vouchsafed to
take our nature upon Him, took both body and
soul together, yet S. Thomas, in asking the question which he purposed to answer by affirming this

sooner than Jeremiah, yet later than Mary, in that he was
sanctified in the 6th month after his conception, when his
mother was visited by the mother of Christ.   But that some
celebrate the conception of the B. V., this is borne with by the
Church, not referring it to the conception of seeds but of natures,
which was in the infusion of the soul; nor do they celebrate it
[the conception of the B. V.] because it was in sin, but by
reason of the sanctification, nearly adjoined to it." (Dion. in
Sent. 3. 3. q. 1. p. 38.)

[1] "In primo instanti conceptionis suæ." Alexander VII. in
the Constit., *Solicitudo omnium Ecclesiarum,* used the more
restricted expression, "animam in primo instanti creationis
atque infusionis in corpus," quoted by Perrone, de Immac.
B. M. V. Conc. p. 48.   The Scholia on Scotus (p. 31) use the
term "in primo instanti *animationis;*" Biel, " in instanti suæ
animationis," and "ante *conceptionem secundam,* qua fuit in
utero matris suæ animata," in 3 dist. 3. q. 1.

[2] Eirenicon, p. 147.

truth, used the words " in the first instant of His Conception," of the conception of His Holy Body. For he put the question thus, " Whether the Body of Christ was animated in the first moment of His Conception ? " The question would have been absurd, had the words, " in the first moment of His Conception," in themselves implied any more than the conception of His Body. For it would have been to ask, " whether His Soul was in His Holy Body, when He took at once His Body and Soul ?" S. Thomas obviously meant to ask, whether, upon that operation of God the Holy Ghost, whereby His Holy Body was formed in the Virgin's womb, His Soul (contrary to what was at that time supposed to be the case in ordinary conception) was present in His Body. For he goes on to argue against the applicability of the Aristotelian grounds for denying that the body was ordinarily animated at the first, to the Conception of our Divine Lord.

While, then, I am truly thankful that Mgr. Dupanloup and yourself still maintain the old distinction, I hope that I shall not seem to you at least, my dearest friend, to be presuming, if I think that, in this too, an explanation, which would remove difficulties from us, would be of service to you, if the Church of Rome wishes the Immaculate Conception, as matter of faith, to be understood of the soul only of the Blessed Virgin, and not of her body also. Without some such explanation, I should have feared that the belief of the

Immaculate Conception among you would be what
to us seems the most natural explanation of the
words of the Bull, that in the Blessed Virgin, as in
her Divine Son, both body and soul were conceived
immaculately, the only difference being, that the
Conception of the body in her case, though in the way
of nature, was immaculate, by virtue of His foreseen
merits; in His case, it was immaculate, there being
nothing to defile it.   You must have heard, from
time to time, of a maxim among Marian writers,
that, of two admissible aspects of doctrine, *that* is to
be preferred which does most honour to the Blessed
Virgin; a maxim which, I suppose, would find its
way here too in popular devotion.

   6. With regard to the larger subject of the Immaculate Conception, as a whole, some explanation
could possibly be given, to soften the apparent contradiction of the doctrine to Holy Scripture, as interpreted by the long tradition in the Church.   The
Scotists did not conceal the apparent contradiction.
Thus, Biel enumerates authorities against the conclusion to which he had come[a]:

   " The second conclusion according to that opinion, ' The
Virgin Mary was not preserved from the contagion of original
sin in the first moment of her animation.'   They endeavour to
prove this by authority and reason.   By authority of the
Apostle, Rom. v. [12], ' In Adam all sinned.'   For he says, ' As
through one man sin came into this world, and death by sin,
and so death passed upon all men, in whom (quo) all sinned,'
all who were in him according to the ' ratio seminalis.'   Also
Rom. iii. [23], ' All have sinned and come short of the glory of
God.'   The Interlineary Gloss says, 'sinned in themselves or in

_____
[a] in Sent. 8. 3. q. 1.

Adam.' Also, 1 Cor. xv. [22], 'As in Adam all die, so in Christ shall all be made alive.' Also, Eph. ii. [3], 'We were all children of wrath.' In all these places, the Apostle speaks universally without exception; therefore under that universality the Virgin is comprised, being a daughter of Adam, and having been born in Adam 'secundem rationem seminalem.' Gregory of Ariminum says here (in ii. dist. 30. q. 2), 'Since by human reason certainty cannot be had on this matter, *that* seems to me rather to be held which is most consonant to sacred scripture, which, wherever it speaks hereon, delivers an universal sentence as to all, without any exception.'

"This same is proved by authority of the saints. For the blessed Augustine in the 'de fide ad Petrum,' c. 23 [S. Fulgentius, Bened. in S. Aug. Opp. vi. p. 18. App.], 'Hold most firmly and no wise doubt, that every man who is conceived by intercourse of man and woman is born with original sin, subject to ungodliness and liable to death, and therefore is by nature born a child of wrath. Of whom the Apostle says, "We too were children of wrath even as others."' Also on that of John i., '"Behold the Lamb of God." He alone was innocent Who did not so come, i. e. by propagation [Tract. iv. n. 10. p. 316. Ben.]. Also de perfect. just. [c. ult. T. x. p. 188], 'Whoever then thinks that there was or is in this life any man or any men, except the One Mediator of God and man, to whom remission of sins was not necessary, contradicts Divine Scripture,' quoting Rom. v. as above. Also de Nupt. et Conc. [i. n. 18], 'Christ willed not to be born of cohabitation; that thence too He might teach, that every one who is born of cohabitation is flesh of sin, since That alone which was not born therefrom, was not flesh of sin,' and consequently the flesh of the Virgin, which was born of cohabitation, was flesh of sin. Also against Julian (ii. 30), who denied that children contracted original sin, he says the same, 'If beyond doubt the Flesh of Christ is not flesh of sin, but like unto flesh of sin, what remains but that we understand that, It excepted, all other human flesh is flesh of sin?' and shortly after [c. 15. n. 52], 'The Body of Christ is thence said to be "in the likeness of flesh of sin," because whosoever denies that all other flesh of

E

man is flesh of sin, and so compares the Flesh of Christ with
the flesh of other men who are born, so as to assert that both
are of the like purity, is found to be a detestable heretic.' And
de Gen. ad lit. x. c. 23 [x. 18. n. 82. Ben.], 'Accordingly the
Body of Christ, although it was taken from the flesh of woman
who had been conceived from that stock of sin, yet, because It
was not so conceived in her, as she had been conceived, neither
was He flesh of sin, but likeness of flesh of sin.' Where it
clearly appears that he thought that the flesh of the Blessed
Virgin was flesh of sin. Also in the de fide ad Pet. [n. 16],
'Because the cohabitation of parents is not without passion,
therefore the conception of the children born of their flesh cannot be without sin, when not propagation, but passion, transmits sin to the little ones.' But it is known that neither the
Blessed Virgin nor any other human being, besides Christ, was
conceived without cohabitation of parents. Also Ambrose on
Luke [L. ii. n. 36, quoted by S. Aug. c. Julian. i. n. 10], 'The
Lord Jesus Alone, of all born of woman, was throughout holy,
Who, by the newness of His Immaculate Birth, did not feel the
contagion of earthly corruption, and by His Heavenly Majesty
dispelled it.' If then 'Christ Alone,' then no others, and so
neither His virgin Mother. And on Isaiah [quoted by S. Aug. de
Nupt. et Concup. i. fin.], 'Therefore He was, as Man, tempted
in all things, and in the likeness of man endured all things.
For all men are liars, and no one is without sin, but God only.
That then is maintained, that from man and woman, i. e. through
that corporeal union, no one should seem free from sin. For
He Who is free from sin, is free also from this mode of conception.' Also Dama, 'The Holy Ghost cleansed her with one
word.' But cleansing is only from sin; therefore she had sin;
not actual; therefore original. And Leo, in a sermon on the
Lord's Nativity, 'As He found none free from guilt, so He
came to free all.' Also Anselm (Cur Deus homo, ii. 16) says,
'Because by His Death which was to be, that Virgin too of
whom He was born and many others were cleansed from sin;'
if then they were cleansed from sin, then she had sin before her
cleansing. And P. Lombard, iii. L. 8: 'It may be said and
believed, according to the agreement of the attestation of the

saints, that the very Flesh of the Word was Itself before
subject to sin, like the rest of the flesh of the Virgin, but
was cleansed by the operation of the Holy Ghost, so that, free
from all contagion, it should be united to the Word.' Lo,
he says, 'that the flesh of the Virgin was subject to sin, and
was cleansed by the operation of the Holy Ghost.' Very
many other like things may be alleged out of the sayings of
the saints." Then, after quoting S. Bernard, he adds, from
the Decretals, de Consecr. dist. iii. c. i. [where the Assumption and Nativity of the Blessed Virgin are enumerated
among the festivals, not the Conception], "It is said in the
gloss: 'Of the Feast of the Conception nothing is said, because it is not to be celebrated as it is in many countries, and
chiefly in England. And this is the reason, because she was
conceived in sin, as also the other saints, except the One
Person of Christ.'"

The quotations from S. Augustine are, I think,
the more remarkable, because of the care which he
took to guard himself against seeming to ascribe
actual sin to the Blessed Virgin. When affirming
against Pelagius, that no one was exempt from
actual sin, he protests that, for reverence to our
Lord, he would not speak of the B. V. (whom
Pelagius had instanced among others) when speaking of sins.

"Except then the holy Virgin Mary, of whom, for the
honour of the Lord, I will that no question whatever should
be had, when sins are treated of;—for whence know we, what
more of grace, for the overcoming of sin altogether, may have
been conferred upon *her*, who obtained to conceive and bear
Him, of whom *it is known* that He had no sin?—excepting then
this Virgin, if we could bring together all the other holy men
and women, while they lived here, and could ask them whether

they were without sin, what can we suppose that they would
answer? what that man [Pelagius] said, or what the Apostle
John said? I pray you, whatever was the eminence of their
sanctity in this body, if they could be asked, would they not
have cried out with one voice, 'If we say that we have no sin,
we deceive ourselves and the truth is not in us'?'"

Now from this very passage, which, with a passage
of S. Anselm, was put forth by the Scotists as the
proof from authority that the B. V. had not original sin, I should have rather inferred that S. Augustine believed that she was not exempted from it.
For he does not pronounce that it was *certain* that
she never had any venial sin.   The subject was
hateful to him, for honour of his Lord, and he
would have nothing to do with it.   But the contrast with the *certainty*, that our Lord had no sin,
leaves *some* shade of uncertainty.   And yet had
he believed that the B. V. was born as exempt
from original sin as our first parents, then any sin
whatever would have been the repetition of Adam's
fall; which were of all things the most unimagi-
nable and abhorrent.   Then too, the expression,
"Whence know we, what more of grace for the
conquering of sin altogether, may have been bestowed upon her?" which some Schoolmen so
strangely quoted, as if it implied exemption from
original sin [5], I should have thought, at least im-

* De Nat. et Grat. c. 36.

[5] Biel says l.c., "We are said to conquer sin, which never
was in us, when we are preserved by grace from it, that it
master us not." Even this we could not say, unless we had

plied the existence of a tendency to sin within, the "fomes peccati." One could speak of "overcoming the world," "overcoming Satan," meaning thereby overcoming the might or the external temptations of Satan or the world. But sin has no temptations except from within. To "overcome sin" must be, one should think, to overcome its risings within one's self.

S. Antonine, I see, insists that S. Augustine, when rejecting all question of sins in regard to the B. V., in honour of our Lord, meant the same sins, which, in contrast with her, he affirms of the rest of mankind, viz., actual sins.

> "* In answer to this authority, it is said according to Thomas [Aquinas] and Durandus, that Augustine is speaking there of actual sins, as is clear and patent from what precedes and follows in that book, and from the authority of John in his first canonical Epistle, which Augustine immediately afterwards adduces: 'If we say that we have no sin, &c.' But all Doctors agree in this, that the Virgin alone among adults was free from venial sin too."

But, apart from this, it seems to me utterly inconceivable, that a writer so careful as S. Augustine, who revised his works and retracted inaccurate expressions of so very slight account, who

some involuntary tendency to the sin; but conception in original sin is antecedent to human will, and no matter for struggle or victory.

* Summa, P. i. Tit. 8. c. 2. de Concept. B. M. i. 552. Verona, 1740.

—+—

guarded his language, and, on the subject of actual
sin, made the specific exception in regard to the
B. V., should have spoken so absolutely and without all exception as to the derivation of original
sin to every one born as we all are born, unless he
had believed that no exception was to be made;
and this the more, since he is speaking, not of our
liability to those consequences of the fall, which
the inheritance of original sin involves, but of the
fact, that Christ Alone *had been* born without sin,
because He alone was born, not of human generation, not in the way in which His blessed Mother
was born. When he is speaking of actual sin, he
does except the Blessed Virgin, out of reverence
to our Lord.

Often as, in consequence of the necessity of
warning his people or the Church against the Pelagians, he had to speak, formally and dogmatically,
of the universality of original sin and of the mode
of its transmission, he never makes more than one
exception, the Person of our Lord. The very pains
which people have been at, to make the occasion in
which he exempts the B. V. from *actual* sins, to
include original sin also, brings out the more the
force of the omission. It is not S. Augustine's
way to allow any grave statement of his belief to
rest on an expression, which does not, according to
the natural force of the terms, contain it. According to modern defenders of the doctrine of the Immaculate Conception, the omission was not a mere

slip of S. Augustine's, upon a subject which was not under discussion, language (inadvertently on his part) too broad and comprehensive.

According to them, he did mean to except the B. V. once, although it does not seem to have occurred to any one that he did, until the Scotists wished to shelter themselves under his authority. But if so, it must have occurred to him that he had not excepted her distinctly even there, and, that every where else he had written, as one would, who did not mean to exclude her. The one work in which he so wrote, was written, A.D. 415, when S. Augustine was 60, fifteen years before his decease. Though circulated, as all his works were, it was written originally to individuals. He could not anticipate that what he had thus written, would be known, as it is now, to all who know his works at all, and to tens of thousands who do not know them. Yet neither in what he wrote subsequently upon the universality of the transmission of original sin to all born after the law of our birth, did he make any exception, nor in his Retractations did he say that he had failed to make that one exception; and yet even in works later than this date, he corrected very minute mistakes.

You, my dear friend, will not think that it is in any spirit of controversy that I put together from the collections of Cardinal de Turrecremata, De Bandelis, and others, a series bearing upon the Immaculate Conception.

The work of Cardinal de Turrecremata (who, when he compiled it, was Magister Palatii at Rome) was no ordinary work. It was executed when he was of mature age (he was 49 when he completed it), with full access to libraries, "at the mandate of the legates of the Apostolic See, then presiding over the Council of Basle ʼ," on the affirmative side, viz., "that the B. V. was conceived in original sin." (The other side was executed by John of Segovia.) Of course, he had difficulties, printing not being yet invented. And so he states that he had omitted very many authorities, which he had seen in libraries, because he could not ascertain the names of the authors; partly too he was hindered by lack of time, and he limited his selection to one hundred authorities. But what he quoted, with the exception of very few passages, he says, that he had seen with his own eyes. His own statement, prepared for the Synod, was :—

"ᵇ Behold, O sacred Synod, 100 witnesses, who, being most profound Doctors in Divine and Canon law, or very learned Fathers, give a most clear testimony to the side of the question for which you have entrusted me with the ministry, viz., that

---

ʼ This is stated in the title, "Tractatus de veritate conceptionis Beatiss. V. pro facienda relatione coram Patribus Conc. Bas. A.D. 1437, mense Julio de mandato Sedis Apostolicæ legatorum, eidem S. Concil. Præsidentium, per R. P. F. Joann. de Turrecremata S.T.P. ord. Præd., tunc S. Apost. Palatii Magistrum, postea S. R. E. Cardinalem Episc. Sabin. Romæ 1547."

ᵇ P. vii. init. extracted in De Alva's Trituratio, pp. 22, 23.

the most Bl. Virgin was in her conception subject to original
sin. To whom it would be easy to add many others, considering that the faith and doctrine of almost all the ancient expositors of the Bible and Doctors of the schools, who are of more
celebrated authority, fame, and opinion, tends to that side of the
question. But, *for the present*, I have been content with this
number, because the number of 100 is held perfect in Holy
Scripture (as the gloss says, Deut. 22). as also because want of
opportunity and multiplicity of occupations did not permit me
to visit several libraries; also, because although I found in
libraries, which I visited, many other Doctors, both on the
Sentences and in expositions of the Bible, and in treatises made
in praise of the most Bl. V., who taught and preached this doctrine, and left it in their writings for instructing the Christian
people, yet, since I often could not know their names, I
decided not to quote the sayings of these many Doctors. But
the testimonies of the 100 Doctors or venerable Fathers, (except
some very few, of whose judgment I had knowledge from the
faithful report of others,) I have seen in their originals with my
own eyes."

These authorities are but a small portion of his
important work[9]. To him was assigned the office

[9] The work is so manifestly one whole, from one mind, at
one time, and that, engaged in close, hand-to-hand, yet peace-
loving, controversy with the opposite party, with continual
reference to each of the opponents, and occasionally to
preachers of sermons at the Synod, and to the fathers of the
Synod itself, with even the recurrence of rare expressions, that
De Alva must have looked very superficially at the book (as his
character was), that he could speak of its citations, at one time,
as the work of Barth. Spina, General of the Order, Prof. of Theol.
and Master of the Apostolic Palace, who directed the publication,
and, while able, laboured on it; at another, of Alb. Duimius,
Domin. Prof. at Rome, who corrected errors which had crept
into the MSS. in the 110 years between its delivery and its
printing. They were merely Editors. Pref. of Alb. Duim. to
De Turr.'s work.

of answering what had been said by the two advocates on the other side, supporting what had been
said by his colleague the Provincial of Lombardy,
to whom the opening of the subject had been committed. He followed the arguments of his opponents, step by step, even at the cost of repetition,
and supported his allegations of Holy Scripture or
his arguments by the traditional interpretations,
and advanced nothing unsupported. His extracts
are conscientiously and carefully made, as one
would expect from him, especially upon such an
occasion. Even De Alva, who is unsparing of his
accusations of those who wrote on that side, and
who often finds fault for inaccuracy, where there is
none to be found, is frequently compelled to own
the authentic way in which Cardinal de Turrecremata cites his authorities, or contrasts it with the
less exact citations of others. De Alva, on the other
hand, who accuses so confidently, falls at times into
the slips, to which self-confidence and suspicious-
ness expose any one. He is useful in checking
citations, but he has need to be checked himself ;
for he declares authors or their works to have been
non-existent or forged, because he could not himself trace them, or two writers to be the same,
because he had not the means of distinguishing
them. Quétif's belief was the same as De Alva's,
yet in his learned " Library of the Dominicans," he
has noticed some of these mistakes of De Alva's in
regard to Dominican writers ; and he uses the ex-

pression, " [1] if it had not been an ascertained thing,
that he (De Alva) ran lightly over the authors
who occurred to him."

The careful study of his elaborate work makes
one think heavily, that, had it ever been read to the
Council, their decision (which was counted exten-
sively as the decision of the Church) might have
been stayed. As it was, they decided under the
influence of unanswered arguments and (of which
De Turrecremata complains) invidious declamation.

De Bandelis [2] appeared to me to have quoted less
exactly [3]. At least, he has sometimes important
words which do not occur in the present texts, and
sometimes gives an epitome of a passage rather

[1] Biblioth. Præl., art. F. Hugo Argentin. i. 470.

[2] "De singulari puritate et prærogativa Conceptionis Salva-
toris nostri Jesu Christi ex auctoritatibus 260 Doctorum illus-
trium."—Printed at Bologna, A.D. 1481.

[3] In such a mass of authorities, he has, I may say, of course,
made mistakes. As the list in Melchior Canus (referred to,
"Eirenicon," p. 178) rests doubtless on his authority, I would
say he was probably mistaken about S. Bernardine; the sermon
which he ascribes to S. Antony of Padua has not been found,
although S. Antony, if I understand him aright, does not express
any opposite belief. S. Erhardus, or Gerardus, Bishop and
Martyr, is the same as a "Bishop and Martyr" quoted by De
Turrecremata. Sometimes, too, De B. has quoted the same
author under two or more names (such as he found probably
in his MSS.), although not so often as De Alva imputes to
him. In the absence of bibliographies it was almost impossible
to avoid it. It was not obvious, e. g., to an Italian, that "Richardus Radulphi [Richard Fitz Ralph], Chancellor of Oxford,"
was the same as "Dom. Armachanus," i.e. Archbishop of
Armagh.

than its exact words⁶. His citations too are often
(in the way of S. Thomas Aquinas in the Catena
Aurea) made up of disjointed sentences, which he
enwreathes into one whole. I have then used his
work as a convenient index, but I have (sometimes
with some labour) given the exact words and a
fuller context, although, in this way, often not so
salient as they stand in his work⁷.

No one can wish more earnestly than myself
that a solution of these authorities⁸ should be found,
and should be authoritatively given. I wish this
as earnestly now, as I *did* wish beforehand, that
the Immaculate Conception should not be made
a matter of faith, but left as a matter of 'pious
opinion;' and I wish it on the self-same grounds;
fifteen years ago, that there might be no fresh diffi-

⁶ I have seen this stated in one case by Deza, his continua-
tor, as quoted by De Alva.

⁷ As the works from which they quote for the first 1100 years,
have been since printed, I have inserted nothing during that
period, which I have not myself verified. Wherever I have subsequently used authorities from Turrecremata, still unprinted, I
have referred to him. Sometimes De Alva himself quotes a
MS. containing De Turrecremata's authority and agreeing with
it except in unimportant variations, or in giving a fuller context,
as De Turrecremata says he understood "compendiousness" to
belong to his office. In these cases, I have translated from De
Alva's extracts. In one or two cases I have found the passage in
Quétif. Later authorities, which rest on Turrecremata alone, I
have, when I have cited them, marked with a †.

⁸ I have weighed carefully what De Alva says, though, his
work being a folio, it would be wearisome to any reader to introduce it in controversy.

culty in the way of re-union; *now*, that, if possible, the definition, made in 1654, should be so explained as not to be an obstacle. But you have no internal ground to give any such solution, since there is no question about the doctrine among you. When the building is raised, the scaffolding is not wanted; nor is any question had about the difficulties experienced in raising it. These become mere matter of history. If, then, there is to be any explanation, (and an explanation is of much moment towards the re-union of Christendom, East and West too,) the impulse must come to you from without. In the view, then, of obtaining an authoritative explanation, I have re-arranged this body of tradition, which cannot, I think, be simply set aside, without destroying altogether the value of tradition as a witness of truth. Whatever this or that Father or middle-age writer may be said *not* to mean, it is of moment, that it should be shown, *what* this concurrent testimony, spread over so many centuries, *does* mean, based, as so much of it is, on words of Holy Scripture, that God sent His Son in "the likeness of flesh of sin."

Perrone, following P. Benedict Piazza, divides the authorities into five classes: "*(1) those testimonies, in which it is asserted that God Alone or Christ Alone is without any sin, without making any mention of original sin; (2) those, which affirm

* De Imm. B. V. Conc. p. 57.

that the whole human race is infected with original
sin, without specially naming the Blessed Virgin;
(3) those, in which Fathers teach, that, *Christ
Alone excepted*, all men are defiled with that original stain; (4) those, which maintain that the flesh
of the Blessed Virgin was *flesh of sin;* (5) those,
in which Fathers assert in plain terms, that the
Blessed Virgin was *sanctified, cleansed, purged.*"

Perrone contents himself with considering some
of the two last classes. I have myself mostly
omitted the first. The force of the third class
Perrone has, I think, naturally understated. To me
its great weight seems to lie, not in the fact of the
contrast alone between our Lord and His redeemed,
but that the exemption of our Lord's Human Nature
from original sin is ascribed to the difference of the
mode of His Conception. All, those Fathers teach,
have been born subject to the original sin, who
received their being after the way of nature; our
Lord's Human Nature *Alone* was not so subjected,
because He was *not* conceived after the way of
nature; He was conceived, not of man, but of the
Holy Ghost. The very nature of the contrast
compels the Fathers to speak of the Blessed Virgin.
Her conception must have been consequently present to their minds. Original sin did not, they
say, pass to our Lord, because He was conceived of
His Mother in a way in which *she* was *not* conceived. Had they thought that she had been excepted, it seems almost impossible, that no one of

them should have made the exception. It is
not a case of oratorical or devotional language, or
of a general confession of our hereditary sinfulness.
They are dogmatic statements, carefully varied.

The earlier Fathers who speak to the subject
belong chiefly to Peculiar's second class. S.
S. Augustine gathers them not met as asserting
the belief of the Church as to the universal transmission of original sin to all naturally born of
Adam. The writers themselves are naturally more
or less full or precise. S. Augustine takes certain expressions (e. g. those of S. Irenaeus as key-
notes of a system of faith which they implied but
which those Fathers did not fully explain. These
I give on S. Augustine's authority, else I should not
have cited them. Yet with such a full statement
as Origen's one cannot doubt even apart from
S. Augustine's authority, that the Catholic writers
before him, whom Pelagius claimed not only held
the doctrine of original sin but the mode of its
transmission, as contained in the fuller statement.
This gleams through in most of the writers quoted.

1. S. Irenaeus lays stress on S. Paul's words,
" *the likeness* of the flesh of sin" as belonging to
our Lord, in contrast with the rest of mankind [a].

[a] No otherwise could men be saved from the ancient wound
of the serpent unless they believe in Him, Who *is the likeness
of flesh of sin*, being lifted up from the earth on the wood of
witness, drew all things to Himself and quickened the dead."

[b] iv. 2 7, quoted by S. Aug. c. Julian. i. 3. Opp. x. 500.

I had perhaps better add Tertullian and Origen here, (although not quoted by S. Augustine,) because the explicitness of their statements (borne out by S. Ambrose and other Catholic writers) shows that, long before the Pelagian controversy, the mode of transmission of original sin was stated in connexion with Psalm li., and that no exception was made.

2. Tertullian, about A.D. 199, wrote—

Satan, "[1] whom we call the angel of wickedness, the contriver of all evil, the corruptor of the whole world, through whom man, being from the beginning beguiled, so that he transgressed the commandments of God, and on that account being given over unto death, hath henceforth made his whole race, that is infected of his seed, the transmitters of his condemnation also."

And, in a work after his fall into Montanism—

"[2] This, too, appertaineth to the faith, that Plato divides the soul into rational and irrational. Which definition we too approve, yet not so, that both be ascribed to nature. For the rational must be believed to be natural, being inborn in the soul from the beginning, as coming from a rational Author. But the irrational is to be understood to be later, as having come from the suggestion of the serpent, that very transgression of theirs which they admitted, and that thenceforth it ingrew and grew up together in the soul, having now a sort of character of nature, because it happened in the very first beginning of nature[3]."

---

[1] De Testim. Anim. 3. p. 135. Oxf. Tr.

[2] De Anima. c. 16.

[3] Lumper (Tertullian, c. 6. art. 10. p. 363) refers in illustration to Bossuet, t. 2, Défense de la Tradition et des Saints Pères, L. 8. c. 29. p. 148.

"'To such a degree is well nigh no nativity clean, viz., of heathens." Then he explains S. Paul (1 Cor. vii. 14) to mean that the children of believers were clean, as "designated for holiness;" "else," he says, "the Apostle well remembered the decision of the Lord, 'Unless one be born of water and the Spirit, he will not enter into the kingdom of God,' i. e. he will not be holy." He proceeds, "So then every soul is so long counted in Adam, until it be counted anew in Christ; so long unclean, until it be so counted anew; and sinful, because unclean, receiving ignominy from the association of the flesh [he means *additional* ignominy, since he goes on to speak of the body as only an instrument of evil]. The evil then of the soul (besides what is built thereon by the intervention of the evil spirit) is antecedent from the fault of origin, being in a manner natural. For, as we said, the corruption of nature is another nature, having its own god and father, viz. the author himself of its corruption, yet so that there is good too in the soul, that which is principal, that which is divine and genuine, and properly natural. For that which is from God is not so much extinguished as overshadowed. For it can be overshadowed, because it is not God; it cannot be extinguished, because it is from God. So then, as light, hindered by some obstacle, abides, but appears not, if the density of the hindrance be adequate, so also the good in the soul, oppressed by the evil, according to the quality of that evil, is either missing altogether, the light suffering occultation, or shines, when allowed, having gained freedom. So some are exceeding evil, some exceeding good, and yet all are one kind of soul. So in the worst, too, there is something of good, and in the best there is something of the worst. For God Alone is without sin, and the only Man without sin is Christ, because Christ is also God."

And in another—

"' For which cause also, we were 'children of wrath,' he saith, but ' by nature,' lest, because the Creator had called the

---

⁴ Ib. c. 39—41.   ⁵ Adv. Marc. v. 17. pp. 608, 609. Rig.

Jews children, the heretic might argue, that the Lord was the creator of wrath. For when he says, 'we were by nature children of wrath,' but the Jews were sons of the Creator, not by nature, but by election of the fathers, he referred their being 'children of wrath' to 'nature,' not to the Creator. Subjoining, as 'also the rest,' who clearly are not sons of God. He appears to ascribe sins and concupiscences of the flesh, and unbelief and anger, to the common nature of all men, yet [he doth so], the devil taking captive nature, which too he himself already infected, by bringing in the seed of transgression."

3. Origen :

" ' But if you would hear what other saints also think of that birth [in the flesh], hear David saying, 'I was conceived in iniquities, and in sins did my mother bear me,' showing that whatsoever soul is born in the flesh is polluted by the defilement of iniquity and sin ; and that therefore is that said, which we have mentioned above, that 'no one is clean from defilement, not even if his life be of one day.' "

" ' Whosoever cometh into this world is said to be made in a certain contamination. Wherefore also Scripture saith, 'No one is clean from defilement, not even if his life be of one day.' For from the very fact, that he was placed in his mother's womb, and takes the matter of his body from the origin of his father's seed, he may be said to be contaminated in father and in mother. Or know you not, that when the male child is forty days old, it is offered at the altar, to be purified there, as having been polluted in the conception itself, either of the paternal seed or the maternal womb ? Every man, then, was polluted in father and in mother, but Jesus, my Lord, Alone entered pure into this generation ; He was not defiled in His mother. For He entered a body undefiled [being a virgin]. For He it was, Who had said long before too through Solomon, 'But rather, being good, I came to a body undefiled.' He was

---

° Orig. in Lev. Hom. 8. n. 3. T. ii. p. 230. ed. De la Rue.
⁷ Ib. Hom. 12. n. 4. Ib. p. 251.

not then defiled in His mother, but neither was He in His
father. For Joseph yielded no part in His generation, except
ministry and love. Wherefore also, for his faithful ministry,
Scripture granted him the name of father. For so Mary herself saith in the Gospel, ' Behold I and Thy father have sought
Thee sorrowing.' So then He alone is the great High Priest,
Who was defiled neither in father nor mother."

"'But of that regeneration [in the world to come, S. Matt.
xix. 28], the prelude is, that which is called in Paul the washing of regeneration, and [the prelude] of that newness is that
which followeth upon the washing of regeneration in that of
renewal of life. But, perhaps, according to birth too, 'no one
is clean from defilement, not if his life be one day,' on account
of the mystery concerning the birth, in regard to which [birth]
each one of all who have come to the birth may say that which
was said by David in the 50th Psalm, thus, that ' I was conceived in transgressions, and in sins was my mother pregnant
of me,' but according to the regeneration from the leaven, every
one who has been born from above of water and the Spirit, is
clean from defilements, to speak boldly, clean ' through a glass
and darkly,' &c."

"'Or, rather, it seemeth that this [Rom. v. 14] ought to be
taken simply, that ' the likeness of Adam's transgression ' ought
to be received without any discussion, so that by this saying all
who are born of Adam, the transgressor, should seem to be
indicated, and to have in themselves the likeness of his transgression, received in themselves, not only from the seed, but
also from education."

4. S. Cyprian and his African Council of sixty-
six Bishops,—in that celebrated response, in which
S. Augustine says that "[10] the question whether it
was lawful for an infant to be baptized before the

* In S. Matt. T. 15. n. 23. Opp. iii. 685, 686.
* In Rom. T. 5. n. i. Opp. iv. 550.
[10] Contr. 2 Epp. Pelag. iv.. 8 n. 23. Opp. x. 481. See other
places of S. Aug. in S. Cyprian's Epistles, p. 195. n. Oxf. Tr.

eighth day, was so handled, as though, through the Providence of God, the Catholic Church were already confuting the Pelagian heretics, who were to rise so long after,"—say,

> " [1] If then to the most grievous offenders, and who had before sinned much against God, when they afterwards believe, remission of sins is granted, and no one is debarred from Baptism and grace, how much more ought not an infant to be debarred, who, being newly born, has in no way sinned, except that, being born after Adam in the flesh, he has by the first birth contracted the contagion of the old death, who is on this very account more easily admitted to receive remission of sins, in that not his own but another's sins are remitted to him."

S. Jerome quotes [2] besides from S. Cyprian's collection of texts of Holy Scripture, arranged under heads, the heading [3], "That *none* is born without defilement and without sin."   In support of which S. Cyprian alleges Ps. li. 5, "Behold I was conceived in iniquities, and in sins did my mother conceive me;" and 1 John i. 8, "If we say that we have no sin, we deceive ourselves, and the truth is not in us."

S. Cyprian unites actual and original sin, and denies the exemption of any from either of them.

5. Reticius, Bp. of Autun, one of the three Bishops appointed by Constantine to judge with

---

[1] S. Cyprian and Afric. Council to Fidus, Ep. 64 fin.
[2] Dial. c. Pelag. n. 32.   Opp. ii. 715. ed. Vall.
[3] Testim. iii. 64.   Treatises, p. 100. Oxf. Tr.

Melchiades Bp. of Rome in the case of the Dona-
tists [1], said of Baptism;

> "[1] Every one knows that this is the chief forgiveness in the
> Church, in which we put off the whole weight of the old sin,
> and blot out the ancient sins of our ignorance, where too we
> put off the old man with our inborn guilt."

S. Augustine dwells on the terms, " weight of
the old sin," " ancient sins," " the old man with
our inborn guilt."

6. Olympius, "[1] a Spanish Bishop of great glory
in the Church and in Christ," said in a sermon,

> " If faith had remained any where on earth uncorrupt, and
> had held its footmarks imprinted, which, when marked, it
> abandoned, never, by the death-bringing transgression of the
> protoplast, would he have infused vice in the germ, so that sin
> should be born with man."

7. S. Hilary, like S. Irenæus, dwells on the expression, " the *likeness* of the flesh of sin," in our
Lord, in contrast with ours [1].

> " Since then He was sent in ' the likeness of flesh of sin,' He
> had not sin too, as He had flesh.   But because all flesh is from
> sin, being derived from sin, i. e. from Adam our parent, He was
> sent in ' the likeness of flesh of sin,' there being in Him not
> sin, but ' the likeness of flesh of sin.' "

---

[1] Eus. H. E. x. 5.   S. Augustine dwells on the fact of his
so judging, as showing that he was " of great authority in the
Church."

[1] Ap. S. Aug. c. Julian. i. 7. p. 501.

[1] Ib. § 8.

[1] From an unknown and lost work in S. Aug. l. c. § 9.

S. Hilary elsewhere [a] speaks of

"The Apostolic faith attesting that 'the Man Christ Jesus was found in fashion as a man,' and was sent in 'the likeness of flesh of sin,' so that, being 'in *fashion* as a man,' He should be in the form of a servant, and not be in the defects of nature; and being in 'the likeness of flesh of sin,' should indeed be the Word-Flesh, yet be in 'the likeness of flesh of sin,' rather than be the flesh of sin itself; and, being the Man Christ Jesus, should be Man, yet so that, in the Man, He could be nothing else than Christ is; and thus that He should both be born Man, by the birth of the body, and yet not be in the faults of man, *not being in the origin;* because 'the Word made Flesh' could not but be the Flesh which It was made, and the Word, although made Flesh, yet did not part with Its being the Word; and while 'the Word, made Flesh,' cannot lack the Nature of His origin, It could not but abide in the origin of His own Nature, that He was the Word; nor yet could the Word not be understood to be truly the Flesh which He was made; yet so that, since He dwelt among us, that Flesh was not the Word, but the Flesh of the Word dwelling in the flesh."

S. Augustine quotes S. Hilary again as con-

[a] De Trin. x. 26. p. 1054. Ben. The Bened. comment on the passage is, "We have in this section the sum of what had been hitherto proved, that the Word, taking Flesh, did not lose what He was, and took the verity of human nature, not its defects. The ground, why Hilary so earnestly maintained the distinction of the Divine and Human Nature in Christ, was to prove that our infirmities, which the heretics ascribed wrongly to the Divine Nature, were incidental only to the Human. But since it was unfitting that the God-united Man should be subject to the dominion of passions, he shows appositely, that Christ knew not the foul beginnings of our conception, and so was not liable to our passions, as far as they are injurious and vicious, and have rule over us."

necting our original sin with the mode of our conception;

" ' My soul shall live and it shall praise Thee, and Thy judgments shall help me.' He doth not think that he lives, in this life, in that he said, ' Behold I was conceived in iniquities, and in sins did my mother bear me.' He knows that he was born under the origin of sin and under the law of sin."

8. From S. Ambrose, besides the passages already cited by Biel[1], S. Augustine quotes his comment on David's words, "Behold I was conceived in wickedness, and in sins did my mother bear me."

" [2] Before we are born, we are stained by contagion; and, before we enjoy the light, we receive the injury of our origin itself, we are conceived in iniquity. He did not express, whether of our parents or our own. 'And in transgressions does his mother generate each.' Nor did he declare, whether the mother generates in her own sins, or whether there be already some transgressions too of the new-born. But see whether both are not to be understood. Neither is the conception without iniquity, since the parents too are not without lapse; and, if even the child of a day old is not without sin, much more are not those days of the maternal conception without sin. We are conceived then in the sin of our parents, and we are born in their iniquities. But the birth itself too has contagions of its own, nor has nature itself one contagion only."—" In Whom [Christ] Alone, there was both a virginal conception and birth, without any defilement of mortal origin. For it was meet, that He, Who was to have no sin of bodily prolapsion, should feel no natural contagion of generation. Rightly then did David mournfully lament in himself the very defilements of nature, that stain begins in man earlier than life."

---

[*] In Ps. cxviii. 175. p. 366. Ben.
[1] Above, p. 66.
[2] Apol. David. c. 11. Opp. i. 694, 695.

" ² One is *our* iniquity, another that of our heel, in which Adam was wounded by the serpent's tooth, and by his own wound left the inheritance of human succession subject thereto, so that we all halt through that wound."

And in language which, though ante-Pelagian, is such as S. Augustine adopted⁴;

"It is declared, that salvation should come to the nations through One, Jesus Christ, Who Alone could not be righteous, whereas every generation erred, unless, being born of a Virgin, He was by no means held by the law, which lay upon a guilty generation. He who was counted righteous above the rest, says, 'Behold I was conceived in wickednesses, and in sin my mother bare me.' Whom then should I now call righteous, save One free from these chains, Whom the chains of the common nature hold not? All are under sin; from Adam over all death reigned. Let Him come, Who Alone was righteous in the sight of God, of Whom it should be said, now no longer with limitation, 'He sinned not in His lips,' but, 'He did no sin.'"

S. Augustine then asks Julian, whether he would venture to say to S. Ambrose too, "that, since he excepted Christ Alone from the bonds of a guilty generation, because He was born of a virgin, whereas all others descended from Adam were born under the bond of sin, which sin the devil sowed, he made the devil the creator of all born from the union of the sexes."

"Confute him" (he says) "as a condemner of marriage, who says that the Virgin's Son was Alone born without sin."

---

² On Ps. xlviii. 6. n. 8. Opp. i. 947, quoted in S. Aug. c. Jul. i. 8.

⁴ Quoted by S. Aug. c. Julian. ii. 2, and cont. 2 Epp. Pelag. iv. n. 29, from S. Ambrose's de Arca Noe, not there now.

He further quotes from S. Ambrose;

"' Christ was therefore immaculate, because neither was He maculate by the wonted condition of birth itself."

"' He [Peter] offered himself for *that* which he, before, thought sin, asking that not his feet only, but his head also should be washed; because he had immediately understood that, by the washing of the feet, which in the first man slipped, the defilement of the guilty succession was done away."

And again, commenting upon the same text, upon which S. Irenæus had touched before, and which S. Augustine expands so often, that "God sent His Son in the likeness of sinful flesh," he connects our Lord's sinlessness with His not being born, as all besides were born.

"' He does not say, 'into the likeness of flesh,' because Christ took the verity, not 'the likeness' of human flesh. Nor does he say, 'into the likeness of sin,' for He did no sin, but was made sin for us. But He came 'into the likeness of flesh of sin,' i. e. He took the likeness of sinful flesh; therefore, 'the likeness,' because it was written, 'And He is a man, and who shall acknowledge Him?' He was a man, in flesh according to man, who should be acknowledged; with virtue above man, who should not be acknowledged. So also He hath our flesh, but hath not the faults [vitia] of this flesh. For He was not generated, as every human being is, of commingling of male and female; but, being born of the Holy Ghost and the Virgin, He had received an immaculate Body, which not only no faults [vitia] had stained, but neither had the injuring concretion of generation or conception offuscated. For all we, the race of man, are born under sin, whose very birth is in fault, as thou

---

' On Isaiah in S. Aug. c. 2. Epp. Pel. iv. 29, p. 488.

' Id. ib.

' De Pœnit. i. 3. Opp. ii. 393, 394. The part "all we . . . guilt" is quoted by S. Aug. ib.

hast it read, when David says, 'Behold I was conceived in iniquities, and in offences did my mother bear me.' Therefore the flesh of Paul was a body of death, as he himself says, 'Who shall deliver me from the body of this death?' But the Flesh of Christ condemned sin, which, being born, He felt not, which, dying, He crucified; so that in our flesh there might be justification by grace, where, before, there was defilement through guilt."

Another passage, which S. Augustine quotes from S. Ambrose as his "teaching, how from that law of sin, (i. e. from the concupiscence of the flesh, carnis,) every man is generated, and therefore contracts original sin," I leave untranslated on account of its strength.

"' Hos filios generans David partus illos corporeæ commixtionis horrebat, et ideo mundari sacri fontis irriguo desiderabat, ut carnalem et terrenam labem gratia spiritualis ablueret. 'Ecce,' inquit, 'in iniquitatibus conceptus sum, et in delictis peperit me mater mea.' Male Eva parturivit, ut partus relinqueret mulieribus hæreditatem, atque unusquisque concupiscentiæ voluptate concretus, et genitalibus visceribus infusus, et coagulatus in sanguine, in pannis involutus, prius subiret delictorum contagium quam vitalis spiritus munus hauriret." S. Augustine explains that the "pannis involutus" is a metaphor, "non utique laneis aut lineis, aut hujuscemodi talibus, qualibus jam nati obvolvuntur infantes, sed pannis vitiatæ originis, tanquam hæreditariis, involutus."

9. From S. Gregory of Nazianzum, speaking of Baptism, S. Augustine quotes [9],

"Let the word of Christ too persuade you of this, when He

---

[8] De Sacramento regenerationis, s. de Philosophia in S. Aug. c. Julian. ii. 6, n. 15.

[9] In S. Aug. c. Julian. i. n. 15. T. x. p. 505. The sermon from which S. Aug. quotes is not extant.

saith, that 'no man can enter the kingdom of heaven, unless he
be reborn of water and the Spirit.' By this are the stains of
the first nativity purged, whereby we 'are conceived in iniquities,
and in sins have our mothers borne us.' "

On the other hand, he speaks of the Blessed
Virgin, as having been "fore-purified" before the
Conception of our Lord;

"¹ He becomes Man in all things, save sin, having been
conceived by the Virgin who had been fore-purified (προκαθαρ-
θείσης) by the Spirit as to both soul and flesh; for it ought to
be that both His generation should be honoured and that virginity should be preferred."

10. From S. Basil, S. Augustine quotes one passage, in which he speaks only of the universality
and the transmission of sin from our first parents:

"² Adam received that first command, 'From the tree of the
knowledge of good and evil ye shall not eat.' If Eve had fasted
from the tree, we should not now need this fast. 'For they
who are whole need not a physician, but they who are sick.'
We have been made sick through sin; let us be healed through
repentance."

Others, perhaps more explicit on the universality
and the transmission of sin, are:

"³ Adam, eating amiss, transmitted the sin."
"⁴ Let him hear the whole truth of the matter, that every

---

¹ Orat. 38. n. 13. p. 671, repeated in Orat. 45. n. 9. pp. 851,
852.
² Hom. i. de jejunio, n. 3. Opp. ii. 3. Ben.
³ Hom. in fam. et sicc. n. 7, fin. Opp. ii. 70. Ben.
⁴ Hom. in Ps. 48. n. 3. Opp. i. p. 180.

human soul was subject to the evil yoke of slavery of the common enemy of all, and, being deprived of the freedom which it had from Him Who created it, was led captive through sin. But every captive has need of ransom for freedom. And in no way has man power towards God, so as to propitiate Him for a sinner, since he himself too is subject to sin. 'For all have sinned, and come short of the glory of God, being justified freely,' &c."

"' Beautiful was I, according to nature, but weak, because I had been put to death by sin, through the plots of the serpent."

.

11. Julian the Pelagian falsified a homily of S. Chrysostom, as though he had said that infants had no *sin*, i.e. not original sin, whereas he had said, that they had " no *sins*," i.e. not actual sins. From him S. Augustine quotes the following passages, in proof that he believed that all were bound by that primeval sin :

"' When Adam sinned that grievous sin and condemned the race of all mankind in common, then was he condemned to toil."

"If Adam," S. Augustine comments on this, "by his great sin condemned the whole human race in

---

³ Hom. in Ps. 20. n. 5. p. 129.   The Benedictine Editors quote also Hom. in Ps. 32. p. 132, d. p. 185, c., and a glowing passage, Ep. 261. n. 2. T. iii. p. 402, in evidence that "S. Augustine maintained nothing else against the Pelagians, except what was certain from the perpetual teaching of the Church." Præf. ad Bas. Opp. T. iii. p. xxxiii.

⁴ Epist. 3 ad Olympiad. n. 3. T. iii. p. 554. Ben.   Quoted by S. Aug. c. Julian. i. n. 24.

common, is the child born uncondemned? And through whom is he delivered save by Christ?"

"[1] Christ cometh once; He found our paternal debt, which Adam contracted: *he* [Adam] brought in the beginning of the debt; *we* increased the usury by our subsequent sins."

S. Augustine marks the expression, that it was "*our* paternal debt," which appertained to us, before we increased it by our subsequent sins. He quotes also a much longer passage from his Commentary on S. Paul's words, "By one man sin entered into the world," which I will give more briefly.

"[2] It is manifest that not this sin, in the transgressing of the law, but that of the disobedience of Adam it was, which ruined every thing. 'Death reigned from Adam to Moses, over those too who did not sin.' How did it reign? in the likeness of the transgression of Adam, 'who is the image of Him to come.' For for this cause is Adam also an image of Christ. How an image? saith one. Because as *he* became, to those born of him, although not eating of the tree, a cause of death, which was brought in through that eating, so also Christ became to those who are from Him, although not having done righteously, the securer of righteousness, which He bestowed upon us all through the Cross.—So that when the Jew saith to thee, How, the one, Christ, doing aright, was the world saved? you may say to him, How, the one, Adam, disobeying, was the world lost? And yet sin and grace are not equal, not equal are death and life, not equal are the devil and God.—But not as the offence, so also the free gift, &c. For what he saith is of this sort. If sin, and that the sin of one man, availed so much, how shall not grace, the grace of God, not of the Father only, but of the Son also, prevail much more?—First he said, that if

---

[1] Hom. ad Neophytos, ib. n. 26.
[2] Hom. 10 in Ep. ad Rom. ib. n. 27. pp. 143—145. ed. Field.

one or some souls but by the soul universally[a], then,—if you can maintain that souls are in such wise foreign to the propagation, as yet, by rightest reason, to be shown to be bound by that debt, which is to be cancelled by the Death of Christ alone, and to appear justly bound, not by being themselves propagated but by this debt of the flesh,—not only maintain this, unhindered by any, but show us too how we may maintain it with you."

But if the fresh creation of the soul could not be maintained without falling into one or other heresy, S. Augustine thought it better to leave its origin as a thing unknown. One Soul, however, and One only, S. Augustine formally excepts, whatever the truth as to the origin of the soul might be.

"But that you, beloved, may hear from me too something defined on this question, it is to be estimated as of no slight moment, nay, it is of chief necessity and to be maintained, that whatsoever be the origin of souls, whether they be propagated from that one or from no other, it is not lawful to doubt that the Soul[b] of the Mediator derived no sin from Adam. For if no soul is propagated from another, when all are held bound by the propagated flesh of sin, how much less is it to be believed that His Soul could come from the propagation of a sinful mother [or soul, peccatricis], Whose Flesh came from a virgin, conceived not by passion but by faith, so that It should be in 'the likeness of flesh of sin,' not in flesh of sin! But if other souls are therefore held bound by the sin of the first soul, because they are propagated from it, That which the Only Begotten fitted for Himself, either did not contract sin thence, or was not derived from it at all. For He, Who loosed our sins, could not but be able to derive to Himself a soul without sin, or He, Who created a new soul for that flesh, which

---

[a] "Universæ animæ," Zosimus' words.

[b] Animam. Animarum is an error, corrected in the edit. Paris, 1836.

without a parent He made from the earth [Adam's], could not but be able to create a new soul for that Flesh, which, without aid of man, He took from a woman."

The omission of any mention of the B. V. here is the more unaccountable, if S. Augustine had believed her Immaculate Conception, because he is arguing that even if our Lord's Soul was derived from her soul [according to Traducianism], He could still have exempted It somehow from the transmission of sin; whereas, had he believed the Blessed Virgin to have been immaculately conceived, the exemption had already taken place in her, and her soul, from which, on the supposed hypothesis of Traducianism, His Soul would have derived Its being, would have been already immaculate, so that there was already no sin, the transmission of which was to be cut off.

As S. Augustine is so often quoted by the later writers, their sayings will be clearer if I set down at length some chief passages of his. Some are given in brief by Biel, as against what he held himself; but controversialists seem so commonly to think that a quotation begins too late or ends too soon, that it is as well to have them with a fuller context, when the context has more on the same subject. The citations are from writings spread over eighteen years of S. Augustine's life, from that which he wrote A.D. 412, soon after the appearance of Pelagianism [s], until his warfare was

[s] The " De peccatorum meritis et remissione." S. Augustine

G

accomplished, A.D. 430, and his last work was left unfinished. There is in them the remarkable uniformity of statement so often observable in S. Augustine. Repeated at such intervals of time, they show his deliberate, unqualified conviction. Concupiscence, the sin of our first parents, is, in his belief, the instrument of transmitting original sin [6]; where it is present in the production of the offspring (as it is in every conception except in the one virgin-birth of our Lord), there it is transmitted to the child. It was fitting that our Lord should be exempt from it also ; therefore He willed not so to be conceived. The Scriptural note which runs throughout is that phrase of Holy Scripture, which occurred in S. Irenæus too, as the characteristic of our Lord, that He came "in the likeness of sinful flesh."

"[7] The Word, Which was made Flesh, was in the beginning, and was God with God. But His very participation of our lower nature, in order that ours might participate of His Higher, held a sort of mediety even in the birth of the flesh, in that we

---

speaks of it as his first work against the new Pelagian heresy (Retract. ii. 23). He had preached sermons against it earlier. But the De bapt. Parv. Serm. 294, was preached A.D. 413. Bened. note, ibid.

[6] Agnosce vitium, unde trahitur originale peccatum. Op. Imp. c. Jul. ii. 122. "The question is now, not as to the nature of the seed but of the fault : for the nature has God for its Author; but from the fault original sin is derived." De nupt. et concep. ii. 8, n. 20.

[7] De Pecc. mer. et rem. ii. 24. n. 38. T. x. pp. 60, 61. Ben.

were born in the flesh of sin, but He ' in the likeness of flesh of sin;' we, not only of flesh and blood, but also of the will of man and the will of the flesh; but He was born, only of flesh and blood, not ' of the will of man, nor of the will of the flesh, but of God.' And therefore we went to death for sin; He went to death for us without sin.—He then *Alone*, even when made Man, abiding God, never had any sin, nor took flesh of sin, although from His mother's flesh of sin. For what of flesh He took from her, He cleansed it, either when He was about to take it, or by taking it [*]."

"[*] Levi was there [in the loins of Abraham] according to that ' ratio seminalis,' whereby he was through concumbency to pass into his mother; in which manner the Flesh of Christ was not there, although, according to it, the flesh of Mary was there. Wherefore neither Levi nor Christ were in the loins of Abraham according to the soul; but according to the flesh both Levi and Christ; yet Levi, according to carnal concupiscence, but Christ, according to the bodily substance alone. For since there is in the seed both visible corpulency and an invisible mode, both continued on from Abraham, nay, from Adam himself to the body of Mary, because it too was conceived and had its origin in that manner. But Christ took the visible substance of flesh from the flesh of the Virgin, yet the mode of His Conception was not from human seed, but it came far differently and from above."

"[1] And what more undefiled than that womb of the Virgin, whose flesh, although it came from the layer of sin, yet did not conceive from the layer of sin, so that that law, which, being in the members of the body of death, warreth against the law of the mind, should not have sowed even the Body of Christ Himself in the womb of Mary.—Accordingly the Body of Christ, although It was taken from the flesh of a woman who had been conceived from that layer of the flesh of sin, yet, because It

---

[*] "Aut suscipiendum mundavit, aut suscipiendo mundavit."
[*] De Gen. ad litt. x. 20. n. 35. T. 3. p. 270.
[1] Ib. 18. n. 32. pp. 268, 269.

was not so conceived in her as she had been conceived, neither was It flesh of sin, but 'likeness of flesh of sin.'"

"² Perhaps he calls the mortality of His flesh sackcloth. Why sackcloth? On account of 'the likeness of the flesh of sin.' For the Apostle says, 'God sent His Son into the likeness of flesh of sin, that from sin He might condemn sin in the flesh.'—Not that there was sin, I say not in the Word of God, but neither, I say, in that Holy Soul and Mind itself of that Man Whom the Word and Wisdom of God had co-aptated to unity of Person with Himself: but neither, again, in that Body Itself was there any sin; but the 'likeness of the flesh of sin ' there was in the Lord; for death is not, save from sin, and that Body was in truth mortal. For unless It were mortal, It would not die; if It died not, It would not rise again; if It did not rise again, It would not show us an example of eternal life. So then death, which is caused by sin, is called sin, as, by 'the Greek tongue,' 'the Latin tongue,' we mean, not the member of the body, but what is done by the member of the body.—So then, sin of the Lord is what is made from sin, because He took flesh thence, from that very mass which had deserved death for sin. For, to speak more concisely, Mary from Adam died on account of sin; Adam died on account of sin, and the Flesh of the Lord from Mary died for the effacing of sins."

"³ Lo, whence original sin is derived (Gen. iii. 7); lo, whence no one is born without sin. Lo, why the Lord did not will so to be conceived, Whom a Virgin conceived. He loosed it, who came without it; He loosed it, Who did not come from it."

"⁴ Christ hath no sin; He neither derived original sin, nor added of His own. He came, apart from the pleasure of carnal passion; no marital embrace was there; from the body of the Virgin He assumed not a wound, but a medicament; He

---

² On Ps. 34. Serm. 2. n. 3. T. iv. 239, 240.
³ Serm. 151. n. 5. p. 720.
⁴ Serm. 294, De bapt. parv. n. 11, p. T. v. 1188.

assumed, not what He should heal, but whence He should heal. I speak as pertains to sin. He then Alone was without sin." "ᵇ Adam first received the bite of the serpent with poison. Therefore (man) born in flesh of sin, is saved in Christ through 'likeness of flesh of sin.' 'For God sent His Son,' not in flesh of sin, but, as it follows, 'in likeness of flesh of sin,' because He came not from marital embrace, but from the Virgin's womb.—Not in the likeness of flesh, for It was true Flesh, but 'in likeness of flesh of sin,' because It was mortal flesh, without any sin whatsoever." "ᶜ The Apostle said, 'We too were at one time by nature children of wrath.' We do not accuse nature. God is the Author of nature. Nature was formed good by God, but by evil will it was vitiated by the serpent. Therefore what in Adam was of fault, not of nature, to us who are propagated is now become of nature. From this fault of nature, with which man is born, none frees, save He Who was born without fault. From this flesh of sin none frees, save He Who was born without sin by 'the likeness of flesh of sin.'" "ᵈ The Apostle, wishing to show that the mass of the human race was poisoned from its origin, therefore set down *him*, from whom we were born [Adam], not *him*, whom we imitated [Satan].—Because, according to the layer of the flesh, we were all in him [Adam] before we were born, we were there, as in a parent, as in the root. So, that tree was poisoned, in which we were."

"ᵉ The heretics [Pelagians] were not yet born, and they were already pointed out. He [John Baptist] cried out against them from the river, against whom he now cries out from the Gospel. Jesus came ; and what saith he ? 'Behold the Lamb of God.' If one innocent is a lamb, John too was a lamb. Was not he too innocent ? But who is innocent ? How far innocent ? All come from that layer, and from that graft, of which David chants groaning, 'I was conceived in iniquity, and in sins did my mother nourish me in the womb.' He then

---

ᵇ Ib. n. 13.   ᶜ Ib. n. 14.   ᵈ Ib. n. 15.
ᵉ In S. Joh. Ev. Tract. iv. n. 10. T. iii. 2. pp. 316, 317.

Alone was a Lamb, Who did not so come. For *He* was not conceived in iniquity; because He was not conceived of mortality; nor did His mother nourish *Him* in sins in the womb, Whom a Virgin conceived, a Virgin bore, because she by faith conceived, and by faith she received. Therefore, 'Behold the Lamb of God.' *He* hath not that layer from Adam; He took only flesh from Adam: He did not take to Him sin. He Who did not take to Him sin from our mass, He it is, Who taketh away our sin. 'Behold the Lamb of God; behold Him Who taketh away the sin of the world.'"

"'From this concupiscence of the flesh, which, although in the regenerate it is no longer accounted as sin, yet doth not happen to nature save from sin; from this concupiscence of the flesh, I say, as the daughter of sin,—whatsoever flesh is born, is bound by original sin, unless it be re-born in Him, Whom, without that concupiscence, a virgin conceived; wherefore, when He vouchsafed to be born in the flesh, He Alone was born without sin."

"'The Pelagian seems to confess that 'Christ came in the flesh,' but, sifted, he is found to deny it. For Christ came in flesh, which was 'the likeness of flesh of sin,' but was not 'flesh of sin.' The Apostle's words are, 'God sent His Son in the likeness of flesh of sin;' not 'in the likeness of flesh of sin,' as though the flesh were not flesh, but, because it was flesh, yet was not flesh of sin. But this Pelagius essays to set all other flesh of every infant on a par with the Flesh of Christ. It is not so, Best-beloved. For 'the likeness of the flesh of sin' would not be set forth as a great thing in Christ, unless all other flesh were flesh of sin."

"'Why toilest thou, by great argumentations, to reach the precipice of impiety, that 'the Flesh of Christ, because He was born of Mary, the flesh of which Virgin, like that of all the rest, had been propagated from Adam, differs nothing from the

---

* De nupt. et concup. i. 24. n. 27. T. x. 294.
¹ Serm. 183. c. 8. T. 5. p. 877. B.
² C. Julian. Pel. v. 15. n. 52. x. 654.

flesh of sin, and the Apostle is believed to have said without
any distinction, that He was sent in the likeness of the flesh
of sin?' yea rather, thou urgest, 'that there is no flesh of sin,
lest Christ's too should be such.' What then is 'likeness of
flesh of sin,' if there is no 'flesh of sin?' Thou sayest that 'I
did not understand this sentence of the Apostle,' yet didst not
thyself explain it, that we might learn from thee, that a thing
can be like another thing, which itself is not. But if this is
senseless, and the Flesh of Christ is, without doubt, not 'flesh
of sin,' but 'like to flesh of sin,' what remains for us to understand, but that, It excepted, all other human flesh is 'flesh of
sin?' And hence it appears that that concupiscence, whereby
Christ would not be conceived, caused in the human race the
propagation of evil, because the body of Mary, although derived
thence, did not transmit it to the Body, Which she did not
thence conceive. But whosoever denies that the Body of Christ
was said to be 'in the likeness of the flesh of sin,' because all
other flesh of men is 'flesh of sin,' and compares the Flesh of
Christ with that of other men who are born, so as to assert that
both are of equal purity, is found to be a detestable heretic."

"'But, as relates to the passing of original sin to all men,
since it passes through concupiscence of the flesh, it could not
pass into that Flesh, which the Virgin did not conceive through it."
Then he blames Julian, that he had quoted imperfectly words
of his ' "that Adam infected all who should come of his stock,"
whereas he had said, "by the hidden infection of carnal concupiscence he infected in himself all who should come of his stock."
He did not then infect that Flesh, in Whose Conception that
infection was not. The Flesh then of Christ derived mortality
from the mortality of His Mother's body, because He found
her body mortal. He did not derive the contagion of original
sin, because He did not find the concupiscence of one having
intercourse. But if He had not taken even mortality, but only
the substance of flesh from His mother, not only could not His

---

³ Ib. n. 54. p. 655.
⁴ From the De pecc. mer. et rem. i. 9. n. 10. T. x. p. 7.

Flesh, not have been flesh of sin, but not even ' the likeness of flesh of sin.' "

" ' The Nature of the Man Christ was not unlike our nature, but was unlike our fault. For He was born Man without fault, which none of mankind was."

" ' God created man upright, being the Author of natures,

' Ib. n. 57. p. 656.

' De Civ. Dei, xiii. 14.   Other passages are de Trin. xiii. 12. n. 16. Opp. viii. pp. 937, 938, "The sin of the first man, passing to all born of the union of the two sexes by reason of their origin [originaliter] and the debt of the first parents binding all their posterity." Ep. 187 (lib. ad Dard.), n. 31. Opp. ii. 688, "Christ willed not that His Flesh should come through such concurrence of male and female; but, from a Virgin, who desired nothing of such sort in His Conception, He took for us ' the likeness of flesh of sin,' whereby the flesh of sin should be cleansed in us. 'For as through the offence of one,' saith the Apostle, 'unto all men to condemnation, so through the justification of One to all men unto justification of life.' For no one is born without carnal concupiscence operating, which is derived from the first man, Adam; and no one is re-born without spiritual grace operating, which is given through the second Man, Who is Christ. Wherefore, if we belong to Adam by birth, to Christ by re-birth, and no one can be re-born before he is born; then He was born in a peculiar way, Who had no need to be re-born, because He passed not from sin, in which He never was, nor ' was He conceived in iniquity, nor did His mother in the womb nourish Him in sins,' because ' the Holy Ghost came upon her, and the virtue of the Highest overshadowed her, wherefore the Holy Thing which was born of her, is called the Son of God.' " The like contrast is in the Enchiridion (after A.D. 421). Of us, he says (c. 26. Opp. vi. 206), "[Adam] after his sin being made an exile, his own race also, which by sinning he had vitiated in himself, as in its root, he bound by the punishment of death and condemnation; so that whatever progeny should be born of himself and his wife, through whom he had sinned and who was with him con-

not of vices; but man, of his own will depraved and justly condemned, generated men depraved and condemned. For we were
all in that one, when we all were that one, who fell into
sin through the woman, who was made from him before sin.
For not as yet was that form, in which we should, each of us,
live, created and distributed to us individually; but there was
already that seminal nature, from which we should be propagated; the which being vitiated on account of sin, and being
bound by the bond of death and justly condemned, man should
be born of man not of another condition."

He uses the same language in that unfinished
work, from the midst of which he was translated
to his reward['], his reply to Julian's insolent attack
on his work, "De nuptiis et concupiscentia." His
immediate subject is, the "great and ineffable" mystery, "penetrable by no understanding, comprehended by no thought," of "the natural laws of
propagation." By these, according to the Scripture
illustration of Levi paying tithes in Abraham,
each man was in his forefathers, but Jesus was excepted from the laws consequent thereon, by reason
of His Virgin-Birth.

demned, by carnal concupiscence, wherein was repaid a punishment like to the disobedience, should derive original sin."
But of our Lord he says, "It is not lawful to say that any
thing of human nature was wanting in that assumption, but
of nature every way free from every bond of sin; not such as
it is born from both sexes, through concupiscence of the flesh,
with the bond of sin, the guilt whereof is washed away by regeneration, but such as it was fitting that He should be born
of a virgin, Whom the faith of His mother, not passion, had
conceived." Ib. c. 34. p. 209. See also on Psal. l. n. 10. p. 467.

['] Prosper, Chron. A. 438.

"[*] But if it be asked, how Christ was not decimated, since He too, it is plain, according to the origin of His Flesh, was in the loins of Abraham, when that father was decimated to Melchisedek, nothing else occurs, save that Mary, His mother, of whom He took flesh, was born of the carnal concupiscence of parents, but not so did she conceive Christ, Whom she conceived not from human seed, but from the Holy Ghost. He then did not appertain to that relation of seed of man, through which *they* were in the loins of Abraham, whom Holy Scripture attests to have been decimated in him."—"Concupiscence of the flesh—there either was not in Adam before he sinned, or it was vitiated in him through sin.—Either then it is itself fault, if there was none before sin, or itself was, without doubt, vitiated by sin; and therefore original sin is derived from it. There was then in the body of Mary the fleshly matter, whence Christ took flesh, but carnal concupiscence did not sow Christ in her. Whence He was born of flesh, with flesh, yet in 'the likeness of flesh of sin,' not, as other men, in flesh of sin, wherefore He dissolved original sin in others by regeneration, He did not Himself contract it by generation. Therefore the one was the first Adam, Christ was the second; for the first was made, the second was born, without concupiscence of the flesh; but the first was only man, the second was both God and Man: and therefore the first could not-sin [i. e. could keep from sin], not, like the Second, could-not sin [i. e. was incapable of sinning]."

S. Augustine's answer to Julian's insolent con-trast of him with Jovinian in this same work, im-plies the same belief. Julian had said, in the course of a series of contrasts between him and the heretic Jovinian, giving the preference to Jo-vinian,

"[*] *He* undid the virginity of Mary, by the condition of her child-bearing; thou transferrest Mary herself to the devil by the condition of birth."

---

[*] Op. Imp. c. Julian. vi. 22.   [*] Ib. iv. 122.

S. Augustine denies this;

"We do not transfer Mary to the devil by the condition of birth; but on this ground, that the condition of birth is dissolved by the grace of re-birth."

S. Augustine does not even give a special answer to the charge.   He gives one answer which applies to all Christians; the ill condition of birth is undone by the grace of re-birth.   This is true of each of us through Holy Baptism.   S. Augustine does not say that the condition of Mary's birth was different from that of others: he only says that it was undone.   But if it was undone, then it was there, to be undone.   This seems to me to lie in S. Augustine's own words, "*but on this ground.*"   He does not deny that such was the result of the condition under which the Blessed Virgin received her existence; but he says, that it was healed.   And the force of his words implies that it was healed by an act subsequent to the reception of her existence.   In her too, "the condition of birth was dissolved by the grace of re-birth."   To be re-born implies having been previously born.

Perrone's comment on the three first of these passages is,

"[1] From which texts it is plain to any one who is not carried away by a spirit of party, that the holy Doctor taught that Christ Alone was to be exempted from the universal contagion of sin; but that the Blessed Virgin, as having derived her being from the ordinary generation of both parents, contracted the

---

[1] l. c. pp. 58, 59.

common stain, and that her flesh was from sin and was flesh of
sin, which (flesh) Christ cleansed, either when about to take it,
or by taking it."

I gave the above authorities, mostly as grouped
together by S. Augustine. Perhaps it will be best
to add some others of the same period, lest this
writing should fall into other hands than those for
whom it is intended, and they might think the evidence of the belief in the transmission of original
sin less strong than it is. At the same time, the
multiplicity of minds who hold the same language,
as to the universality of original sin, and that,
alleging the mode of our birth as the ground of
that universality, or making the exception of our
Lord Alone, seems to me the more to evince the
absence of any tradition that there was any other
exception besides our Lord, or that any one born
according to the law of our birth was excepted.

14. S. Clement of Alexandria [2] [2nd Cent.] contrasts man's *innate* sinfulness with the single exception of our Lord.

"[3] For the Word Himself Alone is without sin; for to sin is
a thing innate (ἔμφυτον) and common" [to all].

---

[2] This and the eight following are quoted by Klee, Dogmatik
ii. 330—336. Of the Immaculate Conception of the B. V., he
said, "Has there not been only a single exception, viz. of the
Holy Virgin, and that in honour of her Son? Did she not by
a very special grace remain untouched by original sin? This
question has no doctrinal quality [A.D. 1830], but there are
many, and there is much, for the affirmative." Ib. 347, 348.

[3] Pæd. iii. 12. T. i. p. 307. Pott.

In another place, in answer to Cassian, who, as a leader of the Docetæ, condemned marriage, he assumes as agreed, that all lay under the common sentence from Adam, but, since there was this evil in all, before actual sin, he says, as an "argumentum ad hominem," that if, on account of this inborn evil, they condemned marriage as giving birth to the body, they must condemn the origin of the soul too (which they did not), since it was more in fault[4].

15. Eusebius of Cæsarea confessed this. He says, on the words, "In sin did my mother conceive me:"

"[5] Like to these words are those in Job, ' Cursed the day in which I was born, and the night wherein they said, Lo, a man child !' For wherefore was it 'cursed,' but that he was conceived in iniquities ? For it was consequent, that curse should follow sin. Jeremiah used the like words, 'Cursed the day in which I was born, and the night in which my mother conceived me.' For it had been blessed, that neither should the

---

[4] " Let them tell when the child just born fornicated; or how did it, who had worked nothing, fall under the curse of Adam. It is left to them, as it seems, to say consistently that the birth was evil, not of the body only, but of the soul also, for the sake of which is the body also. And when David says 'I was conceived in sins, and in transgressions was my mother pregnant of me,' he, as a prophet, calls Eve mother. But Eve was the mother of the living; and if he was conceived in sins, yet he was not himself in sin, nor was he himself *sin*.—He does not accuse Him Who said 'Increase and multiply;' but the first impulses, from our birth according to which we know not God, he calls ungodliness." Strom. iii. 16. T. i. pp. 556, 557. Pott.

[5] Comm. in Psalm l. in Montf. Coll. Nova, i. 211.

first woman, transgressing the commandment, have ministered to the corrupt birth, but should remain in paradise, likened to the angels. ' But through envy of the devil death came into the world.' But the birth through flesh and blood ministered to death for the abiding of the mortal race."

16. S. Athanasius seems to me to explain S. Paul's words, " First-born of many brethren," to mean this, that our Lord's Flesh was first exempted from the effects of Adam's transgression, and, being united with the Word, became a principle of life and holiness. In a writer so accurate as S. Athanasius, I cannot but think that the words that " our Lord's Flesh was *saved* and liberated" must mean, that It was " saved " from that which he had just spoken of, the evil inherited from Adam's transgression, and was first " liberated " from that condition to which it had hitherto been subject, and so in her too from whom It was taken.

" ' When He put on a created nature, and became like us in body, reasonably was He therefore called both our Brother and 'First-born.' For though it was after us that He was made man for us, and our brother by similitude of body, still He is therefore called and is the 'First-born' of us; because, all men being lost according to the transgression of Adam, His Flesh *before all others* was saved and liberated, as being the Lord's Body, and henceforth we, becoming incorporate with It, are saved after His pattern."

17. Didymus of Alexandria, who lived almost throughout the fourth century, mentions the virgin-birth as the ground of our Lord's being free

* C. Arian. Orat, ii. § 61. pp. 367, 368. Oxf. Tr.

from original sin, to which all besides are subject, and that, in controversy with Manichees.

" ' What he [S. Paul in those words, 'the likeness of sinful flesh '] says, is of this sort: The flesh of all men hath its being from fleshly union, except the Protoplast, and He whom the Saviour took. For otherwise it would not be the body of a man, except by union of male and female. Since then the Saviour took from the Virgin alone a Body, not having its origin from intercourse, he called the Flesh of the Lord, 'the likeness of the flesh' which is from intercourse. For he did not say simply that He had 'the likeness of flesh,' but 'the likeness of flesh of sin.' But 'the likeness of flesh of sin' is flesh, differing from other flesh in this alone, that It had Its being without man. But if He had taken a body through fleshly union, not having that which is different, He too would have been held to have been under sentence of that sin, to which we all, who are from Adam, have been subject through succession."

Of us, he says,

. " ' We are all born under sin, since the origin itself is in fault."

18. S. Macarius, of Egypt, a contemporary of S. Athanasius, in strong terms declares the hereditary defilement of the whole human race, as derived from the sin of Adam.

" ' For there is a certain hidden defilement and overflowing darkness of passions, which, contrary to the pure nature of man, through the transgression of Adam, secretly invaded the whole of humanity, and thus muddies and defiles both body and soul."

' C. Manich. n. 8. Gall. vi. 312.
' On 1 John v. 19, Latin, Ib. p. 304.
' De pat. et discr. n. 9. Gall. vii. p. 182.

" ¹ Satan, tossing souls and sifting through a sieve, i. e. through earthly things, the whole sinful race of men, from the fall of Adam, who transgressed the commandment and came under the ruler of wickedness," &c.

" ² For as from one man, Adam, the whole race of men was spread over the earth, so one vice of passions invaded the whole sinful race of men."

19. Mark the Hermit (throughout the fourth century, if the same as Mark Ascetes, else early in the fifth century) puts down as a ground of repentance, that if (which is impossible) any were kept from even lesser sins, still all are under original sin.

" ³ Let us assume that some were found free from these things too [lesser faults], and, from birth, alien from all vice (which indeed is impossible, since Paul saith, ' all have sinned and come short of the glory of God, being justified freely by His grace '), yet even if they were such, still they derive their origin from Adam, and all have come under the sin of the transgression, and therefore have been condemned to the sentenced death, and cannot be saved out of Christ. But Christ having been crucified, and purchasing all therefrom by His own Blood, then are they too redeemed. Then He Himself too, the Redeemer, lays down one all-comprehensive rule for all, and says to the Apostles, ' Say to them, Repent ; for the kingdom of heaven is at hand.' "

20. S. Gregory of Nyssa, A.D. 370, connects the holiness of our Lord's Human Nature with the Birth of a Virgin :

" ⁴ For He Alone, ineffably conceived, and unexplainably borne in the womb, opened the virgin womb, not having been before opened by marriage, guarding the tokens of virginity

---

¹ Hom. V. n. 1. Ib. p. 22.   ² Ib. n. 3. p. 23.
³ Opusc. iii. de Pœnit. n. 10. Gall. viii. 34.
⁴ De occursu Dom. Opp. T. i. pp. 448, 449. Mor.

unimpaired after His miraculous going forth also, and He Alone is believed to be spiritually a male child, contracting nothing of the female sin, whence He is also indeed worthily called Holy; as Gabriel too, bearing to the Deipara the tidings of the life-giving Birth, as it were reminding her of that legislation, which was fore-ordained concerning Him and regarded Him Alone, said, 'Wherefore also that Holy Thing which is born of thee shall be called the Son of God,' in that the title of 'Holy' properly befitted Him Who opened the virgin womb by that Divine miraculous agency."

The immediate subject is the "illæsa virginitas;" but S. Gregory connects this too with the Conception of a Virgin, and his words go beyond the occasion;

"In regard to other first-born, Evangelic accuracy, espying guardedly into the depth of the law, directed that they should be called 'holy,' as obtaining this title by being hallowed to God; but in the case of the First-Begotten of all creation, the Angel called 'Him Who was born, Holy,' as being properly so, as, contemporaneously with His being born, showing, as the prophet saith, that which was indeed holiness, by the rejection of evil and the choice of good."

Our evil, like S. Augustine, he ascribes to the passion which our first parents admitted, and which they transmitted to us by the law of our birth:

"'For if any one were to consider the necessary passions of the soul, he will deem the removal of the evils conjoined therewith impracticable, impossible. Straight from passion our origin begins, and through passion our growth advances, and in passion our life endeth; and, in a way, the evil is mixed up with nature, through those who from the beginning admitted willingly passion, those who, through the disobedience, brought

---

* De beatitud. Or. G. T. i. p. 817. Mor.

H

the disease into their house. For as, in the succession of
animals, born each after its kind to those before them, the
nature is co-transmitted, so that that which cometh to be
is, according to the law of nature, the same as that from
which it is born, so man is born from man, empassioned from
empassioned, sinner from sinner. Wherefore sin is in a
manner co-existent with those born, being co-engendered, and
co-augmenting, and co-terminating with the bound of life."

" ' For man was conceived, as it were, in some womb of
error, through the evil seed, sitting in darkness and the shadow
of death."

21. I may as well add the ancient but unknown
author of the book on Baptism, which used to be
accounted S. Basil's. He only states the universality of our defilement by reason of our birth,
quoting the same texts, which were quoted in later
times in proof that there was no exception:

" ' That word 'anew' (S. John iii. 3) shows, I suppose, the
repairing of the former birth in the defilement of sins; in that
Job says that 'no one is clean from sin, not if his life be of one
day,' and David, mourning and saying, 'I was conceived in
iniquities, and in sins did my mother conceive me,' and the
Apostle protesting that 'all have sinned and come short of the
glory of God,' &c. Wherefore remission of sins is given to
them that believe, as the Lord Himself says (Matt. xxvi. 28),
as the Apostle again attests (Eph. i. 5), that as a statue,
crushed and broken, and having lost the glorious form of the
king, is anew formed by the wise workman and good maker,
exerting himself for the glory of his work, and restoring it to
its ancient splendour, so we too, having suffered on account of
their disobedience of the commandment (according to Ps.
xlviii. 13), might be recalled to the first glory of the image of
God."

---

* De eo, quid sit, ad imag. dei, ii. 29. Mor.
' L. i. n. 7, App. Opp. S. Basil, ii. 634.

22. In the Western Church, S. Pacian, early in the fourth century, states, without exception, save of Christ, that the sin of Adam passed to all his posterity, by reason of their birth of him.

" 'The sin of Adam had passed upon the whole race. ' For by one man (as saith the Apostle) sin entered into the world, and death by sin, and so death passed upon all men.' Therefore also the righteousness of Christ must needs pass over to the whole race, and, as Adam by sin destroyed the race, so must Christ by righteousness give life to all His race. This the Apostle urges (quoting Rom. v. 19. 21). But one says to me, 'but the sin of Adam deservedly passed to his posterity, because they were born of him, and are we then born of Christ, that for His sake we should be saved?' Do not think carnal things: now ye shall see how we are born of Christ as a parent."

23. S. Paulinus declares how Adam's sin was transmitted to his whole race, and that, in special reference to our conception, as spoken of in Psalm li. ;

" 'Unhappy I, who, not even through the wood of the Cross, have digested the poison of the injuring tree. For there remains to me that forefather's poison from Adam, wherewith the first father, transgressing, infected the universality of his race," &c.

" 'For with more ground is that day to be mourned by me, wherein, born into this world, I fell, a sinner, from the womb of a sinful mother², conceived from rank iniquities, so that my mother bore me, already guilty."

 De Bapt. n. 6, 7. pp. 881, 882. Oxf. Tr.
 Ep. 30, ad Sever. n. 2. p. 190. Paris, 1685.
¹ in S. Felic. xiii. 178—182. Gall. viii. 227.
² Peccatricis.

24. The universality of our hereditary death is mentioned also in the writer known as S. Zeno of Verona:

"'That envious accuser—kindled by detestable envy, seducing, since he could not in his own, in another form, persuading to the transgression of the commandment of God, through the woman, miserably slew him; and thenceforth, destroyed by a hereditary condition, the whole human race uniformly perished.''

25. S. Augustine's teaching was handed down, not only directly by his own works or by those whose minds he formed, but through the reproduction of his works in other forms. Cassiodorus mentions a Catena on S. Paul formed out of S. Augustine's writings by Peter, Abbot of the province of Tripoli, who lived probably soon after S. Augustine's decease, since Cassiodorus speaks of the Abbot Peter's work in the past, and in some uncertainty, as to the work [4]. It adds, of course,

---

[3] Tract. xii. n. 2.

[4] "Peter, Abbot of the province of Tripoli, is related to have annotated the Epistles of S. Paul by passages of the works of the blessed Augustine, so as to express by the words of another the hidden meaning of his own heart. These passages he so fitted to each text, that you would rather think it done by the pains of the Blessed Augustine himself" (Cass. de instit. div. lit. c. 8, p. 544). The doubt of Cassiodorus related to the author, not to the work, which he describes, as one who had seen it, and "hoped by the Grace of God to send a copy" to Rome. De Bandelis' citations from Peter of Tripoli occur in the commentary on S. Paul's Epistles in Bede (Opp. T. vi.), which confirms the conjecture of Garnier (on Marius Mercator, p. 378) and Baronius (A. 562, xvi.) that the commentary ascribed to Bede is the Abbot Peter's.

no fresh evidence; being only one more instance of the influence of that great Father's teaching. De Bandelis remarks as to the passages, that they are in fact "the words of S. Augustine." They have been quoted above [s].

26. S. Augustine's teaching was also carried on by writers of sermons, which, before the exact criticism of the Benedictines, used to be accounted his. The next extract is from the sermon of one whom the Benedictines call " [g] a learned and pious author." The denial of *any* exception to the law of our birth is very strong:

" [t] Truly that is the law of sin, which the transgression of its first author brought upon the human race, through *his* sin, upon whom was passed that sentence of the most just Judge. —This is the law, inserted in the members of all mankind, which warreth against the law of our mind and withholds it from the vision of God.—The whole human race is subjected to this law universally, without any exception."

" [s] *He* Alone was born without sin, to Whom, without embrace of man, not concupiscence of the flesh, but obedience of the mind gave birth.—A virgin conceived; she alone could bear a medicine for our wound, who did not bring forth her Holy Offspring from the wound of sin."

27. The Author of the Hypognosticon or Hypomnesticon (who, if he be Marius Mercator [9], was a contemporary of S. Augustine) uses the same

---

[s] "S. Aug. de Trin. xiii., Encheirid., on Psalm 50. Ep. ad Opt., c. Julian.," and there is one from the de Civ. Dei, x.

[g] On Serm. 102. App.

[t] Serm. 103. n. 2. App. S. Aug. T. v.

[s] Serm. 128. n. 1. App. S. Aug. T. v.

[9] See Bened. Pref. to S. Aug. Opp. T. x. App. pp. 2, 3.

argument from the Apostle's words, "in the likeness of the flesh of sin," yet independently.

"[1] What meaneth it, that the Son of God came in 'the likeness of the flesh of sin,' except that the Flesh had no sin, like
ours, as the Apostle Peter saith, 'Who did no sin,' i. e. had it
not, ' neither was guile found in His mouth?' For by saying
'in the likeness of flesh of sin,' he showed that *That* [Flesh]
was without sin, but ours sinful. For He was therefore 'in
the likeness,' because He was not born through passion as we,
but by the mystical inbreathing was born in true flesh from
the virgin's womb. 'And from sin,' he saith, 'He condemned
sin in the flesh,' i. e. from human sinful nature, sinful, I say,
not God being the Author [of sin], but man falling. He
taking Flesh without fault, as I said, and crucifying It guiltless, sin, which through disobedience had condemned us in the
earthly Adam, is condemned in the heavenly Adam, obeying."

28. Ambrosiaster, if he be Hilary the Deacon [2], is also older than S. Augustine:

"[3] To us it was impossible to fulfil the command of the law,
because we were subject to sin. For this cause ' God sent His
Son into the likeness of flesh of sin.' ' The likeness of flesh ' is
this, that, although It was the same Flesh as ours, It was not so
formed in the womb and born, as is our flesh. For it was
sanctified in the womb, and born without sin; nor did He sin
in It. For therefore was a virgin womb chosen for the Birth
of the Lord, that the Flesh of the Lord might differ in holiness
from our flesh ; for in cause It is like, not in the quality of the
sin of the substance. Therefore he said, 'like,' because, being
from the same substance of flesh, It had not the same nativity,
because the Body of the Lord was not subject to sin. For the

---

[1] Hypogn. i. 2. p. 7. ib.

[2] The Benedictines leave it uncertain, stating both sides. So
does Tillemont, H. E. T. x. p. 297.

[3] On Rom. viii. 3, S. Ambr. Opp. ii. App. p. 70.

Flesh of the Lord was cleansed by the Holy Spirit, that He might be born in a Body, such as was Adam's before he sinned, yet under that sentence alone, which was given on Adam" [liability to death].

29. S. Jerome speaks of " sin " in general terms, but affirms that Christ Alone was without it.

"' Of Him [our Lord] *that* is written as His own, 'Who did no sin, neither was guile found in His mouth.' If I too have this in common with Christ, what had He as His own [proprium]?"

"' We follow the authority of Scripture, that no man is without sin, but that God shut up all under sin, that He might have mercy upon all, save Him Alone, 'Who did no sin, neither was guile found in His mouth.'"

"' I grant that they ['countless persons'] are righteous, but, 'altogether without sin,' I assent not. For 'without vice,' (in Greek κακία,) I say that man can be; but 'sinless' (ἀναμάρτητος), I deny. For *that* belongs to God Alone, and every creature is subject to sin, and needs the mercy of God."

"' The elder age [in Nineveh] beginneth [deeds of repentance] and reacheth to the younger, for 'no one is without sin, not if his life be of one day,' and the years of his life easily counted. For if the stars are not clean in the sight of God, how much more a worm and decay, and those who are held bound by the sin of offending Adam !"

30. Rufinus, as an explanation of Isaiah's prophecy, " I have trodden the wine press alone," says,

"' For He Alone did no sin, and took away the sins [others 'sin'] of the world."

---

* Ep. 133 ad Ctes. n. 8. T. i. p. 1029. Vall.
' Ep. 121 ad Algas. c. 8. T. i. p. 868.
* Dial. c. Pelag. L. 2. n. 4. T. ii. p. 730.
' On Jon. iii. 5. Opp. vi. 417. Vall.
* Comm. in Symb. Apost. n. 25. p. 88. Vall.

31. S. Cyril of Alexandria, while rejecting, as ungodly, the idea that the purification of the Blessed Virgin after our Lord's Nativity had any personal reference to the Blessed Virgin, states that all women, except herself, bare in iniquity.

"⁹ First we must inquire, about whom the words 'for their purification' are written. For if any one think that they relate to the holy Deipara, or the blessed Joseph, or the Lord, he will be ungodly. For neither did Joseph know the Blessed Virgin, nor did she conceive in iniquities, like the rest of women, so that they offer for their own cleansing. But she conceived without seed, and bare without corruption; but where there is no intercourse of man and woman, no sleep nor pleasure, no sexual union, what need of cleansing? But neither is it said of the Lord, the Undefiled and above all purity."

"¹ The first man then, Adam, having been taken captive, and held unexpectedly by the handwriting of disobedience and the snares of death, and having, moreover, fallen under sin by the unholy designs of that wicked serpent, the beginner of evil, I mean Satan, and the evil having taken possession of the whole race of Adam," &c.

32. The adherence of Cassian, A.D. 424, is the more remarkable, in that he was a semi-Pelagian. He too is commenting on the same text of S. Paul as S. Augustine;

"³ How too shall that be taken, that the Apostle states that He came 'in the likeness of the flesh of sin,' if we too can have flesh, defiled by no pollution of sin? For this too is stated as

---

⁹ S. Cyril on S. Luke, c. ii. in Mai Nova Bibl. Patr. T. ii. pp. 133, 134.
¹ c. Julian. viii. T. vi. 2. p. 278. Aub.
³ Collat. xxii. 11, 12. pp. 585, 586.

something peculiar in *Him*, Who is Alone without sin. 'God sent His Son into the likeness of flesh of sin,' because He, receiving the true and entire substance of human flesh, is not to be believed to have taken sin itself in it, but 'the likeness of sin.' For likeness is not to be referred to the verity of the flesh (as some heretics wrongly say), but to the image of sin. For there was in Him true flesh, but without sin,—flesh like to sinful flesh. Herein then *that* Man, Who was born of a Virgin, is separated by a great distance from us all who are produced by the commingling of the two sexes, that, whereas we all bear not the likeness, but the reality of sin in the flesh, He took not the reality but the likeness of sin, by assuming real flesh."

He had also just declared absolute sinlessness to belong to Christ alone;

"' We cannot deny that many are holy and righteous, but there is great difference between one holy and one immaculate. For it is one thing that any one should be holy, i. e. consecrated to the worship of God; another, to be without sin, which belongs individually to the Majesty of our One Lord Jesus Christ, of Whom the Apostle too pronounces as something chief and special, 'Who did no sin.' For he would have ascribed to Him, as something incomparable and Divine, a very poor praise and unworthy of His dignity, if we too could pass life, unstained by any sin. Again, the Apostle to the Hebrews says, 'We have not a High Priest, Who cannot be touched with a feeling of our infirmities, but was tempted like as we are (pro similitudine), without sin.' If then there can be that communion of our earthly humility with that great and Divine High Priest, that we too can be tempted without any offence of sin, why did the Apostle look up to this as something alone and singular, and detach His merit by so great a severance from man? By this exception alone then He is distinguished from us all, that it is certain that we are tempted *not* without sin, He was tempted without sin."

' Ib. c. 9. p. 584.

121

33. Eusebius of Gaul, who used to be called Eusebius Emisenus, ascribes original sin in plain terms to the Blessed Virgin;

"' The Beginner of all things has His beginning from thee, and receives from thy body the Blood which was to be shed for the life of the world; and took from thee what He should pay for thee also. For not even the Mother of the Redeemer was free ' from the bond of the primæval sin. He Alone, although born of an indebted'[mother],'is yet not held by the law of the primæval debt."

34. S. Peter Chrysologus, A.D. 433, states the universality and the transmission of original sin, as inherent in us, making no exception, except as to our Lord.

"'Thou sayest, 'If I owe to my kind that I am born, do I also to sin, that nature should make me guilty before [my own] fault?' This thy question, the words of the Apostle answer,

---

⁴ De Nativ. Dom. Hom. 2. Bibl. Patr. T. v. p. 1 f. 545. Col. 1618. T. vi. p. 621. Lugd. 1677. The sermon was omitted in the Antwerp Editions, 1555, 1568, Alva notices.

⁵ Pétau (de Inc. xiv. 2. 5) notices that, *per se*, "in herself," was inserted here in the editions, contrary to the old MSS., making the passage to imply the doctrine of the Immaculate Conception, instead of contradicting it. It was not in Turrecremata's MS.

⁶ Debitrice. This is the reading of Turrecremata's MS. There is a trace of it in the reading of the editions, following that of Gaigny, Paris, 1547, "debito *renascatur*," for "debit*rice* nascatur;" *renascatur*, as applied to our Lord, having no meaning. De Alva thinks it of moment, that there follows in Eusebius, "Thou hast little in common with other *mothers;*" but this relates to the Conception and Birth of our Lord.

⁷ Serm. 111.

'In whom all have sinned.' Whether 'in which man' or 'in
which sin ;' through him and in it all have sinned. Sin then
is not turned into nature, but while sin brings death in, it
exacts the punishment due to it by nature. For God had
made nature, so as to create man to life, which, however, while
it generates to death, owns itself subject to that sin, to whose
punishment it is sown in life. Dost thou embrace this, that
thou art justified through Christ, and reject that, that thou art
condemned through Adam ? And complainest thou, that the
punishment of another was against thee, who seest that the
righteousness of Another healeth thee? Is not the whole tree
in the seed ? The fault then in the seed is the fault of the whole
tree."

35. Vincentius of Lerins, A.D. 434.

" * Who, before his [Pelagius'] monstrous disciple Cælestius,
denied that the whole human race was bound by the guilt of
the offence of Adam."

36. S. Leo I., like S. Augustine and others, ascribes the purity and sinlessness of our Lord's Human Nature to the Virgin-Birth, in that what to all besides, conceived after the way of nature, was "the origin of sin," was absent in Him. This he says, mentioning, yet not excepting from the general law, His Virgin Mother, whom, rather, he states to have been cleansed through her conception of her Son.

" ' One common ground of joy there is for all, because our
Lord, the destroyer of sin and death, as He found none free
from guilt, so He came to free all. The Almighty Lord com-
bateth with our most fierce enemy, not in His own majesty but

---

* Commonitorium c. 24.
' De Nat. Dom. Serm. i. n. i. p. 64. ed. Ball.

in our humility, presenting to Him that same form and that same nature, partaking of our mortality, but free from the whole sin. For that is foreign from this Nativity, which is read of all, 'No one is clean from defilement, not even an infant whose life is of one day on the earth.' Nothing then passed upon that singular Nativity from concupiscence of the flesh; nothing flowed from the law of sin. A royal virgin of David's stock is chosen, who, having to be laden with that sacred Offspring, was to conceive that Divine and Human Son in mind earlier than in body."

"[1] [Satan] would not justly lose the original bondage of the human race, unless he were conquered from that, which he had subdued. That this might be, Christ was without human seed conceived of a virgin, whom not human intercourse, but the Holy Spirit, rendered fruitful. And whereas in all mothers conception does not take place without defilement of sin, she drew her cleansing thence, whence she conceived. For where the transfusion of the paternal seed reached not, there the origin of sin did not mingle itself. Unviolated virginity knew not concupiscence, ministered the substance [of the body]. There was taken from the mother of the Lord, nature, not fault[2]. The form of a servant was created without the condition of a servant, because the new Man was so contempered with the old, as at once to take the reality of the race and exclude the fault of the old man."

"[3] To loose this band of sin and death, the Almighty Son of God, filling all things, containing all things, Equal in all to the Father, and from Him and with Him Co-eternal in One Essence, took on Him human nature; and, the Creator and

---

[1] De Nat. Dom. Serm. 2. n. 3. p. 70.

[2] S. Leo nearly repeated this in the letter to Flavian which was examined and accepted by the General Council of Chalcedon; "But He was born by a new Nativity, because unviolated virginity knew not concupiscence, ministered the substance of flesh. There was taken from the mother of the Lord, nature, not fault." Ep. 28. ad Flavian. c. 4. p. 818. See bel. pp. 434, 435.

[3] De Nat. Dom. Serm. 4. n. 3. pp. 79, 80.

Lord of all things, He vouchsafed to be one of mortals, having chosen to Himself the mother whom He had made, who, her virginity entire, should only minister the bodily substance, so that, the contagion of the human seed ceasing, there should be, in the new Man, both purity and verity [of our nature].—In this Nativity was the word of Isaiah fulfilled, 'Let the earth bud and bring forth a Saviour, and righteousness spring up together.' For the earth of human flesh, which in the first transgressor had been cursed, *in this Birth Alone* from the Blessed Virgin yielded a blessed Fruit, and alien from the fault of His race."

"' Unless the Word of God had become Flesh and dwelt among us, unless the Creator Himself had come down to communion with His creatures, and by His Birth recalled human decay to a new beginning, death would reign from Adam to the end, and an insoluble condemnation would abide upon all men, since, from the condition of birth alone, all would have had one cause of perishing. *Alone* then among the sons of men the Lord Jesus was born innocent, because He Alone was born without the pollution of carnal concupiscence."

37. S. Prosper, A.D. 444, speaks of the universality of original sin, and our Lord as the single exception from it.

"' Against the wound of original sin, whereby in Adam the nature of all men was corrupted and subjected to death, and whence the disease of all concupiscence ingrew, the true and mighty and only remedy is the death of the Son of God, our Lord Jesus Christ, Who, being free from the debt of death and Alone without sin, died for sinners, debtors of death."

"' That men should be born, is the benefit of the Creator; that they should perish, is the merit of the transgressor. For in Adam, in whom the nature of all men was pre-formed, all sin-

---

⁴ Serm. 5. de Nat. Dom. c. 5. p. 86.
⁵ Resp. ad cap. obj. Vincent. c. 1. p 130. Basil. 1783.
⁶ Ib. c. 3. p. 131.

ned; and were bound by the same sentence, which he received. Nor, even if they are without sins of their own, are they freed from this bond, unless they be re-born through the Holy Ghost in the Sacrament of the Death and Resurrection of Christ."

38. Chrysippus, Presbyter of Jerusalem, A.D. 455, disciple of S. Euthymius,

"'' Arise, O Lord, into Thy rest.' For 'Thy rest,' he says is the Virgin, and her womb. 'Thy rest,' because it shall be made to Thee a couch and a habitation. 'Arise, O Lord.' For unless Thou arise from the Bosom of the Father, he saith, our race, long fallen, will not rise again. 'Arise, O Lord;' for, even if Thou arise, Thou shalt not be severed from the glory of the Father, and, having come to us below, Thou shalt not quit the heavens, and, appearing in the Flesh, Thou wilt not lessen Thy ante-mundane might. 'Thou and the ark of Thy strength.' For when Thou, having risen thence, shalt seal the ark of Thy sanctification, then will the ark too [the B. V.] rise with all out of that fall, in which the kindred of Eve set her too."

39. Antipater, Bishop of Bostra, A.D. 460, in a sermon on the Annunciation, addresses the B. V.,

"' Hail, thou who, first and alone, bearest a child free from curse."

---

¹ Serm. de laud. V. Mariæ. Bibl. PP. Gr. Lat. ii. 426. Paris, 1624.

¹ In Ballerini Syll. Monumm. de Imm. B. V. Conc. ii. 19. The expressions to which Ball. draws attention on the other side are, "What mother has persuaded God the Word to dwell manifestly amongst us? And who is this Virgin, who appeared more valued by God than all the powers? Who is it that holdeth in her womb the Uncontainable?" (words put in the mouth of S. John B. when he leaped in the womb),—n. 2, p. 6,—"in whom [i. e. woman] He, angered, cast out the first father, in her, pitying, He sojourned." Ib. p. 8. "But the angel said to her, 'Fear not, Mary, for thou hast found favour (or grace) which the protoplast (woman) lost.'" n. 10, p. 20.

40. Vincentius, Presbyter in Southern Gaul, A.D. 480[9], a contemporary of Gennadius (partly quoting from St. Augustine);

" [1] ' In sin did my mother conceive me,' my mother conceived me with the delectation of sin. I, being conceived, drew with me the iniquity of the original offence. Was David born of adultery, he who was born of Jesse, a just man, and his wife? Why then does he say, that he was ' conceived in iniquities,' save that iniquity is drawn from Adam? No one is born, who doth not draw [from him] fault and the punishment of fault. His word ' behold ' signifies that it is manifest; for all see it, all feel it. Man, living in corruptible flesh, has the defilements of temptations impressed upon himself, because he derived them from his very origin, because, on account of the delectation of the flesh, his conception is uncleanness."

41. Olympiodorus, an Alexandrian commentator, about A.D. 501, speaks of the universality of original sin, and *that*, as derived to us through the mode of our birth.

" [3] The human production is not without defilement and sin, whence also infants are baptized, washing away the defilement, which is through the transgression of Adam. But he says this, because nature is weakened through the transgression in Adam, and is become very liable to slide into sin; and this indeed, on account of our production, which is from love of pleasure, not as if sin had been co-essentiated with us. God forbid ! "

---

[9] See Bened. Pref. to Rufinus, pp. xvi—xviii. Gennad. Virr. Ill. n. 80.

[1] Comm. in lxxv. Dav. Ps. in App. Rufini, p. 255 on Ps. 50 (51), 7.

[3] On Job xiv. 2, in MS. of Nicetas in Potter on S. Clem. Strom. iii. 16, T. i. p. 556. Oxon.

42. S. Gelasius, A.D. 493, does not use S. Augustine's term "concupiscence;" in other respects his teaching is the same, that our disordered nature is transmitted by the law of our birth universally. In his encyclical letter to the Bishops throughout Picenum, A.D. 493, remonstrating with them for conniving at a Pelagian Bishop, he answers the objection of those who accused God of injustice, if children were held guilty of original sin.

"[1] This they put forth as the acutest argument for their dogma, not observing that those first parents of the human race, formed of no parents, but of the harmless matter of clay, and compacted by Divine skill and power, pure and undefiled, and made rational, following, of their own will, the devil their seducer, were infected with perverse desires through the excess of transgression. In whom human nature sinned and was vitiated, receiving doubtless evil which before it had not known; revolting from good and right, it is plain by the course of events itself, that it fell into the love of what was evil and perverse. The first parents then of our nature, having become such, rendered themselves passible and corruptible, violating so far the gifts of the Divine Creator, as to be punished with death. For there is no question but that they were (as) dead on that day when they were made mortal. Accordingly *whatever* those parents produced of their stock, is indeed the work of God, according to the institution of nature, but not without the contagion of that evil which they derived through their own transgression; and as to this same infection of evil, it is clearly certain, that it is not the work of God. Therefore that fault, which nature gathered by its own voluntary motion, is not from the creation of God; yet, even from nature, vitiated by itself, God executeth the institution of His own creation, but the creation produces fault, which it received not

---

[1] Ep. vii. Conc. v. 302 —4. Col.

from the institution of the Creator, but which itself took to itself through the fall of its transgression. For if those first men, born of no parents and formed without any infection, could deprave themselves by the ambition of an illicit presumption, and join on the work of the fraud of the devil in the work of God, what marvel, if they, being depraved, produced a depraved offspring? God formed the human substance free by His creation; but does rot slavery, coming from without, according to human laws, make it, by nature, bound and enslaved? By their origin, men are generated enslaved, and, from a servile condition, they are produced slaves; they become, by law of their birth, slaves before they are born. If this can be, in things which belong not to nature, how much less to be wondered at is it, that it should result from those things, whereby the human substance itself is known to be depraved. And thereby as the human substance, having been created pure, did, by the guilty will of reprobate acts, make itself polluted, so did it yield the offspring and progeny of its nature stained, from the guilty will of its acts, because it produced an offspring of the same sort as it made itself by the excess of transgression. And therefore it not only produces from itself what God formed well, but also what itself, inconsistently and ill, added. But how an interior quality of appetency can change nature, is confirmed by the authority of Divine Scripture." Then, having adduced in illustration the history of Jacob and the cattle (Gen. xxx.), he proceeds, "The Divine testimonies and the very sacraments of the Church and the tradition of Catholic Doctors from the Lord and Saviour Himself, teach, that the beginnings of human generation are polluted. Hence it is, that the prophet cries out, ' Who shall boast that he hath a clean heart, and that he is pure from sin? Not even an infant, whose life is of one day on the earth.' Hence it is, that Holy Scripture also says, 'Who can make clean what is conceived from unclean seed? is it not Thou, Who art Alone?' and elsewhere, 'Because it was a cursed seed;' and David too attests, 'I was conceived in iniquities, and in sin did my mother bear me.' And if he says this, who should assert that he was generated otherwise? The blessed Paul too says, ' We too were once by nature children of wrath, even as

I

the rest.'" Then, quoting S. John iii. 36, he adds, "That
wrath of which it is said, 'thou shalt surely die.' The Lord
Jesus Christ Himself pronounces with a voice from heaven,
' Whoso eateth not the flesh of the Son of man, and drinketh
not His blood, shall not have life in him.' *Where we see no one
is excepted,* nor hath any one dared to say, that a little one
without this saving Sacrament can be brought to eternal life.
Whence, since he is held bound by no guilt from his own act,
there remains nothing but that he is polluted by a vicious
nativity alone."

In his ⁴ sayings against the Pelagian heresy,
Pope S. Gelasius, beginning with the same text,
"No one is clean from defilement," instances
Saints of the Old Testament, and goes through
the chief Apostles, S. James, S. Peter, S. John,
who lay in the bosom of the Lord, S. Paul, to show
that no one is free from sin.

43. Julianus Pomerius, A.D. 498, after stating
that our first parents committed that so great sin,
which both cast themselves out of paradise into the
exile of this penal life, and in them, by virtue of
origin [originaliter], condemned the whole human
race ⁵, says,

" ⁶ Adam subjected us to [obnoxiavit] all evils through his
own guilt, from which the Coming of Christ freed us through
grace. Adam transmitted to us his fault and punishment;
Christ, Who could not take our faults, in that He was conceived
and born without sin, through the taking of our punishment,
abolished at once our fault and punishment."

---

⁴ Gelasii Papæ dicta adv. Pelag. hæresin. Conc. v. 366 — 8. Col.
⁵ De Vita Contempl. ii. 19. ap. S. Prosper
⁶ Ib. c. 20

44. Of S. Fulgentius of Ruspe, A.D. 504, Biel has already furnished two passages [1]. In another place, he, like others, assigns our Lord's Virgin-birth and the consequent absence of concupiscence in His Conception, as the ground of the exemption of His sacred Flesh from original sin, whereas His blessed Mother's, conceived in the natural way, was, he says, "flesh of sin."

"[2]In what words shall the singular excellence of that Flesh be expressed—whose original of birth is unwonted, whereby the Word was so made Flesh, that the Only Begotten and Eternal God should, in one Person with His Flesh, be conceived by His own conception of His own flesh! For it is certain, that the flesh of the rest of mankind is born through human concumbency.—And because, in that mutual commingling of man and woman for the generation of children, the concumbency of the parents is not without passion, therefore the conception of the children, born from their flesh, cannot be without sin; wherein not propagation, but passion transmits sin to the little ones. Nor does fecundity of human nature cause men to be born with sin; but the foulness of passion, which men have from the most just condemnation of that first sin. Therefore the blessed David, although born of a lawful and righteous marriage, wherein could be found neither fault of unfaithfulness nor stain of fornication, yet on account of the original sin (whereby those naturally bound are children of wrath, not only the children of the ungodly, but all they too, who are born of the sanctified flesh of the righteous) exclaims, 'Behold I was conceived in iniquities,' &c. The Only Begotten Son of God then, Who is in the Bosom of the Father, that He might cleanse the flesh and soul of man, was incarnate by taking the flesh and rational soul— in order to take away that sin, which the generation of man contracted in the concumbency of mortal flesh, was conceived in a

---

[1] See above, pp. 65, 66.
[2] De fide ad Pet. ii. 16, 17. in S. Aug. App. T. vi. p. 22.

new manner, God incarnated in a Virgin Mother, without congress of man, without passion of the conceiving Virgin, that so, through God-Man, Whom, being conceived without passion, the uninjured womb of the Virgin bare, that sin might be washed away, which all men, at their birth, drag [with them]."

Some further statements were elicited by a formal letter of some Easterns.

45. Peter the Deacon, Leontius, and others, " being sent to Rome on a matter of faith " (the formula of the Scythian monks, that " unus e Trinitate passus est "), wrote, A.D. 521, a confession of their faith to S. Fulgentius and fourteen other Bishops, in exile for their faith in Sardinia. They say of Adam's sin, and its consequences;

" *Death and immortality were placed in a manner in his free will. For he had a capacity for either, that, if he should keep the commandment, he should, without experience of death, become immortal; if he should despise it, death should forthwith follow. So then, depraved by the cunning of the serpent, he, of free will, was made a transgressor of the Divine law, and so, as had been foretold him, is condemned to the penalty of death by the just judgment of God; and, the whole of him, i.e., in soul and body, being changed for the worse, having lost his own liberty, is made over under the slavery of sin. Thenceforth there is none of mankind, who is not born bound by the bond of this sin, save He, Who was born by a new kind of generation, to loose this bond of sin, ' the Mediator of God and men, the Man Christ Jesus.' For what else could or can be born of a slave, but a slave? For neither did Adam beget children, when he was free, but after he was made 'a servant of sin.' Therefore as every man is from him, so also every man is a servant of sin through him. Hence too the Apostle says,

---

* De Incarn. et grat. c. 6. in S. Fulg. Opp. pp. 282, 283. Paris, 1684, and Gall. xi. 239.

'From one to all men to condemnation.' And again, 'By one man sin entered into the world, and death through sin, and so death passed upon all men, in whom all sinned.' They then are altogether deceived who say, that death alone and not sin also passed to the human race, since the Apostle attests, that both sin and death were brought upon the world through him. From this condemnation and death no one is freed except through the grace of the Redeemer," &c.

The formal answer to this letter from the fifteen Bishops was written by S. Fulgentius, but was the act of all; S. Fulgentius, as being one of the youngest, signing nearly the last. It agrees altogether with the statement of Peter.

"[1] One was the Conception of the Divinity and the Flesh in the womb of the Virgin Mary, and One is Christ the Son of God, conceived in both natures, that He might begin to abolish the stain of the vitiated stock thence, whence it seemed to have its being in every one born. For since all men, born from the union of male and female, have the beginning of conception itself aspersed with the contagion of original sin, because the sin to which the first man, being by nature good but seduced by the malignity of the devil, gave entrance, passed to his posterity, together with the penalty, i.e. death, (which the holy David enunciates in truth, saying, 'Behold I was conceived in iniquities, and in sins did my mother bear me,') it was very necessary that the merciful and just Lord, when He would efface the traces of human iniquity, should vouchsafe, Immaculate, to unite to Himself human nature immaculate in the Conception Itself, where the devil had been wont to claim it to his side and dominion, through the stain of original sin inflicted; of that human nature, whose truth and fulness God the Only Begotten willed to assume, He took also His Conception and Nativity."

---

[1] De Incarn. et grat. ad Petr. Diacon. &c. Ep. 17. c. iii. iv. n. 7, 8. p. 290. Paris, 1684.

"'That wonderful then but true Conception and Birth, according to the flesh, of God-Man,—whereby the Virgin ineffably conceived and bore the God of heaven, and remained an unimpaired virgin mother, she who was truly called by the Angel 'full of grace,' and 'blessed among women,' had this [effect], that by aid of preventing grace and by the work of 'the Holy Ghost supervening in her, and the power of the Highest overshadowing her,' she, when she was to conceive God, the Son of God, neither endured nor willed to have intercourse of man, but, retaining virginity both of mind and body, received from Him, Whom she was to conceive and bear, the gift of unimpaired fruitfulness, and fruitful unimpairedness."

"This is the grace, whereby it was wrought, that God, Who came to take away sin 'because in Him is no sin,' was conceived Man, and was born 'in the likeness of flesh of sin,' from 'flesh of sin.' For the flesh of Mary, which, after the manner of men, had been 'conceived in iniquities,' was indeed 'flesh of sin,' which bare the Son of God into 'the likeness of flesh of sin.' For the Apostle attesteth, 'Because God sent His Son into the likeness of flesh of sin,' Him, 'Who, being in the form of God, thought it not robbery to be equal with God, but emptied Himself, taking the form of a servant.' But therefore was the Son of God 'sent in the likeness of flesh of sin,' the Same, Who was made 'in likeness of men,' that He might both be like unto men in the truth of the flesh which He had Himself created, and that He Who was God, being created in the flesh without sin, might take away our unlikeness, which He saw to be in our flesh, not from His own work, but from our sin. The Son of God, then, being sent, appeared in 'the likeness of the flesh of sin,' because in His true human Flesh there was not the iniquity of man, but his mortality. But when 'the likeness of the flesh of sin' in the Son of God, or rather when the Son of God in 'the likeness of the flesh of sin,' is spoken of, it is to be believed, that the Only Begotten God did not derive from the mortal flesh of the Virgin defilement of sin, but received the entire verity of nature, that there might be that birth of Truth from

---

² Ib. c. vi. vii. n. 12—14. pp. 292, 298.

the earth, which the Bl. David hints at in prophetic speech, saying, 'Truth hath sprung out of the earth.' Truly then Mary conceived God the Word, Whom she bore in flesh of sin, which God received. But she obtained [promeruit] this, that she should conceive and bear Himself, God made Man, *not by any human merits*, but by the vouchsafement of the most High God, conceived and born of her. For unless God the Word, uniting to Himself individually human nature, were born, truly and fully Man, of a Virgin, never would it be granted to us, being carnally born, to be spiritually born of God; but, that a Divine nativity might be given to us being carnal, the Divine majesty of the Only Begotten Son was first conceived and born in the verity of flesh. For 'truth was far from sinners,' and our iniquities had severed us by a great separation from God."

46. Boethius (A.D. 510) writes in a condensed style, and leaves much to be supplied, as being already known ; whence, the comment of Porrée, Bp. of Poitiers (A.D. 1125), is often little more than a paraphrase, filling it out. His argument against Eutyches presupposes the doctrine of the universality of original sin. At the close of his treatise "on the Two Natures and One Person of Christ," he meets the question, how our Lord being born of a race, all of whom were involved in the consequences of the fall and of original sin, could, if He really took flesh of Mary, be freed from them. His answer is, in fact, that Christ took real Manhood, but that, not being born according to the natural laws, He took that Nature, as He willed, subject to death and the sinless infirmities of our nature, yet without sin. The question states the universality of the transmission of original sin, not ex-

cepting the Blessed Virgin, from whom our Lord
took His Human Body; the answer grants that
universality, referring the exception in the case of
our Blessed Lord to the freedom of His Divine
Will.

" ' Another question may be put by those who do not believe
that the Human Body [of Christ] was taken from Mary; but
that *that* was separated and prepared elsewhere, which in
adunation should seem to be generated and produced from the
womb of Mary. For they say, ' If the body was taken from
man, but every man was, from that first transgression, not only
held by sin and death, but was also entangled with the affections
of sins, and *that* was to him the punishment of sin, that, being
held bound by death, he should also be guilty through the will
to sin, why in Christ was there neither sin, nor any will of
sinning ?' Such a question involves a doubt which has to be
noticed. For if the Body of Christ was taken from human
flesh, it may be doubted, what that flesh was, which was taken.
For He saved that man, whose nature He took. But if He
took man, such as Adam was before he sinned, He seems to
have taken human nature in its integrity, yet one which did
not at all need cure. But how could He take man, such as
Adam was, since in Adam there could be will and affection to
sin ?—But in Christ it is not believed that there was even any
will to sin. If too He took the body of man, such as Adam's
was before he sinned, He ought not to have been mortal. For
Adam, had he not sinned, would not have felt death. Since
then Christ did not sin, why did He feel death, if He took a
Body, as Adam's before he sinned ? But if He took a condition of man, such as Adam was after he sinned, then, it
seems that Christ ought not to have been free from being subject to transgressions, &c., since all these punishments Adam
drew on himself by transgression. Against whom we must
answer, that there are three possible states of man. One, that

---

' De duab. Nat. et una Pers. Christi, L. iv. in Boethii Opp.
pp. 1217, 1218. c. 8. p. 321—3. Leyd. 1671.

of Adam, before he sinned, in which although there was no
death, nor had he yet defiled himself with any sin, there might be
in him the will to sin.   Another, whereto he might have been
changed, if he had willed to remain firm in the commands
of God.   For then *that* would be to be added, that he not only
should not sin or will to sin, but neither could he either sin or
will to sin.   The third is the state after the offence, wherein
both death necessarily overtook him and sin itself and the will
to sin.—Of these three states, Christ took into His bodily
Nature, in a manner, the causes of each.   For that He took a
mortal Body, in order that He might chase death from the
human race, is to be set down in that state, which was penally
inflicted after the transgression of Adam.   But that in Him
was no will of sin, was taken from that state, which might have
been, had not Adam given his will to the deceits of the tempter.
There remains the third, that is the middle, state, that which
existed at that time, when there was no death, yet the will to
sin could come.   In this condition Adam was such as to eat,
drink, digest, fall asleep, and the like.   All, things human but
allowed, which brought with them no penalty of death; all
which there is no question but that Christ had."

"Thus far," sums up his Commentator Porrée[1], "he divided
the conditions of Adam, or of those who were engendered
by the law of human generation, i. e. by the sin of original
concupiscence.   Of all which he now proceeds to say that
there was something in Christ, Who took His Body from
sinners, yet not by the law of sin; but nothing whatever of
them had He of necessity, to which the sin of their generation
consigns others, but all of His own will Alone."

47. Cassiodorus (A.D. 514) follows S. Augustine
as to the universal transmission of original sin, with
the single exception of our Lord, by reason of His
Virgin-Birth.

"[2] Some opine, that, as that Almighty Creator extracts the

---

[1] Ib. p. 1272.   [2] De anima, c. 7. ii. 633. Ben.

seed of flesh from our body, so also a new soul can be generated from the quality of the soul; that so it may be shown,
by transmission of fault, to be guilty of that original sin which
the Catholic Church confesses, unless it be absolved by the
grace of Baptism. For in what way ought an infant, who has no
wish to sin, to be found at all guilty, unless, in some way, the fault
should appear to be transfused in the origin itself of the soul?
Whence Father Augustine, commendable for his most religious
doubt, says that nothing is rashly to be affirmed: but that it
rests in His secret, as also many other things, which our medio-
crity cannot know. But this is truly and fixedly to be believed,
that God both creates souls, and, on some hidden ground, most
justly imputes to them, that they should be held indebted to the
sin of the first man. For it is better, in causes so secret, to
confess ignorance, than to assume what may be a perilous boldness, since the Apostle says, ' For who hath known the mind
of the Lord? or who hath been His councillor?' and, 'For we
know in part, and we prophesy in part.'

" But since the tenor of the discussion has led us to this subject, that we should say, that souls generally are guilty through
the transmission of sin, it is meet to make mention of the Soul
of Christ the Lord, lest any one, perverted by calumnious in-
tent, should think that It was held bound by the like condition.
Let us hear then that its origin was prophesied by a worthy
herald to holy Mary ever-Virgin[1]. The Angel saith, ' The Holy
Ghost shall come upon thee, and the power of the most Highest shall overshadow thee; therefore that Holy Thing which
shall be born of thee shall be called the Son of God.' Who, I
ask, in this majesty of birth, could either believe, that there
was any fault of original sin, or suspect any profane injury to
the flesh? Without sin He undoubtedly came, Who was about
to loose the sins of all, conceived by the mystical in-breath-
ing, born of a Virgin. He derived nothing from Adam, Who
came, that the evil of Adam might be overcome. That most long
coil, wherewith we were bound, was broken; the torrent, which
hurried us along, was dried there."

---

[1] Or, "that its holy origin was prophesied to Mary ever-
Virgin," accordingly as we read " sanctæ " or " sanctam."

Cassiodorus makes expression the soul from contracting the Lord's, not the Blessed In another place he asserts that our Lord alone was without sin:

"' This see I here no other can say himself save In Behold the prince of this world cometh, nothing in Me.' For He Alone is perceived to be without sin. This is also shown to have taken away the sin of man.'

He affirms generally the universality of original sin against the Pelagians on Ps. L.[1]

48. The Canons of the second Council of Orange, A.D. 529, were drawn up by S. Caesarius of Arles, sent by him to Pope Felix and by Felix sent to the Council which was assembled for the consecration of a Basilica, "strengthened by his Epistle."[2] They affirm strongly the universality of original sin, and the injury therefrom to soul and body.

"' If any one says that, through the offence of the disobedience of Adam, the whole man, i.e. according to body and soul, was not changed for the worse, but believes that the liberty of will remaining uninjured, the body only was subject to corruption, he, deceived by the error of Pelagius, opposes Scripture, which saith, 'The soul which hath sinned, it shall die.' and 'Know ye not, that to whom ye yield yourselves servants to obey, his servants ye are, whom ye obey?' and, 'By whom a man is overcome by him also is he brought in bondage.'"[3]

---

[1] On Ps. cxxxviii. 23.

[2] Gennadius c. 86, and Pref. to second Council of Orange.

[3] Conc. Araus. ii. cann. 1, 2. Concil. T. v. p. 800, Col. The Council was approved by Boniface in a letter to S. Caesarius, A.D. 530. Ib. p. 830.

" If any assert that Adam's disobedience injured him alone, not his posterity, or that the death of the body, which is the punishment of sin, and not also sin which is the death of the soul, passed through one man to the whole human race, he will ascribe injustice to God, contradicting the Apostle, who saith, ' By one man sin entered into the world, and death by sin, and so death passed upon all men, in whom [in quo] all have sinned.' "

S. Cæsarius himself says;

" ¹ What good had the world done, that God should love it? For Christ our Lord not only found all men evil, but also dead by original sin."

49. Fulgentius Ferraudus (A.D. 533) contrasts the Flesh of Christ, as being free from fault of origin, defileability, liability to sin, with that of His mother :

" ² The Flesh therefore of Christ was taken from His Mother; therefore moreover It is true Flesh; but It is clearly holy, because It was cleansed by the uniting of the Divinity. In the Flesh of Christ, there is the *nature* of our flesh, but the fault of our nature is not found there. So the Flesh of Christ is both like and unlike to the flesh of Mary. Like, because It drew thence Its origin; unlike, because It did not thence contract the contagion of a vitiated origin. Like, because It felt, although voluntary, yet true infirmities; unlike, because, neither through will nor through ignorance, did It commit any iniquities whatsoever. Like, because It was passible and mortal; unlike, because It was undefileable and the quickener even of the dead. Like in kind, unlike in merit; like in form, unlike in virtue. Like, because It is 'the likeness of flesh of sin,' as the Apostle saith, ' God sent His Son into the likeness of flesh of

---

¹ Hom. 7. p. 52. Bal.

² Epist. ad Anatol. de duab. in Christo naturis, n. 4. Bibl. Patr. ix. 503.

sin.' See, how far it is taught that the Flesh of Christ received
from Mary by nature the cause of a new existence, according
to the wont of human birth, apart from any need of marital
intercourse, so that It should *not* be flesh of sin, because It
is Flesh of God; yet should be 'likeness of flesh of sin,'
because It was truly born of mortal flesh; and rightly mortal,
because It drew Its substance from mortal flesh. For through
what door should voluntary death enter into flesh of One Who
'had no sin' whatsoever, unless It were born of *her* flesh, in
whom there could be sin, and through sin, death? Let us
explain this in clear language. The Flesh of Christ was not
'conceived in iniquities.' On what ground then seemeth it,
that It experienced death? We know certainly, that the Son
of God died for us, not out of necessity, but of will. Yet the
Holy Apostle is a witness to the truth, saying truly, 'Through
one man sin entered into the world, and death by sin.' In
That Flesh of Christ sin entered not. Whence did death,
although voluntary, creep in, but because Divine power caused
Him to be born without sin, but Divine mercy caused Him to
die without sin? Yet in that in Him was substance of His
Mother, no proof that Christ took flesh of a mortal mother
is stronger than this, that He suffered death. Thanks be to
Him Who, by taking the nature of human flesh without guilt,
did not yet remove guilt without the penalty; He ended the
penalty, and healed the nature, because He had a nature common with us."

50. Primasius, A.D. 550;

"'He took flesh, like other men, without sin, because It
was born neither of concupiscence, nor through marriage, but
of a Virgin." "*That* was not the flesh of sin, which was not born
of carnal delectation; yet there was in It 'the likeness of flesh
of sin,' because It was mortal flesh."

"''Death passed upon all men.' Death, both of soul and
body, passed too on Abraham, Isaac, Jacob, from original sin,

---

* On Rom. viii. 3. Bibl. P. x. 160.
' On Rom. v. 14. Ib. p. 154.

but they were made alive by the grace of God. Of Whom it is
said, ' He is not a God of the dead.' As the Apostle says, 'to
those also, who have not sinned ;' i. e. sin, bringing sentence of
death [capitale], so passed on men; because not only did *he*
die, who transgressed, but those also, who were begotten from
transgressors, are held guilty by the law of nature; i. e. a corrupted root transmitted its fault through all the branches.
Adam slew: Christ made alive."

51. S. Gregory the Great asserts that the origin
of our Lord was alone without sin, on the same
ground as S. Augustine;

"'No one of the saints, of whatever virtues he may be full,
yet, being gathered from that blackness of the world, can be
equalled to Him of Whom it is written, 'The Holy Thing
which shall be born of thee, shall be called the Son of God.'
For we, although we are made saints, yet are not born saints,
because we are constrained by the very condition of corruptible nature to say with the Prophet, ' Behold I was conceived in iniquities, and in sins did my mother bear me.' But
He *Alone* was truly born holy, Who, that He might overcome
the condition itself of corruptible nature, was not conceived by
the commixture of carnal intercourse."

And, on the text, "'Who can bring a clean thing
out of an unclean?" which is sometimes quoted, in
behalf of the Immaculate Conception of the Blessed
Virgin, he dwells on our Lord's being Alone clean,
on the same ground;

"' He Who by Himself is alone clean, avails to cleanse the
unclean. For man, living in corruptible flesh, has the unclean-
nesses of temptations impressed upon himself; because he de-

---

* On Job, L. xviii. c. 52. n. 84. T. i. p. 598. Ben.
* Job xiv. 4.
' Ib. L. xi. end, T. i. p. 392. Ben.

rived them from his origin. For the very conception of his flesh, for carnal delight, is uncleanness. Whence also the Psalmist saith, ' Behold I was conceived in iniquities, and in sins did my mother bear me.'—But it may be understood in this place, that the blessed Job, contemplating the Incarnation of the Redeemer, saw that that Man Alone in the world was not conceived of unclean seed, Who came into the world from the Virgin in such wise, as to have nothing from unclean conception. For He did not proceed from man and woman, but from the Holy Ghost and the Virgin Mary. He Alone then was truly clean in His flesh, Who could not be touched by delight of flesh, since neither through carnal delight did He come hither.''

Elsewhere he speaks absolutely of our Lord Alone being righteous or the object of God's good pleasure '.

When consulted about the origin of the soul, he answered like S. Augustine,

"'As to the origin of the soul there was no small question agitated among the holy Fathers; but, whether itself descended from Adam, or whether it be given to each, remained uncertain; and they owned that the question is insoluble in this life. For it is a grave question, and cannot be comprehended by man. For if the soul is born with the flesh from the substance of Adam, why does it not die too with the flesh? But, if it is not born with the flesh, why, in that flesh which is derived from Adam, is it bound by sins? But while that is uncertain, *this*

' " In our Redeemer Alone was the Father well pleased, because in Him Alone He found no fault." In Ezek. L. i. Hom. 8. n. 21. " The Redeemer of the human race, made through the flesh the Mediator of God and man, because He alone appeared among men righteous, and yet came, even without sin, to the punishment of sin, reproved man that he should not sin, and stayed God that He should not strike." On Job, L. ix. c. 38. n., 61.

' Ep. ad Secundin. L. ix. Ep. 52. Opp. ii. 970, Ben.

is not uncertain, that unless a man be re-born by the grace of
Holy Baptism, every soul is bound by the bonds of original sin.
For hence it is written, 'There is none clean in His sight,
not even an infant of one day on the earth.' Hence David
saith, 'In iniquities I was conceived, &c.' Hence the Truth
Itself says, 'Except a man be born again of water and the
Holy Ghost, he shall not enter into the kingdom of heaven.'
Hence the Apostle Paul saith, 'As in Adam all die, so also in
Christ shall all be made alive.' Why then cannot an infant,
who hath done nothing, be clean in the sight of Almighty God?
Why was the Psalmist, born from lawful wedlock, conceived
in iniquity? Why is one not clean, unless he have .been
cleansed by the water of Baptism? Why does every man die
in Adam, if he is not held by the bonds of original sin? But
because the human race decayed [putruit] in the first parent,
as in the root, it derived aridity in the branches : and every man
is thence born with sin, whence the first man willed not to
abide without sin."

52. S. Isidore of Seville, A.D. 595;

" [1] After that, through envy of the devil, our first father,
seduced by a vain hope, fell, was forthwith exiled, and, being
lost, transmitted the root of evil-mindedness [malitiæ] and sin
throughout his whole race.—God sent His own Son to be clothed
in flesh, and appear to men, and heal sinners.—He, One and
the Same, was God and Man, in the Nature of God equal
to the Father, in the Nature of Man, made mortal, among us,
for us, from us, remaining what He was, taking what He was
not, to free what He had made."

" [2] Man was, for sin, then delivered to the devil, when it was
said to him, 'Dust thou art, and unto dust shalt thou return.'
—Inward division and struggle in the mind of man is the punishment of sin, propagated from the first man to all his sons.—
This mutability was not created with man, but came to him, as
the reward of that first transgression ; but is now made matter
of nature, because it, as well as death, passes, by virtue of his

---

[1] Sent. i. 11 and 14.   [2] De Offic. i. 26.

origin [originaliter], from the first man upon all men.—Christ, in the form of a servant, for the excellence of His Conception, is Lord of all; because, although He took flesh, He did not take it from the passionate contagion of the flesh."

53. John IV., while Bishop of Rome elect, A.D 620, with three other chief clergy, in the vacancy of the See, answered a letter of five Scotch Bishops, some presbyters, and Abbots of Scotland, to Severinus, his predecessor, about Easter. Hearing too that the Pelagian heresy was reviving, they lay down, in stating the Catholic doctrine, that none can be without sin, except Christ, Who was *conceived* and born without sin, because all must at least be subject to original sin.

"³And, first, it is the foolish talking of blasphemy to say that man is without sin; which no one can any wise be, save the one Mediator between God and man, i.e. the Man Christ Jesus, Who was conceived and born without sin. For the rest of men, being born with original sin, are known, even if they be without actual sin, to bear the testimony of the transgression of Adam, according to the Prophet, who saith, 'For behold I was conceived in iniquities, and in sins did my mother conceive me.'"

54. Sophronius, Patriarch of Jerusalem, A.D. 629, writing a carefully worded Synodical Epistle to the Monothelite Patriarch Sergius, speaks of the actual sanctification of the Blessed Virgin, with a view to her being a fit instrument of the Incar-

---

³ Bede, H. E. ii. 19. Perrone (P. i. Concl. n. iv.) says, that the passage *includes* actual sins. It seems to me to *exclude* them.

nation.   The Epistle was read at the sixth General
Council.

"'He willed to become Man, that by Like He might cleanse
like, and by what was Akin He might save akin, and by what
was Connatural He might beautify connatural.   To this end a
holy Virgin is taken, and is sanctified as to body and spirit,
and so ministers to the Incarnation of the Creator, as being
pure and chaste and undefiled.   From the undefiled, then,
and Virgin blood of the all-holy and undefiled Virgin Mary, the
Word Incarnate, truly Man, although conceived in the virgin
womb, and having fulfilled the times of the legitimate pregnancy,
likened to man in all physical things and those which involve

---

' Ep. ad Ser. in Conc. Const. iii. Act. xi. Conc. T. vii. p.
896, 7. Col.   All the praises, given to the B. V. in his homily
on the Annunciation (Ballerin. Syll. Monumm. ii. pp. 33—131),
bear on the Incarnation, and are an expansion of the Angel's
words, 'Hail, engraced one.'   Sophronius, believing that the
Incarnation took place at the Angel's· word 'Hail,' (as he
makes the Angel say expressly, "Thou hast conceived from the
time I addressed to thee, Hail, and uttered to thee that joy-pro-
ducing voice," n. 86, p. 99. add n. 28, p. 81,) no words could
be too strong, to speak of her pre-eminence *then*.   The words
are put in the mouth of the Angel.   "Thou hast surpassed all
creation, as shining more in purity than all creation, and having
received the Creator of all creation, and bearing Him in the
womb and giving birth to Him, and, out of all creation, having
become the mother of God.   Wherefore I say to thee, 'Hail,
engraced one,' since thou hast been engraced more than all
creation, and of such joy and grace in thee I know the cause,
wherefore I again say aloud, 'The Lord is with thee.'" (n. 18, 19.
i. 63, 64.)   "Wherefore seeing thy pre-eminence in all created
things, I say to thee the greatest things, 'The Lord is with thee.'"
(n. 21. p. 67.)   "Truly blessed art thou among women, because
the blessing of the Father hath through thee dawned upon men,
and has freed them from the ancient curse." (n. 22. pp. 67, 68.)
He uses the same term, "fore-purified," as in his Epistle.

not sin, and not disdaining our most passible poorness, is born
God in human form."

55. Bede, A.D. 701, is well known to have followed S. Augustine;

"⁵'Behold the Lamb of God.' Behold the Innocent, the free
from all sin; in that He took bone from the bones of Adam,
and flesh from the flesh of Adam, but drew no stain of guilt
from sinful flesh (de carne peccatrice)."

"⁶ Lo, the Word of God, co-eternal with the Father, and Light
from Light Begotten before all worlds, shall in the end of the
world take Flesh and soul, weighed down by no weight of sin,
and from the virgin's womb as a Bridegroom from his chamber
shall come forth into the world. 'Therefore also That Holy
Thing, which shall be born of thee, shall be called the Son of
God.' In distinction from our holiness, it is asserted that
Jesus shall be born holy, in a way belonging to Him Alone
[singulariter]. For we, although we are made holy, are not
born holy, because we are held bound by the condition of our
corruptible nature. So that each of us may truly say, groaning with the Prophet, 'For behold I was shapen in iniquities, and in transgressions did my mother bear me.' For He
Alone was truly holy, Who, to overcome the condition of our
corruptible nature, was not conceived by the commingling of
carnal concupiscence."

"⁷ What is said in Matthew, 'in Whom I am well pleased,'
is thus explained:—That every one who, repenting, corrects
things which he has made, thereby that he repents, shows that
he is displeased with himself, in that he amends what he has
made. And because the Almighty Father spoke of sinners, as
He could be understood by men in a human way, 'I repent
that I have made man upon earth,' He was in a manner displeased with Himself as to the sinners whom He created. But
in the Only Begotten Alone, our Lord Jesus Christ, He rested

---

⁵ On S. John i. 29.   ⁶ On S. Luke i. 35.
⁷ On S. Luke iii. 22.

with pleasure. For of Him Alone among men, He did not repent to have created man, in Whom He found no sin whatsoever."

" ' 'Behold I was conceived in iniquities, and in sin did my mother conceive me.' As if he said, ' Lo, how Thou prevailest against all; not such only as I am now after such a deed, but such as I first was, and every man, for Thou hast what Thou canst impute to me and to all, from my very origin.' This he says, speaking in the name of the whole human race. For ' I was conceived in iniquities, as was every man.' For from that righteous man Jesse, and from his lawful wife, was he ' conceived in iniquities,' i. e. in adultery ? By no means. For that chaste act hath in the wife no blame, but yet draws with it the appointed punishment, delectation. Which, since it proceeded from iniquity, i. e. from the transgression of the first man, and because it is in a certain way 'iniquity,' therefore he says, 'in iniquities I was conceived.' But He 'prevaileth,' because He Alone was conceived without delectation ; therefore He Alone was born without pain. And therefore He Alone hath what He may impute to a child even of a day old."

56. S. John Damascene, A.D. 730, like S. Gregory of Nazianzum, speaks of her "cleansing," just antecedent to and preparatory to the Incarnation.

" ' After the assent of the holy Virgin, the Holy Spirit came upon her, according to the word of the Lord which the Angel spake, cleansing her and bestowing upon her a power to receive the Godhead of the Word, and also a conceiving power."

This statement of John Damascene is quoted by S. Thomas Aq.¹ as an alleged ground, why it

---

* On Ps. 50. Opp. T. 8. p. 563.   ' De fide orthod. iii. 2.

¹ 3 p. q. 27. art. 3. ad 3. It is among the counter authorities quoted by Scotus in 3. d. 3. q. 1, and subsequently by G. Biel. See above, p. 66.

should not be thought that the fomes peccati was totally removed from the B. V. until after the Incarnation. He himself thought that the cleansing might be twofold; one, preparatory to the Conception of Christ, not from any impurity of fault or from the fomes, but rather collecting her mind into one; but that, secondly, the Holy Spirit worked a cleansing in her, by means of the Conception of Christ, which is the work of the Holy Spirit. And in this way it might be said, that He cleansed her wholly from the fomes peccati, or the law of our members.

In a sermon among the works of John Damascene, it is said,

"'Her did the Father predestinate, the prophets through the Holy Ghost foretold; the sanctifying power of the Spirit came upon her, and cleansed her and sanctified her, and, as it were, forebedewed her. And then, Thou, the Word of the Father, didst, uncircumscribed, dwell in her."

In like way Bede says,

"'The Holy Spirit coming upon the Virgin showed in her in two ways the efficacy of His Divine power; for He both purified her mind from all defilement of sins (as far as human frailty permits), that so she might be worthy of the heavenly birth, and by His sole operation He created in her womb the holy and venerable Body of our Redeemer.—The virtue of the Most Highest overshadowed the Bl. Mother of God. For the Holy Spirit, when He filled her heart, tempered it from all heat of carnal concupiscence, cleansed it from temporal desires, and consecrated at once her mind and body with heavenly gifts.

' Hom. i. in dormit. B. M. V. n. 8. T. ii. p. 859.
' Hom. in Fest. Ann. Opp. T. 7. p. 337.

'Therefore also that holy Thing which shall be born of thee'
(he saith) 'shall be called the Son of God.' Because thou shalt
conceive from sanctification of the Spirit, That which is born
shall be holy.   The Nativity agrees with the Conception, that
since thou, a Virgin, conceivest against the wont of human
nature, thou shouldest conceive the Son of God above the way
of human nature.   For all we men are conceived in iniquities,
and born in sins.   Our Redeemer Alone, Who vouchsafed to be
incarnate for us, was born at once holy, because He was conceived without iniquity."

57. Alcuin, A.D. 780, or an author nearly contemporary [4], implies that the absence of original sin
in our Lord was owing to the mode of His Birth.

" ' In the end of the ages He [God the Son] took from Mary
Ever-Virgin perfect Man of our nature, and the Word was made
Flesh, by assuming manhood, not by exchanging Divinity, the
Holy Spirit coming in the Blessed Virgin, and the Power of
the Highest overshadowing her.   It is written, ' Wisdom built
her a house,' i. e. created flesh in the womb of the Virgin,
animated by a rational soul.   Whence it is asked rightly, since
the works of the whole Trinity are inseparable, why is the
Holy Ghost alone said to have wrought the creation of the
flesh ? But because sanctification is wrought through the Spirit,
and the same Spirit is in such wise God, as to be also the gift
of God, therefore the Holy Ghost is said to have created the

---

[4] Frobenius placed "The Confession of Faith" among Alcuin's
doubtful works.   Mabillon answered the objections of Daillé
to its genuineness, and showed that it belongs to Alcuin and his
age. The characters of the MS., from which Chifflet published it,
"approach very nearly to the time of Charlemagne, and do not
seem later than the 9th century."   Test. de antiq. cod. Boer.
Opp. T. 2. p. 380.   The only objection is, that the name of
Albinus occurs in lighter ink or an erasure.   Mabillon, ib. p.
372.   But if not Alcuin's, whose could it be in that age ?

[5] Conf. Fid. ii. n. 14. Opp. T. ii. p. 401.

Flesh of Christ in the Virgin's womb, that we may understand that It was so created through sanctification of Divine Grace by the gift of the Holy Ghost that It should both be a Divine work, and, in the unity of the Person of the only Son of God, It should be so assumed without any defilement of original sin, that, sanctified through the Conception itself and united substantially with the Word of God, It should not be able thereafter to admit sin."

In his Comment on Psalm 50, he speaks of the universality of original sin in all naturally conceived.

" 'Accordingly he confesses not only his own present sin, but that of his parents in which he himself was conceived and born, saying, 'Behold I was conceived in iniquities, and in transgressions did my mother conceive me.' For, 'who can make me clean, conceived of unclean seed, save Thou, God, Alone Who art without sin ?' What marvel then, that I did, wherein I confess myself a sinner, who know that from original sin I was already conceived in iniquities, who contracted sins before I had the beginnings of life ? O Lord Jesu, with what praise do we extol Thy mercy, what worthy thanksgiving can we pay Thee, Who didst free us from the debt of this handwriting in Thy Blood, destroying on the Cross our bonds of sins, which were written against us by our first parents ? 'For lo, Thou lovest truth, &c.' As in the former verse he proved by the common transgression, that no one was rendered exempt from sins, &c."

58. Rabanus Maurus (A.D. 847), like those before him, ascribes the sinlessness of our Lord's Human Nature to the mode of His Conception, differing, as it did, from that of all besides, and in fact from that of His Mother.

* Expos. in Ps. Pœnit. Opp. T. i. p. 352.

"'This which he says, 'into the likeness of sinful flesh,' shows that we indeed have 'flesh of sin,' but that the Son of God had 'the *likeness* of flesh of sin,' not 'flesh of sin.' For all we men, who have been conceived of the seed of man coming together with a woman, necessarily employ the words, which David spake, 'for in sin did my mother conceive me.' But, because, not through any contagion of man, but by the Holy Spirit Alone coming upon the Virgin and by the Power of the Most High overshadowing, He came into a body undefiled [i.e. a virgin body], He had indeed the nature of our body, but had not in any way the pollution of sin, which is transmitted to those conceived by the motion of concupiscence. For therefore was a Virgin's womb chosen for the Birth of the Lord, that the Flesh of the Lord might differ in holiness from our flesh. For it was like in the cause, not in the quality of the sin of the substance. On that ground then did he call it 'like ;' because from the same substance of flesh He had not the same Nativity, because the Body of the Lord was not subjected to sin."

59. Haymo of Halberstadt lived to A.D. 853.

"'He Himself is in a special way [singulariter] the True Witness, Who is never changed ; as also He is called specially Holy, whereas there are many other called also holy, who, in comparison with Him Who is without sin, are unrighteous. For although they are holy, yet, because they are mere men, they cannot be without sin, and sometimes 'are liars.' But, Christ is essentially holy and true, because He 'did no sin, neither was guile found in His mouth.'"

"'You must observe narrowly, that he does not say absolutely, that he saw 'the Son of man,' but one 'like the Son of man.' For that Angel bore the person of Christ, who therefore is now not called the Son of man, but 'like the Son of man,' because, having conquered death, He 'now dieth no

---

' On Rom. viii. 3. Opp. T. v. p. 229.

' In Apoc. iii. 14. l. ii. init. f. 45. ed. 1535.

' In Apoc. i. 13. l. i. f. 15.

more, death shall have no more dominion over Him;' or else
He is called 'like unto the Son of Man,' because, although He
took our flesh, yet He did no sin, but appeared in the 'likeness
of flesh of sin.' For it is the property of man, not to be without sin. Whence, since Christ had not sin, therefore it is said
by the Prophet, 'I am a worm and no man.' "

60. Rhemigius (whether of Lyons, A. D. 855,
or Auxerre, A.D. 880) follows S. Augustine:

"[1] Why saith he, that He was 'sent in the likeness of flesh of
sin,' when we must believe in truth that He took a true body,
of flesh and bones? But our body or flesh is 'flesh of sin,'
because it is engendered with passion. Therefore it is conceived with sin, it is born with original sin, and cannot live in
this world without sin. But the Body of Christ did not have
its origin through passionateness of male and female, but by
the work of the Holy Spirit from the seed of woman without
seed of man, and therefore without sin was It conceived, without sin was It born, and without sin passed from this world;
and herein was His Flesh after 'the likeness of flesh of sin,'
because He had true flesh, but without sin which we have."

"[2] Thou 'pre-ventedst' [i. e. shalt pre-vent] 'Him in blessings
of sweetness,' i.e. in immunity from sin. In Adam all were prevented by a curse. He Alone was 'free among the dead.'
Thou pre-ventedst Him, i. e. Thou first bestowedst on Him gifts
of grace, that He might be the first-born among many brethren.
—Truly He was prevented with these blessings, because He was
conceived of the Holy Ghost. For Adam was prevented by fulness of bitterness, in whom all die; Christ was prevented in
blessings of sweetness, in Whom all shall be made alive. Or,
Thou preventedst Him, because there was no one before Him,

---

[1] On Rom. viii. 3. Bibl. Patr. T. 8. p. 914. He repeats the
clause as to the conception of all besides in sin, on Heb. vii.
Ib. p. 1099.

[2] In Ps. 20, B. P. xvi. 1082.

' All have sinned and are in need of the glory of God.'—Since
then such a man could not be found in the human race, lest
man should perish in his sin, the Creator of men, taking flesh
of the most blessed Virgin, was made man without sin, being
conceived without sin in the Virgin's womb, without sin He
conversed in the world.—Lo, now was a Priest, having Himself
no sins, and therefore worthy and able, by offering sacrifice, to
cleanse the sins of others.—Need was, that there should be a
rational sacrifice, which should expiate a rational creature. But
any sinful man, as he was unworthy to offer sacrifice, so also, no
less, himself to be the sacrifice.   What then should our
Priest do ?—Whence should the Mediator of God and men
take a sacrifice of propitiation, to restore peace between God
and man ?   For every earthly creature, if rational, had contracted the virus of sin from the root of the first parent; if
irrational, it could not justify the rational.—What should He
do ? Consider diligently the tenderness of that ineffable piety ;
estimate the immense and priceless weight of the Divine charity.
Because the price for our redemption could not be found in
[created] things, our Redeemer offered Himself to the Father
for us a sacrifice ' for a sweet-smelling savour.'   So He Himself
was made Priest and Sacrifice ; Himself the Redeemer and the
Price."

In another place he states, in plain terms, that
the Blessed Virgin was conceived in original sin,
in illustration of the principle that bad and
Simoniacal priests, although themselves most depraved, did not corrupt the sacraments which they
administered, but could confer good and true sacraments.

" ' Forasmuch as the Mediator Himself of God and men too
derived His origin from sinners, and from the fermented mass
took upon Him the unleaven of sincerity, without any infec-

' Opusc. vi. c. 19. T. iii. p. 49, quoted by Pet. de Inc. xiv. 2. 6.

tion of decay [vetustatis, the old man]; yea, that I may speak more expressly, from that very flesh of the Virgin which was conceived from sin, came forth flesh without sin, which of free-will also effaced the sins of flesh."

Pétau subjoins,

"Manifestly Peter in this place confesses that the Blessed Virgin was affected by the original fault, which he must have meant, as the force and ground of the argument shows."

On the other hand, in the passage quoted in behalf of the Immaculate Conception, S. Peter Damiani (as Pétau says [3] of the same expression in a sermon then attributed to S. Ildephonso) is speaking of the actual stains, which we all contract. This appears from the context. He is applying to the Blessed Virgin the words of the Canticles, "Who is this that cometh up from the wilderness, as a column of smoke, perfumed with myrrh and frankincense?"

"'Myrrh," he says, "consolidates bodies dissolved, and claims to itself the lifeless corpse, that it putrefy not. But frankincense is kindled to God in prayer, as we are taught by manifold testimonies of Scriptures. Under 'myrrh' understand continence; under 'frankincense,' devotion. For the flesh of the Virgin, taken from Adam, did not admit the stains

---

[3] l. c. n. 5. "But the same (Ildephonso) in Serm. xi. on the Assumption of the B. V. says, 'the flesh of the Virgin, taken from Adam, did not admit the stains of Adam.' But, as I opine, he is not speaking of the original stain, but of the faults which stain the descendants of Adam."

[4] Serm. 40. T. p. 93. This is one of the sermons which Nicolas of Clairvaux calls his in his Dedicatory Epistle in Bibl. Carth. iii. 193. It stands there as the 6th, p. 205. But there is no reason to believe one of his character.

of Adam, but a singular purity of continence was changed into the brightness of eternal light. Moreover who could adequately praise her devotion, when he remembers the Archangel sent, the Spirit supervening, the Son conceived, God born, a new star, the glory of the Magi, the grace of the gifts, and, above all these, the testimony of her conscience? These two things are they, which surrounded the Virginal substance with complete virtue, continence and devotion, whereof the one so possessed the flesh, the other, the mind, that the cleanest flesh, the purest mind should consecrate more singularly the Mother of the Lord."

In the same sermon, our Lord is introduced, as applying to her the words, (which in later times were employed to prove the Immaculate Conception,) 'Thou art all fair⁵,' as speaking of her sanctification through the Incarnation.

"'Thou art all beautiful, because thou art all deified. There is no spot in thee, because the Holy Spirit *supervened* in thee, Who cleansed thee."

64. S. Bruno the Carthusian, A.D. 1086, gives the usual statements of the universality of original sin, on Psalm li. 5, and Rom. viii. 3, and does not except the B. V. On the contrary, he speaks of the continuance of all under original sin until the death of our Lord, in a way which seems to include the B. V., the more, since it is in a sermon on her Purification.

"'' Whereas Thou art separate from sin, ' I was conceived in original iniquities,' i. e., I, first existing in original iniquities,

---

⁵ Cant. iv. 7.   ⁶ Ib. p. 91.
⁷ In Ps. l. Opp. i. p. 170. ed. Col. 1611.

was conceived by my mother. As though he would say, 'Before I was conceived by my mother, while I was still in my father's loins, I was already in original sins.' Whence the Apostle says, 'death passed upon all,' i. e. original sin by which men come to death, unless it is purged by Baptism. Not only before the conception was I in original iniquities, but, 'and in sins,' i.e. in original iniquities, 'my mother conceived me,' i.e. but also in the conception itself was I in those very original sins. And all this is as if he would set down briefly, 'In this Thou prevailest against me and all human beings, because Thou art ever separate from sin, but I and all human beings, both before conception and in the conception itself, are weighed down by original iniquities.'"

"''He freed me from the law of sin,' i.e. from the 'fomes' of sin, and from the law 'of death,' from the act of the 'fomes' of sin, lest I should do what that 'fomes' ill-advised me. I am truly 'freed from the law of sin,' for it is by the Son of God. For God sent His Son, not that the Son was absent any where, but, because He Himself, invisible by nature, became, by the flesh united to Himself, visible, He is said to be sent, according to our knowledge. God then sent His Son not into flesh of sin, but 'into the likeness of flesh of sin,' into flesh like sinful flesh. For Christ endured the whole matter of flesh except sin, and by His Son Who was sent He condemned sin, i. e. the 'fomes' of sin, which was in our flesh.—Or thus, He condemned sin, i.e. Satan, for the sin which he wrought on the Flesh of Christ. For the devil had right over all men for original sin, of which since Christ was not guilty (for He was not born of concupiscence of the flesh), the devil used towards Him an unlawful power [in His death]" &c.

"'The two weeks are two periods, under the law and under grace. The one, of the Old, the other of the New Testament. The first from Moses to Christ, the second from the birth of Christ to the end of the world. The good woman, then, that

---

* In Rom. viii. 3. Opp. ii. 45.
* Serm. 3. in Purif. S. M. Opp. T. iii. p. 110.

part of the people which bare male children [i. e. good works, as he had just explained it], exercised itself in good works, but for seven days it was unclean, because, to the Nativity of Christ when that week was finished, it could not be loosed from original sin, either by circumcision, or by generation of sons [good works], or by any other observation of the law whatever. ' For,' as the Apostle saith, ' the law made nothing perfect.' In that whole period, then, that woman could not be called clean who was defiled with such a stain. She hath original sin, and it is impossible that she can be clean. But thou sayest, ' Then when Christ was born, that woman was cleansed, inasmuch as in His Nativity the week was ended.' Not so. Why ? Because she must yet abide thirty-three days in the blood of her purification. For not by the Nativity, but by the Passion and Blood of Christ was original sin remitted. For in the thirty-third year from His Nativity our Saviour suffered, that by thirty-three days we may understand as many years. Then all who kept the law and bore males, i. e. persevered in good works, were cleansed from original sin. The Blood then of Christ redeemed both those who were before Him and those after Him. For whoever before the Passion of Christ held the faith and kept the law were both cleansed and redeemed by the shedding of His Blood."

He excepts Mary : yet not in regard to her own conception, but in regard to her Conception of our Lord.

" ' What has been said of the aforesaid woman does not appear to belong to the B. V. M., although she too observed that same law, especially since it is not said simply, ' the woman which has borne a male child,' but with the limiting addition, ' which shall have conceived seed and borne a male child.' For this was said specially for her sake, since she alone bare, having conceived no seed, who remained a virgin before bearing, a virgin in bearing, a virgin after bearing."

' Ib. p. 111.

On the other hand, he speaks of her conquering Satan, but, by the acceptance of God's will, that she should be the Mother of the Lord. The line of death reached to her (as being herself born in the natural way), but was broken in her, not through her conception, but in the active grace of her humility.

"[1] The first head of this line is Adam; the second is Christ. This line begins in Eve and ends in Mary. In the beginning was death; and in the end is life. Death was caused by Eve: life was restored through Mary. Eve was conquered by the devil; Mary bound and conquered the devil. For since the line is extended from Eve to her, in her at length that Hook was bound and incarnate, through Whom that Leviathan was taken, the old Serpent who is the devil and Satan, that he who entered his kingdom through a woman, should be drawn out of his kingdom through a woman."

According to the common Patristic exposition, our Lord was symbolized in that passage of Job, "[2] Canst thou draw out Leviathan with a hook?" and he was drawn out and bound by the B. V., in that of her *He* was born, Who destroyed his kingdom, and bound the strong man.

In like way, in the one passage pointed out in the Index to S. Bruno, which Perrone quotes [3], he is speaking of her adult grace and freedom from sin.

"[4] The Gentile *people* aforetime dead in sins, *which shall be*

---

[1] Serm. ii. de Nat. B. V. Ib. p. 108.

[2] Job xli. 1, &c.　　　　　　　　[3] p. 108.

[4] In Ps. 101. Opp. i. 400.

L

created through the laver of regeneration, so as to be a new creature, *shall praise the Lord* with a new song for the new Man Who is given to the world, believing Him in the heart, praising Him with the mouth, and confessing Him in works. This generation shall praise the Lord, because the Lord Himself, Who beholdeth lofty things from afar, hath *looked forth*, i. e. looked from afar not only upon the Jews who seemed to be near, but also on the Gentiles, in that by His Incarnation the Day-spring from on high hath visited us; which he explains more evidently, when he subjoins, 'The Lord looked from heaven upon earth,' when from the royal thrones He came to the Virgin's womb. For this is that incorrupt earth, which the Lord hath blessed, and on that ground free from all occasion of sin, through whom we have known the way of life, and have received the promised Truth."

65. S. Bruno Astensis has the same language as to the universality of original sin.

" ' God ' openeth His eyes ' on man, because He narrowly searches out his doings and thoughts. ' Who can make clean what is conceived of unclean seed? Is it not Thou Who art Alone?' He means, ' alone clean.' For because every man is conceived and born in original sin, he is deservedly said to be 'conceived of unclean seed,' whom, however, *He* cleansed by His own Blood and the water of Baptism, 'Who is Alone.' "

" 'Can man be justified, compared with God? or can he appear as clean, who is born of a woman? Thou art, he saith, like the rest of men, nor oughtest thou to deny that thou art born of woman, who is frail and a gate of sin'. Thou art not then clean, nor, compared to God, canst thou be justified, that

---

* On Job xiv. Opp. i. 247. Rome, 1789.

' On Job xxv. Ib. p. 266.

* The editor subjoins from S. Thomas Aq., "He says this markedly; because from this very thing, that man is 'born of woman,' through concupiscence of the flesh, he contracts a stain."

thou hast said, 'let them set equity against me, and let my
judgment come to victory.' 'For lo the moon shineth not, and
the stars are not clean in His sight; how much more corruption,
and the son of man a worm!' For what is meant by the moon
but the Church? or what by stars but the saints? So he
says, the Churches and the stars of the New Testament, i. e.
those renewed by the holy water of Baptism and released from
original sin, are not altogether pure before the eyes of God."

66. S. Anselm (A.D. 1093) in his treatise on the
Incarnation, "Cur Deus homo," introduced the
person at whose instance he wrote the treatise,
asking,

"⁹ In what way out of the sinful mass, i. e. from the human
race, the whole of which was infected with sin, God took a
Man without sin, as it were the unleavened out of the leavened?
For although the Conception of that Man be in itself pure and
without the sin of carnal delectation, yet the Virgin herself, from
whom He was taken, was conceived in iniquity, and was born
with original sin, since she too sinned in Adam, in whom all
sinned.''

"¹⁰ Anselm answering him," Pétau says, " puts this
as a thing admitted, that *That* Man 'was without
sin,' although 'taken from the sinful mass,' and proceeds to explain how this was effected."

S. Anselm's first answer is, that it must be so,
whether we understand it or no.

" Since it is certain that That Man is God and the Reconciler
of sinners, it is beyond doubt, that He is altogether without
sin; but this He cannot be, unless He be taken without sin
from the sinful mass."

His second answer here is, that the redemption

---

⁹ ii. 16.　　　　　¹⁰ De Inc. xiv. 2. 6.

profited those who lived before its accomplishment,
and that the B. V. was one of these.

"That Virgin, from whom was taken that Man, of Whom we
speak, was of those who before His Nativity were cleansed from
sins through Him, and, in *that* her cleanness, He was taken
from her."

A further answer he proposed to give [1], but reserved it for a supplemental treatise, "On the Conception by a Virgin, and original sin [2]." Here he
anew proposes the question for himself, "in what
way God took unto Himself Man out of the sinful
mass of the human race without sin [3]." But had he
believed that the Blessed Virgin had been conceived without original sin, he could not even have
put this question, because the question would have
been solved in her own birth. For, if the transmission of original sin had been stopped in her,
there could have been no difficulty as to its
not being transmitted further. But S. Anselm's
answer includes the Blessed Virgin among those
to whom it was transmitted; for it is, that original
sin is only transmitted to those born after the way
of nature from Adam, and that our Lord was not
so born.

"'We must now consider whether this, as it were, inheritance
of sin and of the punishment of sin, justly passes to the Man,

---

[1] Ib. c. 18. p. 94.   [2] Opp. p. 97.
[3] "Qualiter Deus hominem assumpsit de generis humani
massa peccatrice absque peccato."
[4] De Conc. Virg. c. 11, 12.

Who was descended from Adam through the Virgin." His answer is, " Since Mary, from whom alone Jesus was, was from Adam and Eve, He too must be from them.   For that it was expedient, that He Who should redeem the race of man, should be and should be born of the father and mother of all."   But that " thus too it was not difficult to understand that the Son of the Virgin was not subject to the sin or debt of Adam."   For "Adam could not transmit the evils [which he had brought upon himself] to any person, although propagated from him, in whose generation neither his nature nor his will gave him any power." Further, that it was inconceivable that " ' through the seed, which no created nature, nor will of the creature, nor any power given to any one, produced or seminated, but the will of God Alone, proper for the propagation of man, did, by a new power, sever, clean from sin, from the Blessed Virgin, any necessity of another's sin or debt or punishment should pass to that same Man, even although He were not taken into the Person of God, but came into being as a pure man ;" that the words "in sin did my mother conceive me" did not apply to a conception, in which there was no delectation, and so did not interfere with the grounds for " ' asserting that the seed taken of the Virgin was pure, although it was from the sinful mass ;" that the case of John Baptist and others, born of barren and aged parents, was different, in that, in their case, " ' nothing new was given to the nature of Adam, as it was in the Son of the Virgin," but only the natural powers of the parents were re-paired ; wherefore, he adds, " since they were generated through the natural propagation given to Adam, they cannot and ought not, in the miracle of their conception, to be likened to Him of Whom we are speaking, so that they could be shown to have been freed from the band of original sin."

Even in that passage, part of which is sometimes quoted in proof that S. Anselm thought that the B. V. was exempted from original sin, he speaks of her being cleansed only " by faith before the Con-

---

᾿ Ib. c. 13.   ᾿ c. 14.   ᾿ c. 16.

ception itself" of her Son; but faith being the
act of one, endowed with knowledge and will, this,
of course, implies that S. Anselm did not believe
her to have been exempted in her mother's womb.

"' It was fitting that that Virgin—to whom God the Father
purposed to give His Only-Begotten Son, Whom, being
Begotten Equal to Himself, He loved as Himself, in such wise,
that He should be, by nature, One and the Same, Son of God
the Father and of the Virgin; and whom the Son chose for
Himself to make her substantially His mother, and from
whom the Holy Spirit willed, and purposed to operate, that
He should be conceived and born, from Whom He Himself
proceeded—should gleam with a purity, than which no greater
can be conceived under God. But how that same Virgin was
cleansed *through faith*, before that Conception itself, I have
said ', where also I have given another reason for this very thing,
of which I am here treating."

Albertus Magnus, A. D. 1260, quotes this passage of S. Anselm, as showing that the B. V. was
conceived in original sin, but that she was sanctified
from it in her mother's womb.

"' S. Anselm says, 'the blessed Virgin gleamed with purity,

' Ib. c. 18.

' Referring to the Cur Deus homo, ii. 16, 17.

¹ De laud. Virg., on Missus est, q. 127. Opp. xx. p. 85. S.
Antoninus quotes John of Naples to the same effect, "that
this of Anselm is rather for, than against [the Conception in
original sin]. For it was meet that the purity of the mother
should be beneath the purity of Christ God, Who did not contract original, nor commit actual, sin; and this comes to be
thereby, that the mother committed no actual, but contracted
original sin. But if she had not contracted original sin, then
her purity would be equalled to the purity of Christ, and would
not be beneath it." Again, Guido of Perpignan, in his Con-

than which no greater can be conceived under heaven.' But the purity of Man-God is, neither to have nor ever to have had original sin; the greater after that is to have had original sin, but immediately and altogether to have been cleansed from it. Therefore the B. V. ought indeed to be conceived in original sin, but forthwith to be wholly cleansed from it, therefore she ought to be sanctified in the womb."

67. John Beleth, A.D. 1102, was a contemporary of S. Bernard, and asserts the same ground against the celebration of the Festival of the Conception, that the B. V. was born in original sin.

"ᵃ Some sometimes celebrated the feast of the Conception [of the B. V.], and perchance they still celebrate it; but it is not authentic or approved; nay, indeed, it seems that it should be rather forbidden. And on this ground, that the B. V. was conceived in sin."

68. Rupertus (A.D. 1111), having explained the two "breasts" in the Canticles to be the two gifts of the Holy Spirit, the one, the remission of sins, the other, the distribution of graces, and that these two gifts were signified by the two clauses of the Angelic salutation, "the Holy Ghost shall come upon thee," and "the power of the Highest shall overshadow thee," apostrophized the Blessed Virgin;

cordantia, p. 19, "He [St. A.] does not say 'equally with God,' but 'under God' Christ, because she could not sin either mortally or venially, which we believe to have been granted to none of the saints. But thereby Anselm does not exclude her from original fault," quoting the Cur Deus homo, ii. 16.

ᵃ De div. off. c. 146. de Assump. B. V. f. 561. Lyons, 1565.

"'Thou hadst not experienced the fault of this world, the wine of carnal pleasure, without the intoxication whereof no woman, beside thee, ever could or can conceive, and yet thou couldest judge how much better and more vehement, sweeter and stronger, was the pleasure or love of God, in which thou conceivedst, having been without doubt given to drink of that torrent of pleasure. Thou too couldest truly say, 'Behold I was conceived in iniquities, and in sins did my mother conceive me.' For, being from that mass which was corrupted in Adam, thou lackedst not the hereditary taint of original sin; but before the face of this love neither that nor any other sin could stand; before the face of this fire all chaff perished, that the whole habitation might become holy, in which God during nine whole months should dwell, the whole substance [materia] should become clean, from which the Holy Wisdom of God should build Himself an eternal habitation."

69. A Sermon on the Nativity of S. John Baptist, formerly attributed to S. Bernard, Mabillon thought to be older than S. Bernard [4].

"'The second honour [of S. John B.] is his sanctification

---

[3] In Cant. l. i. init. Opp. i. p. 986. col. 2.
[4]   S. Ber. Opp. T. ii. p. 688.
[5] Ib. n. 3. pp. 689, 690. In a dedication to Count Theobald, his patron, Nicolas of Clairvaux claimed this sermon, with eighteen others, as his own (in Tissier, Bibl. Cist. iii. p. 193). We have no reason to believe a vain man, who was guilty of forging letters in S. Bernard's name for the sake of gain, and twice made counterfeits of his seals (S. Bern. ad Eugen. Ep. 284 and 298). The sermon on our Lord's Nativity (p. 233), in which he professes to have taken much from S. Bernard, and does extract much from S. Bernard's 15th Sermon on the Canticles, may be his. One also was preached in the Convent of Arrimarum, where he was a monk, before he went to Clairvaux. Of this, he omitted the Preface, which stands in it in the works of S. Peter Damiani. In this very sermon on S.

in his mother's womb. For all we, whosoever, from the transgressing mass, enter into the world, draw with us a long coil of
original sin. He Alone is excepted, Who did no sin, Whom the
chamber of the virgin's womb, unknowing of man, poured upon
the earth. For, far otherwise than we and in mode unlike, was
He conceived, the Holy Spirit inundating and cleansing the
Virgin with all His Majesty,—He Who overpassed the wont of
the flesh, the order of nature, the commingling of man! For
so it was meet, that He Who took away sin should not know
sin, should take 'the likeness of flesh of sin,' but not flesh of
sin. Thus since all 'are conceived in iniquities,' we do not
read that any mortal was sanctified in his mother's womb,
except Jeremiah and John Baptist. Although there is no
doubt either as to that singular Virgin, but that she, when
fenced in by her mother's womb, was cleansed by a sublimer
kind of sanctification, as being that sanctuary, in which God,

---

John Baptist, he retains what Mabillon noticed, as a noto of
time, the sentence that "the Church has received the Nativity
of no man, save of God only, to her citadel of authority, excepting his [S. John B.] only." But the Nativity of the B. V.
was kept in S. Bernard's time (Ep. 86 and 174), and, which
is inconsistent, Nic. of Cl. has a sermon on it in this collection.
Yet the addition "et Matri Dei," which was to adapt it
to later times, and which occurs in the Sermon in S. Peter
Damiani's works (Serm. 44, de S. Vict.), does not occur in
Tissier, any more than in the different editions of S. Bernard,
Paris 1609, 1640, 1642, &c. If then the sermon were his, it
must have been, that he took a statement like those of S.
Augustine, carelessly. Yet the ostentatious way in which he
writes to the Count,—" I send to your Glory nineteen sermons,
&c., invented of my own thoughts, dictated by my own pen,
except that, in a few places, I took something from the thoughts
of others, for, still, according to the philosopher, 'alienas sarcinas
adoro.' All these things I dictated in my greener age, before
my pen [stylo] was laid up in the sheath of silence and lost its
splendour and acumen,"—the more indisposes me to believe
him.

the Son of God, was to take flesh. But the sanctification of
Jeremiah was far less than John's. Jeremiah is known to have
been sanctified in his mother's womb ; John to have been filled
with the Holy Ghost. There [in Jeremiah] sanctification means
cleansing; here [in John] filling means inundating.—But it is
far more excellent to be filled with the Holy Ghost, than to be
sanctified.   Observe diligently, with how well ordered an
arrangement that manifold Spirit sanctifies Jeremiah, fills
John, and Mary.   The sanctification of Jeremiah is wonderful, because, although he was conceived in sin, he is born
without sin. For, before he came forth from the belly, he
was sanctified. Nor could *he* be born not holy, who was
sanctified in his mother's womb.   Wondrous thing, unknown
in past ages !   A man conceived in sins, be born without sin !
But a far more glorious power filled John, who was both sanctified from sin and so overflowed by the Holy Spirit, that he
should go forth, both cleansed and filled [with the Holy Ghost].
Truly great before the Lord was he, whom an Angel announces,
God sanctifies, the Spirit fills, his life commends. For in a
more ineffable manner came He upon and into the Virgin
(supervenit in), whom the whole fulness of Divinity over-
poured without measure, that she might receive *Him* wholly,
Who made the whole, so that she is believed not only to have
been washed from sins and filled with the Holy Ghost, but also
to have conceived of the Holy Ghost, because ' what was born
in her, is of the Holy Ghost.'   Hence the Catholic faith confesses that, by a singular prerogative, the Son of God was born
of a Virgin, conceived of the Holy Ghost.—Thou seest by what
higher privilege He, Who was ' fairer than the children of men,'
was severed in His Conception from the children of men.
For *they* were conceived of sins and in sins; *He* in the Spirit
and of the Holy Spirit."

70. S. Bernard (about A.D. 1140), in his celebrated Epistle to the Canons of Lyons[c], blames

* Perrone mentions some, who (as has been so common
in controversy) called the Epistle supposititious. He himself
says, " But Theophilus Raynaud in his Dipt. Mariana (Opp. T.

them for the innovation of celebrating the feast
of the Conception, then denies that it should be
held, because the Conception was not holy, like the
Nativity.   He introduces the blame by praise:

"'Especially in ecclesiastical offices, it [the Church of
Lyons] was never seen hastily to acquiesce in sudden novelties,
nor did a Church full of judgment allow itself at any time to
be disfigured by youthful levity. Whence I greatly marvel that,
at this time, some of you should have thought good to change
this excellent hue, by introducing a new festival, which the
ritual of the Church knows not of, reason approves not, ancient
tradition recommends not.   Are we more learned or more

---

vii. p. 48. Lugd.), candidly acknowledges that this Epistle,
above the rest, must be accounted a genuine production of the
holy Doctor.   He writes, ' Unless we decide to pronounce none
of S. Bernard's Epistles to be his, we are absolutely forbidden to
attribute this (which, most of all, savours of S. Bernard) to
any other, as his genuine production.' "   P. i. c. 1. fin. note v.
Passaglia assumes its genuineness (P. iii. n. 1652 sqq.), and
quotes, as explaining it, equally on the assumption of its
genuineness, Bellarm., Greg. de Valent., Fr. Bivar, Aug.
Manrique, Ben. Plazza.   A. Ballerini labours at great length
to take it from S. Bernard, and ascribes it to his dishonest
scribe, Nicolas of Clairvaux, a worthless but plausible
hypocrite (Syll. Diss. ii. pp. 743—823).   It seems to me
an intense paradox, to maintain that an Epistle should have
been always believed to have been written by such a man,
upon such a subject, to such a body as the Canons of
Lyons, and that, within 20 years after his decease (see below
Peter of Celles), and thenceforth, being itself of such recent
date, should have been cited undoubtingly as his by Albertus
Magnus, Alex. de Hales, S. Bonaventura, S. Thomas Aquinas,
that it should have been ascribed to him in all MSS., and yet
have been forged by one, who had no temptation to forge it.

    ' Ep. 174, ad Canon. Lugd. Opp. i. 169 sqq.

devout than the Fathers? Perilously we venture upon any
thing which their prudence in such things passed over. Nor
is it of such sort, that, unless it ought to be passed over, it
could have escaped altogether the diligence of the Fathers.

"But, you say, 'greatly to be honoured is the Mother of the
Lord.' Good is your admonition; but 'the honour of' the
Queen 'loveth judgment.' The royal virgin needeth not false
honour, having accumulated titles of true honour.—Honour
her unimpaired virginity, her holiness of life; admire fruitfulness in a virgin, venerate her Divine Child. Extol her who
knew not concupiscence in conceiving, or, in bearing, pain.
Extol her, as an object of reverence to Angels, longed for by
the Gentiles, foreknown by Patriarchs and prophets, elect out
of all, preferred to all. Magnify her who found grace, was a
mediatress of salvation, a restorer of worlds; exalt her who is
exalted above the choirs of Angels to the heavenly kingdom.
The Church chants this of her, and has taught me to chant it.
What I have received from her, I fearlessly hold and deliver;
what I have not, I own I should admit with difficulty.

"I have received from the Church, that that day should be
kept with greatest veneration, whereon, taken from an evil
world, she brought festivities of most solemn joys even into
the heavens. Yea, I have learned in the Church too and from
the Church, to keep the birth of the Virgin unhesitatingly festive and holy; most firmly believing with the Church, that she
received in the womb, that she should come forth holy. And
of Jeremiah I read, that, before he went forth, he was sanctified; and of John Baptist I think no otherwise, who from the
womb felt the Lord in the womb. Consider you also whether
this may not be thought of holy David, since he said to God,
'In Thee have I been strengthened from the womb; from my
mother's belly Thou art my protector.' And 'Thou art my
God from my mother's belly; leave me not.' And to Jeremiah
it was so said, 'Before I formed thee in the womb, I knew
thee; and before thou shouldest go forth from the womb, I
sanctified thee.' How beautifully the Divine oracle distinguished between the fashioning *in* the womb and the bearing
from the womb, showing that the one was foreknown only, the

other [the birth] was foreadorned also with the gift of holiness, lest any one should think that the prerogative of the Prophet was to be accounted of foreknowledge or predestination alone.

"But be it, that we grant this of Jeremiah. What shall be answered of John Baptist, of whom the Angel foreannounced that he should be filled with the Holy Ghost, when yet in his mother's womb? I deem not, that this can be referred to predestination or foreknowledge. For the words of the Angel, as he himself foretold, were without doubt fulfilled in their season, and we may not believe, that he, of whom he foresaid that he should be filled with the Holy Ghost, was not so filled; and that, in the place and time which he predicted. But most certainly the Holy Ghost sanctified whom He filled. But how far this very sanctification availed against original sin, either for him or for that Prophet, or if any other was prevented by the like grace, I would not rashly affirm. Yet I would not hesitate to call them sanctified whom God sanctified, or to say that they came forth from the womb with that same sanctification which they received in the womb, and that the guilt which they derived in conception did not any way avail to hinder or tear from their nativity the blessing already bestowed. But who should say that he, who was filled with the Holy Ghost, still remained nevertheless a child of wrath, and, if he had died in the womb with this fulness of the Spirit, should have undergone the pains of damnation? It is hard. Yet I would not dare to define any thing hereon of my own mind. But, however that be, the Church, which judges and proclaims 'precious' not the nativity but 'the death of' the other 'saints,' does, with good reason, by a singular exception, honour with festive joys and venerates *his* birth, of whom, by the message, it is said especially, 'And many shall rejoice in his birth.' For why should not his exit be holy, and so, festive and glad, who could exult even in the womb?

"What then, it is certain, was bestowed even upon a few mortals, we may not suspect to have been denied to so great a Virgin, through whom all mortality emerged to life. Beyond all doubt, the mother of the Lord too was holy before she was born; nor is the Holy Church deceived, accounting the very day of her Nativity holy, and yearly celebrating it with votive

celebration, with the exultation of the whole earth. I suppose
that a more copious blessing of sanctification also descended
upon her, which should not only sanctify her birth, but also
keep all her life thenceforth free from sin. Which is not believed
to have been granted to any other among those born of women.
It was fitting that the Queen of virgins, by a privilege of singular sanctity, should pass her life without any sin, who, by
bearing the Destroyer of death and sin, should obtain for all
the gift of life and righteousness. Holy then was the birth, because immense sanctity, going forth from the womb, made it
holy.

"What should we think is to be added yet to these honours?
They say, ' that the conception, which went before the honoured
birth, should be honoured, because, had that not preceded, this
which is honoured had not been.' What if another, for the
same reason, should assert that festive honours should be paid
to both her parents also? Nay, some one might, for a like
reason, ask the same as to grandfathers, and their fathers, and
so it would go *ad infinitum*, and there would be no limit to festivals. This thronging of joys belongs to our home, not to our
exile; and these numerous festivals are meet for citizens, not
for exiles. But they say, 'a writing is produced of a revelation
from above.' As though any one could not equally produce a
writing, in which the Virgin should seem to command the same
as to her parents too, according to the command of the Lord,
'Honour thy father and thy mother.' I, for my part, easily
satisfy myself not to be moved by such writings, which reason
is not found to supply, nor any certain authority to favour.
For what consequence hath it, that because conception preceded a holy birth, therefore it too should be accounted holy?
Because it preceded it, did it also make it holy? Although it
preceded that it should *be*, it did not, that it should be holy.
For whence had itself that holiness which it should transmit
to what was to follow? Was there not rather need, that since
the conception preceded without holiness, she, being conceived,
should be sanctified, that a holy birth might follow? Did the
earlier borrow holiness from the later? That sanctification,
which was wrought in her when already conceived, could pass

over to the Nativity which followed; it could not by any means
return backward to the conception which had preceded.

" Where then is the holiness of the conception ? Is she said
to have been prevented by sanctification, in such wise that she
should be conceived already holy, and thereby that her conception
too should be holy, as she is said to have been already sanctified
in the womb, that a holy Nativity might follow ? But she
could not be holy before she was," &c.

On this, follows the dogmatic statement already
quoted [*]. S. Bernard speaks of the doctrine held
by the Canons of Lyons as "an error," which he
had "before found in some," but, he says, "I over-
looked it, sparing a devotion which came from a
simple heart and a love for the Virgin. But when
the superstition was discovered among wise men
and in a celebrated and noble Church, of which I
am especially a son, I know not whether I could
pass it by without grave scandal even to you all."
S. Bernard closed the Epistle by declaring his
readiness to correct his opinion by the judgment
of the Roman Church.

[*] See above, pp. 53, 54. The following words were omitted as
not bearing upon the immediate subject, for which it was quoted
there—"Lastly, I read that the Holy Ghost came into her, not
with her, since the Angel says, 'the Holy Ghost shall supervene into thee.' And if I may speak, what the Church thinks,
(and she thinks truly,) I say that the glorious one conceived of
the Holy Ghost, but that she was not so conceived also; I say
that she, a virgin, bare, but was not borne also by a virgin.
Else where will be the prerogative of the mother of the Lord,
by which she is believed alone to exult both in the gift of offspring and in virginity, if you concede the same to her mother
too ? This is not to honour the virgin, but to detract from her
honour."

S. Bernard's Epistle had so much weight afterwards, and, since the tide turned, has been so much
canvassed, that I thought it best to set down all
which bore on the doctrine.

The same teaching appears in two sermons of S.
Bernard on the Assumption of the B. V., which
contain strong passages about her present prerogatives.

" ' Far be it, that this house [the B. V.] should have any
defilement of its own, so that in it the broom of Lazarus
[penitence] should be required. But though she derived the
original stain from her parents, yet Christian piety prohibits
our believing, that she was less sanctified in the womb than
Jeremiah, or not more filled with the Holy Ghost than John;
for neither would she be honoured at her birth with festival
praises, if she were not born holy. Lastly, since it is altogether
clear, that Mary was cleansed by grace alone from the original
contagion, inasmuch as now too, in Baptism, grace alone washes
away this stain, and the sharp stone of circumcision alone
scraped it formerly, if, as is altogether pious to believe, Mary
had no sin of her own, none the less penitence too was absent
from her most innocent heart."

" ¹⁰ None the less bright is also that new mode of conception,
that not in iniquity, as all the rest, but through the supervening of the Holy Spirit and from sanctification alone [i. e. the
hallowing presence of God the Holy Ghost] Mary alone conceived." He does not except S. Anne.

71. Hugo à S. Victore (A.D. 1120) contrasts the
sinless Flesh of Jesus with that of Mary, which was
in her subject to sin, which He cleansed by taking
it

> ' In Ass. B. M. Serm. ii. n. 8. p. 1005. Ben.
> ¹⁰ Serm. inf. oct. Ass. B. M. V. n. 9. p. 1015.

"[1] The definition of the Catholic truth asserts that the Son of God (Who was born for sinners and of sinners) took, from flesh subject to sin, Flesh free from sin; and therefore free from sin, because freed; therefore free, not because It was never under it, but because It ceased at some time to be under it. When It was taken, It was cleansed. By the same grace was human nature cleansed, that it might be united to the Word of God free from sin, whereby a Christian is freed from sin, that he may be united to that same Nature in Christ, his Head. By grace it was effected that that flesh should be cleansed from sin, under which it was from its origin; and, being cleansed in Him, Who in it was to be free from all sin, should be taken free from sin; so that neither should grace prejudice the conception of nature, nor the conception of nature hinder grace."

The explanation, over against which Hugo à S. Victore sets this "definition of the Catholic truth," the more illustrates the difficulty, because it is itself so patently unnatural and unauthorized. *The* question was, how our Lord was exempted from original sin, concerning which there could have been no difficulty at all, had there been any clear tradition that the B. V, had been so exempted.

"[2] Many inquire as to that Flesh, which the Word assumed, in what way It was clean from sin; and, in what way, without sin, It bare the punishment of sin. And in regard to that, in what way It was either clean, or cleansed, from sin, we ought not to withhold the opinion of some—although it seemeth not, that it is [so]; it is believed, that it is not. Some think that that Flesh which was taken by the Word, was in such wise, from the beginning and in our first parents, kept free from the contagion and corruption of sin, when the whole mass of human nature

---

[1] De Sacram. L. ii. p. 1. c. 5. Opp. iii. 590.
[2] Ib. p. 589.

was corrupted by sin, and that It was so transmitted, from the first parent himself down to Its assumption by the Word, free from all sin and clean, that It was never under sin, and therefore was, not *freed* from sin but, *free.* For they say, that that part of human nature, through Which human nature itself was to be freed from sin, when it was held bound to sin, ought not to be itself under sin."

His own belief he expresses again;

" ' In regard to that Flesh, to which the Word was united, it is inquired, whether that Flesh was before, in Mary, subject to sin. Augustine says, that it was', but, in the very act of severance, was cleansed by the Holy Ghost both from sin and the fomes of sin. But Mary He cleansed wholly from sin, not from the fomes of sin, which [fomes] He yet so weakened, that thereafter she is believed not to have sinned." [For this exemption from actual sin, he quotes S. Augustine's celebrated passage'.] "But if the flesh of Christ, in Mary and in others from whom It descended, was subject to sin, how shall that be solved, ' Levi was decimated in Abraham?' S. Augustine solves it thus. Levi was decimated in Abraham, because he descended from him through concupiscence; but Christ was not decimated in him, because He did not descend from him through concupiscence. But did not the same flesh descend into both David and Mary through concupiscence? But not the Flesh of Christ: for this would be to say that it had descended into Christ by concupiscence: which is utterly false. Some choose to say, that as that portion [of flesh] was clean and holy in Adam before sin, so also, after sin, it was preserved in him and in all his suc-

---

' Summa sententiar. Tract. i. c. 16. Opp. iii. 482.

' In the edition Rouen 1648, there is a note on this section. "Here he speaks, *according to the common opinion of his time*, when the Church had not yet defined that we must think differently."

' See above, p. 67.

cessors in a straight line down to Mary. And this they say
they have from Gregory."

72. Eadmer, S. Anselm's disciple, (A. D. 1121,)
imitates S. Anselm in the work "on the excellency
of the Virgin Mary," which R. C. books of devotion
still quote as S. Anselm's.

"'We hold that by faith her heart was so cleansed from all,
if aught yet of original or actual sin remained over, that the
Spirit of God wholly 'rested upon her, being humble and still
and trembling at His words,' accepted her more sweetly than
any holocaust, obeying with most chaste and simple heart the
will of the Lord, and from her, overshadowed with the virtue of
the Most High, incorporated the Son of God."

73. The words in Hervé of Dol, A. D. 1130, as
to the universality of original sin and death through
that sin, are so strong, that some scribe, who believed in the immaculate Conception, inserted the
words "unless she had been exempted by God," and
"excepting the Mother of God," to correct the
supposed mistake'. I doubt not but that he did it
in good faith, in the same way as incomplete state-

---

* De Excell. B. V. M. c. 3. p. 136. ad calc. Opp. S. Anselmi.
' Gerberon, the celebrated Benedictine editor of S. Anselm, pointed out, in his "Censura operum S. Anselmi,"
prefixed to his works, that the words "nisi divinitus exempta
fuisset," and "dempta Matre Dei," had been added, as Estius,
he adds, had suspected. "Ex cujus [cod. MS. qui penes nos
est] etiam fide certo liquet has clausulas, 'nisi divinitus
exempta fuisset' et 'dempta Matre Dei,' esse ab alio insertas,
ut Estius fuerat jam subodoratus. Hæc enim in MS. minime
leguntur." § censura libri De Conceptione B. V.

ments of the doctrine of the Holy Trinity have
been, here and there, filled up in MSS. of St.
Augustine. Still the correction brings out only
the more the force of the original; so that, whereas
Perrone quotes it [a], with the additions, in proof
of the belief in the exemption of the B. V., it shows
that, in the natural meaning of the words, Hervé
included her as involved in the consequences of
Adam's sin.

"[b] If One, Christ, died for all, i. e. that all might live, then it
must needs be, that all died in soul through sin, whose vivifying
was sought by the Death of One, Who Alone was without sin,
nor could be partaker of the death of the soul.—All men died
for sins, no one whatever being excepted [c], whether original
or sins added by the will, whether in ignorance or knowing
and not doing what is just. And for all so dead, One, Christ,
died, i. e. having absolutely no sin, Who Alone was a sufficient
sacrifice for the sins of all," &c.

"[d] He sent Him 'in the likeness of flesh of sin,' not as though
He were not flesh, but because He was Flesh, yet 'flesh of
sin' He was not. For our flesh is flesh of sin, because it is
generated through use of passion. For His Flesh alone was
not flesh of sin, because His mother conceived Him, not
through concupiscence, but through grace. Yet there was
'likeness of flesh of sin,' i. e. passible and mortal, which could
be nourished and hunger and thirst and sleep and be fatigued
and die. For death and weakness are only from sin. And

---

[a] l. c. p. 321. Perrone prints in capitals, the words which
Gorberon avers, and Estius suspected to have been interpolated.

[b] On 2 Cor. v. 14 in S. Anselm's Opp. ii. 196. ed. Col. 1612.

[c] The words "dempta Matre Dei" are interpolated here.
Had Hervé meant to make the exception, he would not have
done so in this form, with the double ablative absolute.

On Rom. viii. 3. Ib. ii. 48.

indeed that Body was mortal and weak, as the bodies of others.
The flesh of sin hath death and sin, but 'the likeness of flesh of
sin' had death without sin. If it had sin, it would be flesh of
sin. If it had not death, it would not be 'likeness of flesh of
sin.' Such the Saviour came, and from sin condemned sin in
the flesh itself, that our spirit, burning with the love of things
eternal, might not be led captive to the consent of passion. For
Adam did not deserve death except by sinning, and Christ took
on Him mortal flesh. So then death is called 'sin,' in that it
came from sin, as we speak of 'the Latin tongue,' 'the Greek
tongue,' not meaning the member itself of the flesh, but what
comes through the member of the flesh. So then the sin of
the Lord is what resulted from sin, because He thence took
flesh from that very mass which had deserved death from sin.
And to speak more concisely, Mary from Adam died for sin[*],
and the flesh of the Lord from Mary died to efface sin."

74. Peter Lombard, A.D. 1141, affirms that the
flesh of our Lord was in Mary subject to sin, but
was purified by the Holy Ghost, previous to His assuming it, and that thenceforth she was freed from
the "fomes" of sin too.

"'It may be said and ought to be believed, according to the
concurrent attestation of the Saints, that It [the Flesh of the
Word before It was conceived] was subject to sin, as well as
the other flesh of the Virgin, but, by the operation of the Holy
Ghost, was so cleansed, as to be united to the Word free from
all contagion of sin, the penalty remaining, not of necessity but

---

[*] The words "nisi divinitus exempta esset" are interpolated
here. They are also ungrammatical. For Hervé says, using
S. Augustine's words, that Mary did die, as a fact; with which
the words, "unless she had been exempted by God," do not
cohere. The whole passage also, from, "So then death is
called," &c., is S. Augustine's. See above, p. 100.

[*] Sent. iii. Dist. iii.

by the Will of Him Who took it. Mary too, the Holy Spirit, forecoming into her, cleansed altogether from sin, either by entirely evacuating the 'fomes' itself, as some think, or by so weakening and extenuating it, that she had afterwards no occasion of sin. But that *thenceforth* the Holy Virgin was free from all sin, Aug. evidently shows, saying in his book on Nature and Grace, 'Except the Virgin Mary, &c.''''

And,

"Since that Flesh, whose singular excellence cannot be expressed in words, was, before it was united with the Word, subject to sin in Mary* and in others from whom it was transmitted by propagation, it may seem not unreasonably to have been subject to sin in Abraham, whose whole flesh was subject to sin. Although Christ was there, [in the loins of Abraham,] yet He did not descend thence according to the common law, viz. through passion of the flesh; as in Adam too all sinned, but not Christ. Whence Aug. on Genesis says, 'As when Adam sinned, they who were in his loins sinned, so, when Abraham gave tithes, they who were in his loins were tithed.' But this does not follow in Christ, although He was in the loins both of Adam and Abraham, in that He did not descend thence by concupiscence of the flesh. Wherefore Christ is said rightly to have taken the first-fruits of our mass, because He took not 'flesh of sin,' but 'the likeness of flesh of sin.' For God sent His Son, as the Apostle said, 'into the likeness of flesh of sin.' For the Word took flesh like to sinful flesh in penalty and not in fault, and therefore not sinful. But all the

---

* See above, pp. 67—69.

⁰ This is the reading in Pet. Lombard, ed. Venice, 1477, ed. Paris, 1504 (revised by Joh. Aleaume, Div. Prof. at Paris); Lovan. 1568 (three MSS. collated) ; Lugd. 1570. This reading, which De B. also has, is obviously right, both on the authority of the editions, and from the "aliisque." My edition of S. Thomas (Antw. 1612) has in P. Lombard's text "materia." The error, I suppose, arose from the dread of connecting sin with the B. V.

other flesh of men is ' flesh of sin ;' His alone is not ' flesh of
sin,' because His mother conceived Him, not by concupiscence,
but by grace. Yet hath He ' the likeness of flesh of sin,' by
liability to suffering and death; because He was hungry, and
athirst, and the like. Although then His Flesh is the same as
ours, It was not formed in the womb, as was ours. For It was
sanctified in the womb and born without sin; neither did He
Himself ever sin in it. In the penalty then It was like our
flesh; not in the quality of sin, because It had not at all that
pollution which is conceived from the motion of concupiscence,
nor was It born of carnal delight."

75. Porrée, Bishop of Poitiers, A.D. 1141, in his
explanation of the treatise of Boethius, " on the Two
Natures of Christ," brings out, as confessed on both
sides, the exemption of Christ Alone from original
sin, and the difficulty raised thereon by the Euty-
chians.

" ' From these [Adam and Eve] and subsequently from male
and female, original concupiscence ministering, was generated
whoever was generated beside Christ. But Christ Himself
was made Man, original concupiscence *not* ministering, but
ineffable and inscrutable Divine grace alone operating."

" ' If any say, that Christ was not Very Man, because, after
the sin of our first parents, He was held by no necessity of
dying, or that, before His resurrection, He was not such as
the blessed will be after the common resurrection of all, because He suffered, this does not follow. For He was not born
of male and female by the law of sin, i. e. human concupiscence
ministering. Therefore He is not held by original guilt, nor
by any necessity of sinning or suffering, either before or after
His Passion; but, as of His own Will He was made flesh, so, of

---

' In Lib. iv. Boeth. de duabus Naturis et Una Persona Christi,
n Boethii Opp. p. 1255.
' Ib. p. 1257.

His own Will, He both suffered and rose again, and shall abide thenceforth without passion."

"⁹ According to him [Eutyches] (if this· was his opinion) there was not assumed in the Incarnation of Christ the sick man, i. e. the human substance, which, in our first parents and thenceforward in all generated from them by concupiscence, was held bound by original guilt, and, being weak through the original fault, suffered by passions."

"¹ They say thus, ' If the Body of Christ was taken from man (as you Catholics believe), but every man, as you say, from the first transgression, i. e. that of our first parents, was not only held by sin, so that he in act did what ought not to be done, and was necessarily dissolved by death, but was entangled, by a sort of necessity, in affections of sin, (this being the punishment of the sin of the first parents, that, being held subject to death, he should be guilty through a certain will of sinning,) why in Christ, Who took such a body, was there neither will nor act of sin?"

"² From this it may be understood, how, although the Body of Christ was taken from man, and every man was, from the first transgression, held both by sin and death, yet in Him was no sin nor any will to sin, and, not sinning, He yet tasted death, which is the punishment of sin."

76. † "Odo, Cistercian, of great reputation for much religion and learning, Abbot of Muris-mundi ³," in the Diocese of Milan, Bishop of Frisingen, A.D. 1138 ⁴:

"³ Lo, it is said of her, ' she stood,' and not incongruously;

---

⁹ Ib. p. 1258.　　　¹ Ib. p. 1273.　　　² Ib. p. 1273.
³ Turr.　　　　　　⁴ Samarthani Gall. Christ. iv. 816.
⁵ "In a most devout homily on the Gospel, ' Stabat juxta crucem,' beginning ' Sicut Christianæ religiouis defectus.'" Turr. P. vi. c. 26. f. 116. v. De Alva said that the sermon had not been found. n. 221. p. 641.

for from what time she was sanctified in the womb from the
sin contracted by origin [originaliter], she remained thenceforth free from all sin. Whence that same excellent Doctor
Augustine saith, 'When the question is of sins, &c.' "

77. The statements of Richard of S. Victor, A.D.
1150, are the more difficult to give concisely, because of the mystical exposition of Holy Scripture,
which he combines with the literal interpretation
of the prophecy, "A Virgin shall conceive and
bear a Son." He dwells largely and glowingly on
the glories of the Blessed Virgin in the Incarnation. But he insists throughout upon her having
been cleansed ; cleansed, he says, by the overshadowing of the Holy Ghost, previous to the Incarnation, and by the Incarnation Itself. Our
Lord Alone could say, "without sin did My mother
conceive Me;" He was clean from His Conception;
she was cleansed by His Conception, and thenceforth the "fomes" too of sin was extinguished in her,
so that she had thenceforth no temptation to sin.

" * There is a threefold promise according to the threefold
loss—Observe therein a threefold sign ; the first, ' A Virgin
shall conceive and bear a Son;' the second, ' And His Name
shall be called Emmanuel;' the third, ' Butter and honey
shall He eat, that He may know to refuse the evil and to
choose the good.' You have then one sign in the Mother,
two in the Child ; a sign of incorruption in the mother; a sign
of recovering dignity and completeness in the Child."

" ' Hear as to the Mother, ' Behold a Virgin shall conceive

---

* De Emmanuele, i. 11.
' Ib. 12.

and bear a Son.'   How great thinkest thou this to be ?—Since
the world was, it has not been heard, that a virgin conceived, a
virgin bare, and, after giving birth, remained inviolate.   Human
nature then received a sort of earnest or first-fruits of its
future incorruptibility, the integrity of the virginal uncor-
ruptedness.   Why, I ask, do we not in this life live without
corruption, but because human nature is not sown without
corruption ?   The root of our corruptibility begins to germinate
from the very hour of our conception.   But behold in the
Blessed Virgin* it is anticipated there whence it seemed to
germinate.   And we know that, when the root is cut off, all
fructifying therefrom is dried up.   'Behold,' he says, 'a Virgin
shall conceive and bear a Son.'   In that it is said, 'a Virgin
shall conceive,' 'a Virgin shall bear,' it is shown plainly, that
both shall be clean, both the flesh which generates, and the
Flesh generated.   The Son then of this birth could Alone in
this respect 'sing a new song unto the Lord,' 'Without
iniquities was I conceived, and without sins did My mother
conceive Me.'   It is therefore plain that *He* came for the
destruction of sin, Who, in His very entrance into the world,
did not bring with Him any stain of sin from His mother's
flesh, but destroyed it.   If then His Conception Alone availed
to destroy the 'fomes' of concupiscence and the whole root of
corruption, what, I pray, could His Nativity, His humility,
circumcision, conversation, patience, obedience, Passion, Crucifixion, avail to the expiation of His Body ?   If what was done
in one hour, yea rather in a little portion of one hour, was of
such avail, what could so many years avail, employed on the
mystery of our redemption ?   He Who could, at the time of
His Conception, through the infusion of His grace, cleanse His
mother's bowels, why should He not be believed to be able to
cleanse those who willed to be partakers of the same grace,
when and how He willed ?   Why should He not be believed to
be able to cleanse that nature in each one of us, which in the
Blessed Virgin He could not only cleanse, but honour too and

---

* i. e. in her Conception of her Son, in a way different from
that, by which sin is transmitted.

glorify? For He glorified her, in that He gave her something above nature. He did in her something which was against nature, something according to nature, something above nature. It was against the infirmity of our nature, that a virgin conceived. It was according to nature, that He was conceived in the womb and formed, and at length born, according to the regular period of birth. Above the nature, not only of our infirmity, but also above that of our first creation was it, that a virgin conceived without seed of man. It belonged to purity, that she could generate without concupiscence; to honour, that she bare a Son Who was pure from all contagion of sin; to glory, that she conceived, not of man, but of the Holy Spirit."

"* And as it is believed as to the inferior sex in the Virgin, that time was when she could sin, and time was when she did not fear to sin; so in the first state of being, every elect until death fears to fall, after death he fears not at all the fall of sin. And as the stronger sex in Christ could not at all sin; so, in the second state, man for ever shall not fear to sin. And it must be observed in the Mother and her Offspring, that in the Mother the flesh was cleansed; in the Offspring, it was not cleansed, but clean: in her it was purged; in Him it was pure. So in the first state our nature is purged; in the second, it is found wholly pure. The first is of purification and sanctification; the second, of purity and glorifying. We have then in the Mother the sign of our purification and sanctification; we have in the Offspring the sign of our future purity and glorifying. Yet we may note in the Virgin Mother alone the sign of each state; the sign of our purification, when she yet had something, which ought to be cleansed; the sign of our purity, when, after the overshadowing of the Holy Ghost, she abode in her purity, the 'fomes' of sin being extinguished."

"¹ Estimate, if you can, what and how great is that magnificence, that the Child of the Virgin should receive all fulness from the hour of His Conception, and in the truth of His Humanity possess the fulness of Divinity. Singular glory, singular grace too of the Blessed Virgin Mary, who bare,

---

* Ib.   ¹ Ib. ii. 25.

retaining the honour of virginity, and bare—not an ordinary
son but—God. Well was it said, well shall it be said, ' Blessed
art thou among women, and blessed is the Fruit of thy womb.'
O what a Fruit! Fruit, how magnificent! glorious Fruit!
desirable Fruit! sublime Fruit! Thou recallest, I doubt
not, what thou readest in the Prophet, ' In that day, the Branch
of the Lord shall be for beauty and glory, and the Fruit of the
earth be for majesty.' And whence came this to our earth,
that it could produce such Fruit ? " " ' Certainly, the Blessed
Virgin Mary was earth according to the flesh then too, when
the Angel said to her, ' Hail, full of grace, behold thou shalt
conceive and bear a Son.' Without doubt, then too was she
earth according to the flesh, and was returning to the earth ; she
was earth through her liability to death, and was going to earth
through death. Whence then could such earth bear such Fruit?
But it is absolutely certain, that unless she had been fully
cleansed, she could not produce such and so sublime a Fruit.
To say more plainly what I have said, unless she had been
utterly cleansed from all contagion of sin, she could not give
birth to God, the Son of God. For that a virgin should conceive, a virgin bear, there was need of the highest purity."

" ' To the Virgin, then, believing but inquiring how this was
to be, it was duly answered by the Angel, ' The Holy Ghost
shall come upon thee, and the Power of the Highest shall overshadow thee.' As though it were said to her plainly, ' That
thou mayest be made meet for such a sacrament, and mayest be
found fit, the Power of the Highest shall overshadow thee,
both to extinguish all concupiscence and to enlighten all ignorance.' " " ' ' Before He shall know,' as though he said more
plainly, ' Before Emmanuel shall be conceived in His mother,'
' the earth ' of our created nature, out of which ' truth springs,'
shall be freed from the twofold root of all sins." " You see
that that remained in the Virgin which was to punishment;
that departed, which was to fault. Vitiosity departed ; pœnality
remained. How marvellous, how stupendous, that her Son, the
Fount itself of pitying love, allowed His mother who was

---

    * Ib. 26.   ‖ Ib. 27.   ‡ Ib. 28.

fully cleansed from all faults to toil under the yoke of our captivity!"

"'From the hour when the Holy Spirit came upon her, from the hour that the Power of the Highest overshadowed her, the blessed Virgin Mary was not only consummated in all grace, but confirmed in every good and gift which she had received. Our Emmanuel, what had He ever in Him, which ought or could be burnt up, Who, receiving all fulness, was from the very hour of His Conception consummated and confirmed in all good? The prophecy then seemeth to be understood of the Virgin Mary alone. For in her the earth of our miserable nature *obtained* full peace from all assaulting of evil."

78. Zacharias, Bishop of Chrysopolis (from Bede), A.D. 1157,

"'We, although we are made holy, are not yet born holy, since the prophet says, 'I was conceived in iniquities.' But Jesus was born holy, in a way belonging to him Alone [singulariter], because He was not conceived by commingling of carnal union."

79. Peter of Celle (afterwards, A.D. 1182, Bishop of Chartres) blamed Nicolas, a monk of S. Alban's, for keeping the Festival of the Conception, as S. Bernard did the Canons of Lyons. The correspondence began, probably, soon after S. Bernard's departure, A.D. 1153'. Peter treated it as "an

---

' Ib. 30.

' Comm. on Ammonius, concord. Evang. on St. Luke i. 35. Bibl. P. T. 19. p. 748.

' The last letter of Peter was, according to Ballerini (Syll. Diss. ii. 770), written when he was Bishop elect, i. e. A.D. 1181. (The word "electus" is not prefixed in his L. ix. Ep. 10. B. P. xxi. 904. Lugd. 1677.) But this was the close of a correspondence, which Peter had resumed upon hearing that Nicolas was

error[8]," unsupported by Scripture[9], and appealed to all before them. He seems to have anticipated no other objection but that of checking the current of devotion to the B. V.[1], about which he declares himself equally zealous with Nicolas. Peter says:

"[2] It is a proverb, 'Old ways are not to be left for new.' Who of the saints, who of the ancients, did not walk on our path? I believe and truly confess, that, had they erred herein, 'God would have revealed this also unto' them. For, had there been any peril therein, would He have kept silence on this only towards those, to whom He revealed His counsels so familiarly, that, even as a supplement to the Gospels, Epistles, and prophets, they enacted canons and decrees[3] to abide for ever, and to be observed almost with the same reverence as the Gospels?"

---

alive, having heard "many years before" (à multis retro annis) that he was departed. (Epp. vi. 6. Ib. p. 872.) In this he inquires, "mindful of the kindly, not displeased, altercation, which we had *long ago*, whether, amended by this imaginary death, he had effaced or softened his error, which came not from ill-feeling, but from a supreme or more than supreme regard for the Virgin of virgins."

[8] Epp. vi. 6, and x. 23, adding, "if it is to be called an error, which proceeds from piety." Also, L. ix. Ep. 10.

[9] "I impugn your phantasies, seducing from an appearance of beauty, but tottering for want of stable foundation. For whatever is not supported by the basis of authorities of Scripture, is stayed by no stable strength." Epp. vi. 23.

[1] "But perhaps you will say to me, 'Dare you, a mere Abbot, to close the wells of a devotion ever to be prolonged, and of a veneration to be dug daily deeper?'" Epp. vi. 23. p. 879.

[2] Epp. vi. 23. Ib. p. 879.

[3] Of General Councils, I suppose.

Nicolas did not answer this, and spoke of the Conception as one of those " Articles, which may be understood either way without injury to the faith on either side '," while he censures Peter strongly for maintaining, that before the Divine Conception, she could feel temptation, which she overcame. Yet he speaks, as if God had revealed that S. Bernard's Epistle on the Conception remained as a dark spot on his breast after death, for which he had to pass, although lightly, through Purgatory '. Such an account, circulated shortly

---

' In Pet. Cell. Epp. ix. 9. init.
' "I venerate the Bl. Confessor Bernard in such wise, as to praise and love his holiness, and yet not love or praise his presumption against the Conception of the Mother of the Lord. And lest you should think that I say what I say, out of an obstinate rather than a good conscience, hear what I have heard from Cistercians themselves, truly religious and loving the Virgin in truth, about the holy Bernard, whose names I hide under a bushel, lest I make them odious to the Community of their brethren. In the monastery of Clairvaux a very religious lay-brother, in a vision of the night, saw Abbot Bernard, clad in snow-white garments, to have a dark spot upon his breast. Saddened and wondering he asked him, ' What is it, father, that I see a black spot in thee ?' He, ' Because I wrote what should not be written about the Conception of our Lady, I bear in my breast the sign of my purgation.' The brother made it known to the convent, and a brother reduced it to writing. It was reported in a general Cistercian Chapter, and, by common advice, the writing perished in the flames, and all the Abbots preferred that the glory of the Virgin should be imperilled, than the estimation [opinionem] of S. Bernard. Not so Paul, not so; who calls himself a blasphemer and injurious, that he might the more extol the glory of the

after S. Bernard's departure, is surely decisive as
to the fact of S. Bernard's having written as he
wrote, and having meant, what his words express.
It has been thought that the Epistle " on the Conception of the B. V." in S. Anselm's works also
alludes to a check given to the devotion of the
simple by the writing of S. Bernard, with the same
tone of disparagement [o].

Redeemer. And certainly, as I believe, the saint, on that
ground, appeared in his own person to a simple man, who knew
nothing of such matters, and made known his fault, that the
discretion of the whole Cistercian Chapter might learn that he
willed that his error should be condemned, and the glory of
the Conception of the Virgin should be extolled. So, if I publish, what I believe he wished to be published, this is not to
extenuate his fame, or evacuate his glory, but to express his
will as to his penitence for his offence. But, after a light transit
through purgatory, he entered into the joy of his Lord," &c.
He mentions S. Bernard's having been "lately canonized,"
which was A.D. 1174.

[o] "To me, desirous of considering the beginning, whence
the salvation of the world held its course, to-day's solemnity
occurs, which is rendered festive in many places by the Conception of the Bl. Mother of God" [or, " which is celebrated by some
at the present time " MS. Corb., one of two MSS.], "and
indeed in old times it was celebrated more commonly, by those
especially, in whom pure simplicity and humble devotion
towards God flourished. But when both greater knowledge
and more influential examination of things imbued and set up
the minds of some, it took away this festival, despising the
simplicity of the poor, and reduced it to nothing, as void of
reason. Whose judgment gained strength, most chiefly because
they who delivered it, were pre-eminent in secular and ecclesiastical authority, and abundance of wealth " (in S. Anselm, Opp.
p. 499. Ben.). The writer has been thought to allude to S.

If so, he must have alluded to others also, since he speaks of the "wealth" also of those who opposed it.

Potho of Prumium about A. D. 1151 used the words of S. Bernard against the introduction of the festival, but alluded very lightly to the grounds[7].

80. Gulielmus Parvus [i. e. Little or Petit] Neubrigensis, Augustinian, dedicated his comment on the Canticles[8] to Abbot Roger Belloland at whose request he wrote it, and who lived about A.D. 1170[9]. He himself died A.D. 1208 at 70. It is a specimen of other works which have been lost. De Alva says that "he said clearly and expressly that the B. V. was conceived in original sin." Del Rio calls him "acute, learned, pious[1]."

Del Rio says that he explained "Thou art all

Bernard's words "paucorum *simplicitas* imperitorum," "devotioni quæ de *simplici* corde et amore Virginis veniebat." Ep. 174 fin.

[7] "We, in all these things, do not derogate from the devotion of the faithful, while we seek a reason, by which we ought to offer to the Lord our reasonable service, lest, perhaps deviating from the right way, we be seduced by a spirit of presumption" (de domo Dei. L. iii. fin. B. P. xxi. 502). In this he must allude to the Festival of the Conception alone; he cannot allude to the two other festivals, to the unauthorized introduction of which he had objected, the Festival of the Holy Trinity and the Transfiguration, since in these there could be no question as to the object of them.

[8] It began "Crebræ petitionis tuæ." De Alva, n. 133. fin. Del Rio used it in a MS. of the College of Louvain.

[9] Polyd. Virg. Hist. Aug. L. 13. in Del Rio.

[1] Isag. in Cant. p. 13.

N

fair," that "¹the B. V. contracted the original contagion from Adam, but was presently sanctified, the
contagion being absorbed."

In the other passage, "One is my Dove," Del
Rio gives a large context, but omits the words in
which Gulielmus expressed his opinion, only saying,
"²Gulielmus thinks that she was conceived in original sin, whom I do not follow, holding that she
was preserved; therefore I have changed all this
[ ], and substituted my own."

81. Sicardus, consecrated Bishop of Cremona
A.D. 1185, "of distinguished learning and piety,"
carries on the objection to the celebration of the
Festival, and on the same grounds, which he expresses in the words of John Beleth :—

"³Some at one time celebrated the Conception of the B. V.,
and perchance some still celebrate it, on account of a revelation which they say was made to a certain Abbot in a shipwreck ; but it is not authentic. Therefore such festival seems
to be to be prohibited⁴, because she was conceived in original
sin."

82. I may as well adduce again the passages

---

¹ On Cant. iv. 7. p. 142.
² On Cant. vi. 8. p. 235.
³ Summa de div. off. (Mitrale) L. ix. c. 43. de Nativ. B. V.
⁴ "Aliquibus," inserted in the Abbé Migne's Patrologia, is
not in De B. It looks like a correction. De Alva doubted
the existence of the book, and alleged as one of his reasons, the
identity of De B.'s citation with that from John Beleth
(above, p. 167). They are so like, that Sicardus probably had
Beleth's book before him. But then it is the more probable
that the two texts agreed.

which I have already given from the works of Innocent III., A.D. 1197 :—

" ' That one (Eve) was produced without fault, but produced unto fault; but this one (Mary) was *produced in fault,*
but produced without fault. That one was said to be *Eva,* to
this one was said *Ave.*"

" ' But forthwith [upon the Angel's words, ' The Holy Ghost
shall come upon thee '] the Holy Ghost came upon her. He
had before come *into her,* when, in her mother's womb, He
cleansed her soul from original sin ; but now too He came
upon her to cleanse her flesh from the 'fomes' of sin, that
she might be altogether without spot or wrinkle. That tyrant
then of the flesh, the sickness of nature, the 'fomes' of sin, as
I think, He altogether extinguished, that *henceforth* any motion from the law of sin should not be able to arise in her
members."

I cannot but think De Alva's interpretation
of the first passage unnatural, viz. that Innocent
meant that " Mary was produced in fault," viz. of
her parents; for, granting that he could have
spoken of an act done to the glory of God, as a
fault, it is contrary to the antithesis. He is speaking of the original sinlessness of Eve, the common
mother of us all, and the sinful nature of her children; and then he contrasts again the Mother and
the Child, the Holy Child born Immaculate, the
mother " produced in fault." In three of the four
cases of this remarkable antithesis, what is spoken
of is the sinfulness or the sinlessness of the being

* In Solemn. Assump. glor. semper Virg. M. Serm. 2. Opp.
T. i. p. 151. Colon. 1575, quoted Eirenicon, p. 316.

' In Solemn. Purif. glor. V. M., Serm. Unic. Opp. i. 107,
quoted ibid.

produced; it seems natural that it should be as to the fourth also. Innocent draws the like contrast between the Conception of our Lord, and that of John Baptist, that "John was conceived in fault, but Christ Alone was conceived without fault:"—

"*Of John the Angel does not speak of the conception but of the birth. But of Jesus he predicts alike the Birth and the Conception. For to Zachariah the father it is predicted, 'Thy wife shall bear thee a son, and thou shalt call his name John,' but to Mary the mother it is predicted, 'Behold, thou shalt conceive in thy womb and bear a Son, and shalt call His Name Jesus.' For John was conceived in fault, but Christ Alone was conceived without fault. But each was born in grace, and therefore the Nativity of each is celebrated, but the Conception of Christ Alone is celebrated."

The second passage speaks of two purifications, the one of the soul after her conception, but before her birth; the other, of the body too, from the material effects of original sin, so that she should have no emotion which could lead to sin.

Upon the first passage the Abbé Migne adds a note: "So could Pope Innocent think as to a matter not as yet defined by the Church, which now is of faith;" the second, which yet contains a doctrine different apparently from that now established, he does not notice. But Innocent III., in the prologue to his sermons, implies that they were written

* Serm. 16. de Sanctis, in fest. Joh. Bapt. i. Baillet, in his Vies des Saints, Dec. 8, quotes this in proof that the Conception of the B. V. was not celebrated then at Rome. T. 8. p. 436.

while he was Pope, and it is stated in his history[9] that they were so preached.

83. De Bandelis (Vincentia and Deza following him) quotes from †Cencius Sabellius (afterwards Honorius III. A.D. 1216) one passage, exactly agreeing with the last of Innocent III., and too characteristic not to be a genuine passage. Cencius Sabellius is known to have written sermons, which he dedicated to S. Dominic[1]. I may as well set down the passage, premising that it was not written by him as Pope, yet by one in high reputation with the two Popes before him:—

"[2] This 'Tabernacle,' the Blessed Virgin, the Most Highest sanctified, because in her mother's womb He cleansed her from original sin. For the Blessed Virgin had this prerogative, that she was not only cleansed from sin, but was also, after that, in the Conception of her Son, freed from the 'fomes' of

---

[9] Gesta Innocentii iii. c. 2.

[1] Fabricius quotes from Lud. Jac. à S. Carolo, Bibl. Pontif. p. 112, a statement that Honorius IIL wrote two collections of sermons. The one was dedicated to S. Dominic. "Others," he says, "I read in MS. in a Cistercian Library, 'to the Clergy and people of Rome,' dedicated to the Convent and Abbot of Cisteaux. They are together with a life of S. Richard of Cisteaux." De Alva said that he could not find any collection of his sermons in the best known libraries, as neither are they in our public libraries.

[2] Sermon on the Purification, Sanctificavit tabernaculum suum. Ps. xlv. 5. Vulg. De Bandelis quotes also what is, probably, a mere summary of what he said in "a sermon on the Assumption," and adds, "He says the same in 'a sermon on John the Baptist,' and 'on Passion Sunday.'" p. 50. He must then have had some collection of his sermons before him.

sin, so that thenceforth she could not sin. And therefore it is subjoined, 'God is in the midst of her, she shall not be moved.' For in the B. V. alone, after the Conception of her Son, God had a hostelry of rest, because thenceforth He found in her neither sin nor fuel of sin. But in other Saints He found a hostelry of commotion; because in them He found at least fuel for sin, from which in this life they were never wholly freed."

84. Turrecremata quotes from † "an ancient opusculum" made from the authorities of the saints, and revised by A. Castellanus, a Dominican, a characteristic passage.

" 'This Virgin was conceived with fault and penalty, and therefore her Conception is not to be celebrated; yet she was sanctified in the womb and cleansed from original sin. Whence also her Nativity is celebrated at this time by the Holy Church. And therefore we say that when the grace of the Holy Ghost came upon her, she was so cleansed from all sin, that the 'fomes' of sin is believed to have been altogether extinguished in her. But the penalty of fault was not removed. Well, then, it is said 'lightened,' not 'exonerated.' For then is a thing 'exonerated,' when the burden is removed altogether; but it is 'lightened' when one part is withdrawn and the other left," &c.

The thirteenth century has two classes of writers who embody tradition, such as it had come to them, the earlier Canonists, commenting on the Decretals, or making "summa's" of their own, and the earlier Schoolmen. They, each in their own way, transmitted the teaching which they embodied, as being the subject of their study, in Canon law, or in the

---

' Serm. on the B. V. on Isa. ix. 1.

discipline of penitence, or in Christian doctrine.
Evidence as to the state of belief is given, in an unexpected way, by some who preached on festivals
of the Blessed Virgin, in that they thought it was
praise of God's great doings to her, that she was
early freed from original sin, whereas, in later times,
the idea that she contracted original sin in the
moment of the infusion of her soul, as the result
of her conception after the ordinary way of nature,
even on the belief that she was freed from it immediately afterwards in her mother's womb, was rejected as a wrong to her, as something abhorrent,
and as a sort of blasphemy.

85. Hugutio or Hugo Bishop of Ferrara (died
A.D. 1212), wrote glosses upon the first short glosses
on the Decretals. His gloss (with his initial, H.)
was adopted by Joannes Semeca Teutonicus (i. e.
the German), of Halberstadt, his disciple, who was
in the favour of Gregory IX. and died A.D. 1243,
and by Bartholomew of Brescia, who died at 84,
A.D. 1250. The two chief glosses bearing on this
subject, were retained in the "amended" edition
of Gratian, published at the command of Gregory
XII., in his preface to which Gregory states that
he had given in charge to some of the Cardinals,
with other learned and pious men, to revise " the
decretum of Gratian with the ancient glosses, whose
authors, being pious men and Catholics, were to be
pardoned, if in some things, either through some

error in them, or because many things had not been defined by the sacred Councils, they spoke too freely, as also in regard to things contrary to Catholic truth, which had been interspersed by impious writers both in the margins and in the body of the Decretum." This, he says, had been done, and the whole Decretum had been revised, together with the glosses. And he provides that " this Canon law, so expurgated, should come unimpaired to all the Christian faithful every where, and that no one should be allowed to add or change or invert any thing in the aforesaid work, or to join on any interpretations, but that it should be for ever preserved entire and uncorrupt, as it is now printed in this our city of Rome." In a later part of the mandate [4], Gregory forbids "all every where, to add, *subtract*, change, or invert any thing in the books of the Canon law, so revised, corrected and expurgated by our mandate" as before [5]. Without, of course, inferring that the Pope was responsible for all contained in so large a book, yet certainly, the glosses so retained, in a work carefully revised and expurgated from what seemed to be unsound, had no longer the mere private weight of a Bishop of Ferrara, however learned and thoughtful.

[4] This mandate is still reprinted in the Corpus Juris Canonici, e. g. Richter, Lips. 1839.

[5] Gregorius Papa XIII. ad futuram rei memoriam, dated "apud S. Petrum sub annulo Piscatoris 1580." I have used the reprint, Paris 1585, "cum licentia" "ad exemplar Romanorum diligenter recognitum."

In this edition so revised, there are two chief glosses of Bishop Hugutio. The first is on the decree, which prescribes what festivals were to be kept by the laity. The often-repeated gloss of Hugo occurs here.

"'Of the festival of the Conception nothing is said, because it is not to be celebrated (as it is in many regions, and especially in England). And this is the ground, because she was conceived in original sin, like the other saints, except the One Person of Christ. In like way it says nothing of the Annunciation of holy Mary, whereas yet it is so celebrated a festival."

The second gloss of Hugutio in this edition, is upon the passage of S. Fulgentius', on the transmission of original sin. There, on the explanation of S. Paul's words "we were by nature children of wrath," "by nature, i. e. from the nativity in the womb," Hugutio added,—

"'That you may better understand this, know that there are two nativities, one 'in the womb,' another 'from the womb.' To be 'born in the womb,' is that the soul should be infused into the body in the womb. To 'be born from the womb,' is to go forth from the womb to the light. Whence the B.V. and John Baptist and Jeremiah were born with original sin in the womb. And this the text means to say in the beginning, that 'every man,' &c., [viz. 'that every man, who is conceived through concumbency of man and woman is born with original sin']. Whence the Conception of the blessed Mary ought not to be celebrated; but her nativity *from* the womb is well cele-

---

* De Cons. dist. iii. c. 1. *Pronuntiandum.*

' See above, p. 65.

* On De Cons. dist. iv. c. 3. *Firmissimè* col. 2436. Paris 1585.

brated, and that of John Baptist, because they were sanctified in the womb, and original sin was forgiven them."

86. The remaining gloss is of Johann. Teutonicus, from whose edition it is retained. It is on the statement quoted from S. Augustine, " [*] For neither is it granted to adults in Baptism, except perhaps by the ineffable miracle of the Most Almighty Creator, that the law of sin which is in the members, warring against the law of the mind, should be utterly extinguished and not be." The gloss says,—

" [1] As in blessed Mary and in John the Apostle, because neither of them could sin. Also the nativity of Mary *in* the womb is not celebrated; but the nativity *from* the womb well."

Besides the fact, that Joh. Teut. adopted the former glosses, the contrast of his saying that there was good reason for celebrating the Nativity of the B. V. *from* the womb, with the statement that her nativity *in* the womb was not celebrated, implies a conviction, that there was a reason for not celebrating it. Perrone mentions, from Strozzi, that there were two other glosses, on the same side; but I have not been able to find them [2]. He adds,

[*] Do pecc. mer. i. ult. in de Cons. dist. iv. c. 2, *Per Baptismum.*

[1] It occurs in Gratian, "with the apparatus of John Theutonicus and the additions of Bartholomew of Brixia." Strasb. 1472.

[2] Perrone says (P. 1. c. 2. note), "Five chapters in the decree of Gratian are counted against the Immaculate Conception," viz. the three given above; "the fourth is, *Placuit*, the

"it is known that the decree of Gratian is not authentic, nor of itself constitutes an authority, nor was even approved by Roman Pontiffs." The mandate of Pope Gregory XIII. is very like an approval.

There is a good deal of repetition among the Canonists, for the occasion of speaking was mostly the same. Yet some were great names. The next, in time, was a Saint, eminent for his holiness.

87. S. Raimund de Penyafort, Penitentiary of Gregory IX., collector of his Decretals, elected third master of the Dominicans A.D. 1238, Doctor of Canon law at Bologna, "³ a man of great holiness, and most perfect in canon and civil law."

He adds only a few words to those of Bp. Hugutio; but grave enough to occasion them to be removed from his works⁴.

fifth is *Quisquis,* which I have only indicated for brevity. Comp. Strozzi (Controversia della Concezione della B. V. M. P. 1. lib.) 3. c. 18. (Palermo 1700)." I have not access to Strozzi's work. Two chapters in the de Consecr. begin, *Quisquis,* "quisquis ex concupiscentia," dist. iv. c. 137, and "quisquis dixerit," ib. c. 155. There are also three Canons of the Council of Carthage under Aurelius against the Pelagians, which begin with *Placuit* (cod. Eccl. Afr. 108—110), de Cons. Dist. iv. c. 152, 153, 154; but I have found nothing definite in any gloss, such as Perrone's reference would lead one to expect.

³ Thol. de Lucha H. E. nov. xxi. 20, in Quétif i. 108.

⁴ "Alva, Sol Verit. Rad. 101, col. 1344, inquires, '*who* took away from all those editions the clause as to the Conception of the B. V. which is read in MSS. ?' The answer is easy. It was taken away by those who presided over the printing, on

"¹ And note that there is no mention of the Annunciation of Holy Mary, whereas yet it is so celebrated a festival; nor of her conception, because this ought not to be celebrated, because she was conceived in sins, as also the other saints except the One Person of Christ, Which was [conceived] not from seed of man, but by the mystical breathing."

88. Henry de Segusio, Bp. of Sisteron A.D. 1250, Cardinal of Ostia A. D. 1262, is known to most of us as "Hostiensis." He was called, Cave says, "Fons et Splendor Juris." He speaks incidentally only; but his statement is remarkable, in that he mentions the sanctification of the B.V. in the womb as the same in kind as that of Jeremiah and John Baptist, and yet, by the titles with which he names her, implies (as of course she is) that she is so far above them.

account of the decree of the Council of Basle, *which also they allowed themselves in many old writers.* The Supreme Pontiffs did not command this as to the ancients who wrote before the Bull of Sixtus IV., but only as to the later. But those editors acted so negligently that, removing the clause from the text, they left a gloss in the margin, whose reclamation manifestly shows that something has been cut out of the text of Raymund. There are almost countless MSS. of this Summa in libraries." Quétif, Scriptt. Ord. Prædic. i. 109, quoted in the Preface to S. Raimund's Summa, p. lii. Veron. 1744. The Latin in Bodl. 64, is, "nec de conceptione ejusdem, quod illud non debet celebrari, eo quod concepta fuerit in peccatis, sicut et cæteri sancti, excepta una Persona Christi, quæ non ex virili semine, sed mistico spiramine [concepta] est." De Alva states that the passage was in old originals and MSS. (he specifies two), but says, that it was removed from the edition of Rome, 1603. Sol Ver. n. 264, p. 706.

¹ Summa P. 1. tit. de feriis, Cod. Bodl. 64. f. 20.

"'Who ought to confess? Every sinner, whoever he be, who has committed actual sin; and this I say, because without original sin was not conceived [genitus] of the seed of man and woman, although some are read to have been sanctified in their mother's womb, as Jeremiah, John Baptist, our blessed and glorious Lady."

89. Durandus Gul. (A.D. 1274), called "Speculator" from his celebrated "Speculum juris," and "Pater practicæ" from his skill in civil and canon law, was a disciple of Card. Hostiensis. He was in the favour of, and in office under, Clement IV., Gregory X., Nicolas III., Martin IV. (a 5th Pope, Boniface VIII., pressed him to accept an Archbishopric), was employed by Gregory to carry some constitutions at the General Council of Lyons. In his later years, he was Bishop of Mende, subsequently to his completion of his Rationale Divinorum Officiorum, with which most of us are more familiar, finished A.D. 1286'. In both works he speaks against the celebration of the Festival, on the ground of the Conception in original sin. In the Speculum, enumerating the festivals on which a process could not be continued, he says,—

"'All the Festivals of the B. V. I do not speak of the Feast of her Conception, because she was conceived in sins,

---

' Summa L. v. tit. de pœn. et rem. § quis debet confiteri init. f. 134. v. Ven. 1538.

' As he says, viii. 0. See Quétif, i. 480—3. Fabr. v. Durandus.

' Speculum P. 2. tit. de feriis fol. 75. Patavii 1479.

although in places it is celebrated out of devotion ; nor do I impeach such devotion."

In his Rationale of the Divine Offices he speaks more at length.   After dwelling on the four festivals, he says,—

"[2] Some also celebrate a fifth feast, of the Conception of the B. V., saying, that, as the death of Saints is celebrated, not on account of their death, but because they were then received in the everlasting nuptials, in like way the feast of the Conception may be celebrated, not because she was conceived, because she was conceived in sin, but because the Mother of the Lord was conceived ; asserting that this [hoc] was revealed to a certain Abbot, in the midst of a shipwreck ; which [account] however is not authentic [1].   Whence it is not to be approved ; since she was conceived in sin ; i. e. through the concumbency of male and female.   But although she was conceived in sin, that original sin was remitted to her, when she was sanctified in the womb, like as both Jeremiah and the blessed John Baptist:

---

[2] Rationale Div. Offic. T. vii. c. cvii. p. 824. Lugd. 1592, collated with the edition of Maintz 1459.

[1] .The unhistorical blunders in the Epistle " de Conceptione B. Virginis," in which this story is related as if by S. Anselm, have been pointed out by Gerberon, in his Censura upon it, prefixed to S. Anselm's works.   It is not only unhistoric, but, professing to be written by S. Anselm, is a forgery.   Gerberon shows that two of the miracles, upon which the celebration of the Festival is rested, are mixed with facts contradicted by history ; that the doctrine contradicts S. Anselm's, and that the account given of the celebration and subsequent suspension of the Feast of the Conception is untrue.   The fiction as to the Abbot Elsinus recurs in the " Miraculum de Conceptione S. Mariæ," which, I should think, is the original form of the fiction.   The Epistle is appended to S. Anselm's works, pp. 505 —507, the " Miraculum, &c." p. 507.

and therefore with good reason are her Nativity and John
Baptist's celebrated; the nativity, I mean, *from* the womb,
when namely they came forth into the light, or into the world.
But their nativity *in* the womb, i. e. when their souls were
infused in their bodies, is not celebrated, as has been premised."

90. Guido de Baiisio, commonly quoted as Archi-
diaconus Bononiensis, or as "Archidiac." in the
Decretum, lectured about A.D. 1280 at Bologna.
The adoption of glosses of his in the Decretals
attests the estimation in which he was held. In
his Rosarium[1], he adopted the words of Hugutio,
referring to his authority.

91. Bartholomæus à S. Concordio, of Pisa, a celebrated Dominican preacher as well as Jurist, must
have belonged to this century (since he died A.D.
1347, having passed nearly 70 years in religion[2],
i. e. since about 1277). His "Summa Confessorum" was a very popular book[3], as appears, both
from the familiar titles which it bore, "Bartholina,"
"Pisana, or Pisanella," "Magistruccia," the number
of its MSS., the frequency of its editions from the
time of the discovery of printing, and its translation
into Spanish[4].

"[3] Of the feast of the Conception of the B. V., it must be

---

[1] Rosarium p. 401. v. Ven. 1601.
[2] Spon Rech. curieuses d'antiquitó, diss. 10, p. 214.
[3] "F. Aug. de Clavasio (died A.D. 1495) acknowledged that
he took all the cases of conscience in his 'Summa Angelica'
from this book." Quótif.
[4] Quétif, i. 623, 624.
[5] In his Summa, v. Feriæ, lit. B. De Alva notes the omission

said, according to Thomas (3 p. q.'7), that, although the Roman
Church does not celebrate it, it tolerates the custom of some
Churches who celebrate that Festival, whence that celebration
is not to be wholly reprobated, yet neither from this, that the
Feast of the Conception is celebrated, is it given to be understood
that she was holy in her conception, but, because it is not
known at what time she was sanctified, the Feast of her
sanctification rather than of her conception is celebrated on the
day of the Conception itself."

92. John Andreæ, the most celebrated jurist,
perhaps, of the next century, who taught at
Bologna from A.D. 1303 to 1348, follows Durand,
both in respecting what was done out of devotion
and in dissuading from the observance of the
Festival.

"' There are four Feasts of the Virgin Mary; the Annunciation in spring; Assumption in summer; Nativity in Au-
tumn; Purification in winter. But the feast of her passive Conception is not included here, although it is celebrated in many
places, out of a devotion which is not to be impeached, as it is
said in the Spec. [Durand's] eod. tit. But do *you* say, that that
Conception, which was of human seed, is not to be venerated.
And this is to be held, that she was conceived in original sin,
as in de Consecr. Dist. 3, c. 1. But immediately after her
Conception she was sanctified, and thence the Church celebrates
the feast of her Nativity."

---

of the whole passage in one old MS. (n. 37), a freedom, which
scribes seem to have taken, or to have been directed to take.
Quétif notices that the library, from whose MS. the passage is
missing, is the same in which De Alva owns that a MS. of
Ægidius of Zamora was altered on the Conception. i. 624.

' In 2 p. Novellæ, Tit. *de feriis* super C. *Conquestus*, T. ii.
f. 56. Ven. 1581.

Other Jurists are referred to by Turrecremata, but, although his references are evidently authentic, the books themselves, probably, for the most part, lie buried in the libraries where he saw them[s].

Of the doctrinal writers of the 13th century, besides the well-known schoolmen, who have impressed their minds on European intellect till now, Turrecremata mentions others, great in their day, who did, in their generation, the work given them to do; some of them even influenced subsequent generations, and now are forgotten on earth, as if they had never been.   Thus,—

93. †One who was once well-known as "an eminent Chancellor of Paris," " William, Chancellor of Paris," is not known, who he is, or when he lived; only Turrecremata knew him to have been "an ancient Doctor."   In explaining the definition, that "Virginity in corruptible flesh is a perpetual meditation on incorruption," he said,—

" ' Or, ' corruptibility ' may be taken thus, that no regard

---

[s] He mentions another "Compilator juris," beginning "omnis qui juste judicat," on c. Firmissimè; John de Friburg (if he be different from John Teutonicus) ; " Compilator speculi juris, called 'summa summarum,' " tit. de feriis q. 8, (different from Durand's) ; Joannes Calderinus A.D. 1360; Peter of Milan ; Petrus de Bracho.   De Bandelis adds " Laurentius, an ancient Glosser;" Bernardus Papiensis, A.D. 1213; another commentator of the Decretum, beg. "ad decorem sponsæ," on c. pronuntiandum; Galvaneus, probably Guelvan de la Flama, about 1310.

[t] In his "Summa, in the matter on Virginity." Turr. P. 6. c.

be had to the condition of warfare, and ' corruptible flesh '
be taken for the corruption of fault or punishment in general;
and that which is of punishment or fault was in Adam and in
us, but in Adam innate, because according to that it was
possible for him to be corrupted; in us otherwise, because
contracted.   In Christ there was only that of penalty from the
beginning, and this taken by Him: in the B. V. before grace,
both sorts of corruptibility *were contracted;* after grace, only
the corruptibility of penalty; and according to this the definition suits alike to Adam and to us and to Christ and to the
B. V.[1]"

94. †Alanus (perhaps Magnus, de Lisle, who died
A.D. 1202, Quétif, i. 194, from Alberic, p. 429.
Leibn.):—

"[2] Some dogmatized that Christ took flesh in the Virgin, not
of the Virgin; some, in the Virgin and of the Virgin; some,
neither in the Virgin nor of the Virgin.   But they who say
that Christ took flesh in the Virgin, not of the Virgin, pay Him
a senseless honour, saying that ' new uncorrupted flesh was

---

28. f. 112.   De Alva found the work in the Royal Library of
S. John of Toledo, under the title " Summa universalis Theo-
logiæ, edita à præcipuo Cancellario Parisiensi."   It began
"Vadam in agrum et colligam," n. 113. p. 451.

[1] De Alva objects to Turr.'s omitting the clause at the end,
"although it[the definition] be not extended to infants on account
of that expression, the ' perpetual meditation.'"   Yet this relates
not to the subject of " corruptibility," but to his definition of
"virginity in corruptible flesh," being " a perpetual *meditation*
of incorruption;" of which, of course, infants are incapable.

[2] Turrecremata quotes " Expos. Symb. Athan.; Serm. Purif.
and de Assumpt. B. V." vi. 26. f. 117; De B. the Expos. Symb.
Ath. only.   Trithemius does not mention the Expos. Symb.
Athan., but says, " he wrote in metre and prose almost countless treatises (opuscula) whereby his memory has been made
immortal with posterity, but a few only have come to my knowledge."

created in heaven,' or that 'the whole flesh of Adam was not corrupted through sin,' but that a certain particle was reserved clean and uncorrupt and was derived by propagation to the Virgin, which Christ took, fearing lest the flesh of Christ should be weak through fault and unclean through vice, if He had taken flesh which was a part of Mary, which in her conception was, like that of the rest, corrupt through fault and guilt; and they do not observe, that, in the remaining generations, flesh is severed from flesh by the agency of concupiscence, whence it is held by the same fault and severed in the same guilt as before its severance. But in Mary, since flesh was severed from flesh by the overshadowing of the Holy Spirit, in that very severance the flesh was cleansed by the Holy Spirit, so that what was corrupt of Mary was clean and uncorrupt in Christ. Whence also the Catholics, well knowing this, say that Christ took flesh, both in the Virgin and of the Virgin."

95. Petrus Præpositus or Præpositivus, Chancellor of Paris, A.D. 1207, "[3] a wonderful man, author of some excellent sermons and postillæ on the sentences:"—

"'First, it is inquired, whether the B. V. was sanctified before the Conception of her flesh was ended. It is to be said, 'not,' because sanctification is cleansing from evil, which cannot be without grace, and because the rational soul is the proper subject of grace. So before the infusion of the rational soul she could not be sanctified. Secondly, it is inquired whether she was sanctified before animation. It is to be said as above, according to the aforesaid in the preceding question, —'not.' But if any one says, that she ought to have been sanctified in her parents, it is not true, because no perfection, belonging to the father, passes to the offspring. But if any one say again, that in the very instant in which the soul

---

[3] Alberic. in Bulæus Hist. Univ. Paris. iii. 706.
[4] On 3. Sent. d. 3, given by De Alva, n. 260. p. 702.

is infused, she was sanctified, it is not true, because then she would not have contracted original sin, and would not have needed the redemption made by Christ, which is false. For this belongs to Christ Alone; but we all are born ' children of wrath.' "

96. Moneta of Cremona, A.D. 1220—1250, one of the first Dominicans, "eminent for holiness and sacred learning.—Roman nobles and other learned men came to hear him teaching at Bologna.—He lost his sight through study and the tears of devotion." Quétif calls his "summa" "opus non satis commendandum [5]."

" [6] Other men [besides our Lord] are therefore called sons of God by the grace of adoption, because, being not sons of God, yea rather children of wrath, as the Apostle says, they were by the grace of God made His sons, not having been sons of God. But Christ, as Man, was alway free from all sin, whence He never was other than the Son of God. Nor was He then made Son of God from not having been Son of God, and therefore He cannot be called a Son of adoption, but rather by grace of union."

97. Gulielmus Arvernus or Alvernus, Bishop of Paris from A.D. 1228 to 1249, is spoken of by Trithemius as "a man learned in Divine Scriptures, not ignorant of secular philosophy, and in knowledge venerable; he composed not a few works of his erudition; in which, showing himself a learned

[5] Leand. Albert., f. 184, a. in Quétif, i. 123.
[6] Summa contra Katharos et Waldenses, L. 3. c. 3. De B.'s quotation, corrected by Quétif (i. 123) from the original. De Alva pronounced the quotation "fictitious, made by Bandelis, as being his image." Ver. 219. p. 630.

and devout master, he made his memory immortal."
Alas for human predictions! Half of his works
are missing. He speaks of our Lord and our first
parents as having been alone exempt from original
sin :—

"'You ought to remember that that grace [decor] is not
found in human souls, save when their powers have been
purged and freed from original perversity and other deformities
of vices; but, before, they are neither graceful nor beautiful,
except the souls of our first parents in their state of innocence
(as we said before), wherein they needed neither cleansing nor
freeing, having still their natural grace; excepting also the Soul
of the Saviour, of which you ought to be most certain, that it
never had any thing whatever of original stain; but in the souls
of our first parents in the aforesaid condition, grace and beauty
were necessarily the same."

98. William of Auxerre, a Paris Theologian,
"nominatissimus et in quæstionibus profundissi-
mus[2]," who died at Rome A.D. 1230, wrote a
"Summa," which was "twice abridged, extracted
by Dionysius the Carthusian, and employed by
Durand." He says,—

"'It is proved, that Christ was, in two ways, in the loins of
Abraham, because the Blessed Virgin, who was His flesh, was,
in two ways, in the loins of Abraham; for she was conceived by
the act of concupiscence, not by the Holy Ghost, and therefore

---

[1] De virt. c. 8. Opp. p. 111, Ven. 1591.

[2] Fabr. Bibl. Lat. v. Gulielmus Antissiod. quoting Alberic,
p. 538.

[3] Summa, L. iii. Tr. i. c. 3. f. 115, 115 v., Paris, 1500, written
between 1220—1230, abridged by Ardego, Bishop of Florence,
and by Herbert, or Aubert, Dean of Auxerre, A.D. 1247. Fabr.

she contracted original sin; and therefore Maurice [1], Bishop of
Paris, forbade the Feast of her Conception to be celebrated in
the Church of Paris."

99. "† John of Paris [1]" [i. e. John Poinlane,
Pungensasinum] Dominican, lectured on the Sentences, at least A.D. 1244, died before 1269 [2]:—

" ' Teaching that the V. M. was conceived in original sin, he
says that the opposite opinion was *against the authorities of
the saints*, and derogates from the dignity of the Son of God
and His Mother, because, according to it, she would not have
belonged to the general redemption of her Son, nor would she
be the Mother of an Universal Redeemer."

To turn to the great writers, who have so impressed posterity;—

100. Alexander de Hales, A.D. 1230, so follows
S. Bernard, that to quote him would be to repeat
extracts from S. Bernard. But he lays down, at
the beginning and distinctly, that " the B.V. must
in her generation contract sin from her parents."
He is meeting the question, which used to be
placed first, whether the B. V. could be sanctified
before her Conception.

[1] Maurice de Soliaco, who was present at the [5th] Council
of Tours, A.D. 1163, died A. 1196. Pagi A. 1164. n. 18. A. 1196.
n. 11.

[2] Quétif, i. 119.

[3] In 3. Sent. d. 3. Turr. P. 6. c. 29. f. 119. v. De Alva, who
had [Ver. 183] ridiculed the citation of " John of Paris, Dominican," as being too vague, owned in a subsequent edition
(Rad. 218. col. 1547) the existence of his work on the Sentences in Belgian libraries, on the authority of G. Carnif. and
J. Bunder. Catal. MSS. f. 340.

"'Sanctification is twofold; of the nature, and of the person. Sanctification of the person is by present grace: sanctification of the nature will only be through future glory, for there, i.e. in glory, nature will be sanctified, as is hinted 1 Cor. xv. For in the resurrection nature itself shall be sanctified, because then shall come to pass the saying which is written, 'Where, O death, is thy victory? Where, O death, is thy sting?' He calls the 'fomes' the 'sting.' But sanctification, which is by Baptism and by present grace, is not a sanctification of nature, but only of the person; but the 'fomes' still remains after Baptism in the nature, and is transferred by generation into the whole nature: wherefore generation is not without sin, because nature is not sanctified, and by generation nature is transfused; therefore it is necessary, that what is generated should in the generation contract sin. And therefore the B. V. could not be sanctified in her parents; rather, it was necessary that in her generation she should contract sin from her parents[a].'"

He sums up,—

---

[a] P. 3. q. ix. membr. 2. art. 1.

[b] De Alva quotes Alanus of Paris, who, he says, wrote before 1390, Michael of Milan (whom Wading supposes to be the same as another of his authorities), A.D. 1480, and others following them, who say that he retracted this (n. 12. p. 261), alleging his Mariale. Turrecremata says, "But what is said of this irrefragable Doctor, that he retracted this conclusion when near death, until sufficient testimony of this be given to this sacred Council (Basle), is accounted to be of no moment; but what some others said, that he retracted it in his Mariale, is manifestly a fiction; yea, in many places of the same book, as when he speaks of the sanctification of the Virgin, he continues and confirms the same doctrine." in Alva, Ib. Alva quotes a citation by Gosch. Hollen on the other side. The two answers of De Alva are contradictory; 1) that the passages alleged do not prove that he denied the Immaculate Conception; 2) that he retracted his denial. His earliest authority is about a century and a half after the death of De Hales, A.D. 1245.

"'It is to be granted, that the glorious Virgin, before her Nativity, after the infusion of the soul in her body, was sanctified in her mother's womb."

Wading' states that he wrote his "Summa" of Scholastic Theology at the command of Innocent IV., that his work was examined and approved by seventy most skilled theologians, commended by Innocent, and set forth by Alexander IV. to be a lecture book in all universities.

101. Albertus Magnus (taught at Cologne, 1238, Aquinas being his disciple among others, was made Bp. of Ratisbon A.D. 1260, by Alexander IV.) puts the question, "Whether the flesh of the B. V. was sanctified before animation or after?" He treats it as a presumption to say that the flesh was forepurified, so as not to infect the soul at the moment of its infusion, and thought it probable that the B. V. was sanctified soon after animation:—

"'It is inquired, whether her flesh was sanctified before animation or after? For some have presumed to say this, that she contracted original sin 'in the cause' and in the matter of her body, but, because the Holy Ghost and the soul came together to the body, and the Holy Ghost is more active than any thing active, therefore He forecame the soul in the entering the body, and cleansed it, so that it might not be able to infect the soul with original guilt."

---

* P. 3. q. ix. memb. 2. art. 4. resol.
' Scriptt. Ord. Min. p. 6.
* In 3 Sent. dist. 3. art. 4. T. xv. 2. p. 26.

His next question is, " Whether she was sanctified *after* the animation, and before the nativity from the womb?" He answers,—

" ' It is to be said, that she was sanctified before the nativity *from* the womb. But on what day or what hour, no man can know, except through revelation ; save that it is more probable, that it was conferred soon after animation, than that it was long awaited."

On S. Luke he says,—

" ' ' Shall overshadow thee.' A shadow hath five things in it; refrigeration, temperament of vision, &c. And to these five are reduced the expositions of the Fathers who have expounded the passage before us. For as to this, that shade implies a certain refrigeration, there are two glosses ; one which says, that to ' overshadow ' is to refrigerate from ' the incentive to vices.' But ' the incentive to vices ' is the ' fomes,' and thus, by the virtue of the Most Highest, the B. V. was purged from the ' fomes.' But you may say, this seems to be false, because she was sanctified in the womb from original sin. To which it is to be said, that she was sanctified in the womb from sin, and from all defilement of original sin, but the ' fomes ' itself was not extinguished in her, but bound, so that it could not be moved to an act either of venial or mortal sin. And afterwards, by the exercise of good works, it was, together with the binding, weakened, so that it was not felt, but in the Conception itself of the Word, it was altogether extinguished, so that it should be altogether none. And this is what the gloss says."

102. S. Bonaventura (A.D. 1255) weighs carefully[2] the grounds alleged in behalf of the opinion

[*] In 3 Sent. dist. 3. art. 5. p. 27.
[1] Postillæ sup. Luc. c. 1. f. 25. Hagenau. 1504.
[2] In Sent. L. iii. dist. iii. q. 2. Opp. T. v. p. 32.

of those, who " will to say that in the soul of the
B.V. the grace of sanctification forecame the stain
of original sin," and those who "laid down, that
the sanctification of the Virgin was subsequent to
the contraction of original sin, and this, because no
one was free from the fault of original sin, save
the Son of the Virgin Alone." He sums up, that
" the grounds proving this last, ' that the sanctification of the Virgin was subsequent to the contraction
of original sin,' are to be conceded." The grounds
which he states, are [3],—

"' 'All sinned in Adam.' But this is only because, according to the ratio seminalis, we were in Adam ; therefore, if the
Virgin was so, it seemeth that she contracted original sin, like
others also.

"Also Augustine [4]; 'no one is freed from the mass of sin,
except in faith of the Redeemer;' therefore all, whosoever are
delivered, are delivered through Christ: but one is not delivered
from sin, who hath it not. Therefore it seemeth that all other
than Christ contracted original sin.

"Also Pope Leo, in a sermon on the Nativity of the Lord;
' Our Lord, the Destroyer of sin and death, as He found none
free from guilt, so He came to free all;' therefore neither did
He find the B. V. free; therefore she contracted original
sin.

"This same seemeth to be so, on ground of reason ; because,
if the B. V. was without original sin, she was without desert of
death : therefore either injustice was done her when she died,
or she died by a dispensation [dispensative] for the salvation
of the human race. The first is a reproach to God; for, were
it true, God were not a just requiter. The second is a con-

---

[3] In Sent. L. iii. dist. iii. q. 2.   Opp. T. v. p. 31.
[4] Rom. v. 6.   [5] De corr. et grat. c. 7.

tumely to Christ; for, were it true, Christ were not a sufficient
Redeemer. Therefore both are false and impossible. It remains, then, that she had original sin.

"Also, no one belongs to the Redemption of Christ, save
one who has fault. If then the B. V. was without original sin,
it seemeth that she belongeth not to the redemption of Christ.
But great is the glory to Christ from the saints whom He redeemed. Therefore, if He did not redeem the B. V., He is
deprived of His noblest glory. If it is profane and impious to
say this, then, &c.

"Also, if the B. V. had not original sin, and the door is shut
against none save by the desert of original sin, it seemeth to
follow that, had she died before Christ, she would have mounted
straight to heaven. Therefore it seemeth not, that the door
was opened to all through Christ. And so the Apostle would say
falsely, ' It pleased Him that all things should be reconciled
by Him, both which are in heaven and on earth.' "

And in his own answer to the arguments,—

"For as the Apostle says, ' All have sinned and need the glory
of God.' The Gloss says, ' All sinners find the grace of Christ,
Who Alone came without sin; and all need the glory of God,
i. e. that He should deliver, Who can; not thou, who needest
deliverance.' And this same thing Augustine says, on John,
treating of the words, ' Behold the Lamb of God,' where he
saith, ' That He Alone could take away the sins of the world,
Who Alone came without sin, because He hath no sin.' *This
mode of speaking is more common and more reasonable and safer.
More common*, because almost all hold, that the B. V. had
original sin; inasmuch as this appears from her manifold suffering of punishment [pœnalitate], which she must not be said to
have suffered for the redemption of others; which also one
must not say that she had by taking them on herself [assump-
tione], but by contracting them [contractione]. *It is more
reasonable*, because the being of nature precedes the being of
grace, either by time or by nature. And therefore Augustine
says, that ' to be born is prior to being re-born;' as being is

prior to well-being: the union of the soul to the flesh is prior
to the infusion of grace into it. If then that flesh was infected,
it was born to infect the soul by original sin through its own
infection: it is therefore necessary to lay down, that the infection of original sin was prior to sanctification. *It is safer,*
because it is more concordant with piety and the authority of
the saints. *It is more concordant with the authority of the
saints,* in that the saints commonly, when they speak of this
subject, except Christ Alone from that universality, wherewith
it is said, 'All have sinned in Adam.' But *there is no one
found, of those whom we have heard of with our ears, who said
that the Virgin Mary was free from original sin.* It is more
concordant also with the piety of faith, because, although the
mother is to be had in reverence, and great devotion ought to
be had towards her, yet much greater is to be had towards the
Son, from Whom all honour and glory comes to her. And
therefore, because this regards the excellent dignity of Christ,
that He is the Redeemer and Saviour of all, and that He opened
the door to all, and that He Alone died for all, the B. V. M. is
in no wise to be excluded from this universality, lest, while the
excellency of the Mother is amplified, the glory of the Son be
diminished, and thus in this the mother be provoked, who
willed that her Son be extolled and honoured more than herself, He the Creator, than her, the creature. Adhering then to
this position, for the honour of Jesus Christ, which in no wise
prejudices the honour of the mother, since the Son incomparably
excels the mother, let us hold, as the common opinion holdeth,
that the sanctification of the Virgin was after the contraction
of original sin '."

---

* Perrone (p. 29) alleges from S. Bonaventura a "Serm. 2.
de B. V. M. Opp. iii. 389, Rom. 1596," maintaining the Immaculate Conception. The editor, however, of S. Bonaventura's
works, ed. Moguntiæ, 1609 (T. Ang. de Rocca, Augustinian,
Sacristan of the Apost. Palace), says, "S. Bonaventura (in lib.
3. Sent. dist. 3. art. i. q. 1 and 2) maintains altogether,
with S. Bernard, S. Thomas, and others, that the B. V. was
conceived in original sin. Hence it must be certainly confessed

103. S.Thomas Aquinas, A.D. 1255, in his Summa Theologiæ, his commentary on the Sentences, his Summa contra Gentiles, and five other works, maintained that the Blessed Virgin was conceived in original sin.   I cite only his Summa, as being one of his two last works.

that this sermon is not S. Bonaventura's, since he himself, in many other places, altogether and steadily maintains the opinion, which he affirmed in the 3rd book of the Sentences." T. iii. p. 355.   And more fully in the notice prefixed to the volume, "I wish to admonish the readers that the second sermon on the B. Mary Ever-Virgin, is either not a genuine work of this holy Doctor (as is said in our marginal note) or that, in regard to the Conception of the B. M. without original sin, something has been added by some modern, *as frequently occurs in many books*.   It is clear that this was done in the 'Compendium Theologiæ' printed formerly, and especially in the chapter 'On Sanctification,' L. iv., as is ascertained from many MSS., from which that Compendium, which was circulated under the name of S. Bonaventura, seems for the most part to differ, an addition being appended contrary to the opinion of this Doctor in the same chapter of the Compendium, and in the Book on the Sentences, 3 d. 3, art. 1, q. 1, 2."   The sermon was inserted subsequently to the first collection of his sermons.   It was not in the edition of Reutlingen, 1484, nor of Hagenau, 1496.   The passage, whosesoever it is, is: "Our Lady was full of preventing grace in her sanctification, i. e. grace preservative against the foulness of original fault, which she would have contracted from the corruption of nature, unless she had been prevented and preserved by special grace.   For the Son of the Virgin Alone was free from original fault, and His Virgin mother.   For we must believe, that by a new kind of sanctification, in the beginning of her Conception, the Holy Spirit redeemed her, and by singular grace preserved her from original sin,—original sin, not which was in her, but which would have been in her."

"' The sanctification of the Blessed Virgin cannot be understood before her animation, on two grounds; first, because the sanctification, of which I am speaking, is nothing but cleansing from original sin. For holiness is perfect cleanness, as Dionysius says. But fault cannot be cleansed except by grace, of which the rational creature alone is the subject. And therefore the Blessed Virgin was not sanctified before the infusion of the rational soul. Secondly, because, since the rational creature alone is susceptible of fault, the offspring conceived, before the infusion of the rational soul, is not capable of fault. And so, in whatever way the Blessed Virgin had been sanctified before animation, she would never have incurred the stain of original fault, and so would not have needed the redemption and salvation which is by Christ, of Whom it is said, ' He shall save His people from their sins.' But this is unfitting, that Christ should not be ' the Saviour of all men ' as is said 1 Tim. ii. It remains then that the sanctification of the Blessed Virgin was after her animation."

"' If the soul of the Blessed Virgin had never been defiled by the contagion of original sin, this would derogate from the dignity of Christ, according to which He is the universal Saviour of all. And therefore under Christ, Who needed not to be saved, as being the universal Saviour, the purity of the Blessed Virgin was the greatest. For Christ in no way contracted original sin, but was holy in His very Conception, according to that of Luke i., ' That Holy Thing which shall be born of thee shall be called the Son of God.' But the Blessed Virgin contracted indeed original sin, yet was cleansed from it, before she was born from the womb."

Then, in answer to the argument that "no festival is celebrated, except as to a holy thing, but *some* celebrate the feast of the Conception of the Blessed Virgin," he answers,—

' 8 p. q. 27. art. 2. c.   ' Ib. ad 2.

"'Although the Roman Church does not celebrate the Conception of the Blessed Virgin, yet it tolerates the custom of some Churches who celebrate that festival; whence such celebration is not to be wholly reprobated. And yet thereby, that the festival of the Conception is celebrated, it is not given to be understood, that she was holy in her Conception; but, because it is not known at what time she was sanctified, the feast of her sanctification rather than of her Conception is celebrated on the day of her Conception."

And in answer to the objection from the text, "If the root be holy, so are the branches;" "but the root of children is their parents; therefore the Blessed Virgin could be sanctified in her parents, before animation," he says,—

"'Sanctification is twofold. The one is of the whole nature, in that the whole human nature is liberated from all corruption of fault and punishment: and this shall be in the resurrection. The other is personal sanctification, which does not pass to the offspring, begotten according to the flesh, because this sanctification regards not the flesh, but the mind. And therefore if the parents of the Blessed Virgin were cleansed from original sin, nevertheless the Blessed Virgin contracted original sin, since she was conceived, according to the concupiscence of the flesh, from the union of male and female. For Augustine says, in his ' de Nuptiis et Concupiscentia,' that all which is born of concumbency [concubitus] is ' flesh of sin.' "

S. Thomas says much the same in two of his books on the Sentences, so that it seems even strange, that a single passage from that work should have been cited, in proof that he believed the Immaculate Conception of the Blessed Virgin.

' Ib. ad 3.   ' Ib. ad 4.

The passage occurs in an answer to an argument derived from a passage of S. Anselm, already quoted [2], that "it was meet that the Virgin, whom God prepared as a Mother for His Only-Begotten Son, should be adorned with *purity*, than which none greater can be conceived under heaven;" therefore, it was argued, "God could create nothing *better* than the Blessed Virgin." S. Thomas answered,—

"[3] Purity is increased by removal from the contrary, and so there may be found a created thing, than which nothing can be *purer* among created things, if it be defiled by no contagion of sin, and such was the purity of the Blessed Virgin, who was free from sin, original and actual. Yet she was below God, in that there was in her the power of sinning; but goodness is increased by approach to the limit, which is at an infinite distance, viz. the Supreme Good; so that something *better* could be made than any finite good."

According to the belief of S. Thomas himself, the Blessed Virgin was cleansed from original sin in her mother's womb; she was then, during her whole life on earth (according to his belief, as he states it in those other places), "free from sin, original and actual." His statement, then, here does not in the least contradict what he had said elsewhere, that she was "conceived in original sin." The answer is given more fully by the author of the "Harmony of the sayings and con-

---

[2] See above, p. 166. [3] i. d. 44. 3. 3m.

clusions of S. Thomas Aquinas," subjoined to his works.

"'I answer, that it is to be said, that there is no repugnance or even apparent contradiction. First, because, in his 1st book of the Sentences, he makes no mention of her Conception, but only speaks of *her*, and her immunity after her sanctification, as appears from the passage cited from S. Anselm which he is there explaining, as also it could be said of any one, sanctified either in the womb or by Baptism, that he was then *free* [im-munis] from all sin, original and actual.

"Secondly, because, although he says that she was 'free,' yet he does not say that she was *always* free, but says it, without any indication of universality, as he says also of other men, that one was at some time without even venial sin in this life, but not always nor long, as is clear, 3ª. q. 79. 4. 2ᵐ., 3. d. 3. q. 3. q. 1 L. 1ᵐ., 4. d. 12. q. 2. art. 2. q. 1. 1ᵐ., d. 21. q. 2. 1. 4ᵐ., Ma. q. 7. 12. 4ᵐ.

"Thirdly, because if any one *will* pertinaciously assert, that the Holy Doctor means to speak of the Conception of the Blessed Virgin, he ought to know that it did not bear upon the matter, of which he was there treating, to insert any thing as to the passive Conception of the Mother of Christ, whereby *she* was conceived, but rather of the passive Conception of Christ, of which he says elsewhere too [that any one who should say] that there was any thing in Adam, not infected by original sin, from which Christ was formed, in the assumption itself [of the flesh], is a heretic, but that the cleansing of His flesh from the preceding infection, at least in idea, preceded its assumption, as is said, 3. d. 3. q. 4. art. 1. O., art. 2. c., 2ᵐ., L. princ°., Jo. 3. lect. 5. But in the first book of the Sentences, there corresponded to the passive Conception of Christ, only something as to the active Conception, whereby the Blessed Virgin conceived Christ, on account of the passage of S. An-selm, introduced there as an authority, wherein it is said that God prepared her for His Only-Begotten, as a Mother.

' Opp. T. xviii. Concordantiæ dictorum et conclusionum D. Thomæ de Aquino, n. 370.

" Fourthly, that S. Thomas says there, as S. Anselm also asserts, that the purity of the Mother of Christ was beneath God, in that in her there was the power of sinning. But this, not through actual sin, as he himself says, Verit. q. 24. 9. 2^m, unless perhaps the Blessed Virgin be considered in her material substance, as he also adduces as to all angels and men, Cont. 3. c°. 109. Therefore, by original sin.

" Fifthly, because he is there explaining the passage alleged from S. Anselm, who every where expressly held, as all the saints commonly affirm, that the Blessed Mother of God was certainly conceived with original sin."

104. This illustrates, and is illustrated by, the saying of the writer of the Sermons [5] " on the Antiphone Salve Regina," who speaks of the Blessed Virgin as having been " *innocent* of both original and actual sins," because he held with S. Bernard that she had been " *absolved* from original sin in her mother's womb." He so explains the words of S. Augustine,—

" ' ' That power was given her to *overcome* sin on all sides,' i. e. on the side of original as well as of actual sins. She then alone excepted, what can all the rest say, but what the Apostle John says, 'If we say that we have no sin, we deceive ourselves, and the truth is not in us'? I too opine with pious belief, that in your Mother's womb you were *absolved* from original sin, nor is the belief vain or the opinion false. Lastly, reasons

---

[5] Cl. de Rota attributed them to Bernard, Archbishop of Toledo; but Mabillon observes that this was an error; since the author in the 3rd Sermon adopts some of S. Bernard's Serm. 16 on the Canticles, but Bernard of Toledo was older than S. Bernard, at the end of the eleventh cent.

[6] In Antiphon. Salve Regina, Serm. 4. Opp. S. Bern. App. ii. 748.

and authorities exist in support of this. Reason thus, If others
were sanctified in their mother's womb, much more thou, the
Mother of the Lord. But Jeremiah and John are read to
have been, the one 'sanctified,' the other filled with the Holy
Ghost, in their mothers' wombs. Thou then too, Mary, Mother
of God, who alone possessedst the whole grace of the Holy
Ghost which others had in part. For the Angel Gabriel called
thee 'full of grace'—Thou camest forth, as dawn, lightsome
and ruddy, because, *original sin being overcome in the mother's
womb*, thou wert born, lightsome with the knowledge of truth,
and ruddy with the love of virtue. Hence it is, that the holy
Church honours with festive celebrations thy holy nativity,
which otherwise she would not do. Lastly, of none beside thee,
save of the Lord thy Son and John Baptist, who were born
holy, does she celebrate the Nativity."

Immediate results of the teaching of S. Bonaventura and S. Thomas were two books which have
ever continued to be reprinted in their works.
The one certainly was most popular, and has been
ascribed to Albertus M., Ægidius de Colonna, S.
Bonaventura, or S. Thomas.

105. Hugo de Argentina, Argentoratensis, Dominican, "[1] real author of the excellent Compendium
Theologicæ Veritatis," A.D. 1270—1290 :—

"[2] There were three sanctifications of the Mother of God.
The first was the sanctification in the womb [3], and this had three
effects, viz. the expiation of original fault, and the infusion of

---

[1] Fabric. iii. 288. Quétif, i. 470, sq. It was attributed
to him by Laur. Pignon, about 1403.

[2] Compend. Theol. Ver. L. iv. c. 4. in S. Bonav. T. 7. p.
740.

[3] John de Combis, Franciscan, has a note on this passage.
"The Doctors do not hold this opinion, nor the Church,

grace, and so great restriction of the fomes, that she could not be led into any sin, although yet the fomes itself remained, according to the essence.   The second sanctification was in the over-

---

which abrogated it in the C. of Basle; whence Scotus (3 d. 3) says, that 'the most Blessed Virgin was holy in the beginning of her conception, in which sanctification she had preservation from original sin and infusion of grace, and extirpation of the fomes, so that it did not remain in her, except causally,' " ad loc. p. 314, Lugd. 1579. A Dominican edition by Seraphyn. Capponi a Porrecta has also a note; "The third 'removes original fault'—i. e., contracted in act, yet abraded as speedily as possible. By the holy Roman Church they are excommunicated ipso facto who brand this opinion with the note of mortal sin or heresy; as they too who in like way presume to condemn the contrary opinion (Sixt. IV. Extrav. Grave nimis).   Hence, stupidly enough, showing their own ignorance, some adduce the Council of Basle as determining against the opinion of the Author. Let such look to Leo X., in the sacred acts of the 2nd Lateran Council, calling the C. of Basle, not a Council, but a Conciliabulum, and be ashamed of such support given them.   Let the sessions, too, be examined, and it will be clear, that at that time they were not with Eugenius, whom the Catholic Church reverenced as undoubted Pope; and who, as being truly owned by her as undoubted Pope, while that their conciliabule of Basle still lasted, gathered together the sacred Council of Florence, of Eastern and Western Fathers. Be this said, not to derogate from the opposite opinion, but to show what is *their* knowledge, who in this matter lean on the broken reed of that which deserved not to be called a Council (as Leo saith there). How could Sixtus himself, who was subsequent to that Council, and favoured that opinion, not have accepted that determination of Basle, if he had seen it to have any force ? How should he, at the end of his Extrav., have said these formal words, ' Since this has not yet been decided by the Roman Church and Apostolic see,' if those of Basle, determining this, had represented the Catholic Church, which is the Roman, &c.," p. 362, Ven. 1588.

shadowing of the Holy Ghost and the Conception of the Son of God, which superadded two to the three premised, viz. the entire extinction of the fomes, and confirmation in good, so that she, who before was only able not to sin, now could not sin. These two effects the Angel expressed, 'The Holy Ghost shall supervene in thee,' as to the first, and 'the power of the Highest shall overshadow thee' as to the second. This confirmation was, not the taking away of free will, but its completion by grace. The third sanctification was in the inhabitation of the Son of God, Who abode nine months in her womb, and added two more effects to all the aforesaid. One, that all the dispositions of the fomes were taken away, as, when a disease is cured, there yet sometimes remains some residue to be cured. The second was a dedication to Divine things.—In the first sanctification, which was in the womb, the B. V. was cleansed from the fomes, as far as the fomes regarded her own person, because nothing remained in her person to be cleansed," &c.

106. **Hannibaldus de Hannibaldis,** 23rd of the Magistri in Theologia of Paris, Cardinal A.D. 1261, "[1] a man of great humility and truth, and a holy man, whom F. Thomas much loved; he wrote on the Sentences a work dedicated to Card. Hannibaldus (his uncle, Cardinal 1237, or 1240) which is nothing else than an abridgment of the sayings of F. Thomas:"—

"[2] The Blessed Virgin was sanctified, neither before her Conception nor in the conception before the infusion of the soul, because the soul is the proper subject of sanctification; nor in the instant itself of the infusion of the soul, because thus she would not have contracted original sin, as neither did Christ,

---

[1] Tholom. de Lucha, H. E. xxii. 23. in Quétif, i. 261.

[2] Scriptum secundum in Sent. ad Annibald. 3. dist. 3. Art. 1. f. 82, in S. Thomas Aq. T. xvii.

and so it would not belong to all to be redeemed by Christ; but she *is believed* only to have been sanctified after the infusion of her soul, because this has been bestowed on other saints. And therefore it was especially fitting, that this should be bestowed on the mother of Wisdom, Whom nothing defiled can touch, as it is in Wisd. vii."

Others exhibit the same traditional system, but independently and alike, to whatever religious order they belonged.

107. Peter de Tarantasia, Professor of Theology at Paris, A.D. 1260 [3]; in 1276, during five months, Innocent V., the first Dominican who was raised to the Papacy:—

"'The nearer any one approaches to the Holy of Holies, so much the greater degree of sanctification ought he to have, for there is no approach to Him, except through sanctification. But the mother approaches more than all to the Son, Who is the Holy of Holies; therefore she ought to have a greater degree of sanctification after her Son. The degree of sanctifi-

---

[3] "On account of his rare learning," Cave says. He was the author of other large works, besides the Compendium Theologiæ and the Comm. on the Sentences, which last De B. quotes. His book on the Sentences was printed at Thoulouse 1652. There is no printed edition at Oxford, Cambridge, or in the British Museum, nor any complete MS. of the work, including the 3rd book, except in the library of Balliol College. As De Band. condenses passages, I have translated the above from the Cod. Bal. 61, to which Mr. Coxe gives the date, "sec. xiv. ineunt." I have collated it with the extract given by S. Antoninus, and that of De Alva, n. 153, who had compared a Thoulouse MS.

[4] In 3 Sent. dist. 3. q. 1. art. 1.

cation may be understood as fourfold: either that one have
sanctity (1) before conception and birth; (2) after conception
and birth; (3) in the conception itself and birth; (4) in birth,
not in conception. For, 'in conception and not in birth' is
impossible. The first degree is not possible, both because personal perfection (like knowledge or virtue) is not transfused
from the parents; and also because in children the being of
grace cannot take place, before the actual being of nature, upon
which it is founded. The second degree is common to all,
according to the common law of sanctification through sacraments. The third is peculiar to the Holy of Holies, in Whom
Alone all sanctification took place at once, conception, sanctification, assumption. There remains then the fourth. But
this has four degrees; because the fœtus, when conceived in
the womb, may be understood to be sanctified either before
animation, or in the animation, or soon after the animation, or long after the animation. The first degree is
impossible, because according to Dionysius (de div. nom.
c. 12) 'Holiness is cleanness free from all defilement,
and perfect and immaculate;' but the uncleanness of fault
is not expelled except through 'grace making gracious'
[acceptable], as darkness by light, of which grace the reasonable creature only is the subject. The second degree was not
suitable to the Virgin, because either she would not have contracted original sin, and so would not have needed the universal
sanctification and redemption of Christ, or if she had contracted
it, grace and fault could not have been in her at once. The
fourth degree also was not suitable to the Virgin, because it
did suit John and Jeremiah, and because it did not suit so
great holiness that she should have lingered long in sin, as
others; but John was sanctified in the sixth month (Luke i.).
But the third seems suitable and piously credible, although it
be not derived from Scripture, that she should have been sanctified, soon after her animation, either on the very day or hour,
although not at the same moment."

"'Greater than this sanctification can none be conceived

---

* Ibid. ad 2.

beneath God, or beneath Christ, Who is God; but had she
been sanctified before, she had not contracted original sin, and
so would have been equal to Christ."

"'Since the Blessed Virgin is intermediate between the
Holy of Holies [Sanctum Sanctorum] and all other holy ones
[Saints], it was meet that she should have a middle degree of
sanctification. Since then Christ was ever free from all sin,
and some Saints were ever free from mortal sin, but not from
venial and original sin, it was meet that the Virgin should
have had original sin, but should never have committed actual
sin; therefore that cleansing was not from sin, but from the
effect and consequence of sin."

108.   Joannes Ægidius of Zamora, a Franciscan,
about A.D. 1274, was one of the most learned and
laborious Spaniards of his day.   He was chosen by
Alphonso "the wise" to be preceptor to his son.
The citation from his "Summa" illustrates how
MSS. were altered naturally to express a subsequent belief, yet not with any idea of falsification;
for the MSS. were for private use only.   In this
case, the substitution of "without" instead of
"with" "original sin" left the passage self-contradictory.

"'Mary, then, although she was ordained from eternity
Mother of grace, according to the true oracles of the Prophets,
yet, since according to the flesh she was propagated of fleshly
parents, we believe that she was conceived with ⁸ sin, and, there-

---

⁶ Ib. q. 2. art. 1.

⁷ In his Summa, cap. de Maria, tom. vi. fol. 55. quater 4.
(Turr. P. 6. c. 23. f. 123.)   De Alva n. 5. p. 243.

⁸ Deza, in what he believed to be the original, in a Franciscan convent, says "that the word 'cum' had been erased, and
'sine' written over it, as is clearer than light to any one, however weak his sight."   Deza continues, "and afterwards he proves

fore the conception of such is not to be celebrated by the Church, but in respect to the sanctification which took place after the conception of natures, i. e. the union of the soul with the body."

109. John de Balbis of Genoa, Dominican. He finished his Catholicon A.D. 1286. From the number of editions, before or between 1460 and 1520, it seems to have been a favourite book, until about 1520, in Italy, France, and Germany. It was also abridged in France. De Balbis also wrote Postills on the four Gospels.

" ' In Syriac, Mary means Lady, and well ; because she bore the Lord of all, and the Virgin Mary was holy, before she was born from the womb. And know, that the sanctification of the B. V. M. was more excellent than all sanctifications of others, which is clear from this. For in the sanctification, which takes place through the common law in the sacraments, the fault is taken away, but the fomes remains, so far as it is inclining to mortal and venial sin ; but in the sanctified from the womb, the fomes remaineth not, so far as inclining to mortal sin, but there only remaineth the inclination of the fomes to venial, as is plain in Jeremiah and John Baptist, who had actual sin, yet not mortal but venial. But in the Bl. V. the inclination of the fomes was altogether taken away, both as to venial and mortal."

" ¹ To one is given grace which should repel, not only all mortal, but all venial sins too, and this is the fulness of that

---

this at length taking formally the words of Bonaventura alleged above, viz. ' this mode is more common, safer, more reasonable.' " De Alva admits that the passage itself is inconsistent with the word " sine," but says a MS. in the Franciscan convent at Zamora had it (p. 244). The work was never printed.

  ⁹ Catholicon v. Maria. Strasburg 1470 (no paging).
  ¹ Ibid. v. Virtus.

special prerogative, which was in the Bl. V., according to which she was full of God; so that also there should be nothing in her which should not be ordered to God. But in Christ there was further given grace, perfecting Him not only as to all virtues, but also as to all uses of virtues, and as to all effects of grace, given gratis, and again as to all emotion of sin, not actual only, but original also, and the power of sinning. For He could not sin; and this is the singular fulness of Christ."

110. Henri de Gandavo [H. Goethals of Ghent], of the Sorbonne, of the Order of the Servites [i. e. of the servants of the B. V.], "Archdeacon of Tournay, a man among all the Doctors of his time the most learned in Holy Scripture, and very subtle in the philosophy of Aristotle, was so highly esteemed in the University of Paris, that he was called 'Doctor Solennis' throughout the Christian world[2]." He lived from A.D. 1217—1293. He was so far from being a follower of S. Thomas, that he scarcely mentions him in his "[3]Book of Illustrious Men."

His was a transition period, in which men, still granting that the B. V. contracted original sin at the moment of the infusion of her soul, were anxious to minimize it to the utmost[4]. I make some short extracts only :—

"The Conception of Christ is rightly to be celebrated on ground of the Conception in regard to the instant of the Conception as such, not only because it was the instant of His

---

[2] Trithem. c. 497. .

[3] Labbe de Script. Eccl. i. 423.

[4] Quodlib. xv. p. 382.

sanctification as Man, but also because His Conception was miraculous by the virtue of the Holy Ghost. But if there passed time between the Conception of the Virgin and her sanctification, I say that the Conception of the Virgin is not to be celebrated, on ground of the Conception, whereby she was conceived to the world, either as to the act of the Conception, because it was not holy, or as to the instant of the Conception, because sanctification did not take place in it, nor in time continuous to it. But, if the Conception of the Virgin, whereby she was so conceived to the world, is to be celebrated, this is only in regard to her future sanctification, and the Conception whereby she was to be conceived to God, that thus, by celebrating the feast of her Conception, reverence may be shown to her person, on account of the dignity of the sanctification, to which she was predestinated by God. And this, as reverence is shown to the person of a king's eldest son, not so much by reason of the royal stock from which he comes, as because he expects to obtain the royal dignity. But because these things relate to facts, of which Holy Scripture says nothing, saints or doctors little, viz., whether Mary was sanctified immediately after the instant of her conception, so that she should have only been infected with original sin for an indivisible instant, or after some interval, so that in all that interval she should have been in original sin, I think that nothing ought to be rashly pronounced—Because it is clear that it is a token of greater love, or a greater token of great love, to endow her quickly, and as soon as she could be endowed, than to wait longer, if then she could be sanctified and cleansed from sin, so that she should have been in the stain of original sin only for an instant, right reason so determining (as it seems to me) this may be piously thought. But what? was it possible, according to nature, that the Virgin, like other mere human beings, should, in the moment when she was conceived, a human being of seed according to the body, and the soul was united to it, have truly contracted original sin, and have remained in it only for an instant? To me, it seems that this is very possible."—P. 382.

"In what I have said of the Virgin, I could not but think what seemed pious and worthy, and, saving the privilege of

Christ, Who Alone was conceived Man in the womb, of clean seed without original sin, I think that the privilege of the Virgin was above all other human beings ; that, although she was conceived in original sin as a human being of unclean seed, yet that she did not remain in it, save for a moment; and so, though she was conceived in sin, she yet was not nourished in sin in her mother's womb.   But all others, even if sanctified in the womb, were not only conceived in sin, but also nourished in the womb for some space of time [in it].   As Innocent III., in a sermon on the Annunciation of the Virgin, expounding what Elizabeth said, the child in my womb leaped for joy, saith this of John Baptist."—P. 383.

111. Ulric of Strasburg [Engelbert] [1], who, " although he was not a Master, having been overtaken by death at Paris, while yet a Bachelor [having been sent by his Order to lecture there], but most renowned both for religion and learning, as the many and glorious works published by him attest evidently, after he had proved that no one could be sanctified in the parents, nor in the conception itself," says,—

" ' We believe that the Mother of God speedily [subito] after her animation was sanctified, so that she could truly say that of Ecclus. 24, ' from the beginning of my duration in my

---

[1] He was a disciple of Albertus Magnus, Prior Provincial of Germany from 1272—1277; " wrote a Summa Theologiæ exceeding good,"—Laur. Pignon, cat. 26, in Quétif, i., 356 ; " the number of famous lecturers who went forth from his schools attests his learning,"—John de Friburg, in the first Prologue to his Summa Confessorum.

[2] Summa, L. v. c. 2, 3, 5, 7, 27 in Turr. P. 6, c. 29, f. 119, and elsewhere.   Alva, n. 312, grants this authority, although he wrongly identifies him with Hugo Argentin.

natural being '—i. e., a little after the beginning of her duration—'and before ages,' as far as relates to priority of dignity,
' I was created,' i. e., produced from the nothing of sin to the
being of the grace of sanctification."

And below, in the same, he says,—

" From this cause of sanctification, the feast is kept in some
places [alicubi]. Although it is not approved by the Church, on
account of the error close by, yet it is endured, that others
should celebrate the Conception of the B. V., not referring
this joy to the conception of seeds, but of natures, which is
in the infusion of the soul, because, as is said, de divor. l.
divortium, ' a wife, returned in brief space, doth not seem even
to have gone away.' Also, it is said in the decret. de pœnit.
dist. i., ' It is accounted not at all to differ, when it differs
little.' "

Dionysius Carthusianus also quotes from his Summa :—

" ' Because that forecoming in the blessings of sweetness
appertains to the praise of Him Who forecomes, it follows
that the more praiseworthy any is made by the greater grace
of sanctification, the more this grace is accelerated in him.
Wherefore we believe that the mother of Christ, most worthy
of all praise, was sanctified soon after the animation—i. e., the
infusion of her soul. But John was sanctified sooner than
Jeremiah, yet later than Mary, viz., in the sixth month from
his conception, when his mother was visited by the mother
of Christ. Yet it is tolerated by the Church, that some
celebrate the Conception of the B. V., referring it to the conception, not of seeds, but of natures, which was at the infusion
of the soul; nor do they celebrate that in itself, because it was

---

' In 3, dist. 3, q. 1. Dionysius himself, regarding the
Council of Basle, even after the withdrawal of the legates of
Eugenius, to have been a " general" Council, held its decision
to be final.

in sin, but by reason of the sanctification near upon it. But
the sanctification of the glorious Virgin was threefold. The
first in her mother's womb; the second in the Conception of
the Son of God, in which the fomes in her was entirely extinguished, and her whole nature, in soul and body, was perfectly
sanctified, that so the Body of Christ might be taken and formed
from her. Her third sanctification was from the indwelling of
the Son of God in her womb, Who, as a consuming fire, rested
in her womb six months, as the fire in the bush, consuming in
her all possibility to evil, confirming her in the good of perfection, that not only could she not decline from good, but could
not pass from more perfect good to a state less perfect; and
thus her whole nature was shone through with the light of
Divinity, and was resplendent with wondrous purity."

112. Richard Middleton (de media Villa) a
Franciscan, who had the honorary titles, "Doctor
solidus et copiosus, fundatissimus et autoratus."
He died about A.D. 1300.

" ' The soul of the B. V., from its union with that flesh, contracted original sin, as Anselm, about the middle of his 2nd
book, Cur Deus homo, says of the B.V., that ' she was conceived
in iniquity, and in sins did her mother conceive her, and with
original sin was she born,' which is to be understood of the
birth in the womb. Augustine too, on Genesis, says of the flesh
of the Virgin, that it was conceived of the stock of the flesh of
sin."   •

' L. iii. d. 3. q. 1. T. iii. p. 27. Brix. 1591. De Alva quotes
a number of authorities, that in advanced age he changed his
opinion and wrote for the immaculate Conception, and also
some lines on the Ave Maria, in which he takes the Scotist
ground of "fittingness." n. 270, pp. 717, 718. If he did
change, it was not on the ground of any contrary tradition, but
of what the Scotists thought most beseeming to Almighty
God.

113. ...

After stating the contrary arguments in the usual way, he says,—

"' But this position cannot hold first, because Augustine in the de bapt. parv. maintains that Christ had not sin. Because He neither contracted original sin, nor added any of His own, whereof he assigns as the reason, that He came apart from the will of carnal desire and embrace of marriage, and adds, that He took from the body of the Virgin not a wound but a medicament, not what was to be healed, but whence He should heal. Whence he concludes in the same place, that He Alone was without sin, and that no member of His was without sin. To say, then,

---

* L. iv. dist. 43. q. 2.
¹ Epitaph in Cavo sub tit.
* Quodlib. vi. q. 20.

that the B. V. was not conceived in original sin, is to say that she was not conceived by passion of the flesh, through marital embrace, because all so born are conceived in sin. It is also to say, that she was not a member of Christ, since Augustine asserts that no member [of Christ] was without sin."

Then he quotes S. Augustine on S. John, "Behold the Lamb of God," &c., and makes the same inference. "The B. V. then, because she was conceived according to marital embrace like the rest of mankind, was also conceived in original sin."

Subsequently, arguing that between opposite motions there is an interval ; if a stone fall on the ground, there must yet be an interval between the downward and upward motions, during which interval it must be on the ground, he adds,—

"Now let us see herein the great praise of the Virgin therefrom, that we lay down that she was conceived under original sin, whether she was in such original sin for an instant only, or for an imperceptible time. For a short and imperceptible time is accounted as an instant, and because it is more reasonable, that a thing cannot proceed from one opposite to another without intervening time, and not through other time than imperceptible ; we shall hold it as said more reasonably that the B. V. was conceived under original sin, and in her conception—marital embrace intervened, and under its original fault she was during some time, although it is very credible that that time was very brief, and as it were imperceptible."

"Let us then commend the Blessed Virgin, yet not so, as to deny her to have been a member of Christ; yea, it rather appertains to the great privilege of her singular excellence, that she was the only one who bore a man conceived without original sin. But if the B. V. had been conceived without original sin, this privilege would not belong singularly to her, but to S. Anne also, who bore her."

He holds that the Feast of the Conception might still be fittingly held :—

"We shall say that a thing is praiseworthy in an inferior, which is not so in a superior. For in Christ it would not have been praiseworthy to have been born in original sin, because He was not conceived by marital embrace; but in those who are so conceived, because in this way they become members of Christ, as freed from original sin by grace, although to be in original sin is not in itself praiseworthy, yet it appertaineth to praise as they become members of Christ. For one doth not become a member of Christ otherwise than as he is freed from original sin by Christ. Whence also Aug. in the de Bapt. parv., setting forth the likeness of the serpent lifted up in the wilderness as a type of Christ, says, ' If innocency in your own case moves you, deny not that guilt was contracted from the first parent."

114. †"Reginald, Franciscan, Archbishop of Rouen;" i.e. Odo Rigaldi. According to the Sammarthani[3], his holiness of life gained him the title of "regula vivendi." He died A.D. 1275, or 1276.

" ' As impurity, if it had not been sanctified, would derogate from the Virgin herself, whose privilege it was that she alone sine viro conceived (as Bernard says), and therefore did not transmit original sin to her offspring, so if the virgin had been conceived without original sin, it would have derogated from her Son Himself."

115. †Hugo Gallicus, an eminent Dominican, Archbishop and Cardinal of Ostia.

[3] Gall. Christ. xi. 7. They mention also his work on the Sentences. See also on him, Wading A. 1236. n. 6. A. 1276. n. 5.

[4] In 3. Sent. d. 3. Turr. P. 6. c. 30. f. 121. v. He wrote commentaries on the Sentences, beginning, " Quæritur utrum plures sint veritates ab æterno," &c. (Oudin. iii. 451), and so, different from that of Rigaltus Diacon. beg. " Veteris et novæ legis," which De Alva (n. 266. p. 711) alleged to be the same.

Q

"'From the corruption of original sin the B. V. was cleansed in her mother's womb, as relates to infection and guilt, because she would still have descended into limbus, had she departed before the Conception of the Son of God, from the debt of original sin which was never fully purged before the Coming of Christ. Whence, at His Coming, being filled with the grace of the Holy Spirit, she was altogether cleansed from that corruption, and so was twice sanctified."

116. John of Naples, "Doctor solennis Parisiensis," taught at Paris, A.D. 1315 ; died probably A.D. 1330. "He had lived most holily, was remarkable for his life, learning, eloquence[6]." S. Antoninus quotes him several times in answer to the arguments alleged for the Imm. Conc.[7]

He retorted the argument drawn from S. Anselm's saying, that it was meet that the B. V. should have the highest purity beneath God, that if the B. V. had not contracted original sin, her purity would be, not beneath, but equal to that of her Son, Who is God[8], adding,—

"Nor does the instance from the good Angels hold, for in them there cannot be sin contracted from origination, but all are created immediately by God."

To another argument from fittingness, he retorted,—

[6] "In 3. Sent. d. 3." Turrecr. Part. 6. c. 29. fol. 118 v. The writer cannot be identified. "Hugo Metensis" lectured on the Sentences at the same time as S. Thom. Aq. Bulæus. Hist. Univ. Par. iii. 216.

[7] Quétif, i. 567.

[8] Summa Theol. Tit. 8. c. 2. t. i. 551—554.

[9] See ab. p. 166.

"It was not fitting, that the natural conception of any human being, not even of the Virgin-mother, should in immunity from original sin be equalled to the supernatural Conception of Christ."

To the argument that she would be "freed and redeemed in a more noble way than others, if it were provided that she should not fall into slavery, than that she should be raised when fallen and be redeemed, being a servant of sin," S. Antonine says, John of Naples and others answer,—

"Redemption or salvation is only of one existing. For as nothing properly has being, when it exists only in its cause, unless it has being in itself, so neither can one be said properly to be redeemed or saved, being under spiritual slavery, which exists only by fault in the parents, and not in the person himself[*]. However much the Virgin might have been preserved from original sin, she could not be said to have been redeemed and saved, unless she had at some time been subject to [original] sin, not in the person of her parents only, but in her own."

The ground, adds S. Antonine, according to him and John of Policrates, is this:—

"A thing, which was once mine and afterwards is not, is said to be redeemed [bought back]; but a thing which never was mine is said to be bought. But a thing which always was and is mine, cannot be said to be bought, or to be bought back (or redeemed). If, then, the B. V. was never subject to any sin, then she was always God's, and so was not [bought back

---

[*] A child already existing in her mother's womb might be said to be redeemed, and would be redeemed, if her mother was redeemed from slavery. One could not say so of one conceived many years afterwards, although, if the mother had remained in slavery, it too would have been born a slave.

or] redeemed. And the same as to salvation, because it pre-supposes the fall or infirmity of sin."

In answer to the argument from the festival of the Conception of the B. V., he said (according to the physics of that time),—

" The festival is not the festival of her Conception, as those say, since it is nine months before her Nativity, on which day the soul, which is the subject of sanctity, was not infused. But rather it is a feast of thanksgiving (as in the old law was the feast of Pentecost, and in the new the feast of Epiphany), whereas no new holiness was conferred, but the Church gives thanks for benefits, and so in that in question."

In answer to the [alleged] revelation and vision as to S. Bernard, &c., John of Naples says, that " they are fantastic visions, which are not to be believed."

In answer to the objection, that one who refused to celebrate the Conception was not devout to the B. V., he answered, " [19] the Roman Church is supposed to be a true lover of the Virgin, and yet it does not celebrate this solemnity."

Turrecremata quotes him, " [1] having, in his Quodlibet [vi.] q. 11, narrated both opinions, he says thus, The opinion of those who say that the B. V. was conceived in original sin, I hold for the present, as more consonant to Holy Scripture."

De Bandelis gave the summary thus: " The

[19] Catharinus Opusc. 3, test. 4, f. 59 in Alva Sol Verit. n.182. p. 547.

[1] Turr. [L. vi.] c. 29. f. 119 v., quoting from a MS. of his Quodlibets in the Dominican Convent at Naples.

B. V. was conceived in original sin, both because she was descended seminally from Adam, and because Scripture excepteth none but Jesus Christ; also because Augustine, Gregory, Pope Leo, Anselm, Bernard, expressly to the letter, say this²." De Alva owned them to be correct.

117. Guido of Perpignan, General of the Carmelites 1318, made "General Inquisitor of the Faith" 1321, Bishop of Majorca, afterwards of Elne (Perpignan).

Alegre says³ he was also called "Guido of Paris, because at Paris he received the honour of the Doctorate amid such admiration of the doctors of the city and university, on ground of his singular and unheard-of wisdom, that he was called 'Doctor Parisiensis' as a title of his own. He was, as Heverard the Carthusian attests, among the wisest fathers of his time, remarkable for his wisdom, virtue, and most transparent religion." Alegre mentions his eight books of Physics, his "De Anima," a work on the Sentences, Quodlibets, and

² Quétif (i. 567) says that De Alva, in a later edition of his work, Rad. 273, col. 1898—1906, gave his "Quodlibet vi. q. 11, on the Conception of the B. V., owning that he was quoted rightly by Turrecremata, De Bandelis, and their followers." In the edition of 1660, ver. 182, Alva had denied it, supposing that the Quodlibets had been published at Naples in 1618, whereas they were the "Quæstiones Variæ" which were there published, in which the passages quoted from the Quodlibets naturally did not occur.

³ Parad. Carmel. æt. 14, c. 58.

a book to Pope John XXII., against Heresies, "whose teaching all Doctors of the better stamp highly value, and his own wisdom, as if he had come down from above."

"'Is Christ, Who is the Virtue of the most Highest and Very God, Son of the Father, born holy, because He was conceived not of human seed, but of the operation of the Holy Ghost? Read we that Jeremiah was sanctified in his mother's womb, and John, yet in his mother's womb, was filled with the Holy Spirit, and consequently born holy? And yet it is known that they were conceived by carnal concumbency from human seed. We believe also that the Bl. Mary was sanctified in her mother's womb. And if John is sanctified in his mother's womb, because he was elected to be the Forerunner of Christ, to point Him out, much more was the Virgin to be sanctified, who was elected to be the Mother of God and the Tabernacle which the Most High sanctified. But Christ is born holy in one way, others otherwise; because Christ is so born holy, that in His Conception He contracted no original fault; but others, even the Virgin Mary, although sanctified in her mother's womb, were so born holy, that they yet contracted original fault[4]. For the Angel concluded that Christ is born holy, because not from knowledge of man, but from the operation of the Holy Ghost, the Virgin Mary, in whom the virtue of God overshadowed Himself, conceived Christ Himself. And this ground Augustine pursues (De Nupt. et Conc. i. 6),

---

[4] Quatuor unum, i.e. quatuor Evangelistarum Concordia on S. Luke i. 35, pp. 18, 19. Col. 1631. S. Antonine of Florence alleges him as saying that the B. V. was conceived in original sin, in his 3rd Quodlibet.

[5] In a note, the editor says, "The opinion which the most reverend author here defends with all his might according to the exigency of his age, in which he lived and wrote, although it is not at this time very scholastic and regular, we did not think it allowable, for reverence towards him, to limit or expunge." P. 19.

and Ambrose (on Luke ii. c. 7), and Augustine (De Nupt. et
Conc. i. fin. and on Gen. ad iii. x. 18) 'Fulgentius' De Fid. ad
Pet. [Aug.] Hom. 4 on John, and De Nat. et Gratiâ, treating
on Rom. 3, 'All have sinned, and need the glory of God,' he
excepts none, neither the Bl. V.; nay, he includes all under
sin and as needing the grace of Christ, 'The grace of Christ
finds all sinners, Who came Alone without sin. Again, Augustine, De Civ. Dei, treating of that of the Apostle, Rom. v.,
'Therefore all were dead, and one died for all.' Also good is
the saying of the Apostle, Rom. v., 'Because through the first
man sin entered unto all and death by sin;' whence, according
to Aug., no one died who did not contract original sin, except
Christ Alone, Who, being conceived, without seed of man, of
the Holy Ghost, did not contract sin. Whence Rom. v., 'as
the sin of one passed upon all to condemnation, so the
righteousness of One passeth upon all to justification,' where
the gloss saith, that as, besides Adam, there was no one who
was not born [in sin], so, besides Christ, there is none who was
not re-born from fault. Therefore he says 'all' and 'all.'"

In the course of his answer to the one passage
alleged from S. Anselm, he says,—

"It was the privilege of the Son to be conceived of a virgin
without man, and so, according to the saints, without original
fault. Therefore, as it was becoming that the Bl. Mary should
not be conceived of a virgin without man, in order that this
purity might be reserved to Christ Alone, so it was not becoming that she should be conceived without sin, whence
Bernard says, because she was conceived of man, therefore she
was conceived in original sin."

118. Hervæus Natalis, called by S. Antonino [a]
"most subtle in logic and philosophy;" Licentiate of
Theology at Paris, 1307 ; Provincial of the Dominicans, 1309 ; General, 1318; died 1323 [b].

[a] Summa Hist. xxiii. 11. 2. T. 3, p. 681.
[b] Quétif i. 583, 584.

The positions which he has to combat are abstract :—

" ⁕ 1) That whatever excellence *can* be attributed to the B. V. without prejudice to the Faith and Holy Scripture, and the authority of the saints, ought to be attributed to her ; 2) that it is not irreconcilable (as it appears) that she should be at the same time in original sin and in grace ; nay, that this seems necessary, because that which expels and that which is expelled are together ; but grace expels fault ; so then, in the same instant of the creation of the soul, the B. V. could incur original fault and be sanctified by grace. 3) The B. V. ought to be sanctified as soon as possible ; but this would not have been, had she not been sanctified in the first instant of her creation.

" But that to lay down that, in the instant of the creation of the soul, she was sanctified, is not repugnant to any of these."

The arguments from fittingness he meets with arguments equally abstract :—

" Although the purity of the mother pertains to the honour of the Son, yet it pertaineth more to the honour of God, that the whole human nature, descending from Adam by generation, should need redemption by Him, than that some should need it, some or some one should not need it. And it more pertaineth to His honour, that He Alone should have died, not owing death, but the Deliverer of all from death by His Death, than that any one should be assumed not to owe death, nor to need to be redeemed from death by the Death of Christ. These things appertain more to the honour of Christ than the purity of His mother as relates to the avoiding of original sin. For, 1) that appertains most to the honour of Christ which appertains to the general influence of His goodness to others, &c. 2) That that appertains most to the glory of Christ, which appertains to His honour, as He is God. But the general influence of the Redemption appertains directly to the

---

⁕ Quodl. iv. q. ult. Venice, 1486.

honour of Christ, as He is God; because this universality is
laid down as the reason why a Divine Person was incarnate;
but the purity of His Mother appertaineth directly to the
honour of Christ, as He is Man, because, although the B. V. is
the Mother of God, she is not the mother of God as God.

" If it be said here that she would have been redeemed by
Christ—granted, that she was without original sin, because
she would have been freed from the future captivity of fault, it
does not hold; for, although it could be said that any thing
was preserved from a future evil, yet one cannot be said properly to have been redeemed or liberated, unless he had been
in act first sold or subjugated to that evil."

But "that it is in fact to be held that the B. V.
was conceived in original sin," he says, "it is
proved, because that is to be held in fact in this
matter, which is most fitting, and most agrees with
the sayings of the saints and of the Scriptures, such
as Rom. v., and for the saints S. Bernard, Fulgentius, c. 23, 40."

119. †John de Poliaco, a Doctor of Paris about
1320. His teaching, that those who had confessed
to the regulars, having a general licence for hearing
confessions, must confess again to their parish
priest, and that the Pope could not dispense with
this, founded on his interpretation of the Lateran
Council, "Omnes utriusque sexus," as being a
general Council, was condemned by John XXII.,
A.D. 1321, and retracted by him (Raynald A. 1321,
n. 37). I know not on what ground he is said to
be the same as John Policratis, whom S. Antonine
joins with " Ægidius, the most excellent Doctor of
the Order of the Eremites, and Guido of the

Order of Carmelites," and adds, "who all adduce the authority of the Apostle in Rom. iii., 'All have sinned,' and they assign their reasons[1]."

Turrecremata cites him thus: "Magister John de Poliaco, a secular, a Magister of Paris, says in his Quodl. 3, q. 3,—

" '' It seems to me that it could not be held by any one as an opinion, but should rather be accounted as a heresy, that the B. V. did not contract original sin, since it is against Holy Scripture and the sayings of the saints.' And, after many allegations of H. Scripture and Doctors, as Rom. 3, 'All have sinned,' with the gloss of Augustine, and Rom. 5, 'As through one man sin entered into the world,' with the gloss, and Eph. 2, adding many sayings of Augustine and S. Thomas in 3, he subjoins,—

"Since then that which is against all Scripture cannot be held probably as an opinion, nay, as far as it is against Holy Scripture, ought to be held as heretical, who is of such presumption and boldness, as to presume to assert the contrary of the aforesaid testimonies, which are grounded for ever? But if any one were to presume, he must be proceeded with, not by argument, but in some other way."

120. John de Bacon, or Baconthorpe, Provincial of the Carmelites in England from A.D. 1329 ; died A.D. 1346. " Doctor resolutus, a man most learned in the Divine Scriptures, excellently learned both in civil law and secular philosophy, distinguished in the University of Paris for conversation as well as learning[3]."

[1] Summa, P. 1, Tit. 8, c. 3, p. 551.
[2] In Turr., P. 6, c. 28, p. 112.
[3] Trithem. c. 615. See also Alegre, Parad. Carmel. iv. 98.

"'The authorities of Augustine against Pelagius prove that all contracted original sin, except the Son of the King Alone, i. e. Christ; and it is certain that, in that whole process, he argues about actual contracting or not contracting, which follows on the union of the soul, because he speaks of the contracting of the person, but the person includes the soul; therefore, &c.

"2. Also, Augustine, arguing against the Pelagians, who simply denied original sin, and that it was not formally in any one, proves against them, that original sin passes to posterity, by means of authorities, which denote the generation of the person by propagation. 'Behold I was conceived in iniquities,' &c., 'Man born of a woman.' But it is certain that the Person of Christ Alone was conceived without propagation; therefore Christ Alone was He who did not formally contract it.

"3. The error of the Pelagians was, that little ones are baptized, not because they contracted original fault, but because they would be able to sin, when they should come to the use of free will. Against these he argues, 'That then Christ did not come to save all, but only adults.' Then I argue, 'Aug. means, that if there were only some necessity or proneness to sin in the persons of infants, and not original sin formally, then Christ was not the Saviour of all. But these mean this as to the B. V.; therefore Christ was not her Saviour, i.e. not the Saviour of all, which is an error.'

"Then, too, a mode of arguing is not to be allowed as to the B. V., whereby, with the like or greater probability, the Pelagians could maintain their error against Aug. But the Pelagians would say, that as in her there was a necessity of contracting it, but on account of preventing grace she did not contract it, so in infants; and it follows, 'But on ground of preventing and perpetual righteousness, they did not contract it, until they should come to the use of free-will, because then first they could be just or unjust.'

"4. On the 'authority of Fulgentius' [and the same applies

' In 3. d. 30, q. 1, art. 2.

to other places], 'are born with original sin,' he observes, 'He speaks of the birth of the person, not of the conception of seeds only,' and so 'all have sinned, and all need the grace of God.' 'Observe,' he says, 'that every man is subject to wickedness.' He speaks of a fact, not of a necessity of contracting original sin; and this is clear by the authority which he cites, which is of fact. 'All have sinned;' he speaks of a fact."

De Bacon argues further against the Scotist solution [5], that she would have contracted it, but for the redemption by Christ; that this "preservation" is not redemption; that it could not be said that there was any necessity of contracting original sin; and argues,—

"It is an abuse, yea a peril to faith, to adopt a mode of arguing which might, if applied to cases ex simili, be the occasion of great heresies; but if, when Scripture spoke absolutely, it was to be explained of something potential only, then it might be said of our Saviour, that He did not suffer in fact those penalties of sin, hunger, thirst, weariness, but the Scripture only said this, on account of the necessity of suffering, i.e. that He had our unhappy nature, which of necessity suffers these things. In like way, as to His being 'very heavy and sorrowful, even unto death,' or of the Passion and Death itself, that He did not in fact suffer. Also of the Baptism of infants, with the Pelagians, that in fact they do not contract [original sin], but that the Scriptures, which prove this, only say that they contracted them, on account of the necessity of contracting them; and countless absurdities might be adduced.

"Also, as P. Lombard proved that Christ did not contract original [sin], because, although that nature which He took of the B. V. was first subject to original sin, and so that there

---

[5] In Aureolus.

was a necessity of contracting it, but that it was therefore sanctified, that He should not contract it; so, in order that the authorities of the saints might not be to us a cause of error, they ought to have made the distinction as to the B. V., that there was in her first a necessity of contracting ·it, but that she did not, in fact, contract it, because she was sanctified in the first instant; but this neither the Master (Peter Lombard) nor the authorities alleged above hint, and that is much."

121. †Joannes Ricardi, Bishop of Dragonara, or Tragonara, in S. Italy, a Franciscan, between A.D. 1311—1340[5].

"'The first sanctification of the V. M. was in her mother's womb, which had three effects; viz. the expiation of the original fault, and infusion of grace, and so much restriction of the 'fomes' that she could not be led into any sin, although the fomes itself remained in Mary, according to its essence[6].'"

122. In 1340, Alvarus Pelagius, a Franciscan, and a Portuguese Bishop, and, at an earlier period, Apostolic Penitentiary, could still speak of the belief in the Immaculate Conception of the B. V. as modern. He was writing against the heresies of the Beghardi.

[5] Quétif, i. 470, in answer to De Alva.

[6] Compend. Theol. beginning "Veteris et novæ Legis." L. iv. in the rubric "on the sanctification of the B. V." in Turr. P. 6. c. 80. f. 122. He took much from Hugo de Argentina, Quétif.

[7] De Bandelis adds, "And therefore the feast of the Nativity is celebrated, not that of her Conception, except by reason of the sanctification, in some parts."

"'In regard to the most blessed Mother [of Christ] the
saints hold, and especially Augustine, that she did not sin even
venially in this life; yet she was conceived in original sin, just
as other human beings, because from that saying of her father
David, 'Behold I was conceived in iniquities,' no one is excepted save Christ, Who was conceived, not of human seed, but
of the Holy Ghost, and in the womb of the Virgin, which was
already sanctified. But our Lady was conceived of the seed of
both parents, Joachim and Anna, as all other women, not of
the Holy Ghost, as her Son. And therefore she was conceived
in original sin, as Bernard proves at length in the Epistle
which he wrote to the Canons of Lyons, in which he censures
them for celebrating the feast of our Lady, which ought not to
be done, or, if done, should be referred to her sanctification in
the womb; for, according to Bernard, she was holy before she
was born, whence Augustine too [S. Fulgentius], De Fide,
ad Petr. (see ab.). For this maketh what is read De Cons. Di. iv.
c. 2 in verbo miraculo, gloss., 'ut in beata Maria,' and Di. iii. c. 1
in gloss. de festo, and caus. xxvii. q. ii. c. 10 [S. Aug. De Nupt.
et Conc. i. 11]; and all the old Theologians hold this judgment,
viz. Alexander [de Hales], Thomas [Aquinas], in his iv[th]. and
ii[nd]. book, Bonaventura, and Richard [à S. Victore]. Although
some new Theologians, departing from the common mind of the
Church, endeavour to hold the contrary, being really indevout
to our Lady, but wishing to appear, her devotees, comparing
her thus in a manner to God and to His Son. Whose novel
and fantastic opinion be utterly cancelled from the faithful!
For it denies the sanctification, against that which the Church
holds, that there was that sanctification, and so, according to
Bernard, she was holy, i. e. sanctified in the womb, before she
was born out of the womb. For if she had not been conceived

---

* De Planctu Ecclesiæ, L. ii. art. 52. B. fol. 169. Lugduni,
1517. He revised the work twice, in 1335 and 1340. Subscription of the author:—"With my own hand I corrected it
A.D. 1335, in Algarva of Portugal, where I am Bishop. A
second time I corrected it, in S. James of Compostella, A.D.
1340."

in original sin, which is contracted in the infusion of the soul
(De Cons. Di. iv. c. 146 in gloss ii.), sanctification would not
have been necessary, as neither in Christ. And therefore. the
Roman Church does not keep the feast of the Conception,
although it tolerates that it be held in some places, especially in England ; but it does not approve it. For what is permitted is not approved (iv. d. c. 6 fin.), or that feast ought to
be referred to the sanctification of the Virgin, not to her Conception, as was said. And so says the prayer, which is said in
this feast at Rome in S. Mary major, ' Deus, qui sanctificationem
Virginis,' &c., as I saw and heard when I preached there on
that sanctification, upon that feast of the Sanctification, which
takes place in December, fifteen days before the feast of the
Nativity.' For this truth, maketh that of Solomon, Prov.

' The passage is absolutely unquestionable.. Turrecremata
quoted, not the one statement about the Church of St. Mary
Major, but the whole context from a MS. (for the work was
not published until six years after his death, A.D. 1468) ; and
De Alva, who quoted also the whole at length, found fault only
(as his way was) with minute details in Turrecremata's citation,
and says, " I have seen it in many libraries in MS." Further,
it occurred in the first edition of Alvarus' works, Ulm, 1474,
in the carefully revised edition, Lyons, 1517, and in that of
Venice, 1560 (as I have seen). 1) It is no argument against this,
that in some 3 MSS. the words are omitted, since we have had
many instances, in which persons, bonâ fide, expunged on this
subject from MSS. what was not consonant with the current
belief. 2) With regard to Alvarus' accuracy, it is to be
observed, that when he wrote his celebrated work, "De
Planctu Ecclesiæ," he was Penitentiary at the Court of Rome.
The work was revised only in Portugal and addressed to Card.
Gomez. Wading cites a statement of his as authentic, because
he was then " present in the Court." He is spoken of as " a
most celebrated Doctor of Spain, most known from that distinguished work of his, ' De Planctu Ecclesiæ.' " If we were
to be called upon to disbelieve what such a man says that he
" saw and heard " in public worship, in which he was himself

xxv. 4, 'Take away the rust from the silver, and a most
pure vessel shall go forth.' That most pure vessel was the
Virgin, which, the rust of original sin having been washed
away [abluta, probably 'taken away,' ablata], by sanctification
wrought in the womb, went forth most pure from the womb.
And Psalm xlv. [xlvi.] 5, 'The Most High sanctified His
tabernacle.' The Virgin Mary was that sanctified tabernacle of
God, according to Ecclus. xxiv. 8. 'And He Who created me
rested in my tabernacle.' Aug. makes for this in the sermon

---

the preacher, because it could not be found in any book, nearly
300 years afterwards, ear- and eye-witness would not count
for much. 3) In regard to the statement itself, it should be
observed, that Alvarus does not say that those at Rome called
"the Feast of the Conception of the B. V." by the name, "the
Feast of the Sanctification." He himself calls it what he held
it to be. So far, then, the statement of De Alva, whom Perrone
quotes (De Imm. B.V. Concept. c. xv. § 3. Pareri, p. 426), "that
in countless Breviaries or Missals, whether Roman or other, he
had not found any, in which the Feast of the Conception was
entitled 'the Feast of the Sanctification,'" is irrelevant.
Alvarus does not say that it was. What Alvarus does allege
is, that there was in his time a collect, used at Rome on the
Festival, beginning, "O God, Who the sanctification of the
Virgin," &c., where the word "Conception" would have stood
in later times. But there is nothing strange that the word
"Sanctification" should be obliterated. Nay, when ordered to
be disused, it would be obliterated of course. The later Carthusian statutes directed the word "Conception" to be substituted for that of "Sanctification." They would then, of necessity, obliterate in their Breviaries a word which was to be
disused. But what is disused, speedily disappears. In despite
of the commonness of printing, the Latin ritual from which
Luther translated into German his first Baptismal office, has
long since entirely disappeared, and, with it, the original of the
2nd collect in our own service. It disappeared in a much shorter
time than that between the time of Alvarus and the search
made by direction of Paul V. See too Carthus. Stat. bel. p. 368.

on the Purification, ' He Alone was born without sin, to Whom without embrace of man, not the concupiscence of the flesh, but obedience of the mind, gave being[1].' This also Aug. determines on Gen. ad lit., and [the decretal] d. ii. si enim, at the end. And we have taught that, God excepted, every creature is under fault, &c. The Master of the Sentences holds the same."

123. †Paulus Salucius de Perusio, "a most celebrated Doctor of the Carmelites," about A.D. 1350. "[2] His book on the Sentences is praised by all." "[3] He was a Professor and most eminent expositor of both civil and canon law; and knew Greek and Latin perfectly," &c.

"[4] It is firmly to be held, that the B. V. was conceived in original sin, both because she was born by concumbency of male and female, and because Christ Alone was conceived without sin, as Augustine and Jerome say; also, because she derived the desert of death, as Augustine says; also, because she was redeemed by the Death of Christ, as the rest."

De Bandelis adds the following illustration, which is too characteristic not to be an original:—

"Yet the Conception of the Virgin might be considered in a two-fold way; first, in the order to the contraction of original sin, and thus it is not to be celebrated. And in this way Bernard understands it, and the gloss on the decree de Consecr. Dist. 3. c. 1. In another way, it may be considered in the order to the future sanctification and the Incarnation of Christ;

---

[1] The thought is common in S. Aug.; the words are from a sermon, put together out of S. Aug., App. v. 128, Ben.

[2] De Alva, n. 238. He says, "I could not find it at Rome or Perugia."

[3] Trith., n. 634.

[4] "In 3 Sent. dist. 8." Turr. P. 6. c. 3. f. 124.

R

and then it may be celebrated. As medicine, as far as it is bitter, is odious and detestable, but, as far as it is inducive of health, is loveable and praiseworthy. And a Church is venerated, not as it is of stone, but as it is consecrated and dedicated to God. And a Prelate, as a sinner, is worthy of vituperation, but, as having jurisdiction and sitting on Moses' seat, is to be honoured."

124. †Nicolas Treveth, an Oxford Doctor, died A.D. 1328, about 70.

" ' The day of her Conception then is not so celebrated, as if it were to be supposed that the B. V. completed her Conception without original sin. For this would be erroneous, whether for that time, when in act she contracted original sin, or in regard to that whereby she was in the potentia to contract it."

125. Durandus à S. Porciano, "Doctor resolutissimus," although a Dominican, can hardly be counted as influenced by S. Thomas, because " ' having first been a follower of the doctrine of S. Thomas, he afterwards wrote against it." He began his work when young, finished it when old. He was Magister of the Apostolic Palace under John XXII. and Bp. of Puy and Meaux, A.D. 1320.

He meets the abstract arguments, such as were

' Quodlib. 3. q. 4. in Turr. p. 6. c. 29. f. 119 v. De Alva, n. 227, doubted the existence of the Quodlibeta. Quétif (i. 563) says that they were quoted by Henry of Erfurt, who died A. 1370, and were still extant in the time of Bunderius.

' S. Antonin. Summa Hist. Tit. xxiii. c. xi. § 2. S. Antonin. mentions there the nephew of Durandus, known as Durandellus, who defended S. Thomas against Durandus. He too is quoted as holding the same doctrine as to the Immac. Conc.

used by Scotus, that it was "fitting" that the Conception of the B.V. should be Immaculate, by
arguments, in form equally abstract, but still
turning on the difference in the mode of Conception, so often insisted upon by those before him.

"'Although the B.V. could have been preserved from sin, it
was not fitting that she should be preserved. The reason
whereof is, that a singular Conception ought to be endowed
with a singular privilege; but the Son of God, according to
His Humanity, had a singular Conception, because He was
conceived not of man but of the Holy Spirit. Therefore He
ought to have a singular privilege; but He would not have
had it, unless His Conception Alone had been without original
sin: therefore it was not fitting that the Conception of any
other, even His mother, should be endowed with the same
privilege. And this is confirmed; because, as it is said
(John iii.), 'that which is born of flesh is flesh, and that which
is born of the Spirit is spirit,' so, in like way, what is
conceived of flesh is flesh, and what is conceived of Spirit
is spirit. Since then Christ Alone was conceived of the
Spirit, but the B.V. and all the rest were conceived of
flesh, i.e. according to the common way of the flesh, it was
fitting that the Conception of Christ Alone should have
nothing contrary to the Spirit. But the B.V. and all the
rest, as they were not privileged to be conceived of the Holy
Spirit, so they had original fault which wars against the
Spirit, and thereby the answer to the reasons of others is plain."
He says that he has read no other authority of S. Anselm than
this, "which yet, rightly understood, makes for us."

Having, then, met the abstract arguments and
retorted the inference drawn from the statement of
S. Anselm, he argues that the B.V. was *not* preserved from original sin, upon authority, alleging

' L. 3. dist. 8. q. 1.

Romans v., S. Fulgentius, and S. Augustine.. On the words, " in whom all have sinned," he says,—

" But he who says, 'all,' excepts nothing. And if it be said, 'therefore Christ was not excepted,' it does not follow, because the Apostle is speaking of those who descend in the way of nature from Adam; moreover the Apostle himself excepts Christ in that same chapter, that, 'as through the sin of one man many were made sinners, so, through the righteousness of One shall many be made righteous.' "

Then, in answer to the objection, " the Church holds no festival, except as to what is holy, but *many Churches* make a festival of the Conception of the Bl. Mary," he says,—

" [a] As to the festival of her Conception, it is either not rightly kept or not rightly named. For a feast may be held of her sanctification, yet, on the ground that it is not altogether certain when she was *sanctified* (as will be said afterwards), but it is certain when she was *conceived*, therefore, putting what is certain for what is uncertain, that is called the feast of her conception which ought to be called the feast of her sanctification."

126. Gregory of Ariminum, a Paris Doctor, General of the Augustinian Eremites, A.D. 1357 :—

" [b] The question is not, whether it was possible for the B. V. to be conceived without original sin, but whether in fact she was conceived without it. Since no certainty can be had hereon through human reason, *that* appears to me in this matter to be preferably to be held, which is more consonant to Holy Scripture and to the sayings of the saints; and therefore, without prejudice to any better opinion, and saving always the reverence to the Mother of God, it seems to me, that it is to be said, that she was conceived with original sin. But to this

---

[a] L. 3. dist. 3. q. 1.

[b] In 2 Sent. d. 30. q. 2. Art. i.

I am moved, first because Scripture, whenever it speaks of this, pronounces universally of all without exception, and is understood by all expositors universally of all who are born in the way of nature; from which it seemeth to follow, that to except any one therefrom is to contradict sacred Scripture. This is confirmed by the authority of S. Augustine (De Perf. Just. v. fin., De Gratia Christi et Pecc. Orig.), S. Ambrose (on S. Luke c. 39, 'Jesus Alone was throughout holy of those born of women,' and on Isa. in S. Aug.), S. Aug. De Nupt. et Concup., Jul. L. v. c. on the contrast between the caro peccati and the caro similis carni peccati, the sup. Gen.; [Fulgentius,] de Fido ad Petrum; [Aug.] c. Julian. vi. 4, that else Christ did not die for her."

He quotes also S. Anselm, Cur Deus Homo, and answers the arguments of the Scotists.

Of such as wrote sermons on the Festivals of the B.V., the following have been quoted, as stating that her sanctification was subsequent to her Conception:—

127. Richard of S. Laurence, Cistercian, Penitentiary at Rouen, A.D. 1230:—

"'"In the beginning God created,' &c., 'In the beginning,' i.e. of the restoration of man, 'God' (Whose special work Mary is, whence the Psalm says to Him, 'Thou createdst the dawn,' i.e. Mary, and, from her, the Sun of righteousness) 'created the heaven and the earth,' i.e. the soul and body; but this 'earth was empty and void,' before the grace of sanctification; 'and darkness was upon the face of the deep,' i.e. she was conceived in original sin, 'and God said,' as it were predestinating her, 'let there be light, and there was light,' when He sanctified her.—Dawn is the first brightness of the day. For she was

---

¹ De Laud. V. M. L. vii. f. 466. in Turr. P. vi. c. 85, f. 125, text corrected by Alva, u. 22. p. 279.

the beginning of the day of grace, which day began from her sanctification. She was partly obscure, partly lightsome; obscure through original sin, as to the Nativity *in* the womb; lightsome through the Nativity *from* the womb by sanctification."

" ¹ Before we come to treat of the twelve special prerogatives of the B.V., we must consider the dignities and privileges of her virgin flesh. And first we must observe, that some derive flesh [caro] from wanting [carendo], because manifold was that glorious wanting or glorious defect in her flesh. The flesh of Mary lacked original sin in her sanctification, whence ' the Most High sanctified His tabernacle ' (Ps. xlvi.) when He cleansed it from original sin, so that it should be born wholly pure. For then the Father seemeth, as it were, to have said to the Holy Spirit that of Proverbs (c. xxv.), ' Take away the rust from the silver, and a most pure vessel shall come forth.' For then that worker in gold, i. e. the Holy Spirit, Who is the artificer of all (Wisd. vii.), took away from the silver of the Virgin's flesh the whole rust of original fault, and then was the flesh itself silver, tried by the fire of the Holy Spirit, purged of earth, i. e. from earthly thought, and purged sevenfold, i. e. through sevenfold grace ; and all this, that the vessel of the Virgin's body might go forth most pure, to receive graces and virtues, and to become a condign material, from which God the Father should prepare a glorious Body for His Only Begotten Son."

128. †De Bandelis alleged two passages from a " Bishop of Lincoln," the one upon Boethius, the other upon a Psalm, the reference to which he did not fill up. " Episcopus Lincolniensis," " Dominus Lincolniensis," or " Lincolniensis," are titles by which Grosthead or " Grosteste" is commonly designated in MSS. ², as well as by the fuller titles

---

¹ Ib. L. iii. f. 175.

² As in Cod. Lincoln. lvi. cv. Merton. xlvii. 26. Or. xx. 1. 3. Univ. lxii. 1. clx. 5. "reverendus Lincolniensis," Ball. cccxx. 3. &c. Coxe, Cat. Codd. MSS. Coll. Oxon.

" Robertus Lincolniensis," or with the use of his surname. He was consecrated A.D. 1235. He had been " a lecturer in the Schools of Theology," was "a preacher among the people," and "in great reputation for learning and holiness." His death was that of a saint.

The sermon on the Psalm was doubtless one of a collection of sermons which he says (in contradistinction to those to the Clergy), " ' I delivered to all generally, and first on the glorious Virgin, the infallible pattern of all living." The passage is a characteristic one, but expresses only what was said by others also of his date :—

" ' More than others did the B. V. shine in this life through uprightness, from which, *after the Conception of Jesus Christ*, she did not decline, even by venial sin. For after she cast away the darkness of original sin, she was so clad with armour of light, that in no part was she obscured by the cloud of venial sin. But Christ never departed, because He had no sin. But neither did the B. V., after the Conception of Christ, ever go back by venial sin; whereas the other saints sometimes go back either by remitting the fervour of charity, or by sinning venially."

' " Finiunt hi sermones quos ad clerum solum proposui. Incipiunt et alii sermones quos generaliter ad omnes protuli," &c. Mert. lxxxii. n. 3.

' " Super Psal. . . . circa principium " de B. p. 62. The passage, said to be taken from a comment on Boethius de duabus naturis et una Persona Christi, has nothing remarkable, nor do I find any trace of such a work by him. It is, " Christ took flesh from the Blessed Virgin, which from the primeval transgression of our first parent was sinful."

129. †Joannes de Rupella (de la Rochelle), Franciscan, a hearer of Alexander de Hales, "[6] a religious and learned man." He "[7] wrote on the Sentences, a Summa of virtues and vices, on the soul." About A.D. 1242.

"[8] Mary, in the origin of her conception, had the bitterness of original corruption ; but, while she was yet in her mother's womb, was sweetened by the grace of sanctification, so as to be born in the sweetness of sanctity."

130. Odo de Castro Rodulphi[9], an ancient Doctor. He was made Cardinal and Bishop of Tusculum by Innocent IV., A.D. 1244.

"[1] A threefold Nativity is celebrated by the Church ; viz. of John Baptist, the B. V., and the Saviour.—Neither the Conception of the B. V. nor that of any other saint is celebrated, but only that of the Saviour. For the B. V. drew with her [in her conception[2]] both fault and punishment; yet she was sanctified in her mother's womb ; but, when ? we know not. But that she could afterwards sin venially, we believe ; but whether she sinned ? we know not. But in the Conception of the Saviour, the Holy Spirit so overshadowed her, that thereafter she did not sin, nor could sin."

------

[6] Wading, Ann. A.D. 1242, n. 2. p. 153.　[7] Trithem. c. 459.

[8] In Serm. Nativ. Virg. in Turr. L. vi. c. 32. f. 123.

[9] In the Toledo MS. he is called "Odo de Castro Rodulphi, D.D. Chancellor of Paris, afterwards a Cistercian Abbot." De Alva Ver. 228, pp. 638, 9.

[1] I have translated from an extract of a Sermon on the Nativity of the B. V. given by De Alva (Lux veritatis Ver. 230, p. 642), from a Toledo and an Escurial MS.

[2] Alva says that the words "in conceptione" are not in the Escurial MS., and in the Toledo MS. are inserted by a much later hand. I suppose that they were inserted to prevent the idea of any later period than the Conception.

131. †Lucas of Padua, Franciscan, a companion and disciple of S. Antony of Padua. Died A.D. 1245.

"³ In his sermon on the Baptism of Christ, 'This is My Beloved Son, in Whom," &c., he says, that the Father commends Christ on four grounds : 1st, from His Aloneness [singularitas], when He says, 'This,' as being separate from others, to Whom none is like. And specially in three things. First, in the fulness of gifts. Secondly, in the immunity from sin, that He neither did sin, *nor contracted it.* And, alleging Heb. vii., 'separate from sinners,' he says He was 'separate, because His flesh was taken from the sinful mass and cleansed.' "

132. †Gulielmus Peraldus [Perault], some say Abp. of Lyons, Dominican. S. Antoninus set him first among the Dominican preachers, and says that his " Summa⁴ on virtues and vices was useful to preachers." He is said to have died before 1250.

"⁵ For the water of a fountain hath bitterness, when it went forth from the sea, but before it is drawn, it loseth it; therefore

---

³ Turr. P. 6. c. 32. f. 123. He quotes also "a sermon on the Nativity of the B. V.," "a star shall arise," in which, after dividing the threefold beauty, he says thus : " Her first beauty was cleanness of original sin ; the second, virginal continency ; the third, heavenly conversation." He quoted it, I doubt not, because the subject being the Nativity, and the text, at " the *rising* of the stars," corresponding to that nativity, the cleanness of original sin referred, according to the context, to her cleanness at her birth, and that cleanness, being at her birth, and not, as far as appears, previously, involved cleansing.

⁴ Summa Hist. tit. 23. c. 11. n. 2. T. iii. 682.

⁵ Serm. 4. de Nativ. B.V. sub them. " fons hortorum." Turr. Par. 6. c. 29. f. 120. Alva could not find the sermon, n. 112. p. 450.

the water, when it is drawn, is sweet. So the Bl. V., going forth from her parents, had in her conception the bitterness of original sin, but when she was sanctified in the womb before her Nativity she lost it, and received the sweetness of grace; therefore in her Nativity she was pleasing to God."

133. Martinus Polonus, Dominican, Penitentiary of Nicolas III., consecrated Archbishop of Gnesen, A.D. 1277, and died. He was author of the Chronicle, of the Summa of the Canon law, called from him Martiniana, &c.

" 'The prophet shows that God disposed her birth, when he says, 'The Lord shall send forth a rod' (Is. xi.); for He sent her forth in the birth of conception and in the birth of Nativity, because God is shown to have promoted both. For He promoted conception, as to nature; nativity, as to grace. For Jerome writes, that Anne her mother and Joachim her father were barren; so that, despairing of offspring, they did not propose to come together any more. Whence, when Joachim had retired from Anne, he is bidden by the Angel to return. It is intimated that a child should be born, God helping nature. But God promoted too the birth of nativity by sanctification; for she was not born, according to the common law, with original fault, but, sanctified in the womb, she was born with abundant grace."

"Here then the true Bezaleel made an ark, i. e. the B. V., of sittim wood, which are like white thorn, incombustible, incorruptible, all which agrees with the Bl. Virgin. For she

---

* Serm. 277. ed. Strasburg, 1484 (no pagin.). A note says, "the author of this book says, 'Mary was a thorn on account of original sin in her conception,' but the opposite is held now." [1484]. Martin speaks of her being " sanctified most fully in the Conception of the Son of God, because afterwards she is believed not to have sinned even venially. Whence Aug. 'cum de peccatis agitur,' " &c.

was a 'thorn' on account of original sin in her conception; white, because of sanctification in the nativity; incombustible, on account of the extinction of the fomes; incorruptible, on account of the observance of virginity."

" ' 'Take away rust from the silver, and a most pure vessel shall go forth'.' In these words, as they may be adapted to the B. V., two things are touched on; the Conception of the B. V. in sin, when he says, 'take away the rust from the silver,' and her sanctification in the womb, when he says, 'a most pure vessel shall go forth.' "

Then, after speaking of the silver, as white through virginity and purity, ductile through obedience, musical through the words, " be it unto me according to thy word," he adds, " But this silver was at one time sprinkled with the rust of original sin, viz. in the conception, because she was conceived in original sin, which, on account of the ancient waste of human nature, is called 'rust.' Observe, her conception (as neither of other saints, who all were conceived in original sin), is not celebrated, except the Conception of Jesus Christ, which was without sin. Showing then the consumption* of original fault, setting, after the way of the prophets, the present for the future, he says, 'take away the rust from the silver,' and afterwards he hints at her sanctification, when he says, 'and there shall go forth a most pure vessel.'—He does not say pure or purer, but 'most pure,' as a difference from other saints. For Jeremiah, on account of the sanctification in his nativity, was a pure vessel; but John Baptist purer, but the B. V. purest; not without reason, for *He* was to dwell in her, Who purifies others. Yet, since we are not only conceived but are born also 'children of wrath,'

' Serm. 278. The same annotator says, "In the sermon immediately preceding, the author of this book says that Mary was conceived in original sin, and her conception was not celebrated; but now in the Church the opposite is preached and celebrated."

' De Alva, n. 214, found some corresponding words on the same text in a Toledo MS. and hinted falsification.

' Consumptionem; Turr. had "assumptionem."

lo, the Church celebrates the nativity of no saint, unless he was sanctified in the womb. Whence, since the sanctification of the B. V. could not be proved by the text [of Scripture] as that of Jeremiah and John Baptist, therefore her nativity was not celebrated of old [then he gives the account of its being revealed by angels] whence it was celebrated throughout the world and rightly; because, as Solomon had predicted, 'the rust of sin having been taken away, this most pure vessel had gone forth' in her nativity."

134. †Conrad (Holzinger) of Saxony, Franciscan. Turr. speaks of his "de salutat. Angelica" as a "notable and most devout work." [A Conrad of Saxony was murdered A. D. 1282, Wading Ann.]

"'Take away the rust from silver, and a most pure vessel will go forth.' The most pure vessel was the B. V., who, when the rust of original sin had been taken away through sanctification in the womb, came forth this day, holy and most pure. Bernard. 'The mother of God was without all doubt holy before she was born.'"

135. Jacobus de Voragine, General of the Dominicans, a Bishop of Genoa A. D. 1290. He is said to have known almost all S. Augustine by heart², Author of the "Golden Legend."

¹ Serm. 2 on the Nativity of the B. V. from the Franciscan Library at Basle. Turr. L. 6. c. 32. f. 123. v. De Alva says that the words "peccati originalis" were wanting in a MS. in old characters in the Escurial, (n. 62. p. 384). But they must have been intentionally omitted, 1) because there was no other "rust" from which it could be held that the B. V. was cleansed; 2) because the interpretation of this text of the cleansing of the B. V. from original sin is known and familiar in other writers.

² Cave sub tit. A.D. 1290.

"' 'Who is this that cometh forth, &c.?' They marvel at her, in regard to her fourfold state. First, as to her birth, when they say, 'arising like the dawn.' For she was then 'like the dawn,' being purged from all darkness of sin and overstreamed with the light of Divine grace. For all other saints are conceived and born with original sin; but Christ was conceived without original sin and was born without original sin. But the V. M. holds a middle place, because she was conceived with original sin, and born without original sin.' "

And then with a mystical interpretation of Job iii. :—

"This threefold difference is referred to in Job iii., when it is said of the day of original fault, which began when the eyes of Adam were opened, 'Let the stars be obtenebrated by its darkness.' For the stars and the other saints were obtenebrated by that day of original fault, because they were conceived and born with original [fault]. 'Let it wait for the Light, i.e. Christ, and see it not.' For that day of fault did not see Christ, neither in His conception or birth nor the dawn of the rising morn. It saw the morn, i. c. the Virgin as to her conception, but it did not see her as to her rising."

"' She is called a star, because she had no corruption, neither in birth, nor in life, nor in death. For in her Nativity she had not the corruption of original [sin], and this is shown by example, because this same is asserted of Jeremiah and John Baptist, of whom one was a prophet of Christ, the other the precursor of Christ; much more is it believed of her who was the mother of Christ."

"' This house was in light; for, as it is said (Cant. vi.), 'the

---

* De Ass. B. M. V. Serm. 4. Alph. xvi. p. 123. Augustæ, 1482.

' Nativ. Serm. 3. Strasb. 1484. Serm. 2. p. 146, Augustæ, 1484.

" De Nat. Serm. 2. Strasb. 1484. and ed. sino loc. et ann. f. 155.

light of the dawn shone in her' when the Holy Spirit sanctified her, because then He took away and removed from her the darkness of original sin."

"' 'Thou art ever with me.' For Christ was ever with the Virgin, in her threefold state, viz. when she was in her mother's womb, when she was living in the world, and when she departed from the world. For when she was in her mother's womb, He sanctified her; while she was living in the world, He preserved her from all sin; when she departed from the world, He made her wholly glorious and luminous. First then ' He sanctified her.' For there are three conceptions and nativities; one, whereby one is conceived without sin, and born without sin; and in this way no one was conceived and born without sin, except Christ Alone. Another, whereby one is conceived with sin and is born with sin; and this is our conception and our nativity, because we are conceived with sin and are born with sin. For there is a middle way, whereby one is conceived with sin and is born without sin, and, according to Bernard, such was the Conception and Nativity of the B. V. For she was (as he asserts in his Epistle to the Canons of Lyons) conceived in original sin and born without sin, because she was sanctified by the Holy Spirit and cleansed from all sin; and therefore, according to Bernard, ' she was holy, earlier than she was born.' This threefold difference is touched upon, Job iii., where he speaks of the night of original fault, saying, ' Let the day perish on which I was born, and the night in which it was said, a man-child was conceived,' and afterwards, ' Let the stars be obtenebrated by its darkness, let it wait for the light and not see it, nor the dawn of the rising morn.' In that he here names light, dawn, and stars; by the sun, Christ is meant; by the dawn, the Virgin Mary; by the stars, the other saints. The night therefore of original fault did not see Christ, either as to the Conception, or His Birth; therefore it is said, ' Let it wait for the Light and not see it.' ' The dawn,' i. e. the B. V., it saw

---

' Serm. on Job iii., on Sat. before 3rd Sunday in Lent, referred to by Turrecremata, c. 29. p. 119, given by Alva, n. 140; not in ed. Paris, 1583.

as to the Conception, but not as to the rising. Therefore it is said, 'nor the dawn of the rising morn.' But the stars, i. e. holy men, that same night of original concupiscence saw, both in conception and the birth, and therefore they were wholly obtenebrated, and have both a tenebrous conception and a tenebrous birth ; and therefore it is said, ' Let the stars be ob-tenebrated by its darkness.' "

136. Thomas de Ales, English Franciscan, "Doctor of the Sorbonne, whose piety and learning gained him a great name, remarkably erudite in human and Divine philosophy, a most acute dis-putant in the schools, a most celebrated preacher of the Divine Word among the people, and on these grounds well known throughout, not England only, but France and Italy [6]."

" [7] In his devout treatise on the life of the blessed and glorious Ever-Virgin Mother of God, Mary, in c. 5, on the Conc. of the B.V., where, having related the history of her conception, he adduced in proof that saying of Aug., 10 sup. Gen. ad lit., ' But since there is in the seed both a visible corpulence and an in-visible mode (ratio) both continued from Abraham or even from Adam himself to the body of Mary, because she also was conceived and had her origin in the same way.' Then, in c. 12, on the sanctification of the same sacred Virgin, he adduces Bernard (Ep. ad Lugd.) and Anselm, saying that she was of those who, before the Nativity of her Son, J. C., by believing His true death, were cleansed from sin, &c."

137. Jacobus, or Jacoponus de Benedictis, Fran-ciscan, died A.D. 1306, author of seven books of Italian hymns, of the "Cur mundus militat sub vana gloria?" and (some thought) of the "Stabat Mater;" although this is now said to be older.

[6] Wadding, Scriptt. Ord. Min. 12, 220.
[7] Turr. vi. 30, p. 122.

"' O virgin, more than woman, | Holy Virgin Mary, | More than woman, I say, | By Scripture I explain ; | While enclosed in the womb, | Soon was the soul infused into thee ; | Virtuous power has sanctified thee ; | Divine union | Sanctified thee; | from all contagion, | Thou remainedst undefiled ; | Original sin, | Which Adam sowed, | Every man is born with this. | Thou wert *cleansed* therefrom | No mortal sin | Assailed thy will ; | And from the venial | Thou alone art immaculate."

138. James of Lausanne, Dominican Provincial in France, A.D. 1318, died 1321; "'a man of vast knowledge, and vast literature, and especially in Holy Scripture ;" "'of distinguished knowledge in things human and Divine."

"'The B. V. was born wholly holy, and without all vileness of sin ; and this is what 'rises' imports. For therefore is she said to be born or generate, as though it meant to begin to be without corruption, as sun and stars rise. Therefore the B. V. is honourable, being sanctified. But this was wonderful, when she was *born* without sin. For to make a new vessel of putrid matter is a great thing. For human nature, from which the body of the B. V. was formed, was all corrupt; and how, then, could she be *born* without sin? See an instance. When a lily is generated within the earth and conceived, it is in vile-

---

' Odi iii. 6. His editor would have it, that Jacopone used "mondata," "cleansed," for "monda," "clean." But, besides the difficulty of supposing that Jacopone would purposely use a word, which in its natural sense would contradict his belief, had he believed in the Imm. Conc., it would then only declare that she was free from it, not that she had been free from it in her conception. Jacopone reserves the word "immaculate" for exemption from every stain even of venial sin.

' Leander, f. 120 v. in Quétif, i. 548.

' Sixt. Sen. ib. Trithemius, c. 659.

' Serm. 2, on the Nativ. of B. V. in Toledo Library. Alva, n. 135, pp. 486, 487.

ness and mire; but when it is elevated and hath gone forth
from the earth, it is all white and without spot. The reason
whereof is, that the virtue of heaven, whereby it is formed,
separates pure from impure. For it parts with the impure in
the earth, and what is pure it maketh to go forth from the
earth, and therefore the lily is born beautiful, although vile and
foul while conceived. The B. V. calls herself a lily. 'I am a
flower of the field, a lily of the valleys' (in the Canticles), i. e.
a lily which yields a sweet odour, because the lily of her virginity was planted into two valleys, viz. of heart and body; and
so, as the lily is conceived in uncleanness, so the B. V. in her
mother's womb was conceived in the uncleanness of original
sin, when soon after, by the virtue of the Holy Spirit, she was
whitened and cleansed, according to which she was born altogether holy."

" ³It is committed to the Holy Spirit by the whole Trinity,
Who is the Author of all purity and holiness, to purify and
cleanse the B. V., when He says, 'Take away the rust from the
silver.' In evidence whereof, he says, that it is to be noted
that the B.V. contracted the rust of the original sin in her
conception and animation, which original fault is well described
after the manner of rust." And below, " None of women escaped
this rust, and no man save Christ, according to Eccl. vii."

139. Card. Bertrand de Turre, Doctor famosus, A.D 1316, also a Franciscan: lived to 1343, " a grave author, wrote very many sermons ⁴."

" ⁵ The first beginning of those ways, i. e. of the works, was

---

³ In a sermon on the Nativ. of B. V. in Turr., Par. 5, c. i.
f. 82 [misprinted 84] v.

⁴ Alva, l. c.

⁵ Serm. de Nat. B. V. on Prov. 8, in Turr. P. 6, c. 30. f. 122,
allowed by De Alva, Ver. 42, p. 337. Turr. also quoted from
his expos. of the Gospels on that " the power of the Highest."
"According to the gloss, it shall cool against the heat of the
fomes, and according to Gregory (Moral. 33), the flesh of

a holy work, which God Himself made, in the first person belonging to the New Testament, which was the B. V. And that first work, according to him, was the Conception of the Virgin herself; not indeed the first, which was in the transfusion of the seeds; nor the second Conception of the Virgin, which was in the infusion of her soul in the already organized body, which was with the contraction of original fault, when her soul was infused into her body; but the third Conception, which was in the infusion of grace, through her sanctification and cleansing from original sin."

140. Jordanes de Quedlinborch (by some called John of Saxony) A.D. 1325, an Augustinian, a Reader of Theology at Magdeburg, and a celebrated writer :—

" ‘It is to be observed that the Conception of the B. Virgin was fourfold. The first, the eternal, of which it is said, Prov. viii., ‘Not as yet was the abyss when I was conceived.’ But this does not bear on the present question. The three others were in time; seminis, hominis, flaminis. In the first of these neither was fault contracted nor grace infused, because it was an inanimate mass, but the soul alone is capable of fault and grace. In the second, viz. in the infusion of the soul, original sin is contracted. For although in that mass there is no fault (as was said), nor is the soul in itself stained, because it

Mary was overshadowed by the power of the Most Highest, because in her womb incorporeal Light took a body, from which obumbration she received in herself all refrigeration of flesh and mind " (P. 5, c. 2. f. 83 v.). And on the Ave Maria: " For she was exempted in birth from the woe of infection; because she was singularly sanctified ; and in the second sanctification, when she conceived the Son of God, there came into her such abundance of grace, that it not only restrained in her the fomes of sin, but totally rent it from her " (Serm. on the Annunc.).

* Serm. i. in Conc. B. V. Turr. P. 6. c. 33. f. 124. De Alva, Ver. 198, p. 585.

is created pure and immaculate, there is yet in that mass a morbid infection, on account of which, so soon as the soul is infused, it contracts original sin. To take a familiar instance, in lime, which being formally hot, of water, which is in itself cold, heat results therein, on account of the heat fore-existing in the lime. So here. In the third Conception, habitual grace is infused, viz. when any one is sanctified in the womb. To this Conception of the Virgin ought the intention of one who celebrates this Feast to be referred; not to the first, which was foul; nor to the second, because in it she contracted original sin, according to the holy Doctors; although some essay to deny this, out of devotion to the Virgin. Whence, if in that Conception she contracted original sin, yet immediately, and if perhaps not on the instant, on account of the repugnance, since that suddenness is impossible by nature, she was cleansed or sanctified," &c.

"'By epicycle understand sin, whereby we are subjected to retrogradation from our heavenly country; but Christ Alone was without sin, and if we be urged as to the B. V., it is to be said that she was not without original sin, at least for a very brief moment, according to the common opinion."

141. S. Vincent Ferrier, A.D. 1414. S. Anto-ninus gives a sermon of his as a specimen[8] of the way in which the Conception should be preached upon, "avoiding all censure of the opposite party, because it was a matter which occasioned scandal among the people, since, owl-like, they cannot bear such a ray of truth, and it would carry away no

---

[7] Post. prima Domin. Adventus f. 1. col. 2. in De Alva. Turrecr. quotes it, "But if it be urged as to the B. V. that she never deviated from right in either way, it is to be said that she was not without original sin, at least for a very short moment, according to the more common opinion of all Doctors." Ib.
[8] Summa Tit. 8 c. 2. fin.

fruit." In that sermon S. Vincent explained[1]
the words "divided the light from the darkness,"
"swiftly purifying that soul from original sin." He
puts down the three purifications :—

" [1] First, when the boy is going forth of his mother's womb;
and this was Jeremiah's, according to that, 'before thou
wentest forth from the womb (i.e. fully), I sanctified thee.' The
second is when the child is still wholly in the womb ; as John
Baptist, who was sanctified in the sixth month, when the Virgin
Mary, having conceived the Son of God, saluted Elizabeth.
The third is as it were in a moment, after the creation and
infusion of the soul ; for the body of the Virgin having been
formed, being conceived of Anna and Joachim, not of the Holy
Ghost (for to say this were heretical, for Christ Alone had
this), the soul of the Virgin having been created and infused
by God, she was suddenly sanctified on the same day, according to that, 'the Most High sanctified His tabernacle.' "

The festival of the Conception was still, at the
beginning of the 15th century, infrequent. For S.
Vincent says, " And *some* make a festival of this."
He says the like, in another sermon on the Conception of the B. V.

" [2] Of no saints is the feast of the Conception held, except
of Christ and the Virgin Mary. But of the Virgin on three
grounds; 1) because she was worthily impetrated; 2) because she was sanctified loftily; 3) because she was preserved
firmly. In the second observe six modes of sanctification ;

---

[1] Summa Tit. 8, c. 3. col. 557.

[1] Ib. col. 558.

[2] Serm. de Sanctt. pp. 19—21, Antw. 1573. De B. refers
also to a Sermon on S. Anne, "the body having been formed
and the spirit created by God, on the same day and hour she
was sanctified.—Ib. p. 283, and on the Nativity of the B. V.
p. 359.

three before nativity, and three after nativity. The fourth in the mother's womb, as Jeremiah. The fifth is greater, and is only read of S. John Baptist, because he was sanctified three months before his nativity. The sixth, and above all these, is the sanctification of the V. M., because, not when she was to be born, nor in the last day, or week, or month, but in the same day and hour when her body had been formed, and her soul created (for then she was rational and capable of sanctification), she was sanctified. When the body of the glorious Virgin was organized and lineated, and the soul joined to her body by creation, then the Most High sanctified His tabernacle. You know, how when a church has been builded, but not before, the Bishop enters to consecrate. So of the Virgin Mary, the body having been organized and the soul infused, the Bishop, i. e. the Holy Spirit came, Who sanctified her."

Of commentators of the same period there have been quoted,—

142. †John de Varsiaco (of Varsy near Auxerre) "[3] a Magister in Paris and a preacher celebrated for learning and eloquence, about 1270."

" ' He commented on many books of the Bible; and in his exposition of the Canticles[4], treating on that, ' Who is this, that cometh forth like the rising dawn?' says, ' The rising dawn.' In the Nativity, the dawn is cold and humid. So the Bl. V., illustrious from the nobility of her race, whence it is sung of her, ' Clara ex stirpe David,' was cold through the, repression of the ' fomes,' or its extirpation according to others ; Luke i.: ' The virtue of the Highest shall overshadow thee.' "

---

[3] Quétif i. 373.

[4] Turr. P. 6. c. 29, f. 12. v. quoting his Postilla on Cant.

[5] Quétif, after speaking of his Postills on Wisdom and Canticles in a Basle MS., says, "Hence you may easily refute F. P. De Alva, who (Sol verit. Rad. 255, Col. 1616) endeavours with all his might to prove that this our John is a fictitious person, and that there are no writings of his" (i. 373).

143. Hugo de S. Caro, Cardinal, A.D. 1245, celebrated for his comments on Holy Scripture, and employed by Gregory IX. to bring about the union with the Greeks, draws out what has, for very many years, seemed to me the deepest meaning of Ecclesiastes vii. 27, 28. " This have I found, saith the preacher, counting one by one, to find out the account : which yet my soul seeketh, but I find not : one man among a thousand have I found; but a woman among those have I not found."

"⁕ Mystically this is explained of Christ, Who Alone is external to that universality, of which it is said, ''All have sinned, and need the glory of God,' and ''In many things we all offend.' Whence, in the Psalm, ''There is none that doeth good, there is not, up to One,' i. e. Christ, Who did no sin whatever, nor had any. ' But a woman have I not found,' who had not something of womanly fault, at least by origin [originaliter]. Even the Blessed Virgin had original sin, wherefore

---

⁕ ad loc. Opp. T. iii. p. 92.
⁷ Rom. iii. 23.
⁸ St. James iii. 2.
⁹ Psalm xiv. 2. 4; liii. 2. 4. Turrecremata quotes †Garicus, a Paris Doctor, as saying the same thing on Eccl. ad loc. "'A woman of all, have I not found,' because none was without original sin" (in De Alva n. 84, p. 413). Turr. P. 6, c. 29, f. 120, v. And †James of Lausanne, a Parisian Doctor, Dominican, "Among all men he found One only altogether clean from all concupiscence, viz. Christ, but among women none, because the B. V. was stained with original sin." Turr. P. 5, c. 1, f. 84, v. ; P. 6, c. 29, f. 119, v.

S. Antoninus quotes Joannes Dominici, whose disciple he was, "That Man was Christ; but the number, a thousand, is put, after the manner of Scripture, a determined for an indetermined number, i.e. for the whole company of the saints,

her Conception is not celebrated; yet they who celebrate it, ought to have respect to her sanctification, whereby she was sanctified in her mother's womb."

"¹ 'And the virtue of the Highest' i.e. the Holy Spirit or the grace of the Holy Spirit 'shall overshadow thee,' i.e. shall refrigerate thee by extinguishing the 'fomes.' Whence the gloss, 'The Spirit supervening into the Virgin shall both cleanse her mind from the defilement of vices.' And observe that 'from the defilement of vices,' can be intransitive, i.e. from vices which are defilement, or transitive, that the meaning should be from the defilement, i.e. from the fomes of vices, whence the Interlinear says, 'against all incentives of vices.'"

He believed that the "fomes" was extinguished at the Conception of our Lord.

144. William of Alton, an Englishman, but a Paris Doctor, about A.D. 1265, explains Ecclesiastes vii. 27, 28 in the same way.

"¹ 'I have found a man of a thousand,' i. e. Christ, in Whom this concupiscence was not, because He had neither original sin [originale], nor inclination to actual sin [actuale]. 'A woman of all have I not found,' viz. in whom there was not original sin."

145. Nicolas de Lyra, Franciscan, Parisian Doctor, Author of the great Commentary on the Bible, which he began in 1292, finished A.D. 1330, still spoke of the belief of "the *cleansing* from original sin" as the "more common."

among whom Christ Alone was found without any sin, not any woman." "So," he says, "explains Joannes Dominici on Ecclesiastes, where also he proves the proposition by many originals of ancient saints and by reasons." Summa, P. 1. Tit. 8, c. 2.

¹ On S. Luke i.
¹ Quétif i. 245, 6.

· "Well did he say, 'shall supervene upon thee,' because the Holy Ghost had before come upon the Virgin when yet in her mother's womb, cleansing her from original sin, as is more commonly said [1]. But in the Conception of the Son of God, the Holy Ghost 'supervened,' i. e. 'came again' to confer on her greater fulness of grace, which consecrated not the mind only but the belly, or, according to some [or (by another reading, probably a correction,) "others "], by preserving her from original sin."

At the close of his Preface to the Gospels, in explaining as to the four Evangelists the symbols of the Cherubim in Ezekiel's vision, he speaks absolutely of our Lord, as being Alone Innocent, and that, as not being, like all others, derived from the root of sin.

"He says, 'before the face of a man,' because, before the consideration of the Evangelist Matthew, as his special object, was placed the likeness of Another Man, i.e. Christ, Whose Humanity he chiefly considers. And Christ is well called 'Another Man,' because He was 'other' than all other men, for *all others proceeded from a root of sin.* He Alone was Innocent, through Whom others were brought back to righteousness, according to which it is written to the Romans, 'For as through the disobedience of one,' &c."

---

[1] Such was the original printed text in the editio princeps of Rome, 1471, 2; Venice, 1482 and 1491; Nuremberg, 1493; one sine loco et anno; also in the MSS. Mert. 165, Oriel 45, Madg. 42 (all of the XIVth century), New Coll. 12, beg. of the XVth cent. Turrecremata also quotes it so on the Decretals. In the edition of Antwerp, 1617, the word "communius" was changed into "communiter," and the words "ut communiter etiam dicitur" were interpolated to express the then state of opinion. "Alios" was also probably substituted for "aliquos."

And on the Thessalonians he answers the exposition of some who thought that S. Paul meant, that those who should be found alive at the Coming of Christ would meet Him without dying.

"'This exposition first fails herein, that it says that some pass without death to immortality, whereas *all, who descend from Adam, except Christ*[1], *incurred original sin*, whose penalty is death, and therefore all will pay the debt of death."

146. Ludolf of Saxony, Author of the "Life of Christ," Dominican A.D. 1300, Carthusian 1338. His work has been probably one of the most popular for above 500 years, as appears from the multitude of the MSS. and editions, and from the early translations[c].

[1] On 1 Thess. iv. 15, § 6, p. 653, 4, ed. Antwerp, 1634, first by Douay Theologians, and then "ex iterata recensione" by D. Leander de S. Martino, Benedictine.

[2] De Alva (n. 226, p. 637) mentions editions in which it stands "præter Christum *et matrem ejus*;" but this is doubtless an interpolation, such as we have had other instances of. The critical edition of 1634 rightly omitted them. The words are not in the XIVth cent. MSS, Oriel 45, Mert. 165, or in New Coll. 13, or in the Bodl. edition, s. l. et a. The instance which De Alva adduces from De Lyra on 3 Esdr. iv. 37, "Wicked are kings, wicked are women, wicked are all the sons of men, and wicked are all their works, and there is no truth in them," relates to actual sin. De Lyra distinguishes greater and lesser sins. "For many kings, women, and men have done iniquities, taking iniquity for enormous crime; and so it is a hyperbole, as they say 'All from the city went to such a spectacle,' i.e. many; but if 'iniquity' be taken for any sin, all are called generally 'iniqui,' except Christ and the B. V., of whom Zorobabel did not speak."

[3] Fabr. mentions 7 editions in the 15th century (in addition

"[7] But she [Mary] was cleansed by some singular privilege from original [sin] in her mother's womb," quoting S. Bernard [Ep. 174, n. 5] and, as from S. Augustine, "The B. V. was sanctified before the Conception of the Son of God, so that she could sin venially; but after the Conception of the Son of God, she could sin neither mortally nor venially."

The writer of notes on the edition of Paris, 1509, thought it necessary to correct this, saying, "[8] Mary is asserted [viz. by Ludolf] to have been purged, *but rather preserved*, from original sin."

He states the universality of original sin, in all born after the way of nature, on the 51st Psalm:—

"[9] 'For lo! I was conceived in iniquities,' i.e. in original sin, 'and in sins did my mother conceive me,' i.e. in the concupiscence of passion; as though he would say, 'My mother conceived me with the delectation of passion; I, being conceived, brought with me the iniquity of original sin, from which I suffer difficulty to good and proneness to evil, on which ground the sin of man is more remissible, and so there is ground that Thou shouldest hear me, seeking Thy mercy.' Lo, a naked and humble confession! He is reproved as to one, and he confesses all, not only actual but original also."

147. †Petrus de Palma [Baume] was appointed to read on the Sentences at Paris in 1322, in a general chapter at Florence, A.D. 1321[1].

to the ancient editions without place and year), 21 editions in the 16th, 3 in the 17th; also an Italian translation and two French. There was also a Dutch transl., Antwerp, 1487.

[7] c. 2.

[8] f. iv. v., not in the edition of Strasb. 1474 or of 1483.

[9] On Ps. 50 f. k. 2. ed. Spire, 1491 f.

[1] Quétif i. 615.

" ' He it is Who by the Holy Ghost extinguished what remained over [superfluitas] of the fomes in His Mother; whence Bede said this in the gloss : ' The Holy Spirit supervening into the Virgin, purified her mind from all defilement of vices.' "

148. " Stephen, an ancient Postillator and Doctor of Paris,"—

" ' On Rom. vii., in regard to the fourth doubt which he raises, viz., ' how original sin is remitted by Baptism,' he says thus : ' But the corruption of soul is called original sin, which is remitted in Baptism, not because corruption or that fomes remains in soul or flesh ; but it is said to be remitted, on two grounds, because God effaces it, as relates to fault, and because that fomes is mitigated. For it does not so reign after Baptism, but is gradually diminished, but is never altogether destroyed, except by miracle, as we believe to have been done in the glorious Virgin Mary,' and below, ' But the union of the soul could not take place without sin, save in Christ alone.' And he is of the same mind on Heb. vii. on the subject of paying tithes."

149. A venerable father of the Cistercian order, Englishman, of Fountain Abbey.

" 'The Bl. V. Mary is compared to the moon by reason of the beauty which it hath from the irradiation of the sun. For

---

¹ Postilla on S. Luke i. Turr. P. 6, c. 29. f. 120.

² Turr. P. 6, c. 35, f. 125 v.

³ In his Tripartite on the Canticles, which begins " Tres sunt qui dant testimonium in cœlo." Turr. P. 6. c. 35, f. 125. De Alva could not identify it. The exposition which he mentions of Thomas Cisterciens. is divided differently (as he says) into ten (not three) parts, begins differently (" Osculetur me osculo oris sui, quæ vox sinagogæ est "), and the passage which he cites from it is wholly unlike (n. 138, pp. 482, 483), so that the one could not be a corruption of the other.

the Virgin Mary had a threefold degree of beauty from the Sun
of righteousness. For she was beautiful in her ingress, like
the new moon, by the gift of the grace of sanctification, which
cleansed her from the original stain. More beautiful in progress, through the gift of the grace of fecundity which purged
her from the fomes of the flesh. But most beautiful was she
in her egress, as it were conjoined to the sun through the gift
of elevating grace, whence she was not only freed from the
original stain, but also from all punishment and temporal
misery."

I will close this list with an eminent Saint of the
15th century, who survived the Council of Basle,
and perhaps saw in the decision of that Council,
after the withdrawal of the legates of Eugenius, an
earnest that the Western Church would thereafter
decide in the way contrary to his own convictions.

150. S. Antoninus, Abp. of Florence, A. D.
1446 :—

"If the Scriptures and the sayings of ancient and modern
Doctors who were most devoted to the glorious Virgin are well
considered, it is manifestly plain from their words that she was
conceived in original sin. But they who hold the contrary
opinion, twist their sayings contrary to the intention of the
speakers," l. c.

He gives at great length the authorities against
the Immaculate Conception, and answers the arguments of Scotus in its behalf, going out of his way,
as he seems to say[s], on occasion of the disputes on

---

[s] "Since mention has been made of original sin, be there
here set down a matter or question, on which curious persons
daily and fruitlessly dispute, viz. of the Conception of the
glorious Virgin, setting down those things which doctors, both

the other side. The authorities are much the same
as have been quoted already; but he takes occasion to speak of them, as having " been approved
by the Church[e]." Of S. Anselm he says, that he
cannot be explained away. Of S. Bernard, "who
wrote more devoutly and fully of the Virgin than
the rest." He separates the later doctors, of whom
he says, that "the chief (potissimi) say the same,
declaring the matter more in detail," notices that
Divines, of all orders, agreed herein, giving
large extracts from Peter de Tarantasia, Dominican, afterwards Pope, viz. Innocent V., with
whom agreed Hervæus [Natalis], Henry of Ghent,
Durandus, Durandellus, and other " doctores solennes " of the Dominicans. He also quotes S.
Bonaventura at large. "Many also of the most
excellent order of the Franciscans say the same,
and especially the most devoted above all, Bonaventura, afterwards Cardinal, and other 'solennes
doctores' of the Franciscans, Richard de Media

ancient and modern, have thought thereon, leaving the determination to holy Church. For although it is not determined
by the Church, that the Virgin was conceived in original sin,
or not; on which ground each may hold either opinion which
pleases him, without prejudice to salvation, yet if the Scriptures," &c. (as in the text).

[e] " The holy doctors, also, and they whose doctrines have
been approved by the Church, say this clearly, quoting S.
Augustine, S. Gregory, S. Leo, S. Ambrose, S. Hilary, &c."
" S. Thomas, whose doctrines also have been approved by the
Church."

Villa, Alexander de Ales, Rigal., and Bernard, in
sermons on the Prophets, in the Serm. ' Egredietur
Virga,' &c." He subjoins " Ægidius, a most excellent
Doctor of the Eremites, Guido of the Carmelites,
and John de Policratis."

Having given the arguments on the other side
from Scotus, and their answers to the arguments
against the Immaculate Conception, he says,—

"But all these are easily answered, clearly, not in a forced
way. 1) To that of the Canticles, 'Thou art all fair, and
there is no spot in thee,'—this is understood properly of the
Church, but only as transferred (transsumtivè) of the Virgin,
after she had been sanctified ; whence it is sung in her Assumption. So Durandellus. 2) Of S. Augustine's words, ' of whom,
in the question as to sin, I wish to make no mention for the
honour of the Lord,' it is said, according to Thomas and
Durandus, that Augustine there speaks of actual sin, as is
evident from the context before and after, and from the authority of 1 John i., which Augustine subjoins immediately, 'If
we say that we have no sin.' But in this all Doctors agree,
that the Virgin alone of adults was free from venial sins.
3) To the argument from S. Anselm about the purity of the
B. V., after giving the answer of John of Naples, he subjoins
his own, ' Or better ; as it may equally be said, that the air
is more lightful [than other], whether it was before dark or no
(for the air which hath more of light, is more lightful, although
it at some time was dark), so in this case, since spiritual purity
arises from the absence of the impurity of fault, which purity
the light of the grace of God causeth, it ought to be said
of the Virgin, who had more of the light of grace than any other
pure creature whatsoever, that she shone with greater purity
than any creature whatsoever, granted that she was at one
time subject to original fault."

In answer to the answers of the Scotists, that

the words "all sinned in Adam" are said generally; but that the contrary is said specifically of
the B. V.; and also, that whenever the soul of
Christ is spoken of alone, the soul of the Virgin is
also understood. He says,—

"The first answer does not avail, viz. that the doctors speak
in common, and according to the common course, not intending
to say that of the Virgin; for he who says 'the whole' excludes nothing, and he who says 'every one' excludes no one,
and he who says 'no one,' excepts every one; but in the aforesaid authorities it is said, not indefinitely, but universally, that
every one propagated from Adam universally incurs original
sin. Then, the saints intend to except no one, not even the
Virgin Mary, since moreover she herself is expressly mentioned in some authorities here and elsewhere. But the philosophers and saints, speaking of any matter in common, treat
that matter, commonly speaking, indefinitely and not universally, if what they say on that matter in common, have an
exception in some special person.

"But as to what is said, that it is understood of Christ only
and His mother, there is no constraining ground for this; nay,
many express authorities exclude Christ from original sin, and
include His mother. For neither is the union between Christ
and His mother such as between the Divine Persons, that, as
we say that, when any thing is said of One Person, appertaining
to the Substance, even when said exclusively, it is to be understood of Another also, (as when Christ says, 'No one knoweth
the Father, save the Son,' &c., the Holy Ghost is not excluded),
so, it should need be, that what is said of Christ, should be
said of the Virgin, inasmuch as the Son, even as Man, was,
beyond comparison, of greater sanctity."

The answers as to S. Bernard he treats as
expedients to escape what could not be explained
away:—

"To that of Bernard, since it cannot be glossed, some simple

persons say, that in a vision he appeared with a spot on his
breast, or that he retracted."

In regard to the visions of some mulierculæ, he
says,—

"If it is said that some saints had a revelation of this sort,
as S. Brigit, it should be known that other saints, illustrious
for miracles, as S. Catherine of Sienna, had a revelation of the
contrary ; and since even true prophets sometimes think that
they have some things from revelation of the Holy Ghost,
which they say of themselves, it hath no inconvenience to say
that such revelations were not from God, but were human
dreams. An instance is in Nathan the prophet speaking to
David [2 Sam. vii.], who believed that he answered David out
of the spirit of prophecy ; and yet it was not so, as the event
showed."

He sums up,—

"In conclusion as to this matter, a man ought so to cleave
to one of these opinions, or rather to the first, that the B. V.
was conceived in original sin, for the reason aforesaid, as to be
prepared to hold the contrary, if the Church should determine
the contrary, and before such determination should not judge
any heretical, or impious, or wicked, who holdeth the other, and
should abstain from preaching this matter before the people,
with gainsaying of the opposite, &c."

Such is the evidence, for the most part collected with great diligence, before the discovery of
printing, from the MSS. in different parts of
Europe by John de Turrecremata, when Master of
the Palace at Rome, being sent by Pope Eugenius
to the Council of Basle. He was much employed
by successive Popes, was made Cardinal by Eugenius, received the high titles of "Defender and

Protector of the Faith " from Pius II. Of course
he did not receive those titles for that work, but
the work was no hindrance to his receiving them.
He relates that he was commissioned to write
for the Council of Basle, but was prevented from
presenting what he had written by the withdrawal of those who held with Eugenius IV. from
the Council'.

In his work on the Decretals he gives the
grounds on both sides: first, he supports the
arguments against the Immaculate Conception
elaborately by the texts of Scripture commonly
alleged, and by authorities of the Fathers who so
expounded them. He then states that each opinion
was held, but that "the way of speaking, that the
Blessed Virgin was included in original sin, seems
to some to be that which ought to be embraced
by all, on account of the three grounds given by
Cardinal Bonaventura, who for his excellence and
devotion is called the ' Seraphic Doctor.'" "True
indeed is what this most illustrious Doctor says,
that this is the more common opinion among the
more learned, who have been of greatest reputation
in Theology. This will be most clear, if any wish
to examine the sayings of the most excellent Doctors,
whether those who wrote on the Sentences or expounded Holy Scripture; he will find that, as it
were, all so hold." Then, after having speci-

' On the Decret. de Consecr. c. 4, cap. *Firmissime.*

T

fied some, beginning with Peter Lombard, he adds,—

" And many others, whom I have collected to the number of a hundred, hold the same opinion, whose sentences and passages I noted in the book which I wrote ' on the truth of the Conception*,' being appointed at Basle, when the sacred Council was celebrated there, to make relation on the affirmative side, which was committed to me by the fathers of the Council; which relation, although I offered myself as prepared to make it in the public Congregation, as a public instrument made to this effect, was hindered, because certain, at the instigation of the devil, the father of schism and discord, attempting in the same Council divers scandals, the Presidents of Pope Eugenius of holy memory departing, I too had to depart, both at the command of my superiors, and lest by my presence I should seem to countenance the counsels of the ungodly."

The Council of Basle, after his withdrawal, and that of the other Dominicans (except, I believe, two), passed the well-known decree, in favour of the Immaculate Conception, the cause unheard. The decree, though received in France, was ignored at Rome, and it seems no improbable conjecture that the language of Eugenius, in his decree for the Jacobines, was occasioned by this decree of the Conciliabulum of Basle in conjunction with Felix its Antipope. At least Pope Eugenius uses the remarkable word "liberavit," which (like those on whose force S. Antonine and others

---

* See above, p. 72 sqq. Barthol. Spina, when he presided over the publication of Turrecremata's work, was " S. Palatii Apostolici Magister."—Card. de Lambertini de Fest. ii. xv. n. 18.

dwell, " redempta," " salvata "), rather implies that she had been conceived in that original sin, from which she is declared to have been "liberated." One who had never been subject to it, could hardly have been said to have been "freed" from it.

" * The Holy Roman Church firmly believes, professes, and teaches, that no one, ever conceived of man and woman, was freed from the dominion of the devil, except through the merit of the Mediator of God and man, Jesus Christ our Lord, Who, being conceived without sin, born and dying, Alone by His Death prostrated the enemy of mankind by effacing our sins, and opened the entrance into the kingdom of heaven, which the first man with his whole succession had lost through his own sin."

I wish I could see any strength in the evidence in behalf of the Immaculate Conception. It was not, like the tradition against it, the ground of the belief which it is brought to support. The tide was turned, not by setting up a counter-tradition, but by an appeal to feeling. The only authorities which Scotus adduces are that well-known passage of S. Augustine, which speaks of "sins," and the context of which certainly relates to actual sins, and one passage of S. Anselm, which (as Albertus Magnus and others observed) even by itself goes the other way. He himself admits that the common opinion at that time was that the B.V. was conceived in original sin.

* Conc. Flor. P. iii. Conc. T. 18. p. 1224. Col.

T 2

" [1] It is *commonly* said, that she [the B. V.] was [conceived in original sin], on account of the authorities alleged, and for reasons taken from two media, one of which is the excellence of her Son. For He, as the universal Redeemer, opened the door to all; but if the B. V. had not contracted original sin, she would not have needed a redeemer, nor would He have opened the door to her, because it would not have been closed against her. For it is not closed except for sin, and chiefly for original sin. The second is from things which appear in the B. V. For she was propagated by the common law, and consequently her body was propagated and formed of infected seed, and thus there was the same reason of infection in her body which there was in the body of another so propagated, and since the soul is infected from the infected body, there was the same ground of infection in her soul as there was in the souls of others propagated in the common way."

To the first abstract argument he opposes one yet more purely abstract, that Christ would not have been an absolutely perfect Redeemer, Reconciler, Mediator, unless He had, to some one person, been so in the most perfect possible degree. But that this was to preserve her even from original sin.

He sets forth three ways of her Conception, as equally possible :—

" 1) God could effect that she should never have been in original sin ; 2) He could also effect that she should only be in one instant in original sin; 3) He could also effect that she should be for some time in sin, and at the last instant of that time should be cleansed."

On the first he says,—

" Grace is equivalent to original righteousness, as far as

---

[1] Scotus iii. dist. 3. q. 1.

relates to the Divine acceptance, so that the soul which has grace should not have original sin. For God could, in the first instant of that soul, infuse into it so much grace, as into another soul in Circumcision or Baptism. Therefore in that instant the soul would not have had original sin, as neither would it, if it had been afterwards baptized. And if even there was infection of the flesh there, in the first instant, yet it was not a necessary cause of the infection of the soul, as neither after Baptism, when, according to many, it remains, and the infection of the soul does not remain. Or the flesh could be cleansed before the infusion of the soul, so that, in that instant, it should not be infected [1]."

On the second,—

"When a soul is in sin it can, through Divine power, be in grace; but in the time when she was conceived she *could* be in sin, and was, according to you; therefore, similarly, she could be in grace. Nor was it necessary, then, that she should have been in grace in the first instant of that time."

He summed up thus hesitatingly,—

"Which of these three, which have been shown to be possible, was done, God knoweth; if it be not repugnant to the authority of the Church or of Scripture, it seemeth probable to attribute to Mary what is more excellent."

In a later place of the same book [2] (whatever be the solution) he simply assumes, what he has said before, "God only knew."

"The B. V., the Mother of God, who was never an enemy by reason of actual sin, nor by reason of original (yet she would have been unless she had been preserved)."

In his answers to the abstract arguments,

[1] l. c. n. 9.
[2] D. 18. q. 1. n. 13.

Scotus is of course invincible, as far as he lays down that "with God all things are possible." Thus, even on the supposition that the creation and infusion of the soul were contemporaneous with the first conception of the seed, he answers, in this way, rightly,—

"'Granted that the creation of the soul had been in the conception of the seed, there would have been nothing inconvenient, that grace should have been then infused into the soul, on account of which the soul would not have contracted any infection from the flesh, though seminated with passion; for as after the first instant of Baptism the infection of the body contracted through propagation could abide together with grace in the cleansed soul, so it may in the first instant, if God then created grace in the soul of Mary."

His weak side is the absence of all authority of Scripture or tradition for what he states to be possible; and, as we have seen already in some of the opponents of his followers, that when Scripture and tradition assert things as a fact, they were to be interpreted, not as declaring a fact, but only a liability to that fact.

"'Every son of Adam is naturally debtor of original righteousness, and from the demerits of Adam lacks it, and therefore every such has whence he should contract original sin; but if, in the first instant of the creation of the soul, grace were given to him, he, although he lacks original righteousness, is never a debtor of it, because, through the merit of another preventing the sin, grace is given to him, which, as regards Divine acceptance, is equivalent to that righteousness, yea

---

' l. c. q. 1. fin.   ' Resp. n. 14.

exceeds it; therefore, in himself every one would have original sin, unless another prevented it by meriting; and so are to be explained the authorities, that all, naturally propagated from Adam, are sinners i.e. in that way in which they have their nature from Adam, whence they lack the due righteousness, unless it be bestowed upon them from without, but as He could bestow grace upon him after the first instant, so He could in the first instant."

The followers of Scotus (as far as I have observed) relied on their inferences from those same two passages of S. Augustine and S. Anselm, and on a narrow application of the principle, that a festival was not kept except in regard to that which is holy; for, plainly, the celebration of the Conception of *her*, who was to be the Mother of the Redeemer of the world, must have been in itself with reference to holiness, whether she was sanctified in the first instant or afterwards.

In regard to the evidence since produced, Pétau, by one just observation, sweeps away a great part of what used to be alleged.

" ' In most of them [the writings in behalf of the Immaculate Conception], while I am wont to approve of the piety, and the effort and zeal to adorn the most holy Mother of God, I miss diligence and critical sagacity in the treatment of this question. For they do not employ faithfulness and discrimination in citing authors, which is, of all things, most necessary; and, as to those which they bring from antiquity, qualified to speak (idoneos), they distort their sayings by false interpretations, alien from their meaning. There is no need to speak of them here individually. It is enough to give warning in general

---

' De Inc. xiv. 3. 9.

terms as to one special head of their error, which has occupied
large part of such lucubrations. For if among the ancients,
especially the Greeks, there occur any thing which sounds, as
to the B. V., like ἄχραντος, ἄφθαρτος, ἀμίαντος, i.e. 'undefiled,
uncorrupted, unpolluted,' and more of this sort, they fly upon
it eagerly, as a Godsend, and adapt it to their purpose. But
it does not follow. For those too, who think that the B.V.
was infected [contactum] with the original stain, yet think
that, in part in the womb itself before she was born, in part,
just at the Conception of the Redeemer, she was overflowed
with such copious grace and holiness, that all the remains of
the original disease, together with the 'fomes,' as it is called,
of concupiscence, were healed or held down in perpetuity, as I
have just shown from S. Thomas, and other Theologians. For
which reason she might be called ' immaculate ' and ' undefiled,'
although she had been overstreamed with the original fault.
For they too are called in Scripture ' undefiled ' and ' innocents,'
who, at the time present, are endued with righteousness and
holiness, though they were not exempt from original sin. So in
the 17th [18th] Psalm, he, who had owned himself ' conceived in
iniquities,' says, 'I shall be undefiled before Him.' .... Paul too
says that we are elect, ' that we may be holy and immaculate.'
And in the Revelation of John, he saith of virgins, that they
' are without spot before the throne of God ; ' and many more
of the same sort. They then are mistaken, who, from those
and the like words, which signify the highest purity and
integrity in the B.V., think that their task is done, and employ
those, in whom they find these expressions, in witness of the
intact and immaculate Conception, which they wish to prove."

Perrone[7] " admits readily the warning," saying,
however, that he thinks that " it is not to be taken
so broadly, but restrained within certain bounds."
He does not say, *what* " bounds." Most of the
passages which he alleges, seem to me precisely of

[7] l. c. p. 80.

that sort against which Pétau justly excepts, in that a meaning is imported into them which they have not naturally.

1. The first, which he cites, would, if certainly genuine, have the same authority as Holy Scripture. For they are words, ascribed to S. Andrew, an inspired Apostle, in answer to the Prefect, in which one should look for a special fulfilment of our Lord's promise to the twelve[*], "When they deliver you up, take no thought how or what ye shall speak : for it shall be given you in that same hour what ye shall speak. For it is not ye that speak, but the Spirit of your Father which speaketh in you." Had the words alleged been certainly S. Andrew's, and had they certainly had this meaning, the case would have been ended, as much, I suppose, as if they had stood in one of the Gospels. They are,—

"[*] The first man through the word of transgression brought death, and it was necessary that, through the word of the Passion, death which had entered in should be cast out. And, because the first man came of spotless earth, it was necessary that the perfect Man should be conceived of a spotless virgin, that the Son of God, Who formerly made man, should repair that eternal life which man had lost through Adam."

But I know not why the term " spotless Virgin," should relate to any thing beyond the actual state of great grace, *when* she conceived of the Holy

[*] S. Matt. x. 19, 20.

[*] Ep. Presb. et diac. Achaiæ de martyr. S. Andr. c. 5. Gall. i. 136.

Ghost. If, as they say, the earth, of which Adam was formed, was called "spotless," because it was not yet subject to the curse on Adam's fall, then the spotlessness of the B. V. would, from the parallel, relate to that spotlessness which she had, when "the Holy Ghost had come upon" her, and "the Power of the Highest had overshadowed" her, and she conceived Jesus. The parallel is between the earth, *when* Adam was formed from it, and Mary, *when* Jesus took His Human nature from her. All which went before, is simply irrelevant to this point.

In like way, it appears to me, that none of the passages which Perrone alleges, go beyond proving a belief in her actual immaculateness, except Paschasius Radbertus, who implies a sanctification in her mother's womb, as would S. Maximus of Turin, if, which I doubt, the present text is correct.

2. Without entering into the question as to the genuineness of the two works quoted as S. Dionysius' of Alexandria, I do not think that it would occur to any one, who had not a thesis to maintain, that they even bore on the Immaculate Conception [1].

---

[1] They are, 1. "Many mothers shall be found; but one only Virgin, daughter of life, bore the living Word, Self-subsistent, uncreate and Creator." Ep. adv. Paul. Samos. p. 212 ed. Rom. 1796. 2. "He (Christ) did not dwell in a servant, but in His own holy tabernacle not made with hands, which is Mary the Theotokos. There, in her, our King, the King of Glory, became a High Priest; and He, having once entered into the holy place, abides for ever." Resp. ad quæst. vii. Paul. Sam. p. 261. 3. "He came down to Moses to deliver the

3. The two homilies, ascribed by the original collector[2] to Origen, have long been known not to

people, and now in these last days coming for our sakes, not in a figure of fire, but conceived in the womb of the Virgin Mary (the Holy Spirit coming down upon her) and preserving His Mother uncorrupt, blessed from her feet to her head, as He Alone knows the mode of His own Conception and Birth. This is she, whom Isaac, foreseeing, said to Jacob, 'The Lord give thee the blessing of heaven from above, and the blessing of the earth which hath all things.' For He Who descended from heaven, the Only-Begotten God the Word, having been borne in the womb, which hath all things: viz. the Holy Spirit upon her; the power of the Highest overshadowing, and the Holy Child Jesus born of the virginal Paradise." Resp. ad qu. x. p. 278. 4. "For from what time the King of Peace vouchsafed to become to us a Priest of Peace, no one, God forbid, is seen who succeeded to this Priesthood; nor did any one go out, save the Lord only ; and the door of the tabernacle was sealed safe and unbroken and undefiled; for it was pitched by the Hand of God and sealed by His finger. Nor was our High Priest ordained by hand of man, or His tabernacle formed by men, but was fixed by the Holy Spirit, and by the virtue of the Most Highest is that ever memorable tabernacle of God, Mary Theotokos and Virgin, protected." Resp. ad qu. v. p. 240. Of these; the first, "daughter of life," is entirely vague. The second relates to the glory accruing to her from the Incarnation ; the words "tabernacle not made with hands," if they were pressed, would rather imply that she was created in the womb of S. Anne, as our Lord's Human Body was in hers. The third rather relates to, what the Fathers so often insist upon, her illæsa Virginitas, by and after the Birth of our Lord. The fourth relates to her perpetual Virginity, the figure of the Eastern door (Ezek. xliv. 1—8), which was shut except for the Prince only, being often used by the Fathers as symbolizing the perpetual virginity.

[2] Merlin, in the Latin edition, Paris, 1512.

be his. Of the first, Huet says[3], "Let any one guess the author, who loves to divine. It occurs in an old Lectionary of the Royal Library." "Neither in doctrine nor style is it like Origen." "The style shows that the writer was a Latin." So, in his judgment, is the second, and of "a writer later than S. Jerome." But, further, the passages affirm the actual sinlessness, without any reference to her own Conception, and with reference to that of our Lord. They fall under Pétau's canon, that "Immaculate" cannot betoken any thing exclusively of the B.V., since it is used in Holy Scripture of those not absolutely without sin[4].

[3] Origeniana, App. n. 5.

[4] "Of this Only-Begotten of God, this Virgin Mary is called the Mother, worthy [Mother] of Worthy, immaculate of Holy Immaculate, one of One, unique of Unique. For no other only-begotten came upon earth, nor did any other virgin conceive the Only-begotten" (Orig. Opp. T. iii. fol. 115. v. Paris, 1512). The second occurs in a supposed address of an angel to Joseph, to allay his suspicions as to her innocency; "receive her then as a heavenly treasure commended to you, treasure of Deity, as fullest sanctity, as perfect righteousness: receive her as the mansion of the Only-Begotten, as an honourable temple, as a house of God, as belonging to the Creator of all, as the undefiled house of the King, the heavenly Bridegroom" (fol. 116). Standing in contrast with suspicion of unrighteousness, probably the words ought not to be taken as affirming any doctrine at all. The third is an address to other mothers who had conceived in concupiscence. "Hear ye, that a virgin will be with child, not conceiving through concupiscence, who was neither deceived by persuasion of the serpent, nor infected by his venomous breath, but a virgin shall be with child, receiving the announcement of the angel, taking the testimonies of the prophets" (f. 116. v.).

4. S. Hippolytus, as Perrone himself owns, is
speaking of the marvellous Conception of our Lord
without defiling human agency. The image of the
" incorruptible wood ³ " implies, at most (which all
must believe), her actual holiness, when Christ our
Lord was conceived of her by operation of the Holy
Ghost.

5. S. Ephraim simply calls the B. V. " guileless,"
much in the sense of the English word ⁴. The

The fourth is a comment on the words of the angel, "Take the
child and His mother." "Thou art not father to this Child,
but the Virgin alone is mother to this Child. He needeth not
a father upon earth; for He hath a Father Incorruptible on
high. He needeth not a mother in heaven; He hath an immaculate and chaste mother on earth, this much-blessed Virgin
Mary, as one saith, 'without mother and without father, like
unto the Son of God.' So that He is understood to be the
Son of God, complete without father on earth, without
mother in heaven; without father as to the body; without
mother as to the Deity " (f. 120. v.). We have here simply
the word "immaculate," and that, united to the word " chaste ;"
which is often especially used of the Virginal conception.

³ "The ark of wood, which could not decay, was the Saviour
Himself. For hereby His tabernacle, incapable of decay or
corruption, was signified, which engendered no decay of sin.
But the Lord was without sin, and from wood, not liable to
putrefaction, in His human nature, i. e. of the Virgin and the
Holy Ghost, encompassed, within and without, as it were, with
the purest gold of the Word of God."—On Ps. xxiv., "The
Lord is my Shepherd," in Gall. ii. 496, Fragm. vi.

⁴ Opp. Syr. ii. 327, where the hymn, the beginning of which
Perrone quotes from Assem. Proleg. Opp. Gr. T. ii. p. lvii., is
given at length. The exact rendering is, "Both guileless
(berirotho), both simple (peshitotho) ; Mary and Eve are
put in comparison : one was the cause of our death, the other
of our life."

quality which he ascribes to her here, is the same which our Lord exhorts to cherish, " Be ye wise as serpents, simple as doves ;" it is a " simplicity " which needs the check of " prudence " to prevent its degenerating into a fault.   For so he explains himself'.

He speaks also of her having a second birth from our Lord', of her being purified by the Light indwelling in her, when He dwelt in her'.

I have not dwelt upon the Greek prayers to the Blessed Virgin, ascribed by Voss to St. Ephraim, because, (1.) They are beyond question neither his nor of an early date; some look to me like later adaptations of prayers once addressed to God.

' S. Ephraim uses the two equivalents *beriro* and *peshito*.   He says, " Eve's *simplicity* (peshitutho) was without *prudence* ('arimutho) ; Mary made *prudence* ('arimutho) the salt of her *simplicity* (peshitutho); and there is no taste in the word of *guilelessness* (berirutho) without *prudence* ('arimutho), nor any confidence in cleverness (nekilutho) without *simplicity* (peshitutho).   For fault is near akin to all *guilelessness* (berirutho), and sin is nigh again to all cunning (tzeniûtho):" and, after a few words, "let *guilelessness* (berirutho) season cunning (tzeniûtho); let *prudence* ('arimutho) give zest to *simplicity* (peshitutho) ; let *prudence* ('arimutho) be *guileless* (beriro), *simplicity* (peshitutho) prudent ('arimo)."   Perrone (p. 312) was misled by the Latin translation " SINE NOXA," as he prints it.

' " As by a second birth [i. e. in time, contrasted with His eternal generation] I brought Him forth, so did He bring me forth by a second birth ; because He put His Mother's garment on, she clothed her body with His glory."   Select Works, p. 51, Oxf. Tr.

' Opp. Syr. ii. 328, quoted Ib. p. 86, n. f.

(2.) Although they have a large variety of terms, expressive of her *actual* undefiledness [1], there is not one which has any bearing on the doctrine of the Immaculate Conception. The only semblance of such bearing has been gained through an inaccurate Latin translation, which has given an idea of past time [2], where even the Greek only speaks of the present. Even had the Greek writer spoken of the undefiledness of the B.V. in the past (which he does not), such a statement as "who was ever perfect and immaculate both in body and spirit," would naturally only express, that, what she was, *that* she had been from the first. A declaration that the actual holiness of any saint had dated back from the first, would naturally imply that such had been the case ever since the first use of free-will. The question of the Immaculate Conception obviously lies beyond this. No prolongation back-

---

[1] The expressions are "all-holy" (παναγία, Opp. Gr. iii. pp. 542, 543, ed. Ass.), "my all-holy one" (παναγία μου, p. 540), "all-blameless" (πανάμωμε, pp. 528. 540), "all-unblamed" (παναμώμητε, p. 535), "all-unstained" (πανάχραντε, pp. 526. 542. 545), "alone all-unstained" (μόνη πανάχραντε), "all-unspotted" (πανάσπιλε), "all-undefiled" (παναμόλυντε), "all-uncorrupted" (πανάφθορε), "all-unhurt" (πανακήρατε, p. 528), "all-hallowed" (πάναγνε, pp. 541, 542. 546).

[2] The expression upon which Perrone lays special emphasis, "SEMPER BENEDICTAM," (as he prints it), simply represents παντευλόγητε, "all-blessed" (p. 535), which, of course, does not involve any idea of time. Time is also represented in the "Quæ semper *fuit* tum corpore tum anima integra et immaculata," which is not in the Greek. (See below, in note 6, p. 308.)

wards of actual holiness can have any bearing
upon that which preceded the power of choice, the
condition of the unborn babe in her mother's womb.
A Marian writer owns this, even as to the Greek
prayers attributed to S. Ephraim.

" [3] S. Ephraim, if I remember right, never speaks
on this doctrine [the Immaculate Conception]
distinctly, but he calls Mary 'the wholly undefiled,'
'wholly uncorrupted,' 'wholly removed from all
stain of sin,' 'fully pure [4].' He compares her with
a pearl, which, ever free from all stain, reflects the
light of the sun [5]."

But these are the very terms from which Pétau
observes that wrong, irrelevant inferences were
made [6]. Nay, the very accumulation of such terms,

---

[3] Zingerle, Marien Rosen aus Damascus, p. viii. ed. 2.

[4] These represent some of the Greek words in p. 303, note 1.

[5] This is founded on a passage versified by Zingerle, p. 64,
in prose thus, "Like the pearl, which free from spots, glistens
in the sun, is the maiden who bore to us the Son of God.
Turn it round on every side and ever [i. e. in every part] the
blinding light beams forth, which beams forth from heaven."
The sun is our Lord Himself, as St. Ephr. says to the
pearl, "Perhaps thy mystery hath respect to the womb
which bare the light." Margarit. Serm. 2. T. iii. p. 155. Syr.
S. Ephraim compares our Lord's generation to that of the
pearl (Select Works, p. 88) ; the light within it, which flashes
forth from it, is His own Deity, when He vouchsafed to lie
hid in the Virgin's womb, "then glistened from her His
gracious shining" (pp. 85, 86, comp. p. 95 ib.). The "ever"
in the sense of time, does not occur in Zingerle's own version.
He does not say whence he took the passage.

[6] See above, p. 296.

without any one hint as to any thing beyond actual holiness, implies the more that the thought was not in the mind of the writer. Some of the terms as to her actual holiness would be hyperbolic[7] if they related to her personally; some of them are terms employed of God alone[8]; their dogmatic meaning seems to be (as is almost said in one place[9]), that by virtue of the Incarnation, the B. V. had a holiness imparted to her, above the holiness of any created being. This is, of course, true; but then, since *this* holiness came to her after years of preparation, it is the more manifest that it has nothing to do with the doctrine of the Immaculate Conception.

S. Ephraim uses, of an ordinary religious birth, terms which, had they been used of the B.V., would

---

[7] ὑπεραγία, "hyper-holy" (p. 528); ὑπερπανάγαθε, "hyper-all-good" (p. 545); "hyper-purer than the rays of the sun" (ib.). ὑπερκάθαρος and ὑπεράγιος are epithets of God. Eust. Opusc. p. 235. 270.

[8] παναγία, πανάχραντε. πανάγιος is given in Stephen's Lex. (ed. Dindorf.) as a title of Jesus, of the Holy Ghost, of the Holy Trinity; παναγία, of the Host.

[9] This connexion is pointed out in the "thence" of the following address (Ib. p. 524). "All-holy (παναγία) lady, mother of God, who alone art most pure both in soul and body; who alone art above all purity and chastity and virginity, who alone becamest, all of thee (ὅλη), the dwelling-place of the whole grace of the All-holy (παναγίου) Spirit, and *thence* incomparably surpassing even the immaterial powers themselves in purity and sanctification of mind and body" (Ib. p. 524). The time relates to the Incarnation; "becamest," i. e. what she before had not been.

U

in a Latin translation), he is contrasting her innocence, in part with no very high standard of
female character, in part with the disobedience of
Eve, of which contrast I hope to say something
hereafter.   Else he is speaking only of her adult
graces [5].

Himself, when He willed to be united with human nature.
Hast thou seen how wondrous the mystery became, transcending
the order of nature ?   Hast thou seen the thing which is above
nature, wrought by the sole power of God ?"   Hom. in Nativ.
J. C. in Conc. Eph. Par. i. c. ix. p. 151, 2, ed. Col. quoted by
Perrone, pp. 318, 19.

[5] " For the serpent, the author of evil, who had brought grief
into the world, the Archangel, bringing glad tidings of joy,
precedes the descent of the Lord from heaven ; instead of him
who thought it gain to be equal with God, He, Who is by
nature God and Lord, is Author of the regeneration of that
nature which He had made ; for her who had been a minister of
death, the virgin Eve, there is chosen for the service of life a
Virgin, most acceptable to God and full of the grace of God ;
a Virgin comprehended in the female sex but apart from female
wickedness, a Virgin, innocent, spotless, free from all fault,
unstained, undefiled (probably ἄσπιλος, πανάμωμος, ἄχραντος,
ἀμόλυντος, or the like, see above, p. 303), holy in mind and body
(1 Cor. vii. 34), as a lily flowering in the midst of thorns (Cant.
ii. 2), not taught the evils of Eve, not defiled by human vanity,
not instructed in old wives' fables, her ears unpolluted with
evil words, her tongue undefiled with dishonest language, her
eyes uninfected by illicit sight ; who had not fouled her native
colour by adventitious tints of luxury, or painted her cheeks
&c., but who, while yet unborn, was consecrated to God her
Maker, and when born, was offered as a memorial of gratitude,
to remain as a sacred guest in the shrine and temple, &c.
Her, worthy of her Maker, Divine Providence gave us, to gain
good ; not to incite to disobedience, but a leader to obedience ;
nor to hold forth a deadly fruit, but to give Bread of life, &c."

9. The writer, formerly known as S. Chrysostom, is dwelling wholly on marvels of the Incarnation [1].

10. The passages of S. Proclus, and whoever be the author of the 6th Homily (whether he or another), are answers to men's marvellings at the mystery of the Incarnation; that it was no degradation to God. Two of the passages have not any seeming bearing even on the actual immaculateness of the B.V. We must needs believe much more than they express. No thinking person can doubt that the Blessed Virgin was created by God in special view of the Incarnation. It is inseparable

---

[1] "He is born of a virgin who knew not the matter; for neither did she co-operate to that which took place, nor did she contribute to what was done, but she was the mere organ of His ineffable power, knowing only, what she learnt when she inquired of Gabriel, 'How shall this be to me, since I know not a man?' And he said, 'Wouldest thou learn this? The Holy Ghost shall come upon thee, and the power of the Highest shall overshadow thee.' And how was He with her and a little after from her? As an architect, having found most useful material, worketh therefrom a most beautiful vessel, so also Christ, having found the soul and body of the Virgin, holy, adorned for Himself a living shrine. Having formed Man in the Virgin, in what way He willed, and having clad Himself with Him, He came forth to day, not ashamed of the deformity of the nature. For neither did it bring disgrace to Him, to bear His own work, and His creation reaped the greatest glory, becoming the raiment of the Creator. For as in the first formation man could not be, until the clay came into His hands, so also it was impossible that the corrupted vessel should be re-made, unless it became the clothing of its Maker " (in Nat. Christi diem, Opp. vi. 395).

from the very thought of God, that He did and doeth all which He doeth or has done, all and every thing, with a special fitness to its end. We believe that, such as we are individually, He has made us with that special combination of qualities, which is fittest for our development by His grace. We would not desire one quality, or gift, or endowment of nature more, believing that He made us more wisely than we could make ourselves. How much more, when He willed to make one for an office, alone in His whole creation ; in her to unite Himself with His creation, and to take our human nature into God! The Incarnation, from its extreme condescension, was and is a special offence to human intellect, which Christians had to clear from censure [8].

The second passage is so strong, that if the imagery were pressed at all (which it ought not to be), it would rather imply some human defilement and disease of our sick nature in the Blessed Virgin [9].

---

[8] "Be not ashamed, O man, of this parturition ; for it has become to us the occasion of salvation. For had He not been born of a woman, He had not died; if He had not died, He would not through His Death have destroyed him who hath the power of death, i. e. the devil. It is no reproach to the Architect to abide in what He has constructed ; the clay defiles not the potter, renewing the vessel which he made. So neither does it pollute the Undefiled God to come forth from the Virgin's womb ; for what He was not defiled by making, He was not defiled coming forth from it." Orat. i. n. 3. Gall. ix. 615.

[9] Our Lord is introduced, saying to the B.V., "I shall not

But then the less ought the allusion in the third passage to the clay of which Adam was made, to be pressed on the other side [1]. Proclus could use the image of " good clay " of one born of good parents.

11. The lines of Sedulius, A.D. 434, if pressed, would rather imply the contrary, as De Bandelis alleged them [2]. They speak of her, in her actual grace, as unlike the rest of mankind, but they speak also of the stain of the old man being first put aside by the Birth of Christ [3]. He too, like

---

defile, as thou thinkest, the royal sandal, if I tread on a creature of clay. I shall not dishonour My uncreated dignity if I indwell the house created by Myself. For neither do the muddy masses injure the rays of the sun, nor again do the diseased wounds soil the hands of the physician. Know that God proceedeth from thee, He doth not begin from thee," &c. Orat. vi. n. 14. Gall. ix. 642.

[1] " Let us learn what meaning had this ignorance of Joseph. He knew not the mystery which was being accomplished in the Virgin, of what marvel she was the minister. He knew not that the Christ prophesied-of was being gendered of the woman espoused to himself; he knew not that the prophet like unto Moses was coming forth from the maiden who knew not marriage; he knew not that she could become a temple of God, who was formed of good [" pure " one MS.] clay; he knew not that by the undefiled hands of the Lord, the second Adam is being again formed from the Virgin Eden; he knew not that the Author of the dry ground is created without seed." Proclus, Orat. vi. n. 8, p. 687.

[2] P. 57.

[3] His verse, rendered word for word into prose, runs thus:—
" And as the soft rose riseth from the sharp thorns,
   Having nothing which hurts, and in honour obscureth its
     mother,

St. Bruno[4], or rather like St. Paul, speaks of the
two lines of the human race, the one, beginning with
Adam, the other, with Christ. Mary was at once
the end of the old, in that she was conceived after
the way of nature, and the beginning of the new,
in that she gave birth to *Him* Who was " incarnate of the Holy Ghost and born of " her ; *Him,*
the Beginning of our new creation. Taken literally, Sedulius says, in fact, that that old vitiated
nature was not re-born, until the birth of Christ.

12. The Manichee, whom the post-Augustinian
author of " the treatise against the five heresies" is
answering, objected to the mystery of the Incarnation in itself. The writer insists, 1) that there

> So, from the stem of Eve the Sacred Mary coming,
> A new Virgin should the old virgin's misdeed expiate;
> That, since the former nature vitiated was lying
> Under death's domain, Christ being born, man might be
> re-born,
> And lay aside the stain of the ancient flesh."
>
> Carm. Pasch. ii. vv. 28, sqq.

In the prose in which Sedulius afterwards re-wrote the Car-
men Paschale, he says, "As the rose, sweet and most soft,
comes from the thorny sod, not to injure its mother which by the
grace of sweetness it obscures, so, from the stem of injuring
Eve Mary coming with sacred Light, the subsequent Virgin
might efface the destructiveness of the first virgin, that the former
nature, which, stained with vices, was subjected to the condition
of hard death, when Christ was born through man, man also
might be re-born through Christ, to lay aside the foulness of
the original stain by the renewal of the oldness of the body."
Pasch. Op. L. ii. c. 1, Gall. ix. 574.

[4] See above, pp. 159, 160.

could be no defilement in a Virgin-birth, where
there had been no passion; 2) that God had Himself both formed and purified *her* of whom He
vouchsafed to be born; i. e. first formed, then
purified[5]. One would not argue from an incidental
expression; else this language would rather imply,
in conformity with St. Augustine's teaching, that,
had there been passion, there might have been
defilement. But, at the least, he does not say that
God created her free from all sin. He does say two
things, 1) that He Himself was not defiled in
creating the B. V., nor in being born of her; 2)
that He purified her for His own Coming.

[5] "The Creator of man, the Son of man, saith to him,
' What is it which moveth thee in My Birth? I was not conceived by the cupidity of passion. I made the mother, of whom
I was to be born; I prepared and cleansed the way for My
Coming. She whom thou despisest, Manichæan, is My mother,
but was made by My hand. If I could be defiled when I made
her, I could be defiled when I was born of her. As her virginity was not injured by My passage, so was My Majesty not
stained there. As the sun's rays can dry up the defilements of
sewers, but cannot be defiled by them, how much more can the
Brightness of the Eternal Light, which no defilement reacheth,
cleanse, wherever it irradiates, Itself cannot be defiled! Fool!
whence came defilement in a virgin-mother, where there was
no concumbency with man, a father? Whence defilement in
her, who, neither in conceiving experienced passion, nor, in
bearing, pangs? Whence defilement in a house which no in-
habitant approached? Its Maker and Lord alone came into
it, arrayed Himself with the garment which He had not" [our
human nature], "and left it closed, as He found it." Cont. 5
Hæreses, n. 7, App. Opp. S. Aug. viii. p. 6.

13. S. Peter Chrysologus, A.D. 433, affirms only that she was pledged to Christ in her mother's womb [s], which expresses only what we must all believe, that she was then, as in all eternity, pre-destined to be the Mother of God. But this can the less prove the Immaculate Conception, in that so many, who did not believe it, believed her yet to have been sanctified in her mother's womb.

14. We have not any ground to think that we have any definite thing which was certainly S. Sabba's. His Typicon or Directory was destroyed in a barbarian invasion, and was re-written by S. John Damascene [7]. But further the ode, which the

[s] "The speeding messenger flies to the spouse, to remove the spouse of God from human espousal and to suspend her affections, not to take away the Virgin from Joseph but to restore her to Christ, to Whom she was pledged [pignorata] in the womb, when being formed. Christ therefore receives His spouse, does not carry off another's; nor does He make a severance, when He joins His own creature in one body wholly to Himself." Serm. 140 de Annunt. B. M. V. Bibl. Patr. vii. 953, col. 1, quoted by Perr. p. 312. Perrone prints "CUM FIERET," "when being formed," in capitals; but, since the whole period in the womb is one course of formation (Psalm cxxxix. 15, 16) "cum fieret" cannot be limited to the one moment of the infusion of her soul, even if the being "pledged" to Christ expressed any spiritual gift.

[7] Simeon of Thessalonica relates, that "it had almost dis-appeared, after the place had been destroyed by the barbarians; that Sophronius, Patriarch of the Holy City, put it forth, having bestowed much pains upon it; and after him John Damascene renewed, and having written, delivered it." Dial. c. Hær. (in Leo Allat. de libb. Eccl. Gr. Div. 1. p. 5. in Fabr. Bibl. Gr. T. v. Hamb. 1712). In another place he speaks of S. Sabba and

Bollandists quote, is referred to anonymously in the Typicon, is given anonymously in the Greek hymn-books, the Anthologion and the Biblion, and all notice of it is omitted in the two MSS. to which I have access⁶. Further, Leo Allatius complains specifically of the interpolations in the Typicon⁹. I know not then, on what authority the Bollandists state the ode, which they quote in Latin, to be S. Sabba's¹. But it has no bearing on the Immaculate Conception².

John Damascene as joint "writers and legislators." "The two composed the Typicon; for the great John, after that from the divine Sabba had been destroyed by the incursion of the barbarians, composed and cast [διετυπώσατο] it throughout from the beginning according to the order from the first."

⁶ In a Wake MS. at Christ Church, of the 12th century, of the Typicon of the Lavra of S. Sabba in Jerusalem, there is no mention of this ode, which begins, κεκρυμμένον τὸ μυστήριον, under March 24. There occurs only the ὡς γενναῖον ἐν μάρτυσιν, upon which, in the printed books, the other hymn is to follow. There is equally no reference to the hymn in a Lincoln Coll. MS. of the 16th century, which is independent of that of Christ Church.

⁹ Leo Allatius subjoins to his account of the Typicon, "Would that we could apply ourselves to the Divine service of Christ from those first fountains, as being more correct and pure! So should we distinguish the tares, sown subsequently by the enemy." P. 8.

¹ On March 25.

² It is, "Gabriel the Archangel is entrusted with the hidden mystery, unknown to Angels, and will now come to thee, the only undefiled and beautiful dove, and the recalling [ἀνάκλησιν, the Bollandists have 'reformationem,' as though there had stood ἀνάπλασιν] of the race, and shall soon cry aloud to thee, all-holy one, the 'hail.' Prepare thou through the word to receive God the Word in thy flanks."

Of the other passages (which are cited as S. Sabba's, in Latin only, by books to which I have no access[3], nor to the Greek original), the one doubtless owes the force ascribed to it, to the paraphrastic character of the Latin translation[4]; the second relates probably to the Incarnation, in which sin was destroyed and its reign checked, of which her being was the earnest, since for this she was created[5]; the third relates to personal blamelessness only[6].

15. The Psalter, which Vallars ascribes to S. Columban, A.D. 589, speaks in the most absolute way of the conception of the whole human race in original sin.

"This verse (Ps. iv. 5) explains the fall of the whole human

---

[3] The second passage is cited in Perrone from Hypp. Marracci in Mariali S. Germani, Rom. 1650; the two others from Vangnereck, Pietas Mariæ, p. 212. Neither is in the Bodleian or British Museum.

[4] "In thee, who never wast akin to any fault, I place all my hope. None is equally blameless as thou, Lady, nor is any undefiled beside thee, O thou subject to no stain." As "in omni genere sanctitatis perfecta" represents παναγία, so doubtless the "NULLI UNQUAM CULPÆ AFFINIS" (as Perrone prints it) ἄμωμον, or some similar Greek word.

[5] "In thee the lapse of the first parent stood still, the power of further progress being taken away."

[6] "O Joachim, breathed on by divine beauty; thou too, Anna, divinely bright. Ye are two torches, from whom arose the lamp, around which we see no trace of shadow." My son, after a long search, could not find any of them in places which seemed the most promising.

race, as in Job, 'Not even if a day old upon the earth, can he be clean from the defilement of sin.' For he is conceived and born in original sin, which is derived from Adam, but is purified by Baptism through the grace of Christ."

It is nothing contradictory to this, that, applying the symbol so often used of our Lord or the Blessed Virgin, he says on the Psalm, "He led them in a cloud of day,"

"'Lo, the Lord comes to Egypt in a light cloud.' The light cloud we ought either to understand properly to be the Body of the Saviour, because It was light and weighed down by no sin; or else we ought to understand the light cloud to be holy Mary, nullo semine humano prægravatam. Lo, the Lord came to the Egypt of this world, on a light cloud, the Virgin. 'And He led them in a cloud of day.' Well did he say of '*day*,' for that cloud was not in darkness, but always in light."

Even ordinary Christians are called children of the light, so there is nothing to imply more than actual sinlessness. But, beyond this, the contrast between our Lord's Body and the Blessed Virgin, as marked by the words, "nullo—prægravatam," seems to imply that he did not believe the Blessed Virgin to be free from all sin, i. e., not from original sin. He gives the force of the word "light," to be "not weighed down by." Of our Lord he says, that He was "not weighed down by sin;" of the B.V., in contrast with this, he does not say that she was not weighed down by sin, but by something else. In our Lord he extols the absolute sinlessness; in the B. V. her Conception of our Lord, not by man, but by the Holy Ghost.

16. Whoever Hesychius, *Presbyter* of Jerusalem was, or whatever his age, he was manifestly speaking of the actual graces of the Blessed Virgin in conquering Satan's assaults.

" ' ' Lo, a Virgin shall conceive and bear a Son, and they shall call His Name, Emmanuel.' 'Lo, a Virgin!' What Virgin? She who is the chosen of women, the elect of Virgins, the excellent ornament of our race, the boast of our clay, who freed Eve from shame and Adam from threat, who cut off the boast of the dragon, when the smoke of desire and the word of soft pleasure hurt her not."

17, 18. It seems doubtful whether any of the passages quoted by Perrone belong to Andrew of Crete[1], A.D. 635.   The homilies, quoted as his, and those attributed to Germanus, A.D. 715, mutually illustrate one another. The strongest words quoted in proof of the Immaculate Conception only bear upon it through a faulty rendering of a faulty text. They

[1] Hom. 2 in Virg. M. Bibl. Gr. Lat. Paris, 1624, T. ii. p. 423.

[2] The first is from a homily on the Zone of the B. V. beginning τίς ὁ φαιδρὸς σύλλογος, which Ballerini (Diss. de homiliis Germano adscriptis, Pareri, x. 259) claims for S. Germanus; the second and third are from the Hom. i. de Nativ. B. V., ἀρχὴ μὲν ἡμῖν ἑορτῶν (Combefis Auct. i. 1295) ; but, if the second homily on the Nativity of the B. V., εἰ μετρεῖται γῆ σπιθαμῇ is Germanus's (as it is claimed in the Bibl. Patr. Gr. Lat. Paris, 1624, ii. 456), then I should think the first is so too.   Leo Allatius ascribes the homily, beginning εἰ μετρεῖται, to George of Nicomedia, A.D. 880, "on the authority of the oldest MSS." (Diss. de Georgiis in Fabric. Bibl. Gr. L. v. T. x. p. 611, Hamb. 1737).   There can, I think, be no doubt that they belong to the same writer.

relate, according to the genuine text, to our Blessed
Lord's Incarnation[9].   In the second homily on the

[9] "To-day the created has been built a temple of the Creator
of all, and the creature is being prepared after a new fashion,
a Divine habitation for the Creator.   To-day, the nature, which
was before put forth from earth, receives a beginning of deifying (comp. 2 S. Pet. i. 4), and the dust hastens to run aloft on
high to the supremest glory.   To-day, from us, for us, Adam,
offering a first-fruit to God, maketh Mary a first-fruit, and the
Leaven of the whole lump, having been first kneaded through
her, is made Bread for the re-formation of the race."   Hom. i.
in Nat. B. M. V. in Combefis, Nov. Auctar. i. col. 1293, 96,
Paris, 1648.   The Greek text is τοῦ ὅλου φυράματος ἡ ζύμη προφυραθεῖσα δι' αὐτῆς ἀρτοποιεῖται πρὸς τὴν τοῦ γένους ἀνάπλασιν.
The only question which can arise is, whether the "leaven" is
our Lord's Flesh, which was first her's, "having been fore-
kneaded through her," or whether he speaks of it as first existing in her, and calls it "leaven" because it was the flesh which,
in Him, was to be "the Bread which came down from heaven"
"to give life to the world."   This is favoured by the like passage in the second homily.   On the other hand, in the homily
"on the falling asleep of the B. V.," attributed to Germanus,
he addresses the B. V., "Thou art the mother of the indeed
true Life; thou art the leaven of the re-formation of Adam"
(Hom. 2, in dormit. B. V. init. Bibl. P. Gr. Lat. ii. 459, Paris,
1622), and in another, on the Annunciation, also given to him,
he says, "Hail, holy virgin-earth, from which was the new
Adam, by an ineffable divine formation, that He might
save the old: hail, holy, Divinely-perfect leaven, from which the
whole lump of the human race was re-leavened, and from the
One Body of Christ, the wonderful commingling, being made
Bread, came into one" (Gall. xiii. p. 102).   Since, in this case
too, the leaven is the *flesh* of the B. V., which our Lord took,
it has no bearing on the doctrine of the Immaculate Conception.   Perrone (p. 316) follows the earlier and unamended
text of Combefis, 1644, and prints in capitals Η ΜΗ ΦΥΡΑ-
ΘΕΙΣΑ, as the text, for ἡ ζύμη προφυραθεῖσα, and renders

Nativity, the writer uses exactly the same image of the Incarnation, so that no one can doubt it[1]. In the first two, he is speaking of the Nativity of the Blessed Virgin as the preparation for the Incarnation. But in no way can the passage be brought to bear on the doctrine of the Immaculate Conception.

The second passage, which Perrone says illustrates the comparison in the Epistle of the Church of Achaia, brings out *this*, that, in the comparison with the virgin-earth, of which Adam was made, the virginity is the prominent idea. The earth of the garden of Eden yielded its fruits without aid of man. He calls it "virgin and untouched," in the same way as Theodotus compares the Blessed Virgin with the garden of Eden, because it brought

---

it " tota massa fermentata, **ıa non fermentata**, per ipsam conficitur panis ;" φυραθεῖσα, too, is "kneaded," not "leavened." But this does not represent even his own text, which indeed cannot be grammatically rendered. Combefis amended the text in 1648 throughout from a MS. of Card. Mazarin. Gallandi (T. xiii. p. 95) unluckily reprinted the un-amended text.

[1] "'Blessed art thou among women,' the spiritual Bethlehem, who, by appointment and by nature, becomest and art called the spiritual house of 'the Bread of life.' For indwelling in thee, in what way He knoweth, and commingled unconfusedly with our lump, He new-leavened the whole Adam with Himself, that He might become a living and heavenly Bread." Hom. 2, in Comb. Ib. i. col. 1309, 12. The same words recur, here τῷ ἡμετέρῳ συμφυραθεὶς ἀφύρτως φυράματι ἀνεζύμωσεν—ἵνα ἄρτος γένηται. Perrone notices that Combefis interpreted the passage, in the first homily, of our Lord.

forth trees at the simple command of God, through "the husbandry of God," without layers placed by man. Both passages speak of her spotlessness; but this, according to the context, relates rather to the time when our Lord was conceived of her [2].

In a third passage, the writer is applying the types of the Old Testament, and considers the entrance of the High Priest once in the year into the holy of holies a type of the Incarnation of Him Who became thereby our great High Priest. In so doing, He calls the B. V. "a tabernacle not formed with hands [3]." Human beings are made, not by a human architect, but by God. If the language were pressed further, it would prove, not the Immaculate Conception, but a Conception like our Lord's, without human agency, by God the

---

[2] "For the Redeemer of our race, willing, as I said, to exhibit a new birth and re-formation of man instead of the former, as there He moulded the first Adam, having first taken clay from the virgin and untouched (ἀνιπτάφου) earth, so here too, Himself operating His own Incarnation, instead of other earth, so to speak, having chosen this pure and exceeding spotless Virgin out of the whole kind, and having new-made in her our nature from ourselves, the Moulder of Adam became a new Adam, that the New, but above all time, might save the old." Hom. 1 in Nat. S. M., Combefis, Auct. i. 1300.

[3] "Hail, tabernacle not formed with hands and formed of God, into which, once in the end of the world, God the High Priest first and alone entered, to operate in thee, after a hidden mystery, the service for all." In Nat. S. Mariæ, Combef. Auct. i. 1324, Paris, 1648, and in the Bibl. Pat. Gr. Lat.,Paris, 1624, ii. 457 as S. Germanus's.

Holy Ghost. The word "Alone" shows that the writer was thinking of the perpetual Virginity of the Blessed Virgin.

In a fourth passage, the writer is contrasting the B. V. with other saints, of whom relics were left on earth, and so is speaking of her actual holiness[4]; in a fifth, he uses two of the titles which express exceeding actual holiness, by reason of the Incarnation; he has no reference to her own conception[5].

19. Damascene, A.D. 731, when alleging as "a diviner ground" why the B. V. was born of barren parents, that "nature waited for grace[6]," is speak-

---

[4] " But not in like wise hath the Incomprehensible been apprehended to do as to the all-undefiled Virgin and Mother, but removing her wholly from death to life, as being loftier than all sin and defilement, and taking up her soul with her body to the spiritual and heavenly altar." Encom. in depos. Zonæ B. M. in Combef. Auct. ii. 791, beg. τίς ὁ φαιδρὸς σύλλογος.

[5] "' Glorious things are spoken of thee, thou city of God,' the Divine David sang to us in mystery in the Spirit, again truly most evidently calling 'the city of the Great King,' of whom glorious things are spoken, her, I deem most clearly and irrefutably, who was indeed elected and superior to all, not in eminence of building nor in height of crested eminences, but her who was raised above others by the nobility of her Divine virtues, eminent in purity, the exceeding pure and exceeding spotless Mother of God; in whom He Who is indeed 'King of kings and Lord of lords' tabernacled, or rather in whom the fulness of the Godhead dwelt bodily." in Encœn. ædis Deip. init. in Combef. Manip. rer. Const. p. 232, beg. δεδοξασμένα ἐλαλήθη.

[6] " But I can bring another higher and diviner ground [of the

ing of the miraculous intervention of God, Who,
he believed, gave to the B. V.'s mother, being
barren (as He did to Sarah), power of giving
birth. If the word "grace" were pressed to mean
the Immaculate Conception, it would prove this as
to the body too, that the Conception of the B. V.'s
body, too, was a work of Divine grace, i. e., that
she was conceived of the Holy Ghost. But the
context shows further, that he uses the word
"grace," not in respect to holiness but of the
gracious interference of God, in making one
hitherto barren fruitful. For as the ground why
"nature waited for grace," he subjoins not any
thing as to holiness, but the fitness that *she* should
be Anne's first-born, who was to be the mother of
the First-born of all creation. "Nature then
waited for grace," in that no child was born of
Joachim and Anne after the way of nature, nor
until, upon prayer, God gave life to the barren
womb of Anne.

The other passage of Damascene expresses only
her exemption from actual sin, and the Virgin-birth

B. V. being born of one barren]. For nature has yielded to
grace, and stands in suspense, not daring to go further. For
since the Virgin Theotokos was to be born of Anne, nature did
not dare anticipate the scion of grace, but remained unfruitful,
until grace should yield her fruit. *For* need was, that *she*
should be born the first-born, who should bear the First-born
of all creation, in whom all things consist." Hom. 1 in Nat.
M. V. Opp. ii. 842, ed. Le Qu.

of our Lord'.   His statement of the later sanctification of the B. V. has been given already '.

20. The writer of a homily, once thought to
be Alcuin's, is of little account '. Yet he also,
equally with the Synodical Epistle of the Council of
Frankfort, A.D. 795, dwells on the actual immaculateness of the B. V. when our Lord was born of
her.   Perrone says '',—

" If the Virgin earth was better than that virgin earth of
which the body of the first Adam was formed, yea was immaculate according to the fathers of Frankfort, it is clear that,
according to their mind, she was *ever* free from stain."

The Bishops of the Council lay stress on the

' " In this [Eden] the serpent found no stealthy entrance,
desiring whose false deifying, we were likened to the senseless
brutes. For the Only Begotten Son of God Himself, being
God and of the same Substance with the Father, formed Himself Man of this virgin and pure field." Hom. ii. in Dormit.
B. V., Opp. ii. 869. He subjoins, " To-day the undefiled Virgin, who had no intercourse with earthly passions, but was
nourished with heavenly thoughts, &c."

' See ab. p. 148.

' " And truly didst thou fulfil the office of the dawn. For the
Sun of Righteousness Himself, Who was to come forth from
thee, anticipating His rising by a sort of matin irradiation,
abundantly transfused into thee the rays of His light, whereby
He turned to flight the powers of the darkness which Eve had
brought on. Thou art beautiful as the moon, yea more beautiful than the moon, because thou art wholly beautiful, and
there is no spot in thee nor shadow of turning." Homily on
the Nativity of the B.V. ascribed to Alcuin, in the Bibl. Virgin.
P. Alva, i. 631. Matriti 1648 in Perrone. It is excluded from
critical editions of Alcuin.

'' p. 818.

" animate " as well as the " immaculate [1]." A body, whose soul is in grace, is far higher than the inanimate earth. Present spotlessness does not involve, of any necessity, spotlessness in the past, much less the absence of even a temporary subjection to original sin in the mother's womb. Peter and the rest of the Apostles were " full of the Holy Ghost" after the day of Pentecost. This does not imply that they were so before our Lord's Crucifixion, when Apostles fled and Peter denied his Lord. No more does Mary's actual immaculateness, when our Lord was to be born of her, imply any thing as to the past.

21. Theodorus, Patriarch of Jerusalem, just before the 2nd Council of Nice, speaks of her exceeding dignity by reason of the Incarnation and of her being created for that dignity, not of her Conception [2].

---

[1] " This too we would hear of you, whether Adam the first father of the human race, who was created of Virgin earth, was created free or a servant. If a servant, how was he then the image of God ? If free, why then was Christ not free, born of a virgin ? He was made man by operation of the Holy Ghost, of better earth, even animate and immaculate, as the Apostle saith : ' The first man was made of the earth, earthy ; the second, from Heaven, Heavenly.' If we confess that the earthy was created free, why do we not much more confess the Heavenly to have been free ? For whence was Adam made a servant, save from sin ?" Synodical Epistle of Council of Frankfort to the Felicians, A.D. 795. Conc. T. ix. 85 ed. Colet.

[2] " Who is truly mother of God, Virgin before and after bearing, created sublimer than the glory and brightness of all nature,

22—24. Joseph the hymn-writer, George of Nicomedia, Peter Chorepiscopus, writers of the ninth century, whom B. Plazza dwells upon, and Perrone alludes to, use the same terms which we have already met with[1], as to her actual holiness, or that derived from our Lord's Presence in her. Those in George of Nicomedia relate to her, as believed to have been presented in the temple when three years old, and so manifestly do not bear on her Conception. But, in fact, the titles are such as had become received titles of the B. V., and are given to her, irrespective of her actual circumstances, as she might then too be called "Theotokos," although the Incarnation, whence she had the title, followed some years later. It is even an argument that George of Nicomedia did not know of the doctrine of the Immaculate Conception, that, dwelling, as he does in three long sermons, on the Conception of S. Anne, he expatiates on the miracle of the removal of her barrenness, on the greatness of the destination of *her* to whom she was to give birth, the removal of S. Anne's barrenness being a forerunner of the greater miracle of the Virgin-Conception, but he has not

sensible or immaterial." Quoted in the 2ad Council of Nice. Concil. T. viii. p. 829. Col.

[1] In George of Nicomedia I find ἄχραντος Hom. in S. M. Præsent. (Migne C. p. 1415), ἀμόλυντος, ἄσπιλος (Ib. p. 1418.) ἄμωμος, ἀκηλίδωτος, ἀκοινώνητος τῆς ἁμαρτίας, ππανάσπιλος, pp. 1419—1453. πάναγνος, ἀμίαντος, p. 1448.

one word as to the immaculateness of her own Conception, upon which Conception he dwells.

25. The writer of the Sermon on the Conception, some Sophronius, of the same period (as it is supposed), dwells on the fulness of grace in her, her many virtues of *merits* by gifts of the Holy Ghost, and so shows that the immaculateness, of which he speaks, is an endowment, the fruit of the use of grace [4].

26. In John Geometra, about A.D. 980, the verse upon which Perrone insists so much [5], belongs to the

[4] " For she was whitened and brightened with many virtues of *merits*, whiter than snow by gifts of the Holy Spirit; and therefore immaculate, because in none corrupt. Although it is believed that there was grace in the holy fathers, yet it was not so far full. But upon Mary came the fulness of all grace which is in Christ, although otherwise. And therefore he says, 'Blessed art thou among women,' i. e. more blessed than all women. And thereby [viz. through the Incarnation] whatever curse was infused through Eve, the blessing of Mary took away the whole." In Opp. S. Hieron. T. xi. p. 96.

[5] I give the whole series of couplets (hexameters and pentameters), of which Perrone joins the first and the last.

" Hail, O form, framed from above, from the starry heaven,
   Drawing nothing of daily evil;
Hail, O form, tempered hitherto (ἄχρι) undefiled in each
   way;
Of beauty aerial, of beauty from this earth;
Hail, O form, like a chariot of fire, hiding another Sun,
   The everliving Lord of the sun;
Hail, grace, Mother of Wisdom, of Light, of Word, of
   Might,
Mother of the Father, daughter of thy Son;
Hail, delight of God, new chariot of the Allwise,
   Where the sun ran its course to our setting;

Latin versifier, who substitutes something of his

> Hail, thou pregnant of the welcomed Word, self-produced,
>   Of the self-engendering light, the primæval Nature;
> Hail, thou who gavest bodily substance to God, and again
>   Hail, thou who cleansedst from grievous grossness
>   unto God."

—Hymn 3 in Lectii Poetæ Græci, T. ii. pp. 748, 9.   Colon.
1614.

The line, which Perrone prints in capitals, " Gaude, PRIMÆVI
LIBERA LABE PATRIS," replaces this last line without any authority from the Greek.   It relates entirely to the Incarnation,
that the B. V. gave our (so to say) coarse bodily substance
(coarse, because bodily) to God (παχυναμένη θεὸν); on the
other hand, that she refined what was mortal, and so, gross
(ἀργαλέου παχέος) he ventures to call it, so that in our
Lord's Person it was deified.   He says, fifteen lines later,
in the like contrast—

> " Hail, who mortalizedst (βροτωσαμένη) God,"

and again, conversely—

" Hail, who Deifiedst (θεωσαμένη) from thine own blood."

In the Sermon of John Geometra, published by Ballerini
(Syll. Monumm. ii. 142—209), I equally find traces only of
actual immaculateness.   Such are the passages on which Ballerini insists, " On account of the woman, a woman is elected,
and on account of Eve, life; on account of the corrupted, a
virgin; on account of the deceived, one not carried away with
[the rest]; on account of her who fell from Eden, she who was
brought to the temple; on account of her who was caught by
pleasure, she who was not defiled even in thought; on account
of her who held evil whispers with the devil, she who conversed with God and meditated on the Divine words" (n. 8,
pp. 153, 154).   " O that nature, which was above nature, not
of soul only, but of body too, which also drew down, more than
the holy souls in others, the operation of the Spirit.   For in
them scarcely were even the souls, being themselves exceedingly cleansed through the Spirit, a very little irradiated; but in
her the flesh too became the dwelling-place of the whole Spirit

own, not to Geometra. His testimony, on the contrary side, has been already quoted [6].

27. The latest authority cited by Perrone, Ful-
bertus of Chartres, A.D. 1007, begins his sermon by
speaking of "the festival" being "suspected," extols
it on account of the eminence of the B. V. over the
rest of mankind, praises the holiness of the parents
who gave her birth, speaks of the guardianship of
the holy angels over them during her conception.
All this looks like apology for celebrating a conception, which was after the way of nature, mini-
mizing the "blessed fault," extolling the care, that
there should be as little human about it as possible.
It is not the clear outspoken language of one who
believed the Immaculate Conception, or who spoke
to those who believed it. In regard to the B. V.
herself, he only says, that it is inconceivable that
the Holy Ghost should have been "absent from that
excellent maiden," a phrase which could hardly be
used of one unborn. He praises her for her actual
graces, her "merits," her "chastity." Finally, he
apologizes for the absence of any traditional knowledge of "the temporal beginnings of this aforesaid
Virgin," which he supposes to have been concealed,
for fear of some heresy which might arise [7].

and the workshop of the Son, yea rather supplying Him with
the matter itself also and commingled through cleansing"
(Ib. 10, pp. 157, 158).

[6] N. 61, p. 154.

[7] "For blessed was the fault, but holy the conjugal society,

I have reserved to the end those passages about which I felt a doubt, those of S. Maximus of Turin and Paschasius Radbertus, as also the question whether the contrast of the B. V. with Eve in earlier fathers bears on this doctrine, as Perrone too thought.

which poured forth in the world such and so great and special and singular an ornament, from the permitted nuptial intercourse. In her necessary conception, no doubt that the vivifying and ardent Spirit filled both parents with a singular gift, and that the guardianship or visitation of the holy angels never departed from them. Deservedly are the most holy progenitors of this holy Virgin much to be praised and extolled, who in all their ways showed themselves such, that not undeservedly should such a succession come forth from their stock, which should, to ancient and subsequent ages, be an example of all goodness.—Truly happy, and to be had in all veneration, and to be extolled for a certain sacred privilege, is the mother of this saint, who surpasses the mothers of all in conceiving and generating *her*, who should generate the Creator of herself and of all. Rejoice and be glad, O happy in such a daughter, since thou wert endowed with such a dowry. What provision of holy angels was there around parents, so exceeding acceptable to God, from the beginning of their procreation, and what watching over so great an offspring! Is it to be believed that the Holy Spirit was absent from that excellent maiden, which He was purposing to overshadow with His power? No faithful can doubt, that all the multitude of the heavenly hosts watched around her, inasmuch as they doubted not that she was to be exalted above them. O exceedingly above others Blessed Virgin, who is to be compared to no merit, nor co-equalled in title of chastity! Truly blessed were those ages, which deserved to receive thee in their time from the consecrated womb. Truly if any, with anxious mind and studious investigation, seek why the memories of preceding saints did not adorn in detail

28. The one expression of S. Maximus of Turin, "originali gratia," is obscure. "Virginali" for "originali" would correspond with the whole context[1], both before and afterwards, which relates to the Virgin-Conception, the unimpairedness of that virginity by the birth of Jesus, the fitness that it should be so, since He came to confer the virginity of Baptism ; the word "originali" comes in abruptly. Yet even if "originali" be the reading, it would betoken no more than that she had grace from her birth, like Jeremiah and St. John Baptist, which we must all believe. One, *born* with grace, would surely be endowed with

the temporal beginnings of this aforesaid Virgin to their faithful followers, so as to publish them to the knowledge of all, let them know, that they were not ignorant of the heresy which would arise, in respect to (pro) the eminent and admirable panegyric of this sacred maiden, and therefore, if they put forward any thing of her birth, they decided that it was to be concealed with sagacious industry from the envious and unbelievers, lest the blind garrulity of the perfidious should find materials for scourging the maternal bosom of the Church by their manifold fallacy." Serm. 6 in ortu almæ V. M. inviolatæ, in Migne, T. cxli. pp. 326, 827.

[1] The context is: "A Virgin conceived, ignorant of consort of man ; the womb is filled, impaired by no embrace, and the chaste womb received the Holy Ghost, Whom the pure limbs retained, the innocent body bore. See ye the miracle of the Mother of the Lord. She is a virgin when she conceives ; a virgin when she bears ; a virgin after bearing. Glorious virginity and excellent fruitfulness! The Virtue of the world is born, and there are no groans from her who gives birth. The womb is emptied, the child is received, virginity is uninjured. For it was meet that, when God is born, the merit

"originalis gratia," in contrast to that "originale peccatum," with which *we* come into the world.

29. Paschasius Radbertus[9], A.D. 844, seems to have

of chastity should grow, and that integrity should not be violated by *His* Coming, Who had come to heal what was corrupted; nor should the chastity of body be injured by Him, through whom the virginity of baptism is bestowed on the unchaste. The Child then, when born, is placed in the crib, and this is the earliest cradle of God; nor does the King of heaven disdain this narrow space, Whose dwelling-place had been the Virgin's womb. Mary was a fitting habitation of Christ, not for her bodily form, but for original grace [virgin? grace.] So then Mary, unburdened of her Blessed Burden, gladly knows herself a mother, who knew not herself to be a wife; and is glorious from her Child, who is ignorant of a husband; and marvels that she had borne an infant, attesting that she had received the Holy Ghost; nor is she terrified because, unmarried, she bore, having the testimony of her virginity and of the Child. For the Child indicates that His Father was the Lord; her virginity is a defence against the suspicion of the amazed."—Serm. V. Nat. Dom. p. 18, Rom. 1784. The idea that "originalis" is an error for "virginalis," is my son's.

⁹ "But the Blessed Mary, although she was born and generated from 'flesh of sin,' and although she herself was 'flesh of sin,' is she not then already, from the prævenient grace of the Holy Ghost, called by the Angel, 'Blessed above all women?' 'The Holy Ghost shall come upon thee, and the power of the Highest shall overshadow thee.' Else if she was not sanctified and *cleansed* by the same Spirit, how was her flesh not 'flesh of sin?' And if her flesh came from the mass of the first transgression, how was Christ the Word Flesh without sin, Who took Flesh of 'flesh of sin,' save that the Word, which was made Flesh, first overshadowed her, into whom the Holy Ghost supervened (in quam—supervenit), and the power of the Highest wholly possessed her. Wherefore her flesh was *now* truly not flesh of sin, in which God infused Himself

held that the B. V. was sanctified in her mother's womb; but his text, as it now stands, has difficul-

wholly, and the Word, which was made Flesh, came to us without sin ; Who, duly, not only did not, *when born*, follow the law of •vitiated nature, but not even that of our first original, which women would have, had Eve, the mother of all, kept the commandment in Paradise. Else how, when the Holy Spirit filled her, was she not without original sin, whose glorious Nativity too is proclaimed happy and blessed by all, in every Catholic Church of Christ ? For if it were not blessed and glorious, nowise would the Festival be celebrated every where by all. But, because it is celebrated so solemnly, it is clear from the authority of the Church, that, when she was born, she was subject to no sins, nor, being sanctified in the womb, did she bring with her [contraxit] original sin. Whence, although the day of Jeremiah and Job, viz. the day of their nativity, is pronounced accursed " [rather, they themselves cursed it. Job iii. 8, sqq. Jer. xx. 14, sqq. The reference to Jeremiah is, moreover, inconsistent, since Jeremiah was sanctified in his mother's womb (Jer. i. 5)], " yet the day when the happy Nativity of Mary was begun is pronounced blessed, and is celebrated religiously enough. But had it been in sin, it might be rightly called cursed and lamentable rather than blessed, when it was announced to her father that she was born in the world. But now, because the B. V. M. by her Blessing illumines the Universal Church, it is not undeservedly celebrated as venerable, sanctified in the Holy Spirit. For the Nativity of no one is celebrated in the world except Christ's, and hers, and the blessed John's ; John's, because he too is read to have been sanctified in the womb. So also the B. V., unless she had been sanctified in her mother's womb, her Nativity would in no wise be celebrated. But now, because on the authority of the whole Church it is venerated, it is known that it was clear of all original sin, through which not only was the curse of mother Eve dissolved, but also blessing was bestowed on us all. But if the illustrious Nativity of the most

---

• Feu-Ardent's MS. in the Bib. Pat. had " invitiatæ."

ties to all.　De Bandelis[1] and Pétau[2] quote him, under the name of S. Ildephonso, as holding the

sacred Virgin is, universally, rightly so observed and venerated, as so holy and glorious, how much more herself, when she is saluted so respectfully by the Angel as being now 'full of grace.'　For when he says to her 'Hail,' he shows to her the heavenly respect of veneration.　But when he says, 'full of grace,' he both shows that wrath is entirely shut out, and grace restored.　When he says, 'Blessed art thou,' he shows the fruit of benediction, that, when the Holy Spirit came into her, He cleansed and refined the whole Virgin from defilement, so that she should be holier than the stars of heaven."—Bibl. Patr. xii. 566, published there as S. Ildephonso's.　I have used in my translation the better text in the works of S. Ildephonso (Collectio SS. PP. Toletanorum, t. i. p. 298, sq.), where the editors hold it to be probably Paschasius's.

In the sequel, which Perrone cites, Paschasius had been dwelling at great length, and in great nakedness of language, upon her sacred child-bearing, and the absence of any effect upon her bodily frame, and apologizes for so doing.　"But it is the honour of excellent reverence, and the glory of virtue to extol to you the chastity of the most Blessed Virgin, and to confess that it was alien from all contagion of our first origin" (Ib. p. 567, col. 2, in SS. Patr. Tol. i. 303).　These last words, which Perrone prints in capitals, "ET AB OMNI CONTAGIONE PRIMÆ ORIGINIS CONFITERI ALIENAM," relate not to the B. V. herself simply, but to her "pudicitia," and mean that this virgin Birth from her was free from all those effects of child-bearing which follow upon conception in the way of nature.

[1] Pp. 47 and 163, examining Leonard de Nogaroli's Office for her Conception.　De B. observes that the argument "unless she had been sanctified in her mother's womb, her Nativity would not be celebrated " would be faulty, if " sanctified " were made to refer to her Conception, " because John Baptist was not so sanctified, and yet his Nativity is celebrated."　P. 164.

[2] De Incarn. 14. 2. 5.

sanctification in her mother's womb, after the conception in original sin; Perrone would have it, that
he held the Immaculate Conception [3]. The context
of the passage, and its similarity to other passages,
leave me no doubt, that he held that *her* flesh,
equally with that of those before her, was " flesh of
sin ;" he has the same difficulty as so many others,
how our Lord's flesh, being derived from hers,
could be other than " flesh of sin ;" he meets this
in the same way, that hers was cleansed by the
overshadowing of the Holy Ghost before the Incarnation.   In consequence of this overshadowing, he
says, that her flesh was no longer "flesh of sin."
According to this (which is Augustinian language),
her flesh, which was "flesh of sin" before, ceased
to be such through the overshadowing of the Holy
Ghost, which the Angel announced to her, just
before the Incarnation.   As, in any case, the guilt
of original sin had long since been remitted to her,
this relates, I suppose, to the material effects of
original sin upon the frame, the "fomes peccati."
Paschasius then goes on to the argument from the
celebration of the Nativity of the B. V. to the
belief of her sanctification in her mother's womb,
but only equally with S. John Baptist. All which
he says in this respect might be said equally of S.
John Baptist ; and Perrone's expedient, that he is
speaking of what some Schoolmen spoke of, the

---

[3] P. 98, note.

Nativity *in* the womb, i.e. the infusion of the soul, is absolutely excluded by the parallel of the celebration of her Nativity with that of S. John Baptist, which he, in common with others, employs. Since *his* Nativity, which was celebrated, was his actual birth into the world, as was also that of our Lord, there can be no doubt that such was the Nativity of the B.V., which he compares with theirs. It is equally impossible, to take so positive a statement, that hers *was* "flesh of sin," to mean (according to an expedient of others, which Perrone alike approves) that hers was *liable* to be such. Nor would one who believed her Conception to have been immaculate, have argued back from the celebration of her Nativity, since this proved only what had been equally bestowed on S. John Baptist, with whose Nativity he compares hers. Further, Paschasius himself lays the stress upon the freedom of the B. V. from sin at her birth ; "she was subject to no sins, *when she was born*." I think, then, that it is the least difficulty to understand the words, not in the technical sense which "contraxit" had, "contracted original sin," but (as De B. does) of "carrying it with " her. This alone gives the natural sense also to the words, "nor did she, being sanctified in the womb." For they presuppose that she was already there (not her body only, but her soul) when she was sanctified.

Ballerini adds to these passages of Perrone

three Latin authorities:—1) the Charta of dona-
tion of Ugo de Summo to the "Church of S.
Mary Mother'," with a date "A.D. 1047, on the
Feast of Holy and Immaculate Conception of the
B. V. M.;" 2) A "trope '," "on a small parchment,
sewn on to the above charta '," saluting the B. V.
as "conceived without stain;" and 3) a hymn,
found in MSS. of the Breviary, formerly used by
the Monks of Monte-Casino, at the Festival of the
Assumption. Two of these MSS. belong to the
close of the 9th, or the beginning of the 10th
century '. In one of them, a St. Germain MS.,
the hymn is ascribed to S. Ambrose '.

1) What may be the origin or history of this
Charta of Ugo, I know not. But the language of
Sicardus, who was, for 30 years, Bishop of
Cremona, from 1185—1215', is absolutely irreconcilable with the date which it bears. Words
of Muratori have been quoted, that Sicardus was
"not at home, even as to domestic matters '."

' Syll. Monum. i. 11—23.

' Ib. pp. 23—25.   ' Ib. p. 3.   ' Ib. p. 27.   ' Ib. p. 29.

' He says that he was elected Bishop A.D. 1185, Chron.,
quoted by Muratori, Rerr. Ital. Scr. T. vii. p. 526, who says
that he died A.D. 1215. Ib. p. 525.

¹ "Domi suæ hospitem se prodit." Sicardi made a Luyso
Bishop of Cremona under Otho I. (died A.D. 973), distinct
from Luitprand under Otho II., being the same. But Muratori adds, "whence you may understand, how easily historians
slipped in those rude ages, in matters remote from their own
age, when contemporary authors failed them. But," he adds,
"what I have hitherto adduced, no way hinders that the work

Y

Muratori was speaking, not of any ignorance of Sicardus as to events of his own time, but of a mistake which he made as to an event two centuries before him. He was speaking expressly of the " liability to mistake, in those rude ages, *in matters remote from their own age*," and that, in the absence of contemporary authority. But Muratori speaks in the same place of the value of the authority of Sicardus for his own time. This lies in the very nature of things. It is not uncommon that annalists who are unreliable or uncertain authorities for times at a distance from their own, are yet most perfectly accurate when they are speaking of their own. Every one acknowledges the extreme value of contemporary statements. But, in regard to the Feast of the Conception, they are of his own times that Sicardus is speaking. " Some at one time celebrated the Conception of the B.V., and perchance still celebrate it," is language wholly irreconcilable with its having been celebrated for the last century and a half in the city of which Sicardus, " ' a man of distinguished piety," was for 30 years a Bishop. The Charta then must at least be subsequent to the death of Sicardus, at the beginning of the 13th century, even if his successor introduced the

---

of Sicard, added to others older, may contribute supports of its own to learning, *and chiefly when he relates what was done in his own times, or those a little before.*"—P. 527.

' See above, p. 194.

Festival, and that, not only as the Feast of the Conception, but as "the Feast of the Immaculate Conception," of which we know nothing. We only know that it cannot be a genuine document.

2) The " Trope " bears no date. It is probably of the same date as the Charta. For the Charta directs a Trope to be sung "yearly on the Feast of the Immaculate Conception of the B. Mary, Mother of God ;" and the sewing this Trope on the Charta implies that this Trope was that chosen, at some time, to be sung. But since the date of the Charta is uncertain and must be late, so must be that of the "trope [3]."

3) The hymn is of a different measure from that of the twelve which the Benedictines acknowledge as S. Ambrose's [4], and of any other attributed to him ; and a metrical licence occurs twice [5], which implies a change in the principles

---

[3] "Tropes" are spoken of, in a life of S. Notker, as "composed by his companions and brothers in the monastery of St. Gall," i.e. at the end of the 9th or the beginning of the 10th century (Ballerini, Syll. Diss. T. i. p. 22, quoting Du Cange, Gloss. v. Tropus.). So that there is nothing to preclude its being of whatever age the Charta may belong to.

[4] S. Ambrose's hymns are all in Dimeter Iambic; this metre consists of the repetition of the two first lines of an Alcaic. This is not an accidental difference. The Dimeter Iambic—our "long measure" (as far as in our heavy consonantal language we can imitate it)—is a stately measure ; this adaptation of part of the Alcaic, in which each verse ends with two dactyles, is a very tripping one.

[5] "Reddita vita est," v. 4, "ortus in orbe est," v. 22, as

of rhythm, since S. Ambrose's time. The measure, also, is itself very rare, and is an adaptation of part of an old classical measure, probably devised by Prudentius [6], who began writing sacred poetry after the decease of S. Ambrose. But the only expression which can be quoted as bearing on the subject,—God, " seeing the womb of the Virgin, ignorant of guilt,"—must relate to that which is the subject of the whole context [7], the " Virginity." The writer had used the same poetic but unusual word, of the virginity, five lines before, " the un-married womb," lit. bowel. On any other ground

---

dactyles. S. Ambrose in this respect adheres to the old rules. The omission of the elision is one of the marks of a later date. A similar omission in Iambic verse " cæli fenestra facta es " occurs in a hymn, ascribed indeed by Card. Thomasi (Opp. ii. 304) to Venantius Fortunatus, " O gloriosa femina," but which is not in the MSS. of his collective works. Card. Thomasi follows in other places the authority of a single MS., and is corrected by subsequent writers.

[6] Prudentius' hymn on S. Agnes (Perist. Hymn. xiv.) is written in this measure ; Ennodius Bp. of Ticino (A.D. 511) wrote in it a hymn on S Euphemia (B. P. ix. 424). Daniel in his Thes. Hymn. has only one instance of the like measure (T. i. p. 100). Mone, in his 1215 hymns (including Troparia and Sequences), has, I think, only one more, which its rhymes show to be late.—N. 573, T. ii. p. 386.

[7] " Inscia Cernens piacli viscera Virginis," vv. 13, 14; " Virgo puerpera," v. 5 ; " hortus superno germine consitus," v. 6 ; " signatus fons sacer," v. 7 ; " viscere cœlibi," v. 8 ; " innubæ-Virgini," vv. 17, 18 ; " Intacta Mater," v. 21 ; " virgi-nalis vincula permanent—pudoris," vv. 25, 26. So also vv. 27—32.

the emphasis laid on the "guiltless *womb*" would be inexplicable. No one would speak of a "guiltless *womb*" to express a "sinless being;" and even then it would not imply her own immaculate Conception.

The force of the extracts from the Greek writers published by Ballerini, from John, Bishop of Euboea, A.D. 744, to Isidore of Thessalonica, A.D. 1400 (Antipater[s], Sophronius[s], and even Isidore of Thessalonica[l], go the other way), seems to me to turn upon three points:—1) the use, sometimes accumulated, of those words which Pétau held to have been misleading, ἄχραντος, πανάχραντος, &c.; 2) the question, whether the use of those titles of the Blessed Virgin by any writer when speaking of her Conception, implies that he means that her Conception itself was Immaculate; 3) whether, when a writer spoke of the presence or co-operation of the Holy Spirit at the time of the "active conception" of the B.V., he thought that it not only hallowed the parents, and, through their sanctification, in some measure worked upon the natural qualities of the child, or whether he held that the Holy Spirit was given also to the child itself.

On the first question, I cannot but prefer the judgment of Pétau. But neither can I think that

---

[s] See ab. p. 126.　　　　　　　　Ab. pp. 145, 146.
[l] See below, pp. 349, 350.

any dogmatic inference can be derived from the
passages under the second head; and that, both
because words relating to the Incarnation, and so
necessarily to a later period of life in grace, are
joined with the words which imply immaculateness,
and also on the ground of the use of language
generally. It was believed of her, that she alone
among women was ever exempt from all actual
sin; and hence those titles πανάχραντος, &c., became
a sort of proper name belonging to her. As she
alone was *Theotokos*, so she alone was "all-undefiled," &c., in regard to all actual sin. When,
then, one speaks of "the generation of the all-
undefiled and God-bearing Mary[1]," since the 2nd
title "Theotokos" relates to her living being in
this world, so also, I think, does the "all-undefiled."
It is not "the all-undefiled generation of the
Mother of God," but "the generation of her, the
all-undefiled and Theotokos." Western writers have
not hesitated to call herself "Immaculate," who did
not believe her Conception to have been such.
What else could any one call her, believing her to
have been, during her life, sinless, unstained by
sin? "The all-undefiled maiden," was as much
a title of the Blessed Virgin as the "Theotokos."

---

[1] τῆς παναχράντου καὶ θεοτόκου Μαρίας, Joh. Eub. n. 10. Ball.
i. 68. τῆς παναμώμου κόρης καὶ θεοτόκου, Ib. n. 14. Ib. p. 76.
I observed other instances.

I need not repeat what I said before, that the greatest terms seem to be given to the Blessed Virgin, because she was the Mother of God. God had dwelt within her, as He had dwelt in no created being. The Sun of Righteousness had hidden His rays, but had dwelt in her sacred womb. They speak of her as what she became. So we do in all language. We might say, " On this day, the great philosopher, Sir Isaac Newton, was born ;" but he was no philosopher when born, nor had he any title. In like way, when the Conception of S. John Baptist is mentioned in the Menologies as " The Conception of the holy Elizabeth, when she conceived the holy John, the Baptist," they do not mean that he was holy when conceived, but that *he* was conceived, who became so great a saint and " the Baptist." John of Euboea speaks of the " last and great day of the feast, on which the All-holy Spirit came down upon the holy disciples and Apostles of our Lord Jesus Christ." But it was that descent of the Holy Ghost which filled them with Himself, and made them " the *holy* Apostles." So it is plain that, when S. Andrew of Crete says to God, " ¹ Thou hast given them" [Anne and Joachim] " a fruit which bear*eth* Thee, pure," he speaks of what was then future as being, because it was absolutely

¹ Hymn. i. Od. i. n. 2 in Hymnol. de Imm. Deip. Conc. è codd. Cryptoferr., p. 5, Rom. 1862.

certain. So again, when he says, "' the God-filled
pair of the holy ones produces as a fruit the
venerable mother of the Lord ;" "' Anne, escaping
now the reproach of barrenness, containeth the
spacious place of God" [i. e. where He should
dwell]; or "' how is she contained in the womb,
who contained God! how is she produced, who
produced Christ in the flesh !" or "' thou bearest
her who bare the true Lawgiver ;" or "' the
Conception of the pure, the undefiled virgin and the
only Theotokos being announced ;" or "' from thy
(Joachim's) thigh the all-holy throne of Christ is
prepared." Indeed, when it had once become the
custom to give those additional titles, "the all-
undefiled," and the like, to the Blessed Deipara, as
it had before the Feast of the Conception was
instituted, it would seem unnatural not to use
them whenever or however she was mentioned.
I have observed, that the title " pure " or "chaste '"

' Hymn. i. Od. ii. n. 1, p. 7, as in Andr. Cret. Or. in Annunc.
Deip. p. 18, quoted Ib.
' Ib. Od. vi. n. 1, p. 16.
' Ib. Od. iii. n. 8, p. 10.
' Hymn. iii. Od. v. n. 8, p. 49.
' Hymn. iv. Od. v. n. 2, p. 70.
' "Born from an all-chaste virgin," Sophronius in Mai
Spicil. iv. 54 (Hymnol. p. 8) ; " the all-chaste mother of God,"
Nicephorus Apol. Ib. p. 12, "the chaste mother of God,"
Ode iii. p. 9. Mai Nov. Bibl. v. 68. S. Nilus, N. Cryptof.
in Can. S. Bened. Od. 5. "To bear and preserve the womb
chaste (ἁγνὴν) was not shown to any but thee, O engraced
of God," Hymnol. p. 12, note 4. I see that Combefis ob-

or "all-pure" is given to her especially in reference to the Virgin-Birth.

The 3rd question goes deep into the natural mysteries of human re-production. The relation of the parents to the natural mental qualities of the child is so acknowledged as to have become proverbial, even among the heathen, "Fortes creantur fortibus et bonis." There is a yet deeper mystery when this is contravened, and from good parents a child is born, not in original sin only (as we all are), but with natural qualities, of sensuality or others, more than usually predominant. Without entering into a province which God alone knows, this has, at least, been in some degree ascertained : "animi affectus in parentibus, quo tempore liberis operam dant, liberorum iude genitorum ingenia plurimum, sive in bonam, sive in malam partem afficere." Of course, I am speaking only of natural qualities,—still, natural qualities, good or bad. Some of the schoolmen dwelt on the fact, that the act on the part of the parents might be an act, not only blameless but to the glory of God, if fulfilled with a view to His glory. Still, they stated that conception was not

served the same reference in the words ἀγνή, πάναγνος, ὑπέραγνος (in Ballerini, who disapproves of it, Syll. ii. 387), add Ode i. n. 3, p. 6, Ode 5, Theot. p. 15. Hymn. ii. Ode i. 1, p. 27. Ode 3, n. 3, p. 29; Ode 5, n. 1, p. 31. Hymn. iv. Od. vi. Theot. p. 71; Hymn. v. Od. 5, Theot. p. 87; "in thy Conception, O pure bride of God," Ib. n. 1, p. 86; "all-pure bride, blessed mother," S. Joh. Damasc. Ib. p. 87, note.

without concupiscentia, " non parentum, sed naturæ[1]." That extreme purity, which there doubtless was, could only have been by Divine grace
present with her parents then, and had, we must
believe, an effect upon the framing of that sacred
tabernacle, wherein God purposed to vouchsafe to
dwell. But this would not preclude the transmission of original sin ; else in the case of other
pious parents, who desired only that the fruit of
marriage, if given by God, should be to the glory

---

[1] This is expressed in the Oration of Tarasius on the Pre-
sentation of the B. V., n. 5, where he applies to the Conception
of the B. V. what S. John says of all natural birth, "the
barren womb of Anna was made fruitful, 'of the will
of the flesh and of the will of man.'" Ballerini suspects
the negative to have dropped out, partly on the ground that
the common opinion of the ancients requires this, that, in
the conception of the Virgin, " *omnem* carnis concupiscentiam
a genitoribus abfuisse " (Syll. Diss. i. 348). But the alternative
of " the birth of the will of the flesh and of the will of man,"
in S. John, is " of God," i. e. of the Holy Spirit. To have
denied that she was "born of the will of man," would have
been to assert that she, like her Son, was " conceived of the
Holy Ghost," without the operation of man. In a paper in the
Analecta Juris Pontificii (Livraison 75, n. 88, col. 81) which,
I am informed, is quasi-authoritative, and which strongly dis-
courages the circulation of unauthorized private revelations, it is
stated that about 1677 " the Cité Mystique of Marie d'Agréda
affirms, among other things, that concupiscence and ' la délecta-
tion charnelle' had no part in the Conception of the B.V. The
ancient tradition of the Church contradicting this opinion,
Innocent XI. condemned it," " though," the article subjoins,
" one cannot rigorously maintain that it is theologically
erroneous."

of God, original sin would not be transmitted.
The immaculateness of the parents, as sanctified
by the Holy Ghost, upon prayer, may doubtless be
to the gain of the child, but it would not effect
this, that the child also should be conceived immaculate.   This is probably the explanation of the
saying of John of Eubœa, in which he speaks of
the co-operation of God the Holy Ghost at the
Conception of the B. V., since He is present at
all actions which are done holily, seeing they are
done holily only through His co-operation.

"[1] If the dedications of Churches are rightly celebrated,
how ten thousand times more ought we to celebrate this
festival, with earnestness, piety, and the fear of God, in which
not a foundation was laid of stones, nor from the hands of
men was the temple of God builded, i. e. the Holy Mary, the
Theotokos, was conceived in the womb; but, by the good
pleasure of the Father, and the co-operation of the All-holy
and life-giving Spirit, Christ the Son of God, the head Corner-
stone, Himself built and Himself dwelt in her, that He might'
fulfil the law and the prophets, coming to save us."

Peter of Argos in like way insists on the moral
necessity of the greater excellence of the parents of
her who was to "bear God."

"[2] By how much their child incomparably surpassed all other
children, by so much are these [Joachim and Anne] shown to
be superior to all parents.   For since we were compassionated

---

[1] Orat. in Concept. S. Deip., or, in lætum nuncium sanc-
torum justorum, Joachim et Annæ, et in Nativitatem sacro-
sanctæ Mariæ Deip. fin. in Syll. Mon. i. 103, 104.

[2] In Concept. Deip. n. 9, Baller. Syll. i. 186.

by the Incarnation of God, having been condemned to death
and corruption on account of sin, but need was that she who
ministered to so mighty a thing should be better as to purity
than all men, as being to be (oh, marvel!) the mother of God,
need was that the parents too of this Theotokos should be
better than the rest, as being the grandparents of God, Who
was to be born of her. For it was not right that they should
be the parents of any other than of her, or that she should
be named the daughter of others than they."

And James the Monk, at the close of the 11th
century[4]:—

"'Such were the gains and the deeds of the righteous
(Joachim and Anne); such the bright characters of their
virtues, who inflashed the noble beauty of soul brighter than
those who had appeared before them. For need was that
that incomparable gift among those begotten should proceed
from a supereminent election; need was that that hyper-holy
wealth should weigh down from abundant virtues; need was
that such a fruit should be gathered from such pains, that from
a noble root should the noblest germ be put forth; that from
good loins should that best fœtus be yielded, the ever-green
ornament of the race, the most beauteous germ of the nature,
the upstretching stem of the mystery, from which the Flower
of immortality ascending diffused the eternal sweetness, whose
Fruit is made life and incorruption and abidingness to all who
partake of it." "How blessed the election, most blessed
their distinction in virtues, through which the election came
to them; for this it was vouchsafed to them to produce the
Queen of all, as the fruit of piety and strength. For need was
that from royal plantations shouldest thou be yielded, the royal
scion: need was that from abundant virtues shouldest thou,
the abundant wealth of good things, be poured out; need was

---

[4] Ball. ib. i. 161—163.
[5] Orat. in Conc. Sanct. Deip. n. 14. Ib. 192—194.

that thou shouldest be the daughter of such parents, and that they should be the parents of such a daughter. For as thou wast fore-elected before all creation to be mother of God, so was it vouchsafed to them to be preferred to all parents. How more than glorious then is the magnificence of Providence! how more desirable than all objects of desire the excellent things which came *through thee!*"

But that this excellence of the parents, and the religiousness of their act did not prevent the transmission of original sin, is brought out the more by a very late writer, Isidore of Thessalonica, A.D. 1400, who appears to have read and used Peter of Argos. For, using the language of Peter as to the congruity of the parents and child, he still admits (to deny which were heresy) that the sanctified dispositions of the parents did not exempt the child from the prophetic saying, " In sin did my mother conceive me." For in that he says, " it did so, *as far as was possible,*" he shows his belief that it did not altogether[6]. The passage is,—

" [7] It was meet that neither should they [Joachim and Anne] who had become so noble in soul, who had so advanced to the height of righteousness, who had so preferred God to every thing

---

[6] Ballerini (by one of those slips to which we are all liable), rendered ὡς οἷόν τε ἦν, " quemadmodum consentaneum erat," instead of " as far as was possible," thus giving the passage exactly the opposite to its real meaning. Syll. Diss. i. 434. Ballerini frequently refers to Isidore's supposed belief as to the exemption of the B. V., as ii. 387, 393, 396, 413.

[7] Serm. in præsent. Deip. n. 13. Syll. Monn. i. 443—445.

under heaven, so God-enlightened in mind, be the parents of
any other than her [the B.V.], nor that the blessed one, whose
venerableness my speech omits, being unable to express, should
be the daughter of others than these. Moreover [it was meet
that] neither of that intercourse which was the cause of conception to the Virgin, should any thing else be the first cause
and leading impulse than the intercourse with God; that,
as far as was possible, the all-pure one might be able alone both
to escape that prophetic saying, and to say of herself, ' I was
not conceived in iniquities, not in sins did my mother conceive
me alone,' this, too, being comprehended in that list of the
great things which the Mighty did for me. But this the
parents showed from what they did, coming down from what
intercourse from God, they came together to that intercourse,
the cause of child-producing. Excellently then did this too,
being well, concur in the circle of the wonderful things
about her."

In another place, Isidore speaks of the body of
the B. V. as " a vessel of clay, broken by the fall ;"
which he contrasts with her soul in its mature
graces at the time of the Annunciation.

" * As to the body then, when she considered it as of the
things below and of clay, and the produce of that father who
transgressed, she thought that lofty message fearful, and was
wholly full of amazement, how a vessel of clay, and such as the
fall brake, should contain within, such an One, the Uncontainable; and her musing was altogether from that thought; but
when she considered her soul, how she had kept it unspotted,
hyper-pure, how she surpassed every wing, flying by the lofty
ascent of her heart to the heavenly heights, she allowed the
amazement to give way, and yielded undisturbed to the indication, and cried out, ' Behold the handmaid of the Lord, be it
unto me according to thy word.' "

---

* In Deip. Annunt. n. 14. Ib. ii. 413, 414.

III. Perrone follows the Scotists in making the Festival of the Conception of the B.V. to be in itself a proof of the Church's belief in its immaculateness, upon a narrow application of the principle that the Church keeps no festival except in reference to holiness. For 1) the Conception of the B.V., the Mother of our Lord, would have a reference to holiness, even though she, like others conceived as she was, was conceived in original sin, which original sin (as in S. John Baptist and Jeremiah) was to be purged away before her birth. 2) The conception of Anne by Joachim was, according to all, believed to be altogether holy on their part, being, as the story stated, upon prayer and in obedience to the command of God.

The festival of the Conception of the B.V. certainly had, in its beginnings, no.reference to its immaculateness. I do not, of course, mean to assume that they who first celebrated it did not believe it to be immaculate (for this would be to beg the question). I only mean, that it was celebrated on grounds wholly distinct from its immaculateness; and that, if the immaculateness had been the ground of the celebration, it would have been the immaculateness of the active, more prominently than of the passive, conception. It was the Conception itself as a whole, which was celebrated; but the belief as to the history of that Conception brought the active conception into prominence.

The Greeks had not the distinction of active and passive conception, which we find adopted among the Latins from the Physical philosophers[9]. S. Gregory of Nyssa rejected alike the priority of soul or body, and held that the being of both was received contemporaneously [1]. Nor is there, I believe, any trace of any other opinion among the Greeks. The Greeks, in a most marked way, express that what they celebrate is (what one would naturally imagine to have been the occasion of that Festival) the first beginning of *her* being, who was to

---

[9] Cassiodorus mentions two opinions, both of which seem to involve some interval of time. "We read in the creation, that as soon as the body was formed of the dust of the earth, the Lord forthwith breathed into it, and that Adam was made a living soul. Some, following this, said, that as soon as the human seed was coagulated into a vital substance, forthwith created souls, distinct and perfect, are given to the bodies. But those skilled in medicine say, that the human and mortal animal receives the soul on the 40th day, when it begins to move itself in its mother's womb." De Anima, c. 7. Opp. pp. 632, 633. Peter Lombard recognises the distinction, as urged by persons who denied the transmission of original sin. "In the conception itself, where sin is said to be transmitted, the flesh is propagated, and yet, according to the physicists, the soul is not then infused, but when the body has received its lineaments." ii. d. 31. This the objectors rested upon an inference from a mistranslation of Exod. xxi. 22, 23, in the old Latin Version (see in S. Aug. Qu. 86 in Exod. Opp. iii. i. 448), which was corrected in the Vulg. The distinction is formally recognized in Innocent III.

[1] De anima et resurr. T. ii. pp. 673, 674. S. Basil accounts abortion, whether before or after formation, murder. Ep. 188, can. 2. T. iii. p. 271. A.B.

be the Mother of the Saviour of the world. This was the more marked among the Greeks, because they received at that time too the legend of Joachim's childlessness and Anne's barrenness, and that Mary was promised by an Angel to them when bearing reproach for their childlessness, and praying apart for a child which they promised to God, being themselves in advanced age, and dead in body. The Greeks then celebrated at once the miracle wrought on S. Anne, and the conception of the Mother of our Redeemer. S. Anne's miraculous release from barrenness naturally was looked on as a sort of prelude to the Birth, wholly above nature, of our Lord. The festival was at once, "the Conception of S. Anne," and the "Conception of the Blessed Deipara."

We find this in the earliest authority quoted by Perrone, in proof of the early date of the festival of the Conception of the B.V. It assigns just the ground which one naturally imagined to have been the occasion of that festival, and that which S. Bonaventura mentions, viz., that it was the first beginning of *her* being, who was to be the Mother of the Saviour of the world.

"'O religious Anne, to-day we celebrate thy conception, that, freed from the bonds of barrenness, thou conceivedst *her* in the womb, who contained Him, the Uncontainable."

' Ode, ascribed to S. Andrew of Crete. Bibl. Patr. T. x.

The same two subjects run through the other four hymns belonging to the 9th or 10th century, lately published [3]. What, in the later West, is called the active Conception, is mentioned in precise physical terms [4]. They occur in all the sorts of shorter hymns in use in the Greek Church [5].

In like way, as to the Greek sermons on the festival of the Conception. A large proportion of the sermon is given to the legend of Joachim and Anne, and their release from barrenness ; so that there can be no question, but that the Conception celebrated is that of the B. V. in the hitherto barren womb ; the joy of the festival is, of course, that it was the pledge and prelude of the Birth of our Redeemer.

p. 685. Opp. p. 252, ed. Combef. If his, this would place the festival about the 6th General Council, which he survived. John of Eubœa (about A D. 744) speaks of the festival " as not known to all " (Orat. n. 23, Ball. Syll. i. 102). George of Nicomedia, two centuries afterwards, speaks of it "not, as of later date, ad-invented, but as being connumerate with the distinguished feasts," in Combefis Auct. i. 1016.

[3] De Immac. Deip. Conc. Hymnol. Græc. Rom. 1862. Chiefly in the three first, pp. 27—78 ; but in that of the vigil too, the conception contrary to hope is mentioned, pp. 82. 90; the barrenness, pp. 84. 91. 92.

[4] Pp. 36. 62. 63. 68. 69. 77.

[5] Stich. 3. 5. 7. 8. 9. 10. 11. 12. 13. 15. 16. 18. 19. 20. 22. 23. 25. 26. Suntoma, 2. 6. 8. 10. 11. Kath. 1. 5. 6. 7. 8. 9. Cond. 1. 2. 3. 4. Exap. 2. 3. Trop. 1. 2. 4. The miraculousness of the Conception in S. Joh. Damasc. in Deip. Nativ. Orat. i. n. 2, p. 842, " the strange and unexpected conception," Jacob. Monach. Combef. Auct. i. 1248.

And in like way, in a discourse attributed to George of Nicomedia, A.D. 886 :—

"'Since to-day's festival is, by reason of the wonders accomplished in it, a forerunner to all the more illustrious festivals, and, underlying them as a sort of foundation and basis, gathers together under itself the whole of the mysteries which were diversely dispensed, it is meet that we should hallow to it reverence and joy, as the beginning and cause of all good."

He speaks of the "[7] unhoped for conception of her, who, in a new way, worked the supernatural and unspeakable Conception."

John, Bishop of Eubœa, assigns as the ground of the joy of the festival, that the ark which was to receive God was formed on that day.

"'This is the beginning of the new covenant, of the new and God-receiving (θεοδόχου) ark, formed in the womb of Anne, of the root of Judah, Jesse and David. For the prophet says, 'I will raise up the tabernacle of David which was fallen down, and will build up its ruins.' So the tabernacle of David is raised up in the conception and procreation of his daughter; for she it is, of whom first of all, Jacob, prophesying, blessed Judah thus, 'Judah, thy brethren have praised thee.' Truly happy are ye, Joachim and Anne, for ye are from Judah and Jesse and David, and she is from you, and from her is the Lawgiver, and Lord of the prophets, and in the last times the fulfiller of the law, Christ the Lord."

Peter, Bishop of Argos, of the 9th century (as it

[6] Bibl. Patr. xii. 695, col. 2; Greek in Combefis, Nov. Auct. T. i. p. 1018.

[7] Orat. 3. Combef. Auct. i. 1064.

[8] Orat. in Conc. Deip. n. xi. in Ballerini Syll. Monum. T. i. pp. 71, 72.

is supposed), sets forth the Festival, as the " *indi-cations* of our reconciliation with God," the con-ception of her who will become the cause of all our joys, through the Incarnation.

" * Seeing many and strange marvels, forerunners of the greatest, I greatly rejoice, gladdened in my heart, and am amazed at the tender mercy of the Lord towards us, and His exceeding forethought. For to-day are the *indications* of our reconciliation with God ; to-day our outcast race, beholding *the preludes of our recall*, rejoiced ; to-day, the forefathers of our return to earth, hearing that the sentence was about to be dissolved, as not heretofore, rejoice. Now, being evan-gelized, that the most fragrant rose, planted in the unfruitful ground [her barren parent], was about to smell sweetly to all which is under the sun, and to expel the foul smell of the transgression, they rejoice. Now, the whole creation, seeing the purest temple of the All-ruling Christ being founded, bounds for joy.—Let us all rejoice then and shout in psalmody, seeing the nobility of our race beginning to be planted in the womb of Anne, and let us make spiritual choirs, celebrating the con-ception of her who will become the cause of all our gladness and the agent of joy unutterable. Sing we harmoniously to our God, sing we, as being, through Anne and Joachim, enriched with the agent of our freedom, who were enslaved to sin, the Virgin, all-spotless Lady. We, who offended, are freed from condemnation ; we, the disobedient, are received ; we, who laded ourselves with the unbearable burden of our sins, are called to rest. Of all these things and of all the rest, the present feast is the beginning and cause, as a day-star arising before the sun, and by itself indicating all [feasts]."

And further on :—

" ¹ Wherefore all things to-day rejoice with joy, and our

---

* Orat. in Conc. S. Deip. n. 1. 2. Syll. Mon. i. pp. 121—126.
¹ Ib. n. 10. Syll. i. 136—138.

nature bringeth voices of thanksgiving to God, saying, 'I
thank thee, O Lord, that Thou hast raised me, barren and unfruitful, to child-bearing; that Thou hast begun to clear away
the thorns of the condemnation, and hast through the divine
Anne and Joachim levelled me for cultivation. I thank Thee
Who didst chasten and dost again receive me. What shall I
repay Thee, Who didst for the transgression condemn me
to bear in sorrows, and again through a birth, evangelizest *the
indications of joy?* Now a rose from me appearing, Mary, in
the womb of Anne, removes out of the way the ill-savour from
my corruption, and giving her own good-savour, makes me
share divine exultation. Through a woman am I hitherto unhappy; through a woman have I now become happy. For I
see the things, foretold by Thy prophets concerning Thee,
beginning to be accomplished, and I expect to see the end
thereof, as not heretofore. Now is the Virgin, who shall have
and bear Thee, the Emmanuel, planted in the womb of the
barren, and the light cloud [on which God should come, Isa.
xix. 1] is being formed ; and the rod is rooted, whereon I shall
be stayed [Isa. xi. 1]. Now is the door, looking Eastward
according to Ezekiel, and reserved for Thee Alone for entrance,
being formed."

Nicon, a Greek monk, who lived about A.D. 1060,
under three Patriarchs of Antioch whom he mentions, John, Nicolas, Peter, in an Arabic Typicon
in 40 chapters, exhibits the Greek Feasts, as they
were in his day in the Patriarchate of Antioch, and
has Dec. 9, "the Conception of S. Anne, when she
conceived the B. V. M. Theotokos [1]."

In like way her Nativity itself was celebrated as
the prelude of the Incarnation, the first earthly
moment of the Mother of the Redeemer of the
world.

[1] In Bibl. Or. i. 620, quoted by Ass. Kal. v. 434.

"'Of this so bright and most glorious advent of God to men, there must needs be some vestibule of joys, through which the great gift of salvation advances towards us. And such is the present festival, having, as its prelude, the birth of the Theotokos, and as its term, the destined concretion of the Word with the flesh."

And Photius :—

"'As we know that the root is the cause of the branches and trunk and fruit and flowers, although the care and pains bestowed on the rest is for the fruit's sake, and none of the rest spring forth apart from the root, so, without the Virgin's festival, no one of those things which spring from her come to light. For the Resurrection is, because there was Death; and Death, because Crucifixion—and the Birth of Christ, to speak briefly and well, was, because of the Virgin's birth. So, the Virgin's festival, fulfilling the office of root, or fountain, or foundation, or whatever could be said more appropriate, is brightened by all those festivals, and is distinguished by many gifts, and is known as the day of the salvation of the whole world. For to-day the Virgin Mother is born from a barren mother, and the palace of the Lord's sojourning is prepared."

The evidence of the Greek Calendars and Icons also shows that the subject of the Festival is the Conception of the Blessed Virgin, in those first beginnings. The festival is entitled "'The Conception of Anne," "'The Conception of the holy Anne, the mother of the Theotokos." The

---

* Andr. Cret. in Nat. B. M. Combef. Auct. i. 1289. 1292.
* Hom. in S. Mariæ Nativ. in Combef. ib. pp. 1584. 1586.
* "Both Vatican Codd. Russ. and Fasti Græco-Moschi." —Assem. Kal. T. v. p. 432.
* "Basilian and ordinary Greek Menologies."—Ib.

Icons embrace three stages': 1) the Angel appearing to Joachim praying, announcing to him the Conception of his daughter ; 2) another Angel to Anne, signifying the same ; 3) Joachim and Anne embracing one another, " signifying that Mary, their daughter, was conceived," or " as a symbol of the fact of her conception '."

This is further illustrated by the fact, that the Conception of S. John Baptist was also celebrated by the same Churches which celebrated the Conception of the B.V.' The festival was known in the Russian Church as " the Conception of S. John the forerunner ';" in the Basilian and ordinary Greek Menologies it is called " the Conception of the holy Elizabeth when she conceived the Holy John the Baptist ';" and so in the marble

---

' Assem. ib. p. 252, from an Anthology in Culcinius. "In all, both Greek and Ruthenian pictures, Joachim is represented in the Temple, or rather adorned chamber, embracing and kissing Anne his wife. So also in the smaller triptych in Papebroch, p. lx., with the inscription above, ' Conception of S. Anne,' and at each side in the lower margin the names ' Anna,' ' Joachim.' "—Ib. p. 432.

' Assem. Kal. v. 252.

' From Assem. Kal. Eccl. Univ. T. v. p. 250, on Sept. 23.

' Tab. Papebroch.

' Menol. Basilian., p. 63, ib. Assem. adds, "the Codd. Vaticani Ruthenici," and "a metrical September of the Greeks," "but on the 23rd the womb received the forerunner within." In a Greek Mosc. picture, the Angel Gabriel is represented announcing to Zechariah that Elizabeth should have a son.— Ass. v. 250. Sollier adds, "Kalendarium Constantinop., Kal.

Calendar of the Neapolitan Church, which is the
earliest notice of the Feast of the Conception of
the Blessed Virgin in the West; "for," Assemanni
says, "that Church Grecised of old." The Armenian Bishop, whose testimony is quoted for
the existence of the festival of the Conception
of the B. V. in Armenia, mentioned at the same
time the fact of the celebration of the Conception
of S. John Baptist. "Being asked whether the
Conception of the B. V. was celebrated in his parts,
he answered, 'It is celebrated, and this is the
reason: because the Conception itself took place,
the angel announcing to Joachim grieving, and at
that time living in the desert. In like way also
the Conception of the Bl. John Baptist, for the like
reason. But of the Conception of the Lord which
took place, the Angel announcing it to Mary, who
conceived of the Holy Ghost, none of the faithful
doubt [3].'" It seems, from the form of speech, that
the faithful must have doubted about the others,
since of the Conception of the Lord alone he
says, "of it none of the faithful doubt."

The Syrians called the Conception of S. John
Baptist " the Annunciation to Zechariah [4]."

In the West, the Feast of the Conception of
the B. V. was brought by the Greeks with them,

Eccl. Neap., Usuard in omnibus omnino antiquis Martyro-
logiis," in adj. obss. p. 555 in Bolland. T. vii. Jun.

[3] Matth. Paris., ad ann. 1228.

[4] Assem. Kal. T. v. p. 433.

first to Sicily and Naples[5]; and so was held on the
same day upon which they themselves celebrated
it, that upon which (the Nativity being fixed for
September 8) the Blessed Virgin must first have
received in her mother's womb the rudiments of
her body. It seems to have been propagated
further by private devotion, probably by religious;
at least, we find it first among the Canons of
Lyons; then, that Matthew Paris relates that the
16th Abbot of S. Alban's (Geoffroy, Abbot from
1119 to 1146), enjoined that the Conception, with
some other feasts, should be kept festively in copes[6].
The inquiries, which he relates to have been made in
A.D. 1228, of the Armenian Bishop, were made by
Monks, and imply that it was both celebrated in
England, although not universally, and was doubted

---

[5] Assemanni (Kalend. Eccl. Univ. v. 458) speaks of the
Conception of the Holy Deipara being received from the
Greeks, and says that it was received at Naples first, "yet
after the manner received from the Greeks, viz. on Dec. 9,
appealing to a marble Neapolitan Calendar of the 9th century,
and Mazocchi in vetus Marmoreum S. Neap. Eccl. Comm. Neap.
1744. F. Ballerini has shown that Peter of Argos, who
preached on the Conception in Sicily, became Bishop of Argos
at some time after A.D. 879 (De Petr. Arg. Episc. Hist. disq.
n. 3—12. Syll. Diss. i. 107—118.

[6] "The feast of St. Giles, and the Conception of the B.V.,
and the feast of S. Catharine, for reverence to God and His
saints, be ordered to be celebrated festively in copes." Matth.
Paris vitæ 23 S. Alban. Abbat. p. 64. I do not think that the
narrative implies that this was not the first appointment of the
festivals.

of'. With this it agrees, that those who first
speak of it, to condemn it, speak of it as the act
of a few. "Some sometimes celebrated, and perhaps still celebrate it," says Beleth (Rector of the
Theological School at Paris, A.D. 1162). S. Bernard treats of it as a novel and unauthorized act of
the Canons of Lyons. Sicardus, in Italy, A.D. 1185,
repeats Beleth's words. Bp. Hugutio, the Canonist,
about 1260, speaks of "a celebration in many
regions, and especially in England," but equally
condemns it. John de Friburg [Joannes Theuto-
nicus], A.D. 1250, repeats him. S. Raymund de
Penyafort, Penitentiary of Gregory IX., notes its
absence from the Decretals, and approves its omission. Durandus, eminent both as a Canonist and
writer on ritual, in the special confidence of
Gregory X., A.D. 1274, states the grounds of those
who celebrated it to be the same as among the
Greeks, that "the Mother of the Lord was conceived," but rejected it.

Hugo de S. Caro, A.D. 1245, spoke of its not
not being celebrated (authoritatively, I suppose),
yet suggests that such as kept it, should keep it in
view of the subsequent sanctification. S. Bonaventura, who died A.D. 1274, mentions some who,
out of special devotion, celebrated it ; and, although
not considering it safe, suggests the same ground.

' Assemanni thinks that both inferences are true, and that
this doubt is a proof that there was no Council under Anselm.
Kalendar. v. 455.

" 'The Church celebrates the feast of the Conception of no one, save the Son of God Alone in the Annunciation to the B. V. M. Yet there are some who, out of a special devotion, celebrate the Conception of the B. V., whom I dare not either altogether praise, nor simply blame. I dare not altogether praise, because holy Fathers, who, by the teaching of the Holy Spirit, appointed other feasts of the Virgin, who also were great lovers and venerators of the B.V., did not teach to solemnize her Conception. The Bl. Bernard, too, a chief lover of the Virgin and zealot for her honour, reprehends those who celebrate her Conception. All the statutes of the universal Church about the festivals of the saints are founded on sanctity, so that on no day does she hold any solemnity for any saint, in which or for which it was not a holy person to whom that honour is paid. If, then, holiness was not in the Virgin before the infusion of the soul, it does not seem altogether safe to celebrate the festival of her Conception. Nor yet dare I altogether reprehend it, because, as some say, this festival began, not by human invention but by Divine revelation; which, if it be true, without doubt it is good to hold festival on her Conception. But since this is not authentic, we are not compelled to believe it; also, since it is not against right faith, we are not compelled to deny it. It may also be, that that festival is referred to the day of the Sanctification, rather than of the Conception. And since the day of the Conception is certain, and the day of the Sanctification uncertain (as will appear below), therefore not unreasonably the festival of the day of Sanctification may be placed on the day of Conception, nor without ground : because, although the day of the Conception ought not to be celebrated, on the ground that there was not holiness in what was conceived, they may yet irreprehensibly rejoice for the holy soul for what was then begun. For who, hearing that the Virgin, from whom the salvation of the whole world came forth, was conceived, would neglect to return thanks to God, and omit to 'exult in God his Saviour,' save one who felt less devoutly towards the glorious Virgin, and who

---

' 3 dist. iii. P. i. art. i. q. 1.

considered the present more than the future, the deficiency of
good rather than its foundation? For if a king's son be born
lame, being, in process of time, to be delivered from that lameness, men would not have to grieve for the lameness, but rather
to rejoice at the birth. In this way, if any one keeps feast on
the day of her Conception, regarding rather her future Sanctification than her present Conception, he does not seem de-
serving of reproof, and therefore I said that I dare neither
blame nor praise those who so do."

Ægidius of Rome[9], after having spoken of the
Conception of the B. V. in original sin, mentions
two ways in which the Festival of the Conception
might be kept:—

"We will distinguish, then, as some distinguish and well,
that the B. V. was conceived to the world according to the
flesh, and conceived to God according to grace. At the time,
then, when she was conceived according to the flesh, we may
celebrate her feast by referring it to the conception according
to grace. For of many festivals we make an Octave, as, e. g.,
of the Nativity of the Lord; we say through the whole Octave,
'To-day Christ was born'—i. e. on such a day we celebrate the
Nativity of Christ. In like way we can say, 'To-day was the
Blessed Virgin conceived according to grace'—i. e. on such a day
we celebrate such a feast of the Conception. As, then, on the
day in which Christ was not born, we say, 'To-day Christ was
born,' referring this to the day of the Nativity, so in the day of
the Conception of the B. V. according to the flesh, in which
she was not conceived according to grace, we may keep the
feast of the Conception of the Virgin, referring this to the
Conception according to grace. And as to many saints we celebrate the feast of the deposition of the body, not at the time
of the deposition, either because this is unknown, or from some
other cause. If, therefore, we celebrate the time of the deposi-

---

[9] Quodlib. vi. 20, f. 93, Ven. 1504.

tion, we can say notwithstanding, 'To-day was the deposition of such a saint,' not at the time of the deposition, i. e. ' To-day is reverenced and celebrated the day when the deposition of such body took place.' Or we may say, as some say, and well, that a more excellent honour and reverence are shown to the king's eldest son too, because it is expected that he shall be in such excellent dignity. In like way, the B. V., being conceived to the world according to the flesh, was to be conceived to God according to such excellence of grace. So that we can celebrate her Conception according to the flesh, not because she was in this way conceived holy, but because she was to be very holy, so that there should be no celebration of any thing, except in relation to holiness. For such was the excellence of her holiness, that before she was holy reverence might be exhibited to her, by reason of such excellence of holiness which was to be in her. For we should not reprobate him who shows reverence to raiment which any one had used, even before he was a saint, if only he referred this to holiness."

The first known direction for the observance of the Festival of the Conception of the B. V. in this country,—the Constitution of Archbishop Mepham, published in a Provincial Council of Canterbury, A.D. 1328,—set forth this, as *the* ground, that God had appointed " her predestinated Conception for the temporal origin of His Only-Begotten and the salvation of all," " the beginning of our salvation, however remote." Had the Abp. been right in regard to S. Anselm, we should have an instance that one, who did not himself believe the immaculateness of the Conception, instituted the Festival. The Decree ran,—

" ¹ Moreover, since, among all saints, the memory of the most

---

¹ Wilkins, Conc. ii. 552. The feast does not occur in the

Bl. Virgin and Mother of the Lord is the more frequently and
more festively celebrated, the greater grace she obtained with
God, Who truly ordered her predestinated Conception for the
temporal origin of His Only-Begotten and the salvation of all,
that thereby the beginning of our salvation, however remote,
wherein matter for spirituals occurs for devout minds, may
increase the joyous devotion and salvation of all, we, following
the steps of the venerable Anselm our predecessor, who, after
some older solemnities, thought it meet to superadd the festival of her Conception, decree and firmly enjoin that the
festival of the aforesaid Conception should be for the future
festively and solemnly celebrated in all Churches of our Province of Canterbury."

S. Thomas speaks of the Church of Rome as
tolerating but not celebrating the festival, and

full list of feasts prescribed in the Synod of Worcester, A.D.
1240 (Wilkins, Conc. i. 677, 678), nor in the Synod of Exeter,
in 1287 (c. 23. Ib. ii. 146). Lupus' statement, that " Stephen,
in his Synod of Oxford, celebrated under Honorius III., A.D.
1188 [1222], enacted, ' Let all festivals of Mary be kept with
all veneration, except the Feast of the Conception, as to the
observance of which no necessity is imposed " (Notes on
Leo IX. Concil. Mogunt., p. 497), rests on a single Belgian
MS. from which Surius inserted the Canon in his Concilia. It
did not exist in the Cotton MS., from which Sir H. Spelman
published the Council, nor in that which Lyndwode used in his
Provinciale Angliæ, Paris, 1502.   The tone of that canon is also
altogether different from the other Constitutions of Stephen
Langton, then promulgated.   For these embody mostly some
scriptural or religious ground (Wilkins, Conc. i. 585, sqq.) ;
the canon, added in the one MS., is a dry enumeration of
festivals.   The English MSS. are naturally more reliable than
the scarcely decipherable Belgian MS., from which Surius took
the canon.   Moreover, had the Festival been mentioned by
Langton, it could hardly have been omitted in the lists of 1240
and 1287.   It was prescribed A.D. 1362, by Abp. Simon
Islip, and about 1400 by Abp. Arundel.

assigns the same ground : the objection which he answers, only stated that "some" celebrated it. Ralph de Rivo (who died at Rome, A.D. 1390) under Urban VI., still speaks of only three days of the B. V. being in the Roman Office[2]. But Alvarus Pelagius, who died some time after 1340, mentions that the festival (which he calls the festival of "the Sanctification of the B. V.") was held in the Church of S. Mary Major; and John Bacon, a Carmelite, who died A.D. 1350, says, that "[3]it had long been celebrated in the house of the brothers of the order of the Bl. Mary of Carmel, with the venerable congregation of the Cardinals, and so had lasted in the time of many Roman Pontiffs to the present time." He himself argues at length that the festival of the Conception was to be celebrated on Dec. 8.

"[4]Although she contracted original sin, as a daughter of Adam, yet that day of her Conception is venerable, on account of the Sanctification, which was ordained from eternity, and in relation to her subsequent consent."

But the Church of S. Mary Major was no insulated case.

In the first Carthusian statutes, or Customs of Guigo, the 5th Prior, there is no mention of the

[2] De Canon. Observ. Prop. 12.   Bibl. P. xxvi. 300.
[3] In Sent. iv. d. 2. art. 3. fin.
[4] Ib. art. 2. p. 315.

Feast, only of the Purification, Annunciation, Assumption, Nativity [5].

In some old Carthusian statutes [6], without date, but probably soon after 1264, as one refers to (as it seems) the recent institution of the Festival of Corpus Christi by Urban IV [7]., there is a statute, " [8] In the Feast as to the Conception of Bl. Mary, in place of Conception, let it be said, Sanctification."

Turrecremata gives, in addition, the beginning of the first Collect, " Hear, O merciful Lord, the supplication of Thy servants, that we, who are gathered together in the sanctification of the Virgin Mother of God [9]," &c.

---

[5] c. 8. n. 7 (about 1120—1137), Basle 1510. In the Statuta Nova, P. 2. c. 4. n. 26, abstinence is enjoined on the vigils of the five festivals of the Bl. Virg., but they are not named in the statute.

[6] In Mabillon, Ann. Bened. vi. App. p. 685, sqq.

[7] " Since our Lord, the Sovereign Pontiff, has ordained and strictly charged, in virtue of holy obedience, that the Festival of Corpus Christi should be solemnly celebrated by all, we, for reverence to God and the sacred precept, ordain and enjoin, in the same way as is enjoined in the decretal, that the festival be held in our order," &c., n. 4.

[8] n. 45. At the same time permission was granted to the Prior and convent of Liminati, and to others who should be so pleased, to celebrate solemnly the feast of the Conception of the B. V., and that the office should be as in the Nativity, substituting the name ' Conception' for that of ' Nativity.' " n. 26.

[9] " Supplicationem servorum tuorum, Deus miserator, exaudi, ut qui in sanctificatione Dei genetricis et Virginis congre-

In the "New Constitutions of the Carthusian Order, promulgated by William Rainald, Prior A.D. 1368 [1]," the observation was prescribed, but under the name, "the Feast of the Sanctification of the B. Mary."

" [2] In the Feast, the Sanctification of the Bl. Mary, let the Office be as in her Nativity, the name of the Nativity being changed into the name of ' Sanctification.' "

And this was not repealed for nearly a century and a half—141 years. In the third Compilation of Statutes, promulgated by Francis de Puteo, 1509, it is enacted,—

" [3] Let the feast of the glorious Virgin Mary, which is solemnly celebrated on the 6th of the Ides of December, be *henceforth* celebrated throughout the whole Order, under the name of the Conception, according to the determination of the Church, the statute making mention of the ' sanctification' notwithstanding."

---

gamur," &c., Turr. P. 6. c. 35, de Ord. Carthus., quoted by De Alva, n. 231, p. 647. The Breviary, printed in the Carthusian monastery at Ferrara, A.D. 1503, from which De Alva quotes the same prayer with the word " Conception," is stated to have been "diligently amended." De Alva states that rubrics in a Carthusian Breviary, Venice, 1491, used the title " The Conception of the B.V." (n. 231, p. 647). But in the " declaration of the Chapter " A. 1470, which he quotes, there is no mention of the *name* of the Festival, and in the declaration of the Chapter A. 1418, it is only said, that on the Festival the " Gloria in excelsis " should be said. The Paris Breviary, 1511, is two years after the statute directing the change.

[1] Prolog.

[2] Statuta nova Pars i. c. 2. n. 8. Basle, 1510.

[3] c. 1. f. b 5. Reference is made to the c. 2, 3 part. n. 17, as abrogated ; but, being abrogated, it has disappeared.

Of his own time, De Turrecremata says[4],—

" Of no slight authority is the testimony of the most sacred
Cartbusian Order, which, throughout the world, celebrates this
Festival, only under the name of the Sanctification, saying in
the first Collect " (as above).

In an old Dominican service-book there is no
mention of any Festival, whether of the Conception or Sanctification[5]. Another stage, apparently,
was that the Festival of the Sanctification was
mentioned in the Calendar, but it did not appear
in its place among the Feasts[6]. In another, the
feast of the Sanctification occurs generally, without
any specific mention of original sin ; and this seems
to have been used both before and after that published through the influence of Bandellus[7]. Some-

---

[4] l. c.

[5] As in a Breviary and a Missal, both printed in Venice,
1484. (The office-books not specified as being in the Bodleian
are in the Brit. Mus., and have been kindly examined for me
by the Rev. E. Hoskins.)   Quétif says, " The Feast of the Sanctification of the B. V. was unknown in our Calendars and
Breviaries before 1388, when in a General Chapter held at
Rhodez, it was directed that it should be celebrated the day
after S. Matthias, Feb. 25.   No special office for this festival
adapted to our use occurs to me till now before the Pontificate
of Sixtus IV " (A.D. 1471—1484), i. 724.

[6] As in a Missal printed at Venice, A. D. 1482, and another
at Lubeck, A. 1507 [both Bodl.].   In like way, in a Cistercian
Missal [sine loco] A. 1487 [Bodl.], the Conception stands in
the Calendar, no direction as to the office occurs in the body
of the Missal.

[7] In a Breviary printed at Nuremberg, A. D. 1485, the Antiphone at the first vespers is, " Christ, before the creation of

what later, in a Breviary revised under Card. Aug. Gallamin, Brasicholénsis, General, A.D. 1608, "amended, approved, and confirmed by Apostolic authority" [Paul V.], published at Rome A. 1611, and ordered to be used exclusively in the Order, "the Sanctification of the B. V." stands in the Calendar, and the rubric directs, " ⁕ in the Sancti-

the world, provided the health-giving sanctification of His mother." The Collect is the same as that of the Carthusians (above, p. 368). (The sequel of the Collect is printed out in the Missal of Venice, 1496, "may, through her intercession, be by Thee from imminent perils delivered. Through Him, &c.") The invitatory at Matins is, "Come, the Son of the Virgin let us all adore, and for the sanctification of the Virgin let us all jubilate." The first Antiphone in the Venice Office is, "Let us all rejoice in the Lord, celebrating the Festival under the honour of the Virgin Mary, at whose sanctification Angels rejoice and praise the Son of God." In the Missal, A. 1562, "reformed according to the decrees of the general Chapter held at Salamanca, A. D. 1551, and approved by Apostolic authority, as may be seen in the following leaf," there stands in the Collect, "in the sanctification of the Mother [Genitricis] of God and Virgin," for "in the sanctification of the Bl. Virgin." This was reprinted, Venice, 1579, and also Venice, 1596, in the Dominican Missal, "under the most reverend Father Br. Hippolytus Maria Beccaria a Monteregali, General of the whole Order, A. D. 1595, reformed, enlarged, and confirmed and approved by Apostolic authority" [Clement VIII.]. In the Missal edited by command of the most reverend F. Br. Antonine Cloche, Paris, 1721 (after the copy published at Rome, A. 1705), the "Gaudeamus omnes in Domino" is retained, but "conception" is throughout substituted for "sanctification."

⁕ Die viii. Decembris. In sanctificatione B. M. V. totum duplex omnia, præter lectiones infra scriptas de Officio Nativi-

fication of the B. V., let all, except the lessons below, be taken from the Office of Nativity, the name 'Nativity' being changed into that of 'Sanctification.'" The lessons are,—Noct. i., Ecclus. xiv.; Noct. ii., S. Ambr. de Virgin. ii. init.; Noct. iii., S. Aug. de cons. Ev. c. 1. All reference to the Conception is thus avoided.

The same is repeated in an Office also published at Rome in 1615, "reformed and approved by Apostolic authority," but under a different General [1].

The Office known as that of Vincentius Bandellus was published while Joachim Turrianus was General and Bandellus was only President of the Congregation in Lombardy, 1493. The Office had then been recently composed [2]. It was framed to bring out in a marked way the doctrine, that our Lord Alone was conceived without stain, and that in the Blessed Virgin the original stain was removed by the copious grace of subsequent sanctification.

The first Antiphone is, " She is beautiful among the daughters of Jerusalem, as ye have seen her,

---

tatis ipsius assumantur, mutato Nativitatis vocabulo in Sanctificationem. [Bodl.]

[1] Breviarium juxta ritum Sacri Ordinis FF. Præd. S.P.N. Dominici, auctoritate Apostolica reformatum et approbatum, jussu vero editum R. P. Fr. Seraphini Sicci Papiensis, totius ordinis præfati Ord. Generalis Magistri. Romæ, 1615.

[2] Note in red letters at the end of the Breviary, Venice, 1494.

full of charity and love, so, too, in her mother's
womb she was by the copious gift of sanctification
cleansed from all defilements of sin." In a versicle
and response is the text so often quoted by mediæval
writers ; V. "Take away the rust from the silver,"
R. "And a most pure vessel shall go forth." In
the Antiphone on the Magnificat are the words,
"Thou art all beautiful, because through the grace
of sanctification no stain remained in thee."

The Collect is, "O God, Who after the infusion
of the soul, didst, through the copious gifts of grace,
wonderfully cleanse the most blessed Virgin Mary
from all stain of sin, and didst afterwards confirm
her in the purity of holiness, grant, we beseech
Thee, that we who are gathered together in honour
of her Sanctification, may through her intercession
be by Thee delivered from the impending dangers.
Through, &c.[3]." The invitatory at Matins was,
"The sanctification of the Virgin Mary let us
celebrate: Christ her Son the Lord let us adore."
A hymn addresses our Lord as being "Alone

---

[3] The same Collect occurs in "the Missal, Venice, 1506 and
1512. Mass on the Sanctification of the most Bl. Virgin,
edited by the most reverend Father Vincentius Bandellus de
Castro novo," and even in Paris, 1519, in two editions ; the
one in the Paris Academy. The statement of Spondanus,
then, must have referred to something temporary and local,
when he says (Ann. T. 2. ad Ann. 1387, n. 7), that in that year
the Dominicans were induced by the King of France to celebrate the Feast of the Conception, in consequence of the commotion raised in that year through the theses of John de
Montesono.

conceived without stain ;" and speaks of His sanctifying His Mother.

Bernardine de Bustis doubtless alluded to this
Breviary when he used the strong term,—

> "' I composed an office of the innocence of the most pure
> Virgin, not, as a certain man did, of her contamination and
> corruption."

The Office from the Breviary of the Church of
Gironne, in Catalonia, gave in its lessons the doctrinal statement, that the. sanctification followed
immediately after the infusion of the soul [5].

> " The great Artificer, Who willeth that none should perish,
> by that love wherewith He pitied exceedingly man whom He
> had created and made, though undeserving, built Himself a
> house, where He should personally reside in this world, and
> thence take fitting arms to war against the devil, who had
> fraudulently taken captive the whole human race.   This house
> was the Bl. V. Mary, of which Solomon thus speaks in the
> Proverbs : ' Wisdom built her an house, she hewed out seven
> pillars.'   This house also not only did the Almighty Lord
> build, when, on the 80th day from her carnal Conception in the
> womb of her mother Anne, He infused into her a soul, yea
> moreover more fully did He there immediately [6] sanctify her.

---

[4] Serm. 9. p. 1. f. 109, col. 2, quoted by De Alva, Ver. 231,
p. 651. Rosarium iii. 102.

[5] Turrecremata says, that what he quotes had been "extracted from Breviaries of that same Church, which I have had
from some Fathers of this same sacred Council, who, in singing
the hours, observe the custom of the aforesaid Church."
P. 6. c. 14, f. 106 v.

[6] De Alva censures Card. de Turrecremata for omitting here
the word "statim."   The word makes no difference as to the
meaning ; for the "forthwith" is in fact contained in the

For of this may be understood what is written in 2 Kings,
'' Immediately she was sanctified from her uncleanness,' i.e.
from original fault.   But it must be understood that this feast
ought not to be referred to the Conception of the Bl. Mary,
which was from the flesh, since no one, conceived from human
seed, was ever free from original sin, ' not even an infant of one
day, if his life shall be upon the earth.'   Whence also Augustine on John says, ' Who is innocent,' i.e. from the stain of original sin, ' except Christ, Who was not conceived of mortality ? '
And he adds, ' All come from that root and from that stock,
of which David says, " I was conceived in iniquities, and in sins
did my mother nourish me." '·   For when David said this of
himself, he excused no one conceived of human seed.   Yet the
Bl. V., by special privilege of God, was fully sanctified in the
womb of her mother.   And this is declared when it is said,
' Of the aromas of myrrh and frankincense, and all the odours
of the spiceman ;' for as the aromas, placed under coals, trans-
mute the evil of the smoke, so that the smoke which was before
hurtful, before the placing of the aromas thereon, after they
have been placed, is odoriferous and comforting, so the stain
of original sin transmitted to her with her mortal life was, by
the grace of sanctification, absorbed [9]."

The Collect referred to the sanctification of the
Conception, not to the Conception, as though this
were in itself immaculate.

"[9] Grant to us, we beseech Thee, Almighty and merciful
God, that we, who commemorate the sanctification of the
Conception of the B. Mary, Ever-Virgin, in the womb of her
mother, wrought by Thee, may, by aid of her merit and inter-

---

history of Bathsheba, which is mystically explained of it.
MSS., however, may have varied.

[7] 2 Sam. xi. 4.

[8] Transcribed by Alva, n. 231, in correction of Turrecremata's.

[9] l. c.

cessions, be found worthy to rejoice with Thee without end in heaven."

Turrecremata prefaces his · extracts by the words,—

"The most famous Church of Gironne, in the kingdom of Catalonia, professeth the faith most manifestly in the Office which it sings yearly in the Feast of the Sanctification of the Conception of the B. V., in whose Feast the whole Office, which is put together from authorities of Holy Scripture and sayings of Aug., Jerome, and other saints, alike in the little chapters, the responsories, the hymns, and the orison, say that she was sanctified from original sin, to which she had been subjected."

The whole, although an insulated case, is the more remarkable, as occurring in Spain.

The other office, which Card. Turrecremata mentions, as chanted "[1] in many parts of Germany," coincides with what we have found in Theologians, the belief that the B. V. was sanctified in her mother's womb, but that the consequences of original sin still continued, until extinguished by the overshadowing of the Holy Ghost at the Incarnation.

"[2] Also, what the Church chants in many parts of Germany, in the Feast of S. Elizabeth (as ancient Breviaries attest), whose Matin Office in the lessons is as follows :"—

---

[1] I quoted this in my " Eirenicon," " in the office then used in Germany in the Feast of Elizabeth." Perrone says in the same way, " Officium in Germania receptum " (De Imm. B.V. Conc. i. 15. 3. Pareri. p. 425). I had not then access to Turr.'s exact words.

[2] l. c. Alva, n. 231.

"Who shall find a strong woman? Far and from the
utmost bounds is her price. Ingushing in the senses of man
the ancient streams of corruption and fault, it pours itself
more in the weaker vessels [*], according to that, 'One man out
of a thousand have I found, a woman in all those have I not
found.' 'One,' i.e. Christ, one out of a thousand, generated
without the fomes. Of Whom Jeremiah saith, 'The Lord
shall do a new thing upon the earth.' 'But a woman out of
all have I not found.' For the Bl. Virgin, though full of
grace, was born with the fomes, which yet the virtue of the
Most Highest extinguished at the very time of the Conception of Christ, according to that, 'The Holy Ghost shall
supervene into thee, and the virtue of the Most Highest
shall overshadow thee.' For the refrigeration of this overshadowing repelled from her the incentive of the whole
fomes."

Besides these specific Breviaries, Turrecremata
claims the authority of a much wider practice, as
evidenced in the Office of the *Nativity* of the B. V.
He introduces the citations from them thus :—

"To the same effect seems to be the profession of the
Universal Church, which commonly on the Day of the Nativity
of the most Bl. Virgin in many Churches diffused throughout
the world, among the matin lessons, mentions at the beginning
that of Bernard on the Feast of her Assumption (as quoted
above), viz. that 'it is altogether clear that the Bl. Virgin was
cleansed from original contagion,' from which it clearly follows
that she was at one time subject to it. Whence the Universal
Church, using these words of the Bl. Bernard in the aforesaid
Feast, seems to canonize the doctrine of the Bl. Bernard in this
matter; whose doctrine most manifestly containeth that the
Conception of the B. V. was in original sin, as is manifest
above by manifold testimony."

---

[*] "Masculis," in De Alva, is a mistake for the "vasculis"
in Turr.

Clement VI., A.D. 1339, while yet Cardinal and
Archbishop of Rouen[4], allowing that the Blessed
Virgin certainly "had original sin in the cause," and
leaving it an open question whether she had it "in
form" also, says, that in either case, the festival of the
Conception might be celebrated, since those too who
held that she was, in form also, in original sin, believe that she was soon sanctified. In the opinion,
then, of this Cardinal, who some five years afterwards was elected Pope, the festival of the Conception did not necessarily involve its immaculateness.

"[5] But before I divide the theme, it seemeth that that Conception ought not to be celebrated, first, on the authority of
Bernard, who, in his Epistle to the Lyonnese [canons], gravely
reprehends them, because they had received the feast and held
it solemnly. Because no feast ought to be celebrated, except
for reverence of the sanctity of the person as to whom it is
celebrated, since such honour is shown to saints on account of
the [relation] which they have to God above others; but this
is on account of holiness; and not actual sin only, but original
sin also [separates[6]] from God. But the B.V. was conceived
in original sin, as many saints seem to say, and may be proved
by many grounds. It seems that the Church ought not to
hold a festival of her Conception. Here, being unwilling to
dispute, I say briefly that one thing is clear, that the B.V.
contracted original sin in the cause. The cause and reason is
this, that, as being conceived from the coming together of man

---

[4] He is so entitled in the Jesus College MS., which contains
this and some other of his sermons.

[5] In a sermon, "Signa erunt in sole." I have filled out De
Bandelis' citation here and there from the Jesus Coll. MS.

[6] The word in the Jesus Coll. MS. is "designat," which
must be an error.

and woman, she was conceived through passion, and therefore she had original sin in the cause, which her Son had not, because He was not conceived of seed of man, but through the mystic breathing (Luke i.), 'The Holy Spirit shall come upon thee.' And therefore not to have original sin is a singular privilege of Christ Alone. But whether she had 'in form' original sin, or was by Divine virtue preserved, there are different opinions among Doctors. But however it was, I say, that if, in form and not in cause only, she had original sin, we may still very reasonably keep festival of her Conception, supposing that, according to all most opposed, it was but a little hour that she was in original sin, because according to all she was sanctified as soon as she could be sanctified."

So far from the celebration of the Festival of the Conception of the B.V. involving necessarily any belief that her Conception was Immaculate, Clement XI., so late as the beginning of last century, expressly guarded himself against the supposition, that, in enjoining the observation of the Festival, he meant to rule any thing about the controversy. In his Constitution on the Feast of the Conception, Dec. 6, 1708, "Cujus Conceptio gaudium annunciavit universo mundo," lest any should think that he meant "ipso facto" to define the controverted article, he does not call it "the feast of the Immaculate Conception of the Blessed Virgin Mary," but "the feast of the Conception of herself, the Blessed Mary Virgin, Immaculate" [i.e. he so framed the sentence', that the word "Immaculate" could not be united with Con-

' This was pointed out by Card. Gotti, in his "La vera Chiesa," against G. Picenino (De Inv. Sanct.) n. 83.

ception.   He said, not "festum Conceptionis immaculatæ B. M. Virginis," but "festum Conceptionis ipsius B. M. Virginis immaculatæ "].   Lambertini (Benedict XIV.), who quotes him, adds,—

"*Nay, when that Bull was printed in a certain city of·
Italy with the title, 'That the Feast of the Immaculate Conception of the Bl. Mary,' &c., that great Pontiff vehemently
complained of it, and, on Oct. 12, 1789, commanded the
Ordinary of the place sharply to reprehend those who had that
Bull printed with a falsified title, and commanded that it, so
printed, should be suppressed and prohibited from appearing."

Bellarmine, who piously believed the Immaculate
Conception, still asserts that it was "not the *chief*
foundation of the Festival."

"*The chief foundation of this festival is not the Immaculate
Conception of her who was to be the Mother of God.   For
whatsoever that Conception may have been, from the very fact
that it was the Conception of the Mother of God, the memory
of it bringeth singular joy to the world.   For then first had we
the certain pledge of redemption, especially since, not without

---

* De Fest. Christi et B. M. V., ii. 15, p. 472.
* De Cultu Sanctt. iii. 16.   Bellarmine adds, "There is a
great difference between the Mother of God and His forerunner, and between the conception of each.   For since the
greater part of the Church piously believe the Immaculate
Conception, the same Church had an occasion for instituting
this festival, which occasion it had not to institute a festival
on the Conception of John Baptist."   But the *present* belief
(1586) of the [Roman] Church accounts for the spread
of the Festival, not for its institution.   It would be also
to argue in a circle : "the Church's belief in the Imm. Conc.
was a ground of its institution," and "the Institution of the
Festival proves its immaculateness."

a miracle, was she conceived of a barren mother. So then they too, who believe that the Virgin was conceived in sin, celebrate this festival."

In answer to the objection, " In this way the Conception of John Baptist too could be celebrated," Bellarmine answers,—

"It could, as the Greeks do. For in the Greek Calendar, on the 23rd of September, there is marked ' The feast of the Conception of John Baptist.' But the Latin Church did not see good to multiply so many festivals."

In 1679, Natalis Alexander, Dominican,— in answer to the objection that " The Church maintained the Immaculate Conception of the B.V. as a dogma of faith, to which, however, the consent of the Fathers is opposed; therefore the consent of the Fathers does not prove that any thing is to be believed with divine faith,"—denied that the Church had laid down that it was so; and, in regard to the celebration of the festival, he answered,—

" [1] The Feast of the Conception does not prove the immunity of the B.V. from original sin in the beginning of her Conception. For the Feast of the Conception of S. John Baptist is inserted in the old martyrologies, the Roman, Usuard's, and Adon's; and yet he was not conceived without the stain of original sin : and the Conception of the B.V. is celebrated, not on account of its own holiness, but on account of the holiness and dignity of the person conceived, who was predestined in eternity and conceived in time, to be the Mother of God. On which dignity all her privileges are founded, and in regard to which all those graces and prerogatives are ordered, and especially that purity, than which none greater under God can be conceived."

---

[1] Hist. Eccl. Sæc. ii. Diss. xvi. § 21, p. 488.

On the Office for the Conception by L. Noga-
rellus, which was approved by Sixtus IV., he
says,—

> "It was approved by Sixtus IV., not as an evidence of faith,
> but as a testimony and profession of piety; but was judged by
> Pius V. unworthy to be read in the Church, as being entirely
> made up of fictitious authorities from the Fathers and eccle-
> siastical testimonies, which, moreover, were nowhere found in
> their works; nor did it meet the mind of the Church : where-
> fore this holy Pontiff suppressed it.   But now in the office of the
> Roman Church, there is not the slightest word [verbulum]
> whereby the Immaculate Conception of the B.V. is indicated."

IV. In regard to any authority from Holy Scripture for the Immaculate Conception, I referred, in
my "Eirenicon," but very briefly to what Perrone
speaks of as the only Scriptural ground[2] of the Immaculate Conception, the "Protevangelium," where,
according to the present Vulgate, the crushing of
the serpent's head is ascribed immediately and
directly to the woman, "she shall bruise thy head,"

[2] "The chief and almost unique testimony [produced by the
supporters of the Imm. Conc.] you may say to be Gen. iii. 14,
15. The other passages of the Bible which are wont to be
brought for the pious opinion from the O. T. especially, touch
thereon only in the mystical sense, and have their whole force
either from the exposition of Doctors, or from the use of the
Church, which is wont to accommodate to the B.V. not a few
texts, which in their literal and proper sense are said of Divine
Wisdom or of the Divine Word. But much less can those be
urged which are taken from types and figures. For although
they are nowise to be despised by a Catholic, yet they are un-
suited to the object which I have proposed to myself, to inquire
as to the foundations for a dogmatic definition."   P. 1. c. 9.
pp. 365, 368.

for "It," or "He shall bruise thy head." The
argument, as you know, is, that, "if the woman
were to crush the head of the serpent or Satan, it
is inconceivable that she should for a moment, by
original sin, have been subject to him." Now, in
this argument there is, I think, a good deal of
exaggeration [3]. For the question among those who
wrote on that Conception came to be, not at all as
to the responsible being, after she was born into
this world, but as to the fœtus existing, soul and
body, in its mother's womb, yet not having, as far as
we know, consciousness, or will, or any capacity of
good or evil. To have consciousness in the Virgin's
womb, used to be treated of as a special prerogative
of our Lord, because He was not Man only, but
God [4]. In S. Bernard's time, or before, it was

[3] De Turrecremata mentions incidentally in his work the
"declamation," the exaggerated and sometimes coarse (f. 201)
language, used by the maintainers of the Imm. Conc., to
describe what they held to be involved in the doctrine which
they opposed ; as, that the B. V. had been " the dwelling-place
of the demon, the captive of hell, the slave of devils, the handmaid of the devil " (f. 234 v.,—236 v.), or that "she was
odious and hated by God " (f. 272 v.), "infected with malice "
(f. 273). He speaks of these revilings (convicia) as being the
chief arguments on that side (ib.). He says (f. 201), that
"such terms ought not to have been used by those who, by the
most sacred constitution of the sacred Council, were appointed
to inquire into the truth, not to inveigh, and provoke the minds
of the simple, by certain (salva pace) false witnesses, since
they who say that she was subject to original sin, do not say
that," &c.

[4] Vazquez (in 3 P. q. 27, cc. 3, 4) and Suarez (in 3 P. q. 27,

granted that, from the first moment of her existence on this earth, the B.V. was free from original
sin, having been cleansed from it in her mother's
womb.   At a later time, some, who yet maintained
the transmission of original sin to her, as having
been naturally descended from Adam, minimized
the time in which she remained under it as much
as possible.   They felt themselves bound by the
tradition which they had received, to hold that she
had not been exempted from it, but conceived that
she was freed from it in her mother's womb at the
earliest possible period consistent with her having,
by the law of her conception, contracted it at all.
The language, then, of maintainers of the Immaculate Conception does seem to me exaggerated,
when they say, that if conceived in original sin,
she was "under the power of the devil," because
of this momentary interval, in which the unborn
and, as far as we know, unconscious being was
conceived with that taint, from which God, it was
held, freed her immediately.   We should not speak
of S. John Baptist or Jeremiah as having been

sectt. 7, 8) hold " that the B. V. had the use of reason from the
beginning of her Conception, and supernatural knowledge ; and
that her sanctification was wrought through an act of her own
free-will, loving God above all things, through the grace given
to her."   This they ground on the miracle wrought on John
Baptist in his mother's womb, whereby, at the presence of
Jesus, he "leaped for joy " (arguing that more would be given
to the Mother of the Lord) ; and Suarez also, on the authority
of S. Bernardine.

under the power of the devil; as many, at least, as
believe that they were sanctified in their mothers'
wombs; and yet in them no one doubts that what
to us who, by infant-Baptism, are freed from the
guilt of original sin, is the heaviest consequence
of it, viz. "that the flesh lusteth contrary to the
spirit," remained.

However, if the "Protevangelium" is to prove
that she personally bruised the serpent's head, it
must be that this is said of her personally, as it
would be if the reading of the Vulgate were
right, "ipsa conteret caput tuum." I referred
before, as in a very simple matter, to the authority
of the great Roman Catholic critic, De Rossi;
and now, since his book is not in every one's
hands, I will set down his arguments in proof
that the reading "ipsa" is wrong. I would only
premise that, whereas in languages in which the
gender of the pronoun is marked and not that
of the verb, the question necessarily turns on the
pronoun, not on the verb; contrariwise in Hebrew,
the question turns on the verb only, it being one
of the observed archaisms of the Pentateuch; that
הוא, the masculine form, is used of the feminine
also. But although הוא might represent alike
"ipse" or "ipsa," yet when joined with a masculine
verb, ישופך, no one who knows any thing of Hebrew
could doubt that it ought to be rendered "he" or
"it," not "she." To turn, however, to De Rossi's
summary:—

B b

"'Few, doubtful and altogether unreliable are the Hebrew MSS. in support of it (היא), in which *yod* is perhaps a little *vau* (י for ו) and with shurek or the vowel of the masculine: uncertain and deviating from the reliableness of all the rest is that Greek (whether interpreter or scholiast), perhaps only indicating the reading of Latin MSS. or some Father: solitary and to be set aside is that copy of Onkelos. The reading of the Vulgate, though much better supported, is not yet sufficiently certain, on account of the dissent of the MSS. and Jerome; nor is it of any certain, but rather of altogether doubtful and even (as we shall see below) suspected origin, so that it is rather to be accounted among the errors in that version; and the most learned expositors and critics among Catholics so in fact account it.

"But for the masculine הוא there stand—1) the consent and testimony of almost all Hebrew MSS.; 2) the analogy of the sacred context, in which the verb which follows and the pronoun suffixed are masculine; 3) the Samaritan text and Samaritan version; 4) the Greek version of the LXX., all the MSS. Editions and Versions derived from it, Ethiopic, Coptic, and old Latin, and those who used it, whether Greek-speaking Jews, as Philo, or Christian writers, agreeing; 5) all the Chaldee paraphrases, Onkelos, Jonathan, and the Jerusalem; 6) all the other Versions of the East, the oldest Syriac, the Arabic of Saadias, the Mauritanian Arabic of Erpenius, the Persian of Tawos; 7) some MSS. of the Vulgate, as the Oblong of S. Germain and the Correctorium Sorbonicum, Stephen's Biblia, Paris, 1540 and 1546, ad marg., the Biblia Lovan. of Henten, and the *Notationes* of Lucas Brugensis—Lindanus adds four Louvain MSS., and I doubt not that others would coincide, if there should be a fresh and more accurate collation of Latin MSS. on the place; 8) many editions of the Vulgate on the margin, before those of Sixtus and Clement; 9) the pure version of Jerome in the *Bibliotheca Divina*, edited by the Benedictines of S. Maur, Opp. T. 1; 10) Jerome, who, besides his version, reads *Ipse* in his Quæstt. Heb., on Ezek. xlvii, on

---

* Varr. Lectt. Vet. Test. Vol. iv. App. pp. 208, 209.

Isa. lviii; 11) Irenæus [iv. 40; v. 21], Cyprian [Test. ii. 9], Lucifer Calaritanus [Bibl. P. iv. 182], Chrysostomus [Hom. xvii. in Gen. n. 7, Opp. iv. 143.], Petrus Chrysologus [Bibl. Patr. vii. 976. H.], Eucherius [B. P. vi. 834, H.], Procopius Gazæus [ad loc. p. 70], S. Leo [Serm. ii. in Nat. Dom. p. 67], also Moses Bar Cepha [De Paradiso, P. i. cap. 28, p. 157, ed. Mas.], S. Ephr. Syr. [ad loc.], and all the Fathers who used the Greek or Syriac; 12) lastly, the masculine reading is better, by which the bruising of the serpent is ascribed immediately and alone to the Seed of the woman, and from which the redemption, power, Divinity of the Messiah are plainly elicited.

"Which original authorities and witnesses, being most exceedingly grave and insurmountable, evidently demonstrate that the true reading of the sacred text is הוא, *hu, ipse, ipsum :* and countless Catholic authors, both before and since the Council of Trent, follow this reading as the truer, and prefer it to the feminine."

He enumerates thirty-five, refers to "others" generally, adding that the words of most of them, and the places where they occur, are given by Coster[6] and Natalis Alexander[7]. De Rossi sums up,—

"[8] To whomsoever, then, the present reading of the Vulgate belongs, whether to the interpreter, or (which is more probable) to the amanuensis, it ought to be amended from the Hebrew and Greek fountain-heads, and to be referred (as I have said formerly, 'De præcipuis causis negl. hebr. litt.' p. 94) to those passages of the Clementine edition, which yet can and ought to be conformed to the Hebrew text, and to be amended by the authority of the Church."

---

[6] Vindex loci Gen. iii. 15 c. xi.
[7] Hist. Eccl. Diss. xl. T. viii. p. 271.
[8] l. c. p. 211.

Perrone, indeed, would have it "that it is all one, whether you read ipsa, or ipse, or ipsum," [i. e. whether it is foretold that the B.V., or Christ, or the Seed of the woman should bruise the serpent's head]—

"*For since the woman, not by her own power, but by the merits of her Son, was to bruise the head of the serpent or the devil, if it shall be read *ipsa*, it is to be understood 'through Him,' i. e. the Seed, or the Son; but if *ipse* or *ipsum*, the meaning will be, that the Son or Seed of the woman, *together with the woman*, should bruise the head of the serpent or the devil. But analogy seems rather to favour the woman than the Seed; or, if any prefer it, to both together; so that the woman with her Seed, i. e. her Son, was to triumph over the devil and sin."

But the text speaks of none but " the Seed of the woman." It speaks of our Lord's direct and personal crushing of the serpent's head. He was " the Seed of the woman;" but the crushing is ascribed, not to her, nor to Him in conjunction with her, but to Him Alone. The argument, then, for the Immaculate Conception, derived from the passage, being, that " She who was said to crush Satan could never have been, for a moment, even in her mother's womb, under original sin;" the major premiss of the argument is gone, when it appears that nothing is said here of any personal victory of hers. It was God Incarnate, not any mere human being, Who crushed our enemy, though, thereafter, He has and shall crush him under our feet also.

* Imm. Conc. P. i. c. 9 (Pareri, pp. 366, 367).

V. There is yet one Patristic evidence of Perrone,
which has seemed to you too, my dear friend, satisfactory as to the one side of original sin, the transmission
of the guilt, viz. the parallel drawn by some of the
Fathers between the Blessed Virgin and Eve. I cannot (although I should wish to do so) see its force. It
was, indeed, part of God's marvellous condescension
in our redemption, that since man and woman,
our first parents, fell, He willed to give to both a
place in our redemption, in that He who was
" Very God " became " Very Man," and was, as
Holy Scripture emphasizes it, " born of a woman."
And this He did, first engracing *her*, of whom He
vouchsafed to be born.   The quotations which you
give from the Fathers, are most valid against *that*,
which you somehow thought that I held, that " the
Blessed Virgin was only a physical instrument in
our redemption."   And, of course, she could be a
" moral instrument " only through Divine grace.
But then we must not, I think, stretch the parallel
drawn by the Fathers beyond what they themselves
say.   Nay, contrariwise, their agreement up to a
certain point, and their uniform omission of something which lies beyond that point, seems to me to
imply, that they had not that other point in their
minds.   If they had had it, why should no one
of them have expressed it?   The correspondence
indeed between S. Justin, S. Irenæus, Tertullian,
is so exact, that I cannot but think here (what
in some other points I have been obliged, some

time since, against my will, to think), that they are
not independent witnesses, but that S. Irenæus had
seen S. Justin's works, Tertullian, those of one or
both of his predecessors.   All three insist on these
points of correspondence or of contrast; that each,
Eve and Mary, was a virgin; that the one believed
the serpent, the other the Angel; the one was
disobedient, the other obedient : through the one
came death, through the other life, in that, on her
faith and obedience she bare God within her, the
Author of life.   And in these points, the other
Fathers agree with more or less of fulness; S. Cyril
of Jerusalem, S. Ephraim, S. Epiphanius, S. Augustine, S. Peter Chrysologus, S. Fulgentius of Ruspe.
But then, it is even remarkable that while, as you
say, these Fathers dwell on the graces of the Blessed
Virgin, her faith, joy, obedience, graces of a soul
pre-eminent in grace, not one has the most distant
allusion to the question, *when* that eminent sanctification began in her.   They set her before us, in
that moment of her life for which God created her,
when Eve's disobedience and our curse were about
to be undone through her obedience, and she was
to become, to herself and to the whole human race,
the cause of salvation by becoming the Mother of
the Saviour.   How she became fitted for that
office, they are as silent as Scripture itself.   They
betoken a traditional parallel between Eve and
Mary, in those points, wherein they contrast them;
they imply an entire unconsciousness of any other

parallel; and the minuteness of the one series of parallels or contrasts makes it almost certain that they would have added that of their being, in their first and earliest origin,—the first moment, not of birth, or of conscious existence, but in the first original of their being,—alike free from original sin, alike clothed in that original righteousness, had they inherited the belief from the Apostles or from the Blessed Virgin herself. Nay more, the context rather implies that, up to the Incarnation, the full effects of Eve's disobedience continued, of which the transmission of original sin was the centre and the mainspring.

I intended nothing less, when I began this letter, than such an investigation as this, which I have now concluded. Yet it seemed to me to be for the interest of truth, to have the whole case before us. What I desire is, such an explanation of the doctrine as we could receive, made authoritatively. I trust that, in some way or other, one side of the doctrine only has been presented in the Bull "Ineffabilis." And in order to obtain some such explanation, I have put the difficulty in regard to the tradition in its full force. To some of your controversialists this will seem simply polemical. They will think it a mere contumacious re-opening of the question, decided for the Roman Communion by the tacit acquiescence in the Bull "Ineffabilis."

Others, I hope, will see that what I have written has a twofold aspect. Among my own people, it will tend to lead many to think upon a subject, which does not ordinarily occupy their thoughts. And reflection will, I think, bring them to believe, what was believed on this subject by S. Bonaventura. For no one, who thinks, can well doubt that as much (if not more) was vouchsafed to the Mother of his Redeemer, as was granted to Jeremiah or S. John Baptist. Since then they were, according to Holy Scripture, sanctified in their mother's womb, it is intrinsically probable that so was the Blessed Virgin, because she had a nearness to our Lord, such as no other created being could have. Although then (as some of the older of those who maintain it say) not stated in Holy Scripture, it seems almost involved in the belief as to Jeremiah and S. John Baptist, which is so contained. It will, I trust, be a gain to our own people, to have had the subject thus brought before them, since the very dwelling on the negative side,—the difficulties as to the Immaculate Conception,—brings with it a necessity of dwelling on the positive side, the greatness of the Blessed Virgin herself, the wondrousness of the graces vouchsafed to her, the probability of her exemption from actual sin. The question itself was brought down almost to a point by the later Schoolmen; but that point involved the whole doctrine of the transmission of original sin, whether it were transmitted to all

who were conceived in the natural way of our disordered nature. The tradition on this subject
constitutes the difficulty, that it is so often stated,
in such a long tradition, that Christ Alone was
born without sin, because He Alone was born by a
Virgin-birth. Other grounds, that the Blessed
Virgin, unless born in original sin, would not be of
the number of Christ's redeemed, would not have
needed redemption, are met in that Bull, which
affirms that she was exempted "on the ground of
the foreseen merits of Christ." If it could be laid
down by authority, that all which was meant by
the Bull was, that "to the Blessed Virgin grace
came, not three months merely before her birth,
[as to S. John Baptist] but from the first moment
of her being, as it had been given to Eve," much
misgiving as to the doctrine would cease.

Difficulty would still remain as to the tradition,
what the Fathers did mean by all that concurrent
testimony. Your Divines, as well as ours, are
interested in the maintenance of the "quod ubique, quod semper, quod ab omnibus." It is a great
principle of fixity amid fleeting opinions and heresies. It is the very principle, stringently laid
down in the Tridentine doctrine of Tradition.
Antecedently to the decision, several of your
Bishops expressed themselves concerned, lest the
value of that principle should be endangered. The
facts remain as before, and need explanation as
before. Such concordant testimony must have a

solid meaning. It will not meet the exigencies of
the case, to state simply that they do not contradict the Bull "Ineffabilis." Members of the
Roman Communion must have full confidence as
to this. But the question is, *in what way* it does
not. It does not, I think, meet the case, to say that
the writers were speaking generally only, as to what
the Blessed Virgin *would have been* subject to,
had she not been exempted. For they are speaking, not of principles, but of facts, why our Lord
only *was* conceived without sin. The prerogative
of the Blessed Virgin, according to some, has a
relation to that of her Divine Son; that as He
Alone, of all human sons, was conceived without sin
in Him, so she was the only mother who conceived
one without sin,—not of her own, for conception,
sanctified by grace, has no sin in the parents, but—
sin transmitted to the child.

Some, indeed, of your Bishops (with all respect
to them) made short work of the Vincentian rule.
To them it seemed sufficient evidence of an Apostolic tradition, that the doctrine was (though without the direct authority of the Church) taught
every where at that time. They held that this
agreement of its priests in teaching the doctrine
so committed the Church, that, if the doctrine
were only a pious opinion, not a certain truth, the
Church would be involved in error, if her separate
and individual teachers taught it as certain truth.
In the old terms. of Vincentius, the "quod ubi-

que" and "quod semper" ceased to be two concurrent marks of genuine traditions.   According
to these Bishops, in order to establish that any
belief rested on genuine tradition, it needed not to
show that it had been "always" taught: it suf-
ficed that it should be taught, at this moment,
"every where" in the Roman communion.   In
their minds, the "quod ubique" in itself involved
the "quod semper."   Others, of a stricter school,
insisted on the necessity that, for any thing which
should be constituted an Article of Faith, there
should be evidence that it had "always" been
taught.   They, like our own Divines, required the
"quod semper" as well as the "quod ubique,"
and, thus far, agreed with us.   This was laid down
with great clearness, among others, by the Bishop
of Cervia; "That saying of Vincent of Lerins
must move me, received as a rule by *all* Theologians and constantly observed, whenever it was
the question of distinguishing or defining dogmas
of faith, 'what was always, every where, by all,
received as a dogma of faith, and has been believed
till now.'   Every Catholic dogma, being a fact
manifest to us by Divine revelation, can neither
be known or proved, save by the Word of God,
written or handed down; and since God could,
either expressly or implicitly, by Scripture or tradition, reveal a truth unattainable by human intellect or reason, the Church never proposes as a
dogma to be received and believed by all under

pain of anathema or heresy, unless it be contained
explicitly, or at least implicitly, in the Word of
God, written or handed down. But some Theologians contend that this could scarcely be affirmed
as to the proposed truth. For had it been expressly or implicitly revealed in Scripture or tradition, how should older Fathers and Doctors,
Theologians, and the whole order of Dominicans,
and the whole school of the Thomists, not only be
ignorant of it, but venture with all their might
and vehement abundance of argument to assail it,
the Supreme Pontiffs conniving, or at least not
condemning as heretics those who for many ages
opposed with their whole strength the Conception
immaculate at the first instant [1] ? "

---

[1] Pareri ii. 217, 218. "Eirenicon," pp. 388, 389. The same
argument from the "quod semper," or the absence of tradition,
was used by the late Archbishop of Paris (Pareri ii. 26. Dub.
1, 2, 4. Eiren. p. 354) ; the late Abp. of Rouen (Par. i. 357.
Eir. p. 360) ; the late Bp. of Coutances ("could with the
greatest difficulty be derived from Holy Scripture or tradition,"—Par. i. 363. Eir. p. 362) ; the Bp. of Evreux (Par. i. 101.
Eir. p. 363) ; the Archbishop of Bourges, agreeing with his
Theologians (Par. i. 498. Eir. p. 368) ; the Abp. of Cham-
béry (Par. i. 411. Eir. p. 370) ; "the more erudite in Germany,"
reported by the Abp. of Bamberg (Par. ii. 59. Eir. p. 371) ;
the Abp. of Salzburg, as "an opinion fixed in the minds of
very many" (Par. i. 326. Eir. p. 374) ; the Bp. of Adria
(Par. i. 317. Eir. p. 385) ; the Bp. of Mondovi doubted (iii. 144.
Eir. p. 385) ; Bp. of Majorca at length (Par. ii. 157, sqq.
Eir. p. 392, sqq.) ; Bp. of Lugo (ii. 98. Eir. p. 396) ; "learned
theologians " quoted by Bp. of Iaca (Par. i. 480. Eir. p. 397) ;
some alluded to by the Bp. of Santander (Par. i. 424, 425.

So many and grave Bishops also held this conviction,—that in order to prove a tradition to be
Apostolic, it was requisite that the evidence should
be traceable, and that it did not suffice that it
should be taught at this moment "every where"
in the Roman Catholic Church,—that the rule of
Vincentius still, I suppose, has its supporters.

You say, that the difficulty lies in the difference
between the Catholic and Protestant doctrine of
original sin. I hope it may prove so. For then it
will not lie with us. The doctrine, as it has been
stated or applied by the writers whom I have
quoted so largely, comes to this, that the soul is
infected with original sin by its union with the
body, when conceived in the way of nature, which
(however good and pure the parents were) is inseparable from concupiscence of nature; that, before the soul is infused into the body (whenever
that infusion may take place), there is neither good
nor evil, for there is only an irrational substance,
incapable of good or evil; that original sin is contracted in the infusion of the rational soul; that it
is transmitted to all who were in Adam, according
to the "ratio seminalis," and are conceived in the

Eir. pp. 398, 399); the Bp. of Chiapo, quoting Suarez,
S. Thomas, Pétau, (Par. T. ix. App. i. 19, 20. Eir. pp. 399,
400); Vic. Ap. of Mysore (Par. iii. 353. Eir. p. 401); V. Ap.
of Coimbatore (iii. 354, 355. Eir. pp. 402, 403); V. A. of
Constantinople (Par. i. 266. Eir. p. 136); V. A. of Patna
doubtful (Par. ii. 385. Eir. p. 137).

way of our disordered nature. S. Thomas distinguished, further, the material and formal causes of original sin ; the formal, upon which you have chiefly dwelt, viz. "the privation of original righteousness, it being incumbent upon us to have it;" and the material, viz. "concupiscence, or the inordination of the soul," to which you allude under the term, "the consequences of that deprivation." Our Article contains the same doctrine as to its transmission, "of every man, that naturally is engendered of the offspring of Adam ;" it states the loss of "original righteousness;" but it dwells chiefly on that, with which we, who are baptized, have alone to do, the *phronema sarkos*, the concupiscence, which "remains in us who are regenerated." Ever since I have been acquainted with the Council of Trent, I have been convinced that the doctrine stated in our Articles, while it is opposed to that of Luther and Calvin, virtually agrees with that of the Council of Trent, in that it presents only a different aspect of the same truth. For our Article which states that "the concupiscence, which remains in the regenerate, has *in itself* the nature of sin," is clearly at variance with statements, which were the object of the condemnation of the Council of Trent, such as, that "[1] sin is of the essence of man;" or more strongly, that

---

[1] Luth. in Gen. iii. quoted by Möhler, Symbol. i. 6. p. 72 [p. 84 Eng. Tr.].

"'the essence of man is sin;" that "'the nature of man is to sin," "'man himself is sin;" that " original sin is that very thing which is born of father and mother;" that "'the conception and the growth and the accretion of man, while he is in his mother's womb and is not yet born, before we altogether become human beings', —that is, all, one with another, sin;" that "man, as he is born of his father and mother, to-gether with his whole nature and essence, is not only a sinner, but sin itself;" or that "'concu-piscence' [the Patristic word adopted in our Articles] was not so very alien a word, if only it were added (which is not allowed by most: viz., Catholics) that whatever is in man is sin, that from the intellect to the will, from the soul to the flesh, he is stained and filled with this concu-piscence." But our Article only presents a dif-ferent aspect of the doctrine of Trent. The Council had to condemn the error of Luther, that concupiscence was *truly and properly sin;* but plainly it would not have used the term "*truly and properly* sin," unless it had held that it had something of sin about it. The English Church, on the other hand, would not have used the words,

---

' Sayings of Luther, collected and excused by Quenstedt, Theol. did. polem. P. ii. pp. 134, 135, Witt. 1669, quoted by Möbler. Ib. p. 74 [p. 86 Eng. Tr.].

' Der 51 Ps. P. ii. Witt. 1539, German by G. Major.

' "Ehe wir rechte Menschen sind."

' Calv. Inst. ii. 1. 8, Ib. p. 62 [108 Eng. Tr.].

"the nature of sin," had it meant that it was "truly sin '."

But I know that our people have not observed the expression, "deprivation" (viz. "of that supernatural unmerited grace which Adam and Eve had on their creation") "and *its conse-quences*;" and hence they have thought your statements of original sin novel (at least of late years) and inadequate. They would not have thought so, had they remembered the words of the Council of Trent, which condemns, under anathema, "any who does not confess that the whole Adam was changed for the worse in body and soul," and that "this sin of Adam, which in origin is one, is transfused into all by propagation, not by imitation;" that "all men by the disobedi-ence of Adam lost innocence, being made unclean,

---

' "The Holy Synod confesses and is sensible, that in the baptized there *remains concupiscence*, or an incentive [fomes] (to sin), which, whereas it is left for our exercise, *cannot injure* those who consent not, but resist manfully by the grace of Jesus Christ; yea, he who shall have 'striven lawfully' shall be crowned. This concupiscence, which the Apostle some-times calls sin (Rom. vi. viii.), the holy Synod declares that the Catholic Church has never understood to be called sin, as being *truly and properly* sin in those born again, but because it is of sin, and inclines to sin." Conc. Trid. Sess. v. n. 5, p. 24 Waterw. Tr. "This infection of nature doth remain, yea, in them that are regenerated, whereby the lust of the flesh is not subject to the law of God. And although there is *no condemnation* for them that believe and are baptized, yet the Apostle doth confess, that concupiscence and lust hath, *in itself*, the nature of sin." Art. ix.

and, as the Apostle says, 'by nature children of wrath,' servants of sin and under the power of the devil and of death;" that "free will was not indeed extinguished in them, but was weakened and bound." For this you included under the words, "its consequences." For if Adam's sin had only involved the "deprivation of supernatural unmerited grace" (as these understood you to mean), then our re-creation in Christ would have entirely effaced the evil effects of the fall, since we are brought into a closer nearness to God, being made members of His Son, than Adam was, when invested with the robe of original righteousness.

While the transmission of original sin is certain, clear from Holy Scripture, from uniform Christian tradition, from nature itself, the mode of its transmission is, I believe, an inscrutable mystery, insoluble by man. The "privation of original righteousness" does not, by itself, account for all the phenomena. "Who," asks Möhler, "comprehends evil in itself? Who has ever penetrated that deep connexion between moral and physical evil? Who has explored the bands which unite body and soul? Who knows the relation of the sexes, and can tell what is life and the generation of life [a]?" Möhler points out the inadequacy of every attempt to solve it. Traducianism, i. e. the derivation of soul from soul, would have given an

[a] Symbolik, c. 2, § 5, p. 63.

easy solution. S. Augustine, while owning his ignorance, leant towards it, apparently on that ground.
The Church has held it to be too material.   On the
belief that each soul is created anew, and, of course,
created pure by God when He infuses it into the
body, Möhler points out the difficulties of the two
chief theories, either that,—1) "by the fall of Adam,
a destructive, infectious quality was introduced into
the body, which, propagated through generation,
seized on the soul at the moment of its union with
the body, drew it down to itself, and imparted disorder to it;" or,—2) " that fallen man, apart from
the hereditary guilt, was born just as Adam, considered without supernatural gifts, i. e. with all
natural properties, powers, and qualities of the
paradisaic man, as also without any quality in
itself evil;" and " that the evil of the corrupt condition in which man is now born, is to be regarded
as this, that in Adam he deserved to be deprived of
that righteousness, which was bestowed on him
through the supernatural gift of grace, i. e. to feel
the rebellion of the flesh against the spirit.   What
nature would have been, without the supernatural
gift of grace, *that* is, on account of the self-in-
curred loss of this gift, the punishment of all born
of Adam."

To the former, Möhler objects, that—

" Apart from the fact that the origination of a positive evil
quality is itself an enigma, nay inconceivable, this explanation
represented evil as something very material." " How," he

asks, "could the propagation of such a material poison impart
to the spirit the elements of all *that*, which constitutes self-
seeking in its whole vast compass—rebellion against God, pride
and envy towards men, vanity and self-complacency in himself?"

To the second he objects,—

"In that this theory does not explain and cannot explain
the perversity of will wherewith we are born, it too is unsatis-
factory. It speaks only of a conflict between the sensual and
the rational principle, which, without that which was Divine,
would have occurred as an event of nature. But the question,
above all others, is, to explain the wounds of the spirit, especially the perversity of the will. Would the spirit of man,
simply because it is an essence distinct from God, considered
in itself,—i. e. without the supernatural gift of grace,—as a
naked finite being, stand in that position over against God and
all which is holy, in which man is now born? Then would
man, as a finite being, be of himself inclined to sin, and he would
not first become so through misuse of his freedom. The
supernatural Divine principle can assuredly not have as its
destination, to remove the inclination, existing in man as a
creature, to opposition to its Creator, or rather merely to
hinder its coming to an outbreak. Through the absence of
this supernatural gift of grace, without which all are now
born, man is not as yet perverted in will: he may become so,
and will without doubt readily become so; but in the moment
of his formation he is not."

The two theories, then, appear to me to have
exactly the same difficulty; viz. how the soul,
created pure by God, should, in the first beginning
of its existence, before the use of reason, have in
itself the disposition to evil. A child, a few
months old, will wilfully bite the mother who is

nursing him[9].   What I thought to be the meaning
of those writers who dwell so much on concupiscence as the channel of the transmission of original sin, was, that the passion of nature which,
in consequence of Adam's sin, became, in some
degree (however sanctified by grace to the parents),
an absolutely necessary condition of the reproduction of our race, became also the means of
disordering the body and, through it, the soul.

Pope Innocent III. expresses this more concisely
in a work which he wrote, as a Deacon, the " De
Contemptu Mundi," than he did in one written
amid the cares and distractions of the Papacy[1],
his " Comment on the Penitential Psalms," in which,
however, he expands his former statement, writing,
as he hoped, " *Himself inspiring*, Whose Spirit
bloweth where It listeth."   It is the work of a

---

[9] Of course, such a child could not altogether know what it
was doing; yet he never did it when his mother's eye was on
him: he left off, when she again looked at him.

[1] He begins his Preface to his Commentary on the Penitential Psalms, " Lest, amid the manifold occupations and
vehement anxieties which I endure beyond my strength, not
only from the *cares of rule*, but also from the malice of the
times, I should be wholly swallowed up by the deep, I gladly
steal from myself some brief hours, wherein, in order to recall
my spirit to itself, lest it should be altogether divided and
alienated from itself, it may meditate something in the law of
the Lord, which may profit hereto, Himself inspiring, Whose
Spirit bloweth where It listeth, that I may not evermore be
so made over to others, as never to be restored to myself," &c.
Opp. i. 208.

remarkable Pope, who was elected at thirty-seven; and, although all good thoughts come from God's holy inspiration, such words, I suppose, make what is so written a somewhat formal teaching of the Pope. His object in the passage of the " De Contemptu Mundi" was to inspire humility, on the ground of the original of man. He supposes a person to think better of himself so far, in that he was not made directly of the dust, as Adam was. He answers,—

"[1] Yet *he* was formed from earth, but that, virgin earth; *thou* wert procreated from seed, but that unclean. For 'who can make that clean, which is conceived of unclean seed?' For 'what is man, that he should be spotless, or how should he appear righteous, who was born of a woman?' For 'behold, I was conceived in iniquities, and in sins did my mother conceive me.' Not in one iniquity only, nor in one delinquency only, but in many iniquities and in many delinquencies; in delinquencies and iniquities of mine own; in delinquencies and iniquities of others. For conception is twofold; one of seeds, the other of natures. The first takes place in [faults[2]] committed, the second takes place in [faults] con-

---

[1] De Contemptu Mundi, L. i. cc. 3, 4. T. i. p. 422.

[2] In his comment on Ps. li., where Innocent repeats the passage, nearly verbally, expanding it here and there, he words it, "The parents commit actual fault [actualem culpam] in the first, and the offspring contracts original fault [originalem] in the second; wherefore he says, For lo! 'I was conceived in iniquities,' which, in the conception of seeds, my parents committed; 'and my mother conceived me in delinquencies,' which, in the conception of nature, I myself contracted. Far be the thought, that it should be said on this occasion that David was conceived in adultery, since Jesse, his father, begat him of his lawful wife." T. i. p. 268.

tracted.   For the parents commit [fault] in the first; the
offspring contracts [original fault] in the second.   For who
knows not, that even conjugal concumbency is never altogether
committed 'sine pruritu carnis, sine fervore luxuriæ, sine
fœtore libidinis.'   Whence the seeds conceived are defiled,
stained, and vitiated; from which [seeds '] the soul, at length
infused, contracts the defilement of sin, the stain of fault, the
filth of iniquity; as from a corrupted vessel liquid poured in
is corrupted, and, coming in contact with what is polluted,
is polluted by the very contact. For the soul has three natural
powers—the rational, that it may discern between good and
evil; the irascible, that it may reject evil; the concupiscible,
that it may desire good.   Those three powers are corrupted in
the origin itself [originaliter] by three opposite vices.   The
reasoning power by ignorance, that it should not distinguish
between good and evil.   The irascible power by anger, that it
should reject good.   The concupiscible power by concupiscence,
that it should desire evil.   The first generates delinquency;
the last bringeth forth sin; the middle generates both delinquency and sin.   For delinquency is, not to do what ought to
be done; sin is, to do what is not to be done.   These three
faults are contracted from the corrupted flesh, through three
natural entanglements.   For in carnal intercourse, the percep-
tion of reason is laid asleep, so that ignorance should be propagated; the irritation of lust is stimulated, so that anger is
propagated; the feeling of pleasure is satiated, so that concupiscence is contracted.   This is the tyrant of the flesh, the

---

' "Ex quibus," the only antecedent being " seminibus."
On Ps. 51, it is "ex seminibus ergo fœdatis atque corruptis,
there is conceived a body in like way fouled and corrupted,
whereinto the soul at length infused is corrupted and fouled,
not from the integrity and cleanness which it had, but from
the integrity and cleanness which it would have, if it were not
united to a body fouled and corrupted, since it is both infused
by creating and created by infusing.   For as from a corrupted," &c. as in text.   Ib.

law of the members, the incentive of sin, the sickness of
nature, the nutriment of death, without which no one is born,
without which no one dies, which, if ever it passes away as to
guilt, yet ever remains in act. For 'if we say, that we have
no sin, we deceive ourselves, and the truth is not in us.'
Oh, heavy necessity, unhappy condition! Before we sin, we
are bound by sin; and before we fail [delinquimus], we are
held by delinquency. 'By one man sin entered into this
world, and through sin death passes upon all men.' 'Have
not the fathers eaten the sour grapes, and the children's teeth
are set on edge?'"

Perhaps this doctrine of Pope Innocent III.
would afford an easier and more natural solution
of much of the traditional language, than that of
the Scotists, that "original sin is *only* the absence
of original righteousness in those who ought to
have it." For, according to that doctrine, there
is nothing in the human being which has to be
remedied ; nothing which should make it other
than Almighty God originally willed it to be.
Almighty God has not, indeed, bestowed upon it
any gift to replace that gift of original righteousness which Adam forfeited for us; but neither
is there any scope for that gift, until the
child, being born, have a choice of good or evil.
There is nothing, according to this doctrine, inherent in the child itself ; and so, in the conception of the B.V., on this theory there was
nothing to be removed, but only a superadded gift
of grace to be added (analogous to the gift in
infant baptism) which should be equivalent to,
yea exceed as to Divine acceptance, that original

gift of righteousness. On the doctrine of Pope Innocent III., original sin did, in the language of Pope Clement VI., exist in the Blessed Virgin "in the cause;" and therefore, there was not only something from which she had to be "preserved," but something also which was to be removed from her inchoate being. This would allow a natural sense to be given to those expressions, "freed," "delivered," &c., which, as was noticed above by several writers, imply the actual existence of something from which she was delivered. It would allow also of a meaning to those many passages, in which the Fathers contrast the Virgin-Conception of her Son with her own, in that in His Conception there was no concupiscence, whereas in hers there was. For that doctrine of Innocent III. presupposes that, through that concupiscence, something disordering was transmitted, which, unless it were removed, would infect the soul. And this disordering would, again, be something positive to be removed. In whatever way the tradition be accounted for, the difficulty as to the doctrine of transmission of original sin to all conceived as she too was, would be removed by the acknowledgment, in Pope Clement VI.'s language, that "the B. V. had original sin in the cause."

It is still, I think, an open question whether the material cause of original sin remained in the B.V., in regard to which S. Thomas says[5], that the

[5] 3 p. q. 27. art. 3.

incentive to sin [fomes peccati, "concupiscence"] was "bound" in the B.V. when she was sanctified in her mother's womb, so that it should not burst forth into actual sin, but that it was "wholly withdrawn" from her by the overshadowing of the Holy Ghost at the Annunciation, "in the Conception of the Flesh of Christ, wherein her immunity from sin ought to be reflected, redounding from her Child to the mother."

I must make up my mind, as before, that your controversialists will censure details, give sweeping answers, speak of my accusing the Church of God, and the like. As far as I myself am concerned, this is not hard to bear; for, with the judgment-seat of Christ so near at hand, human praise or blame are but a breath, except as they dispose or indispose men's minds to long for that blessed reunion of Christendom, for which all would long, if they did but hope it. But this sort of controversy does not tend to heal deep wounds. It rather aggravates them. It may serve its temporary end of raising in some minds suspicions as to myself. It will leave things in the main as before. This difficulty lies deep in thoughtful minds. Happy he who could remove it!

And now let me, in closing this long letter, revert to that subject, with which I set out, the expostulation, with which you close yours, "'Have you not been touching us on a very tender point in a very

* Letter, p. 121.

rude way ? Is not the effect of what you have said
to expose her to scorn and obloquy, who is dearer
to us than any other creature?" God forbid! I
have not spoken, I trust, any thing which could be
construed into derogation of *her*, who is the Mother
of Jesus, my Lord and God. I have not spoken, as
those fathers spake, for whom you apologize and
whose language you explain. I could neither use
it nor cite it, and I marvel that they used it. I
meant to speak only of an office, popularly assigned
to her, but of which the Roman Communion too
has, I believe, pronounced nothing to be " of faith."
They are not any expressions of love, or reverence,
or admiration, which I have stated to be our difficulties. I know not how any could be too great, if
they had not a dogmatic basis, beyond what we
believe God to have revealed. And here too,
if God had clearly revealed, what some among
you believe, there would be no further question,
just as we who believe that God has given authority to the priest to pronounce forgiveness in His
Name, and that He Himself confirms to the penitent what is so pronounced in His Name, do not
think that the priest comes between us and God;
and we know that we ourselves are wrongly accused
of " substituting the Sacraments for Christ," i. e.
the modes of His operation, or, in the Holy Eucharist, His Presence, for Himself.

But, negatively, I own that we have been in this
respect in an unnatural state. Our hearts have

been cramped. We have not, many of us, been able to give full scope to our feelings, nor have ventured to dwell on the mysteries connected with the Mother of our Lord and God. I know not whether you found it so when among us, that even your tender heart dared not pour out its tenderness, just in this special subject, where it would flow most naturally. I know not, and do not wish to draw out any thing from your heart's sanctuary. If it was not so, you were, in this too, an exception. Most of us seem to look on a wide sea before us, with strong tides and eddies and currents, and we see that these carry off others, whither we dare not follow, and so we stop short and thrust not out from the land. Habitually, I suppose, we gaze on our Dear Lord on the Cross, and scarce dare think of the sword which pierced His Mother's soul, and enhanced His grief. Perhaps, we are taken up with our own sins, and the Price which He paid for our souls then, and our fresh crucifixion of Him, and how our sins pierced Him; and so it comes most natural to us, to think more on S. Mary Magdalene there, as being most like us and a pattern for us, and emboldening us to touch His sacred Cross, or cling to His Sacred Feet. Or, hearts of love have again dwelt, perhaps, more on the Disciple whom Jesus loved, whose Divine Gospel reveals to us so much of His Love, than on His Holy Mother, because they have felt safer thus, and no one has claimed that Apostles should be our one

way and access to Him. As I said at the outset,
this is, I believe, our one fear. But as usual, the
fear passed its bounds, and men—I mean, of course,
not Protestants, but those who have dwelt on the
unfathomable mystery of the Incarnation and confess what lies in the word Theotokos, and in what
we daily say to our Lord and God, "When Thou
didst vouchsafe to deliver man, Thou didst not abhor the Virgin's womb,"—hold back from thinking
of the rest of her life, not out of want of reverence
or love for her, but for the fear of what is de-
manded in her name. Faber, in those lines which
you quote, and in which he expresses so tenderly
his love for her ', must have had a different class of
minds before him. Plainly, we could not love too
much *her*, from whom Jesus vouchsafed to receive a
mother's care, who loved Him, the All-Holy and
her Redeemer too, as no other mother could love
her son; whom He loved with a Divine, but also
with Deified human love; love, with which no other
son could love his mother. The love of the mother
and Son were essentially different from all other

' But scornful men have coldly said,
  Thy love was leading me from God;
And yet in this I did but tread
  The very path my Saviour trod.

They know but little of thy worth,
  Who speak these heartless words to me;
For what did Jesus love on earth
  One half so tenderly as thee?

love, because He was her Son after the Flesh, but also Almighty God. And that same love must continue on now, only that her God-enabled power of love, in the beatific vision of His Godhead, must be unspeakably intensified. They are cold words to say, that it is not the amount of love for the mother of our Redeemer and our God (how could it be?), but the mode of its expression, to which any of us have objected.

And the more we can be set free from this fear (as your words help thereto, should they prevail, by God's blessing, and be heard among your people), the more you will promote the love and honour of her, whom, next to Jesus and for the sake of Jesus, your own soul loves.

There is an earnest of this in writers among us of very different characters of mind, as the pious and affectionate Bishop Hall, notwithstanding his Puritan descent, or the exact and theological Bishop Pearson, or the learned but controversial Bishop Hickes, or our dear departed friend's predecessor in sacred poetry, the pious, learned, and imaginative George Herbert. I might premise to these our good Bishop Andrewes, who, in those devotions which, after his departure, were found "moistened with his pious tears," and which you aided to restore to us, uses the prayer of the Greek Church, "Making mention of the all-holy, undefiled, and more than blessed Mary, Mother of God and ever-Virgin, with all Saints, let us commend ourselves and each other, and all our life to Christ our God⁸." He who so prayed, must often have had her in his thoughts.

Let me add the rest, not as denoting any devotedness, but as expressing this, that no love could be too great, if it did not manifest itself in ways which we think unallowed.

So Bishop Hall⁹:—

"But how gladly doe we second the Angell in the praise of her, which was more ours than his! How justly doe we blesse her, whom the Angell pronounceth blessed! How worthily is she honoured of men, whom the Angell proclaimeth beloved of God! O blessed Mary, he cannot blesse thee, he cannot honour thee too much, that deifies thee not! That which the Angell said of thee, thou hast prophesied of thy selfe; we beleeve the Angell, and thee : ' All generations shall call thee blessed,' by the Fruit of whose wombe all generations are blessed."

And Bp. Pearson, who is recommended, I suppose, by all our Bishops to be studied by candidates for Holy Orders:—

"¹ The necessity of believing our Saviour thus to be ' born of the Virgin Mary,' will appear both in respect of her who was the mother, and of Him Who was the Son.

"In respect of her it was therefore necessary, that we might perpetually preserve an esteem of her person, proportionable to so high a dignity. It was her own prediction, ' From henceforth all generations shall call me blessed ;' but the obligation

---

⁸ Tracts for the Times, No. 88, p. 60.   Greek Lat. p. 132. ed. 1828.

⁹ Contemplations, L. i., The Annunc. of Christ.

¹ On the Creed, Art. 3, " Born of the Virgin Mary."

is ours, to call her, to esteem her so. If Elizabeth cried out 'with' so 'loud a voice, Blessed art thou among women,' when Christ was but newly conceived in her womb, what expressions of honour and admiration can we think sufficient, now that Christ is in heaven, and that mother with Him? Far be it from any Christian to derogate from that special privilege granted her, which is incommunicable to any other. We cannot bear too reverend a regard unto the 'mother of our Lord,' so long as we give her not that worship which is due unto the Lord Himself. Let us keep the language of the primitive Church: "Let her be honoured and esteemed; let Him be worshipped and adored."

Bishop, then Dr., Hicks, in a controversial tract, expressly intended to enable persons to judge "whether the Roman Catholics do indeed no more than pray to the saints in heaven, as they do to their brethren on earth, to pray for them in the name and mediation of Jesus Christ," has such passages as these following. There is poor language throughout, yet there is also theological language and theological inferences here and there, which indicate how, but for this fear, he would have spoken :—

"It may be showed in general that she was a very holy person from the word κεχαριτωμένη, whether it be rendered, 'Thou that art highly favoured,' or 'Thou that art full of grace.' It is not to be imagined that such an Angel should be sent from God, to give such a title to any man or woman, but who was a saint of the first rank. But it is much more evident, that she was such an one from the matter of his message or Annunciation, which was to tell her, that she should conceive and bring forth Jesus, the Saviour of the world, and

---

¹ S. Epiph. Hæres. lxxix. § 7.

that 'the Holy Ghost' to that end should 'come upon her,' and that 'the Power of the Highest overshadow' her; and that the Holy Child, which should be born of her, should be the Son of God. Certainly, the Holy Ghost would come upon none but a pure saint; He that affects the symbols of innocence and purity, in all His appearances, and cannot 'enter into a malicious soul, nor dwell in the body that is subject unto sin,' would not have come in that manner and for that mighty purpose upon any daughter of Adam, but who had 'cleansed herself from all filthiness of flesh and spirit, and perfected holiness in the fear of God.'

"Nay, God the Father, Who was to prepare a Body for His Eternal Son, as it is written, 'a Body hast Thou prepared Me,' would not form it of the substance of a sinful woman; but His own essential Holiness, as well as the mysterious decency of the dispensation, would prompt Him to form It of the substance of one, that, like the king's daughter in the Psalm, was 'all-glorious within,' and a pure and spotless Virgin, both in body and mind. The fulness of the Godhead would not dwell bodily in a wicked woman, nor would *she* be deceived and led away by the serpent, whose heel was to bruise the serpent's head. To be chosen for the Mother of God, was the greatest honour and favour that ever God conferred upon any human creature. None of the special honours and favours that He did to any of the saints before or since are equivalent to the honour of being the Mother of God. And, therefore we may be sure that God Who said, 'Them that honour Me, I will honour,' would not have done so great an honour to any daughter of Abraham, but to one who best deserved it—who had no superior for holiness upon earth. If we had no particular account of her graces, we might rationally conclude all this of her from the history of our Lord's Incarnation; for nothing less than a superlative holiness could receive such a testimony of Divine honour from the Holy Trinity. She was as it were the spouse of God, Co-parent with Him of the wonderful Immanuel, Who was God and man, 'God of the substance of the Father, begotten before the worlds; and man of the substance of His Holy Mother, born in the world,' 'Perfect God and perfect Man,' 'yet not two but one Christ.'

"Though we read of no other graces in her [than purity, humility, faith], yet we may be sure she had all the rest, that could render her righteous and acceptable in the sight of God. And therefore (3) It is our duty, who have the benefit of her example, to honour and celebrate her name and commemorate her virtues, and set forth her praises, in whom there was a concurrence of so many Divine accomplishments, &c. If the names of other saints are distinguished with miniature, hers ought to shine with gold, especially, if we consider that she, of all the virgin daughters of Israel, had the honour to be chosen by the Holy Trinity for the mother of our Lord. 'What shall be done to the woman, whom the King of kings delighteth to honour?' Certainly if we should hold our peace and refuse to praise her among women, the stones of the Church would cry out, 'the stone shall cry out of the wall, and the beam of the timber shall answer it.' Wheresoever the Gospel is preached, that which she hath done and suffered for our Lord ought to be spoken of for a memorial of her, from whom He took that very Body which was crucified, and that precious Blood which was shed for the remission of our sin." Spec. B. Virg. Serm. T. 2, pp. 65—72. London, 1713.

I may the rather add another name, because little known; one who spent sixteen years as a Confessor, in the times of the Republic. He may be the better specimen of others now forgotten.

"¹ I shall not need to tell you who this 'she,' or who this

---

¹ Dr. Frank, Sermon on Christmas Day. "She brought forth her first-born Son, and wrapped Him in swaddling clothes, and laid Him in a manger." Sermons. T. i. p. 77. Ang. Cath. Lib. "But if He would be born of a woman, could He not have chosen another greater than 'she,' than a poor carpenter's wife? Some great queen or lady had been fitter for to have been made, as it were, the Queen of heaven," &c. Ib. p. 79.

'Him.' The day rises with it in its wings. The day wrote it with the first ray of the morning-sun upon the posts of the world. The angels sung it in their choirs, the morning stars together in their courses. The Virgin Mother, the Eternal Son! The most blessed among women, the fairest of the sons of men. The woman clothed with the sun, the Sun compassed with a woman; she the gate of heaven; He the King of Glory, that came forth. She, the Mother of the ever-lasting God: He, God without a mother; God blessed for evermore. Great persons as ever met upon a day."

You will appreciate the yearnings of George Herbert :—

> "'I would address
> My vows to thee most gladly, blessed Maid,
> And mother of my God, in my distress.
>
> "Thou art the holy mine, whence came the gold,
> The great restoration for all decay
> In young and old.
> Thou art the cabinet where the jewel lay—
> Chiefly to thee would I my soul unfold.
>
> "But now, alas! I dare not: for our King,
> Whom we do all jointly adore and praise,
> Bids no such thing:
> And where His pleasure no injunction lays
> ('Tis your own case), ye never move a wing."

Whether our dear friend, from whom we have been lately parted, did, in those early days, lay a special emphasis on the exception, "All but *adoring* love may claim," and meant thereby to allow of any "love," except what involved "latreia" or the worship due to God alone, I never

---

⁴ George Herbert. The Church: To all Angels and Saints.

asked him, and I know not. Yet the exception, strictly taken, is just that of Bp. Pearson, whom he had studied. The beauty and tenderness of the lines are all his own. Yet he, through whom God so attuned men's hearts for the living belief of truths, which at that time were held but too drily, taught what he had learned from those before him. How many hearts those words have spoken to, cannot be told on earth.

> " ' Ave Maria! Blessed Maid!
> Lily of Eden's fragrant shade,
>   Who can express the love,
> That nurtured thee so pure and sweet,
> Making thy heart a shelter meet
>   For Jesus' Holy Dove?
>
> " Ave Maria! Mother blest,
> To whom, caressing and caress'd,
>   Clings the Eternal Child:
> Favour'd beyond Archangels' dream,
> When first on thee with tenderest gleam
>   Thy new-born Saviour smiled.
>
> " Ave Maria! Thou whose name
> All but adoring love may claim,
>   Yet may we reach thy shrine;
> For He, thy Son and Saviour, vows
> To crown all lowly lofty brows
>   With love and joy like thine."

With his words, then, I close. Pleasant and mournful at once has it been thus publicly to write to you, my dearest friend. I would rather have written to you upon other subjects, than these

' " The Christian Year:" The Annunciation.

which have occupied me; on my hopes for the
future ; on the terms upon which union might be
effected ; on articles which might be framed, which
the Roman Church could admit as sufficient, and
which, if our people could believe them to be sufficient for so great an end as the re-union of Christendom, the practical English mind would look at
steadily in the face, and pray to God, and, by His
grace, embrace them.   But it is a delicate matter
on your side (alas! that I must use these terms), as
on ours.   For there are in the Roman Communion
those who wish to exaggerate differences, who decry
" explanations " under the term of " concessions,"
who think that it is beneath its grandeur to enter
into negotiations with those whom they account as
rebels.   There are too, who wish that the present
popular system should take deeper root and put
forth fresh germs, and who would regard us (loyal if
they were obliged to own us in matters of faith) an
" element of weakness," because we do not go along
with them in these devotions.   What then I would
say on these subjects I must bring out, if so please
God, apart from your loved name.   Shrinking as I
do from any thing like controversy with yourself, in
memory of those days when we took sweet counsel
together and walked in the house of God as friends,
and every thought, feeling, desire, longing of our
souls was one, I will enter into no topic which I
can help, which might expose you perhaps to suspicion, because you love me with the deep love of

your large loving heart, or which might occasion a jar, where I long that all should be harmony. I will then only accept your own almost parting words, as expressing accurately my own convictions, when you say to me, "' Whereas it was said twenty-five years ago in the British Critic, ' Till Rome ceases to be. what practically she is, union is *impossible* between her and England,' you declare on the contrary, ' Union *is possible*, as soon as Italy and England, having the same faith and the same centre of unity, are allowed to hold severally their own theological opinions.'"

I do think this. I do not think it necessary that we should extend or contract our several systems to one Procrustean length. Faith is one; and on what is "of faith," we must be agreed. I think that, not by "concessions" on your part, but by mutual explanations as to what is "of faith," we can be at one in all which is really "of faith," if only, as to that large system which lies outside that centre of faith, neither we have a quarrel with you, because the majority of your people practically hold it, nor you require of us, that, in case of re-union, our people should be practically taught it.

"With God all things are possible." The marvels of His past mercies are earnests of greater marvels hereafter. The first crack of the ice is not so sure a token of the coming thaw, as love, infused by God, is of larger gifts of love. We have one

* Letter, pp. 121, 122.

common Enemy. His instruments on earth are
banded together at least by one common hatred of
the truth, which Jesus revealed or sealed, which
Apostles, taught by the Holy Ghost, proclaimed,
which the Church has, by a continuous succession,
taught, and which the Holy Ghost teaches in her.
Satan seems to have organized his armies more,
and to have learned from the Church the necessity
of union. Devil does not cast out devil. And
shall not we, who hold together the same body of
faith, who believe the same mysteries of the All-
Holy Trinity, of the Incarnation of our Lord and
God, of the operations of God the Holy Ghost in
man's regeneration and restoration, the same Word
of God, inspired by Him; the same offices of the
Ministry instituted by Him; the same authority
given to the Church to bear witness to, uphold,
maintain, transmit the same truth; the same Real
Presence of our Lord's Body and Blood, the same
Atoning Sacrifice of the Cross, the same pleading
of that One Meritorious Sacrifice on earth, as He,
our Great High Priest, evermore pleads It in
heaven—shall not we seek to be at one in the rest
too? Shall we not seek and pray to understand
one another, require of each other the least which
fealty to our God requireth, that so—not as some
have misrepresented, through outward means, but
—through our united testimony to the truths revealed to the Church, through our confession of
our God-given faith, through the might of union,

cemented by the One Holy Spirit of Love, we may resist this swelling tide of unbelief, and win to the truth, through the power of God, those who can be won of its manifold opponents? Shall the enemies of the faith be united by their common hatred of the faith, and we, who have the same faith, not be united by our love of God Who gave it? You, who have so much of that love, will do what God shall enable you; may He, in His mercy, grant that my undeserts may not interfere with His work!

Yours most affectionately,

E. B. PUSEY.

CHRIST CHURCH,
Feast of All Saints, 1866.

P. S.—I had begun a second Letter upon those happier subjects, which I thought two years and a half ago I must not address to you. But this Letter has been so long delayed, amid doubt whether to finish it at all, and the difficulty of completing several things at once, that one object of it—viz. to bring before the Bishops of the Roman Communion so much of the work of one of their learned writers, Card. de Turrecremata, as I could, before the approaching Council—would be lost by waiting for the rest. I publish, then, this long-written Letter, though with reluctance, because your controversialists will think that my object in so writing is simply controversial. The Cardinal's work has been one more of the varied instances of human labour, fruitless for this world. Written for the Council of Basle, at the command of the Papal legate its President; withdrawn with its author, through the divisions of a thenceforth disallowed Council, although needed to complete the case, on one side of the question which the Council had to decide upon, and which the residue of the Council, now a Conciliabulum, did under the auspices of John of Segovia, the chief proponent on the opposite side, decide, without hearing it, while professing to have heard both sides [7]; then lying hid and neglected [8] for 110 years, and, after it was printed, notwithstanding all its learning, almost as unknown as before. Alas for human toil!

Lent, 1869.

---

[7] "We, having diligently inspected the authorities and grounds, which have been alleged now for many years in public relations on the side of either doctrine before this sacred synod, and have seen and weighed with mature consideration many others on this matter," &c.—Conc. Bas. Sess. 36, Conc. T. 17. p. 394. Col.

[8] "A work so pure and conformable to Christian piety, that there nowhere appears the darkness of human invention, or any feeling for his own opinion, but every where there seemeth to gleam the clear brightness of evangelic truth. A work very necessary, but hitherto most rare, and also, through the unskilfulness of transcribers, bespread and deformed with countless mistakes, it was wholly made over to neglect."—Pref. of Alb. Duimius, Rome, 1547.

ON THE GREEK LITURGIES.

My own studies not having lain in the Greek Liturgies, I consulted my friend the Rev. G. Williams, King's College, Cambridge, and append some observations which he addresses to me. They coincide with some which I had myself made as to the appearance of interpolation on this very same subject.

"It cannot, I think, be denied that the Orthodox Greek Church does 'even surpass' the Church of Rome 'in their exaltation of the Blessed Virgin¹' in their devotions; and all that I can say is, that on this point the Orientals, generally 'so jealous of antiquity,' have innovated on the practice of earlier and what we hold to be purer times. This, we shall presently find, is mere matter of history.

"But when it is added that this practice has gone the length of 'the substitution of the Name of Mary for the Name of Jesus at the end of the collects and petitions' in the Office Books and 'in the formal prayers of the Greek Eucharistic Service,' in which petitions are offered, not 'in the name of Jesus Christ,' but 'of the Theotocos,' the statement seems to me to require qualification; for the word 'substitution' would

---

¹ Dr. Newman's Letter, p. 95.

convey the impression to most minds that the name of 'Jesus Christ' had been removed to make way for that of the 'Blessed Virgin,' which, of course, is à necessary element in the parallel of the alteration of the 'Te Deum to her honour in private devotion.'

"I am not aware that there is any proof of such substitution or alteration of the pleadings in the prayers of the Greek Church, although there is, as you know, distinct evidence of the date of the introduction of those pleadings, and of the author of that innovation; for the last of the 'four most excellent inventions,' which Peter Gnapheus, the heretical Patriarch of Antioch, is reported to have introduced into the Catholic Church is this: ἐν πάσῃ εὐχῇ τὴν θεοτόκον κατονομάζεσθαι καὶ ταύτης τὴν θείαν κλῆσιν ἐπικαλεῖσθαι[*], and although the sole authority for this statement, so far as I am aware, is very late (cir. A.D. 1320), yet there can be no doubt that it is made by Nicephorus on the authority of earlier ritualists, and is confirmed by all we know, from other sources, of the adulteration of the Greek Office Books. For this we cannot have a more competent witness than Leo Allatius, who, in his work on the Church Books of the Greeks, complains in no measured terms of the perpetual accretion of their offices, and describes the process whereby 'maximam librorum copiam majorem fecit, et, novis semper additis, molem in immensum auxit.' He mentions many authors of these additions, of all ages, and adds, in words with which we must heartily sympathize: 'Sed utinam liceret nobis ex primis illis fontibus tamquam integrioribus et purioribus, divino Christi servitio incumbere; næ illis superseminata ab homine nequam zizania dignosceremus.'

"Thus much about the Church Books of the Greeks in general. Then, as to the Liturgies in particular, there is a general conviction among all who have examined them and had the opportunity of collecting copies, that they have been very much tampered with by way of interpolation.

"Let me here say, by the way, that the passage which we

---

[*] Nicephorus Callistus, Hist. Eccles. Lib. xv. 28, ad fin. Vol. ii. p. 634.

looked at together in the Bodleian ², and which is cited by Dr. Newman (in Note D. to his Letter, No. 13, p. 150) as occurring 'at the Offertory of the Mass,' according to the 'Rite of S. Chrysostom,' in which the Sacrifice of the Altar is offered through the intercession of the Theotocos, is in fact no part of the Liturgy of S. Chrysostom, though so reckoned apparently by Goar. In the Greek Liturgies, that introductory portion in which that passage occurs is not even ascribed to S. Chrysostom, whose Liturgy proper begins with the εὐχὴ τῆς προθέσεως, which follows *without a break* on the introduction, in Goar p. 68. But with regard to the Liturgy proper, Goar declares that the variations, not only in the editions, but in the ancient MSS. which he had consulted, were so great that he was deterred from the task of collation (p. 108).

"While, then, the present state of the Greek Liturgies and other Offices must be admitted to be good as a proof of the actual practice of the Orthodox Church, which I presume is all that Dr. Newman intended, it would require a far more extensive acquaintance with the history of these accretions than even Goar or Leo Allatius possessed, to ascertain how far they are available as a proof of the antiquity of the forms which they contain."

---

² In Fabricii Bib. Græc. tom. v. p. 8, Hamburg, 1712.

APPENDIX.

WHEN I formed the Catena in my "Letter" by aid of Card. de Turrecremata's work, I had only access to it through De Alva's work against it. De Alva gives the authorities quoted by Card. de Turrecremata in what is now Part 6 of his work, accurately and precisely, and sometimes enlarges them by aid of MSS. in which he saw them. Some twenty-three of those authorities I omitted, since, however strong was my impression of the accuracy of the Cardinal's citations, there seemed, by De Alva's account, to be a certain residue, which might, during the 110 years between his compilation of his authorities and their publication, have come from some other hand. The careful study of the Cardinal's work has so satisfied me that it is one very accurate whole, that I have subjoined some few authors whom I omitted in the Catena, and have added an analysis of the whole. I regret that it is but a skeleton, and can give no idea of the extreme carefulness and ready learning with which it is written, or of the way in which every statement is supported by authority. As a specimen of his painstaking, I may mention how he tells simply that he had read through the acts and decrees of the Council of Ephesus for an alleged quotation of two lines from a tract of S. Cyril against Nestorius, which he could not find[1]. In another place he speaks of having read through homilies of S. Bernard, to find an alleged passage, in vain. Elsewhere he mentions having sent (I think, to Spain) to verify an authority by the original, which he expected before the end of the Council. He says he could not give the precise words of Ægidius of Zamora, "[2] on account of the distance of Zamora, where his books are kept, from Basle, where he was writing," but says that the meaning is certain. But, since the subject will probably occupy the attention of the approaching Council, I have been anxious, in what degree I could in the time, to bring before the Bishops the thoughts of one of their most careful writers.

The following passages of S. Augustine, which Card. de Turrecremata alleges, ought to have been quoted before :—

"[3] God judged it better, both to take from that very race which had been conquered, the Man through Whom He should conquer the enemy of the human race, and yet from a virgin, Whose Conception Spirit, not flesh, preceded; faith, not passion. Nor was there present any concupiscence of flesh, whereby the rest are sown and conceived, who derive [trahunt] original sin; but this being most utterly removed, the holy virginity

---

[1] P. 12, c. 11, f. 156.   [2] P. 6, c. 32, f. 123.
[3] De Trin. xiii. c. 18, n. 23.

was fecundated by believing, not by concumbency; that what was born of the stock of the first man might derive its origin of the race only, not also of criminality. There was born, then, not a nature vitiated by the contagion of transgression, but the sole medicine of all such faultinesses. A Man was born, I say, having no sin, never in the least to have it, through Whom should be re-born those to be freed from sin who *could not* be born without sin. *For*, although conjugal chastity employeth well carnal concupiscence, which is in membris genitalibus, habet tamen motus non voluntarios, whereby it shows that it either could not have existed at all in Paradise before sin was, or, if it were, was not such that it could sometimes resist the will. Need was there, then, that that carnal concupiscence should not be at all there, when was conceived the Virgin's Son, in Whom the author of death was to find nothing worthy of death, and yet to slay Him, himself to be conquered by the Death of the Author of Life, conqueror of the first Adam and holding the human race, conquered by the Second Adam and losing the Christian race, which was freed from human crime out of the human race, through Him Who was not in the crime, though He was from the race, so that that deceiver should be conquered from that race, which he had conquered by crime."

" ' He, the Son of Man, was made the same as thou, that we may be made sons of God. He was 'made flesh.' Whence the flesh? From Mary. Whence the Virgin Mary? From Adam. Then from that first captive; and the flesh of Christ was from the mass of the captivity."

" ' That one sin, which, being so great, was admitted in a place and condition of so great felicity, so that in one man in the origin and (so to speak) from the root [originaliter atque radicaliter] the whole race of man was condemned, is not loosed or cleansed, except by the One Mediator of God and men, the Man Christ Jesus, Who Alone *could* be so born, as not to have need to be re-born."

---

⁴ In Ps. lxx. Serm. 2. n. 10.

⁵ Ench. n. 14. c. 48. Opp. vi. 214, quoted with other passages of the Ench. Turr. iii. 5. f. 44 v.

These two corresponding statements, "man" born after the way of nature, "could not be born without sin," "Christ Alone *could* be born, so as not to need to be re-born," have a strength of evidence of their own, in so careful a writer as S. Augustine.

151. From S. Maximus of Turin, he quotes,—

" ' Although Mary, herself a daughter of Eve, had borne Christ, she had not conceived Him of Adam. When, then, the enemy of God saw the Son produced through so many miracles, he revolved with himself, I deem, and said wondering, ' Who is this, Who, without my knowing, has come into the world ? I know that He is born of a woman, but whence conceived, I know not. His mother is here; but His father I cannot search out.' " And below, " ' Since the world was, it never befell me, that any should be born man, and have nothing of human fault. What is this generation, so new, so mighty ? Born among sinners and ungodly, derived too from a mortal mother, He appears to me cleaner than all who are born, and purer than heaven itself.' "

A passage was quoted against him from "a Sermon on the Assumption," then attributed to S. Maximus ; which also he says his opponent had (as so frequently besides) alleged imperfectly, but which does not occur even in the Appendix to the Benedictine edition of S. Maximus. The two sermons, so entitled, are (they say) on the Annunciation, Serm. xi. xii., App. col. 43, 45, De Turr. He says (which is plain), that the passage relates to the Nativity, not to the Conc. of the

* Hom. 37, de quadr. 1, col. 106, 107.

B. V.; it being a comment on Isa. xi. 1, which
was interpreted of the Nativity, and was read at
the festival of her Nativity, and the word being
"prodiit." "[7] From a vitiated root there went
forth (prodiit) a rod, which is understood of the
Virgin Mary, as Isaiah testifieth, ' a rod, &c.'"

Petavius [8] alleges from a homily of S. Maximus,
an expression which, he thinks, could only have been
used by one who believed that the B. V. was subject to human infirmity. The Roman editor of
S. Maximus thinks otherwise [9].

I cannot verify an authority in which the name
was probably wrongly deciphered, as "S. Cyril in
his tract against the Manichees," who, in the
heading of the chapter, is called by the editor,
Chrysostom (with whom " the chosen vessel " is a
favourite title for S. Paul). Anyhow, it is evi-

---

[7] P. xii. c. 8. f. 253 v.

[8] De Inc. xiv. 1. 6.

[9] The words are, " Ait Illi beatissima Mater, ' vinum non
habent,' cui, velut indignans, respondit Jesus, ' Quid mihi et
tibi est, mulier ? ' Hæc verba indignantis esse, quis dubitat ?
Sed idcirco, ut reor, quia tam temerè ei mater de defectu car-
nalis poculi suggerebat, qui veniret totius orbis gentibus
novum salutis æternæ calicem propinare." Hom. 23 (De
Epiph. Dom. 7) col. 68, Romæ. " Temerè " must, I suppose,
mean "inconsiderately." To me, the meaning of S. Maximus
seems to turn, not simply on the word "temerè" alone, but
much more on the words " *tam* temerè," with the comment,
" hæc verba indignantis esse quis dubitat ? " I doubt whether
any modern writer would use them; much less one who
believed in the Imm. Conc.

dently a real authority, whom Turrecremata was extracting,—

" ¹ The Lord Alone came in the likeness of sinful flesh; He Alone was like sinners in the nature of the flesh which He took, but was not a sinner by conversation. He Alone acquired a new glory of the flesh (as the chosen vessel stated), that He should be accounted not a sinner but like a sinner." And below, "His was the likeness of sinful flesh, Who knew not the verity of sin." And below, "This being so, One and Alone is our Lord, Who both united the flesh with the spirit for the salvation of the flesh, and bore the likeness of sinful flesh with uninjured and inviolate holiness of spirit."

From S. Cyril (in answer to the passage alleged from "a treatise against Nestorius" which he could not find, " After Christ, it is rash to place in Mary spot or sin " (which would also, he says, relate to actual, not original sin), he quotes S. Cyril's anathema :—

" ² Whoso says that He, i. e. Christ, offered an oblation for Himself also, and not rather for us alone, for He needed not an oblation for Himself, Who altogether knew not sin, let him be anathema" (Ep. ad Nest. Opp. T. 5. P. 2, p. 77).

I may add two citations from De Bandelis, of which the first is like S. Cyril :—

" ³ When the Saviour came, there was no just man upon earth, as the Ap. teaches, saying, 'For there is no difference, for all have sinned and need the glory of God, i. e. Christ, Who Alone was without sin '" (on S. Luke).

and—

" ³ Peace was made on earth through Christ, because taking

---

¹ Turr. P. 3. c. 6. f. 45 v. ² L. xii. c. 11. f. 256.
³ De Bandelis, p. 89.

away from the midst the enmity which was against us, He reconciled us all with the Father. And therefore His Name was well called Jesus, i. e. Saviour, because He was incarnate for the salvation of the whole human race."

From S. Leo I chiefly adduced his sermons on the Nativity. Turrecremata chiefly urges the authority of the Epistle to Flavian, as having been stamped, moreover, by the authority of the Council of Chalcedon.

" 'To the same concurs the most blessed Leo I., in that his Epistle which he wrote to Flavian on the faith, of whose authority, in the cap. *S. Rom. Eccl. di.* 15 [c. 3] where works of the holy Fathers which are received as Catholic in the Church are mentioned, it is said, ' Also the Epistle of S. Leo, directed to Bp. Flavian, in the Council of Chalcedon, whose text if any one dispute to one iota, and receive it not reverently, let him be anathema.' In this Epistle he thus speaks : ' For if man, when made in the image and likeness of God, had abode in the honour of his nature, and had not, through concupiscence, being deceived by fraud of the devil, departed from the law imposed upon him, the Creator of the world would not become a creature, nor the Everlasting take what belonged to time, nor the Son of God, equal to God the Father, assume the form of a servant, or the likeness of flesh of sin. But because, "through envy of the devil, death entered into the world," and the captivity of man could not be loosed, unless He should so undertake our cause as, without injury to His own majesty, to become Very Man, and should Alone not have the contagion of sin,' &c. "

Thus far is (through whatever accident) from S. Leo's third sermon on Pentecost [5]; the rest, which is marked as from the conclusion of the

---

[4] Turr. vi. 1, f. 96 v.
[5] Serm. 77, de Pent. 3, c. 2, f. 309, ed. Ball.

" Sermo," from the Epistle to Flavian, and occurs also, though not consecutively, in his second sermon on the Nativity.

"The Son of God enters into these lower parts of the world, coming down from heaven, and not departing from the glory of the Father, generated by a new order, by a new nativity. 'By a new order,' because, invisible in His own [abode] He was made visible in ours ; He, the Incomprehensible, willed to be comprehended ; abiding before all time, He took beginning in time ; the Lord of the universe, shrouding the Infinity of His majesty, took on Him the form of a servant ; the Impassible God disdained not to be passible Man, and the Immortal to be subject to the laws of death. 'Generated by a new Nativity,' because inviolate Virginity knew not concupiscence, ministered the substance of the flesh. Then was taken from the Mother of the Lord, nature, not fault."

On S. John Damascene, T. observes, that P. Lombard (iii. d. 3) and S. Thomas (in 3 p. q 27 ad ult.) refer " the cleansing of which he speaks, to the cleansing of the fomes, which cleansing takes place in those only who have had or have orig. sin (as above). Therefore it follows as before " (f. 97).

S. Gerard [s], Bp. of Csanad and Martyr, A.D. 1048.

"'Although the B. V. was born from the mass of sin, yet because her own conversation was uniformly most holy, nor

---

[s] S. Bernard (in de Turr.) is doubtless a misprint for " B. Erhard" (as Prof. Stubbs conjectures). De Band. has "B. Herardus Ep. et Mart.," and in the marg. " F. Gerard." He wrote a book " on the praises of the B. V. M. ; Lenten Sermons ; Homilies for the great days of the whole year," which were preserved in the library of the Sagredos at Venice. Mabillon Acta SS. O. Ben. Sæc. vi. T. 1, p. 627. De Turr. quotes from a serm. on the Nat. of the B. V.

doth she remember any offence whatsoever, she was altogether free from the chain of sin. For God cleansed her from all offence, from the most pure beginning of her nativity.' And below, ' O happy maiden, which weeps in the cradle, and is so elect in heaven; which, being conceived from sin, is purified from all sin, and, conceiving without sin of the Holy Spirit, bore God the Word most ineffable ' " (f. 100 v.).

From S. Bernard, De T. also quotes,—

" ' Behold, I beseech you, of what sort is this; how new, how admirable, how lovable, how delightsome! For what more beautiful, than a pure generation? What more glorious, than a holy and spotless Conception, wherein is nothing of shame, nothing of defilement, nothing of corruption? For that conception is not only glorious in its, as it were, outward beauty, but also precious in inward power, so that (as is written), in the left hand of the Lord glory and riches are found together, riches, I say, of salvation, with glory of newness. For ' who can make clean what is conceived of unclean seed,' save He Who was Alone conceived without fallen [illicita] and unclean pleasure? In my very root and origin I was infected and defiled. Unclean is my conception; but there is, by Whom that confusion should be removed. He takes it away, on Whom Alone it falleth not. I have riches of salvation, whereby I may redeem the impurity of my own conception—the most pure Conception of Christ. Thou hast yet greater riches, thou hast ampler glory. The Mother is without corruption of virginity, the Son without all stain of sin. There falleth not on the Mother the curse of Eve; there falleth not on the Child that general condition, whereof it is said by the Prophets, ' None is clean from defilement, not an infant, whose life on the earth is of one day.' Lo an Infant without defilement, Alone among men, True, yea too, the Truth itself. ' Behold the Lamb without spot, Who taketh away the sins of the world!' For who should better take away sins, than He on Whom sin falleth not? He can undoubtedly wash me, of Whom it is certain that He was not defiled. Let this Hand

---

⁷ In Vigil. Nat. Dom. Serm. 4, n. 2. 3. 5. col. 772, 773.

cleanse my mud-blinded eye, Which Alone was without dust !
Let Him take away the mote of my eye, Who hath no beam
in His own; rather, let Him take away the beam out of mine,
Who hath not even a little dust in His own ! "

De Alva objects to the authority from Peter
Comestor [1], that the style is different, and that a
writer a little later than De Turr. quotes as from
Pet. Comestor the words, " A lily, white without
streak of sin. A beautiful mirror, without original
stain." But if his, it says no more than the passage
itself, that she was cleansed from original sin in the
womb, though "conceived with fault and penalty."

Omitted authorities are,—

152. "[2] Ancient Doctor of Paris following Pet. Lomb. and

---

[1] Cited above (p. 198), as taken from Castellanus, on De
Alva's conjecture. De Turr. quotes it : "The venerable Father,
master of histories, called Peter Comestor, in a sermon on the
Nativity of the B. V." (P. 6, c. 26, f. 117). Labbe mentions
a report, "A sermon [of his] on the Immaculate Conception
of the B. V. M., is *said to have been printed* at Antwerp by
G. Westermann, A. 1536, extracted from an old MS. in
England." Scr. Eccl. ii. 200. But there is no proof—1) that
it was printed ; 2) that it was his; 3) that it did teach the
Imm. Conc., since so many passages are alleged for it, and
which only express belief of her immaculateness at the birth.
The Decastichon, quoted by Vinc. Bellov. (Spec. his. 29, 1),
and from him by S. Antoninus (Chron. tit. 13, c. 8, T. 3,
p. 77), relates only to her greatness. De Turr. says the same
(xiii. 2, f. 263 v., 264), and that the passage has no force,
against his saying to the contrary.

[2] Turr. vi. 28, f. 117 v. De Alva would have this to be the
work of Armachanus, and so only a multiplication of authorities ; but Armachanus' Summa begins "Fides est substantia

Hugo; but no name is expressed in the book which we have, his Summa, which begins ' Primum principium omnium sive Deum esse sic ostendimus.' In L. iii., answering the question, ' Whether the Flesh of Christ, before it was united to the Word, was, in the B. V., subject to sin ? ' he answers, ' It must be said, yes; but not in as far as it was the Flesh of Christ, but, before it was united to the Word, it was, by the operation of the Holy Ghost, cleansed from all contagion.' And below ; ' The corruption of fault was in the flesh of the V., when the Angel came to her, according to which she could sin. But in the coming of the Holy Ghost, the flesh was filled with grace and purged from that corruption, and thus she was twice sanctified,' " &c.

153. Richardus Armachanus, i. e. Richard Fitz-Ralph, A.D. 1347, a disciple of John Baconthorpe, Divinity Prof. and Chancellor of Oxford.

"[10]In 3 Sent. di. 3, he says the same, as appears by the testimony of some, who hold the contrary. Magister John, who zealously stirred this matter in this sacred Council, expressly relates this in his sermon on the Conception. But as to what is said, that he of Armagh retracted this in a sermon, viz. ' Wisdom built her a house,' until this be shown, by trustworthy attestation which should be satisfactory to this sacred Synod, it is not to be believed, especially since John Vitalis, who first stated this in his little tract hereon, is known most certainly to have spoken falsely in many like things, which he said of other Doctors, as of Alex. de Ales, St. Thomas, and Alexander Neckham."

Dominicans.—154. Peter de Palude (de la Palu), Master of Paris, Dominican Patriarch of Jerusalem, died A.D. 1342. " He wrote on the whole of Scr. as well as on the book of the Sentences [1]." " A great

rerum, non apparentium ;" and he proceeds to assign to human grounds a province inferior to faith.

[10] vi. 28, f. 118.   [1] Quétif i. 607.

ornament of his order, nation, age, highly commended by almost all writers[2]." He was sent by John XXII. as Nuncio to Flanders.

After having given at great length the grounds on both sides, he sums up[3],—

[2] Ib. 603.

[3] De Alva alleges on the contrary, some sermons published first anonymously, then under his name. Quétif says, "Although there are many praiseworthy things in these sermons, there are intermingled so many and such great puerilities, savouring of the simplicity and levity of the author, that it is a great wrong to our De Palude to ascribe them to him, being a man, not only of erudite and most eloquent discourse, but of clear and discriminating judgment. In editions subsequent to that of Nuremberg, 1496, many sermons were cut out, fabulous and puerile histories were removed, almost all heads of sermons cut off, yet many things were left, alien from De Palude, and so they appeared at Paris (F. Reynault, 1572, 1573. 8), and were called 'the productions of an anonymous erudite Theologian, and of no mean judgment' (Quétif i. 607). So they were restored to their anonymousness. Quétif observes (besides that—1) they were at first published anonymously; and that, 2) when published under the name of De Palude, no ground was assigned for ascribing him to them), that, 3) several authors are quoted in them later than De Palude—Simon de Cassia, died A. 1348; Th. de Argentina, Augustinian, died A. 1357; Peter de Candia, Franciscan, elected Alexander V., A. 1409. 4) That he cites Franciscans rather than Dominicans, and abandons S. Thomas for Scotus; and on the question, "whether Christ would have come, had there not been sin," abandons the H. Doctor in his Summa, asserts nakedly that he was deceived, and embraces the opinion of S. Bonaventura, which was also that of Scotus; and maintains at length, that Christ would then have come in impassible flesh—the opposite whereof, Alva says, De Palude holds in the Sentences. The reference to the Council of Basle in the first edition, might, Quétif says,

"'The third on the opposite side is to be granted, and the three following, which prove that she was conceived in original sin."

155. Thomasinus of Ferrara, Dominican. "'He wrote a compendium of S. Thomas on the Sentences, using throughout the very words of the holy Doctor, omitting much, yet giving the chief things, sometimes in a different order, adding some little from time to time, especially when new questions had arisen in his own day, as on the Conception of the B. V., to clear and defend the sentiment of the saints. Sometimes also things are noted in the margin from the Summa, when the matter is treated there more clearly or certainly."

"' On iii. Sent. di. 3, he speaks in these exact words, agreeing with Thomas; 'Before the infusion of the soul, the B. V. could not be sanctified; nor was she sanctified at the very instant of her conception, so that grace should preserve her from original sin, that she should not be infected by it. For Christ hath this exclusively in human nature, that He needed not redemption, because He is our Head, but to all of us belongeth to be redeemed by Him. This would not have been, had there been any soul uninfected by original sin. And therefore it cannot be said that the B. V. was sanctified in the first moment of her infusion.' "

---

have been inserted by the Editor. But on these and other grounds, Alva [I suppose in a later work] concludes that "the author was a Franciscan, not a Dominican;" and so, of course, not De Palude; and of the fifteenth, not the fourteenth century, very probably after the Council of Basle.

' L. 3. d. 3. q. 1. f. 23 v.
' Quétif i. 700.
' Turr. vi. 29, f. 119 v.

156. Bernard de Gannato, of Clermont, Dominican, "a very famous master of Paris [7]," lived
about the close of Cent. 13 and beginning of the
14th, "was often cited by John Capreolus on the
Sentences [8]."

"[9] In his criticisms of Henri of Ghent in the Quodlibet 15,
q. 13, he says, 'It is certain that the B. V. contracted original
sin, both because she proceeded from the corrupt mass, even as
others, and because she herself belonged to the universal redemption made by her Son, even as others. 'For all have
sinned and need the glory of God' (Rom. 3 and Eph. 3). 'We
were by nature children of wrath.' Whence neither was she
excluded. Therefore it is to be held that she contracted orig.
sin.' "

157. Robert de Holcot, a Dominican, Doctor
and Professor of Theology at Oxford, "a man of
acutest genius, most studious of learning, human
and Divine, of much labour, incredible industry,
and of such reading, as to have gone through
almost all the older theologians of note." Died
1349. He wrote largely on Holy Scripture, as
well as on the Sentences.

"[1] On the Book of Wisdom, Lect. 161, treating of that of
Wisdom 14, 'men trust their souls to a little wood,' and pur-
suing the thought, how Christ is the wood of life, says, 'As
wood, planted in the earth, consolidates the earth on all sides,
and by its roots binds and holds it together, that it fall not off;
so Christ, planted in the V. M. His mother, consolidated her
by virtues, and so bound her by graces that she could never

---

[7] Turr.
[9] Turr. vi. 29, f. 119 v. 120.
[8] Quétif i. 402.
[1] Turr. vi. 29, f. 120.

fall off through sin, mortal or venial. For she was so sanctified in the womb, that she was cleansed from original sin, and the fomes was so bound in her, that it never inclined her to sin. And this was the first sanctification in her mother's womb[2]. But the second was in the Conception of her Son, in which the fomes was taken away, according to its essence, and grace was superadded, and determined the free-will inflexibly to good, so that from that time she could in no way be bent to evil, whence she was then established in such way as she could be on the way " [i. e. not having yet attained].

158. **Thomas de Walleis**, English Dominican, Master in Theology, imprisoned A.D. 1332 by John XXII. for charging him with heresy for denying

[2] " In the printed editions (as Basle, 1586, Lect. 58, p. 532), sixteen lines are inserted, directly contradicting the preceding statement, affirming that she was not conceived in original sin. But Deza says that they were uniformly absent from MSS., of which he had seen 'six very old.' Even De Alva owns that 'they were absent from all MSS. except two;' but he does not add," Quétif says, " whether they were on the margin or in the body of the MSS., whether in the same hand, or whether before or after the Council of Basle. Certainly they are not in old MSS. of the fifteenth century. So, on the ground of the decree of that Council, the editors of the first edition at Spires, A.D. 1483, falsely ascribed those lines to the author, which, whether it was rightly done, be the Sovereign Pontiff the judge. The Roman Index, however, had not allowed this in authors anterior to the Bull of Sixtus IV., commanding that they should remain intact " (Quétif i. 630). The interpolation is not in any of the Oxford MSS., viz. Bodl. 279 [14th cent.]; Merton, 161 [14th cent.]; Ball. 27 [end of 14th cent.]; Merton, 162 [beg. of 15th]; Lincoln, 110 [15th cent.]; Magd. 148 [15th cent.]. The Bodl., Mert. 161, Magd. 148, are, however, probably not independent of each other, since, owing probably to the ὁμοιοτέλευτον, they all omit the words between the " fomes," l. 3 of the text above, and the " fomes " l. 6. All the MSS. omit " mortal or venial," l. 1.

that the souls of the faithful see God before the Resurrection ; released at the prayer of the king of France and University of Paris. He "wrote a good Postill on the Psalms of the two first nocturns [3] " (i. e. Psalms 1—37).

" ' In his postill, treating on Ps. 17, 'My God, His way is perfect,' says, 'The way, whereby God came to us, was the Bl. V. She was an undefiled way, because she was clean in the Conception of her Son. For the Sun of Righteousness, coming into the Virgin, took away wholly all fomes of sin. Therefore, saith S. Jerome in the Sermon on the Assumption, ' All which was wrought in her was purity and simplicity, all was truth and grace, all was righteousness and mercy which looked down from heaven.' ' "

He is often confused with Thomas Jorsius or Joyce (died A.D. 1310), who wrote on "the Psalms of the first nocturn" i. e. Psalms 1—25, each being commonly called Thomas Anglicus. De Alva quotes from Th. Walleis. He gives this fuller extract, which perhaps may be an expansion of the comment of the first writer in the second :—

"In the Conception, because it is said (Ps. 77), 'Thy way is on the sea,' 'mari,' i. e. Mary, and in her conversation. Ambrose says somewhere, 'The ship passeth in the sea, and there are no traces in the wave.' Christ cometh from heaven, and is conceived through the ear, and the Word is formed in the womb. Such Mary remained. She was also an undefiled way in her whole conversation. The cause was, that she ever had the Sun of Righteousness, going on and drying up, in her sight. Moreover, she long-time had Him bodily within her,

---

[3] Laur. Pignon, n. 107.   [4] vi. 29. f. 120.

and therefore no spot of mud could be in her; yea, if it had been, it had been consumed in the instant, because, were the sun infinite, it would act in an instant. But the Sun of Righteousness is infinite. And therefore, coming into the Virgin and acting through His light and heat, immediately in the same instant, He consumed all source of grief in her. For He extinguished and removed the fomes of sin too bodily. Wherefore S. Jerome says, in his book on the Assumption[a], 'Whatever in her,' &c."

159. Nicolas Gorram, "Postillator of the whole Bible." "In the interpretation of H. Scripture and preaching of the Word of God he was so eminent in his times as to be second to none; a man of piety, sound learning, eloquence, practical wisdom, and every gift which can be desired. Died about A. 1285." Quétif i. 438.

"'All which things being considered, a most clear testimony seemeth to be collected from the aforesaid saying of the Angel, that the most sacred V. was conceived in original sin; since the fomes itself is, materially, original sin, as appeared above. Whence Augustine, in his book of retractations (De Verbis Ap.), as the Master of the Sentences adduceth (in ii. di. 30) saith:— 'There is ever fighting in the body of this death, because concupiscence itself, wherewith we are born, cannot be ended; which concupiscence, wherewith we are born, is a vice which

---

[a] In the Opp. Suppositia, T. xi. p. 100 ed. Vallars, who calls the book a fraud, as it personates S. Jerome, as if written to Paula and Eustochium.

[b] P. 5. c. 2. ff. 83 v. 84, referred to in P. 6. c. 29 f. 120, "Mag. Nic. Gorran on Luke: 'The Holy Ghost shall supervene in thee,' &c., which, as was said above, refers to the extinction of the fomes of sin." De Alva, not looking to the place referred to by Turr., says that he does not give Gorram's words.

maketh the little one capable of concupiscence, but rendereth
the adult concupiscent.' For which words of Aug., the Mag.
Sent. saith, it is given to be understood, what is original sin,
i. e. the vice of concupiscence, which through Adam entered
into all born through concupiscence, and vitiated them (which
also he confirmeth by testimony of Augustine), saying, ' Whence
Aug. in the book De Bapt. Parv., Adam, besides the example
of imitation, did also by a hidden corruption of his carnal concupiscence, corrupt in himself all who should come of his
stock.' "

160. Vincentius Historialis, i. e. Bellovacensis, lectured privately at Paris, A. 1228. Died A.D. 1264.
One of the first Dominicans. For love of study he
declined all dignities. Chaplain to S. Louis
(Quétif i. 212, q. 97).

" ' In a glorious tract which he compiled in praise of the
Virgin, worked together from authorities of the Saints, in the
chapter on the sanctification of the B. V., in proof that she was
sanctified in the womb from original sin, among other things,
he adduces that of Bernard on the Assumption of the same most
sacred Ever-Virgin, which is a manifest proof of the proposition, ' it is altogether clear that the B. V. was cleansed by grace
alone from the original contagion ' " (See ab. p. 176).

161. James of Beneventum, Dominican, about
A. 1360, wrote commentaries on S. Luke and
S. John, treatises and sermons [8].

" ' In his notable and copious work of sermons on the
seasons and the Saints, in his sermon on the Nativity of the

---

[7] De Turr., f. 120 v. In P. 13, c. 2, f. 263 he answers the
allegation on the other side, saying, 1) that in his L. 8, c. 121,
he alleges nothing of his own, and 2) that Ildephonso (i. e.
Paschasius Radbertus), whom he quotes, is speaking only of
the Nativity.

[8] Quétif i. 648.   [9] Turr. l. c.

B. V., on the text ' Vas admirabile opus Excelsi,' in proof of her
sanctification from original sin, he adduces Prov. 25.   ' Take
away the rust from the gold, and a most pure vessel shall come
forth.' "

162. John Pickardi, of Luxemburg, Domi-
nican, Bachelor of Paris about 1708, " [1] most illustrious for religion, doctrine, and practical wisdom."

"[2] In his sermon on the Nativ. of the B. V. on the text, ' A
little fountain which grew into a river' (Esther x.), he says, 'This
river was little, because it was conceived in original sin ; but it
grew in its sanctification in the womb, and its increase was in a
fourfold way.   First was the sanctification in the womb, which
was greater than the sanctification of Jeremiah and John
Baptist.' "

163. John Steringacius, Teutonicus (de Sperne-
gasse Laur. Pignon n. 39, de Sterngasse Leander,
f. 136 v.), Doctor of Paris about 1390, wrote on
the Sentences, Questions on Nat. Phil., Sermons
on the seasons and on Saints [3].

"[4] On the Sent. 3. d. 3, he says thus, ' The B. V. was not
sanctified, either before the conception, nor in the conception
before the infusion of the soul, because the rational soul is the
proper subject of sanctifying grace ; nor again in the instant of
the infusion of the soul, because so she would not have contracted original sin, as neither did Christ, and so it would not
belong to all to be redeemed by Christ; but she is believed
only to have been sanctified after the infusion of the soul.' "

---

[1] Quétif i. 522.   [2] Turr. l. c.   [3] Quétif i. 700.
[4] Turr. l. c.   De Alva assumes the passage to belong to the
Compendium of Hannibaldus (ab. p. 229), on account of the
identity of the words; but it is a common formula, and " Bunderius had seen the book." Quétif.

Franciscans.—164. Robert Conton or Cothon, English Franciscan, Oxford and Paris, Doctor of the Sorbonne, "a man of acuteness and solid judgment[5]." About 1340. "He was called Doctor Amœnus."

"[6] In his L. 3. q. 9, inquiring whether the B. V. contracted original sin, having recited the opinion of those who hold the negative with some of their arguments, he uses these words, 'But although this opinion is probable, yet, since the contrary opinion seems to be of the mind of the saints, therefore I hold it. And I say that the arguments alleged conclude as to the B. V. more than as to any other. And I grant that, if any one was preserved, it is more in harmony as to the mother of Christ than as to others.'"

165. Bartholomæus de Pisis, Franciscan. The only Bartholomew of Pisa mentioned by Wading is Barth. Albicius, A.D. 1372, who wrote "Conformitates B. Mariæ V. cum D.N. Jesu C.," or "six books on the life and praises of the B. V." De Alva says that he could not find the passage in the Quadragesimale of Barth. Albicius, printed at Milan 1498, and adduces a passage from Serm. 37, where B. Alb. speaks of "the infusion of grace bestowed by God in the conjunction of the soul with the flesh," and from his Mariale (Ven. 1590) tract. 7, in which he speaks of the preservation of her conception from original sin as a "pious belief." We have had

[5] Pitseus (de Ill. Aug. Scriptt. p. 443), who says that he was wont eagerly to maintain the Imm. Conc. Bale says, "They are wont to adduce him as a witness, that Mary contracted a stain (macula) in her conception." Cent. 5, n. 65, p. 424.

[6] Turr. vi. 82, f. 123.

instances of the omission of passages adverse to that belief, and also we have had instances of the insertion of passages favouring it. One hundred and twenty-six years had intervened before the publication of the Quadragesimale, 218 before the appearance of the Mariale. If the passages in Barth. Albicius are his, the "Barth. de Pisis" of Card. de Turr. must be another Franciscan.

"¹ In his Lent sermons, on the Gospel, 'There was a dedication-feast in Jerusalem' (John x.), inquiring whether, de facto, when any one is sanctified, he is made impeccable, he lays down a fourfold difference of sanctification. He says thus: 'In the fourth way, a person is sanctified by a sanctification, whereby a faculty is given of avoiding both venial and mortal sin, by removal of the fomes or overcoming (superationem). And in that way the glorious mother of Christ was sanctified in the second sanctification, which was in the Incarnation of the Son of God,' adducing Alex. de Ales, in 3."

166. "⁸ To the same effect is the fath. br. Jacobus de Casali, of the same order, in a treatise which he wrote on that matter."

Augustinians.—167. Bernard Oliveri, Mag. of Paris, Provincial of the Augustinians A.D. 1330, Bishop of Tortosa, "the most eminent man of his age in Spain, and most eminent theologian of his time." Th. de Herrera in Ossinger, Biblioth. Aug., p. 642.

¹ Turr. vi. 32, f. 123.
⁸ Turr. vi. 32, f. 123 v. He wrote " Learned Questions on Philosophy and Theology," Wading (Script. Ord. Min. p. 798), who also mentions him alone as *the* eminent writer in the monastery of Casalis in the custodia of Montferrat (Ann. Min. ix. p. 105).

"'In his sixth Quodlibet, q. pen., which he framed on the Conception of the B.V., he is of the same sentiment as Ægidius Romanus."

168. "John Teutonicus, Augustinian ¹, both in his postills on 'Missus est' and his sermons on the Conception of the B.V."

"² In his Serm. 2 (beg. 'Lauda ac lætare, filia Sion') he says, 'It is to be held that the B. V. was conceived in original sin, because in her Conc. virtus virilis seminis et amplexus maritalis intervened; and under that original fault she was for some (aliquod) time, although it is credible that that time was very short, and, as it were, imperceptible. Nor does it derogate from the praise of the B. V. that she was conceived in original sin."

169. Henry de Vrimaria, or Frimaria ³, Augustinian Doctor of Theology at Paris about A.D. 1334, well-studied in H. Scr. and the Aristotelic Philosophy; distinguished for personal piety and charity (Pamph. Chron. Ord. Erem. p. 40, Possevini Appar. T. 1, p. 733).

"⁴ In his work de Sanctis, in his sermon on the Nativity, he is altogether of the same opinion [as Jordanes Teutonicus].

' Turr. vi. 33, f. 114, De Alva admits the passage, but says that he did not write Quodlibets, but only revised, amended, and perfected those of his master, Ægidius Romanus (n. 46).

¹ Among the Dominicans, three persons were known as Joannes Teutonicus. I do not find any in Ossinger.

² Turr. l. c.

³ Ossinger says (p. 953) that P. de Alva published a treatise of his for the Conception of the B. V. with nineteen others (Lov. 1664). No such work is mentioned in Pamphilus, who enumerates twenty works of his, or by Ellsius. Probably it is the very sermon which De Alva thinks to make for him.

⁴ T. vi. 33, f. 124.

De Alva gives some words of his, as if they made for him.

"Her singular dedication was this; her internal sanctification was swifter and more copious than others. It is clear as to swiftness, because the sanctification of John was in the 6th month, that of Jeremiah still later, but the Bl. V., as it were, in imperceptible time, so that some say, that in the same instant in which she contracted original sin, she was sanctified by grace. Shall we not say more holily, rightly, and better, that, being prevented through the grace of sanctification, she was preserved from original sin? Certainly it is more reasonably and honestly said, than that in the same instant she was both stained and purged and sanctified."

But this seems only to say, that it would be better to say at once that the B. V. was preserved from original sin, than to assert a self-contradictory proposition in order to seem to maintain the universal transmission of orig. sin, and yet absolutely to exempt her from it.

In the 4th sermon De Vrimaria said,—

"I say, first, that the B. V. is called a tender rod through the purity of innocence; for she was sanctified by grace in her mother's womb, and then through the exercise of virtues," &c.

De Alva said that "both parties owned the sanctification in her mother's womb;" but, in fact, both the comparison to the sanctification of John B. and Jeremiah, and, I think also, the term "sanctified in her mother's womb" belong to writers who did not believe her to have been "preserved from orig. sin." For to be "sanctified" is a gift to one who already exists; but the preservation from orig. sin was held to be by grace infused simultaneously with the gift of existence.

De Alva raises a doubt as to two sermons on the Conception in the same collection, in the first of which De Vrimaria speaks (according to De A.) of the opinion of the Conception in orig. sin as the more probable, in the second directly asserts it; but he questions them only as contradicting the first sermon on the Nativity, as he understood it. In the second of these sermons De Vrimaria speaks of the "three conceptions—of the seed, of the soul, and of grace, whereof the first is not to be celebrated, because, being inanimate, it is not susceptible of grace, nor the second, on account of the soul being infected by contact with the body." He says that "the opinion of certain doctors, that the B. V. contracted not original sin, is repugnant to H. Scripture, and takes away the greater reverence for Christ Himself." Then he argues, as in the first sermon of the Nat., that "she could not have been purified in the same instant, because two opposites do not take place in the same instant," and sums up, "And therefore others say more probably, that not in the same instant, in which she was infected by original sin, but in another proximate instant, in such wise as was possible to nature, she was purged and sanctified by grace."

171. John Clivoth, of Saxony [in Turr.'s printed work it stands ‘Liniros⁵,’ through mis-

---

⁵ Turr. vi. 33, f. 124. In vi. 28, f. 218 v., by a misreading

reading, doubtless, of his MS.; Clivoth is in De
B.], "lived in the 13th cent. a very celebrated
writer and most eloquent preacher" (Oss. p. 235).

"On iii. d. 3, he adduces many authorities of the saints, the
first of which is Aug. on Ps. 34, where Aug. says that the
B. V. M. died on account of the sin of Adam, adding that it
cannot be explained of death from Adam, which is the penalty,
for that death was common with Christ. Aug. infers the
same, c. Julian. ii., de Nupt. et Conc., and many others."

172. John Stringarius, S. T. P., Augustinian,
chosen A.D. 1434, with fourteen other Theologians
of the Eremites, to be present at the Council of
Florence, where he disputed earnestly against the
Greeks and Arminians[6]. He must then, unless
there was some other Augustinian of that name,
have been a (perhaps older) contemporary of De
Turrecremata.

"'To the same is f. Magr. John Steringarius[8] on 3 Scnt.,

John Beleth is printed as "Mag. Joannes *Valleti* in his Summa
on Divine Offices." He quotes Beleth's words, "That *festival*
is not authentic." De Alva, identifying the Augustinian with
the Dominican (p. 446), would claim both to be Hannibaldus
under another name. But, although the first part, which is
almost the same formula, occurs in all, the sequel (as to the
'fomes') is not identical with Hannibaldus, as De Alva says,
although it is on the same subject.

    [6] Oss. p. 879.

    [7] P. vi. c. 43. f. 124.

    [8] I have adopted the orthography of De B. for Steringacius
in Turr., supposing it to be one of the orthographical mistakes
in the MS., of which Duimius complains. De Alva would have
it, that it is the same authority as the Dominican Steringarius,

saying that the B. V., neither before Conc. nor in Conc.
before the infusion of the soul, was sanctified, because the soul
is the proper subject of sanctifying grace. Nor again in the
instant of the infusion of the soul, because thus she would not
have contracted original sin, as neither did Christ. But she is
only believed to have been sanctified after the infusion of the
soul. For this was given to other saints also, as to Jeremiah,
who foresignified Christ, and John Baptist, who pointed out
Christ. Therefore it was specially meet that this should be
conferred on the mother of Wisdom, to Which nothing defiled
can enter."

Also, a little below,—

" Nor can it be said, that the fomes was totally taken away
from the B. V. by the grace of sanctification, as was granted to
Adam thro' original righteousness before he sinned, viz. that
the lower powers should never be moved without the will of
reason. For this derogates from the dignity of Christ, that,
before His Incarnation, in Whom the immunity from condemnation was first to appear, any one should, according to the
flesh, be freed from the first condemnation. And therefore it
seems that it ought to be said, that by sanctification in the
womb the fomes was not taken away from the Virgin according
to the flesh, but remained bound. But afterwards, at the very
Conception of the Flesh of Christ, it is to be believed that the
total withdrawal of the fomes redounded from the Child to
the mother."

Cistercians.—173. John Calcar, Cistercian (perhaps a corrupted name). De B. has a Joh. de
Cervo, Cistercian, who wrote on that side in 3 Sent.
dist. 3.

" * In a book, which he called ' Collection of Ears of Corn,'
which begins, ' The Angel said to the shepherds,' in Serm. 78

---

but De B. is far too accurate to place the same person
among Dominicans and Augustinians within seven pages.

  * Turr. vi. 35. f. 125.

on the Nativity of our Lady, on the text 'The morning arose,' Gen. 32, he said, ' Where is a distinction of a treble grade of sanctification. The first is, when it takes place not immediately in the Conception, but immediately after the infusion of the rational soul; and this degree befits the B. V. For it was not fitting that she should remain long under the original stain, that the Conception of Christ should be from a most pure mother."

174. "[1] John Monachus, Cistercian, in his iii. d. 3."

C. 175. "Sermones Soccii," sermons for the whole year, by a Cistercian Prof. of Theology, of the Convent of Marienrayd, who in humility did not publish them. They were found in his "socci," after his decease, and published under this title, as a memorial of his humility. " Able, mighty in Scripture, most fluent writer of sermons " (C. de Visch, Scriptt. Cist. p. 239).

"[2] In his notable work on the Saints, in the Serm. on the Nativity of the B. V., on the text, ' I have prepared a lantern for Mine Anointed,' he says thus : ' But that she might obtain the highest purity, she was purified thrice ; first in the mother's womb from original sin, which purification so far restrained the fomes, that she was able not to sin, yet it left in her the fomes in its essence.' And he is of the same opinion in other sermons on the same festival."

De Alva (Ver. 287) allows this passage, but thinks he may have meant the "depuratio materiæ

---

[1] Ib. "Joannes Monachus, Cistercian, Paris Theologian, wrote on the Sentences, according to Sylvester Maurolycus, Maris Occani, L. ii." De Visch, p. 171.

[2] vi. 35, f. 125.

ante animationem." He quotes from Andreas de Peruzzinis, a saying from the 30th sermon: "There is a treble væ from which she was liberated,—the væ of original sin, the væ of venial sin, the væ of mortal sin." But since, according to Turr., he taught the same in several sermons, this may naturally mean, that she was "liberated" from it, after its contraction, in her mother's womb.

176. "Mag. Garric, whether secular or regular I cannot know." "[3] A profound Theologian, a Master of Paris."

"[1] In his Postill to the Romans, treating of Rom. 7:— 'So the law and commandment are holy,' on occasion of what Gregory says in his Sermon on the Assumption of the B.V.M.[2], 'Nor could she be bowed down by the bands of death,' says, 'It is asked, as to the B.V., since she had original sin, Why could she not be bowed down by the bands of death? and having distinguished a threefold band, the first whereof is the leaving the body, the second, the return of the body to ashes, the third, the descent into hell, he pursues the solution of the question. But what he says on Eccl. 7, I have alleged above" (see p. 278).

---

[1] Id. v. 1, f. 84 [82] v. [2] Id. vi. 35, f. 125.
[3] There is no such sermon in his works.

ANALYSIS

Of Cardinal de Turrecremata's "Treatise on the Truth of the Conception of the most Blessed Virgin, as a relation to be made before the Fathers of the Council of Basle, July, a.d. 1437, compiled at the mandate of the Legates of the Apostolic See presiding over the said Council [1]."

PART I.

C. 1. Card. de Turrecremata first lays down certain fundamental rules to be observed in the judgment on that question. These rules are:—1) That in the definitive judgment of a General Council, testimonies and sayings of Holy Scripture are chiefly to be weighed and considered; 2) That, next to the authority of Holy Scripture, in the definitive judgment of this present cause, as of any other cause of faith, those holy Doctors are most to be considered and embraced by the Council, whose sayings in matters of faith have been most approved by the Universal Church. 3) That the testimonies of the Fathers to be adduced should be viewed in their originals (so as to be considered in their context). 4) That if any doubt should arise as to the meaning of any text of Holy Scripture, the

[1] The division made by Card. de Turrecremata has been followed, as marked in the beginning of the volume, because without it his references to his earlier chapters in the later parts would be unintelligible. The division into thirteen Parts, marked at the commencement of each Part, was made by the Editor, Alb. Duimius. The subordinate chapters, into which Duimius divided each of those Parts, have not been noted, since the double notation would be confusing, and the folios sufficiently indicate the place in the work.

aforesaid Fathers should be chiefly regarded in the exposition thereof. 5) That those scholastic Doctors are to be preferred, both in the exposition and understanding of Holy Scripture, and in defining matter of faith, who most expressly and formally resolve their meanings to Holy Scripture and the doctrine of the Fathers. These rules he supports largely by authority.

The opponents urged—Obj. 1) Two maxims from a treatise alleged as S. Aug.'s [2], but wrongly. " Great things are to be handled the more cautiously if they cannot be corroborated by *special* authorities ;" and " When Scripture tells us nothing, we must seek by reason, what is most agreeable to truth." Inference. Since there is no express authority as to the Conc., we must go by reason. Ans. 1) " special " not in S. Aug [3]. But what is said of all, is said of each; so S. Aug. ag. Pelag. Reason may clear faith, cannot prove it. If no proof of Scr., then, like the Assumption, it must be matter of opinion. Ans. 2) There *are* many testimonies to Conc. in orig. sin. Obj. 2) 1 Pet. 3, " Be ready to give a reason of the faith." Rom. 12, " Prophesy according to the ratio fidei." Ans. Not, as these say, full reason and knowledge, but proof from testimony of Scr. or from principles of faith. " Perilous to make human reason the rule and measure of understanding Scr. in determining verities of faith " (ff. 2.—8).

C. 2. Exposition of terms of the question proposed by Council, " Whether it is more pious to believe that the soul of the most Bl. Mother of God was, at the instant of its infusion in the body, preserved from orig. sin, than to believe that the Virgin herself was conceived in orig. sin," viz. " pious," " conception," " orig. sin." *a*) " Pious " may mean—1) belonging to Divine cultus ; or, 2) most reverential to the B. V. as a mother ; or, 3) most according to Catholic faith ; or, 4) piously to be believed. *b*) " Conception " = animation or nativity *in* womb, as opposed to nativity *from* womb, viz. birth. *c*) " Orig. sin," " wanting of orig. righteousness, which ought to be in us, contracted through vicious origin." So all chief doctors of schools,

---

[2] It is the De Assumptione B. M. V. which, the Benedictines say, is " auctoris incerti et pii," but which is not of any assignable date. Opp. S. Aug. T. vi. App. p. 250.

[3] It is in the treatise, as the Benedictines have printed it.

Alex. de Ales, &c. Opposite definition, "a damnable fault or offence against God." Ans. This fits better actual sin. If it implies that one offends God, false; for no free-will in orig. sin. Orig. sin, not mortal sin, as contended on the other side. Divine imputation concurs not as formal cause of orig. sin. Transmission of orig. sin, bec. all in Adam (ff. 8 v.—11 v.).

- C. 3. Opp. holds, that "sentence of Divine law concurs, hemming in [coarctans] to contraction of orig. sin." Ans. Law of God cannot be to sin. S. Paul contrasts law of God and law of sin. Scr. alleged proves law of punishment, not of fault. Gen. 2, "Thou shalt die;" "Thou shalt return to the dust." Rom. 8, "Our body is dead bec. of sin," Col. 2, "the handwriting against us." Even the "fomes" is not from Divine law (ff. 11 v.—14).

C. 4. Corol. "Original sin, although a great evil, is, in those conceived in it, as to fault, the least sin, because it has least of will, i. e. not in the person, but in the principle of the nature." It may not be said of one in orig. sin, "This soul sins," or "deserves death." Cor., that the opprobrium that one conceived in orig. sin is foul, stained, tenebrous, &c., said in declamatory terms, as an appeal to feelings against opinion that B. V. was conceived in orig. sin, unfounded (ff. 14 v.—15).

PART II.

Second part of the work, in which are put the authorities of the Old and New Testament according to the glosses and expositions of the Saints, denying that Christ Alone was free from original sin in His Conception; and refutations of the general ways of answering on the opposite side, solving also many of their arguments.

C. 5. Authorities from O. T., with their glosses and declarations, that Christ Alone was conceived without orig. sin (the force is in the gloss oftener than in the text). *a.* Gloss on Num. 19, on "red heifer." *b.* Job 14, "Who can make that clean," &c.; *c.* Wisd. 1, "Christ brighter than the sun," &c. *d.* Ps. 21, "Thou hast prevented him with blessings of goodness." *e. f.* Ps. 22 and 85, "Deliver my only one," &c.

g. Ps. 22, " On Thee have I been cast from the womb." *h.* Ps. 45, "Fairer than the sons of men." *i.* Ps. 51, gloss on " Against Thee only," and on " That thou mayest overcome, when," &c. *k.* Ps. 88, "Free among the dead." *l.* Cant. 2, "I am the flower," &c. *m.* Cant. 5, " Elect out of a thousand." *n.* Isa. 4, " Seven women," &c. *o.* Isa. 53, " Who did no sin." *p.* Ezek. 9, " Called a Man," &c. (ff. 15, 16).

C. 6. Auth. out of N. T.—Matt. 3, Luke 3, "This is My beloved Son." Luke 1, " That Holy thing born of thee," and "Blessed is the fruit of thy womb." John 1, " Behold the Lamb of God." John 3, " He who is from heaven is above all." John 8, "The Son abideth ever." Ib. " Which of you convinceth Me of sin ?" Heb. 1 and Ps. 45, " God hath anointed Thee," &c. (ff. 16, 17).

Refutation of eight ways of answering these authorities.

C. 7. *Way* 1.—That Christ might be said to be excepted principally, another less principally, as Deut. 6, Matt. 4, " Thou shalt serve God alone," excludes not 1 Tim. 6, " Serve their masters." Ans. *a)* To God latria is due, to man service. *b)* Argt. might be extended to all (f. 17).

C. 8. *Way* 2.—That Christ might be said to be exempted of Himself, the B. V. by grace, as Matt. 10, " None is good, save God only." Rev. 15, " Thou only art holy." 1 Tim. 2, " To God Alone," &c. Ans. *a)* (as bef.), it would apply to all, not to B. V. only ; *b)* many authorities say explicitly, that all besides Christ contracted orig. sin. It could not be said, " Christ Alone was blessed, *and all saints unblessed*, because God and Christ Alone have incommunicable bliss." " Holy," " good," *do* belong to God only (ff. 17 v.—18 v.).

C. 9. *Way* 3.—The exclusion would not hold against evidence of reason. Ans. This begs the question. As to instance of eating the shew-bread, " doctrine does not admit exception ; practice may, from circumstances " (f. 18 v.).

C. 10. *Way* 4.—As to facts, judgments of prophets, unless specially enlightened by God, may rest on probability, not on truth, as in Elijah's opinion of Israel. Ans. *a)* Not doctors only, but H. Ghost, the Teacher and Inspirer of truth, said it. *b)* Too many, too great, holy doctors so spoke (f. 19).

C. 11. *Way* 5.—That, if the same reason belongs in a degree to another, that person is not excluded ; as, "No man knoweth the Father save the Son," but the H. Gh. knoweth Him. Christ ought to be without sin, because Mediator ; so the B. V. also, by reason of her marriage-bond with Christ her Spouse, being first Mediatrix and reconciliatrix. Ans. *a*) Rule does not hold, save in unity of Divine Persons. *b*) Christ is the Mediator of all, including the B. V. (f. 19 v.).

C. 12. *Way* 6.—That they allege *as* universally, that Christ Alone was without actual sin, and was Alone *born* without sin. Ans. *a*) Doctors rest that exception of Christ on what belongs to Him only, viz. that He was conceived, not "ex virili semine, sed mystico spiramine," and that He came as the Purifier and Redeemer of the whole human race, and so, not to be cleansed Himself. *b*) S. Aug., Anselm, Bern., *do* except actual sin as to the B. V. *c*) "Birth" did not mean mere birth from the womb, since Jeremiah and John B. known to have been born without sin. *d*) Christ Alone born without "fomes" (f. 20).

C. 13. *Way* 7.—Since Christ *could* not be conceived under orig. sin, the exception of Him did not include all others under it, any more than the saying, "All men, except angels, are incorruptible." Ans. (as bef.) *a*) It would prove too much; *b*) Christ *was* Man (f. 20 v.).

C. 14. *Way* 8.—That the B. V. was so united with Christ that when He is excepted, she is excepted. Ans. *a*) Christ is so excepted by Fathers as to exclude all else. *b*) On grounds, excluding all else. The Proposition, "Christ Alone was free from orig. sin," resolves itself logically into two—"Christ was in His Conc. free from orig. sin," "no one else was" (f. 21).

Answers to seventeen reasons corroborating *Way* 8, as to the inclusion of the B. V. with Christ.

C. 15. *Reason* 1.—"As the operation of the B. V., in her Conc. and Birth of Christ, was exempted from the common law, so was her person." Ans. *a*) Actions of a person being excepted, so is the person as to those actions, yet not as to past time. B. V. was excepted from time of her sanctif., not before. *b*) Argt. would include too many, the objects of miracles, as Sarah, S. Anne, or the workers of miracles. *c*) Operation in the Conc. of Christ, not that of B. V., but of the Holy Ghost. *Reason* 2.—" Flesh of Christ and of B. V. was one." Ans. *a*) Orig. sin is in soul, not in flesh. *b*) Flesh of Son of God and of B.V. not as whole and part, nor identically the same, though His was formed of her most pure blood, and at her own Conc. the flesh of the B. V. had no relation to the Flesh of Christ. *c*) The Church is said to be one flesh with Christ, yet this does not follow. Absence of orig. sin in Christ is ascribed to causes peculiar to Himself. *d*) Other like sayings, " Christ Alone was born of a Virgin," " Christ Alone was conceived of the Holy Ghost," " Christ Alone was at His Conception Blessed," &c., admit not of exception (ff. 22, 23 v.).

C. 16. *Reasons* 3, 4.—" The B. V. being Queen and spouse of Christ, as He was King, His exemptions and prerogatives were hers." Ans. *a*) Not Queen, &c., at her Conc. *b*) Church also His spouse ; but to affirm exemption of it, would be to deny Christ's redemption. *c*) Although B. V. was spouse of God most High, and Mother, yet not one primal principle with Christ of our redemption, but she was herself redeemed by the redemption made by the one Saviour (ff. 23 v.—25 v.).

C. 17. *Reason* 5.—" The B.V. being with Christ one principle in spiritual regeneration, she must be included in Christ's exemption from orig. sin." Ans. Spiritual regeneration is— *a*) wrought by One, God, through grace; *b*) for the merits of Christ; *c*) B.V. cannot concur as one principle; for God Alone can infuse grace; Christ Alone can merit. She is one of the redeemed. *d*) The Church is the mother of the sons of God—1) by Sacramental birth through Baptism ; 2) nourishes by doctrine and example. B. V. their mother, bec. she *a*) bare their Regenerator; *b*) cares greatly for each soul; *c*) in a certain manner she by charity co-operated to faithful being born in Church. Past spot injures not present purity (ff. 25 v.—28 v.).

C. 18. *Reason* 6.—" Christ and the Bl. V. the first principle of all living, in spiritual being and life ; such first principle could not have been spiritually dead." Ans. Same expanded. Also, Christ, not B. V., Head of the Church, but influences are from the Head. Reply. *a*) Prov. 8, Ecclus. 24, read on her

feasts, so speak of wisdom. *b*) Prayers of Church, "vitam
datam per virginem," "vitam præsta puram," &c. Ans. *a*) Prov.
Eccl. literally of Christ; *b*) mystically of B. V. or Church.
They cannot mean *this*, since Christ alone principle of grace;
as God, as its Author; as Man, ministerially; apply to B. V.
as bearing Him Who is fountain of life; fulness of grace different in B. V. and Christ; in Christ, redounds to others; the
B. V. is " gratiæ non datrix sed impetratrix " (ff. 28 v.—30).

C. 19. *Reason* 7.—" B. V. was mother of Adam and his principle in spiritual being, therefore could not have been corrupted
from him." *Reason* 8.—" She was first Mediatrix, therefore
never had any thing for which she needed reconciliation or
Reconciler; and so not orig. sin." *Reason* 9.—" She was first
mother of grace and mercy, so never child of wrath." Ans.—
1 Tim. 2, " One Mediator between God and men ;" Col. 1,
"Reconciled all things by Him ;" Luke 2, B. V. says, "My
spirit rejoiceth in God my Saviour." B. V. mother of grace,
as bearing Author of grace, co-operating by prayers to gain
grace (ff. 30—31).

C. 20. *Reason* 10.—" All things were re-made through B. V.,
nothing without her; so she did not need re-making." Arg.
" By 'through' is meant secondary cause; as God moves
heaven through angels, enlightens world through sun, so she
concurred with Christ in meritorious operation, whereby man
was restored. Christ Alone is not to be called the Redeemer,
but also B. V. ; nor did He redeem the world, save through
her." Ans. This cannot stand with integrity of Christian
faith. Gal. 8, " a mediator," &c. 1 Tim. 2, " One Mediator,"
&c.; S. Peter, Acts 4, " no other name," " no redemption
except by His Blood." Assigns to B. V. proper office of the
Humanity of Christ. She herself would not have been redeemed; worthy satisfaction can only be made through hypostatic union. The re-making of the human race was by merit
of Passion and Death of Christ. But B. V. did not concur
with Christ in suffering and dying for mankind, &c. Opposed
Arg. 1. "Since Christ remits sin and saves His own
through Church meritoriously, much more might B. V. be
said to have concurred with Christ to redemption of man."
Ans. " All *receive* influences of redemption, not working it."

Tit. 3, " not by works of righteousness," &c. Eph. 2, " saved
by faith, not of yourselves." Incarnation, the principle of grace,
could not be merited. John 1, " Grace and truth by J. C."
Good of one mere man cannot be cause of good to whole
nature. Arg. 2. If men " fellow-workers with God " (1 Cor. 3),
much more B. V. could concur, as helper of God, in causality
of redemption of man. Co-operation fourfold,—1) giving help ;
2) counsel (neither towards God) ; 3) as His instrument (in
some things, not all); 4) by disposing to receive the effects of
work of the Agent, as by teaching or by administering sacraments. These do not bear out concurrence in causality.
Arg. 3. " We receive every thing now through Mary, so she
concurred with Christ in causality of grace." Ans. In that
One meritorious Sacrifice, B. V. concurred not as priest offering,
but as one for whom it was offered. Arg. 4. " As Eve concurred with Adam in bringing in sin, so Mary with Christ in
restoring our salvation." Ans. Both sexes concur, but not
causally or effectively. To bring in sin lay within natural power
of first parents ; restoration only by operation of Soul of Christ,
united with Divinity. Things were re-made through B. V.,
only in that she bare the Re-maker of all. Obj. The words,
" by her and with her," import more of causality and likeness of concurrence with Christ in mystery of redemption.
Ans. Hyperbolical language of devout minds not to be taken
rigorously as language of schools. " Through " to be understood, not in regard to the Passion of Christ, but of her Conc.
of the Redcemer (ff. 31—34).

C. 21. *Reasons* 11 and 12. " S. Anselm says, ' B. V. mother
of things created, and of restoration of all things,' so she needed
not re-creation." Ans. S. Anselm himself explains this of her
having borne Him, by Whom all things were saved (f. 34).

C. 22. *Reason* 13.—From Eph. 5, " If Christ loved B. V. as
Himself, He should have preserved her from orig. sin." Ans.
a) The whole Church the spouse of Christ, of whom it could
not be said. *b*) B. V. not spouse of Christ at her Conc.
c) Christ did reserve some things to Himself. *Reason* 14.—
" Flesh of B. V. flesh of Christ, but no one hateth his own
flesh." Ans. Same as before, as to the Church and the time of
Concep. Hatred in God, not as in man, since God is love ;

nor are little ones in orig. sin shut out from love of God, but
only from completest participation of His love, in vision of His
Essence, forfeited in Adam. *Reason* 15.—" The Church, the
spouse of Christ, was to be without spot and blemish ; much
more B. V." Ans., as before. Christ *did* reserve to Himself
what belonged to His office as Redeemer, not to be born of
human seed, whereby orig. sin contracted, and therein did,
ipso facto, reserve the not being born in orig. sin (ff. 34 v.—
36).

C. 23. *Reason* 16.—" The B. V. was not subject to Christ
in His Humanity, as the Church was." Ans. This alien from
the faith of the Catholic Church as to the Saviour J. C., God
and Man. Ps. 8, " Thou hast put all things under His Feet ;"
1 Cor. 15, " All things shall be put under His Feet," did " not
except any thing." Obj. Contrary to evidence of reason ; so
B. V. was not included in that "all." For Scr. does not say
specially that she was, but does say, she is at His Right Hand.
Ans. False, *a*) That it is against reason that B. V. was subjected to our Lord and Saviour Christ. For Scr. says,
" nothing is excepted." *b*) Ps. 45, said literally of the Church.
Humanity of Christ, through hypostatic union, closest to
God. The B. V. subject to Christ's Humanity, as member to
Head. Christ, the Head of the whole Hierarchy. Christ
merited His exaltation through infinite Virtue of His Passion.
Christ Alone Son by nature ; all else, adopted. Obj. *a*) " spouse
and mother not under feet of Spouse and Son." Ans. The
Feet of Christ signifying His dominion, subjection of spouse
to husband is of Divine, natural, Apostolic institution. Gen. 3,
1 Pet. 3, Col. 3. Spiritual espousal to our Saviour, God and
Man, different from espousal to man, the wife's companion.
b) Earthly mothers subject to sons, as Pope or Prince, much
more to King of kings (ff. 36—38 v.).

C. 25. *Reason* 17.—" That she is in a manner set over Christ
Himself" (Ipsi Christo principatur) ; Luke 2, " and was subject
unto them." Ans. 1.) but also to Joseph, who was not only
conceived in orig. sin, but had venial sins ; 2) S. Luke's words
seem to relate to Childhood of Christ ; 3) Christ's subjection
" of piety, not necessity." Her present princedom over Him
contradicts His session at Right Hand of God, i. e. His pos-

session of all good things of God. "That the B. V. after the Ascension was not subject to supreme pontiff contrary to faith" (ff. 38 v.—39 v.).

PART III.

Wherein are put the authorities of Holy Scripture, according to the glosses of the holy Fathers, saying that every man semi-nally propagated from Adam is conceived in original sin, with many authorities of many Saints, lights of the Church, asserting the same, of necessity of faith. And the ways of answering on the opposite side are refuted.

C. 26. Authorities of O. and N. T., with their glosses and declarations, that all besides Christ incurred orig. sin. In O. T., Gen. 17, "He hath broken My covenant," with gloss; Lev. 17, uncleanness and sin-offering after child was born. Job 3, "Perish the day in which I was born." Ib. 15, "What is man, that he should be clean, born of a woman?" Ib. 17, "I will say to corruption, thou art my father;" Ib. 25, "How can he be clean, who is born of a woman?" Ps. 32, "Thou hast forgiven the iniquity of my sin;" Ps. 51, "In sins," &c.; Ps. 53, "There is none that doeth good;" Prov. 20, "Who can say, my heart is clean?" Ps. 142, "In Thy sight shall no man living," &c.; Isa. 53, "All we, like sheep," &c.; "The Lord hath laid on Him," &c.; Isa. 64, "Thou wert angry, and we sinned," &c.; Matt. 18, Luke 15, "If a man have a hundred sheep," &c.; John 1, "Behold the Lamb of God;" Rom. 3, "By the works of the law shall no flesh be justified before Him." "The righteousness of God through faith in J. C., there is no difference, for all have sinned," &c.; Rom. 5, "As by one man," &c.; 1 .Cor. 1. 15, "As in Adam all die," &c. S. Aug. adds others, in c. Julian L. i. (ff. 40—42).

C. 27. Authorities from SS. Hilary, Chrysostom, Jerome, Ambrose, Augustine, Leo, Cyril, Remigius, Bede, Anselm, Gregory Great, Bernard, that all men, besides Christ, were conceived in orig. sin (ff. 42—46 v.).

C. 28. Authorities from the saints, and chiefly S. Aug., that it appertains to the Catholic faith to believe that all seminally

propagated from Adam were conceived in orig. sin. Council of
Milevis, S. Fulg., S. Aug., S. Anselm, S. Leo, S. Thomas
(ff. 46 v.—48 v.).

Refutation of seven modes of answering authorities of Scr.
and doctors, as to universality of orig. sin in conception of all
seminally derived from Adam.

C. 29. *Mode* 1.—" In ambiguous passages, Scr. admits of
any rational exposition. The word 'all,' then, in authorities
alleging that 'all, seminally coming from Adam, are conceived in
orig. sin,' is not to be understood of a logical but of a political
universality."

Ans. 1. Very perilous to introduce this distinction in passages where most evident necessity of Scr. or reason requires it
not. It might be argued, that "all things were made by Him,"
or "all things are naked and open to Him," &c., or " He careth
for all things;" or " No fornicator or unclean person," &c.; or,
"Lend, hoping for nothing again;" or, "Depart, ye cursed,
into everlasting fire," prove not universality of creation by
the Word, or of God's knowledge or Providence, or deadliness
of fornication, or wrongness of usury, or eternity of punishment. So here, where no evidence of reason requires the contrary, it is against glory of God to deny universality of redemption. E. g. " All men are liars," " are all under sin, " none
that doeth good," imply logical universality of corruption ; and
that "righteousness of God cometh unto all," states universal efficacy. Authorities ;—S. Aug. repeatedly, S. Amb.,
S. Anselm, S. Bernard, say " orig. sin is to be understood of
all without exception." 2) The same ruled by Council of Milevis,
that universality of original sin was always held by Catholic
Church every where. So S. Aug., quoting most distinguished
Bishops before him. Obj. "The Church says, in Ath. Creed, 'all
shall rise with their bodies,' " but B.V. shall not then rise.
Ans. 1) H. Scr. had mentioned those who rose at death of
Christ; so not to be understood universally ; but as to orig.
sin it denies exceptions. Grounds why logical universality
to be held; 1) Whole argument of so many Fathers against
Pelagians would fail, as to orig. sin ; 2) It would throw
doubt on truth of H. Scr. ; 3) Scripture excepts none, save
Christ ; 4) Universal proposition would be turned into parti-

cular; 5) In fact, B. V. is nowhere expressly excluded, but *is* expressly included by holy doctors. Why are these authorities to be taken in logical universality, and others not ? 1) Many give as rule, "An unfigurative universal in H. Scr. is to be extended to each included in the subject of the proposition, and not to be restrained to some only, unless the non-restriction be expressly or deducibly contrary to H. Scr." Instances objected (some childish) answered. 2) Fathers frequently repeat, that all seminally derived from Adam incur orig. sin, and Christ Alone excepted. 3) Authority of Apostolic See in Zosimus, "none can be said to be redeemed, not before captive under sin." 4) Large authorities of most illumined and devout doctors (ff. 48 v.—55).

C. 30. *Mode* 2.—"Universal rule not to be applied to individuals, exempted by prerogative or dignity, as *a*) no argument from human bodies here to that of Christ, or the B. V., or glorified bodies. *b*) Esther was exempted. *c*) First principle of a being never said to be subject to its contrary, as first luminous body to darkness. But B. V. is first principle in spiritual life of all men. *d*) Causative power does not descend from what is posterior, but contrariwise. B. V. not so much daughter of Adam, as his mother; then corruptive force could not have descended to her." Ans. to *a*: True, if prerogative belongs to the same time; but B. V. not Mother of God at her conception. To *b*: Same, Esther was Queen, passage misunderstood; *c* untrue (as ab.); and *d* fallacy. B. V. was lineally descended from Adam, though prior in dignity; causative power of regeneration not in B. V., but in Christ (ff. 55, 56).

C. 31. *Mode* 3.—"Universal rule not to extend to one, of whom the contrary is primarily or consequentially expressed, especially if any thing be said in favour of one." Ans. But no contradiction as to time of conception. Not true (as alleged) that praise in Holy Scripture requires us to explain away things blameworthy, as to Abraham, Jacob, Sarah, or Egyptian midwives. The more Scripture praises, the more it blames what is blamable, as in David, Solomon (ff. 56—59 v.).

C. 32. *Mode* 4 much the same as 2; that "the rule is not to be extended to privileged person, who (they assert) was pre-

served by singular grace." Ans. The minor assumes the point
at issue. It could only be grounded by *a*) authentic Scripture,
b) determination of Church, *c*) testimony of most approved
doctors and Fathers. Reply. Not necessary to show any privilege of the B. V.; *a*) because every thing to her praise might
be assumed; *b*) because of the Divine maternity, on ground of
which other privileges, not mentioned in holy Scripture, are
believed of her; *c*) that it would be self-evident to any not
prejudiced against it. Ans. to *a* : But it would be to her
praise to believe that she was conceived of the Holy Ghost,
and in possession of everlasting bliss from her conception, &c.;
to *b* : That other prerogatives are either expressly contained in
holy Scripture, or derived from it by necessary consequence, as
attested by holy doctors; to *c* : This would imply that the chief
teachers of the Church believed what was contrary to sound
sense. Freedom of Christ from original sin, in itself indubitable, is asserted in holy Scripture; much more would
that of B. V., which is not self-evident. Proof as to Christ
(ff. 59 v.—63).

C. 33. *Mode 5.*—"The above propositions of holy Scripture
prove that the B. V. contracted orig. sin 'de jure,' not 'de
facto.'" Ans. *a*) Expression wrong, since there can be no
"jus" to sin. *b*) Debt is to have orig. righteousness. *c*) Divine
justice does not punish for doing or contracting what is due.
Holy Scripture speaks not of "jus," but of fact. Obj. It is
meant that she would have contracted it, had she not been
preserved. Ans. Obligation to contract, does not imply fulfilment. No one would say "one was damned," because he
would have been, had he not been preserved. Contradiction to
say, that she contracted "de jure," and the "jus" did not extend
to her. Consistent to say "she did not contract orig. sin, but
would, had she not been preserved;" not " she contracted it not
in fact, and did contract it de debito vel jure" (ff. 63—
66 v.).

C. 34. *Mode 6.*—"The authorities are to be understood
causally, or virtually, or aptitudinally, that every one seminally
descended from Adam contracts original sin, causally, when conceived in the way of our corrupt nature, formally, when the
soul of the offspring conceived, by its union with the flesh,

contracts the stain. And that God could stop the second." Ans. Scripture could not say that one *was* guilty, if he was so only potentially, &c. If it might be said of one, it might be said of all. If soul of B. V. was prevented by grace in first instant, then it never had any cause, or virtue, or aptitude to contract orig. sin (ff. 66 v.—67 v.).

C. 35. *Mode* 7.—"That orig. sin was contracted 'antecedently,' having in their causes all things necessary to incur sin, not 'consequently,' i. e. completely and in fact." (This explanation in a sermon in the Council.) Ans. the same, but specific as to illustrations (ff. 67 v. 68 v.).

One answer to all these last. They admit, on authority of Holy Scripture and the Saints, that the B. V., in some way, do jure et debito, or habitudinaliter, or causaliter, or antecedenter, contracted original sin, and are thereby open to all the objections which they urge (ff. 68 v. 69).

PART IV.

" Confutation of answers to authorities of Holy Scripture adduced by my colleague in his relation."

C. 36. *Auth.* 1.—Rom. 3, "All have sinned, &c." Obj. 1. "Said only of actual sins." Ans. from S. Aug.; "not true of 'all,' unless infants included, who have no actual sin." Obj. 2. "Glosses say the contrary." Ans. Not so; authors cited (P. Lomb., Nic. de Lyra, Nic. de Gorran, Mag. Henry in his postill, Steph. of Paris). Obj. 3. "If 'all' is taken of actual sin, not true of infants; if of orig., not true of Adam and Eve." Ans. True of both together (ff. 69—71).

C. 37. *Auth.* 2.—Rom. 5, "By one man," &c. Arg. "All propagated from Adam sinned in his sin. But B. V. carnally propagated from Adam. Therefore." Obj. "Sons are said to sin in parents, who suffer punishment for parents' sin (Lam. 5. 7; Ps. 106. 6; Dan. 3 and 9)." Ans. *a*) Then it might be said "Christ sinned in Adam," Ps. 59. 5. *b*) Authorities imply that the sons also sinned. *c*) The contrary evident from text itself and Fathers on it. *d*) If said of any, it might be said of all; contrary to faith. Reply. Meaning of the same predicate often varies according to the subject. *a*) "Dead to sin" (Rom. 6) said otherwise of Christ and of us. *b*) "We are dead"—of Christ, actual death; of us, aptitude or necessity. *c*) God true, devil a liar; God essentially true; Satan sometimes says true. *d*) Jews and Greeks all under sin, but different sins in Rom. 1 and 2. Ans. Meaning of predicate varies as to different subjects, not of individuals, contained in one subject. Christ dead to or through sin, cannot mean the same as our being "dead to sin," because Christ was exempted from sin. "All men are liars;" surely against faith to argue that saints in heaven are so; on earth has one common meaning: actual sins vary; original sin is one in all (ff. 71—74).

C. 38. *Auth.* 3.—Rom. 5, "As by the offence of one." Obj. *a*) A wrong allegation of S. Aug. de Nat. et Grat., as though he said, all were not included in sin of first man. *b*) The sentence of condemnation one thing; its execution another. B. V. would be exempted. Ans. (as before) Orig. sin not by sentence of God, but from sin of first parents (ff. 74 v.—75 v.).

C. 39. *Auth.* 4.—Gal. 3, "Scripture concluded all under sin." Obj. Said of Moses' law only, which showed sin, did not justify, and of actual sin. Ans. Moses' law taught it truly; authorities include orig. sin (ff. 75 v. 76).

Auth. 5.—Matt. 9. "They that are whole," &c. Obj. The great employ physicians to prevent illness. Ans. 1) Christ says it of all men. 2) Angels who were preserved needed not physician. 3) Grace given ordinarily both to heal and to prevent (*this*, de fide). Arg. as to the great, proves not that they are more sick than others. Auth. of S. Aug., on the universality of this need of healing, defended (ff. 76, 77).

C. 40. *Auth.* 6.—Luke 19, "The Son of Man came to seek and to save that which was lost." Obj. 1. "Lost," to be taken aptitudinally. Obj. 2. One preserved from sin is equally "saved" as one set free from sin committed. Obj. 3. Text relates to calling sinners to repentance, and so not to B. V. Ans. to 1 : Our Lord speaks absolutely ; to 2 : presupposes sin in those healed ; to 3 : the words cannot be so restrained. So S. Aug.

Auth. 7.—1 Tim. 1, "Christ Jesus came into the world to save sinners." Obj. This holds equally, if in such multitudes one or two were preserved from sin. Ans. (as before) S. Aug. argues absolutely (ff. 77, 77 v.).

C. 41. *Auth.* 8.—1 Tim. 2, "There is One God, and One Mediator between God and man, Who gave Himself a ransom for all." Obj. answered below.

Auth. 9.—2 Cor. 5, " If one died for all, then were all dead." Obj. 1. Expos. of words " all dead" manifold. Ans. This hinders not, that exposition " all dead in sin " is right; defended out of S. Aug., who holds it essential to Catholic faith. Obj. 2. Where said specially, that Christ died for Bl. V. M. as sinner? Ans. Where said of Joachim, Anne, Joseph, His brethren? If of them, then of B. V. too, conceived as they. Exception not proved. Obj. 3. " Christ," S. Bern. says, " was crucified for angels ;" so not for sinners only. Ans. Fact denied (proof later). All S. Aug.'s arguments for orig. sin would fail. Obj. 4. S. Aug. exempted B. V. from sins. Ans. From actual, not from orig. sin. Obj. 5. Death, as to B. V., might be aptitudinal death ; else inconsistent with her being reparatrix and vivificatrix. Ans. *a*) S. Paul and S. Aug. speak of actual death. *b*) If.preserved in first moment of existence, no aptitudinal death. *c*) Interferes not with title reparatrix, vivificatrix, in sense in which these are understood (ff. 77 v.— 79 v.).

C. 42. Reply to authorities of S. Aug. S. Aug. had to do with deniers of grace, objected not to preservation from sin, if owned to be of grace. Ans. Pelags. denied, 1) original sin, 2) necessity of grace. S. Aug. absolutely affirms orig. sin in all, leaves it open only, whether one might keep free from actual sin by grace. If S. Aug. only meant not to object to preservation from orig. sin by virtue of nature, why do advocates of Immaculate Conception so seek to show that B. V. was not included in those general sayings, in which, according to them, she would be included, since by virtue of nature she could not be free from orig. sin, &c. And other answers (ff. 79 v.—83 v.).

PART V.

In which are put the authorities of Holy Scripture from which, according to the glosses and expositions both of the Saints and other doctors, it is gathered specifically that the B. V. contracted original sin.

C. 43. In O. T. *a*) Type of tabernacle, first formed, then hallowed; as interpreted by S. Thom. Aq. *b*) Job 3, " Let the stars be obscured in the darkness of the night thereof," as interpreted by S. Thom. Aq. and S. Bern. *c*) Eccl. 7, " One man of a thousand," &c., as interpreted by Gloss. Ord., Card. Hugo, Mag. Garric, James of Lausanne. *d*) Prov. 25, " Take away the rust," &c., as in Albert. M., James Laus. and many other postillators.

In N. T. S. Luke i. " The Holy Ghost shall come upon thee," &c. as in S. Amb., S. Aug., S. John Dam., S. Fulg., S. Greg., S. Bern., Bede, Hugo de S. V., P. Lomb., Card. Hugo, Albert. M., S. Thom. Aq., S. Bonav., Bertr. de Turre, Ulric., Mag. Nic. Gorram (ff. 82 [misprinted 84]—84).

C. 44. Obj. 1) That the fomes or concupiscentia implies not the previous existence of original sin. Ans. 1) From the definition of the fomes. 2) From the names given to it—viz. *a*) fomes, as fomentum peccati; *b*) concupiscentia; *c*) concupiscibilitas; *d*) languor naturæ; *e*) tyrannus; *f*) lex carnis; *g*) lex peccati (as origin of all); *h*) lex membrorum. 3) from answer of S. Aug. to Pelagians and from S. Ambrose; 4) from grounds given by Saints, why the fomes was not in Christ.

Arguments in support of obj. may be reduced to three: 1) that if two things so exist that one may be separated from the other, but not conversely, one may be in the subject without the other; but the fomes may exist in the baptized and original sin not, and fomes prior in order and more common and universal. Ans. Briefly (omitting much), *a*) The 'fomes' is not prior nor the cause of original sin in the same subject. The disordering of the inferior powers, or the material cause of orig. sin, is the result of the disordering of the will from God. *b*) Though the fomes exists in more than original sin *is*, not

in more than it has been. Arg. 2) "Absence of original righteousness, formal cause of orig. sin, fomes or concupiscence, its
material cause," granted; but the "material" is the less, the
"formal" the more principal. In original righteousness, the
formal cause was the rectitude of will; the material, the impression of that rectitude on the inferior powers; by loss of the
formal, the material was lost; aversion of will then from God is
principal cause, rebellion of inferior powers is the effect. Arg. 3)
That the fomes, as well as the necessity of dying and the like
penalties, are the punishment, not of original sin, personally contracted, but of that which was in the first parent. Ans. Contrary
to Holy Scripture, Fathers, Schoolmen, authority of Bl. V.
herself. S. Luke 1. "My spirit hath rejoiced in God my
Saviour," according to S. Bernard, Hugo de S. V., S. Aug.
(ff. 84- -87).

C. 45. Authorities of doctors, who specially attest that the
B. V. M. contracted orig. sin, and 1st. of S. Aug., with refutation of nine answers of some to the contrary (f. 87).

1) De Gen. ad lit. c. 10, "What was more undefiled" [see ab.
p. 99], which contains—*a*) that the Flesh of the B.V. came from
the propago of sin; *b*) that she did not conceive Christ from
the propago of sin; *c*) that therefore the law in the body of
death, opposed to the law of the mind, did not rage in Him;
therefore, according to S. Aug., it did in all else. 2) De Gen.
ad lit. ib. "Accordingly, the Body of Christ, although It
was taken from the Flesh of woman, which was conceived from
that very propago of the flesh of sin, was yet not so conceived
in her, as she too was conceived, nor was It flesh of sin, but
'likeness of flesh of sin.'" 3) "According to the seminal
ground, Levi was there," &c. [see ab. p. 99]. 4) Cont. Jul. L. ii.
[ab. p. 65]. 5) Cont. Jul. L. v. [ab. p. 102]. 6) de Bapt.
Parv. L. ii. [ab. p. 98]. 7) de Trin. L. xiii. [ab. pp. 429—435].
8) Serm. Nat. Dom. beg. "L'om. N. J. C." ["made out of various
passages of S. Aug. unceatly strung together," Ben. Serm.
128. App. T. v.]. 9) contra quinque Hœrr. L. v. [ab. p. 312,
313]. 10) on Ps. 34 [see ab. p. 100]. 11) on Ps. 70
[ab. p. 430]. 12) on Joh. Hom. v. "Behold the Lamb of
God" [see ab. p. 65] (ff. 87—96 v.).

;PART VI.

*In which are, to the same effect, authorities of other holy
doctors after Augustine, and other excellent Theologians.*

C. 46. Eus. Emis. [Gall.] de Nat. Dom. [ab. p. 122.] S. Leo
Ep. ad Flavian. [ab. pp. 434, 435], written to and accepted after
examination by the Council of Chalcedon, contains these four
propositions to our purpose; 1) that Christ Alone had not the
contagion; 2) that from the Bl. Virgin was taken nature, not
fault; 3) that Christ Alone was conceived without concupiscence; 4) that in Christ Alone man found himself innocent.
Also from two sermons on the Nativity [ab. pp. 123—125]
with answers (ff. 96 v.—97 v.).

C. 47. S. John Damasc. [ab. p. 148, and p. 435] S. Anselm,
Cur Deus Homo [ab. p. 163]. Obj. 1. The saying was Boso's.
Ans. 1) S. Anselm accepts it. 2) He says the same in his own
person. Obj. 2. It is un-Catholic, saying she was *born* in orig.
sin. Ans. True as to fomes (as in S. Aug., Gloss., Bede,
S. Thom., P. Lomb.). Ans. to passages alleged from de Conc.
Virg. c. 10 [ab. pp. 366, 367] (ff. 97 v.—99 v.).

C. 48. S. Maximus Taurin. [ab. p. 431] Boethius [ab. pp. 335—
337].

S. Gregory, in Ezek. Hom. 8, M. Mor. L. xxv. c. 1.   xi. fin.
[ab. p. 142] (ff. 99 v.—100 v.).

C. 49. Hugo de S. Vict. de Sacr. L. i. p. 8 [see more ab.
pp. 177, 178]. A S. Bernard [?], a Bishop [ab. p. 435].

S. Bernard, in serm. on the Assumpt. [ab. p. 176].

Obj. 1. S. Bernard spoke conditionally, "Quod si." Ans.
But, anyhow, positively, in context and elsewhere.

Obj. 2. That on the part of the parents the B. V. was so
conceived. Ans. 1) Intention of parents holy; 2) S. Bern.
says it of her own person; 3) that she was cleansed.

Obj. 3. That "trahere" is different from "contrahere."
Ans. Denied. Fulg. uses "trahere" as "contrahere." One
descended from lepers, could not be said "traxisse lepram," if
preserved from it.

Obj. 4. S. Bern. said, Mary had no sin "proprium," but
orig. sin is "proprium." Ans. "Proprium" in S. Bern. is
manifestly actual sin.

Serm. on Nat. of S. John B. in S. Bern. [ab. pp. 168, 197].

Serm. in Vig. of Nat. of our Lord [see ab. p. 436] (ff. 100 v.—102).

C. 50. Ep. to Canons of Lyons [ab. pp. 171—175] (f. 102 v.).

C. 51. Obj. 1.—Story of black spot [ab. pp. 191, 192]. Ans. Contrary to history, and other answers.

Obj. 2. That he did not assert it, since he submitted the whole to Apost. See. Others so submitted, what still they asserted.

Obj. 3. That it related to the Conc. seminis, not naturarum. Ans. The contrary is evident (ff. 103, 104).

C. 52. S. Thomas Aq., with commendation of his doctrine from Univ. Paris. He quotes iii. d. 3. art. 1. 3 P. q. 27. art. 2. Quodl. 6. q. 7. Comp. Theol., beg. Æterni Patris verbum, cap. de sanctif. matr. Dei, c. 22. Expos. salutat. Aug. [In fol. 104 v. he speaks of " *six* passages " of S. Thomas, as meaning apparently to quote them, but there are only five, including the Comp. Theol.] (ff. 104 v.—108 v.).

C. 53. Offices of many Churches [ab. pp. 255, 256; 374—377] (ff. 106, 107 v.).

C. 54. Distinctions alleged: H. Scr., in ambiguous passages, for its harmonizing and sound understanding, admits fourfold distinction in—1) difference of time; 2) office; 3) person; and 4) disposition. Instances: statements as to ark, 1 Kings 8, and Heb. 9; John B. prophet and not prophet; Elias and not Elias. In " All gone out of the way," not of acts, but of habitual or necessary disposition or inclination of corrupt nature thereto. So, "Every man a liar," commonly. "All we like sheep," &c. Innoc. III., in decretal, limited " He that believeth not shall be damned," to adults, as alone capable of belief. So it may be said, that B. V. was conceived in sin, taking—1) conception as " commixtio seminum," and " peccatum " largely, as Bern. seems, for fervor libidinis, or vitiosa corruptio carnis; or, 2) original sin, for penalty of sin, i. e. vicious corruption of nature, not for " wanting of orig. righteousness;" or, 3) from likeness in mode of conception and its penalties; or, 4) aptitudinally, i. e. taking orig. sin largely, as a necessary disposition on the part of corrupt nature thereto. And this might be said as to the past, on account of a certain aptitude in itself, though not in act. So angels said, Job 10, not to be "stabiles," not being so by mere nature, as God Alone to have immortality, i. e. by His own Nature; and under the words, "To whom much is forgiven, he loveth much," those preserved from sin are included, as having had it remitted. Specific answers to Ep. of S. Bern.

The arguments reducible to five :—

Obj. 1. That H. Scr. admits that what it speaks of as done [actum], should be referred, not to the actual, but the habitual disposition of the person, whether past or future.

Obj. 2. That one may be said to be conceived in orig. sin by reason only of the aptitudinal disposition to contract it, although in act he never contracted it.

Obj. 3. That sometimes a disposition to sin, or some morbid quality in the seed or in the flesh, is called original sin.

Obj. 4. That a thing, on account of its natural disposition alone to another thing, takes the name of that thing whereto it disposes.

Obj. 5. That, on the ground of the likeness of penalties to those who contract original sin, it may be granted that she was conceived in original sin.

Ans. to 1) No such instance in H. Scr. Glosses include orig. sin in its sayings, Innoc. only reciting opinion. On same principle all orig. sin might be denied, while only admissible if contrary said in clearer places of Scr. If grace given to B. V. at first instant, there was no such habitual disposition; to 2) S. Anselm speaks not of aptitudinal disposition, but of certainty that child, when it receives its soul, will have defilement of sin; to 3) Meaning of S. Anselm and S. Bernard the same as the rest, that since, in punishment of the Fall, conception is not without passion, thence children born with orig. sin; 4) involves manifold absurdities. Any saint might so be called wicked, as having the dispositions inclining thereto. As to instances, Hezekiah could not have been said to have died, nor Nineveh to have been overthrown; "mobilis" or "instabilis," as said of angels, expresses liability, not act. S. Aug. only says, that those preserved from sin owed to God same thankfulness as those forgiven; 5) would, *a*) open the door to Pelagianism; *b*) Christ Alone had *likeness* of sinful flesh only; *c*) sin being

in the soul, those resemblances to others in the body no ground
for saying that she contracted not orig. sin; *d*) no one derives
penalty without sin. T. sums up these answers.—" It will be
of no little use to consider and weigh with what zeal, labour,
ability, the proposer on the other side strove to seek out so
many various ways of speech, whereby it could be granted
that the B. V. contracted original sin, saying, now, that she
contracted it by condition of nature ; now, from the mode of
propagation; now, taking original sin largely ; now, taking conception for conception of seeds; now, putatively; now, by
assimilation. And why this variety of speech ? Plainly in
order, by one or the other way, to escape those very plain
sayings of Scripture and the holy Fathers " (ff. 107 v.—113 v.).

To attempts to explain away S. Bernard, he alleges that
Alex. de Hales, Albertus M., S. Thomas Aq., S. Bonav.,
understood him to deny that B. V. was sanctified in conception, and argues from the Ep. itself (ff. 114—115 v.).

C. 55. Bede [ab. pp. 147, 148] ; Cassiodorus [ab. pp. 137—
139] ; Hugo à S. Vict. [ab. pp. 176—178] ; Rich. de S. Vict.
[ab. pp. 185—189] ; Abbot Odo [ab. p. 184] ; Peter Comestor
[ab. p. 437] ; Alanus in expos. of Athan. Creed [ab. pp. 210,
211] ; P. Lombard [ab. pp. 181—183] ; Joh. Valleti, i. e.
Beleth [ab. p. 167] ; Anonym. in his Summa [ab. p. 437] ;
William Bp. of Auxerre [ab. p. 213] ; Præpositivus [ab.
pp. 211, 212] ; William, Chanc. of Paris [ab. p. 209] ; Henry
of Ghent [ab. pp. 234—236] ; Abp. of Armagh [ab. p. 438] ;
Joh. de Poliaco [ab. pp. 249, 250] ; Wm. Durand [ab. pp. 205
—207] (ff. 116—118 v.).

C. 56. *Dominicans.*—Card. Hugo de S. Caro [ab. pp. 278,
279] ; Hugo Gallicus, Abp. and Card. of Ostia [ab. pp. 241,
242] ; Albertus M. [ab. pp. 166, 216, 217] ; Peter de Tarantasia
[ab. pp. 230—232] ; James de Voragine [ab. p. 268] ; Ulricus
Arg. [ab. pp. 236—238] ; Peter de Palude [ab. p. 438] ; James
of Lausanne [ab. pp. 272, 273] ; John of Paris [ab. p. 214] ;
John of Naples [ab. pp. 242—245] ; Thomasinus [ab. p. 440] ;
Hugo de Arg. [ab. p. 227] ; Nic. Treveth [ab. p. 258] ; Bernard of Clermont [ab. p. 441] (f. 119 v.). Rob. Holcoth
[ab. p. 441] ; Thomas de Walleis, Angl. [ab. p. 442] ; Peter de
Palma [ab. p. 282] ; Martin. Polon. [ab. pp. 266—268] ; Nic.

Gorram. [ab. p. 444]; Wm., Abp. of Lyons [ab. p. 265];
John of Genoa [ab. pp. 233, 234]; Wm. of Alton [ab. p. 279];
Vincent. Historialis [ab. p. 445]; James of Beneventum [Ib.];
Joh. de Verdiaco [Varsiaco, ab. pp. 277, 278]; Joh. of Luxem-
burg [ab. p. 446]; Joh. Steringacius Teutonicus [Sterngasse,
or Sperngasse, [Ib.] (ff. 118 v.—120 v.).

C. 57. *Franciscans.*—Alex. de Ales [ab. p. 214—216]; S.
Bonaventura [ab. pp. 217—220]; Rich. Middleton [ab. p. 238];
Reginald, Abp. of Rouen [ab. p. 241]; Thom. de Ales [p. 271];
Joh. Ricardi [ab. p. 253]; Bertrand de Turre [ab. pp. 273,
274]; Nic. de Lyra [ab. pp. 275—277]; Alvarus Pelag. [ab.
pp. 253—257]; Ægidius Zamor. [ab. p. 232]; John of La
Rochelle [ab. p. 264]; Rob. Conton [ab. p. 447]; Br. Lucas Pad.
[ab. p. 265]; Barth. de Pisis [ab. p. 447]; Gerard. Odonis (i. q.
Odo de Castro Rodulphi) [ab. p. 264]; James de Casali
[ab. p. 448]; Conrad Sax. [ab. p. 268] (ff. 120 v.—123 v.).

C. 58. *Augustinians.*—Ægidius Rom. [ab. pp. 239—241];
Greg. de Arim. [ab. p. 260]; Bernard Oliveri [ab. p. 448];
John Teut. [ab. p. 449]; Jordanes Teut. [ab. p. 274]; Henri
de Vrimaria [ab. pp. 449, 450]; John Liniros [prob. Clivoth]
of Saxony [ab. p. 451]; John Setringarius [ab. p. 452] (ff.
123 v.—124 v.).

C. 59. *Carmelites.*—Guido of Perpignan [pp. 245—247];
Paul de Perusio [ab. pp. 257, 258] (f. 124 v.).

Cistercians.—Ludolphus Sax. [ab. pp. 271, 272]; John
Calcar. [ab. p. 453]; F. of Fountain Abbey [ab. pp. 283, 284];
Author of Sermones Soccii [ab. p. 454]; Anonym. (Richard
of S. Laur.) [ab. pp. 261, 262]; Jo. Monachus [ab. p. 454];
Mag. Garricus [ab. p. 455]; Hannibaldus [ab. pp. 229, 230];
Mag. Stephanus [ab. p. 283] (ff. 124 v.—125 v.).

C. 60. *Canonists.*—John Teutonicus [ab. p. 202]; Barth.
Brix. [ab. p. 199]; Mag. Joh. [ab. p. 209]; Hugo [ab. p. 199];
Raimund [ab. p. 203]; Hostiensis [ab. p. 204]; Gul. Duran. [ab.
p. 205]; Jo. Andr. [ab. p. 208]; Guido Archidiac. [ab. p. 207];
John de Calderinis [ab. p. 209]; Peter de Prato ["Braco"
de B.]; Peter of Milan; Joan. (Summa, l. i. tit. 12), Barth.
de Concordio [ab. p. 207] (ff. 125 v.—126).

PART VII.

Value of these authorities.

C. 61. Many more expositors, writers on the Sentences, writers in praise of B. V., not alleged, because names not known. Obj. Authority of doctors far below that of Councils, therefore other nameless authorities on opposite side of the same value. Ans. 1) Canon law says, gravity of witnesses is to be weighed. 2) Authorities, cited by T., alleged in General Councils and in this against Bohemians. Obj. Knowledge of faith and of H. Scr., like every other science, is increased in time. Ans. *a*) In sciences, substance of knowledge increases; in Theology, later articles are implicitly contained in earlier. *This* is not the revelation of things unknown (which were possible), but contradiction (which is impossible). Obj. In the Clementines, sayings of Saints and modern Doctors of Theology singled out. Ans. Not in contrast with old, against Scr. Prov. 22, Zosim., Decretals, &c. *b*) These "moderns" were P. Lomb., Alex. Ales, S. Thomas, who are on this side (ff. 126 v.—128).

C. 62. Grounds of Dominicans, although devoted to B. V. 1) Prerog. of Christ, to be alone conceived without orig. sin. 2) Scr., that all born in way of nature are conceived in orig. sin. 3) The fathers. 4) The faith of the Church, as shown in Breviaries. 5) General representative Councils. Letter of Pope Leo, accepted by Council of Chalc. 6) Apostol. See, Pope Zosimus. 7) Most Doctors of Theol. and Canon law. 8) Zeal for the integrity of honour of God our Saviour, and so of His V. M. 9) Teaching of S. Dominic, to hold to Scr., the Fathers, and common doctrine of Church. 10) Opposite doctrine not expressly founded on Scr. or Fathers, but opposed to both (ff. 128, 129 v.).

C. 63. Grounds from twenty prerogatives of Christ. 1) Alone not conceived of unclean seed, Job 24; 2) Fairer than the sons of men, Ps. 45, Heb. 1; 3) "Anointed above His fellows," *ib.*; 4) "Free among the dead," Ps. 88; 5) "Who among the sons of God is like unto God?" Ps. 89; 6) Cant. 2. 1; 7) Isa. 4. 2; 8) Isa. 11. 1; 9) Jer. 31. 22; 10) "The holy of holies," Dan. 9; 11) "Born of the Holy Ghost," Matt. 1; 12) "My

well-beloved Son, in Whom," &c. Matt. 3. 17; 13) "The Holy
Thing born of thee," Luke 1; 14) "Lamb of God," John 1;
15) "He Who is from above," &c. John 3. 31; 16) "Likeness
of sinful flesh," Rom. 8; 17) "Firstborn among many brethren," *ib.*; 18) "One new man," Eph. 2. 15; 19) Rom. 7. 2;
20) "Lord of lords," Rev. 19 (largely supported by Fathers
and middle-age writers) (ff. 130—134 v.).

C. 64. Grounds for the same, derived from prerogatives of
the Conception of Christ in H. Scr.

1) "Sinless, because from a virgin," Isa. 7. 2) Ground from
Isa. 19. 1; 53. 2. Rev. 7. 2 (as explained in Gloss); 3) Of the
Holy Ghost, Matt. 1, Luke 1; (coll. John 12); 4) The newness as being alone free from sin (coll. S. Leo and S. Bern.);
5) The first which was clean (coll. S. Greg.); 6) Its aloneness.
Obj. It would have had prerogatives still, notwithstanding
Imm. Conc. Ans. True as to Himself, not as to His parent
or His own Conception. Hence purity is the basis of all
(ff. 134 v.—136 v.).

C. 65. Grounds from special prerogatives ascribed to B. V.
1) Purity of her conception of Christ; 2) Blessedness of Fruit
of her womb through immunity from sin; 3) Her sanctification.
[Obj. She could be said to be purged and sanctified, though
spotless, coll. *a*) John 15. 2, Luke 2. 22, Acts 21. 26; *b*) S. Ans.
"B. V. purified by faith of Incarnation;" *c*) Heb. 7. 26
of Christ; *d*) Dionys. Areop. of angels. Ans. B. V. not said
simply to be purified, but purified from orig. sin; use as to Bl.
Angels different in kind: use of word assumed contrary to
received language. Our Bl. Lord is said not to be " purified,"
but "separate from sinners"]; 4) sanctified from fomes in
Conception of Christ; but this implies fore-existence of orig.
sin (ff. 136 v.—140 v.).

C. 66. From the condition of her propagation from our first
parents; 1) because conceived in ordinary way; 2) because
carnally conceived, as John 3. 6, "That which is born of
flesh is flesh," with authorities and refut. of contrary; 3) from
being tithed in loins of Abr., according to S. Aug., &c. (ff. 141
—146).

C. 67. From penalties, to which B. V. was subject.

1) The ordinary sufferings of mortality, even before use of

reason (argt. of Aug. against Pelagians) ; 2) her mortality ;
3) (in support of this) her death, not being for the sins of
men ; 4) she died for sin of Adam, Rom. 8.   5) Christ Alone
died, being free from debt of death ; 6) pœna damni, i. e. loss of
Divine vision, unless Christ had opened heaven ; 7) (in confirmation).   " Had the B. V. died before Death of Christ, she
would not have entered heaven *then* " (authorities, Aug. Innocent III.).   Obj. Man naturally mortal ; even Christ would have
died of old age, if not crucified.   Ans. Man, before sin, mortal,
but would not have died (Rom. 5, 6).   Christ did not contract,
i. e. derive, these penalties together with the cause thereof, but
assumed them, that He might suffer.   Obj. Pœna damni, alone
due to original sin.   Ans. Pœna sensus in time ; pœna damni
in eternity.   Obj. God leaves the penalty, though He forgives
orig. sin to the baptized ; so, although He preserved the B. V.
from it.   Ans. It is just to leave penalties of forgiven sin, not
of sin not contracted.   Obj. to 7. But Moses saw God in this
life, and Christ from the instant of His Conception.   But
Moses's vision passing, not habitual ; to Christ, heaven was not
shut, since He did not sin in Adam (ff. 146 v.—151 v.).

PART VIII.

C. 68. Arguments from some titles of Christ, indicating the
universality of His saving influence, in respect of the whole
human race.   Few only of these names taken, for conciseness.
1) Jesus, or Saviour, *a*) " Who shall save His People," i. e. the
whole world, "from their sin."   Whence S. Aug. argues that
infants have orig. sin, having no other to be saved from.
b) He " came to seek and to save that which was lost ;" but to
be preserved from sin, is not to be saved from sin, as, to be preserved from perishing is not to be saved, having perished : also
Isa. 49. 25.   But texts must be explained of all alike ; else no
limits to exception.   2) Redeemer ; but all for whom He gave
Himself for a redemption had some sin, from which they were
redeemed (ff. 151 v.—152 v.).

C. 69. *a*) From force of term " redemption," opposed to man's
being " sold under sin ;" but from this we were bought by

H h

the precious Blood of Christ; for to redeem, i.e. buy back, implies alienation; we, having been God's, had by sin become Satan's. Obj. 1) Redemption may be only gift of grace to one who had lost it; 2) Redemption and preservation not contrasted; for *a*) redemption implies continued preservation. *b*) Angels said to have been redeemed; 3) Micah 6, people said to have been redeemed who never were in Egypt. Unborn children manumitted. Ans. to 1, anyhow redemption from slavery cannot be; to 2, redemption and preservation at the same time are contradictories; angels not said to be redeemed as man was; to 3, corporate body was redeemed, which remains the same, though members change. Manumission not redemption, for *a*) redemption only of living thing; *b*) manumission, freeing of one's own; redemption, recovery of what is another's.

b) Redemption so used in H. Scr. Luke 1, "Sent redemption to His people;" Gal. 5, "To redeem those under the law;" Tit. 2, "To redeem us from all iniquity." *c*) On authority of Pope Zosimus. "No one can be said to be redeemed, who was not before really captive of sin." *d*) Gloss. Pope S. Greg., S. Bern. "Thomas Aq. and common consent, that no one is redeemed by the Blood and Satisfaction of Christ, who was not before captive of sin" (ff. 153—159).

C. 70. Obj. There are six modes of redemption from sin; 1) from actual mortal sin; 2) from venial sin; 3) from original sin, by Baptism or sanctification in the womb; 4) by being preserved from falling into mortal sin, or 5) into venial sin, or 6) into original sin. Auth. for 4: Ps. 33, "The Lord shall redeem the souls of His saints" (by the Blood of Christ), "and they who hope in Him shall not fail." So authorities. Obj. 2. "The more one gains from the fruit of redemption, the more may he be said to be redeemed;" or, "if redemption be from actual sins, the more sins, the more redeemed," fallacies. Redemption single act; such not more redeemed, but redeemed from more; to receive more of the grace of God after redemption does not imply being more redeemed. Ans. to 5 and 6 follows from 4. Obj. "Unless B. V. was preserved from orig. sin, she was not most perfectly redeemed, nor would Christ have been the most perfect Redeemer." Ans. Preservation no redemption at all; then, too, Christ would not be the most perfect

Redeemer of world, which He did not so redeem, and many
other corollaries, as "the world would have been more perfectly
redeemed by Christ, had it been preserved from sin," &c.; contrariwise, the B. V. most perfectly redeemed by fore-deliverance
from orig. sin.   Mode of redemption of man most perfect, on
six grounds; 1) the most perfect Person of Redeemer, God-
Man; 2) the most precious Price; 3) the most perfect love;
4) the most perfect institution and reintegration of dignity of
man; 5) the multitude redeemed, all redeemed most perfectly;
and 6) from all.   So our Lord and Saviour J. C. is to be adored,
Who, being the most perfect, with most perfect love did by most
perfect Price redeem the whole human race from all evil.   If
preservation from orig. sin the most perfect, then more perfect
still is preservation from its penalties, more perfect to preserve
all mankind from it (ff. 159—162).

C. 71. Arg. 1. "If the one extreme exists, therefore the other.
But there are, who have always been and will be vessels of wrath,
therefore was one, who was always vessel of mercy."   But
fallacy in "always;" for to be vessel of mercy is to be made
such, and so had beginning, as to have been reconciled, healed,
redeemed, washed, of which one could not say, he was so always
(f. 162 v.).

Arg. 2. "If both extremes exist, therefore the mean.   But
Christ, Who neither had nor could have orig. sin, one extreme;
man, who could have and had it, the other.   Therefore the mean,
the B. V., who could have had it, but had it not.   Ans. But conception is either supernatural, as our Lord's, or natural; but
orig. sin follows natural conception.

C. 72. "All mankind would think it a more perfect redemption, if the human race had been restored to, and confirmed
by grace in, a state of innocence, and souls were born in
original righteousness.   Redemption, then, may be preservation
from future evil."   But redemption is of individual soul, and
implies change in it.   Such, then, could not be said to be
redeemed as we are (f. 163).

C. 73. Arg. from instances: 1) unborn offspring redeemed; 2)
fruits of 2nd or 3rd year, if mortgaged; or, 3) one adjudged to
death, if pardoned.   (1 and 2 irrelevant to redemption by Christ;
3 inaccurate, freed but not redeemed.)   4) " Christ redeemed us

from everlasting death, and so from something future." Ans.
We are redeemed from the guilt and due of eternal death,
which is past; but orig. sin could not be due, since it is contrary
to due, nor could the B. V. have this debt before her conception,
since she was not; nor, on the hypothesis, in first instant of
conception, since (ex hypoth.) she was in grace. Also, if B. V.
was redeemed from eternal death, she had orig. sin, since it is
only due to sin. So as to temporal punishment, redemption was
completed at Resurrection, and so we are "redeemed in hope"
of its completion; but to approach thus the end of perfected
redemption, and to be preserved from all sin, are contradictions
(ff. 164—166).

C. 74. From reason: 1) He is redeemed more efficaciously,
who is more freed from servitude, who is forecome from being
slave, than he who is first allowed to be under slavery, and
then freed. 2) The more accelerated is passive redemption,
the more efficacious. Ans. Such not redeemed at all. 3) Christ
redeemed us from the curse of the law; but we were never
under it; Ans. Nor were any but Jews at any time. 4) Satan
is bound now, and has less power; are we less redeemed?
Ans. Satan has less power, because we are redeemed from
sin, which made us his captives (ff. 166, 167).

C. 75. Scripture passages alleged, in proof that "redeemed"
may mean simply preserved, 2 Kings 7, Exod. 13, God redeemed
Himself a people; (answered as before), of real deliverance
from actual servitude. Ps. 49 and 30, "God shall redeem my soul
from the power of hell. Thou hast brought my soul out of hell."
Isa. 43, "I have redeemed thee." Hos. 13, "I will redeem thee
from death." Ans. Redemption by Christ. Ps. 23, "Shalt
deliver his soul from hell," not redemption by price (ff. 167—
168 v.).

C. 76. Church and Angels only redeemed by being preserved.

Ans. As to Church: It has been redeemed from sin in all its
members, being subject to sin, though not all at once. Coll.
Luke 3, "Redeemed His people." Matt. 1, "Shall save His
people from their sins." Eph. 8, "He is the Saviour of the
body. Christ loved the Church, and gave Himself for her"
(ff. 168 v.—169 v.).

Ans. As to Angels: Redemption used by S. Bernard in different sense. Christ died and was crucified for the B. V. as for the whole human race, not for the Angels (though opponents said it, it is marvellous whence they had it), or gave ransom for them, or reconciled them. Christ's redemption of man filled up ranks of Angels, &c. (ff. 169 v., 170 v.).

C. 77. Minute objections to passage of S. Thomas.

Why said S. Thomas that the exemption of any one would derogate from the honour of the passion of Christ? Ans. As contradicting S. Paul, " He is the Saviour of all men," and the like (ff. 170 v.—172 v.).

PART IX.

C. 78. *Mediator.*—All for whom Christ was a Mediator, must have had some sin. Office of mediator to reconcile two estranged. Obj. " Christ would not be most perfect Mediator, unless He preserved one," repeated in different forms. Mediation between those estranged, and preservation from being estranged, incompatible.

Reconciler.—2 Cor. 5, " God was in Christ, reconciling the world to Himself;" and Rom. 5, " We were reconciled to God by the Death of His Son."

Physician.—Whom Christ healed by medicine of His Passion must have been sick. " By His stripes," &c. " They that are whole," &c.

Justifier.—Jer. 23, Rom. 3. Obj. To be justified does not imply previous guilt (instances cited relative to God, Ps. 51, Eccles. 18, Ps. 50, Luke 7, *bis :* and of man, Rev. 22, " And let him that is just be yet more justified." Ans. The justification here spoken of was through the Blood of Christ.

Sanctifier.—1 Cor. 1, " made to us Sanctification," &c.; 1 Cor. 6, " But ye have been sanctified;" Heb. 13, " That He might sanctify His people by His Blood."

Cleanser.—Mal. 3, Ps. 51, Rev. 1, " cleansed us from our sins with His own Blood;" Rev. 7, " washed their robes in Blood of the Lamb." But the clean not washed by preservation from defilement.

Shepherd.—But He came to seek the sheep which were gone astray—the whole human race.

Priest.—Heb. 9, " By His own Blood He entered once into the holy place," &c., quoting Council of Eph. (ff. 172—175 v.).

C. 79. Grounds on which some doctors thought her conception in orig. sin true and Catholic assertion, from Hugo de S. V., P. Lombard, S. Thomas, S. Bonaventura, and the rest.

That assertion is to be held true, the opposite of which contradicts—1) H. Scripture; 2) the determination of the whole Church [the Council of Milevis]; 4) sayings of H. Scripture, as understood by holy doctors; 5) determination of Apostolic See [Pope Zosimus]; or, 6) which follows by necessary inference from what holy doctors pronounce to be indubitable, and bid to be firmly held, and which as such is placed in the body of Decretals; or, 7) the opposite of which derogates from the dignity of Christ and His privileges (ff. 175 v.—177 v.).

C. 80. Answer to objections to the conclusions of C. 79.

i. " It is nowhere expressly said in special terms, that the B. V. was conceived in original sin." Ans. 1. No more are many other Catholic truths. Perilous principle to affirm that those things only are Catholic faith, which are comprehended in express and special terms in H. Scr. or determinations of the Church. For countless others are elicited from them equally firm. Nor is it absurd (as alleged) to make no difference herein between the B. V. and the worst of men; for the Ap. says, Rom. 3, " There is no difference; all lack the glory of God." Nor is it necessary (as is alleged) that the deduction should be as evidently known to all, as that wherefrom it is deduced, except perhaps in things to be believed explicitly. Also, it is one thing to say that a saying is Catholic, another, that all Christians are bound to believe it of necessity of faith. One has not to believe every assertion said to be Catholic, unless it be expressly laid down in H. Scr., or plainly deduced from it, or determined by the Church to be such. Ans. 2. It is expressed in equivalent terms in Scr. authorities, so explained by the Fathers.

ii. " Since ' one doubtful in faith is an infidel,' all who doubt of this would have to be called infidels." Ans. The maxim belongs to things expressed in H. Scr., or determined by the Church to be held explicitly.

iii. "Who does not bring back from errors, when he can, shows that he errs himself. But Roman Church and general Councils have used no diligence to bring people back from belief in Imm. Conc." Ans. The saying relates to manifest error against express Scr. or determination of Church.

iv. "Sermons on Imm. Conc. preached yearly on this Fest. in many parts of Christian religion in presence of Clergy and people, unhindered (as before). Rom. Ch., then, and general Councils, not opposing this, approved it, and so Church for many centuries continuously was in error as to faith." Ans. 1) as before. 2) Imm. Conc. not preached for many centuries (as often stated), since Card. Bonaventura says he had never heard of it (see ab. p. 220). So then, neither at Rome nor Univ. of Paris.

v. "Cardinals, Bishops, and all the chiefs of curia at Rome, celebrate annually F. of Conc. under name of Conc., and sermons preached on it as being Immaculate."

Ans. 1) Roman Church or Apostolic See has not instituted, canonized, pronounced, or celebrated it, or had it marked in the Calendar. Not what Cardinals, &c. do, acts of Rom. Ch., but when supreme Pontiff, with College of Cardinals, publicly celebrates and keeps the Feast. Roman Ch., then, has rather refused to keep the Feast. Ans. 2) It is to be supposed that Card., &c. keep F. as F. of the Sanctification, which is believed to have followed the Conc. after slight delay, quoting Alvarus, " for many years Penitentiary in Roman Court." The Sanctification must the more be object of festival, not Conception, since Conc. on Dec. 8 was Conc. seminum, and the B. V. (i. e. her soul) as yet was not. It might as well be argued, that Church encouraged belief that B. V. was sanctified before animation (condemned by Bern. and Univ. Paris).

vi. "The Council of Basle itself had sanctioned it by having the office and Sermons for Imm. Conc." Ans. These were acts of individual fathers; the contrary also done, and many exorbitances against the Pope.

vii. "Held commonly that the F. of Nativity of B. V. celebrated her sanctification. If F. of Conc. the same, two Festivals on same subject." Ans. 1) Church has instituted F. of Nat., only permitted *this;* in many Churches this is not F. of Conc., nor is the sanctification the direct object of F. of Nativ.; held also that F. of Conc. was a F. of thanksgiving (John of Naples, ab. p. 244). Custom no ground against opposed teaching in the Church, " Jesus said, ' I am the truth,' not ' I am custom,' " Greg. VII.

viii. "It *was* argued, 'Roman Church does not keep F. of Conc., therefore the B. V. conceived in orig. sin ;' now Rom. Ch. does celebrate it, argument reversed." Ans. Argt. not used, nor fact true.

ix. "S. Bernard referred question to Roman See; therefore not already article of faith." Ans. No; but it might be Catholic truth.

x. Same argument from its being proposed at C. of Basle (ff. 177 v—181 v.).

C. 81. Answers to arguments for Imm. Conc. from Divine power.

Arg. 1) that she could; 2) that it was most fitting; 3) that she ought; 4) that she was so preserved.

Ans. Wrong definition of "potentia ordinata" of God, viz. "a certain congruity of the Divine goodness (according to the exigency or attingency of our reason) nowise narrowing the Divine Will, that it should not justly and reasonably do the opposite, though our intellect cannot equally see both." For 1) our reason no measure; 2) since these congruities vary, there would be as many potentiæ ordinatæ, which no school admits; 3) variety of opinion on this very point. Better to say absolute power of God is whatever does not involve contradiction, or tend to defect of power; "potentia ordinata" is, what He not only can do absolutely, but wills in His wisdom to do. Hence power of God absolute or conditioned, that it be not 1) against the law which in His goodness He placed in us (as, to reward the wicked, punish the bad); 2) against the order which His wisdom has constituted and laid down for us in H. Scr. Thus, supposing the pre-ordination of Passion of Christ, impossible that man should be redeemed in any other way; supposing He willed that Christ should be Redeemer, impossible that any should not have sin. Authorities.

Obj. 1. " God might give dispensation, as all makers of law, or Ahasuerus to Esther, or sovereign Pontiff, or God as to His positive laws." Ans. " It does not hold, that if some law may be dispensed with, all may. If B. V. could be dispensed, a great multitude might." Laws of first table could not, as containing relation of creature to Creator. Evidence of reason taken from H. Scr. supports, not this, but the contrary. There is no law, instituted by God, as to contracting orig. sin.

Obj. 2. " If God could not preserve the B. V., it must be by reason of His wisdom, or justice, or omnipotence. But not for lack of any. Ans. Division insufficient; contrary not to these, but to the order instituted by Divine Wisdom.

Obj. 3. Luke 1, " With God nothing is impossible :" Ans. Spoken of God's absolute power, not of " potentia ordinata." Impossible the whole Trinity should be incarnate, or that men should be saved, otherwise than by the Death of the Son of God (ff. 184, 185).

C. 82. Answer to arguments, that it was " becoming " that the B. V. should be so preserved. " Becoming " defined, though inadequately, " beauty befitting, not necessary to condition."

Ground from first prerogative, " because she is virgo virginum ;" distinction, because a thing is becoming, it does not therefore become God to give it.

Immunity from orig. sin not necessary ornament of virginity, else none would have it. Christ Alone the Lamb, not whose spot has been wiped away, but who had no spot. What *is* essential to virginity ? " Integritas carnis cum integritate mentis."

Arg. 2. If B. V. had not been so preserved, her virginity would have been not perfect, but minished. For virginity of mind is corrupted by any mortal sin. Ans. *a*) No virginity antecedent to original sin; for soul created when infused : *b*) original sin, not mortal.

Arg. 3. Virginity of mind, as of body, cannot be restored. Ans. Not true, else there would be no virgin.

Arg. 4. Perfect innocence becomes virginity, such as Christ's ; hers, then, should be like His. Ans. *a*) Christ Alone in likeness of sinful flesh ; *b*) purity of Reconciler and reconciled not the same, since reconciled from sin.

Arg. 5. The Church a virgin in such wise that there 'never was nor shall be in her spot or wrinkle;' so also B. V. Ans. *a*) Pure, for Christ washed it with His Blood (Eph. 5; Rev. 1), yet all from Abel had original sin. *b*) Freedom of Church from all spot relates to life to come, since Church made up of its members; and "if we say we have no sin," &c.; Church indeed free from stain of mortal sin in true members.

Arg. 6. From S. Bernard, In Rev. the moon under her feet means the Church or corruption. Ans. 1) S. Bernard's meaning to be sought from his plain words, not from obscure or metaphoric; 2) S. Bern., from context, is speaking of time of Incarn.; as to Church, as above. Reply. If B. V. not immaculately conceived, why so singularly praised? Ans. 1) Her loftier sanctification; 2) her virginity first dedicated; 3) mother of all virgins, because without precept, counsel, example; 4) fecundity united with it; 5) transfused to those who saw her; 6) most adorned with virtues (ff. 187—189).

C. 83. From second prerogative, "spouse of God."

Ans. But 1) Church also the bride, yet her members born in orig. sin; 2) so also individual virgins; 3) not true that God loves less those who *have* sinned; nor, 4) that any is called a sinner from the past, or that saints in heaven are called sinners (as alleged).

Arg. 1. Unbefitting that spouse of Prince should have been maidservant and slave of his enemy. But 1) so as to any friend of Prince or her parents; 2) one thing what is fitting for us, another, what befits God to permit. 3) Contrary to Scr., which speaks of Israel as slave (Isa. 52, &c.; Jer., Ezek.), and calls to Him sinful soul, Cant. 6.

Arg. 2. Spouse always loved, could not have been hateful or hated (this arg. much rested on); 1) when in orig. sin, not spouse or Mother of God; 2) *that* does not defile which is without the will; 3) souls of all righteous, spouses of God (2 Cor. 11); 4) love of God, eternal love, therefore consistent with having had sin, or what God hates. God, at once "amat quod fecit, odit quod facimus," "amata est fœda, ne remaneret fœda."

Arg. 3. "Once to have sinned withdraws from perfect love." Ans. i. e. from his being perfectly lovable; but this only in Christ. But not from God's love; "where sin abounded, grace super-abounded." Prodigal son restored to perfect love. "We shall be like unto the angels," who never sinned. Nay, many who have sinned have more love from God than many angels. God must needs love Christ in His Humanity, more than all creatures together: therefore fitting that Christ should have diligibility beyond B. V.

Arg. 4. "Christ loved His mother more than any other son his, therefore it fitted that He should make her simply worthy of love of all." Ans. 1) At her Conc. she was not His mother; 2) fitting that Christ should have a lovableness incommunicable to any creature, never to have had any thing displeasing to God: the B. V. next, not to have had any thing of her own will (ff. 189—192).

C. 84. Prerogative 3, "full of grace." Arg. From saying of S. Jer.[1]; "To others grace is given in part; into Mary the whole fulness of grace empoured itself;" "into Mary came the fulness of the whole grace which is in Christ, although otherwise." Therefore innocence was, being a gift of Divine grace which was in Christ. Some explain this, as though Christ and B. V. were equal in grace, and so that she too had not orig. sin. Ans. This un-Catholic; 1) contrary to Scr., as Ps. 45, "anointed above Thy fellows—fairer than the children of men;" "He Who is from heaven is above all." He is the Word. .The Spirit was "not given by measure to Him." 2) From determin. of Church: Those condemned, who held that one in this life can be so perfected as to become impeccable, and incapable of advancing in grace. Alvarus, "some pseudo-religious, pretending to be devout to Mary, said she was as full of grace and the H. Sp. as C. J., and could not be more perfect in this life, or grow in grace, or was more perfect in death than in life." Had S. Jerome thought this, he would not have doubted her assumption, or said the Soul of Christ was Alone free from sin. "Fulness of grace," in schools, manifold; 1) sufficient to salvation—1 Cor. 1, Eph. 4; 2) fulness of comparison—of Apostles and S. Stephen; 3) fulness in whole Church, no grace which is not in some one—Eph. 4; 4) in mother of God, to avoid all actual sin; 5) which makes all sin, orig. and actual, impossible, and disposes to excellence of union with Divinity—

---

[1] Not S. Jer. ab. p. 444.

in Christ Alone; or, 6, *a*) fulness of grace in final cause
union with God, in Christ, union of Person; *b*) in efficient
cause, so as to overflow to all others (as bodily light may, 1)
shine, 2) illumine, 3) make others luminous, 4) be sole source of
light) as in formal cause, perfecting Him, not only as to all
virtues, but all uses of virtue and all effects of grace, and
driving away all sin, actual or original, or power of sin.
Again, "fulness of grace," 1) in itself, i. e. as to essence and
virtue and greatest extension to all effects of grace. This,
Christ's only; 2) relatively to office in B. V. to be mother of God;
in Stephen for his office. This is meaning of Jerome, as shown
by context to relate to conception of Jesus. Obj. Sins wounds
of soul; scar remains, even amid glory. Ans. No scars remain,
except glorious scars of martyrs, or of the Passion (ff. 192—
195).

C. 85. Fourth title, "Blessed art thou among women," i.e. more
than all; and so, " whatever curse was infused through Eve, the
blessing of Mary took the whole away." Then she lacked no
virtue which was ever in woman; therefore not innocence which
Eve had. Ans. In this and other authorities, reference is to the
Incarnation. (This most common error as to authorities alleged
on opposite side, that what is said of her sanctification or her Concept. of the Son of God is referred to her passive conception.)
2) Innocence, in the sense of never having been under sin, a
state, not a virtue. For *a*) not a mental habit; *b*) question in
schools, whether man, in state of innocence, had grace; (absurd,
if innocence were virtue). *c*) This innocence not restored
by Death of Christ, but gift of God greater than sin of Adam;
d) all virtues restored through penitence; but not this innocence. 3) Eve's innocence has no relation to original sin;
4) more natural to say that she was born in original righteousness, which is known not to be.

Arg. 2. State of grace excels state of nature; Adam and
Christ both innocent, therefore Eve and Mary. Ans. Innocence, not virtue. Excellence of gifts presupposes not change
of state; Christ was conceived as Reconciler, Mary as one to be
reconciled.

Arg. 3. Mary took away curse, not subject to it. Ans. 1)
" She herself took it not away," else Incarn. useless; 2) She

herself was subject to penalties from the curse of Eve to be removed by her son. Passage of S. Aug.[2], objected, proves the contrary; for, since it was her privilege to conceive One Innocent, then Anne, her mother, did not.

Answer to passage of S. Hildefonso (Paschas. Radb. ab. pp. 332—334). Turr. argues (as above) that the context implies that the immunity from original sin was at her Nativity, since else irrelevant. The use of "contraxit" he explains as "ex origine sua traxit," instancing S. Fulgentius' use of trahere" (ad Petr. c. 27), and S. Aug., that S. Cyprian on his birthday "pecc. orig. contraxit[3]," and that it is used even of actual sins, as by S. Ambr. (Hexaem. vi. 24 n. 88) "culpam suam quam negando contraxerat," and by S. Aug. de Bapt. Parv. i. n. 63, iii. n. 7, that infants had as yet contracted no sin of their own life. Passage of Pasch., so understood by Vinc. Hist. and James de Voragine.

Obj. 1. Orig. sin comes from sentence of Divine law; every one born in orig. sin cursed by God. God, Who gave law against cursing father and mother, would not curse His own. Ans. Like declamations might be used as to His mother's mother and whole kin. Maledixit may be "pronounced evil," but of punishment, not of fault; for God wills no sin, but that all should be saved. Malediction, in this sense, fruit of first parents' sin, not law of God. But under curse as punishment Christ Himself was subject to it. Also at her conception she was not mother of God; and idioms such as "the Lamb slain from the foundation of the world," are to be explained, not extended. Obj. 2. "Blessed art thou among women," i. e. while they were cursed. Ans. *a*) Related not to time of Conc.; *b*) not so understood by authorities (ff. 193—199).

C. 86. From title, "Most worthy of all praise," but innocence is subject of praise. Ans. 1) Title given her by Church in regard to Incarn. "Blessed art thou, sacred Virgin Mary, and worthy of all praise; because from thee arose the Sun of Righteousness, Christ our God." 2) Many praises belong to Christ Alone; and are not ascribed by Church to B. V. There-

---

[2] "Opus imperiti consarcinatoris." Ben. App. S. Aug. T. v. Serm. 194.

[3] "Traxit." Serm. 310 n. 1. ed. Ben., see also Op. Imp. c. Jul. ii. 117, col. 1000 D. "Quod nascentes trahunt." S. Fulg. de fide ad Petr. n. 17, ab. p. 132.

fore this Antiphon cannot mean this. Warning of S. Bonaventura 3 d. 3 and S. Bernard, against false praises of B. V. To say she was conceived in orig. sin, does not detract from her honour, as of no other saint; to deny it, derogates from honour of Christ, and so from hers.

Arg. 2. " Matter of blame to have sinned; stain of sin inconsistent with being most 'worthy of all praise.'" Ans. Blame belongs to things in our own power only.

Arg. 3. Jer. says, " Whatever can be said in human words too poor for her praise, for she was praised by God and angels." But to have been ever innocent no slight praise. Ans. 1) (as before). Not all praise, not what belongs to Christ Alone. 2) He only says we cannot speak adequately of her virtues, as S. Aug. says of S. Jer., S. Jer. of Læta. (ff. 199, 200).

C. 87. From title, " Queen of heaven." Arg. 1. Every excellence of inferiors should exist in the chief. Ans. Not unless she is chief in all things. But B. V. chief in grace, Angels had greater natural gifts, as simplicity of substance, &c. Yet not to have been subject to orig. sin, nature, not grace, in Angels.

Arg. 2. Not fit that the Queen of grace should ever have been guilty of fault, or Queen of angels handmaiden of demon, or oppressed by him through sin. Ans. 1) It follows not, that because a thing would become any, therefore God should give it. 2) King of grace through inflowing, cannot have had any fault; Mary, Queen of grace, not so, but by intercession only. But intercession heard from those who had orig. sin. 3) Terms, such as handmaid of Satan, not to be used. For in Conc. no knowledge or free-will; but handmaid, &c. imply will. False that the soul, contracting orig. sin, " a diabolo veluti virgo a lenone constupratur." Satan does not intervene in orig. sin. Such and like language, used to move minds of the simple, gravely rebuked (ff. 200, 201 v.).

C. 88. From title, " exalted above all choirs of angels." Highest angels have all which lower have. B. V. then, being above them, had this, always to have been innocent. Ans. It would follow, either that no man would be equal to angels, contrary to our Lord (Luke 20, Matt. 22), or that no man sinned. Never held in schools, that equality with angels implied equality of original *state*, but of merits only. Angels in each order, alike in grace and natural gifts. Man placed in them, according to conjunction of spirit with God, and chiefly charity. Freedom from orig. sin, no prerogative in them, because impossible.

Arg. 1. Michael cast down dragon; unfit that woman, who had been his slave and handmaid, should be set over them. Ans. (as before), " who doeth sin, servant of sin ;" but no act in orig. sin. Arg. 2) "B. V. casts down angels," Jer. Ans. Said of evil women [4]. Arg. 3) Since Christ at Right Hand of the Father, according to His Humanity, has best goods of His Father, so B. V. at Right Hand of the Son, has His, and so innocence. Ans. 1) B. V. not at Right Hand in her Conception. 2) Because B. V. *is* most pure and immaculate, not therefore in her Conc. 3) Christ does not possess those goods as Man. Arg. 4) B. V. equal in all things to Christ except in not being God. Ans. Contrary to faith ; for His Humanity object of worship, organ of Divinity, temple wherein Godhead dwells bodily. His love and Passion price of our redemption. Arg. 5) S. Anselm, "Above thee, the B. V., is God alone ; all which is not God, is below thee " (the B. V.). By God, he means Christ in both instances ; else Humanity of Christ below B. V. Arg. 6) S. Bern., "B. V. immersed in light inapproachable, as far as condition of creature allows without personal union." Ans. This expressly sets her below the Humanity, Which *was* personally united. Arg. 7) Aug., " 'What could be more holy than her in human seed ?' But Christ born of human seed, since of the most pure blood of the B. V." Ans. Contrary held by all who believe virgin-birth. Arg. 8) Anselm, " Who surpasseth angels in purity ;" but one once in sin may surpass in virtue, not in purity. Ans. Not true. Prov. " Take away rust, and a most pure vessel shall go forth." Where is greater grace, there greater purity. Ps. 51, " I shall be whiter than snow ;" 1 Tim. 1, " Love out of pure hearts ;" Acts 15, " Faith (i. e. "informed " by love) purifying heart." But those who have been sinners often have greater love. 2) Purity of angels not freedom from orig. sin, which they could not have, as neither could animals, but from actual, and *this* was in B. V. Last Arg. " Christ, being Almighty, gave His mother

[4] Before the Flood.

all befitting her, therefore never to have been hated by her
Son." 1) As before, in her own Conc. not mother of God.
2) To have sin by will, would have been unbefitting her future
prerogative; not to have had orig. sin, esp. pro parvula morula.
3) To have had what is hateful, does not make her to have been
hateful. "Thou hatest nothing which Thou hast made," &c. as
before.

Inferences from the whole—1) It belonged to Christ Alone,
the Universal Redeemer, Mediator of God and men, to have
contracted in His Conception nothing displeasing to the eyes
of His Father, to expiate which, a Sacrifice was necessary.
2) It became not that this should be communicated to another,
which would be inseparably derogatory from glory and dignity
of Christ. 3) Conception in orig. sin noways derogates from
prerogatives of B. V., any more than to be cleansed by His
Blood, and reconciled to the Eternal Father (ff. 201 v.—205).

PART X.

*Answers to authorities and grounds alleged to prove that God
ought to preserve B. V. from orig. sin; and first, answers
to statements as to literal sense of Holy Scripture.*

C. 89. Arg. 1. *That* is the literal sense of H. Scr. which the
Holy Ghost intended, and which we have been told inerrantly to
be its meaning. 2) H. Scr., alleged by Church to prove any thing,
means what it is alleged for. 3) Lessons read on F. of Conc.,
prove that, according to its literal meaning, H. Scr. proved the
Imm. Conc., Ans. Exception to word "ought;" God owes
nothing except by promise. Their definition of literal sense
of H. Scr. contrary to the H. Scr. itself, which distinguishes
what the letter means, and what the things signified by letter
mean, viz. spiritual meaning. Gal. 4 recognizes this. Evident, too, from fact. In many lessons, H. Scr. is used in
applied sense, as on sanctif. of Jeremiah and S. John B.
Church believed that John B. was so sanctified, and thence used
lessons. In Holy Scr., too, truths are illustrated not proved
by mystical senses, as "I will be to him a Father," of Christ.
"A bone of him shall not be broken," because paschal lamb

type of Christ, therefore ordered that its bones be not broken. But spiritual meaning not proof, because grounded on likeness only; but likeness may be partial. Literal sense may be in plain terms or metaphor, and same metaphor used of God and man, as light, day. The same might apply in different degrees, or might belong to different times (ff. 205—209).

Auth. 1. Gen. 3. Arg. Others have conquered Satan, but have not bruised his head; some most singular privilege of B. V. Ans. 1) Not explained of B. V. as literal meaning; bruising his head, resisting the beginning of temptation (Greg. M., Isidore, de Lyra, &c.), so it belongs to all saints; 2) interpreted of the Church (Gloss). 3) If of B. V., not of the time when she had no use of free-will. The sanctified in womb and baptized children are freed from power of devil, do not bruise his head, because there is no co-operation of theirs. 4) Expos. of saints say that it was in her actual graces (Rup. Bern., Isid., &c.). Others, that she bruised his head, because He Who should bruise it was to be born of her. So S. Bern., where alleged to the contrary, "all heretical pravity trampled by her," because all against Incarnation, as, that Christ not of her substance, or that she did not bear but found her Son (non peperisse sed reperisse), or title Theotokos denied. So S. Bern. (ff. 209, 210).

Auth. 2. Ark of shittim wood. Arg. B. V. incorruptible wood. Therefore she was not born in corruption of orig. sin. Ans. Not interpreted of B. V. exclusively, but 1) of flesh of Christ; 2) of the Church; 3) if of B. V., of sanctification after Conc. (as Alb. M.). If argument might be taken from accident of the wood, then contrary might be argued from comparison to things corruptible, as vine, tabernacle, ship. Auth. 3. "A star shall arise," Num. 24; but star brightness; therefore no spot of orig. sin. Ans. Star of wise men. If applied to B. V., argument would have fallacy of equivocation, as in almost all the authorities. If argument held as to B. V., so to all called stars, &c. But Job 3, stars darkened; Job. 23, stars not clean in His sight. "Arising," too, would belong to Nativity, not to Conception. Auth. 4. Esth. 15, "This was not made for thee but for all" applied to orig. sin. Ans. Does not in letter belong to B. V.; would belong to her as Bride, not to Conc.; exception

I i

as to Esther derogated not from king, as would that of B. V.
Auth. 5. Ps. 19, "Day to day uttereth speech." S. Bern.
" Angel announces Incarn. to B.V." If B. V. the day, then her
dawn full of light. Ans. Arg. would apply to all saints, " sons of
light and of the day." S. Bern. says, she is day propter inte-
gritatis virtutem. If it applied at all, sanctification which followed on Conc. Auth. 6. " He placed his tabernacle in the sun ;"
so Conc. not in darkness of orig. sin. Ans. Sun, interpreted of
Church, would involve Imm. Conc. of many more. Auth. 7.
Ps. 45, " The King shall desire thy beauty." Therefore no preceding spot. Ans. Expounded of Church, which was not clean,
but cleansed. Auth. 8. " The Most High hath sanctified His
tabernacle." Her sanctif. greater than others ; but not earlier
than Jeremiah's, c. 1, or Isaiah's, c. 49 ; therefore freedom from
orig. sin. Ans. Literal sense, material tabernacle. Lyra. "The
Church or the Body which the Son of God took." Even if of
the B. V., does not prove as to Conception. For four prerogatives of sanctification of B. V., 1) Prior in time. For " before
I formed thee in the womb, I knew thee " of Jeremiah, is his
eternal predestination. Isaiah in c. 49 is speaking not of himself, as alleged, but of Christ ; would not have been adduced, if
weighed with its Glosses ; 2) in perfection of grace, making not
Nativ. alone, but whole life blameless ; 3) more confirmed in
good, as more united with Christ her Son ; 4) extinguished all
passion in beholders. Auth. 9. Ps. 87. " He was born in her ;
the Most High Himself founded her." Ans. 1) Relates to the
Church ; 2) as to the B. V., explained by de Lyra, as to mortal
and venial sin ; strange that neither Gloss nor de Lyra thought
of orig. sin, had it been meant. Auth. 10. " Holiness becometh
Thy house for ever." Ans. De Lyra, of the Church. Else as
in 8.

Auth. 11. Whole 8th ch. of Prov. under different heads,
chapter being sung in some Churches on F. of Nat. and Conc.
of B. V. Arg. Intelligent agent regards end more than means
to end ; and of means, those which are nearest to end. God then
accounts of B. V. more than all inanimate creation. Incarnation,
i. e. the Man Christ, was the first object of God. Redemption not primary object of Inc. ; for the greater, Christ, not referred to the less, man. B. V., belonging substantially to Inc.,

intended by God prior to first parents and decree of Divine curse in contraction of orig. sin. Conception then of B. V. " before abyss " is, she was conceived without darkness of ignorance and sin. Ans. 1. Prov. 8 literally can be explained only of Christ; in part, only of His Godhead (so Gloss. Nic. de Lyra), same as John i. 1; denotes eternal co-existence, personal distinction from the Father, personal being. Obj. 1. God, not Lord of the Son. Ans. "Lord" used as in Ps. 2. Obj. 2. " Possessed," of inferior. Ans. God called " possession " of Israel. " Order " in Divine Nature, of mode of being, not of time or perfection.

Ans. 2. Prov. 8, in office of one virgin (" as is known to all the fathers, who have the ordinary of the orisons "), yet against faith, so to interpret it. Obj. But great difference between B.V. and other virgins. Ans. Difference as to mystical interpretation, not so as to make it literal. Words declaring eternal generation of the Word, not to be used of human generation. B. V. not "before every work of mercy," else she would have no share in the redemption, work of Divine mercy. Tit. 3, and in Magnificat. All which is read in lesson does not belong to any virgin, but Prov. 8. 32—35 apply to all virgins, specially B. V.

Ans. 3. To say that redemption not chief end of Incarn. against Creed, "Who for us men," &c., and Scr., Matt. 18, The Son of man came to seek, &c.; John 3, God so loved, &c. Gal. 4, God sent His Son, to redeem, &c.; Heb. 2, Took man, through death to destroy, &c.; S. Matt. 1, For He shall save, &c.

Ans. 4. Against reason, too. 1) If redemption not chief end of Inc., then chief end not named in Scr. Reply, What is most needed for fallen man is named more frequently. Ans. Chief end, according to them, not named at all. Injurious too to devotion.

Ans. 5. 1) Since Inc. is for creation any how, inconsistent to urge that greater is not for the less : comparison is not between God and creature, but between two works of God. Expos. that by " abyss " is meant " sin," not supported.

Auth. 12. Prov. 9, " Wisdom built her a house." Arg. Not on a decayed foundation. Ans. To be explained literally of Christ and Church. But members of Church born in orig. sin.

Auth. 13. Prov. ult., " her lamp shall not be put out in darkness." Arg. of orig. sin. Ans. 1) Explained of Christ and
every perfect soul. 2) Cannot be understood of orig. sin, for,
at infusion of soul, no light to be extinguished.

Auth. 15. Cant. 2, " As lily among thorns," explained of
actual purity and chastity. Righteous compared in Scr. to lilies.

Auth. 16. " ' Thou art all fair, my love, and there is no spot in
thee,' being said absolutely, belongs to all her being, and so to
Conc." Ans. Literal sense not of B. V., much besides does not
belong to her. Cant. not prophetic book. No Comm. explains it
as prophecy of her (he had looked to Gloss. Greg., Bern., Will.
of Paris, Alan., Ægid. R., John de Varsiaco, Lyra), nor ancient
doctor. Theol. say, " Her sanctif. in womb to be believed,
though no Scr. proof." This could not have been said, had this
been so understood. Properly explained of Church ; but each
member had orig. sin ; all had had some spot of sin. Obj. To
say that Church of God had been once fœda, against Christian
religion. Ans. (as before) Limitations of time often necessary
to explain Scr. Dignities of B. V., not all of one time. Eph. i.
"God chose us to be blameless." Not of whole life. Ruin of
Jews from explaining prophecies of later time, as to the beginning. Circumcision not observed, though not limited as to
time. Hymn in office of Confessors calls each " pius, prudens,
humilis, &c. ;" all (as S. Aug.) were not always such. Solomon
could not contradict David, who foretold separation of Christ
from others, and Solomon himself, Eccl. 7 (as ab.), " Wholly
pure and always pure," different ; the 2nd belongs to Christ
only. Explained by S. Thomas of absence of actual sin.

Auth. 17. Cant., " One is my dove." Ans. Lit. of Church.

Auth. 18. " Who is this like rising dawn ?" Ans. Explained of
Church. As to B. V., related to her birth (ortus). Not necessary that metaphor should be verified in every thing. " Typus
in parte est, non in toto ;" dawn, too, imperfect light ; so would
prove contrary.

Auth. 19. " Wisdom will not dwell in body subject to sin."
No proof that it relates to first instant of her Conc.

Auth. 20—25. Wisd. 7, Eccl. 24, relate to Uncreated
Wisdom.

Auth. 26. " From the beginning was I created." Ans. Predestination of Incarnation. But if mystically of B. V., enough that she was, *a*) manifoldly foretold under various figures, *b*) speedily sanctified, *c*) Deipara.

Auth. 27. "Ministered in a holy habitation." Ans. 1) Literally Christ; 2) She did not minister at her Conc.

Auth. 28. "I was exalted like cedar." Expl. Of members of Christ, who had orig. sin.

Auth. 29. "I was exalted like palm tree." Ans. The like.

Auth. 30—34. Comparisons to olive, cinnamon, myrrh, rose-tree, Ps. 128; (like answers) some chiefly of Christ, but also of Church.

Auth. 35. "In Me is all grace of virtue and truth." Ans. Of Uncreated Wisdom.

Auth. 36. "I was as a vine." Ans. Of Incarn.

Auth. 37. Ecclus. 24. 41. Words too great for conception of nature, relate to Birth of Christ, Who brought us medicine of salvation.

Auth. 38. Isa. 11. "A rod shall come forth from root of Jesse." Ans. Relates from force of terms to Nativity, in which office it is used. No such sermon of S. Ambrose as alleged (de Gabaonitis), with words "in qua nec nodus origi. nec cortex venialis culpæ fuit," nor quoted by S. Aug. as alleged.

Auth. 39. Angelic salutation, Ave, full of grace, &c. Ave, "absence of woe." Ans. If urged, would belong to women after Resurr. (except of child-birth), "avete." Matt. 28. If væ of pœna, not removed; if of fault, removed at this time. Whole argument faulty, because said at time of overshadowing of the Holy Ghost. Obj. "Gratia plena, benedicta es," as before.

Auth. 40. "My spirit hath rejoiced in God my Saviour; all generations shall call me blessed." Arg. If Conc. in orig. sin, not blessed, but miserable. Ans. Blessing belongs to her adult life ("For He hath beheld," &c.), and to the Incarnation.

Grounds alleged from command to honour parents. Arg. 1) as before. Ans. At her Conception, she was not His mother. This began with His Birth, "born of a woman, born under the law." Son bound to honour her, not absolutely with every thing, but with what fitted. Not fitting that natural Conc. should be like supernatural (S. Ans. de conc. virg. c. 12), &c.

Arg. 2) bound to preserve her from wrath of God. Ans. B. V. was preserved from doing any thing personally, which should be hindrance of Divine love. Orig. sin did not prevent her being the object of God's love. Arg. 3) If Assumption reasonable on this ground, then Imm. Conc. Ans. In Assumption, she was His mother; nor did it derogate from His own honour. Arg. 4) Orig. sin a debt which ought to be remitted to a mother. Ans. as bef. Strange to call orig. sin either debt or deadly sin. Arg. 5) "'The Lord willed not the faith as to His birth to rest on injuries to His mother.' S. Amb. Therefore He willed to pass by what belongs to faith in Him and His glory, to preserve honour of His mother." Ans. S. Amb. meant only, Christ preferred to be thought conceived in marriage, than through sin, which Jews would think. Inference unadvised; against our Lord's precept, S. Matt. x., "He that loveth," &c., and practice; S. Luke ii. 49. Arg. 6) Matt. xi. "Among those born of woman arose not greater than John B." B. V. greater than John B.; so she arose not from orig. sin. Ans. Said of men; not so statement of universality of original sin (ff. 205—230 v.).

PART XI.

Answers to arguments from resurrection and Assumption of B. V.

C. 90. Arg. In S. Aug.'s time, Assumption of B. V. 1) as much matter of doubt, and 2) as difficult to reconcile with H. Scr. as Imm. Conc. now. Ans. to 1: *a)* doubted, as by S. Jer. (ab. p. 444), and S. Bern. on Ass., not denied; *b)* some believe that those who rose (S. Matt. 27) ascended with Christ, but all confessed that Christ alone was conceived without sin. Ans. to 2: Error to take all universal propositions of H. Scr. universally, or to limit all. Prop. as to resurr. limited by S. Matt. 27. No exception to be made to "All things were made by Him;" so neither to His being universal Redeemer; both derogate from Him. Prop. as to orig. sin not simply universal, but one exception, and one only, made—Christ Himself; so disallowing all other exceptions ("great festival made" of this arg.). Arg. in Aug. (Anon.) rested on the points, which, at time of her own

Concep., were not—oneness of her flesh with that of Christ, her maternity, indwelling of Divinity (whence called, throne of God, chamber of Most High, tabernacle of Christ),—integrity in Conc. and birth of Christ. Arg. The same on both sides. To have been under orig. sin did not make B. V. habitation of the dæmon (as alleged, and Satan does not inhabit souls) or captive of hell, or slave of dæmons, handmaid of the devil (slavery not, where there is no will). Obj. Mohammed more considerate of purity of B. V., from Coran : "[1] Mary, God chose thee and purified and chose thee illustrious above women of world." Ans. "Purified" implies something to purify. Tradition, he "heard the messenger of God (Moh.) saying 'none of the sons of Adam is born whom Satan touches not when he is born, and who does not weep at his touch, save Mary and her Son.'" Ans. 1) Moh. could not refer to orig. sin, not believing it ; 2) said of birth, when children weep, not of Conc.; 3) contradicts hymn, the Church and Wisd. 7 explained of Christ. Ibn Musa, "Moh. said, many men perfect, no woman save mother of Jesus." Ans. If said of her life, the belief of all ; if of her Conc., contradicts Eccl. 7. Other argts. repetition (ff. 230 v.—241).

C. 91. Ans. to argts., from her being Mother of God, from comparison of original and venial sin, and from material temples. Arg., Wherever she is mentioned, some prerogative above common implied. Ans. 1) would prove nothing as to her Conc.; 2) fact denied. Instances, Luke 2, "The sword shall pierce." "Thy father and I have sought Thee ;" John 2, "What have I to do with thee ?" &c.; John 19, "Woman, behold thy son" all explained by Gloss and fathers. Arg. 1. "Some say, Jesus made John her son by nature, without previous generation." Ans. Much would follow, contrary to faith—a) One besides Christ had a natural virgin-mother ; b) with no father on earth ; c) that John was our Lord's natural brother ; d) that B. V. had son by nature, not of her substance, not God, a sinner. Confusion of natural and adopted son contrary to

---

[1] Sura iii. 42. They also quoted 45—47, which De Turr. sets aside, as obviously irrelevant. All the citations are together in Martini Pugio Fidei, f. 587, taken from his MS. by Galatinus, L. 7, c. 5. See also in Maracci, Refutat. Alcor. iii. 36, p. 112.

nature. Arg. 2. "If B. V. exempt from venial sin, therefore from orig. sin, as being worse." Ans. Not so; for original sin has no sin of will. "Venial sin is sin of person, proceeding from some disordering of the actual own will of him who sins venially." "Original sin is sin of nature, proceeding from disordering of nature, and is contracted without any act of will of the being conceived." Exaggeration of saying that orig. sin made the being conceived, a traitor (proditor). Not true that "little one conceived in orig. sin, has even more inclination to commit sin of unfaithfulness to God than Adam." Ans. Concupiscence in child, habitual; in Adam actual. Disposition to act makes not one guilty of it; else any might be guilty of any thing. Obj. If universal statements taken without limitation, her exemption from actual sin as repugnant to Scr. as from original. Ans. 1) Exceptions of birth of Jerem. and John B. in H. Scr. Nothing repugnant to it. Authorities say she was privileged as to actual, not as to orig. sin. 2) Proof as to such universal declaration of universality of actual sin fails. Job 15, " Born of a woman," orig. sin; Job 25, " No one is clean, not an infant a day old." The same. Such could not have actual sin. Prov. 20, " Who can say, I have a clean heart?" forbids boasting. Isa. 53," All we, like sheep, have gone astray," includes children. So Ps. 21, " They have all gone out of the way." Ps. 116, " I said in my heart, All men are liars." Rom. 3, " All come short of the glory of God," in themselves or Adam. Authorities from S. Aug. 3) S. Aug. did except B. V. from actual sins.

Arg. 3. The vessels of temple of purest gold; much more should B. V., figured by them, never have been made of fetid flesh, sprinkled with defilement of abominable sin. Ans. 1) Allegorical exposition proves nothing; 2) vessels, chiefly typical of Christ—Isidore, &c.; 3) also typical of faithful, would prove they had no orig. sin; 4) would imply that B. V. not formed of common substance of man, whence (opponents say) " soul is made more abominable to God and angels than temple full of horrid dung;" 5) if B. V. were typified, not proved that it related to her animation (other usual argts.); 6) Gloss on Cant. 1; Murenulas, &c. Ans. 1) No such Gloss; 2) would prove nothing as to Conc. (ff. 241 v.—247).

PART XII.

C. 92. Answer to reasons and authorities that B. V. was by prevenient grace of sanctification preserved from original sin.

First, four propositions stated as belonging to both doctrines and these rejected. 1) That some excellences of accidental glory or dignity, corresponding to works of mercy, found in saints, are not in B. V. Ans. Highest order of heavenly hierarchy have all of lower. 2) That to Christ Himself, the Beatitude and Reward of the saints, from Whom emanates whatever bliss or excellence of essential or accidental glory the saints have, some prerogative and excellence of dignity of glory, accidental or relative, is wanting. 3) That in all true excellence of glory Christ and the B. V. are equal. Ans. " Against Holy Scripture and all reason, are not of the mind of those doctors alleged on the opposite side, as shown above." 4) That the B. V. is believed to have been sanctified in her mother's womb, " as soon as the grace of sanctification could exist in her," corrected, " as soon as was fitting."

Four modes of preservation. 1) " Cleansing of infection, viz. that the semina of the parents, of which the virgin body was formed, should be purified before infusion of rational soul into the clean, not unclean, flesh, so that it should not contract orig. sin;" mentioned in Bonav. 2 d. 34, q. 4. Ans. Rejected by schoolmen and only mentioned by S. Bonav. 2) " By the removal or suspension of the causality, that God should remove from that semen, or suspend, the force causative of sin, because it was conceived ' libidinosè,' as in miracles of S. John Ev. drinking poison, or preserving the three children from fire." Ans. Pet. Lomb. (2 dist. 31) does infer from Ambr. and Aug., that the soul contracts orig. sin from union with flesh, yet not by flesh acting on spirit. 3) That by a special privilege God sanctified Anne and Joachim, not only personally, but as to the power of nature, that they might generare absque libidine et consequenter sine peccato. Ans. This privilege reserved to B. V. "Blessed is the Fruit of thy womb:" so Comm. 4) That she was preserved by grace of dispensation, privilege, or sanctification to child, not to parents, so that it should be graciously granted to

B. V. at first instant of her conception, that she should not be
bound to the law or effect of the law of contraction of orig. sin.
Grounds, 1) her greater purity, that she never was subject to
uncleanness, as of greater wisdom, in which was never ignorance.
Ans. Contrary to Ps. 51, " Thou shalt purge me," and Prov. 25.
" Take away the rust, and most pure vessel," &c. Previous
cleansing diminishes not actual purity, nor former ignorance
actual knowledge. 2) " Since B. V. has singular magnificence
above all pure creatures, fitting that she should have singular
mode of sanctification, and not the homely one, that infants and
flagitious be reconciled after enmity, and so said to be sanctified, because purified from sin." *a*) Sanctif. of B. V. was above
all in greatness, earliness, firmness; *b*) not like that of those
purified from actual sin, for from orig. sin only; *c*) yet dignity
short of that of Christ, and so her Conception. 3) This mode of
sanctif. found in saints and friends of God, and Christ said to be
sanctified, Who was yet never under sin. Ans. *a*) in fact before
[here meaning seemingly mistaken]. 4) All grant that B. V.
was sanctified as soon as possible, then it might have been before
orig. sin. Ans. Only as soon *as fitted.* Henry of Ghent (as
ab. p. 235) (ff. 247 v.—250).

Alleged authorities for preservation of B. V. from orig. sin,—
1) Acts of S. Andrew (ab. pp. 297, 298). Ans. Many called
"immaculate" who yet were born in orig. sin (as Ps. xxxvii. and
cxix. 1, and [not] S. Ambr. serm. 2 on S. Agnes.) 2) In [not]
S. Ambr. serm. de Gabaon. (as ab.). 3) Id. on S. Luke "Maluit
Dom. de suo ortu quam de matris pudore dubitari" (see
ab. p. 502). 4—9) from S. Jerome (forgery, ab. p. 444), de Ass.
Virg. beg. " Cogitis me, Paula et Eust." (answered ab.). 10)
S. Aug. de 5 hæres. (see ab. pp. 312, 313), "Stulte, unde sordes,"
relates to virginity. 11) Ib. " If I could be defiled" (quoted by
opponent, " si potuit inquinari mater mea cum ipsam facerem,"
for " si potui inquinari," gravely censured by T. 12) S. Aug.
[not his] serm. on the Assumption (ans. as ab.). 13) S. Aug. de
Nat. et Grat., exception as to B. V. Ans. 1) Context, both
before and after, includes B. V. in orig. sin ; before, in citing
H. Scr. " All have sinned and lack," &c., else no need to
become Christians. " They that are sick," &c. ; all flesh
except Christ's, "flesh of sin;" afterwards, " the offence

passed to all men," &c.; 2) Aug. excepts only actual sins, for this what heretics objected, and what S. John, whom he cited, alleged; 3) saints would not have to confess that they had orig. sin, it having been washed in Bapt.; 4) borne out by S. Aug. de Perf. Just. c. ult.; 5) to confer grace to conquer sin, must relate to actual sin; "conquer" a personal act; 6) Aug. denies of B. V. what he affirms of the righteous, but this is actual sin. "All the more famous doctors, Mast. of Sent., Alex. de Ales, Albert., S. Thom., Bonav., and others named above, are of the same mind as to S. Aug.'s meaning. 14) Aug., some serm. on the B. V. (misquoted). "As soon as she came into the world by the line of human generation;" *a*) "came into world" is of nativity; *b*) not of infus. of soul, for that is creation of God; nor, *c*) of concept. of seeds, &c. 15) In same serm. "A maiden born of stock of Adam, of sinful stock, instead of curse of Eve, is pronounced blessed above all women." Ans. Refers not to her own Conc., but to that of Christ. Else, "born of sinful stock," and change from curse to blessing would imply orig. sin. 16) S. Maximus (misquoted) relates to Nativity from *a*) word "prodiit;" *b*) contrasts of "fons rudis humani generis," "radix vitiata," and "virga prodiit," *c*) read on Nativ. of B. V. 17) "As thorn the rose, Judæa Mary bare," hymn. "genuit," of actual birth, as in Ant. "To-day she bare (genuit) the Saviour," &c.; generatio used of Nativity of Jesus. S. Aug. Our Saviour (natus) born of the Father. 18) "Purity, than which none can be conceived greater under God" (see ab. p. 166). Ans. *a*) Said of the Conc. of Christ, not of her own. This shown from context. *b*) S. Ans. would not contradict what he has just said. But, c. 12—18, he had ascribed Imm. Conc. of Christ to His Virgin birth; c. 19, he had said she was cleansed. Also, Cur Deus Homo. Not disciple's words only, for not to correct is to connive. So interpreted by Alex. de Ales., Albert., S. Thomas, Bonav., and almost whole school. 19) S. Ans. De Concept. Virg. Ans. *a*) Not his, and contradicts him; *b*) style, idioms, different; *c*) book not named by old Theol. or Vincent. Hist.; *d*) falsehood, that F. of Conc. was kept in S. Ans. time. *e*) Eng. Theol. said, book not held in Eng. to be his, had many suspected doctrines, esp. contradicted Cur Deus Homo. 20) From same; same ans.; also in suæ conc. primordio may mean "soon after," as John 8: "The devil was a murderer from the beg.," i. e. soon after existence; 21) his Ep. to Eng. Bps.: "I hold him not true lover of B. V., who refuses to celebrate F. of her Conc." Ans. 1) If his (ab. p. 206), he may have kept Fest. as of her sanctif. 2) F. is on day of Conc. of seeds, not of animation. 22) S. Cyril Alex., that, in answer to Nestorius saying, "In the time of grace, the curse of fault was not wanting," he is said to have said, "After the Son, it is rash to put on Mary stain or sin. Ans. 1) T. had read through Acts, Decrees of C. of Eph. and S. Cyril's Epp. to Nest. No such passage there; 2) would relate to actual sin; orig. sin is implied in S. Cyr. Ep. to Nestor., "Whoso says that Christ offered Himself as oblation for Himself too, and not for us only, since He needed no oblation for Himself, Who knew no sin, let him be anathema." Then all, for whom that oblation was offered, had sin. 23) S. Bern. on Nat. of S. John B. (ab. pp. 108—170), "that B. V. was cleansed by a higher kind of sanctif.;" but earlier sanct. was not higher kind. Ans. On the contr., he says "she was *cleansed*," and, lower down, "was washed" (mundata, abluta); says of B. V., S. John, and Jerem., "they were conceived of sin; He of the Spirit and in the Holy Spirit." 24) Id. Serm. on Nat. (not of Assump., as they said). "The flesh of the V., taken from Adam, admitted not spots of Adam." Ans. Context and word "admisit" (not "contraxit") shows he meant actual sin. 25) Id. Serm. on Nat. "Fœcundæ Nat.," &c. "Pure humanity in Mary is not only pure from all contagion, but pure by singularity of nature." Ans. From context before and after, of her adult graces. 26) Hom. Vig. Nat. "alone blessed among women, alone free from the general curse, and alien from the pang of mothers." Also in Serm. on Adv. Ans. Relate to her child-bearing. 27) Ib. "To me a brightness flashes, first in the generation of Mary," &c. Ans. In context her descent of David; "singular privilege of sanctity," i. q. "more copious benediction of sanctif.," elsewhere, throughout life, "singulari privilegio," context, of her virgin Conc.; "she alone did not conceive in sin," then her mother did. Obj. "These, then, were great miracles." Ans. S. Bern. says "prefigured by miracles." Yet conc. of barren parents miraculous, as Bern. says of John B. and of B. V.; miracle, nasci (not concipi) sine peccato. 28) Rich. a S. Vict. (ab.

pp. 508 sqq.), " It fitted not that flesh of Mary be subject to any fault." Ans. If correct, of actual sin and of virgin Conc.; from context "pravitas" used of actual sin, not of evil, " malum." 29) S. Thomas, *a*) "purity removal from contrary; so may be creature, than which nothing can be found purer in creation; such purity of Mary, who was free (immunis) from original and actual sin." Ans. Better not have quoted S. Thomas, whose doctrine is so clear in so many places; he only spoke of actual immunity, not past. Doubtful passages to be explained by clear. Greg. No notice of any contradiction in his Concordantia Dictorum; her *depuration* from all sin, whereby she attained highest purity under God, implies orig. sin. *b*) Id. in expos. salut. Ang. "She was most pure as to fault, because she incurred neither original, nor mortal, nor venial sin." Ans. 1) After examining many originals, the words "nec originale" not found. 2) S. Th. had just said contrary; " Christ excelled the B. V. in this, that He was conceived and born without orig. sin, the B. V. was conceived in orig. sin, not born." *c*) Ib. "she was free from all curse (on Adam and Eve) pain in childbirth, labour of brow, returning to dust;" therefore, according to S. Th., from orig. sin. Ans. Arg. not S. Th.'s, for he asserted the contrary.

Summary.—T. had passed over much said on the other side, chiefly as to meanings given to Scr. and h. doctors, and propositions so elicited, as—1) not only new, but often opposed to the old; 2) not founded on Scr. or authentic doctors; 3) for conciseness, yet ready to answer to Synod any thing omitted.

1) Authorities of Scr., rightly understood, as understood by Saints and the most approved doctors, have no force to prove preservation of B. V. by prevenient grace of sanctification. 2) Passages of H. Scr. alleged, rightly understood, as by the Saints and most received doctors, support not doctrine of Imm. Conc.; 3) nor authorities of holy doctors inspected fully, not lopped, as experience shows; 4) nor inferences from H. Scr., sayings of doctors, offices of Church. 5) There being then no authentic ground from Scr., or sayings of authentic doctors, or evidence of reason gathered from foundations of faith, it is truer, sounder, safer (in S. Bonav.'s words), as being supported by Scr., according to Gloss, and express say-

ings of Saints, and irrefragably taught by nearly the whole
school of famous doctors of law, human and Divine, that Christ
Alone was free from orig. sin (ff. 250—261).

PART XIII.

The fifteen propositions of opponents, and where refuted.

C. 93.   1) " That the Bl. Deipara did not contract orig. sin,
but, being endowed by God her Son with singular privilege, and
prevented by gifts of grace, was preserved therefrom," throughout.   2) "That she might still be said to have contracted orig.
sin," specially answered in c. 8 ; 3) " that she might still be said
to have been redeemed by Christ more than others " (refuted
most plainly in c. 21) ; 4, 5) and is truly believed to have been
cleansed (purgata) and sanctified (refuted in c. 18) ; and
0) was subjected to many penalties, which came from that first
sin, yet not voluntarily, but by necessity of nature (refuted
most clearly in c. 20) ; and 7) that her conception fell short of
the privilege of Christ (refuted, as regards immunity from sin,
c. 22) ; and 8) that she could be said to have been tithed
in Abraham (refuted, c. 19) ; and 9) that unless she was so
preserved from orig. sin, Christ would not have been the most
perfect Mediator (refuted, c. 22) ; 10) that if the B. V. had
contracted orig. sin, and only remained an imperceptible time,
or a single instant, in it, it had been worse for her than to have
been damned eternally, with the pœna damni or pœna sensus
(refuted in principle in c. 2, on orig. sin); 11) further grounds.
The B. V. must have chosen rather to lose the Divine vision
(which is worse than the pains of sense) than to be for one
instant in one mortal sin.   Ans. *a)* No " pain of loss " to infant
dying in orig. sin, since not made for Divine vision, nor could
have gained it.   *b)* Better not to have been born, than to be in
mortal sin ; not so, than to die in orig. sin ; orig. sin is not mortal
sin, and could not fall under choice.   Proposition alien from
common doctrine of Theol. or judgment of human reason.
Prop. 12) Had B. V. contracted orig. sin, she would not have
attained her ultimate innocence (confuted c. 26) ; or 13) to

the highest possible grace (confuted c. 29); 14) that to assert her preservation from it, is not contrary to Scr. (contrary shown in many chapters, especially c. 11), or to the holy doctors, (contrary shown in c. 12) (ff. 261 v.—262 v.).

C. 94. Answer as to scholastic doctors alleged by first Magister proponent.

1) S. Dominic said to have said, "Christ was formed of virgin and immaculate earth." Ans. Treatise not known; if his, answer same as to S. Andrew. To be conceived in orig. sin does not derogate from integrity or purity of B. V. 2) S. Thomas Aq. (answered above, cc. 12 and 29). Statement of John Vitalis, that S. Thom. wrote to retract, omitted honestatis causa. 3) Rob. Holcot, treatise, that doctrine of S. Anselm not to be condemned. Ans. S. Anselm held conc. in orig. sin (ab. c. 12), so did Holcot (ab. c. 11); 4) Vincentius Historialis. Ans., says nothing of his own. Passage of S. Ildef. cited, does not prove it. 5) Master of Sent. Ans. Contrary proved from other places and that cited. 6) Alex. de Ales said to have contradicted in last illness what he had said. Ans. No proof of this, contrary doctrine in c. 14. 7) Ric. Middleton, said in his old age to have written on Ave Maria, that the B. V. was not conceived in orig. sin. Ans. Not proved, and, in face of opposite teaching, not to be believed till proved. 8) Scotus, in 3 d. 3. Ans. Spoke doubtfully there. 9) Nic. de Lyra, in answer to Jew. Ans. His doctrine very clear (see c. 14); does not say in tract, that B. V. did not contract orig. sin (ab. c. 28). 10) Armachanus retracted what he said, 3 d. 3, in sermon, "Wisdom built her a house," "no wise man would build house on ruinous foundation." Ans. *a*) In his De Quæstt. Arm. viii. 15, expressly concludes from Scr. that all except Christ had orig. sin, and distinguishing her sanctif. from that of John B. and Jer., says that the B. V. never committed sin. *b*) Assertion unproved; *c*) improbable on grounds so slight. 11) Peter Comestor. Passage alleged, Si fieri posset, &c. does not deny what he had said (ab. c. 14). 12) Alex. Nequam. Ans. His contrary teaching allowed by opponent; no proof of retractation. 13) Rob. Lincoln, De Laud. B. V. Citation (as T. had read in tract) was suspected ; said that he never held that doctrine. 14) Hen. de Hassia, modern

doctor. Ans. Held that neither was to be asserted or condemned. 15) Ant. de Butrio. Ans. Only related, " I hear that
now Church has approved doctrine of Franciscans, and so that
she was not conceived in orig. sin." Untrue, else question
would not be before Council.

8. Franciscans alleged, Peter Aurelii, Tract on the Conc.,
Pet. Thomæ, Ep. to Infanta of Aragon, Fraĥcis de Mairon,
Pet. of Candia (in his obedience, Alex. V.), Francis of Asti,
Ludolph of Naples, Ocham in his Quodl. ; Augustinian, Tho. de
Argentina ; Carmelites, Pet. Thomæ, Patr. of Jerus. de Laud.
B. V. and Bacho., also John of Basle, Bp., and, by last proponent, Fr. de Sambarellis, tit. de feriis. Ans. If granted that
they did, not to be compared to testimonies of H. Scr. and
doctors cited c. 12 (ff. 262 v.—265).

C. 95. Miracles alleged by John Vitalis, that Alex. Nequam,
three other Dom. or Franciscans, had been seized with diseases
(some dying) for asserting Conc. in orig. sin. Ans. Such
miracles fictitious. T. had inquired of aged fathers of his order
in different provinces, had they seen or heard any thing of
this sort ? they ridiculed it. Ans. As to miracles said to be
related by S. Anselm, later (f. 265).

C. 96. Ans. to question proposed by Council; *That* is most
pious, which is most to honour of the Redeemer. *a*) That He
Alone was conceived without orig. sin; *b*) He the Universal Redeemer. Also most maintains faith and devotion to the Passion.
2) Most to the honour of B. V., Mother of the Universal Redeemer; 3) *That* is most piously to be believed which is most conformable to Scr. (ab. c. 11) ; 4) which is so probable through
consequence of Scr. and clearness of reason, that no Scr. or
true reason opposes (esp. c. 25—29). Obj. Commonly in
Church some things are said to be more pious, inflaming affections and instructing intellect; devout piety more regarded than
certain faith; probability enough. Instance, belief that some
of our Lord's Blood remained on the earth after His Resurrection, against S. Thomas. Ans. That is not to be called devotion
which, neglecting the doctrine of the Fathers, rests on teaching
of some few, inferior in authority, repute, and wisdom. Holy
Scr. dictated by Holy Spirit, remains more entire ; necessity of
Divine Incarnation more venerated ; dignity of Christ, and uni-

versality of His Redemption more guarded. People only against the doctrine, because ill-taught (ff. 265 v.—266 v.).

C. 97. On Feast of Conception of B. V.

Three conclusions—1) Conception of B. V. not to be held on its own account. Arg. Chiefly from S. Bern. Concl. 2) That it may be celebrated by reason of sanctification, following proximately on Conc. of nature. S. Thom. (ab. p. 223), S. Bonav. (ab. p. 363). 3) "The festival, if to be celebrated, were better called F. of her Sanctification." 1) Alvarus, an excellent doctor in Canon law, and primarius in Roman curia (as ab.). Ancient custom in Rome, abiding among Carthusians, the most religious Church of Gironne, and many other most sacred places of Christendom, and Dominicans. F. to be kept for that which is supernatural, Sanctification, not what was natural, Conception (ff. 266 v.—269).

C. 98. Obj. 1) The three miracles in Ep. asserted to be S. Anselm's; 2) his alleged Epistle; 3) from the alleged institution of Roman Church; 4) common use and practice of Christian people; 5) that though conceived in orig. sin, *a*) from that mass Christ was to be born; *b*) like foundation-stone of temple; *c*) some special miracle as to the purifying seminum; *d*) Revel. to Anne and Joachim; *e, f*) because certain that her personal Conc. would be in grace.

Ans. to 1, account of miracles not authentic, so S. Bern., S. Bonav. 2) Ep. given to S. Anselm, not genuine; *a*) because it speaks of Wm. Conqueror in the past, and counts it long since; *b*) difference of style; *c*) contradicts S. Bern., who speaks of fest. as new; *d*) unlikely objects of revelation; deacon, married though persuaded by B. V. to abandon it, and adulterous priest; *e*) grounds for celebration, unworthy S. Ans. *f*) doctrine contradicts S. Ans., and, as to union of soul with body, angels intervening, the schools; *g*) no such treatise in Vinc. Histor.; *h*) direction alleged, to substitute Conc. for Nativ., not observed, as shown by many Brev. and Missals. Ans. to 2) not S. Anselm's; to 3) Roman Church tolerates, does not keep it; to 4) "custom without truth, antiquity of error." S. Cypr. Not true, that Church celebrated the Conc. without view to subsequent sanctif.; to 5) then Conc. of John B. might be celebrated (ff. 269—272 v.).

K k

C. 99. Twenty differences between the two doctrines.

1. That to be conceived without orig. sin was a singular prerogative of Christ, denied by maintainers of Imm. Conc. Falsely imputed that B. V. was odious and hated by God, which could not be without actual sin. To have had for some time or moment something displeasing to God, true, yet nothing opprobrious or blameworthy to the person so conceived, nor " infected with malice," nor "most worthy of all blame," nor "handmaid or servant of the devil " (ab. C. 28),—the chief arms of opponents.

2. This doctrine is zealous to maintain entire the prerogatives of Christ, which the H. Ghost, through Scripture or the holy Fathers, designated as belonging to Christ Alone.

3. It confesses Christ, as incomparably superior and more excellent than all the saints.

4. It maintains the true privileges of B. V., as to have conceived a Son without orig. sin.   S. Bern. Theophilus.

5. It is more consonant to faith and piety of ancient Fathers, S. Bonav.

6. It rests on authorities of Scr. in their literal meaning; but the opposite on mystic and parabolic.

7. In adducing authorities, it aims at taking meaning of Scr. according to tradition and exposition of the Fathers, and not to stretch the sense beyond the limits assigned by them.

8. In its reasons and grounds of proof, it rests not (as wrongly imputed) on authorities of H. Scr. which speak only generally, but on special also, borne out by the glosses of the saints; the contrary (as shown above) is rested really on no authority of Scr., either generally or specially, formally or argumentatively founding or corroborating it.

9. It is more conformable to the doctrine of the saints (ab. c. 12); the contrary, well considered, has not one who says directly, that the B. V. was not conceived in orig. sin.   Aug., Anselm., Maxim., S. Ildef. (as adduced), do not support it.

10. It is older, yea the faith (as shown ab.) of all the old Fathers, from the beginning of the Church. False then that not found before Anselm, who asserted it. S. Bernard called the opposite [rather the Festival] a novelty, "presumed upon against the rite of the Church, [a novelty] mother of temerity, sister of superstition, daughter of levity." Bonaventura said

that he had heard of none who asserted immunity of B. V. from orig. sin (ab. p. 220).

11. It has most evidence of reason, founded on the firm rock of the Canon, sayings of Saints, privileges and prerogatives of Christ and the B. V. (as seen in 50 Reasons, c. 16—22). Opposite is grounded only on certain typical, and parabolic or mystical, or evidently false propositions, or unauthentic revelations.

12. It has most favour in the schools of the doctors (c. 14) including all the Canonists; the opposite has very few, novel, and (as compared with the others) of very small reputation and authority.

13. This doctrine (as Bonav. says) being among holy Doctors the more common, more reasonable, the safer and more conformable to the piety of faith, is most acceptable in the case of wise and God-fearing doctors. What is alleged on the contrary, that it is so detested among Christian people, that they do not endure the mention of it, but that the opposite is most grateful to all, is false. For when it is duly explained, assigning its grounds and necessity, it is most acceptable to the Christian. It would be useful to consider, how the opposite doctrine was introduced, whether by the Apostolic See, or by Councils. "No; but in many places it was introduced with violence, threats, defamation, of which I could mention much in detail as to the ways and practices of some in the introduction of the aforesaid doctrine. But I pass it over, honestatis gratia."

14. It asserts that the B. V. was redeemed by the Blood of her Son, and so that Christ was the universal Redeemer; the opposite, denying that the B. V. was ever a captive by the servitude of sin, in fact denies that she was redeemed by Christ at the price of His Blood, and so that Christ was an universal Redeemer (quoting Pope Zosimus in support).

15. It asserts that the B. V. was washed or cleansed by the Blood of Christ (as in Rev. 1); the contrary, asserting that she never had any spot, in fact denies it.

16. It asserts that the B. V. was reconciled by the Death of Christ. The opposite, asserting that she never had any fault, denies that Christ was her Reconciler and Mediator (c. 27).

17. It asserts that the B. V. needed the oblation of Christ, our High Priest (Eph. 5); the opposite, asserting that the B. V. was not subject to any sin, says that she needed not the oblation and Sacrifice of Christ, as was shown (c. 22) from the declaration of the Council of Ephesus.

18. It asserts that the B. V. belonged to that hundredth sheep which perished when the first man went astray, to seek and to save whom the heavenly Shepherd, leaving the ninety-nine, i. e. the heavenly host, came down to earth. The opposite, asserting that she was not conceived in original sin (seeing she committed no actual), implies that she belongs not to these hundred sheep.

19. It asserts that the door of the kingdom of heaven was opened by the key of the Passion of Christ, quoting Inn. III. (in c. majores, extra de bapt.) : the contrary, asserting that the B.V. was never subject to orig. sin, denies that the kingdom of heaven was ever closed to her, and so that it was opened to her by Christ.

20. It is more pleasing to the B. V. than the contrary, since the glorious Virgin, being full of truth and the mother of the Truth, takes no pleasure save in truth (quoting S. Bern. and S. Bonav. (ff. 272 v.—275 v.).

C. 100. Epilogus, apologizing for imperfection through " the multitude of other occupations and shortness of time," and at the same time for its length, on account of,—

1) The fulness of H. Scr. and the Fathers in support; 2) the especial duties of Prof. of Theol. to elucidate, defend, and enlarge the truth; 3) the glory and dignity of our Saviour Jesus Christ, God and Man, Whose glory and the prerogatives of Whose dignity this doctrine zealously strives to maintain uninjured; 4) zeal of devotion to the Blood, the Price of our redemption, the plenitude of whose universality this doctrine defends with the utmost devotion; 5) the question of the prerogatives, dignity, and privileges of the most glorious B.V., which this doctrine is known to strive with most earnest zeal of devotion to maintain. 6) Reverence for saints so great, and scholastic doctors of Divine and human law, whose this doctrine commonly was; 7) the profuseness of the discourse in behalf of the opposite doctrine, whose largeness could not be briefly

answered. Some things however he omitted, many as being plainly said without foundation of truth; many as irrelevant; some as detracting from the authority of the holy doctors, the pillars and ground of the truth; some as injurious, which he omitted *honestatis causa,* wishing " so to fulfil my ministry, in defending the truth of those doctors, that charity should remain unimpaired " (f. 276).

De Turrecremata, at the end of his work, adds to his statement in the work on the "Decretals" (ab. p. 290) these facts :— " When, this work being completed, I, the aforesaid magister John de Turrecremata, master of the Apostolic sacred Palace, in full congregation of the Council of Basle, offered myself as prepared to make the relation enjoined me (as a public instrument was made hereon), I was answered through the most reverend lord Card. of S. Angelo, Apostolic legate and president of our holy Lord; that, since the Fathers of the holy Council were at present much occupied about the arrival of the Greeks, they could not then attend to the aforesaid matter of the Conception of the B. V.; whence they thought that, with good reason, this matter was to be superseded till the arrival of the Greeks. I then, whose business it was to obey the injunctions of my superiors, abstained from any further request for an audience. Yet I remained for several months at Basle, ever ready to make the aforesaid relation, if I should be asked for. At last, when a most grave and scandalous discussion arose between some Fathers residing at Basle, and our holy Lord Eugenius, as to the place whither the Greeks should come, the lords Legates, and presidents, and other good men, whom the temerities of those of Basle very much displeased, departing, I too determined to depart from them, as ill-minded as to the faith of Christ, betaking myself with the book of my relation to the Apostolic See, which is the mistress of faith, and in which (as Jerome says) the Christian religion ever remained undefiled. From all this any well-instructed man will understand most clearly, how void and invalid the determination is, which some say was made at Basle in the aforesaid matter of the Conception of the B. V. after my departure. It is invalid in truth, being made against the plainest testimonies of the holy Fathers of the Church, and against the express doctrine of the principal doctors of Divine and human law, as may be seen, as clear as light, from the aforesaid work. Invalid also and void of all authority is the aforesaid determination, 1) because it was made after the departure of the most reverend Lord Cardinal Legates and Lord President, and so by certain Acephali; 2) because it was made after the translation of the Council from Basle to Bologna, and so not by a synod of the Universal Church (as some lie), but by a certain congregation of Satan and church of malignants; 3) because it was made by those who, for their errors and devilish temerities, were excommunicated and most justly condemned as heretics and schismatics by the Apostolic See and Synod of the holy Universal Church, as appears from the processes made at Bologna and Florence against them (ff. 275 v.—276 v.).

ADDENDA.

P. 257. The extract from Paulus Salusius de Perusio rests on the authority of De Alva, who quotes it from De Turrecremata (note 238), "Turrecremata adduces his authority thus : 'The same holds Mag. Paulus de Perusio in 3 Sent. dist. 3, saying thus, "It is firmly to be held,"' &c." In his work, as published, the references only, not the words, are given. The substance is given much more fully in Dr. Bandelis, pp. 88, 89.

P. 258. De Turr. introduces his quotation from Nicolas Treveth with the praise "A great man, as is inferred from his most celebrated works, speaking of the celebration of the Feast of the Conception of the B. V. which takes place in some Churches, after much more, says that 'the day,' &c." and adds at the close, "For this would be superstitious."

Of John de Monte Nigro, to whom de Turrecremata frequently refers, as his colleague, who had opened the subject on the same side, and whose grounds he maintained against John of Segovia and others, Quétif says (i. 799),—

"He was a man of great parts, a subtle philosopher, profound theologian, skilled in Greek as few, acute and self-possessed in disputation. He was long, from 1483, Provincial of Upper Lombardy, and still held the office a. 1443. In General Councils convened in that period, whereat he was present at the command of the Sovereign Pontiff, and was very distinguished, he is often called Br. John Provincial, without any addition. He was sent first by Eugenius IV. to the Council of Basle, where he showed remarkable instances of his wisdom, in defending the articles of the Catholic faith and the mind of S. Thomas, as also in maintaining the rights of the Sovereign Pontiff."

He too left Basle, when it became a Conciliabulum, was

one of the six Latin deputies chosen to dispute with the Greeks at Ferrara on the Procession of God the Holy Ghost, and took the chief part in the same disputation at Florence. His disputation was much praised by Joseph of Methone, who took the same side against Mark of Ephesus. Quétif quotes from Conc. Flor. col. 698. 702. 710, 711. 715, ed. Labbe.

His work was written in the Council of Basle, A.D. 1435 or 1436. It has lain hid in the Libraries at Basle (Haenel's Catalogue, col. 637. Quétif 1. 800) and Bologna (Ib. 823).

END OF EIRENICON, PART II.

WORKS by the Rev. E. B. PUSEY, D.D.

ELEVEN ADDRESSES DURING a RETREAT of the COMPANIONS of the LOVE of JESUS, engaged in Perpetual Intercession for the Conversion of Sinners. 8vo, cloth, 3s. 6d.

The CHURCH of ENGLAND a PORTION of CHRIST'S ONE HOLY CATHOLIC CHURCH, and a MEANS of RESTORING VISIBLE UNITY: an EIRENICON, in a Letter to the Author of "The Christian Year." 8vo, cloth, 7s. 6d.

The MINOR PROPHETS; with a Commentary Explanatory and Practical, and Introductions to the Several Books. 4to, sewed, 5s. each Part.

Part I. contains HOSEA —JOEL, INTRODUCTION. | Part III. AMOS vi. 7 to MICAH i. 12.
Part II. JOEL, INTRODUCTION—AMOS vi. 6. | Part IV. [In the Press.

DANIEL the PROPHET: Nine Lectures delivered in the Divinity School of the University of Oxford. With a new Preface. *Third Edition.* (*Fifth Thousand.*) 8vo, cloth, 10s. 6d.

The COUNCILS of the CHURCH, from the Council of Jerusalem to the close of the 2nd General Council of Constantinople, A.D. 381. 1857. 10s. 6d.

SCRIPTURAL DOCTRINE of HOLY BAPTISM. Printed in the Tracts for the Times.

The DOCTRINE of the REAL PRESENCE, as contained in the Fathers from the Death of St. John the Evangelist to the Fourth General Council. 1855. 12s.

The REAL PRESENCE the DOCTRINE of the ENGLISH CHURCH; with a Vindication of the Reception by the Wicked, and of the Adoration of our Lord Jesus Christ truly Present. 1857. 9s.

The ROYAL SUPREMACY not an ARBITRARY AUTHO- RITY, but Limited by the Laws of the Church, of which Kings are Members. Ancient Precedents. 8vo, 7s.

CASE as to the LEGAL FORCE of the JUDGMENT of the PRIVY COUNCIL *in re* FENDALL *v.* WILSON; with the Opinion of the ATTORNEY-GENERAL and Sir HUGH CAIRNS, and a Preface to those who Love God and His Truth. 8vo, 6d.

The CHURCH of ENGLAND LEAVES her CHILDREN FREE to whom to OPEN their GRIEFS: a Letter to the Rev. W. U. RICHARDS. 8vo, with Postscript, 5s.

LETTER to the LORD BISHOP of LONDON, in Explanation of some Statements contained in a Letter by the Rev. W. DODSWORTH. (*Fifth Thousand.*) 16mo, 1s.

RENEWED EXPLANATIONS in consequence of Mr. DODSWORTH's Comments on the above. 8vo, 1s.

COLLEGIATE and PROFESSORIAL TEACHING and DISCIPLINE, in answer to Professor VAUGHAN. 5s.

MARRIAGE with a DECEASED WIFE'S SISTER; together with a SPEECH on the same subject by E. BADELEY, Esq. 3s. 6d.

GOD'S PROHIBITION of the MARRIAGE with a DECEASED WIFE'S SISTER (Lev. xviii. 6) not to be set aside by an Inference from His Limitation of Polygamy among the Jews (Lev. xviii. 18). 8vo, 1s.

WORKS Edited by the Rev. E. B. PUSEY, D.D.

VILLAGE SERMONS on the BAPTISMAL SERVICE. By the Rev. J. KEBLE. 8vo, 15s.

TRACT XC. On certain Passages in the XXXIX Articles, by the Rev. J. H. NEWMAN, M.A., 1841; with Historical Preface by E. B. PUSEY, D.D.; and Catholic Subscription to the XXXIX Articles considered in reference to Tract XC., by the Rev. JOHN KEBLE, M.A., 1851. 8vo, sewed, 1s. 6d.

The SPIRITUAL COMBAT; with the PATH of PARADISE; and the SUPPLEMENT; or, The Peace of the Soul. By SCUPOLI. (From the Italian.) (*Sixth Thousand, revised.*) 3s. 6d.

———————————— Cheap Edition, in wrapper, 6d.; fine paper, limp cloth, 1s.

The YEAR of AFFECTIONS; or, Sentiments on the Love of God, drawn from the Canticles, for every Day in the Year. By AVRILLON. (*Second Thousand.*) 6s. 6d.

A GUIDE for PASSING LENT HOLILY. By AVRILLON. 12mo, cloth, price 6s. (*Fourth Edition.*) *In the Press.*

A GUIDE for PASSING ADVENT HOLILY. By AVRILLON. (*New Edition.*) *In the Press.*

The LIFE of JESUS CHRIST in GLORY: Daily Meditations from Easter Day to the Wednesday after Trinity Sunday. By NOUET. 8s. (*Second Thousand.*) Or in Two Parts, at 4s. each.

The FOUNDATIONS of the SPIRITUAL LIFE: a Commentary on Thomas à Kempis. (*Second Thousand.*) By SURIN. 4s. 6d.

PARADISE for the CHRISTIAN SOUL. By HORST. Two Vols. (*Fourth Thousand.*) 6s. 6d.

LENT READINGS from the FATHERS. *In the Press.*

ADVENT READINGS from the FATHERS. (*New Edition.*) *In the Press.* 5s.

MEDITATIONS and SELECT PRAYERS of ST. ANSELM. 5s.

From the " Paradise for the Christian Soul."

DEVOTIONS for HOLY COMMUNION. (*Third Thousand.*) 18mo, 1s.

LITANIES. In the words of Holy Scripture. Royal 32mo, 6d.

SERMONS by the Rev. E. B. PUSEY.

PAROCHIAL SERMONS. Vol. I. (*Fifth Edition.*) 8vo, cloth, 6*s.*

—————————————Vol. II. (*Fourth Edition.*) 8vo, cloth, 6*s.*

ELEVEN SERMONS (with others) preached in the Octave of the Consecration of St. Saviour's, Leeds. (*Second Thousand.*)

SERMONS preached before the University of Oxford, between 1856 and 1865. *In the Press.*

SINGLE OCCASIONAL SERMONS.

I. THE DAY OF JUDGMENT. Preached at St. Paul's Church, Brighton, 1839. (*Fourth Thousand.*) 6*d.*

II. CHRIST THE SOURCE AND RULE OF CHRISTIAN LOVE. Preached at St. Paul's Church, Bristol, 1840. (*Second Thousand.*) 1*s.* 6*d.*

III. THE PREACHING OF THE GOSPEL A PREPARATION FOR OUR LORD'S COMING. Preached at St. Andrew's, Clifton, for the S.P.G., 1841. (*Second Thousand.*) 1*s.*

IV., V. GOD IS LOVE. WHOSO RECEIVETH ONE SUCH LITTLE CHILD IN MY NAME RECEIVETH ME. Two Sermons preached at Ilfracombe, 1844. (*Second Thousand.*) 1*s.* 6*d.*

VI. CHASTISEMENTS NEGLECTED, FORERUNNERS OF GREATER. Preached

at Margaret Chapel, on the General Fast Day, 1847. (*Second Thousand.*) 1*s.*

VII. THE BLASPHEMY AGAINST THE HOLY GHOST. Preached at All Saints', Margaret-street, 1845. 1*s.*

VIII. DO ALL TO THE LORD JESUS. Preached at All Saints', Margaret-street. (*Fifth Thousand.*) 6*d.*

IX., X. THE DANGER OF RICHES. SEEK GOD FIRST, AND YE SHALL HAVE ALL. Two Sermons preached at Bristol, 1850. (*Second Thousand.*) 1*s.* 6*d.*

XI., XII. THE CHURCH THE CONVERTER OF THE HEATHEN: Two Sermons preached at Melcombe Regis, 1838. (*Third Thousand.*) 12mo, 6*d.*

XIII. A SERMON PREACHED AT THE CONSECRATION OF GROVE CHURCH, 1832. *Third Edition.* 6*d.*

The above in one Volume, price 7s. 6d.

LIFE, THE PREPARATION FOR DEATH: a Sermon preached at Great St. Mary's, Cambridge, 1867. 6*d.*

OUR PHARISAISM: a Sermon preached at St. Paul's, Knightsbridge, on Ash-Wednesday, 1868. 6*d.*

SINGLE UNIVERSITY SERMONS.

I. THE HOLY EUCHARIST A COMFORT FOR THE PENITENT. Preached 1843. (*Nineteenth Thousand.*) 1*s.*

II., III. ENTIRE ABSOLUTION OF THE PENITENT: Two Sermons. Preached 1846. (*Fifth Thousand and Second Thousand.*) 1*s.* each.

IV. THE PRESENCE OF CHRIST IN THE HOLY EUCHARIST. Preached 1853. (*Second Thousand.*) 1*s.*

V. JUSTIFICATION. Preached 1853. (*Second Thousand.*) 1*s.*

VI. THE RULE OF FAITH, AS MAINTAINED BY THE FATHERS AND CHURCH OF ENGLAND. Preached 1851. (*Second Thousand.*) 8vo, 1*s.*

VII., VIII. ALL FAITH THE GIFT OF GOD. REAL FAITH ENTIRE. Preached 1855. (*Second Thousand.*) 2*s.*

IX. PATIENCE AND CONFIDENCE THE STRENGTH OF THE CHURCH. Preached on Nov. 5, 1837. (*Third Thousand.*) 1*s.*

The above in one Volume, price 7s. 6d.

EVERLASTING PUNISHMENT: a Sermon preached before the University of Oxford, 1864. 6*d.*

WILL YE ALSO GO AWAY? a Sermon preached before the University of Oxford, 1867. With PREFACE and APPENDIX. 1*s.*

LENTEN SERMONS.

REPENTANCE FROM LOVE OF GOD, LIFELONG: a Sermon preached in St. Mary's Church, Oxford, 1857. 1*s.*

THE THOUGHT OF THE LOVE OF JESUS FOR US THE REMEDY FOR SINS

OF THE BODY: a Sermon for Young Men. Preached 1861. (*Second Thousand.*) 6*d.*

THE SPIRIT COMFORTING. Preached 1863. 1*s.*

𝕷𝖎𝖇𝖗𝖆𝖗𝖞 𝖔𝖋 𝖙𝖍𝖊 𝕱𝖆𝖙𝖍𝖊𝖗𝖘

OF THE HOLY CATHOLIC CHURCH, ANTERIOR TO THE
DIVISION OF THE EAST AND WEST.

Translated by Members of the English Church.

Vol.	VOLUMES PUBLISHED.	Published price. £ s. d.	Subscrib. price. £ s. d.
1.	St. Augustine's Confessions. *Third Edition*	0 9 0	0 7 0
2.	St. Cyril's Lectures. *Third Edition*	0 10 6	0 8 0
3.	St. Cyprian's Treatises. *Second Edition.*	0 10 6	0 8 0
4 & 5.	St. Chrysostom on 1 Cor., 2 vols.	0 18 0	0 14 0
*6.	St. Chrysostom on Galatians and Ephesians.		
*7.	St. Chrysostom on Romans		
8.	St. Athanasius against the Arians	0 9 0	0 7 0
9.	St. Chrysostom, Homilies on the Statues.	0 12 0	0 9 0
10.	Tertullian. *Second Edition*, Vol. I.	0 15 0	0 11 0
11.	St. Chrysostom on St. Matthew. Part I.	0 12 0	0 9 0
12.	——— on Timothy, Titus, and Philemon	0 12 0	0 9 0
13.	St. Athanasius' Historical Tracts. *Reprinting.*		
*14.	St. Chrysostom, Homilies on Philippians, &c.		
15.	———Homilies on St. Matthew. Pt. II.	0 12 0	0 9 0
16.	St. Augustine's Sermons. Vol. I.	0 14 0	0 10 6
17.	St. Cyprian's Epistles	0 12 0	0 9 0
18.	St. Gregory the Great on Job. Vol. I.	0 15 0	0 11 0
19.	St. Athanasius against the Arians. Part II.	0 10 6	0 8 0
20.	St. Augustine's Sermons. Vol. II. *Reprinting.*		
21.	St. Gregory the Great, Morals, &c. Vol. II.	0 15 0	0 11 0
22.	St. Augustine's short Treatises	0 16 0	0 12 0
23.	St. Gregory, Morals, &c. Vol. III. Part I.	0 10 6	0 8 0
24.	St. Augustine on the Psalms. Vol. I.	0 10 6	0 8 0
25.	St. Augustine on the Psalms. Vol. II.	0 10 6	0 8 0
26.	St. Augustine on St. John. Vol. I.	0 14 0	0 10 6
27.	St. Chrysostom on 2 Corinthians	0 10 6	0 8 0
28.	St. Chrysostom on St. John. Vol. I.	0 10 6	0 8 0
29.	St. Augustine on St. John. Vol. II.	0 16 0	0 12 0
30.	St. Augustine on the Psalms. Vol. III.	0 14 0	0 10 6
31.	St. Gregory, Morals, &c. Vol. III. Part II.	0 15 0	0 11 0
32.	St. Augustine on the Psalms. Vol. IV.	0 14 0	0 10 6
33.	St. Chrysostom on the Acts. Part I.	0 10 6	0 8 0
34.	St. Chrysostom on St. Matthew. Part III.	0 12 0	0 9 0
35.	St. Chrysostom on the Acts. Part II.	0 10 6	0 8 0
36.	St. Chrysostom on St. John. Part II.	0 14 0	0 10 6
37.	St. Augustine on the Psalms. Vol. V.	0 12 0	0 9 0
38.	St. Athanasius, Festal Epistles	0 6 0	0 4 6
39	St. Augustine on the Psalms. Vol. VI.	0 14 0	0 10 6
40.	St. Justin Martyr	0 8 0	0 6 0
41.	St. Ephrem's Rhythms (from the Syriac)	0 14 0	0 10 6
42.	St. Irenæus, by the Rev. J. Keble. *In the Press.*		

* In the course of revision after the improved Text by the Rev. F. FIELD.

	Published price. £ s. d.	Subscrib. price. £ s. d.

ST. ATHANASIUS against the Arians. 2 vols. (*Third Thousand.*) (With very full illustrative notes on the history of the times, and the faith in the Trinity and the Incarnation. The most important work published since Bishop Bull) **0 19 6** **0 15 0**

———————— Historical Tracts. (St. Athanasius is *the* historian of the period.) (*Second Thousand*) . . . **0 10 0** **0 8 0**

———————— The Festal Epistles. (The work recently recovered in the Syriac translation) **0 6 0** **0 4 0**

ST. AUGUSTINE'S Confessions. (*Fourth Thousand.* With notes. (Containing his early life and conversion. The notes illustrate the Confessions from St. Augustine himself) . . **0 9 0** **0 7 0**

———————— Sermons on the New Test. 2 vols. (Clear and thoughtful expositions of Holy Scripture to the poor of Hippo, with rhetorical skill in fixing their attention.) (*Second Thousand*) **1 8 0** **1 1 0**

———————— Homilies on the Psalms. 6 vols. (Full of those concise sayings on Christian doctrine and morals, which contain so much truth accurately expressed in few words) . **3 15 0** **2 16 0**

———————— on the Gospel and First Epistle of St. John. 2 vols. (At all times one of the favourite works of St. Augustine) (*Second Thousand*) **1 10 0** **1 2 6**

———————— Practical Treatises (chiefly on the doctrines of Grace) (*Second Thousand*) **0 16 0** **0 12 0**

ST. CHRYSOSTOM on St. Matthew. (*Third Thousand.* 3 vols. **1 16 0** **1 7 0**

———————— on St. John. 2 vols. . **1 4 6** **0 18 6**

———————— on the Acts. 2 vols. . **1 1 0** **0 16 0**

———————— on St. Paul's Epistles (excepting those on the Epistle to the Hebrews, which are completed). 7 vols. in 6. (*Third and Second Thousand*) **4 0 0** **3 0 0**
(These contain the whole of that great Father's exposition of the N.T. still extant, and occupy five vols. folio of the Benedictine Edition. St. Chrysostom, besides the eloquence of his perorations, is remarkable for his care in developing the connexion of Holy Scripture.)

———————— to the People of Antioch. (The celebrated homilies, where St. Chrysostom employed the fears of the people at the Emperor's displeasure to call them to repentance.) (*Second Thousand*). **0 12 0** **0 9 0**

	Published price. £ s. d.	Subscrib. price. £ s. d.

ST. CYPRIAN'S Works. (*Third Thousand.*)
(St. Cyprian, besides his great practical wisdom, states the doctrines of grace as carefully as if he had lived after the Pelagian heresy. He was a great favourite of Dean Milner. He is a witness of the early independence of the several Churches)   **1 2 6**   **0 17 0**

ST. EPHREM'S Rhythms on the Nativity, and on Faith. (From the Syriac. A very devout writer of the mystical school, and full on the doctrine of the Incarnation.) (*Second Thousand*) **0 14 0**   **0 10 6**

ST. GREGORY THE GREAT on Book of Job. 4 vols. (Called the Magna Moralia, from the depth of the observations on human nature of one who lived in close communion with God) .   **2 15 0**   **2 2 0**

TERTULLIAN'S Apologetical and Practical Treatises. (The treatises, especially the Apologetic, have, over and above, much historical information on early Christianity. They are full of those frequent sayings of deep practical truth, for which his name is almost proverbial.) (*Third Thousand*) **0 15 0**   **0 12 0**

ST. JUSTIN THE MARTYR. Works now extant **0 8 0**   **0 6 0**

ST. IRENÆUS, the Works of. Translated by the late Rev. JOHN KEBLE. *In the Press.* .

ORIGINAL TEXTS.

ST. AUGUSTINI Confessiones (revised with the use of some Oxford MSS. and early editions.)

ST. CHRYSOSTOMI in Epist. ad Romanos	0 12 0	0 9 0
——————————————— ad Corinthios I. . .	0 14 0	0 19 6
——————————————— ad Corinthios II. .	0 10 6	0 8 0
——————————————— ad Galatas et Ephesios	0 9 0	0 7 0
——————————————— ad Phil., Coloss., Thes.	0 14 0	0 10 6
——————————————— ad Tim., Tit., Philem.	0 10 6	0 8 0
——————————————— ad Hebræos . .	0 12 0	0 9 0

Or the set .   **£4 10 0**   **3 9 0**

(For this edition all the good MSS. of St. Chrysostom in public libraries in Europe have been collated, and the Rev. F. Field having employed his great critical acumen upon them, the English edition of St. Chrysostom is, so far, the best extant, as Sir H. Savile's was in his day.)

THEODORETI ad Romanos, Cor., et Gal.   **0 10 6**   **0 8 0**

(The second volume, containing the rest of Theodoret's Commentary on St. Paul, was nearly completed by the Rev. C. Marriott, when the Church was suddenly deprived of his unwearied labours. The few remaining sheets, and the collations belonging to them, having now been found among his papers, the volume will shortly be published.)

By the same Author.

In the Press.

EIRENICON. Part III.

A SECOND LETTER TO THE VERY REV. DR. NEWMAN,

On the Possibility of Corporate Re-union and of Explanation
on the part of Rome.

With an Appendix in answer to the Rev. T. Harper's Strictures.

THE MINOR PROPHETS. Part IV.

———◆———

Edited by the same.

THE SUFFERINGS OF OUR LORD
JESUS CHRIST.

By F. THOMAS, from the Portuguese.

2 Vols.

To be published after Trinity Sunday.